CUT FROM THE SAME CLOTH

A TALE OF BORDEAUX

By

Glyn Gowans

Grosvenor House
Publishing Limited

This book is published by
Grosvenor House Publishing Ltd
Link House
140 The Broadway, Tolworth, Surrey, KT6 7HT.
www.grosvenorhousepublishing.co.uk

This book is a work of fiction. Any resemblance to
people or events, past or present, is purely coincidental.

A CIP record for this book
is available from the British Library

ISBN 978-1-83615-340-5
eBook ISBN 978-1-83615-341-2

For Karim, whose golden key opened
all the right doors.

ABOUT THE AUTHOR

Glyn Gowans was born in Newcastle-upon-Tyne and educated at Durham University, where he graduated in Law. After nineteen years specialising in intellectual property with a major UK law firm, he took early retirement to write. His novels *Gloria! Gloria!* and *Infernal Paradise* were published in March and July 2025 respectively.

PREFACE

An apartment in the very centre of Bordeaux was home for two years during the 1990s. The views from its windows were spectacular: every building was neoclassical and constructed from the local mellow stone; nothing postdated the nineteenth century. We were also blessed with delightful and hospitable neighbours – of all ages and backgrounds. A young couple from Paris swiftly emphasised that Bordeaux was not a typical French city. That proved to be an understatement. In truth it's unique – and not merely because wine affects almost every aspect of Bordelais life in some way.

Despite my rusty French, it soon struck me that many Bordelais spoke more clearly than their compatriots in other regions of France – certainly at a slower pace, almost leisurely; indeed, at times I felt I was listening to a refined bilingual Briton. And then there were the smart shops selling the sort of clothes and shoes one would associate with folk who rode to hounds in the Shires. Within a few months, and after visiting a fair number of wine châteaux, it became evident that such clothing was indeed popular among their proprietors; a fair percentage of Bordeaux's burghers aped them.

It was also remarkable just how many Bordelais had – or claimed to have – a 'noble' title, or at least the magic 'de' before their surname. They might only reside in a bedsit, but there'd be a family portrait or two on the walls, and they could rustle up an excellent meal served on fine old porcelain with antique silver cutlery bearing the family's coat of arms. Above all, there'd be surprisingly good – but coyly unidentified – wines poured from treasured crystal decanters. Standards had to be maintained.

GMG, Witham, Essex, 2025

PART 1
CHAPTER 1

In her room at Bordeaux's Hotel Continental, Laura Appleton was sinking into a state of intense depression: Jean-Claude Bourjois, whom she'd invited to dinner weeks ago, had just phoned to say he couldn't make it after all; apparently, his car had died.

'Take a cab!' she'd pleaded in her excellent French.

'*What – all the way from Margaux, Laura? Anyway, I have to wait for the recovery vehicle – and I've got filthy messing around under the hood. I'm really in no state to eat in any respectable establishment, let alone Le Chapon Fin.*'

'Jesus!'

'*Well, you're over from the States for three weeks, aren't you? We'll make it another night ... soon – very soon. I'll be in touch. À bientôt!*'

And, with that, he rang off.

With the mobile still in her hand, Laura remained standing beside the double bed, staring at her own miserable expression in the full-length mirror on the wardrobe door. It just wasn't fair: the Armani trouser suit in charcoal-grey linen fitted her slim figure perfectly, and it was seasonally casual for a warm June evening yet businesslike, striking the right balance for a very special dinner at the exclusive Chapon Fin – the dinner she'd so meticulously planned!

'And I look so sexy,' she muttered as the tears began to roll down her cheeks, '– irresistible!' Of course, Jean-Claude's cancellation wasn't the end of the world, but she'd been convinced that tonight was going to be *the* night – the night when the final pieces of her superbly crafted jigsaw were going to fall perfectly into place – when she would offer him a 'business' partnership! And then, well ...

Laura sat down heavily on the bed and brooded: something wasn't quite right. She trusted Jean-Claude implicitly – she always had. Magic memories came flooding back of their first meeting ten years ago; she could picture it so vividly, as if it had happened yesterday – awesome serendipity! Her Oenology course at Bordeaux University included a *stage* – her vocational student placement – at a prestigious Margaux vineyard, Château La Fayette. As chance would have it, Jean-Claude, at the remarkably young age of twenty-eight, had just succeeded his late father as La Fayette's *maître de chai*, the technical and production director. Her experiences, both then and subsequently, evinced that Jean-Claude was the most honest man she'd ever known. Which was why his story about the car breaking down was troubling her. There was something about his voice which seemed ... well, he'd sounded like an amateur actor nervously trying to repeat some forgotten lines with the aid of an offstage prompter. This mental image rapidly led Laura to conclude that Jean-Claude hadn't, in fact, been phoning from Margaux at all, but from his home at Le Porge on the other side of the Médoc peninsula. And so, the prompter had to be his vile wife, Sophie.

'The bitch!' she hissed, thumping a pillow. It was obvious: he'd told Sophie about the dinner engagement – almost certainly at the last minute, being so terrified of her reaction – and she'd blown a fuse, ordering him back to miserable Le Porge! She could picture the scene: Sophie storming around her so-called studio with typical Gallic hysteria; Jean-Claude protesting that it was all innocent, just business – the sort of dinner that world-famous wine critics like Laura love to have with key *maîtres de chai* – and what sort of excuse could he possibly give her anyway?

'For Christ's sake,' Sophie would have screamed, '– tell her anything! Tell her the goddam car's broken down. And don't give me all that crap about "business". That American whore's been trying to get into your trousers ever since she first set eyes on you. I haven't forgotten what the two of you got up to in the old Margaux house – in *our* cellar!'

On and on she would have ranted. Laura could hear and picture her vividly, even though the disaster had taken place some five years ago.

*

Laura's career was just beginning to take off in a big way. After finishing her studies in Bordeaux, she'd returned to the States and got a job with one of New York's most prestigious wine merchants, Plinth, Toke & Hirsh – PT&H. She liked to think that she'd secured the position solely by reason of her impressive academic and vocational qualifications: a French degree from the University of Pennsylvania, a Masters from Yale Business School, and, of course, her extremely pertinent qualifications gained in Bordeaux. Yet the bulk of the résumé she'd submitted to PT&H hadn't stimulated any particular interest on the part of the firm's directors: each year they received scores of similar curricula vitae from equally dynamic young Americans wanting to make a name in the luxury wine business. In truth, Laura only secured an interview because her father, Bryan Appleton, was the owner-chef of La Maison Blanche, the 'pre-eminent rendez-vous gastronomique' of Los Angeles.

Although a culinary genius, it was Bryan's French-Canadian wife, Hélène – the front-of-house supremo – who'd moulded him into an

2

American icon. And when their daughter was just thirteen, it was also Hélène who'd headhunted a new sommelier from the Paris Ritz – Daniel Mombrier, a young widower who'd recently lost his wife and little girl in a car crash. Laura had quickly developed an infatuation, and during school vacations it became impossible to keep her away from La Maison Blanche, where, after only a few minutes of running errands for her mother, Laura would find her way to the cellar and 'Uncle' Daniel's magical world. When he and his colleagues were tasting, she'd be allowed to sniff the glasses just as they did, and would wonder at the amazing and mystifying fragrances flooding her head – blackcurrants, cherries, peaches, honey, vanilla. And Laura's girlfriends thought she was decidedly odd, collecting and mounting wine labels and corks the way their parents used to collect stamps. But Laura didn't care what they thought, and by the time she was eighteen, she'd set her heart on a career in wine.

Meanwhile, Mombrier had not only been made a La Maison Blanche director, but also a junior partner with a minority stockholding. That had all been Hélène's idea: Daniel had become an institution – the food and wine critics gave him almost as many column inches as Bryan himself – and it would have been a disaster if they'd lost him. Perhaps Bryan would not have been so accommodating had he known that Hélène and Daniel had also become lovers, but then they were very discreet – so discreet that even Laura was unaware of the tryst.

So, when Mr Hirsh of PT&H read the references to La Maison Blanche in Laura's résumé, his mouth fell open and his heart began to race. Only the previous evening, he'd watched Mombrier on NBC's *Good Living* show, waxing lyrical about heavenly red dessert wines from Provence. And, to cap it all, an army of workmen on East Sixty-First Street were, to his knowledge, frantically putting the finishing touches to La Maison Blanche de New York, the latest venture of the gloriously successful Appleton-Mombrier team; even though PT&H had not been granted the honour of stocking the new restaurant's cellars, the ongoing business was still up for grabs.

Within a week, Laura was installed in a claustrophobic office across the hall from Mr Hirsh.

From any objective viewpoint, Laura was attractive – pretty rather than beautiful – with her long oval face, green eyes and auburn hair. And at five feet nine with a svelte figure, thanks to regular workouts and a meticulous interest in her diet, she looked quite the athlete. Immediately assigned to PT&H's wine tastings, her admirable marketing skills delighted the directors. Requests for articles from newspapers and wine periodicals followed, and what started as a trickle rapidly turned into a flood. Then came the TV appearances on shows like *Good Living* – often with Uncle Daniel – and viewers with hitherto little interest in wine would be carried away by their infectious enthusiasm. The publishers of the two great wine gurus of the English-speaking world, Britain's Hugh Johnson and America's Robert Parker, sat up and began to take stock. Johnson and Parker were not getting any younger, they reasoned, and a vast amount of money was at stake: translated into seventeen languages, Johnson's *Pocket Wine Book* alone was selling over 400,000 copies annually – more than any other wine book in history. Young Laura Appleton was clearly a leading candidate for heir presumptive, but when the publishers began bidding for her with offers of royalty advances as if she was a bottle of 1848 Lafite Rothschild up for auction, they found her a tough nut to crack.

This whirlwind of speculative bidding descended upon Laura just as she was about to embark with Mombrier on a six-month sabbatical from PT&H for the purpose of filming *Daniel and Laura in the Temples of Wine*, a ten-part multinational series on what the producers referred to as 'The Top Ten Vineyards of Bordeaux'. After only a few days of shooting around St-Emilion, however, it was obvious that something was wrong with Daniel: he was missing cues, forgetting lines, looking disinterested. Soon, they were seriously behind schedule and tempers were beginning to fray. Unsurprisingly, Laura's joie de vivre evaporated, and her exaggerated smiles and cheerful banter before the cameras were transparently fake. Not a day passed without her making several attempts to find out what was the matter. She feared the worst – that Daniel had been diagnosed with an incurable illness; cancer was at the forefront of her mind. But he swore that, as far as he was aware, nothing was wrong with his health.

Everything came to a head at the end of the second week, on their last day of filming around the village of Margaux. In the original schedule, no less than four days had been allotted to filming at the great Château Margaux itself. And so, it had come as a surprise when, shortly before leaving New York, Laura had 'suggested' that three days would be sufficient, and that the fourth should be devoted to neighbouring Château La Fayette, where she'd trained during her student days, and which, in consequence, had played a significant role in bringing her the success she was now enjoying.

'But La Fayette's not in the Top Ten!' the TV executives had wailed.

Laura, however, had been adamant. There were mutterings of prima donna and even breaches of contract. But in the end, she got her way, thanks to emailed pictures of La Fayette's impressive architecture, and assurances that its proprietor, Baron Guy de Bondé, was not only one of the most influential figures in Bordeaux, but also a delightful 'character'.

Her arguments were not without foundation, and yet she was being disingenuous: Laura was desperate to curry favour with Jean-Claude Bourjois. Her infatuation was still as powerful as it had been during her La Fayette stage – if not stronger – for worshiping him from afar had been an addictive drug; even in the deepest moments of passion with her occasional boyfriends, she would will herself to picture Jean-Claude and imagine that it was he who was having sex with her. Frustration and guilt would inevitably follow. Her lovers couldn't understand the post-coital depressions, and she couldn't bring herself to explain them. The relationships would fizzle out, and Laura would return to her solitary nights of passion with erotic fantasies of Jean-Claude.

Besides, as her career began to blossom and bring her back to Bordeaux with increasing frequency, Laura's professional contacts with Jean-Claude served to provide her with evidence of a mutual attraction. In this she was wholly mistaken, but all-consuming infatuations and chronic self-deception are often complementary bedfellows. And although Jean-Claude had always behaved as a perfect gentleman from the first day of her *stage*, such correctness was, paradoxically, regarded by Laura as proof positive that he had to be attracted to her: no handsome young Frenchman could be so courteous, helpful and caring without some ulterior motive. But then, she was the product of a society and era which were both exceptionally cynical and sexually precocious.

What Laura found particularly galling was that Jean-Claude had married Sophie – a Parisian and the daughter of one of France's most successful businessmen – just months before her own arrival at La Fayette, and, moreover, after a whirlwind romance and the briefest of engagements. Ironically, it was Jean-Claude's desire to provide Sophie with some comradeship through the medium of a vivacious American that had led him to invite Laura into their home. After their first meeting, however, Sophie didn't encourage further contact; all additional socializing by the two women was solely the result of Jean-Claude's naive initiatives. And at the dinner parties, barbecues and beach trips to which Laura would be invited, Sophie would always manage to procure some unattached male who could be expected to lay siege to her for the duration.

Laura's own intuition told her that Jean-Claude's marriage was doomed: Sophie had temporarily got bored with decadent Parisian society and had enjoyed shocking family and friends by taking on the challenge of civilizing a savage from the outback; the novelty would soon wear off. As for Jean-Claude, he'd simply had his head turned by the attentions of a superficially sophisticated and beautiful city girl. And, of course, at the time of his seduction he'd been particularly vulnerable due to his father's terminal cancer. Separation and divorce could not be far away. Indeed, there were many telltale signs, including Sophie's constant moaning about Jean-Claude's small house in Margaux. Yet, her much heralded plans for some kind of 'dream home' near the Ocean were clearly beyond his means. Furthermore, Sophie's assumption that she'd be able to socialize with the Bordelais wine aristocracy on equal terms had been swiftly shattered: her husband's background made this quite impossible, not to mention the open secret of the marriage's alienation of her own family. Above all, when Sophie's pregnancy became common knowledge shortly after Laura commenced her *stage*, she inwardly glowed with the thought that it had been a shotgun marriage: from what she'd seen of Sophie, childbirth and motherhood were unlikely to reconcile her to provincial oblivion.

During her business trips to Bordeaux over the next five years, Laura would always discreetly probe for any hint of marital breakdown or scandal, but the gossipmongers never managed to provide her with more than a few crumbs of comfort: there was still no concrete evidence of the dream house, and Sophie had almost abandoned their only child, Alexandre, in favour of her 'painting'. Nevertheless, Laura remained firmly convinced that she still had a chance of winning what she wanted more than anything else in the world – Jean-Claude's heart, body and soul.

Consequently, as Laura breakfasted with Daniel Mombrier at the Relais de Margaux before the two of them set off for filming at Château La Fayette, she was looking forward to a whole day with Jean-Claude. And thanks to her, millions of viewers would soon be captivated by his beauty and deep sexy voice; *Good Living*'s producers would be eager to have him on the show, and once Stateside, she was sure Jean-Claude would succumb to her best seduction techniques. He'd be desperate to divorce Sophie; if he wanted to bring his son to America – and she doubted that the mother would fight to keep him – she'd even be prepared to play the role of stepmother. After all, Alexandre sounded like quite a nice little boy.

These reveries of romantic bliss dissolved as Laura realized that Daniel was staring strangely at her over his uneaten croissant. He looked worse than ever. *He's going to ruin the day at La Fayette* was her first thought. Then she felt mean and selfish. She reached out and touched his hand.

'For God's sake, Uncle Daniel, I swear to you on Mom's life that if you don't tell me the honest truth about what the hell is wrong with you, we're going straight upstairs to pack our bags and take the first flight home. Come on, tell me – *now* – I can take it.' She thought of La Fayette and Jean-Claude, and prayed for a miracle.

Daniel cleared his throat. 'I ... I've ... I've wanted to ... to tell you, Laura, for a long time – a very long time, but ...'

Laura sat bolt upright with her heart in her mouth; she just knew instinctively life would never be the same again. 'Tell me *what*?' she prompted.

'You've been like a daughter to me, Laura ... since I lost my own, and my wife, before I came to America ... all those years ago. I'd never want to do anything to ... to damage our very *special* relationship, Laura. ... Your mother–'

Laura gasped: it wasn't Daniel who was ill but Mom! 'What's wrong with her?' she croaked.

'Wrong?'

'Her illness – what is it?'

'She's not ill.'

'I'm not following any of–'

'Give me a chance – I'm trying to explain.' For once, Daniel sounded tetchy. There were a few seconds' silence. 'I love your mother very much, Laura, and she loves me. She's finally decided to ask Bryan for a divorce, and as soon as it comes through, we're going to get married.'

Although Laura could hear words and phrases such as 'daughter', 'worship', 'blessing' – several times – and 'eternal friendship', she wasn't paying any attention. She looked at him across the breakfast table as if she was seeing him for the first time. The devil had revealed himself. He was no longer kind, loveable 'Uncle Daniel', but an oily, ingratiating, lecherous fraud who'd bewitched and seduced Mom.

Brought back to reality by the receptionist announcing from the dining room doorway that the minibus had arrived to take them to La Fayette, Laura said: 'So, this – this – *thing* between you and Mom has been going on for some time? How long?'

'"*Thing*"? We're in love, Laura, *chérie*. I'm sure you know what that means. It's not something sordid.'

'Oh, for Christ's sake, don't preach to me! You lost your family and had a breakdown. Dad offered you a new life in a new country. You got a great job in one of America's best restaurants. He welcomed you into his own home. We *all* treated you like one of the family – *Uncle* Daniel! He even made you a partner in his business.'

'Your *parents*' business, Laura. It's been a *team* effort, and Hélène–'

'Exactly! They're a team – a team you're trying to break up.'

'That's not fair. And there's no need to shout.'

'Don't tell me how to behave – you're *not* my father, you asshole.'

'I feared you'd take this badly, but I didn't expect hysteria and obscenities.'

'Oh, excuse me, Mr Wine Waiter!'

A cough halted the row: now the minibus driver – visibly irate – stood in the doorway. '*Excusez-moi, madame et monsieur, mais nous sommes pressés.*'

Laura waived him away with a '*J'arrive!*' as she snatched her shoulder bag off the floor. 'And I'll tell you something for nothing – Dad worships Mom. If she asks for a divorce, he'll be devastated. She means everything to him – *everything*! And if you think he's just going to shake your hand and wish you well when the shit hits the fan, you must be a real dumb son of a bitch.

'I'm going to La Fayette now. I'll inform our long-suffering director that due to irreconcilable differences, you and I can no longer work together in *any* circumstances, but that *I* am prepared to proceed with the series on my own – or with some other acceptable co-presenter. In any event, I don't want to see you ever again.'

'Laura! *Please*! We can't part like this. You need time to digest–'

'I'm sorry if my morality is a bit too conservative for you, Daniel, but that's the way I am. I love *both* my parents, and I don't want to see either of them hurt. You disgust me.'

Laura reached the door just as Daniel began to sob; she didn't look back.

In tears herself, Laura dashed to her room. She wondered whether she should phone Mom, but it would only be around one a.m. in Los Angeles, and she'd be asleep – lying beside Dad. That image made her shake with rage, and she cursed Daniel's name. She'd phone Mom later in the day at La Maison Blanche, when she'd be able to get her alone in her office.

When Laura arrived at La Fayette and told the director of Daniel's excommunication, there were volcanic eruptions of artistic temperament on the gravel drive before the château's grand facade. International phone lines hummed and lawyers were consulted. A bemused throng of estate workers, including Jean-Claude, witnessed the fireworks. Pompous Henri de Bondé, the baron's only son and heir, watched and listened from the top of the monumental steps that led to his front door, fearful – whatever the crisis might be – that he and his inheritance were not going to feature on television after all. In point of fact, Henri had been waiting to tell the TV people that he'd be substituting for his father, who, alas, was unwell and had been ordered by his doctor to rest.

Having dumped her problems on the director and his staff, Laura retreated to Jean-Claude's cramped office in the *chais* – the long, low and windowless stone-built wine stores – and proceeded to share Daniel's confessions with him; he was sympathetic and tactile. Around noon, Henri materialized and, with uncharacteristic charm, asked 'Bourjois' to take an early lunch with Laura. Indeed, he ordered his employee not to spare the expense; he would have acted as host himself were it not for the TV people demanding endless refreshments.

Jean-Claude took Laura to a humble restaurant frequented almost exclusively by locals. It was perched on the marshy banks of the Gironde at the tiny hamlet of Port de Lamarque, about a fifteen-minute drive from Margaux, from whence the ferry to Blaye, some five kilometres distant on the other side of the great river, sailed a few times a day. The food was simple and cheap yet delicious. Over coffee, Jean-Claude phoned the Relais de Margaux to ascertain if Daniel had checked out. Laura had nothing to fear: he'd left around eleven in a taxi booked to take him to Bordeaux Airport. Laura's relief turned to joy when Jean-Claude, as thoughtful and hospitable as ever, suggested that, instead of spending a lonely evening at the hotel, she'd be very welcome to join him for a simple supper at home.

'Shouldn't you check with Sophie if that's OK?' she enquired.

'Oh, Sophie's gone to Toulouse. She's trying to persuade Aérospatiale to buy a few of her paintings – to "brighten up" the meeting rooms and corridors.' They both giggled. 'She's left Alexandre with my aunt in Bordeaux. She won't be back until tomorrow.'

Laura's heart seemed to miss a beat.

Back at the Relais de Margaux, a sheaf of messages awaited Laura, so she spent the rest of the afternoon on the phone. The director told her that she was 'a very naughty girl', but notwithstanding some reluctant voices, the joint venture had decided to continue the project with Laura as sole presenter. Henri de Bondé sounded furtive, and after a lot of beating about the bush, said that he was prepared to pay her fifty thousand francs if she would ensure La Fayette remained in the series and that he got top billing and not Bourjois. Politely, she told him what he could do with his money. Mom scolded her for being so unkind to Daniel; Dad said there were 'no hard feelings' – he was more than happy for Daniel to remain at his post. In fact, as he himself was in love with the head receptionist, they might even make it a double wedding at La Maison Blanche! Laura did not call Daniel on his mobile.

When Jean-Claude picked her up at eight, Laura appeared to be in much better spirits, although he suspected she was putting on a good act for his benefit. He was happy too – 'full of beans' as Laura put it when she probed coquettishly. His explanation that he was just looking forward to sharing with her some very special bottles from his humble cellar didn't sound wholly convincing to her ears. At the cosy Margaux cottage, he set to work in the kitchen preparing garlic butter for the steaks he'd grill, together with a simple green salad of *mâche*. Laura was delegated to set the table. It proved a very enjoyable meal; the steaks were preceded by some delicious foie gras accompanied by a fine old Sauternes. Jean-Claude apologized for the absence of a pudding, but Laura was more than happy with his small but excellent selection of cheeses, which the remainder of a rare bottle of the outstanding 1945 La Fayette complemented admirably. As they chatted amiably and with increasing frankness about common acquaintances in the wine trade, Laura's concerns for her parents' marriage steadily diminished. And, with her inhibitions weakened, she finalized her strategies for achieving the sort of conclusion to the evening she so ardently desired.

Jean-Claude was imagining how wonderful it would be if the rare tête à tête dinners between his wife and himself could be like this, for although Sophie enjoyed drinking wine, she had no other interest in it whatsoever. And when she did cook, everything had to be smothered in some overpoweringly rich sauce, which would make it impossible to enjoy any fine vintage. But, worst of all, were her dinner-table monologues – a constant litany of the inadequacies of their home and the essential possessions which she lacked. Still, all that would soon end: that very afternoon he'd finally procured the finance for the dream house – and from a most unexpected source.

Jean-Claude asked Laura if she'd like a *digestif*: there were some rather special bottles of cognac and Armagnac in the cellar; just one for the road before he ran her back to the hotel. Laura said she really shouldn't, but she'd love to see his cellar: during her *stage*, Sophie had always managed to find her some little tasks to perform whenever Jean-Claude had gone to fetch something.

'It's only a very small cellar,' he warned her. 'Not much to see really.' He scanned her expensive clothes. 'It's very dusty down there. Are you sure–?'

'Jean-Claude Bourjois, poking around in dirty cellars is my bread and butter!'

The cellar was accessed via a door in the kitchen. At the bottom of a steep stone staircase, Laura stood in a barrel-vaulted chamber illuminated by one bare 100-watt bulb. It was certainly compact, but there was still enough space to store a few hundred bottles. Jean-Claude mumbled something dismissive and went in search of his cognac while Laura examined some of the racks. After the fifth 'Oh my God!' she began scolding him about his false modesty: around her lay some of the finest clarets of the twentieth century; the quality certainly made up for any lack of quantity.

'Where the hell did you get all these? Are they insured? Can't imagine Sophie's aware of their value. She'd have auctioned them long ago and got the deposit on that goddam house she wants!'

10

Jean-Claude laughed. 'For Christ's sake, don't tell her. I think she's only been down here once. Luckily for me, she's claustrophobic – that's why she needs a big house – and she thinks there are rats down here.'

Laura shrieked theatrically as Jean-Claude came to stand beside her with a very dusty bottle of cognac. 'There *aren't* rats, are there?'

'Well ... I don't think so. I've never seen one. Maybe a little mouse once in a while.'

Laura spotted a 1928 Château Margaux. 'Jesus Christ! I once managed to drink half a glass of this nectar at a wine tasting for the Great and Good of Philadelphia in some millionaire's colonial mansion. Parker – God bless him! – gives the 1928 ninety-eight points! There are folks back home who'd sell their granny for a bottle of–'

'Money! Parker! *Points!* Most of these bottles were gifts, Laura ... to my father, grandfather, great-grandfather ... from one *maître de chai* to another – birthdays, Christmases, weddings ... years ago. Some – much more recent vintages, of course – were gifts to me. You know, many are like old friends – when only one bottle is left of a particular vintage, I can't bear the idea of opening it.'

'Well, if you ever want to give some away or sell them, think of me first. Mind you, I doubt I could afford to pay the market prices, but ...'

Jean-Claude carefully removed a filthy bottle from one of the racks and, keeping it horizontal, proffered it to Laura. 'You enjoyed the 1928 Margaux. I think, however, that you might just prefer this one.'

'*Another* Château Margaux?' she scoffed, pretending to be blasé. The label was faded and it took her some time to read the year. 'It's not? It can't be?' She shook her head in disbelief. 'Not the 1900? – *the* 1900 that Parker gives a hundred out of a hundred?'

'You Americans and your ridiculous points!'

'Don't mock. Parker's system has even won him medals in *your* country.'

'Ha!'

Laura licked her lips. 'Oh, Jean-Claude, can I hold it, please? Just for a minute.'

He raised his eyebrows. 'Sure.'

As he laid the bottle in her outstretched palms, his skin brushed hers. She looked into his eyes and saw what she wanted to see: it was time for Laura Appleton to offer herself to the Supreme Being.

'Are you all right, Laura? You look ...'

With a beatific smile, Laura began to descend to her knees, still holding the precious bottle. Her intention was to place it on the floor, somewhere out of harm's way, and then to bury her head in the sacred zone – that part of Jean-Claude's blue jeans which caressed his groin. But, as Laura descended to the flagstones, he assumed she was succumbing to alcohol-induced light-headedness and about to pass out. Fearing for his treasured Margaux, he quickly reached down to rescue the bottle before it was too late. Laura misinterpreted the gesture, and saw him reaching to embrace her. Swept away by a tide of emotion, she attempted to reciprocate. The bottle slipped from her hands and smashed on the stone flags.

'*Merde*,' Jean-Claude croaked, '– *merde, merde, **merde**!*'

For a few moments, they both remained frozen to the spot, watching the red liquid trickle across the floor, Laura refusing to believe her crime. Then she realized that all chances of a night of passion had also been destroyed.

'What have I done?' she wailed, tearing at her mass of fussily styled hair. 'Oh, Jesus Christ! How could I? *How?*' She bowed her head, refusing to look at Jean-Claude. But whatever pain he might have felt for his shattered heirloom quickly evaporated as her sobbing became hysterical. Imagining the shame, guilt and remorse racking her tortured mind, his heart went out to her. He knelt down and placed his hands on her shoulders.

'Laura, *please*. It was just wine, for God's sake.' He tried to raise her head. 'Come on, Laura, look at me. Do I look angry? ... *Do* I?' He managed a forced chuckle. 'The wine was probably corked or oxidized. A lot of these old bottles ...'

Laura finally looked up; her face was a tragic picture of tears and running mascara. 'Everything was going so well,' she wailed between the sobs. 'I wanted so much ... It could have been a *perfect* evening.' She looked down again at the pool of thousands of dollars' worth of Château Margaux and shook her head slowly. 'And now you must hate me. I wish I was dead!'

With the sobbing resuming and intensifying, Jean-Claude resolved to get Laura out of the cellar. He pulled a handkerchief out of his pocket. 'Come on, no more crying over – what do the English say? – spilt milk? Let's go back upstairs and have some of this excellent cognac and a cup of good strong coffee. ... Yes?'

Jean-Claude's muscular arms raised Laura to her feet; for a few moments, he held on to her waist, fearing that in her present state of grief and inebriation she might slump back to the floor with its pool of wine and broken glass. She steadied herself, placing her still trembling hands on his hips; he gave her a big brotherly hug.

'Just think, Laura, we'll be laughing about this little accident for years to come. And back in the States you'll probably be able to dine out on the story with all those wine buffs you know. One day, when you're even richer and more famous than you are now, you'll be able to replace–'

Laura gently pushed Jean-Claude away to free herself from his embrace. 'You're an angel,' she said, staring into his eyes. 'You're the sweetest, kindest–' She interrupted herself to kiss him on the cheek. Then she took a step back, smiled and lunged. Before he could react, her lips were tightly pressed against his – her hands caressing his buttocks. Momentarily paralysed, he was about to extricate himself when a floorboard creaked somewhere in the house above. Laura felt his body stiffen.

'Well, this *is* a pretty picture, I must say!' boomed a female voice.

Laura spun round as Jean-Claude simultaneously pushed her away. Sophie stood at the top of the stairs, hands on hips, and a murderous expression on her contorted face.

'Sophie! What are *you* doing here? You should be in Toulouse. I mean – I've been trying to phone since– It's not what you think, Sophie, I – we–'

'Oh? And what *do* I think?' Sophie made no move to descend the steps.

'Well – I ... It might look like ...'

'Yes?'

'I mean ...' He really didn't want to say what it might possibly look like.

'It looks to *me* that while the cat was away, the mice – or should I say *rats*? – were playing, and that, had I not had a very successful trip to Toulouse, with meetings which were not as long as I'd anticipated, and the naive thought that my husband would be thrilled by an unexpected early return so I could give him the good news in person and we could celebrate with a bottle of Krug ... well, Christ only knows what the two of you would have got up to. Thank God I decided to leave Alexandre with your aunt in Bordeaux until tomorrow. If he'd witnessed this ... this *spectacle–*'

'No!' protested Jean-Claude, moving to the bottom of the steps, '– you've got it all wrong, Sophie.' He turned to Laura, who'd still to open her mouth. 'Hasn't she, Laura?'

Laura inhaled deeply. 'Well ...' She appeared to change her mind about what she was going to say. Instead, she just shrugged her shoulders and sighed.

Perplexed by Laura's apparent reluctance to plead their innocence, Jean-Claude embarked upon a rapid but disjointed account of the events which had brought Laura to the house, dinner à deux, the cellar, and the accident. He even ungallantly drew attention to Laura's devastated make-up and his soiled handkerchief. By the time he'd finished, he found himself standing just two steps below Sophie; Laura had remained where she was.

'I *told* you about the filming at La Fayette,' Jean-Claude bleated for the third time. 'I mentioned it again at breakfast this morning. You *knew* Laura was staying in Margaux. You *knew*–'

'You're pathetic, Sophie snapped, flicking a hand as if dismissing an errant servant, '– utterly pa-*thetic*. Can you really be so stupid? That slut has been desperate to get you out of your pants since she first set her cow-like eyes on you. I want her out of my house *now*. She can *walk* back to the hotel. It'll take her twenty minutes. If you drive her, she'll probably try to suck you off.'

'Sophie! That's a disgusting thing to say about–'

'Oh, don't look so shocked, Jean-Claude,' Sophie snarled, turning on her heels and disappearing through the doorway, 'frustrated lust is written all over the bitch's tarty face.'

'Sophie! ... *Sophie*! She can't *walk* back – not at *this* time of night! ... And I've got great news – about the house! I saw Guy–!'

Jean-Claude made to run after his wife, but Laura cried: 'No! Don't make things worse. I'll walk. This is Margaux – not Haarlem.'

An hour later, Laura lay in her bed at the Relais de Margaux, smiling in the darkness. On reflection, the evening might not have been such a disaster after all: Jean-Claude had finally seen a particularly nasty side of Sophie's character; Sophie had been put on notice that he was probably being unfaithful; and, unless she had a vivid imagination, there'd definitely been a stirring in his loins when she kissed him with all the passion she could muster.

*

In her room at the Continental, Laura was still lying on the bed, staring at the ceiling. She shook her head slowly. 'Jesus, just *five* years ago,' she murmured. 'Seems like an eternity. ... So near and yet so far. ... And then it turns out that the reason he was so chirpy that night was because he'd just secured the finance for that fricking "dream house"! How, I'll never know. No wonder Sophie didn't dump him.'

Laura pushed herself up and swung her legs over the side of the bed; the Armani trouser suit was a crumpled mess; she didn't care. It was after ten, and she hadn't phoned Le Chapon Fin to cancel the goddam reservation. She didn't care about that either. ... Food! She hadn't eaten! Did the Continental do room service? ... They didn't. Well, she wasn't hungry anyway; some pills would do. But as she scanned the cluttered dressing table for the blister pack, her eyes focused on the bottle of Château La Fayette she'd brought from New York. She smiled wryly. 'Oh, I'd almost forgotten about you, baby! Welcome home, my little secret weapon.'

CHAPTER 2

In front of Château La Fayette's *chais*, the only remaining car was Jean-Claude's battered Peugeot: every other employee had gone home long ago. But paralysed by indecision, the *maître de chai* sat in the driver's seat, staring through the fly-splattered windscreen.

'God, I wish I was dead!' he muttered. *The shame! – the humiliation! How did Henri ever think he could get away with it? – how?... Or are the American distributors behind it all? Could Henri be innocent? ... Possibly. ... No! – they'd have needed his help. ... Hell! I don't know! Anyway, it's bound to come out – fraud in Bordeaux always does – sooner or later.*

Jean-Claude tried again to decide whether to await Henri de Bondé's return from Paris that evening and have it out with him, or go home and seek Sophie's advice. At least he'd had the sense to cancel dinner with Laura: she'd have known straight away something was wrong and started probing – oh, playfully and good-naturedly – but with that purring American voice and those eyes of hers, she'd have completely disarmed him. And with a few glasses of wine and some good food inside him, his defences would have slowly crumbled, and then ... well, he probably would have revealed the horrifying discovery he'd made just a few hours ago ... But, on the other hand, if he'd told her the whole story, she'd have believed his protestations of innocence, wouldn't she? Perhaps, with all her experience and connections, she could advise him, recommend–

Get real! Who am I fooling? I'm La Fayette's maître de chai, *and most people who know anything about the workings of a vineyard will assume that the* maître *can't be ignorant of anything that goes on there for long, at least if he's doing his job properly. And why didn't I spot what was going on?* **Why?**

Jean-Claude's fists hit the steering wheel. 'I'm a fucking idiot!' he yelled. Half-turning, he lifted his jacket off the back seat: somewhere there was a packet of Gauloises. Sophie would be furious if she knew he'd gone back on his solemn undertaking, but with all the worry and stress ... He grabbed the packet, briskly lit up and inhaled deeply – only to find himself engulfed in choking smoke.

'*Merde!*' he hissed, getting out of the car, '– it's bloody hot!'

It had indeed been a baking day, unseasonably so for early June, and despite all his own problems, he still couldn't help wondering what that might mean for the flowering of the vines. They were late, worryingly late, what with the severe April frosts and then the terrible storms in early May. He pictured Sophie inspecting the damage to their garden at Le Porge one morning, with Richelieu trotting behind protectively with Alexandre – weird really, as the lad never reciprocated the devoted Dalmatian's affection.

'Le Porge!' he snapped bitterly. *A village in the middle of nowhere – well, in the middle of the forest – an awful road to Bordeaux and almost forty kilometres from La Fayette. Why the hell couldn't we have built the sodding house in Margaux, or even one of the neighbouring villages?*

He remembered what everyone had said at La Fayette when he'd told them about the move to Le Porge: 'She's from Paris, of course.' He'd smiled – even laughed – when they'd said that: he'd felt obliged to humour them; he'd known most of the staff all his life. Deep down, he felt he'd betrayed them: there weren't any vines at Le Porge, not one – just forest ... and the sea, of course – well, ten kilometres away at the end of a winding road through the dense conifers. Sophie could cycle there – followed by an arduous trek across huge sand dunes. Forest, sea and bikes: Sophie's idea of a perfect life – or so she'd said – and a large ultramodern house. It had taken over four years from start to finish: finding the land, selecting the architect, approving the designs, the construction, the landscaping, the furnishing. ... It had cost a hell of a lot ... a hell of a lot.

Another wave of panic began to engulf Jean-Claude.

I'll have to leave La Fayette immediately – unless Henri can convince me there's nothing shady going on. ... Maybe the printer put two and two together and made five? ... But if I walk out now, how would that affect all the financial assistance Guy provided to build Le Porge – the loan and the guarantee to the bank for the mortgage?

Jesus! The mortgage! I hadn't thought of that. If I kick up a fuss, Henri could turn real nasty – I'm ninety-nine per cent sure there's a scam and he's in it up to his neck. He'd cancel the guarantee – can he do that? – call in the loan! Would the bank then foreclose? ... How quickly could I get another job? Oh, Christ, what a bloody mess!

What's Le Porge worth anyway? What if I have to go abroad? ... Surely it won't come to that? Dear God! And who'd pay anything like what we've spent on that dump, something that looks like a hi-tech office in a wilderness? – certainly not your average snooty Bordelais, that's for sure. No, that white elephant has 'negative equity' written all over it.

'This is all Sophie's goddam fault!' Jean-Claude's cry reverberated around the cobbled courtyard. With even greater ferocity, he added: 'It's God's punishment for the way I degraded and humiliated myself to procure that sodding money!'

*

Ever since their marriage, Jean-Claude had been telling Sophie that her plans for 'their' dream house were simply beyond their means, but every time the subject came up, her enthusiasm and passion for the project had proved infectious. He'd watch her face light up as she paced around their cramped Margaux cottage, describing with childlike joy how each and every room at Le Porge would look: the classical elegance of the intimate dining room; the space and light of the sitting room with its walls of glass and panoramic views of the garden and forest; Jean-Claude's cosy wood-panelled study; her own studio – at last! – where she'd have the space to paint the vast canvases she'd been dreaming about for so long. And she and Alexandre – when he was a little older, of course – could cycle for hours through the forests without ever meeting a soul; no cars or other vehicles to worry about – no danger of accidents – which meant that the dog – or rather *dogs* as there'd be plenty of space for two or three – would be able to trot along beside them.

Above all – she always mentioned this last – there'd be the sea, not the murky, treacherous waters of the Gironde estuary just down the road from Margaux with its mudbanks, dangerous currents and surging tides, but the Atlantic and the virgin, unpopulated Côte d'Argent. Extending both north and south of Le Porge Océan in a wide silvery band as far as the eye could see, they'd always find an empty kilometre stretch to themselves – even in midsummer. That was an exaggeration – a half-kilometre maybe. She really knew how to cast a spell over him, but then one of the first secrets he'd ever told her about himself was his childhood dream to live beside the sea. It had been in her Paris apartment on their second date.

Jean-Claude had just succeeded his father, Christophe, as La Fayette's *maître de chai*. Christophe's cancer had not been responding to treatment, so Baron Guy de Bondé, the vineyard's owner, had insisted on him going to the very best consultants in France and receiving whatever treatment he was prescribed, all at his expense. Consequently, Christophe was admitted to the renowned Hôtel Dieu hospital in Paris, and his wife, Joséphine, moved into a neighbouring hotel – also paid for by the kind baron. Jean-Claude had visited them every weekend while the treatment lasted, and it was on one of those visits that he'd struck up a conversation with an attractive young brunette in a private gallery in the Rue de Rivoli. He'd just left his father in the Hôtel Dieu – Christophe had spent most of the afternoon talking philosophically about death – but Jean-Claude never could remember how he'd ended up in the gallery, particularly as he had no interest in art. Sophie subsequently told him that he'd spent almost thirty minutes staring at an abstract of red and green interlocking squares entitled *Carré d'Agneau Rouge et Vert* before she plucked up the courage to approach him and enquire whether he liked the work. When he finally awoke from his reverie and she repeated the question, he simply mumbled, 'No – it stinks.' Then she confessed to being the artist and he invited her out to dinner. He'd just celebrated his twenty-eighth birthday; she was two years younger.

After lunch at her apartment the following day, they had sex on the kitchen floor; in the golden afterglow, Jean-Claude told her all about his passion for the Côte d'Argent. Maybe it was the fear that he was about to lose his father which made him recount his magical memories of childhood holidays at the old house his father used to rent for a month each summer at Lacanau – 'the poor man's Arcachon' as Tante Colette, his mother's sister, always called it. Looking back now, they were the happiest days of his life: the worry-free days of swimming, fishing, beach games and adventures in the forests, shared with the innumerable relatives who used to descend on them from all over France – not to mention Tante Colette's wonderful meals.

So, there on Sophie's kitchen floor after their first lovemaking, Jean-Claude had been positively poetic about his wonderful childhood summers. She'd been enchanted and had roused him from his ecstatic nostalgia with a fervent promise that one day he *would* have his dream home by the Atlantic. During the following weeks, events moved rapidly: Christophe died, Sophie became pregnant, and her father – self-made millionaire Paul Charpentier – went ballistic. Jean-Claude and Sophie swiftly married anyway – Monsieur and Madame Charpentier neither attended the civil ceremony nor sent a present – and the newlyweds moved into the Margaux house that had been in Christophe's family for over a century. In less than a year, Jean-Claude's mother was also dead. That had been a relief for Sophie: Joséphine had clearly disliked her; baby Alexandre finally got his own room. Nevertheless, the house was still far too small for Sophie; to be fair, she didn't have much space to paint.

Five years later, Jean-Claude was receiving a decent salary as La Fayette's *maître de chai*, but with barely any savings or capital, except the Margaux cottage, the dream home had still not got off the ground. Sophie was becoming belligerent. Matters were not helped by her unsaleable macabre paintings, or the continued refusal of the Charpentiers to acknowledge Jean-Claude's existence – albeit they were now prepared to receive Sophie and their grandson in Paris. After one particularly stormy row during which Sophie threatened to 'go home', Jean-Claude finally went to see his bank manager. He was very understanding, but the bank had rules, and it really was in Jean-Claude's very best interests that he should not overwhelm himself with debt. The other banks he approached said more or less the same thing, but he just couldn't countenance the thought of disappointing Sophie: he loved her so much.

It was Sophie who suggested seeking a loan from his employer, Guy de Bondé. It was truly the last thing Jean-Claude wanted to do. Guy – the dear man had always insisted on informality and first names – had been like a second father to him since his earliest childhood memories, and although his generosity was legendary throughout the Médoc, to ask Guy to lend his young *maître de chai* two million francs to build a house on the other side of the peninsula! – well, it was impudent. But Sophie egged him on; she was like a dog with a bone.

The interview in Guy's study was a nightmare. After an embarrassed Jean-Claude had detailed the Le Porge project, the baron sat silently for some moments staring into space. Finally, he said: 'You must love Sophie very, very much, my boy. However, to be frank, I don't have that sort of capital lying around. ... But I can lend you half and give a guarantee to the bank for the balance. Just don't tell Henri – you know how he is.'

Jean-Claude was stunned: never in his wildest dreams had he expected such generosity. He dashed to his bank: the baron's munificence, the manager confirmed, was more than adequate to secure the necessary mortgage – naturally! Jean-Claude tried to phone Sophie on her mobile to give her the incredible news, but she was in Toulouse with clients and had switched it off; later, the battery must have gone dead. He'd been expecting a call from her hotel all through the dinner with Laura – he'd been so happy that evening – and then she turned up in the cellar.

So, the Le Porge project began traumatically. The cellar fiasco was bad enough, but barely had Guy signed the second mortgage and the bank's guarantee, when Alzheimer's began to reduce him to a state of horrifying premature senility. Now he was in a private institution in a Bordeaux suburb. More than eighteen months had passed since Jean-Claude had last seen him; it had been too upsetting. By all accounts, Henri had also stopped visiting.

*

'Poor Guy,' Jean-Claude murmured. He lit another Gauloises. Above the roof of the *cuvier*, which housed the château's celebrated oak vats, he could see the top floor of the main house, the magnificent neoclassical stone pile of Château La Fayette itself, where Henri – armed with his power of attorney – together with his wife, Nancy, and their two children, Benoît and Aliette, now lived in style. Jean-Claude sighed: things had definitely taken a turn for the worse since Henri's assumption of the estate's management. In truth, he reminded him of a chemistry master at school who used to interrogate any boy who'd spent more than two minutes in the toilets. What compounded matters was Henri's practice of speaking in the manner so beloved of many upper-class Bordelais – slowly and with a slight English accent, an affectation which even Guy himself had derided, but then their relationship had always been strained. Jean-Claude's parents had urged understanding: poor Henri's mother had died giving birth to him. Jean-Claude's sympathy, however, had been exhausted long ago, and in recent times he'd endeavoured to keep his dealings with Henri to a minimum. Mercifully, he spent much time travelling abroad – particularly in the USA – lavishly entertaining 'celebrities' with a view to getting La Fayette served at their tables.

'Think of Pétrus,' Henri was prone to remark whenever Jean-Claude failed to express sufficient enthusiasm for his marketing philosophy. 'There are still Bordelais who can remember when you could buy Pétrus at the corner shop for a few francs. It wasn't much more than decent, run-of-the-mill plonk. And now, Bourjois, if one can get hold of a bottle of the stuff at all, it will cost an arm and a leg. And do you know why, Bourjois? *Do you?*'

Jean-Claude would always look blank, even though he knew the answer and Henri's Pétrus story by heart.

'Well, I'll tell you. It's because Jean-Pierre Moueix was an inexhaustible promoter of Pétrus in the Sixties and got it served at the White House. Now it's allocated to the world's millionaires. Of course, most of them can't tell the difference between Pétrus and Coca-Cola – let alone Pétrus and La Fayette – but the point is, Bourjois, the only thing that matters to these people is the name on the label – "the brand" – and its image, not what's in the bottle.'

This kind of talk always made Jean-Claude bristle. It was anathema to a man whose roots were in the soil, and who'd had a lifelong love affair with the vine. Just once he'd had the temerity to remind Henri that, whatever its humble origins, Pétrus had been producing superb wine for decades, and certainly long before it ever graced the table of the American president. Old Jean-Pierre Moueix might have shocked the Bordelais with his brazen marketing gimmicks, but when all was said and done, he'd invested massively in his vineyards and had steadily raised the standards of all his wines to superlative levels; if they were not the best in the world, they were certainly amongst the very best. So, Henri couldn't hope to emulate Pétrus – or any of Bordeaux's other astronomically priced stars – unless he was prepared to invest in quality himself. And that meant reducing yields, new vine stock, new presses, new– But Henri would cut him short with a groan and a comment between gritted teeth about a bad workman blaming his tools.

20

It was strange, Jean-Claude reflected, as the stone walls of both the *chais* and *cuvier* became golden in the late evening sunlight, that when he and Henri were kids, Guy had been so keen on their being friends – encouraging them to play together in the house ... up in the attic. And then Henri, who was so wimpish and clearly detested him, had one tantrum too many and–

I always knew it wasn't an accident. Why didn't I tell the truth? Why did I try to protect the stuck-up git? ... Perhaps it would have been better if he had killed me. ...

Jesus! This label fiasco! What the hell am I going to do?

Jean-Claude looked hard at his watch: Henri's train from Paris could be late; he might dine in town, or–

He dropped his cigarette on the cobbles and stubbed it out. *I'm tired. I need to think straight. There's the God-awful Friday 'working lunch' with Henri tomorrow anyway, and perhaps the printer will have the lab report by then. ... Yes, I'll go home and tell Sophie **everything** – ask for her advice. Perhaps she'd love to move to California – especially if I got a better-paid job in one of their top 'wineries'. She'd be in her element with all those West Coast arty-farty people, and, by all accounts, Le Porge seems to hold little attraction for her anymore.*

*She's always saying I'm naive, but we'll sell the house somehow – **and** extinguish Guy's loan – **and** the guarantee. There has to be some idiot – a Parisian with more money than sense – who wants a house like that – 'by' the sea. What's ten kilometres to a Parisian?*

Yes, we'll emigrate and sever all links with La Fayette before the shit hits the fan. I bet Henri'll be over the moon to see the back of me, and then he can screw his inheritance to his heart's delight.

CHAPTER 3

Laura felt surprisingly happy, notwithstanding the miserable, sleepless night she'd endured at the Continental after Jean-Claude had chickened out of their dinner at Le Chapon Fin. But as daylight began to filter through the shutters, she'd told herself to get a grip: she still had the means to ensnare him. With a gurgling stomach reminding her that she'd not eaten since lunch the previous day, she was showered, dressed, and making her way to her favourite breakfast rendezvous by seven; the world's most delicious croissants awaited her at the Café Comédie.

To stroll through the streets of Bordeaux in the warm sunshine of a June morning makes one grateful to be alive, Laura enthused as she rounded the corner of Rue Montesquieu and paused to feast her eyes on Cours de l'Intendance's architectural splendours. The great thoroughfare, flanked on each side by the facades of some of the city's grandest palaces of commerce and former noblemen's townhouses, channelled her gaze eastwards along its gentle descent to the Garonne. Momentarily dazzled by the sunlight, she donned her sunglasses and focused on a delicious contrast of ancient and modern: this morning, the enchanting vista terminated with a towering white-painted cruise liner moored at the quayside, which, in consequence, blocked the usual view of the river's far bank. That this contemporary intrusion into a predominantly neoclassical scene should be a graceful ship, and not an office block demanding attention through calculated unconventionality, exemplified Bordeaux.

It seemed to Laura that every other city she knew in the world was constantly tearing itself apart: beloved landmarks disappeared overnight; bigger and better shopping malls erased entire blocks; highway 'improvements' were constantly under construction; and the locals often appeared as transient as their environment. But not in Bordeaux: hardly anyone or anything ever changed. Whenever she returned, so many familiar faces would greet her – and with all the warmth one would only expect from old friends. Waiters, barmen, store assistants, the Continental's cleaners – year after year they remained at their posts. Did they have jobs for life? Didn't they have ambitions to chance their luck in Paris, or even at a better establishment in Bordeaux itself? It was all so different to New York and Los Angeles – even smaller cities back in the States – where standing still for more than five minutes seemed to be an admission of criminal indifference to self-improvement.

'Stop the world I want to get off!' she whispered with a chuckle as she walked on.

Although many designer clothing boutiques now occupied the ground floors of Cours de l'Intendance's noble edifices, Laura was in no mood for window shopping. Filling her lungs with air richly smelling of freshly-made coffee escaping from the city's innumerable cafés, and of salt and seaweed from the Garonne's tidal waters, she strode purposefully down the street, regenerated as if by a powerful life force radiating from the buildings' golden stone; the angle of the early morning sun, together with its long shadows, highlighted their facades' magnificent details. She passed the house where Goya had spent his last years in painful exile, and then, as she always did, admired the monumental caryatids that supported the massive balconies of the seventeenth-century Hôtel de Pichon across the road; it was in this sumptuous residence that Louis XIV and his bride, Maria Theresa, had rested while travelling to Paris after their marriage at St-Jean-de-Luz on the Franco-Spanish frontier. Almost hypnotized by these splendours, Laura narrowly avoided a collision with a pedestrian-crossing beacon and discovered to her surprise that she'd already reached the Place de la Comédie. She grinned broadly and said aloud and unhesitatingly: 'Bordeaux, I love you! This is where I'm going to live.'

Crossing to the square's south side, she made for the Café Comédie. Clad in the customary white shirt, black trousers and ankle-length white apron, one of the waiters was arranging chairs and tables on the pavement. He looked up as she approached and beamed.

'*Bonjour*! *Quelle bonne surprise*! Welcome back, Miss Appleton. *Ça va*? How long are you staying this time?'

'I'm fine, Fabien,' Laura replied in French, shaking his hand, 'and how are *you*?' They exchanged pleasantries, and then, adopting a solemn expression, she said: 'I hope you've got plenty of croissants this morning – I'm starving.'

The waiter raised his eyebrows. 'And what were you up to last night to give you such an appetite?'

'Fabien!' she cried, pretending to scold him. 'If we were in politically-correct America–'

'You wouldn't be about to drink the delicious *Cuban* coffee we serve here, or savour the fantastic croissants which Madame has just brought from Bordeaux's best *pâtissier*. Ha!' Beaming mischievously at Laura, he opened the café's door for her, but she stood her ground, a look of horror on her face.

'You never told me the coffee was' – she lowered her voice and looked around – '... *Cuban*. Oh, my God!'

'You never asked. I suppose you'll never come back to the Comédie now you know.'

Laura moved to the open door. 'Well, I suppose as long as you don't tell the State Department ...'

Fabien shrugged. 'Er, I don't know. Perhaps we could arrange something. ... Maybe dinner at my place? ... Tonight?'

Laura couldn't contain her laughter any longer. She put her head around the door, spotted 'Madame' behind the counter, and shouted: 'Your waiter's blackmailing me, Jeanne. He says your coffee's Cuban, and that if I don't go out with him–'

Within seconds, Jeanne was at the door, kissing Laura's cheeks and gushing words of welcome.

While coffee, croissants, butter and jams were set before Laura at her favourite table by the window, two middle-aged men came and sat at an outside table, and Fabien went to take their order. Through the open doorway, Laura heard a distinctly haughty English voice bellow: 'Now, David, leave the ordering to me! We don't want a repetition of the near-disaster at the hotel in Tours, do we?'

'Frankly, Philip,' replied David with a note of pique, 'I rather enjoyed our breakfast of hot chocolate, *pain au chocolat*, and chocolate ice cream with hot chocolate sauce. And, judging by the amount you guzzled, so did you.'

For a few moments, Laura studied the two Britishers through the plate glass windows. Both clad in sports jackets, Viyella shirts, woollen ties, beige cavalry-twill trousers and tan Oxford brogues, they looked vaguely familiar – probably London wine merchants doing the rounds and feeling hopelessly naked without their pinstripe suits. 'Philip' and 'David' were going to have a roasting day in Bordeaux; she just prayed they didn't recognize her.

A table on the pavement would also have been Laura's preference on such a lovely morning before the Place de la Comédie became busy with traffic. However, having some important calls to make, she preferred the relative quiet and privacy of the café's air-conditioned interior. She polished off her first croissant, and then, at a few minutes past eight, tapped out the number of Jean-Claude's direct line at La Fayette. He answered almost immediately, just as Laura had anticipated: he was invariably the first person to start work in the *chais*.

'No problems getting to Margaux then this morning?' she snapped.

After a moment's hesitation, Jean-Claude said: '*Oh hello, Laura. How are you this morning?*'

'I'm fine but hungry, not having eaten last night. So, I'm at the Comédie stuffing my face with croissants. And *you?*' There was another brief pause; down the line, Laura thought she detected the sounds of a cigarette being lit. 'Are you smoking, Jean-Claude?'

'*Er ... yes. I'm fine too. Look, I'm sorry – very sorry – about last night, but what with the car and–*'

'Since when did you revert to that disgusting habit?'

'*Christ! You sound like Sophie. ... A while back – bit of pressure – bought a pack of Gauloises, then another. You know how it is.*'

'No, I don't actually, Jean-Claude.' She took a sip of coffee and watched Philip and David outside, eyeing suspiciously some *pains au chocolat* that had been set before them. 'What sort of pressure? I thought you sounded a bit down the last few times I phoned from the States.'

'*Nothing – I mean ... you know – the kind of stuff every* maître *has to worry about – winds, frosts, hail, bugs. It's been a lousy spring, Laura. ... And then there've been problems with the ancient machinery Henri won't replace, and–*'

'You mean the same perennial problems you've experienced ever since you took over from your dad. You've never let them get you down before, Jean-Claude, have you?' There was no response. 'So, what was wrong with the car?'

Having been thrown off guard by Laura's investigation of his smoking habits, he had to grope for an answer. '*Bit technical really.*'

'Try me, even though I'm only a dumb girl.'

'*Come on, Laura, you know I don't ... I'm not ... Carburettor – blocked and damaged filter. Fairly easy to fix – if you know what to unscrew and you've got the right parts handy.*'

'I see. So those breakdown guys had you back on the road quite quickly.'

'*Um, not really. They took ages getting to me – ages.*'

'At Margaux?'

'*Hmm?*'

'Where you broke down.'

Laura heard Jean-Claude suck viciously on his cigarette.

'*Er ...*'

'Or was it your living room at Le Porge?'

Silence.

'*Laura–*'

'Boy! I don't know how you can be so frightened of her, Jean-Claude. I mean, I know she hates my guts and sticks needles into some effigy of me, but your job and my business mean we *have* to meet from time to time, like all other great *maîtres de chai* and famous wine writers.'

'*I'm not a "great–"*'

'Oh, shut up! And where's your sense of humour gone? She can't–'

'*She? What are you talking about?*'

Laura dunked a piece of croissant in her coffee and held it above the cup while the excess drained off. 'For Christ's sake! I'm not stupid, Jean-Claude. Immediately after your call last night I realized Sophie had invented that story about the car breaking down. Honey, you're such a hopeless liar – hopeless! I told you not to tell her you were dining with me when we made the arrangements.'

Jean-Claude breathed a sigh of relief: the mist was clearing. '*It – it just slipped out.*'

'Christ!'

'*I'm sorry. I told her a week ago I'd be dining with Hugh Johnson, along with a few other* maîtres *in Bordeaux, and then at breakfast yesterday she said, "You won't be in for dinner tonight, will you? It's that bloody wine writer ..." And she paused, searching for the name. My mind was elsewhere. I'd forgotten the Hugh Johnson lie and just assumed she was being deliberately insulting – pretending to forget your name. So, I said, "Laura Appleton". She went mad, of course. It took me all day to pluck up the courage to phone you.*'

'I can imagine. Did she smash any of her vile paintings over your head?'

'*No, but she threatened to throw some in the fish pond.*'

'Best place for them, I should imagine. Actually, after salvage they might be quite saleable. Try it – water damage could only improve them.'

Jean-Claude managed a laugh. '*To be fair, you haven't seen her latest works. The collection's called* Les Orifices *– one hundred canvases, each one depicting an orifice – from different species.*'

Laura's hysterical laughter attracted the attention of Philip and David on the other side of the plate glass. They smiled. Looking like two naughty children with their unwiped lips and jowls covered in dark brown chocolate, Laura was wracked by fresh convulsions.

'Are her *Orifices* shocking? I mean–'

After recovering his composure, Jean-Claude said solemnly: '*Not really. To be honest, when Sophie first showed me the collection, I said, "You didn't tell me you'd got a commission from Dunkin Donuts." She could have killed me.*'

With Jeanne bellowing from the bar that her customer would not be allowed to leave without sharing the joke, Laura desperately tried to get back to the serious matters she wanted to discuss.

'We have to meet *very* soon,' she told him earnestly. 'I'm about to make some *really* important decisions – probably the most important of my life. Time is of the essence, Jean-Claude. I need ... I need your advice.'

'*Can't you give me some idea of what this is all about?*'

'Not over the phone. ... It's very personal. We need a couple of hours in private. If only you hadn't cried off last night.'

'*I'm so very sorry.*'

There was a pregnant pause.

'Look, I've got some meetings this morning here in town, but what if I join you for lunch around one? That little place on the river you took me to once ... near Lamarque, the day–'

'*Impossible. I've got a working lunch with the Almighty Henri.*' Jean-Claude's brief feelings of good humour evaporated.

'Dinner tonight?'

Jean-Claude groaned. '*Sorry. No can do. Sophie's invited some damned Parisian down for the weekend – owns one of the top galleries. She's trying to get him to exhibit her–*'

'Don't say that word again!'

'*– her **paintings**. I promised to be there and play the sommelier role at her intimate dinner party.*'

'This time I believe you.'

Jean-Claude thought hard for a few seconds. '*Um, what are you doing tomorrow? If it's fine, Sophie's taking her visitor down to the beach so he can feast his eyes on all the naked young men. I've told her I need to spend a couple of hours at La Fayette to catch up on some paperwork – which is true. You could drop by to taste the two-year-old wine we're bottling – OK, 2001 was not a brilliant year with the cool September and rain but I think some of us Médoc grands crus produced decent wine. Then we could go down to Lamarque for lunch – whatever.*'

Laura jumped at the offer. They agreed to meet at the château around twelve.

Just as she was about to ring off, Laura chirped: 'Oh I nearly forgot!'

'*Yes?*'

'I've brought you a bottle of wine from the States.'

'*Not another Californian Chardonnay? Or is it an Arkansas Cabernet Sauvignon? ... An Alaskan Gewürtztraminer?*'

'Ha, ha, ha! Very funny, you ungrateful snotty Frenchman. As a matter of fact, it's a bit of a puzzle.'

'*Oh?*'

'Hmm. It's a wine *you* should know very well.'

'*French?*'

27

'Uh-huh.'

'*Bordeaux?*'

'Uh-huh.'

'*Médoc?*'

'Getting warm.'

'*Margaux?*'

'Warmer and warmer.'

'*Come on, Laura, I've got work to do.*'

'Oh well! I was going to subject you to a blind tasting tomorrow and see what you came up with, but on reflection I wouldn't want to embarrass you. So, I'll tell you. It's a bottle of *your* wine.'

'*La Fayette?*'

'That's what it says on the label.'

'*Vintage?*'

'2000.'

'Christ! The first bottles were only dispatched to the States a few weeks ago.' Jean-Claude paused. 'What's the problem, Laura?'

She detected a slight hint of alarm in his voice. 'I just thought you'd like to see how your wine reacts to travelling across the Atlantic – and back, of course. I mean, I know all about water being turned into wine, but this is more like the miracle in reverse.'

'*Laura, what the hell are you talking about?*'

'Sorry! Don't want to spoil the fun. All will be revealed tomorrow. Have a nice day. *Ciao!*'

At La Fayette, in his cramped Spartan office carved out of a corner of one of the *chais* through judicious use of plasterboard partition walling, Jean-Claude slowly replaced the receiver and stared at the rows of wine bottles standing proudly to attention on top of his old metal filing cabinets. There were two on each side of the door, a door which was invariably wide open and through which he could look directly into the first-year *chai*. The bottles were for display purposes, like trophies commemorating all his hard work and achievements over many long seasons. There were one-and-a-half litre magnums, standard bottles of seventy-five centilitres, and baby half-bottles. Some contained the two-year-old vintage currently being bottled; others, the three best vintages from the previous ten years.

The bottles on the cabinet to the left of the door bore the restrained yet elegant label – *étiquette* – which had barely changed since the de Bondé family had acquired La Fayette during the 1820s. There were no representations of evocative pastoral scenes or artists' impressions of the noble architecture of the château itself; colourful bunches of grapes did not adorn the borders; the family name of the proprietors was not given top billing. In brief, the label was simplicity itself: the paper was white, and across the centre in fine black copperplate script appeared the name Château La Fayette; above, in gold, was a discreet representation of a baron's coronet; beneath the name was the year of the vintage in red, and below it was the standard nomenclature in black print: '*Grand Cru classé en 1855*' and '*Appellation Margaux Contrôlée*'. Finally, at the very bottom of the label in print worthy of an eye test, were the proprietor's details. It was no exaggeration to say that Jean-Claude loved this label: it admirably complemented the wine within the bottles; style, tradition, quality and breeding were encapsulated within its discreet motifs, print and colouring.

The two equally battered cabinets to the right of the door also doubled as display units, but these were for the estate's so-called 'second' wine. Their labels were almost identical to those of the first wine – the *grand vin* – save that they bore the name '*Maréchal de La Fayette*', and the '*Grand Cru*' statement was omitted. Most of the better vineyards of Bordeaux have long produced two – or even three – grades of wine, whether red or white, for it would be remarkable if a vineyard's grapes would all be of the same quality. Across the estate there are likely to be variations in soil type, drainage, and exposure to sun, wind and rain; pests and diseases may strike some vines but not others; harvesting will take place over many days – even weeks, depending on the size of the vineyard, its resources and the vagaries of the weather – with consequent variations in grape quality and ripeness; older vines generally produce better wine than young ones; and Bordeaux vineyards grow several grape varieties – sometimes up to four – so that when bottled, almost all the red wine, and much of the white, is a blend.

Indeed, it is the magic and mystery of the blending process, the *assemblage*, which constitutes much of the *maître de chai*'s art and genius. Consequently, when the *maître* undertakes the *assemblage* of the wine intended to be the château's highest quality product, there'll always be vats or barrels which fail to meet the required standards. The rest of the vineyard's production, therefore – assuming it's of a sufficient quality to be associated with the château's name at all – may be blended and bottled under one or more subsidiary labels. Otherwise, the wine may be disposed of to a merchant for the production of generic 'Bordeaux' without any other indication on the label as to the wine's source.

However, because of the superlative quality of Bordeaux's greatest vineyards, many of their second wines have generated impressive reputations of their own; in some vintages, they're even finer than the first wines of many renowned châteaux. There is, therefore, nothing second-class about the quality – or prices – of Carruades de Lafite or Les Forts de Latour, the second wines of the Bordeaux megastars Châteaux

Lafite-Rothschild and Latour. A very recent vintage of any one of them might retail at only a third of the price of its big brother, but even in Bordeaux's wine stores, one could still be looking at a price of at least £150 a bottle – in Britain or the States, much more.

Consequently, second wines are a big business. After all, in today's 'global market place' brands and image are everything: consumers regard a product as 'an Armani' be it branded Georgio Armani, Emporio Armani or Armani Jeans; it's much the same in the luxury wine market. And so, when a dinner party's hosts grace their table with a bottle of Forts de Latour, they don't lie when they confirm that it's from the great Château Latour; nor do they insult their guests' intelligence with a lecture about affordable 'second wines'.

As for Château La Fayette, the canny de Bondés began producing their Maréchal as long ago as the 1950s, the name reflecting the military connections of the château's namesake: the vineyard was founded by a relative of the famous Marquis de La Fayette, who, during the American War of Independence, commanded the forces which finally entrapped Lord Cornwallis at Yorktown in July 1780. Now, with the brand firmly established, the estate's one hundred and fifteen acres of vines were producing around eighty thousand bottles of Maréchal annually, just ten thousand fewer than the average production of the first wine – figures which underlined Jean-Claude's efforts to improve the latter's quality. And with Maréchal regularly commanding prices higher than those of many Bordeaux *grands vins*, Jean-Claude could also take pride in his second wine. Yet, despite all Henri de Bondé's marketing strategies and hype, even La Fayette's *grand vin* still didn't command the prices of Bordeaux's Premier Division megastars, even though many critics opined that in its best vintages it could almost match the latter in quality terms. So, in downtown Bordeaux, a good recent vintage was retailing at around the equivalent of £50 a bottle.

Still staring at the displays of his two wines, Jean-Claude shook his head from side to side. Then he closed his eyes and sighed heavily. If only Sophie had come home last night, he reflected, his worries would now be shared, and he'd no longer be wandering alone in this living nightmare. But the house had been empty when he finally arrived at Le Porge. Sophie phoned around ten to say she was staying in Bordeaux with her antique-dealer friend Cathérine, with whom she'd just enjoyed the latest Pedro Almodovar movie at the Gaumont; Jean-Claude had no idea who 'Almodovar' might be. As it was late, and tomorrow she had to collect Alexandre from his boarding school *and* her Parisian art dealer from the station, she'd decided that it made sense to accept Cathérine's offer to stay over. Jean-Claude raised no objections.

Although he'd always disliked Cathérine, whom he regarded as shallow and mercenary, it was somewhat irrational to blame her for exacerbating his predicament. But he still felt angry that she'd helped to keep Sophie away from him at this critical juncture. And now he was compounding his problems with more lies to Laura – although he didn't seem to be such a bad liar after all: she'd been completely taken in by his story of Sophie's 'jealousy' – almost as if she'd wanted to believe it! But how many more lies would he have to tell?

Jean-Claude opened his eyes and focused once more on his beloved bottles. 'Château La Fayette … and Maréchal de La Fayette,' he whispered sadly. Then he buried his face in his hands. 'Laura knows!' he cried, '– she's worked it out! … I'll kill Henri for this.'

CHAPTER 4

It was almost eleven-thirty when Laura reached the venue for her next appointment, 136 Cours Georges Clemenceau, and scanned the professional plates on either side of the impressive gated entrance. She was hot and thirsty: the sun was now fierce and the temperature had soared since her delicious breakfast at the Café Comédie. Rushing from one *immobilier* – estate agent – to another around the city had compounded her exhaustion, but she was a stickler for punctuality, even if Bordeaux's realtors were not. Nor did they seem to possess much in the way of proactive commerciality. In truth, her mounting frustration was being exacerbated not only by the heat, but also by the depressing realization that there were very few properties on the market of the type she was looking for, and, moreover, at a price she could afford.

Laura finally located a brass plate – ominously in need of a good polish – announcing that the firm of Lampre & Fils was situated on the fourth floor. A stone-vaulted passageway led from the busy street into the cobbled courtyard of a grand eighteenth-century town house. After passing through a pair of open French windows, she was presented with two means of access to the fourth floor – an uncarpeted stone spiral staircase and a miniscule lift of uncertain age; she chose the stairs. It was a depressing ascent: everything was dusty and grubby; the woodwork and bare walls were in desperate need of a lick of paint; unshaded bulbs dangled from the ceilings, activated in typical French fashion by occasional wall-mounted switches; and, as if to underline the building's apparently straightened circumstances, the air was rank with the odours of dampness. While mounting the final flight to the fourth floor, the lights went out, and no amount of button pressing would reactivate them. She began to wonder what sort of lawyers, doctors, dentists and realtors could inhabit such a dump.

A notice on Lampre & Fils's frosted glass door instructed visitors to ring and enter. Having complied, Laura found herself in a drab reception area where two secretaries – both smoking – sat before vintage word processors. Her heart sank: there was little in the way of standard real-estate paraphernalia in evidence, such as glossy colour brochures of prime properties on the agency's books, or artists' impressions of new developments.

'*Oui?*' murmured one of the secretaries, without looking away from her screen. Assuming she was addressing someone else, Laura didn't respond. She was about to introduce herself when the same secretary tutted, looked up, stared at her malevolently and barked in French: 'Well, do you want something?'

Laura's hackles rose. In perfect French, she said: 'Yes. I'm Laura Appleton. I have an appointment with Monsieur Pierre Lampre. Perhaps you'd be kind enough to inform him I'm here?'

The secretary pointed to an open door. 'Go straight through. He's expecting you.'

Although Monsieur Lampre's office was no better furnished, there were some faded artists' impressions of an out-of-town shopping development on his walls. But, judging by the French family-saloons dotted around its landscaped exterior, and the fashions of the happy shoppers, the premises – if ever completed – would have now been standing for over thirty years. Lampre, who was intently reading some papers on his cluttered desk, looked about sixty. Yet, with a full head of thick silver hair, finely chiselled features and tanned skin, he was still a good-looking man. His clothes were redolent of a university senior common room – striped shirt, paisley tie, and lightweight blue summer blazer; the pipe he held in one hand enhanced the professorial image. Perhaps he could be of some use after all, Laura mused: his offices might be the pits, but several Bordeaux contacts had strongly recommended him. 'He knows everyone,' she'd been told more than once; someone had said enigmatically that he was 'a bit of a fixer'.

'Bonjour, Monsieur Lampre,' Laura bellowed from the doorway as she strode purposefully towards him, right hand outstretched.

Lampre shot up from his desk, revealing to Laura's surprise that he sported dark blue jeans. He was tall and had the air of a man who was determined to keep in shape.

'Ah, Mademoiselle Appleton! Please forgive me. I was engrossed in something *rather* important. Do sit down. You really should have been announced. Hopeless secretaries! So difficult to find the right sort these days. Must apologize. Is French all right? I do speak a spot of English, but–'

'French is fine, Monsieur Lampre.'

'*Pierre*, please.'

Laura smiled. 'Pierre. And I'm Laura.'

After a few more pleasantries and some weather trivia, Lampre got down to business; there was no offer of refreshments.

'So, you want to buy a vineyard, preferably in the Médoc, but failing that, you'd settle on something in St-Emilion or even Pomerol. Your last choice would be an estate in Graves – Pessac-Léognan to be precise.' Lampre stared at Laura with a twinkle in his eye. 'Do you know anything about wine or vineyards, my dear?'

In less than five minutes, Lampre received a succinct summary of Laura's career; there was no false modesty.

'That's *very* interesting,' he said with what Laura thought was a note of irony, 'but, in brief, you don't have any experience of *owning* or *managing* a vineyard – of *producing* wine, do you?'

'I–'

'Of course, in a sense I have a vested interest in selling you any old thing and making a nice commission – the more expensive the property the better. Dear me, it's such a fad at present, such a status symbol. Insurance companies, banks, fashion houses, clothes designers, film stars – even popular musicians – they all want to get in on the act. They think there's something wonderfully upmarket – one is tempted to say "noble" – even "aristocratic" – about owning a plot of soil laid out with rows of vines, especially if there's a large old house tied up with them. Such vanity! But then so many of these estates – at least in *our* part of the world – *are* associated with some titled family or other, as well you know. I would even hazard to suggest that some people believe they can buy respectability simply by acquiring a vineyard, a sort of magical entrance ticket to society. It's strange, isn't it, how the sentence "I own a vineyard" can have such an extraordinary effect on people – particularly the sort of people who introduce themselves with that ghastly question, "And what do you do for a living?". I don't know about you, my dear, but I always seem to end up sitting next to such people on trains and planes. Luckily, when I tell them I'm an estate agent, that's usually the end of the conversation. If I'm feeling particularly antisocial, I say I'm an accountant.'

Laura's blood was beginning to boil. 'I don't need a *vineyard* to buy my way into society, Pierre. Wine is my life. I want to produce it – good wine – excellent wine – the best.'

'Yes, yes! I'm sure! But in my rambling way, I'm just trying to make two points. First, because so many fools from all four corners of the earth have invaded Bordeaux in the last twenty years or so, prices have rocketed for the sort of estate you're looking for. Frankly, for what you're prepared to pay, Laura, you wouldn't be able to buy a cabbage patch in the Médoc – or, indeed, in any of your other preferred locations. Even the Graves region is riding high now. To be blunt, you've missed the boat. If only you'd come knocking on my door a decade ago. ... Mind you, if you're prepared to start from scratch – you know, buy some barren plot of land, plant new vines and wait several years until you have a marketable product, like the Rothschilds at Château Clarke back in the Seventies ... but then you'll have no income – let alone profits – for years and years.'

'I couldn't operate on that basis, Pierre. I need to buy a going concern.'

'I thought so. Incidentally, my dear, did you know Lafite didn't make a profit until 1948, a century after the Rothschilds bought it?'

Laura thought Lampre was beginning to sound more and more like a bank manager. 'What was your second point, Pierre?' she enquired glumly.

'My second point? ... Ah, yes. Well, perhaps – just perhaps, Laura – you're allowing your heart to rule your head. You're a very successful woman. Maybe you should stick with what you know best, and not risk all your capital on a highly speculative venture in a foreign country. I mean, if you're *really* set on a change of direction, why aren't you thinking of a vineyard in the USA?'

Laura smiled enigmatically. 'I have my reasons, Pierre. In any event, Bordeaux is simply the best.'

'Well, I can't disagree with you on *that* point! A most refreshing admission from an American, I must say, although I suspect from a few telltale signs that ... Well, as a man old enough to be your grandfather and who's been married three times, *and* who's had more mistresses than was good for him, I think I know a few things about affairs of the heart.' He sighed. 'Anyway, these little signs suggest to me that your desire to invest in Bordeaux also has something to do with a romantic attachment. Am I right?'

Laura blushed. 'I ... I really don't think–'

'Enough said! Well, that proves my point about hearts ruling heads, doesn't it?' Lampre tutted. 'You must be practical – realistic. Yes, you're wealthy, but not so rich that you can afford to lose all your capital. And if you want to make a name for yourself as a wine producer, you're going to have to devote almost all – if not *all* – of your time and efforts to your vineyard ... at least for a few years. You can forget about writing, TV shows and all that sort of stuff, I'm afraid.

'And what about a *maître de chai*?' he continued. 'You certainly can't do *that* job. You'll need a damned good chap, believe me, unless you're happy to produce plonk – which I'm sure you're not.'

'I'm *not*. ... As a matter of fact, I have a brilliant *maître* in mind. He's – he's almost agreed to join me.'

'"*Almost*"?'

Rising from her seat, Laura snapped: 'Monsieur Lampre – Pierre – I'm grateful for all your advice and concern about my future, but my mind is made up. By hook or by crook I'm going to own a vineyard and make fine wine if it's the last thing I do, and whether you help me or not. So, if you've no properties on your books–'

'Excellent! What spirit! Just what I wanted to hear. Now sit down and listen.' Lampre glanced at his watch. 'Good Lord! Two minutes to twelve already! I'll be late for lunch. The lady will be *most* upset.'

Laura sat down with a groan. 'Lunch! You French and your stomachs! I've travelled almost four thousand miles for an eleven-thirty appointment and now you tell me that–'

'Premières Côtes de Bordeaux!' Lampre blasted, rocketing out of his chair like a jack-in-the-box. He bounded across the room to a pile of papers perched precariously on the mantelpiece of an impressive marble fireplace.

Startled by the sudden activity, Laura followed his movements with obvious bemusement. 'What about Premières–?' she began irritably, but Lampre had no time for interruptions.

'Just a minute!'

Having found what he was looking for, he yanked a piece of paper out of the pile causing a minor avalanche, and marched towards Laura waving it enthusiastically.

'Very attractive area on the other side of the Garonne – south-east of Bordeaux – around Langoiran and Cadillac. Quite hilly. Reminds me a bit of the English Cotswolds. Do you know the Cotswolds, Laura?'

'I–'

'Huge changes there – the Premières Côtes, not the Cotswolds of course. The vineyards are upgrading sharply. Quality and value are the key words. Largely merlot grapes for the red, you know, like Pomerol. Look at Château Reynon, for example. Are you familiar with Reynon?'

'Er, no. I–'

'Marvellous! – both the red and white. Oh, the *white*! So fragrant – from old Sauvignon vines, you know. Château de Haux is now Danish owned, while Château Carsin's new owners are Finns, would you believe?' Lampre thrust his piece of paper into Laura's hands. 'I think this could be the perfect place for you, my dear – *perfect!*'

'But I really don't want to be in the Premières Côtes. No one in the States has ever heard of–'

'But that's the whole point, Laura. Don't you see? It's just being discovered – *now*. You've a chance to get your feet on the first rung of the ladder. Properties there are still affordable, and the potential for making excellent wine is staggering.' He violently tapped the paper he'd given her. 'Read that – the particulars of Château Belle-Mère.'

'Château *Mother-in-Law*!' spluttered Laura in English. 'You must be joking!'

'I jest not, dear lady. Thirty-five hectares – about eighty-six English acres – of excellent vines, sixteen of red and nineteen of white, producing superb red, white and rosé wines. Of course, you may wish to rationalize. Stunning eighteenth-century house at the heart of the estate. Excellent new equipment in the *cuvier*. Option to buy adjoining land for expansion. Anyway, it's all there in black and white. Go and have a good lunch, read and digest, and then if you're interested – as I'm sure you will be – we can make an appointment and pop out to see the place.'

Before she realized what was happening or could protest, Lampre was lifting Laura by the elbow from her chair and steering her towards the door.

'But I really don't want ... I mean ... How much are they asking for this place and why are they selling?'

Dismissively, Lampre waved a hand in the air as they rushed through the secretaries' domain – the two women were also in the process of frantically vacating the premises – and struck an expression of mild shock. 'It's *very* affordable! Slap bang in your price range. Oh, you may need a *small* loan, but we can sort that out. I know many bank managers.'

They'd reached the lift and Lampre jabbed the call button.

'What do you mean, "a small loan"?' asked Laura suspiciously. 'How small?'

Lampre snorted. 'Damned lift! Takes for ever. I'm sure your prospective *maître de chai* will adore Belle-Mère. I don't suppose he's currently employed at your alma mater, so to speak, Château La Fayette, is he? You did say you'd studied there, didn't you?'

Laura's mouth fell open. 'I – I–'

The lift groaned to a halt, and, as its door creaked open, Lampre pushed her in.

'Bourjois is indeed a brilliant young man, my dear. Henri de Bondé would be quite lost without him. So sad about poor Guy, of course.'

Laura stared wide-eyed at Lampre, who remained standing in the corridor. 'Jean-Claude – Monsieur Bourjois – knows *nothing* of my plans, Pierre, I assure you. Look, I trust our discussions will be kept confidential?'

Lampre struck an expression of exaggerated outrage. '*Naturally*! Good Lord, I've been in practice in this city for almost forty years, dear lady! I am a man of honour. And now I bade you *à bientôt*. No doubt you'll be in touch after lunch.'

Laura was confused. 'Aren't you coming down in the elevator? And why *are* the owners selling?'

37

Lampre rolled his eyes. 'Use the elevator? Certainly not! At my age I need all the exercise I can get. Anyway, it's always breaking down. ... They've gone bust – the owners. The bank's foreclosed.'

And then the door creaked shut, Lampre disappeared, and Laura found herself in total darkness: the light bulb in the lift, like everything else at 136 Cours Georges Clemenceau, needed replacing.

As the lift descended, Laura could hear rapid footsteps clattering down the stone spiral staircase and assumed she'd intercept Lampre on the ground floor. However, when the door opened and she emerged into the sunlight streaming through the French windows, there was neither sight nor sound of him. Determined to catch him up, she rushed across the courtyard and through the vaulted passageway, but when she reached Cours Georges Clemenceau, he was nowhere to be seen. Hot, frustrated and thirsty, she decided to go somewhere for a drink and possibly a bite to eat. Anyway, with almost its entire population at lunch, the city would be dead for the next two hours. 'When in Rome,' she muttered. A groan followed: she realized she was still clutching Château Belle-Mère's particulars. Irritably, she thrust them into her portmanteau, and, on the spur of the moment, decided to treat herself at the Café Régent; it was just a couple of minutes away at the corner of Clemenceau and Place Gambetta.

When Laura arrived, the terrace was already packed, but in view of the heat and the noise from the seething traffic, she was more than happy to sit in the air-conditioned interior. An impeccably attired waiter showed her to a table towards the rear of the wood-panelled restaurant, where she gratefully sank into the proffered chair and ordered a bottle of Badoit, her favourite sparkling water. Within seconds, the waiter was filling her glass with as much ceremony as if serving a great wine. She gulped it down and picked up the menu.

The table to her right had been free when she arrived, but as she studied the salads which the Régent had to offer, she heard a waiter say: 'Well, monsieur, is *this* table any better?'

'I suppose so,' a man's voice boomed. 'I really cannot abide sitting underneath air conditioning units which attack one with such violent and freezing gusts that one might just as well be lunching alfresco at the North Pole. Christophe would have known that. Now, be a good chap and ask Christophe to bring me a *coupe de champagne* before I die of thirst.'

The French was excellent but spoken with an unmistakable English accent. It was a voice which Laura knew all too well. 'There goes my quiet lunch,' she murmured with mixed feelings as she peeked over the top of her menu. She sighed and put it down. 'Hello, Quincy. What a very ... *pleasant* surprise. I was wondering when we'd bump into each other.'

Quincy Dubloon was in his mid-fifties, but at six-foot four and weighing around fourteen stone, he still looked like a man who could put up a creditable performance on the rugby field with players half his age. And with thick dark hair, sparkling chestnut eyes and a ruddy outdoor complexion, many people would have found him handsome. Born and raised in East Africa during the final days of Empire, Quincy had been led down the prosaic route of English public school and Cambridge. At undistinguished Lloyd College, which selected him solely for the purpose of boosting its mediocre rugby team, Dubloon chose to read geology: he had vague ideas of prospecting in exotic parts of the globe; the life would be tough, exciting and occasionally dangerous. But geology turned out to be a rather difficult subject, while his fellow geologists were a frighteningly academic bunch devoted to hiking and youth hostels.

But for his first season of May Balls, Dubloon could easily have degenerated into a fully paid-up member of the beer-swilling rugby fraternity. Requiring a female partner, big-boned Pam Hudson came to the rescue. A first-year geology undergraduate who fitted the department's ethos perfectly, Pam played hockey for Newnham; persons of a generous disposition might have described her as 'comely'. When Quincy swallowed his pride and invited Pam to Lloyd's ball, she accepted heartily. And, thanks to her foresight in securing the key to Newnham's boathouse – she'd had no qualms in exploiting the Captain of Rowing's crush on her – Quincy was finally able to lose his virginity, once they'd tired of the dancing.

There was no romance on either side, simply lust. After all, they'd nothing in common – certainly not their preferences for alcoholic beverages: Pam was a dedicated wine drinker. Frankly, she would never have considered membership of the Wine Society but for its dashing chairman's proactive recruitment drive during her first week at Cambridge. Vincent de Forgeron, as the eldest son of the fifteenth Marquis de Forgeron, was the heir to more than three hundred acres of assorted vineyards around Bordeaux. After introducing herself at his freshers' event 'stall' and making polite enquiries about membership, Pam was pleasantly surprised to discover that he was not at all stuck-up; on the contrary, he was positively charming and appeared keen to befriend her. He also emitted all the vibrations of a man who wanted to be dominated by a strong woman. Within a few hours, Pam was sampling various Forgeron wines in the sitting room of the small but elegant house which Vincent's anglophile father had rented for him in the neighbouring village of Grantchester. When she was sufficiently tipsy and ready for sex, Vincent tentatively suggested that some strokes across his buttocks with a leather belt could be pleasurable. Unhesitatingly, Pam obliged. A few weeks later, she was installed as Secretary of the Wine Society.

By the time Quincy was introduced to the carnal delights Pam had to offer, she and Vincent were actively seeking fresh blood to liven up their Grantchester sessions. So, one evening, Pam persuaded Quincy to accompany her to a Wine Society meeting. He found Vincent charming and witty, a welcome change from the geology department's tedious bores. And as Quincy tried to learn how to hold a wine glass properly and the correct way to spit, he analysed his current status and concluded that he really had to broaden his circle of friends and his intellectual pursuits. Yes, he loved sport, but even at the rugby-crowd parties there were people who talked about books, music and art, firing names at him like Hesse, Sartre, Stockhausen and Klimt. And when some of his friends ridiculed such people afterwards with baffling comments like, 'Steppenwolf is crap, if you ask me,' or 'Cassals makes Rostropovitch sound like an amateur in his recording of the Elgar,' Quincy realized that they weren't the philistines they pretended to be. Such observations compounded his fears that his place at Cambridge had been a horrible administrative error which might at any time be discovered by an overzealous clerk.

When the wine tasting concluded, Quincy offered to help with the clearing up; Vincent expressed his gratitude by inviting him and Pam to dine at Grantchester the following Saturday. Thanks to Vincent's culinary skills, it was an excellent meal, and some very fine wines were served. Later, after brandy and cigars had been consumed by all three diners, Quincy discovered that in certain respects he actually enjoyed sex with an extra participant, albeit he suspected two women would be a lot better.

That summer, while Pam spent her vacation working in her father's chain of off-licences in and around Canterbury – Mr Hudson expected his daughter to earn her keep – Quincy found himself swimming, sunbathing and sailing with his new French friend at the Forgerons' Cap Ferret summer house. There were all the ingredients for a truly hedonistic experience: youth, wealth, privilege, sun and sea – not to mention drugs and plenty of sex. At the beginning of September, thanks to the hot, dry summer having accelerated the ripening of the grapes, Quincy joined Vincent and the rest of the Forgeron family in St-Julien to prepare for the grape harvest, the vendange. The Médoc enchanted Quincy – so unlike the dull, bourgeois world of his retired and repatriated parents in Twickenham, with their meals of over-roasted meats and boiled vegetables, golf club dinner dances and bridge parties. The Médoc was a glorious anachronism, an almost feudal society of patrician aristocratic landowners in their grand residences loyally served by earthy folk united by a common purpose – the production of wine, including the world's greatest, wines that were seducing him with ever increasing power. It was, he concluded, an outpost of civilization in a vulgar world.

By the time the *vendange* finally began, Quincy felt he'd found his Arcady. He envied Vincent so much that he would have done anything to change places with him – even better, to join him in the Médoc. In truth, he could only bear the thought of returning to England and his geology studies because Vincent would be accompanying him, coupled with the not unreasonable assumption that, if he played his cards right, he'd be returning to Bordeaux on a regular basis.

When Vincent graduated the following summer, the Wine Society's members unanimously elected Quincy as his successor; Pam was content to remain the faithful secretary. He continued to play rugby, and the combination of sporting prowess, good looks, and Wine Society chairmanship proved a winning formula for attracting female admirers. Consequently, Pam became redundant. In any event, she'd been adopted by an existing *ménage à trois* of postgraduate philosophers – two males and one female – who shared a terraced house. It had resulted in her spraying aerosol paint on women sporting fur coats.

Back in France, Vincent also found new friends and partners. In consequence, the phone calls between Bordeaux and Cambridge diminished. When Quincy took the initiative and tentatively sought an invitation to St-Julien, none was proffered: Vincent talked about his tremendous workload. After three months' silence, Quincy finally realised the friendship was over. He was hurt, but his memories of Bordeaux were not wholly tarnished.

Early in his final year, Quincy began to investigate the possibility of a wine-related job after graduation. He swiftly secured interviews with some leading London merchants; there was even an offer from one. But Quincy's father baulked at both the idea of his son starting his career as a junior salesman at Berry Brothers on St. James's Street, as well as the initial salary. Strings were pulled and a position was procured in merchant banking. Thus, after scraping home with a Third, Quincy moved on to the City.

It was on the Tube one evening, returning to his glum Hammersmith flat after a particularly tedious day at the bank, that Quincy found himself sitting opposite Pam Hudson. He was embarrassed; she was not. Only eighteen months had passed since they'd received their degrees – hers was a First – but Pam had changed dramatically: she could now have been a candidate for Business Woman of the Year. In just a few minutes Quincy learned that Pam's mother had murdered her father with a kitchen knife and then killed herself with an overdose. In consequence, Pam had inherited not only the family home in Canterbury, but also the Hudson chain of off-licences. She'd just spent an afternoon with her City solicitors; they were handling the sale of the off-licences to a national chain.

'What are you going to do?' asked Quincy in shock, '... travel the world, I suppose.'

'Certainly not!' snapped Pam indignantly. 'I'm negotiating to buy Boxcar & Greenbacks, the Pall Mall wine merchants – you know – founded in 1760 and all that. They've got a Royal Warrant, and–'

'Yes, Pam, I know B & G.'

'And I'm launching a new magazine for wine buffs. I'm thinking of calling it *Wine Wisdom*. Want a job, Quincy?'

And so it was that at the age of twenty-three, Quincy became *Wine Wisdom*'s editor and Pam's employee.

With complete confidence in his abilities, Pam gave Quincy a free hand in running *Wine Wisdom* while she concentrated on bringing Boxcar & Greenbacks into the twentieth century. Quincy did not disappoint her: liberated from his banking straitjacket, he embarked upon his new career with boundless enthusiasm. It only took a couple of years for *Wine Wisdom* to become the market leader in its field, thereby knocking its two main competitors, *Carafe* and *Goblet*, from their staid pedestals. Their gentlemanly styles had no place in the pages of *Wine Wisdom*: Quincy was going to call a spade a spade; diplomatic epithets and coded messages would not be used to describe second- or third-rate wines from once great vineyards that had been coasting for years; wines from the New World would be investigated thoroughly and objectively and not treated with undisguised condescension; and wine-world gossip would also play a significant part in generating *Wine Wisdom*'s healthy circulation figures. Unsurprisingly, Quincy was soon charming viewers of the BBC's *Wine and Dine* programme; young, dynamic, handsome and with a deep, sonorous 'Oxbridge' voice, the ratings soared! Then came his highly successful series of pocket-size *How To* books: *How to Buy Wine, How to Store Wine, How to Serve Wine* and *How to Wine and Dine*. And wherever he lunched or dined – gratis, naturally – he was invariably accompanied by a beautiful young woman – often a celebrity in her own right.

Meanwhile, a powerful combination of marketing whizz-kids, financial consultants and venture capitalists had persuaded Pam that after two hundred years of impeccable trading as suppliers of fine wines to the monarchy, Boxcar & Greenbacks possessed almost inexhaustible reserves of valuable yet unexploited goodwill. Accordingly, an extensive chain of 'B&G' wine shops stocking the finest wines was launched across England. But with overextended borrowings when the banking crisis hit, Pam's empire went into receivership, the Royal Warrant was revoked, and what was left of Boxcar & Greenbacks' goodwill evaporated. Following a nervous breakdown, Pam retreated to a former crofter's cottage in the Outer Hebrides; Quincy bought *Wine Wisdom*. He went on to host his own television programme, *Let's Open A Bottle!*, and to acquire Woopston Parva Hall – a William-and-Mary manor house in Wiltshire – and an apartment in one of Bordeaux's grandest eighteenth-century residences on exclusive Cours de Tournon.

Asserting that he enjoyed his freedom too much, Quincy remained a bachelor; certainly, he appeared to have an insatiable desire for young attractive women. And yet, after a few months – if not sooner – even the most sexually adventurous female would begin to bore him; the chase was always so much more exciting than the kill, he claimed. Laura Appleton bewitched him from the moment he first set eyes on her while she was still a junior employee at Plinth, Toke & Hirsh: she'd been assisting at a wine tasting in New York; he was the guest speaker. Used to getting his own way, he was put out when she declined his dinner invitation. Over the years, when their paths crossed, he'd made several further attempts to start the seduction process, but all had proved unsuccessful. And, as is often the way with such things, the more she rebuffed him, the greater became his obsession to conquer her. It never crossed his mind that she had no sexual interest in him whatsoever.

*

At the Régent, Quincy's heart had gone into overdrive; he didn't even need to put a face to the voice, such was the way Laura's self-confident yet sonorous American tones had always affected him. In truth, it was one of the most erotic voices he'd ever heard.

'Laura! How absolutely *marvellous*!' Heads turned as Quincy rose rapidly from his seat and darted to her side with impressive agility. They kissed each other's cheeks. '*Marvellous*!' he repeated, shaking his head from side to side with joyous incredulity. 'What luck! What providence! Would you do me the honour of allowing me to lunch with you, my dear?'

He towered over her, she thought, like a vulture about to swoop upon its unsuspecting prey. 'Of course, Quincy.' She really had no option.

'Capital! Capital!'

As Quincy took his seat, Laura felt the table shrink, as if transmogrifying into something designed for a child's nursery, a feeling compounded by the spectacle of Quincy's huge hands absent-mindedly rearranging the cutlery before him.

A waiter materialized with a glass of champagne. 'Ah, at *last*!' bellowed Quincy. 'Where *have* you been hiding, Christophe? *Ça va*? What are you drinking, Laura?' he added before the waiter could reply. He spied the water. 'Good Lord! No aperitif? You're not on one of those faddy American diets, I hope? Champagne? – a Lillet? – or do you want to go straight in with a bottle of the old vino? My treat, of course.'

Laura sighed. 'I've got a lot on today, Quincy. I need a clear head – especially in this heat.'

'Tish and tosh! Come on, a *coupe de champagne* won't harm you. If anything, it'll *clear* your head and boost your decision-making faculties.'

'Really, Quincy, I–'

'Bloody hell! You're supposed to be a wine buff, Laura. You're in Bordeaux!'

She knew Dubloon: there'd be no peace until he got his way. She'd just take a few sips of the champagne. And she didn't like those words 'supposed to be'.

'Oh, all right, Quincy. I'll–'

'Good girl! A *coupe de champagne* for madame,' he roared triumphantly at Christophe. 'Now,' he continued like an excited child on a birthday treat to an ice cream parlour, 'what are we *eating*?'

Laura stared pointlessly at the menu: she'd already chosen but feared Dubloon would veto that choice as well. She looked up to discover that her breasts appeared to be hypnotizing him; he didn't avert his gaze.

'You're more beautiful than ever, my dear.'

'And you never change, Quincy. I'm having the salad with *gésiers*.'

'Excellent choice! And to follow?'

The waiter set a glass of champagne beside Laura's right hand; her nails were drumming a violent rhythm on the white tablecloth. 'That's it,' she said resignedly. 'I'm just having a salad.' She lifted her glass. 'Cheers!'

'Cheers – and may your visit to Bordeaux be a *great* success!' Quincy flashed a smile and took a healthy mouthful of champagne. 'Ah, jolly good! I feel better already. Now, this salad nonsense – the rack of lamb's *very* good here, you know. I can thoroughly–'

'I'm having a salad, Quincy.'

He pouted unconvincingly. 'Oh, very well. I'll have the *carré d'agneau* and forego one of the Régent's delicious starters.'

'For heaven's sake, have what you want! You haven't even looked at the menu yet.'

'Don't need to – know it like the back of my hand. Maybe I'll persuade you to have a pudding.'

Laura groaned.

'Now, as you're having duck – well, duck *salad* – and I'm having lamb, I think a good Médoc – nothing extravagant mind you – would be in order. How about–?'

'Quincy! I've already told you. Today I'm–'

'Good gracious! You Americans can be so excitable ... and inflexible. All right, no wine for the Great American Wine Expert. ... I'll never be able to drink a whole bottle on my own.'

'Jesus! Sometimes you're like a spoilt child, Quincy. Have a *half*-bottle.'

'Sticks and stones, my dear.'

'Stop saying "my dear" all the time. It's so ... *chau*vinistic – so *patron*izing. You weren't born in the nineteenth century, were you? And you're not my grandfather, although you're old enough–'

The waiter was hovering to take their order.

When Quincy came to the choice of wine he said: 'Now, young man, don't try to convince me that you have any excellent half-bottles, because I've tried them all and know better.'

'Yes, Monsieur Dubloon.'

'And madame doesn't desire wine today – even though she's one of America's *greatest* wine experts – so there's no point in choosing something splendid or expensive which you and your colleagues will end up guzzling in the kitchens.'

Laura pretended to play a violin. 'Oh, come off it, Quincy!' she sniggered. 'I've never known you to drink less than a bottle at *any* meal.'

'Wicked child! If we weren't friends I'd be tempted to sue.'

Laura was on the point of riposting when the waiter looked sadly at her and said in English: 'I'm so sorry, Miss Appleton, that there is nothing on our list of wines which appeals to your refined senses.'

Quincy guffawed. Laura scowled at him and then smiled sweetly at the waiter, who she now realized was really rather attractive. 'You know my name?'

'But of course! I recognized you immediately upon your entrance to our establishment. I have all your DVDs. The *Temples du Vin* series is *formidable*! They also have been helping with my English.'

'It's excellent.'

'Thank you.'

Quincy groaned. 'Oh *please*! May I order the wine now?'

'Yes, yes! – of course, Monsieur Dubloon.'

'Thank you. ...Well, I'm very tempted by the 1990 Labégorce Zédé.'

'An excellent Margaux,' the waiter agreed.

'It *is*,' Laura added rather lamely, realizing what she'd be missing.

'However,' Quincy continued, glancing mischievously at Laura, 'I think your price is ridiculous.'

'I'm sorry you should think so, Monsieur Dubloon.'

'I know so, Christophe. No – there's a super little bargain lurking in this list. It's only a second wine, but what a second! Rather young, I grant you, but it's drinking well already.'

The waiter attended expectantly. 'Yes?'

Quincy drained his champagne. 'I'll try a bottle of the Maréchal de la Fayette 2000.'

Christophe beamed. 'Very good, monsieur. An inspired choice, if I may say.'

'You may, young man, but on condition you give me three good reasons.'

The waiter turned to Laura. 'Because,' he said staring into her eyes, 'it is a fine wine, like its big brother. Secondly, 2000 was a good year for Margaux. And thirdly, as you are no doubt aware, monsieur, La Fayette was where madame studied before she became so famous. So, it is a wine which must bring to her always the fondest of memories.'

Quincy slammed the table with the palm of his right hand. 'Good Lord! Was it *really*? Was it, Laura?'

'Of course it was. Don't pretend you didn't know.'

'I'd quite forgotten – utterly slipped my mind. Well, I suppose you must know the wine inside out. At least you won't be missing anything, will you?'

There's that mischievous grin of his again. What's he up to? If he's trying to get me into his bed, he's going about it in a very odd way.

Ten minutes later, Laura had to admit that in small doses at least, Quincy was good company. He could tell a story so well that, at the end of it, one's body ached from the laughter. He radiated energy and self-confidence. He spoke his mind and didn't mince words, which in this day and age of political correctness was something she admired, even if she didn't always agree with his opinions. Normally, she'd have been content to lunch with him; it was just that today she'd wanted to study Belle-Mère's details in peace and quiet. But as she sat sipping her champagne and nibbling olives while Quincy recounted straight faced how he'd lost his trousers on the sleeper train from Nice a few weeks earlier, her laughter became louder and louder. If only he wasn't so lecherous – if only she didn't have the constant feeling that everything Quincy did and said was for some ulterior sexual motive – well, they could be really good friends.

'... but because of the derailment outside Toulouse, Laura, I only had ten minutes to get to the Hôtel de Ville. So, there was no time to go to my apartment and change. Well, as chairman of the conference I couldn't be late, could I? – not with Monsieur le Maire, dear Alain Juppé – so charming but *too* clever – *and* the Rothschild crowd, *and* the Dubourdieus – I mean, just *everyone* who is anyone in Bordeaux assembled en masse and, no doubt, bristling with indignation that yours truly – an Englishman of all things! – should be in the driving seat of their great seminar on the future of Bordeaux wine.'

'How come you got chosen anyway?'

'I was the compromise candidate – with their petty jealousies, the Bordelais couldn't agree on any of themselves doing the job. Anyway, can you imagine their faces when I arrived on the dot of ten in that beautiful eighteenth-century room full of people looking like models out of Burberry or Escada catalogues, and strode to my place on the platform next to Juppé wearing my pinstripe suit's jacket, striped shirt, Liberty silk tie, and a pair of sleeping-car conductor's blue serge trousers with gold stripes down the seams that didn't even reach my ankles?'

'Jesus! I wish I'd been there.'

'Why weren't you?'

'Commitments – filming in Australia.'

'Feeble excuse! Such a cocky lot the Australians – always have been. They're arrogant enough about their wine successes without you getting them to sing their own praises in a TV series. Now they'll be insufferable.'

'You do exaggerate, Quincy. Did anyone make a wisecrack about the pants, or were the Bordeaux social register doing their "let's-pretend-we're-English act"? Did you ever get your own back?'

'No, of course not. Pinched – a thief must have crept into my birth in the middle of the night. As for the conference crowd, most of them were frightfully diplomatic. However, there was one awful woman – you may know her – turns up everywhere like a bad penny trying to promote her pedestrian little wines ... from Entre-deux-Mers, I think. Mind you, she always starts off by saying her château is "near St-Emilion" – which it is, about ten miles away to be exact. ... Château Garonne? ... Dordogne? ... Loire? Well, it's got something to do with rivers.'

'But she's not within the *appellation*?'

'Exactly. Barges her way into any conversation, prattling on about her triumphs and hurling brochures and business cards at one like confetti.'

'God! That rings a bell. She's not English, is she?'

'Yes, with a terrified mouse of a Belgian husband. Can't remember her bloody name. Should do – she's always emailing some nonsense or other to me at *Wine Wisdom* seeking free promotion.'

'Likewise. ... Susan? ... Sue? ... Sue Olivier!'

'That's the one! What a cow – if you'll excuse the language. She's always mistaking me for Hugh Johnson.'

'Poor Hugh!'

'Charming! Anyway, during the coffee break I was chatting to dear Nancy de Bourrelier of Château de Valise, when all of a sudden, I – and everyone else in the room I should think – heard this rather coarse female voice with a cockney accent declaim, "If you ask me, Laura, they must 'ave shrinked in the wash. You'd think that with all the bleedin' millions 'e gets from that naff *Pocket Wine Book* thing 'e could afford a decent pair of pants."'

Laura exploded. 'I can just picture her. Who was the "Laura" she was buttonholing?'

'You, of course.'

'But–'

'In reality, our dear colleague poor Jancis Robinson. Old "Sue" has got us *all* mixed up.'

'But I don't look anything like Jancis,' Laura responded indignantly, 'or talk like her. She's English for Christ's sake and wears those huge specs.'

'And I don't resemble Hugh Johnson.'

'She's mad – Sue, not Jancis.' Laura smiled mischievously. 'Come on, Quincy. I know you. Out with it. What was your put-down?'

'Nothing too clever I'm afraid. Didn't want to cause a scene, of course. I just turned round, greeted Jancis, smiled at the dreaded Sue, looked her up and down and said, "Hello! I think we've met before, Mrs ...? No, I'm wrong. It's your *outfit* I've seen before. So popular some years ago, wasn't it?" I then did a sort of male model pirouette, waved one leg at her and added, "Like them? Armani's such a genius, isn't he? Just got back from Barolo this morning. Grabbed these in Milan – all the vogue in Italy."'

With Laura laughing hysterically, Christophe arrived with their food and poured Quincy a small amount of the Maréchal de La Fayette to taste. As was his custom, Quincy did nothing elaborate – a quick sniff, a swirl, a gulp. He nodded his approval.

'Care for a little, Laura?'

Seemingly hypnotized by the bottle with its familiar label, she had flashes of her conversation with Jean-Claude only a few hours earlier. 'Oh, all right, you ... you *agent provocateur*.'

Quincy and Christophe looked at each other momentarily; Laura thought she saw the waiter wink at him. Then smiling broadly, he poured her some wine, topped up her water, and wished both diners *'bon appétit'*.

As he walked away, Laura said: 'Come to think of it, Quincy, you gave the 2000 Maréchal quite a rave review in *Wine Wisdom* a couple of months back, didn't you? In fact, every time I pick up a copy of your enchanting little publication these days, one or other of La Fayette's wines is getting praised. I'd no idea you were such an admirer of my alma mater.'

'Oh come, come! I've always been fond of the Bourjois style – as well you know.'

'It's taken you long enough to admit it!'

'Nonsense! We at *Wine Wisdom–*'

'– have always been "correct". Now you gush.'

'"*Gush*?" ... My dear Laura, *Wine Wisdom* does not "gush". It's not at all our style. You'll be accusing me of taking bribes next, or–'

'Oh *please*! All I said was–'

'And what about *you*? For years you've been singing the praises of La Fayette as though your life depended on it.' But before Laura had a chance to frame a suitable reply, Quincy launched into an animated account of a bizarre interview he'd had recently with a BBC producer who wanted to make a documentary about the history of the corkscrew.

Some minutes later, and as he continued with more anecdotes, Laura glanced around the restaurant. All the clients gave every indication of enjoying their lunch. And thanks to her long acquaintance with Bordeaux, she knew that it wasn't simply the consumption of good food and wine which generated this general air of well-being and contentment: the very sounds, sights and smells of a restaurant – clattering cutlery, clinking glasses, popping wine corks, chattering clients engulfed in a heady incense of cooking odours – appeared in themselves to have a remarkably revitalizing effect on the Bordelais.

At some point it dawned on her that Christophe kept replenishing her glass, and that it didn't bother her. 'Bordeaux's a wonderful city, Quincy,' she heard herself say with perhaps more passion than she'd intended.

'Unique'

'Exactly.'

'An outpost of civilization in an otherwise vulgar world.'

Laura nodded her approval vigorously as she chewed a mouthful of lettuce and endive. 'So well put.' She groaned as if on the point of orgasm.

Quincy stared at her open-mouthed and suspended his attack on the *carré d'agneau*.

'Take this vinaigrette, for example,' Laura enthused. 'If only they'd give me the recipe. It's ... it's the vinaigrette of the Gods.'

Quincy resumed his offensive with a chuckle. 'So, Laura,' he said without looking up from his plate, 'what are you up to in Bordeaux?'

She was about to stab a *gésier* with her fork but froze in mid thrust. 'I'm not "up to" anything, Quince,' she replied somewhat defensively.

'"*Quince*"! It's a long time since you called me that ... not since–'

'I mean,' she added swiftly and with a warm smile, 'I'm here – like you, no doubt – for my usual round of tastings and châteaux visits ... keeping myself up to date ... *au fait* ... *au courant*.'

'Yes, of course. That's why you have to keep "a clear head" as you put it earlier on.'

'You got it, buddy.'

'You've a lot on, you said.'

'I have.'

'Who did you visit this morning? Taste anything spectacular? Been to Haut Brion yet? You must taste their latest effort – *very* interesting. Dear Robert Parker will be gushing with all his most exotic epithets – "burly", "brawny", "lusty" – even "sexy" perhaps. On the other hand, I might be in a minority of one – it wouldn't be the first time. Robert might hate the stuff and award it only seventy-eight and a *half* points. Points! It's the half points I can never understand. Can you? I mean–'

'Let's not have the points argument, Quincy.'

'Kill joy!' He scraped the minute remaining traces of meat from the *carré d'agneau* and then stretched back in his chair. 'So?'

'So?'

'Oh, for heaven's sake, Laura! What have you tasted since your arrival? – or is it a bloody state secret?'

'Don't be childish, Quince.' She reached for her wine glass and almost knocked it over. 'The Maréchal is *very* good – despite being so young.'

'Ah! So, you've been out to Margaux?'

'No – I mean *this* Maréchal – the one we're drinking now. I haven't had time to drive all the way to Margaux yet.'

'Really? It's not *that* far. How long have you been here? – three days? ... four?'

'Three. Look, what is this? – the Inquisition?'

Quincy held up his hands in mock surrender. 'My, my, *my*! We *are* sensitive about something, aren't we? I don't suppose that might have something to do with your visits to various estate agents in this fair city, would it?'

For a few seconds, suspicions of spying and breaches of confidence raced through Laura's mind. Then came panic as she pictured *Wine Wisdom*'s gossip pages revealing her plans to acquire a vineyard. Her publishers would have a fit; her father would ceaselessly beg her not to emigrate; people from all over the world would try and interest her in their lousy vineyards at inflated prices; and – horror of horrors! – old Quincy might start blabbing immediately – now! – today! – in Bordeaux! In a matter of hours, the whole wine fraternity would know, including Jean-Claude and his employer. She could see all her plans disintegrating. Quincy had suddenly become a dangerous bitchy wolf in sheep's clothing. The pretty waiter, the champagne, the ever-so-innocent choice of La Fayette – it had been a conspiracy! Quincy had followed her to the Régent. It was no coincidence – sitting at the next table, indeed! She had to speak to Jean-Claude before–

'You're not listening to a word I'm saying, are you, Laura?'

'How *could* you?' she snapped, scowling.

'How could I what?'

'Spy, snoop–'

'Don't be so paranoid. I've just told you – bloody hell, you *weren't* listening! My neighbours – you met them at that party I gave at the apartment during the 1997 Vin Expo – you've probably forgotten them. He owns a chain of dry cleaners and she works at the Grand Théâtre – lovely couple. ... Anyway, their son André's long-standing girlfriend – she was at the party too – works at Brussaut, the estate agents just around the corner. She told André that you'd emailed them recently asking about properties in Bordeaux – all very hush-hush – and that she remembered you from the party. I was chatting to André in the lift yesterday and he dropped it into the conversation.'

Laura glared at him suspiciously. 'And the others?' she hissed.

'"Others"?'

'Come on! You said I'd been to "*various* estate agents".'

Quincy beamed smugly. 'Pure deduction, old thing. I mean, no one looking for an apartment goes to just *one* estate agent, do they?'

Laura's brain reeled. *Apartment?* ... *What apartment?* Christophe's sudden appearance distracted her. 'Ah, here's your fellow conspirator,' she muttered, still attempting to sound cross. 'I guess the next phase of your plan is to ply me with brandy.'

'Don't be ridiculous. We'd counted on your having the fresh strawberries – a particular favourite of yours, I believe. Christophe was going to lace them with a truth serum he gets from a cousin in the Foreign Legion. It usually works like a treat.'

By the time Christophe returned with the strawberries and an *île flottante* for Quincy, Laura was back on an even keel, having apologized for her behaviour; she'd even begged forgiveness for her earlier remark about grandfathers and Quincy's age.

'So, why all the cloak-and-dagger stuff, Laura? I mean, we've been friends for *years*. You should have got in touch. I'd have been more than happy to recommend some people – suggest some properties even. To be absolutely honest with you, I'm seriously thinking of selling my own apartment.'

Laura looked shocked. 'But why? It's beautiful ... so convenient – and you spend so much time in Bordeaux.'

'All true, but the property taxes are escalating all the time and ... Well, actually, I don't come as often as I used to. There's so much good wine these days – from the Americas, your beloved Australia, South Africa – that us wine folk have to travel across the globe more and more. When I started in this business thirty years ago, the British were only interested in Bordeaux, Burgundy and German whites. Last year I used the apartment for only ten weeks. Frankly, it's a luxury.'

'I see.'

'Which is why I'm puzzled by your wish to have a base here.'

Laura shifted uncomfortably. 'Well ... I ... I–'

'Got it! You're going to write a mega work on Bordeaux – at last, a real competitor for Parker – and you need a base. You'll keep your apartment in New York, I assume. ... Or is it a jumbo TV series on Bordeaux? ... Maybe you could *rent* my place? Now there's a thought. You haven't committed yourself yet, have you?'

'No. I–'

'Splendid! Of course, I'd want the right to stay a few weeks each year. That wouldn't be a problem, would it? Would you want it for more than a year?'

'I–'

'I can't imagine you'd expect me to stay in a hotel – I would if you insisted, of course. I'd need to check the tax implications of renting but –'

'Quincy–'

'Don't tell me you'd prefer to be in the suburbs – or by the sea? Forget Arcachon – between September and May you'd find more life at Skegness – oh, you won't know it – a hellhole on Lincolnshire's bleak North Sea coast. Where *are* you looking? ... The Jardin Public? Frightfully expensive! Place des Quinconces? Stunning but too noisy. And please, don't be a gullible Yank and get seduced by the poetic medieval decay of the Old Town.'

Laura felt she was being battered by a tornado. So many questions and assumptions – so much guilt on her part – and all that wine!

'Come on,' Quincy roared, '– out with it!'

She couldn't think; she didn't think. 'Premières Côtes de Bordeaux.'

CHAPTER 5

Having spent the night in Bordeaux at the home of her *antiquaire* friend, Cathérine Gravelier, Sophie Bourjois had subjected herself to a hectic morning of procuring provisions for her weekend houseguest, the Parisian art dealer Dominique Buffet. Sophie had been thrilled by Buffet's sudden acceptance of her long-standing invitation to stay at Le Porge, and she'd expended much time, effort and money during the past week to ensure it would be a memorable occasion. She'd discovered his favourite food and drink, his preferred toiletries – with which she'd already stuffed the guest bathroom – and the sort of people to whom he was attracted. From her own observations in Paris, it had come as no surprise to receive confirmation that the latter were exclusively male and under thirty with blond hair, blue eyes, and bodies fit for an Armani underwear advertisement. One of her gallery friends in Bordeaux had procured three eminently suitable art students, and they'd agreed to exhibit themselves at the Le Porge beach on the Saturday afternoon of Buffet's visit, when Sophie and her guest would stumble upon them as if by accident.

Sophie had been warned that Buffet was a gluttonous gourmand with table manners to match; indeed, eating with him in public could prove embarrassing, such was the squalor he created. It was rare, however, for any aspiring artist to protest: an exhibition at his gallery – arguably the most prestigious in France – guaranteed the sale of at least one work at an astronomical price to a nouveau riche tycoon or rock star, whereupon the artist's works would instantly become collectable commodities, irrespective of artistic merit. Yet, Buffet wouldn't permit any old thing to be exhibited on his premises: his genius lay in identifying general trends in the lifestyles of his potential clients and marrying them to what was on offer in the art world. Gloom, brutal realism and nightmarish fantasy were currently the order of the day; hence Buffet's interest in Sophie's *Orifices*. And over the telephone, he'd been gripped by her professed passion for dead creatures washed up along the shore near Le Porge.

So, while Laura Appleton had her brief meeting with Pierre Lampre, Sophie was throwing caution and economy to the wind, making her final purchases. The *traiteur* tempted her with quails stuffed with truffles elegantly bedded down in vol-au-vent nests, which, she was assured, would be perfect heated up in the oven. From the best *pâtisserie* in town she chose two monumental gateaux smothered with *pruneaux d'Agen*, oozing

Armagnac. And her preferred *fruitier* witnessed a near total exhaustion of his stocks of *fraises des bois* and tropical fruits; luckily for Sophie, he also had on display one of Buffet's all-time favourites, the peerless red bananas of Zanzibar.

Having arranged to collect all her purchases in the late afternoon on the way to the station to pick up Buffet, a very elegant Sophie, sensibly dressed in a cool silk trouser suit, made her way through the scorching midday heat – without haste but with a trace of anticipation – to Cathérine's antique shop in the Rue des Remparts. Cathérine would have preferred premises in the neighbouring Rue Bouffard, where most of the city's more prestigious antique shops were located, but she comforted herself with the knowledge that she'd not done too badly for a forty-six-year-old mother of two teenagers who'd found herself bereaved and almost destitute three years earlier when her husband, a residential property developer, had shot himself upon being declared bankrupt.

Cathérine had never previously worked; nor had she possessed any obvious qualifications for any particular employment. But an acquaintance had drawn attention to her ability to find remarkable objets d'art at local *brocante* markets and to negotiate their purchase at bargain prices from ignorant dealers. With some reluctance, she was persuaded to give it a try professionally. Armed with the proceeds of an unsolicited whip-round by her closest friends, she'd been able to purchase an initial stock of bric-a-brac and to rent a decrepit little shop in the St-Michel quarter, surrounded by other similar establishments – not to mention the food shops and eateries of Bordeaux's North African population.

Looking ten years younger than her age, Cathérine was also blessed with a ruthless determination to prosper: never again would she be financially dependent on another, or be reduced to such ignominies as dressing her children and herself in second-hand clothing. Within a year she'd moved to the infinitely more salubrious Rue des Remparts – just minutes from the palatial Hôtel de Ville – and begun specializing in Empire furniture. Thanks to her zealous socializing and passion for the Internet, she now possessed an impressive client list, including prestigious dealers in London, New York and Shanghai. Friendships were cultivated or maintained solely to further her business; if and when it became obvious that the 'friend' was no longer of any financial value to her, he or she simply ceased to register in Cathérine's thoughts. On the other hand, being wholly mercenary, an outcast could just as easily and quickly be welcomed back to the fold through the procurement of some transaction which benefited her bank balance.

Sophie had first met Cathérine some eighteen months ago at a vernissage of her canvasses staged by a small gallery in Rue des Remparts. The paintings were not at all to Cathérine's taste, but she kept her opinions to herself – like most of those attending. Instead, she purported to empathize with the metaphysical verbiage Sophie spouted about the sublime import of the vicious brush strokes of acrylic orange which criss-crossed montages of pages ripped from *Paris Match*. Pursuing her usual subtle interrogation techniques, Cathérine quickly discovered that Sophie came from a wealthy Parisian family, that her husband was someone 'terribly important' at Château La Fayette – the name rang a distant bell – and that there was a 'fantastic' modern house 'by the Ocean'; it got better and better. After a while, Sophie felt obliged to engage in some form of reciprocity, and to Cathérine's relief, the artist finally asked the question she'd been awaiting.

'And what do you do, er ...?' Sophie had never excelled at remembering names.

Humbly describing her 'little hobby' and pointing to the shop across the street, Cathérine struck gold. Sophie gushed with enthusiasm over the Empire style – 'Mama and Papa have some wonderful pieces at their place in Normandy,' she boasted – and went on to say she'd long felt that an Empire table would look absolutely perfect in her hall. A seemingly profound friendship swiftly blossomed. Luckily for Cathérine, Sophie's birthday was in the offing, and her father, Paul Charpentier, was in a generous mood. So, Sophie got her Empire table, Cathérine disposed of an item of stock which she'd begun to fear would never sell, and Jean-Claude came home one day from work to find yet another vast piece of furniture cluttering his home.

Sophie found her new friend such wonderful fun: it was almost like the old days in Paris – a continuous round of lunches, receptions, dinners and parties with other *antiquaires* and associated professionals. Cathérine, for her part, finally had an entrée into the contemporary Bordeaux art world; she'd long been acutely aware that many wealthy people liked to decorate their homes eclectically with bold contrasts of ancient and modern. The first six months or so of their relationship, therefore, saw Cathérine's business reaching new levels of success. Sophie, on the other hand, did not sell any paintings, but she began to think that life in Bordeaux could be tolerable after all.

Alas, almost exactly a year ago, after the two of them had attended a performance of *Les Pêcheurs de Perles* at the Grand Théâtre, Cathérine did a stocktaking and concluded that her considerable investment in the friendship was no longer paying sufficient dividends: Sophie had already introduced her to everyone she knew who was of any value; Jean-Claude, a mere *maître de chai*, was a philistine with no money; the Le Porge house was unlikely to be furnished with any more items from her shop; and Sophie's parents sourced their antiques in Paris, knew the value of their own Empire collections, and had no desire or need to sell anything. To cap it all, Sophie's paintings were infantile daubs – pretending otherwise had become a chore.

The following day, Sophie's phasing-out process commenced. Cathérine cancelled their lunch engagement with the excuse that an American client had turned up out of the blue and was insisting on giving her a Michelin-star lunch at the St-James. A week later, Sophie visited the shop and was introduced to a Madame Castelnau, a smartly dressed thin woman in her fifties, whose husband, Sophie was informed, owned half a dozen vineyards around St-Emilion.

'Eight to be precise,' Madame Castelnau bleated with a significant glance at her gold and diamond Cartier watch, whereupon Cathérine started rushing around shutting up the shop because 'dear Madame Castelnau' had invited her to lunch at Le Noailles. Sophie prayed for the invitation to be extended, but the other women made their brusque farewells outside the shop and then marched off without even asking Sophie whether she was going in the same direction. Fuming with jealousy, she vowed to await Cathérine's call begging forgiveness. No call came.

And then, a few months ago, while trudging to an undistinguished gallery on the wrong side of town which was exhibiting a few of her works, Sophie had taken a short cut along Rue des Remparts. As she passed Cathérine's shop, her former friend was arranging some items in the window. Despite all her solemn resolutions, Sophie unhesitatingly opened the door. Her immediate reaction was one of intense regret: at the back of the shop was Madame Castelnau waxing lyrical about her latest shopping expedition to Paris.

Cathérine, however, seemed pleased to see Sophie. With her back to Madame Castelnau, she pulled a face and whispered: 'Don't dash off. The old cow will be gone in a tick. I've a customer upstairs, but I don't think he's interested in anything.'

After five minutes, however, Madame Castelnau, who'd not even acknowledged Sophie's existence, was still in full flow about her new wardrobe; nor had the customer materialized. Sophie longed to escape: nothing had changed, save that Madame Castelnau's use-by date had also expired. It was as Sophie was saying goodbye and moving towards the door with Cathérine opining about the need to keep in touch, that she heard the stairs creak. Out of the corner of her eye, she glimpsed a tall man with dark curly hair and bronzed skin dressed in a suit. That, in truth, was the extent of her impression of him.

The rest of the afternoon went from bad to worse. At the gallery, Sophie discovered that her paintings were no longer on display, but lying on the floor in a pile at the side of the proprietor's desk. Her allotted wall space was now adorned with a dozen large and almost identical watercolours of a vegetable garden painted by an Englishwoman living in the Dordogne. Sophie could barely restrain her anger. She referred to her contract – her exhibition still had three weeks to run – and hoped that it wouldn't be necessary for her to seek legal advice. The proprietor was blunt: Sophie's paintings were 'crap'; he'd made a terrible mistake in agreeing to exhibit them; she could sue and be damned.

When Sophie got home that evening, Jean-Claude was sitting at the kitchen table with a plate of cold cuts and cheeses surrounded by labelling-machine brochures. She slumped into the chair opposite him, poured herself a glass of white Graves, and began to unburden herself. But as she recounted the gallery owner's treachery, Sophie couldn't escape noticing that her husband's eyes kept returning to the brochures. After downing three glasses of wine in less than ten minutes, her boilers were well fired up; Jean-Claude turned over one page too many.

'Can't you forget your bloody vineyard for one bloody second?' she screamed, flinging the pile of brochures on the floor.

She was still ranting when the telephone rang five minutes later.

'Yes!'

'*Sophie? It's Cathérine. Is this a bad time?*'

'Yes!'

'*Oh. It's just that I've got a customer who's very interested in your work. Fancy lunch tomorrow?*'

And that was how Sophie's affair with Dr Geoffroy de Tiquetorte commenced.

*

It had been Tiquetorte's very first visit to Cathérine's shop when Sophie made her unscheduled visit. He'd no knowledge of its proprietress; nor did he know Jean-Claude's wife, even though he was one of Henri de Bondé's oldest friends and a minority shareholder in Château La Fayette. But then Tiquetorte didn't socialize with *maîtres de chai* or their spouses. He'd only walked over to Rue des Remparts from his surgery in Allées de Tourny during a welcome hour's gap between appointments because he was looking for a set of six Empire dining chairs, and a friend of a friend had recommended Cathérine's niche establishment. Initially, he'd regretted his visit: the first person he saw on entering was one of his most irksome patients, Madame Castelnau. Compounding the horror, her proprietorial swagger led him to believe that she was the *antiquaire*.

Swiftly putting him right, Cathérine directed him to the first floor, where, she said, 'Monsieur de Tiquetorte' would find exactly what he was looking for. She'd follow 'in a tick': Madame Castelnau was on the point of leaving, she assured him, fixing her with an icy stare. When Tiquetorte grew irritated by the owner's failure to materialize – Madame Castelnau was determined to stand her ground and procure a free consultation about a twitch in her left eyelid – he descended to the ground floor just in time to see an attractive woman exiting the front door. It was only a fleeting glimpse, but he liked what he saw. Then Madame Castelnau launched into a dramatic account of the development of her eye-twitching symptoms, whereupon Cathérine interrupted forcefully, grabbing Tiquetorte's arm.

'My dear doctor, I'm so terribly sorry to have kept you waiting. I was just on my way up when a dear friend – one of the leading lights in the contemporary art scene – popped in to invite me to her latest exhibition. Wasn't that sweet? Now let's go and have a look at those *wonderful* chairs. Aren't they spectacular?' As they approached the foot of the stairs, Cathérine half-turned. 'We've got business to discuss, Martine. I'll ring you, OK? ... Now, Dr de Tiquetorte, do you require six chairs or eight,' – there was a tremendous bang as Madame Castelnau slammed the front door – 'and did you see my Empire bed *à bateau*? Isn't it a treasure?'

Tiquetorte had not only seen the monumental bed – he'd fallen in love with it instantly, picturing it in the master bedroom of his magnificent Rue d'Aviau townhouse. And now that his wife, Cassandre, resided permanently at her medieval manor house near Périgueux – breading Labradors with a girlfriend – she could hardly object to his removal of the tasteless twin divans she'd demanded. There followed a tough bargaining session, during which Tiquetorte had to wrestle with playing several conflicting roles. First and foremost, he desperately wanted the bed: it was precisely what he'd been seeking for more than two years; he'd even pay Gravelier's asking price of twenty thousand euros – if necessary.

'The bed's a fine piece, madame, but I'm looking for *chairs*,' he said dismissively.

True enough, but dining chairs for the townhouse were not absolutely essential: the dining room was already graced by a decent table and six chairs of Louis Philippe vintage. On the other hand, Gravelier's set were very smart – very smart indeed – even if they weren't Empire. And somehow, in the course of all this wheeling and dealing, he wanted to find out about the pretty artist. It was probably a foolish fantasy, but nothing ventured nothing gained. In fact, in order to give the impression that he wasn't really fussed about buying anything, Tiquetorte had started talking about her as soon as they reached the first floor.

'I thought she looked familiar,' he said as they made their way towards the dining chairs.

'Who?'

'The painter.' Cathérine looked blank. 'Downstairs ... your friend.'

'Ah, Sophie Bourjois – a *great* artist – *so* sought after. Perhaps you've seen her on the telly. ... Now look at that for craftsmanship!'

With calculated apathy, Tiquetorte studied the chair Cathérine was patting like a beloved pet. 'Sophie Bourjois? ... That rings a bell. ... Sophie–'

'It's very difficult to find a set of six in such perfect condition,' Cathérine repeated for the third time.

'Indeed. It's a pity they're not Empire, however.'

'Oh but, Doctor, I assure you–!'

'They're *Restauration* – early *Restauration* I grant you ... 1820 perhaps.' He began shaking his head. 'Over a thousand euros a piece for *Restauration*–!'

'With all due respect, Monsieur de Tiquetorte, I'm afraid you're wrong. They *are* Empire – *late* Empire. They were in the ownership of the Comtes de Loupiac for over a hundred and fifty years – at Château Faux Pas and–'

'*Really*? I know the Loupiacs *and* the house *awfully* well. Good God! Now that you mention it, they *do* look familiar.' Tiquetorte sighed. 'Poor Cécile. I knew Frédéric had left a lot of debts when he passed away last year, but I'd no idea she was having to sell stuff.' As if thinking aloud, he added: 'I really ought to go and see her ... this weekend perhaps.'

In the event, Tiquetorte was offered the 'late Empire'/'early *Restauration*' chairs for seven hundred and fifty euros each.

'I'm not sure, Madame Gravelier,' he said, walking around the room, glancing at the chairs from all directions and pretending not to look at the gorgeous bed. 'I just don't know. Maybe I'm being silly. I mean, I have a lovely set of Louis Philippe chairs at Rue d'Aviau and–'

'Rue d'Aviau! How divine! Such beautiful architecture! And those heavenly *little* gardens overlooking the Jardin Public! Why, the Empire style is an absolute must for Rue d'Aviau – it's the right period.'

Tiquetorte chose not to point out that the fine terraces along the Jardin Public's east side were closer to the era of Louis Philippe than Napoleon I. He merely shrugged his shoulders. 'I don't know,' he repeated. 'I need to think about it.'

Cathérine didn't like the sound of that. She briefly contemplated a further reduction. After all, the senile Comtesse de Loupiac had almost given her the chairs.

Tiquetorte had gravitated to the bed. 'This is a nice piece of furniture,' he said matter-of-factly as if noticing it for the first time, adding quickly: 'Where did you say Madame ... er ... Bourjois was exhibiting?'

'Sophie? Oh, not far away. The bed is quite something, isn't it? I have an American client who's *very* interested. It would be a shame to see it leave the country, don't you think?'

Against his better judgment, Tiquetorte found himself nodding in agreement. 'Just out of interest,' he queried, looking over the bed with a critical eye, 'what price are you asking? ... Oh! There's a nasty chip down the side here.'

As Cathérine made light of the defect, the doctor continued to point out miniscule scratches and other trivial blemishes in the almost two-hundred-year-old piece of furniture. Down on his hands and knees, examining the base, he suddenly looked up and asked: 'Does Sophie Bourjois live in Bordeaux, Madame Gravelier? I feel sure I've seen–'

'Sorry? ... Sophie?' Cathérine was irritated by the way her ex-friend kept constantly drifting into the conversation. 'No! I mean she's often in town visiting some gallery or other, but she lives in the country – glorious house – so avant-garde. And her studio!' She raised her eyes and sighed. 'Believe me, Doctor, it's like something out of California. Of course, it wouldn't be *your* style, I'm sure – although Sophie does have some superb antiques – mostly gifts from her family, the Charpentiers. You know, Paul Charpentier, the industrialist ... plastics, I think.' She lowered her voice. '*Terribly* wealthy.'

Tiquetorte nodded his head knowledgeably: the name Charpentier was vaguely familiar. 'Ah, yes, *Paul* Charpentier.' He stood up, pretending to lose interest in the bed.

Just for a split second, Cathérine detected something in Tiquetorte's demeanour – possibly a gleam in his eye or maybe the tone of his voice, but definitely something which suggested that his interest in Sophie was ... well ... She looked him straight in the eye. Her mind began to run riot with strategies for selling both the bed and the bloody *Restauration* chairs.

'Sophie's house,' Cathérine fizzed, 'is spectacularly situated in the forest just minutes from the sea. Breathtaking!'

'Arcachon?'

'No, the Cap Ferret side of the Bassin.'

'*Really*! I have a place there. I probably know the house. Where exactly?'

Cathérine shook her head. 'I doubt it – *very* remote. It's *near* Cap Ferret' – she waved an arm vaguely – '*that* way ... quite obscure actually. To be honest with you, Doctor, she's rather passionate about her privacy. You know what these artist types are like. When she's painting, she needs absolute peace and quiet. That's why the boy's in a boarding school – here in town.'

A child! Damn! Tiquetorte remained expressionless.

'And a young attractive woman alone all day, kilometres from anywhere ... well, I think *I'd* be just a little anxious ... stuck out there ... in the forest ... and everything.'

'What about her ... her husband, or is she–?'

Catherine rolled her eyes. 'He's hardly ever there! Well, that's half the poor girl's problem. Jean-Claude's a complete workaholic – has a vineyard. Well, you know what these wine people are like – they never stop – sunrise to sunset. ... Château La Fayette actually.' She spoke the name as if uttering a household brand as prestigious as Rolls-Royce.

Tiquetorte desperately tried to think straight; it wasn't easy with this ghastly woman droning on about 'the dynamic contrapuntal aesthetics of juxtaposing ancient and modern artefacts'. *Jean-Claude Bourjois! – Henri's bête noire! – the unknown quantity in our current transatlantic venture! It's too fantastic for words! An affair with his wife! What a glorious challenge! Killing two birds with one stone, so to speak. If I pull it off, Henri'd love the irony – Alain de Carbon Blanc too as a fellow La Fayette shareholder and Henri's lawyer. If she's as good-looking as I suspect, they'll also be salivating with envy. And being an invisible fly on the wall – what a vulgar analogy! – in the Bourjois household, they'd be eternally in my debt. Fate, that's what it is! Thank you, God. And if I play my cards right, I'll get the chairs, Bourjois's wife, and the bed to screw her in!*

'... no guarantees, Doctor, but as we're really very, very old friends and terribly close, I might be able ... I mean, she may be in the middle of a huge canvas at the moment and not want to be disturbed. But I could try ... if you wanted ... if you're *really* interested in her ... *style.* I like to do little favours for my clients – my very *special* clients, that is.'

Cathérine looked at her Empire bed with genuine fondness. 'You know, Doctor, I'll be sorry to see it go. There's been many an afternoon during the past few months when I've had a delightful siesta up here after lunch – I generally shut the shop between noon and four. I've felt like the Empress Joséphine on that bed.'

Tiquetorte raised his eyebrows.

They managed to sort out a deal with remarkable expedition. He acquired both the bed and the chairs for twenty thousand euros *in toto*!

He paid a ten per cent deposit by cheque there and then. The balance, less a retainer of one thousand euros, was to be paid prior to delivery; the retainer would be handed over if and when Sophie accepted an invitation to lunch at Tiquetorte's Cap Ferret villa, or invited him to a 'private viewing' at her Le Porge studio, whichever first occurred.

In the event, the contract was fully performed far sooner than either party could have hoped for: when Cathérine telephoned with her lunch invitation, Sophie was so mad with Jean-Claude over the labelling-machine brochures that she unhesitatingly accepted, even though she'd resolved to spend a few days at Le Porge in order to complete her *Orifices* portfolio. Cathérine painted a glorious portrait of Dr de Tiquetorte – handsome, rich, cultured, and with houses dotted all over Aquitaine. She also managed to slip in a few oblique references to the separation from his wife. Due to her rage, however, Sophie came away from the telephone remembering almost nothing about the conversation.

On her drive into Bordeaux the next day, Sophie was still in a foul mood, wishing that she'd not succumbed to Cathérine's carrot during a moment of weakness. In all the time she'd known her, Cathérine had never procured a single customer for her paintings – not even a signed print – notwithstanding her mantra about 'the dynamic counterpoint of the aesthetic juxtaposition of ancient and contemporary art'. Sophie's difficulties in finding a parking place near the Café Bordelais in Allées de Tourny did not improve her temper. When she finally arrived at the bistro fifteen minutes late, Cathérine was already sipping a Lillet at their reserved table. She nodded enigmatically at her gentleman companion. Tiquetorte looked over his shoulder towards the door, smiled broadly and rose from his seat. He held Sophie's hand for a few seconds longer than usual for a customary polite greeting as Cathérine effected introductions; he'd not been deceived by that brief glimpse in the antique shop.

Cathérine was soon telling herself that she'd made a brilliant choice of venue for performing her new role as matchmaker. She loved the food at the Café Bordelais – it was nothing special for the others – and its unpretentious relaxed atmosphere thanks to folksy decor, casually dressed young staff, and jazz mood music. And how well everything was proceeding, but then poor Sophie was probably desperate for a relationship, particularly with a man who possessed all the graces, charm and sophistication which Jean-Claude so patently lacked. Tiquetorte talked wittily about Bordelais society; Sophie reminisced about Paris. On the periphery of their conversation, Cathérine kept smiling – and praying that Sophie wouldn't get too heavy about her art, despite Tiquetorte's disingenuous claim that he was longing to see her 'exciting work' thanks to 'dear Cathérine's unbridled praise'.

By the time they reached coffee, Sophie felt positively uplifted – almost reborn; Cathérine had certainly redeemed herself. 'Geoffroy' was – Sophie weighed up numerous superlatives – lovely, as simple as that. He was lovely. Maybe it was the wine, but, frankly, she didn't give a damn whether he bought one of her paintings or not. Just to have him as a friend would do fine. At last, after all the years of exile in the Gironde, a member of one of *the* Bordelais families had treated her like an equal – had laughed and joked with her, referred to her as 'madame' when giving the order with consummate panache to the waiter, had stood up when she went to powder her nose *and* upon her return. He could open Bordeaux's magic doors. She'd join his circle, meet all the others – oh the parties! – at their châteaux and summer houses around the Bassin, the yachts at Arcachon. ... And she could reciprocate with some tremendous receptions at Le Porge, with a marquee on the lawn and–

Sophie's heart sank as she pictured Jean-Claude – a wallflower – out of his depth – at a loss for words.

As if reading her mind, Tiquetorte said: 'I'm not sure you should tell your husband you've had lunch with me.' He smiled mischievously.

Sophie suddenly experienced a sickening premonition that her expectations of a thrilling new life were about to be dashed.

'Poor Jean-Claude,' Cathérine chirped. 'We seem to have forgotten all about him. I wonder why.' There was a pregnant pause.

'I – I don't quite follow, Geoffroy,' Sophie said nervously. 'Do you know Jean-Claude, my–?'

'Don't look so worried, Sophie,' he interjected laughing. 'It's just that I don't think I'm your husband's favourite person.' Her heart seemed to miss a beat. 'Has he never mentioned me? I'm Guy de Bondé's physician.'

'Oh! ... And?'

'Well, you know about his illness, don't you?'

'Alzheimer's, isn't it?' whispered Cathérine with masterly gravitas. Sophie nodded.

'I understand that your husband wasn't very happy with my treatment – made a few critical remarks to Henri.'

'Jean-Claude did? ... Surely not?'

'I gather his view was that Guy should have been hospitalized earlier.'

'I do remember my husband saying something about him being in an attic, but that was ages ago.'

Cathérine snorted. 'In an *attic*? How ridiculous! I can't imagine where Jean-Claude gets these dotty ideas from.'

Feeling dizzy, Sophie said: 'I don't think he'd make up something like that, Cathérine. He's extremely fond of Guy, you know.' She turned to

Tiquetorte. 'The illness upset my husband terribly. He was such a lovely man – Guy, I mean.'

Tiquetorte nodded. 'Indeed. The family were devastated. They couldn't bear the idea of Guy going into one of those terrible geriatric hospitals, so, in consultation with me, they converted the château's top floor into a sort of clinic for him – complete with a full-time nurse.'

'How *mar*vellous!' gushed Cathérine. 'I can't imagine anyone in their right mind calling the top floor of something like Château La Fayette "an attic".'

'Your husband, on the other hand, Sophie, seemed to believe – at least I think that's what Henri told me – that Guy should have been surrounded by a veritable battery of doctors, nurses and high-tech equipment and not–'

'Maybe I should have a word with him,' Sophie suggested anxiously, her face crimson with embarrassment. 'He can be so bloody tactless. I can't believe he'd tackle Henri de Bondé–'

'I'd rather you didn't, Sophie. It's all in the past and I think it would be best to let sleeping dogs lie. After all,' – Tiquetorte broke into a smile – 'if you're going to help me remodel my Cap Ferret villa, we'll need to see quite a bit of one another, won't we? Presumably, I'll have to come over to your studio and pick out some paintings. Actually, I have in mind some trompe l'oeil murals. Is that in your line?'

Sophie was speechless for a few seconds. 'I – I ...'

'I'll take that for a yes. Anyway, as a sort of persona non grata on the Jean-Claude front, maybe your ... *relationship* with me shouldn't be rammed down his throat, hmm?'

'Geoffroy's *so* right, darling,' affirmed Cathérine, pursing her lips. 'You know what he can be like.'

In fact, Sophie had no idea what she meant. Jean-Claude had never been the jealous husband type – far from it. But then, he'd never had the least cause to be jealous. On the other hand, he had appeared to resent her increasingly frequent trips into Bordeaux during the last twelve months or so. Be that as it may, there was no way she'd give him the slightest opportunity to foul up her new friendship. Geoffroy would be her secret, her enigmatic mystery client. The joke was that if she were to tell Jean-Claude about Geoffroy, he probably wouldn't take the least notice. But she wasn't going to tempt fate.

Sophie could feel her equanimity returning. She grinned impishly at Geoffroy. 'I think I'll have to give you a nom de guerre – if that's the right phrase.'

'Very appropriate,' Cathérine chortled, helping herself to another chocolate mint.

'But please don't think I expect you to buy something, Geoffroy,' Sophie said earnestly. 'You haven't seen any of my work in the flesh yet. You may hate it!'

'Don't worry on that score, Sophie. I'm not known to hold any punches when talking about art. I can be quite a stern critic, believe you me. So, watch out!'

All three of them laughed heartily. Their mirth attracted the attention of a passing waiter, and Tiquetorte asked for the bill.

A few days later, Sophie joined Tiquetorte at his Cap Ferret villa. It was a cold but sunny Saturday morning in late March, and he'd lit a log fire in the sitting room. He was still in the process of opening the shutters when Sophie arrived; the house, like Cap Ferret itself, had been almost deserted since the end of the previous summer. Cathérine was to have driven out from Bordeaux too, but as Sophie motored the final kilometres down the wooded peninsula, Cathérine called her mobile. She was at the shop: a neighbour had phoned to say he could smell gas. She was now waiting for the man from Gaz de Bordeaux to make an appearance. Sophie heaved a huge sigh of relief.

The villa was liberally furnished with rustic Aquitaine antiques. From what Sophie could see, artistic works were limited to nineteenth-century family portraits, various paintings of Anglo-French naval battles, and a surfeit of eighteenth-century aquatints of assorted tropical fruits and vegetables. There was certainly not much of a seaside holiday atmosphere – more like a retired admiral's residence, albeit such was the density of the pine woods, it was impossible to get even a glimpse of the sea. Nevertheless, one could smell the salt and detect a distant pounding of waves.

Commencing his conducted tour, Tiquetorte announced that he had in mind 'a complete clear out'; he was set on a more 'Mediterranean look' with contemporary furniture and bold modern art bursting with dazzling colours. Sophie pictured her *Orifices* and cringed; they wouldn't do at all. Tucked away somewhere at Le Porge, however, were some small canvasses reminiscent of Kandinsky; they might do for starters. Later, before the roaring log fire, Tiquetorte served a choice lunch of foie gras, cold pigeon and *tarte tatin*. As they stared into the flames during a lull in the conversation and sipped the final drops of a 1990 Sigalas-Rabaud, Tiquetorte placed an arm around Sophie's shoulders and kissed her cheek. Within seconds they were tearing at each other's clothes; the hedonistic golden Sauternes had rarely failed to wear down the defences of even his most reluctant of prospective mistresses.

Although Tiquetorte suggested the idea, it was Sophie who, a few days later, asked Cathérine if she and Geoffroy could use her first-floor salon for their lunchtime Bordeaux rendezvous. It was so discreet and much more convenient than traipsing all the way to Rue d'Aviau. Cathérine readily consented, but after the first tryst she telephoned Tiquetorte and made it quite clear that she'd henceforth expect to be exiled to the Café Bordelais at *his* expense – not to a neighbouring brasserie for a sandwich at her own expense. She also hoped that he could see his way to making the occasional purchase.

After three months, Sophie tried not to dwell on the negative aspects of their relationship. Above all, she'd yet to meet any of Geoffroy's friends. Her mild protestations in this respect were met with seemingly rational explanations. First and foremost, they had to be very careful about where, when and how they were seen together. Anyway, as an eminent physician, he was an extremely busy man. He wished they could meet more often, but it just wasn't humanly possible. Sophie was also forced to admit that Geoffroy had talked a lot of sense about her paintings – that before launching herself into the 'Mediterranean style' he desired, she should finish *Les Orifices*: on completion they'd undoubtedly be the subject of a major exhibition. To her intense relief, there'd been no more talk of trompe l'oeil: that really wasn't her sort of thing at all. The sex, however, was sublime. Furthermore, she could have real conversations with Geoffroy. He was a wonderful listener – so understanding when it came to her married life; it was like having a good gossip with a long-standing girlfriend. Indeed, Jean-Claude's tedious routines, their tiffs and scenes – all the sad minutiae of a marriage which had long ago run out of steam – appeared to fascinate him.

*

As Sophie entered the Rue des Remparts shop, just hours before Buffet's anticipated arrival, and smelled again the intoxicating odour of wax polish, a frisson of erotic expectations exploded within her. Cathérine was standing beside her desk, peering into the mirror of her compact.

'Hello, Cathérine. Café Bordelais as usual?'

Without looking up, Cathérine said: 'Hello. Lover boy's already upstairs. Seems like you've got champagne today. And I think I detected a whiff of smoked salmon. … As a matter of fact, Sophie, Madame Castelnau has invited me to Jean Ramet. I think she's desperate to get back into my good books. She was in here yesterday, taking a keen interest in a seven-thousand-euro escritoire. Wants the hubby to get it for their wedding anniversary. She was babbling on about her old ten per cent discount. I suppose *I'd* offer someone lunch at Jean Ramet to save seven hundred euros.'

Sophie moved to the foot of the stairs; she really wasn't interested in Cathérine's bitching. 'Oh well,' she said brightly, 'the food's *very* good at Ramet – it certainly deserves its Michelin star. I'm sure you'll have a lovely meal.'

Cathérine grimaced. 'With that leach of a woman? You must be joking! Anyway, don't forget to lock the door behind you if you finish before I get back.'

Sophie willed herself to keep smiling: she hated the way Cathérine always said the same thing week after week and made their lovemaking sound so mechanical. 'Do we ever?' she muttered under her breath.

'And enjoy your weekend with that fat old queen from Paris. I'm sure Buffet and Jean-Claude will get on like a house on fire!'

Sophie heard a floorboard creak above her and looked up. Geoffroy was standing at the top of the stairs pretending to impersonate Cathérine, silently moving his mouth like a ventriloquist's dummy. He held a glass of champagne in each hand and from his unzipped flies protruded a formidable erection. The front door banged shut and the lovers burst out laughing.

CHAPTER 6

As Jean-Claude droned on and on about the progress of the new wine's second racking, Henri de Bondé stared directly into his eyes. All he could think about, however, was Geoffroy's unbelievable luck: at this very moment, he'd be savouring the delights of Sophie Bourjois's body – and in an antique shop of all places. What a glorious paradox! Not for the first time, he wondered whether Bourjois had the slightest suspicion that his wife might be having an affair. Geoffroy's view, based on Sophie's observations and gut feeling, was that the dimwit didn't have a clue, which was par for the course as far as Henri was concerned. On the other hand, after three months of intimacy with Sophie, Geoffroy was wholly convinced that her husband had never even hinted at the least suspicion of anything untoward going on at La Fayette. She had, nonetheless, witnessed a change in his character during the course of the year. She'd first detected it sometime in late January – or possibly early February – when Jean-Claude had become even more introverted; trying to have a conversation with him these days, she'd confided, was like getting blood out of a stone. She'd even admitted that sex was now something of a rarity, although since the commencement of their affair, it was not a deprivation which caused her any loss of sleep.

With a hint of a smile, Henri continued to stare at Jean-Claude, who, somewhat embarrassed, looked down at his notes and pretended to seek confirmation for the barrage of facts on the vines' health and the progress of spraying for oidium with powdered sulphur. In truth, Henri's constant eye contact and supercilious facial expressions were making the weekly working lunch in the study even more unpleasant than usual. Thanks to the tension, he'd not touched any of the food laid out on the sideboard – a minimalist selection of assorted cheeses and hams plus a thickly sliced baguette – such a contrast to the lavish spreads Guy used to provide. Henri, however, had already downed a healthy plateful, plus two glasses of Pavillon Blanc de Château Margaux, probably the Médoc's best white wine; La Fayette, like most Médoc vineyards, only produced red. Jean-Claude had restricted himself to mineral water: having resolved to confront Henri, he needed to keep his wits about him.

Henri had started tapping the desk: he was bored stiff; he really couldn't pretend to be interested in the technical side of things. And anyway, wasn't that what Bourjois and his minions were paid to handle?

Frankly, as long as people did their jobs and made sure that there was a good crop of top-class fruit ready for picking come September, he couldn't give a fig about oidium or any of the other diseases which might attack the vines. But his father had instituted these tiresome weekly sessions with the *maître* and Henri supposed that it did keep people like Bourjois on their toes. He liked to stare out of the window once in a while and make the little tick think he wasn't paying attention. Then he'd suddenly fire off some pertinent question; he was thinking of one now. He'd wait until Bourjois moved on to his personnel report and then pounce with ... well, something like:

'*By the way, Bourjois, during the last four weeks what has been the cost per hectare of oidium spraying, and how does it compare with the same period last year?*'

He prayed Bourjois wouldn't have the answer – he really couldn't bear listening to any more drivel about powdered sulphur – and that the tedious bore would apologize and promise to let him have a written note of the figures as soon as he got back to his office.

Henri glanced at his watch: Bourjois really ought to have got to 'personnel' by now. He had quite a way to drive for his next appointment – Bordeaux's Jardin Botanique – how ridiculous! These cloak-and-dagger assignations were getting rather farcical. He felt sure the man was paranoid – 'Albion' indeed! What a stupid pseudonym! He really couldn't understand why 'Albion' wouldn't come to the château for their little meetings. After all, he had a perfectly legitimate excuse to pay regular visits – at least once in a while. Or they could meet in a restaurant in Bordeaux – anywhere. But there was just no arguing with Albion. ... What did it mean anyway, 'Albion'? ... Probably something classical, but he'd never been too hot on the classics at school. Maybe he should look it up some time. Yes, this afternoon, before setting off he'd–

It suddenly dawned on Henri that the room was strangely silent. He stopped fiddling with his empty wine glass and glanced at Bourjois. To his surprise, the prat was now staring at *him*, and, to be quite frank, he felt slightly uncomfortable about the expression on his face: if he wasn't mistaken, it looked remarkably like contempt.

'Yes, Bourjois? You've said all there is to say about oidium, I assume? Personnel ... hmm? I've got to make a move very shortly – important meeting in town. Keep it brief, there's a good chap.'

Jean-Claude shuffled his papers. 'I ... I ...'

'Yes? Nobody's died, have they? That pest – what's-his-name – the one who's always falling off ladders and things, he's not gone and cut off another finger, has he? Should never have employed him. Knew he'd be trouble as soon as–'

'I *know*,' Jean-Claude interrupted, '– I know about ...' He shifted uncomfortably in his seat and closed his eyes.

Henri furrowed his brow and sighed impatiently. 'Sorry? Know *what*? Get on with it, man. I can't spend all day–'

'I know about Maréchal.' Jean-Claude leaned back in his chair and sighed loudly as if a great weight had been removed from his shoulders. Henri, however, gave every indication of being even more confused.

'Bourjois, I really don't have time to play guessing games. What the hell are you gibbering about?'

'I'm not stupid, Henri. From the start I didn't like the idea of shipping bottles unlabelled to the States. Nor did I approve of your strategy for marketing Maréchal under a different name there. You don't have to be a genius to see how that waters down the goodwill. And ... and the opportunities for fraud with unlabelled bottles are–'

Henri thumped the desk angrily and set his plate and knife rattling. 'Now look, Bourjois, I thought we'd buried this old chestnut long ago. I can't believe you've got the audacity to raise it again. I don't tell you how or when to rack the bloody wine, do I? I don't tell you how or when to spray the vines for sodding oidium. Believe me, Bourjois, a lot of proprietors would. They'd be fussing around you all day long giving orders – "Spray this! Pick that! Prune now! Clean the vats! Scour out the *cuvier*!" Not me. I let you get on with your job. Christ, you virtually have carte blanche to do what you bloody like!'

'Perhaps you *should* take more interest,' Jean-Claude muttered.

'Don't be so bloody impertinent! ... The point is, I *don't* tell you how to do *your* job. Frankly, Bourjois, I wouldn't presume to do so. And yet *you*, someone who couldn't sell a glass of water to a man dying of thirst in the desert, have the damned cheek – the effrontery – to tell me how to market my wine. *My* wine, Bourjois, not yours.

'Have you ever been to the bloody States, Bourjois? ... Well, *have* you?' Henri waved his hands dismissively. 'I don't give a damn whether you have or not. They're ignorant, Bourjois – Americans are pig ignorant. They know nothing of France or the French language. A few can just about pronounce the word "*château*", although I suspect they think it's French for "winery". So, those dunces are never going to get their big mouths around "*maréchal*". Believe me, Bourjois, even Yanks who *have* heard of Château La Fayette aren't bright enough to connect it with Maréchal de La Fayette. And they'd never make the connection between our second wine's name and the hero of their little revolution against the English. For a start, they write his name as one word, L-A-F-A-Y-E-T-T-E, and call him "General Lafayette".'

'I know,' Jean-Claude admitted hesitantly. 'You've told me before. And I *did* read the report from those marketing consultants you hired in New York.'

Henri hit the desk once more; this time the knife clattered off the plate. 'Well then, why the hell are we having this bloody conversation again, Bourjois? They firmly advised that General Lafayette is a better brand name for the North America market – much better than Maréchal de La Fayette. It's as simple as that. And I thought we were all agreed that if we had stocks of both brands lying around here, there was the danger of those half-witted villagers we employ mixing the two up. It's sod's law. Can you imagine the nightmare scenario of hundreds of cases of General Lafayette going to the Paris Ritz and thousands of bottles of Maréchal turning up in New York? Can you? My God, it doesn't even bear thinking about!'

Henri looked again at his watch and stood up. '*Merde*! I've got to fly.' To his surprise, Jean-Claude remained glued to his chair. 'So, Bourjois, that's why Maréchal goes unlabelled to our U.S. distributor. They pop the General labels on at their New York warehouse. It's all done very professionally – if that's what's worrying you. ... All right? Anyway, good old General is selling over there like hot cakes. It's appealing to their best patriotic instincts!

'Sorry we haven't got time to discuss personnel, Bourjois,' Henri snapped unconvincingly as he moved towards the door with the intention of dismissing his *maître de chai*. 'Send a memo over if there's anything important. ... Bourjois?' Jean-Claude swivelled round in his chair to face him. 'Good bye, Bourjois.'

Mustering all his courage, Jean-Claude bided his time for a few seconds. Then, with untypical resolution, he said: 'So, Henri, you've watched them – the New York distributors – labelling our Maréchal with those 'General' labels we have printed by Monsieur Ducasse at Pauillac. Good labelling machine, is it?'

Henri fumed with exasperation. '*What*? I don't give a damn about the ... Oh, dear Lord, give me strength! ... Yes, Bourjois, it's state of the art. Now, *please*–'

'And presumably you don't know anything about them affixing Château La Fayette labels to our second wine ... do you, Henri?'

*

'Sorry to have kept you waiting, Bourjois,' Henri said in a voice which even sounded faintly apologetic. 'I've managed to ... to put back my next appointment.'

As Henri shut the study door and returned to his desk, Jean-Claude wondered why he simply hadn't used his mobile or the landline, just an arm's length away, to rearrange the appointment instead of going off to some other part of the house.

'Now, what's all this about what's-his-name – Ducasse? ... Are you sure you wouldn't like a glass of Pavillon Blanc, just a ...? Henri's half-hearted question faded away as he helped himself.

Jean-Claude politely declined. *Be firm!*

'Where were we?'

'Jean-Luc Ducasse.'

'Ah yes. Ducasse and Miami.'

'Orlando.'

'Orlando? Didn't you say something about Florida? I mean, you were babbling so quickly, I really couldn't begin–'

'Orlando *is* in Florida.'

'Oh.'

'Near Disney World and Epcot and–'

'Epcot?'

'It's another theme park.'

'Ah.'

'He went with his wife Mathilde, their son Stéphane, Stéphane's wife and their kids – his grandchildren – Jean-Luc's grandchildren, that is. ... They all stayed at the Orlando Marriot and–'

'Jean-Luc?'

'Our printer – Jean-Luc Ducasse.' Jean-Claude couldn't stop himself from tutting. 'The Ducasse family have been printing La Fayette's labels for over a century, Henri. You met Jean-Luc only a few months ago when commissioning the new labels for Maréchal – I mean General–'

'Yes, yes. I remember. ... Funny little man. ... And this Ducasse bought a bottle of General Lafayette in Miami?'

'No, *not* General – well, whatever it was, they had it at the Marriott in Orlando. Like I said before, Jean-Luc decided to treat his family to a holiday in Florida using the twins' – his grandchildren's – tenth birthday as an excuse.'

'How extraordinary! More money than sense, these people.'

'Anyway, one evening they had a slap-up meal at the Marriott's top restaurant, and, to his delight, Jean-Luc found his favourite wine – well, he told me it's his favourite – on the wine list.'

'General Lafayette?'

'*No*, Château La Fayette itself.'

Henri sat bolt upright. '*Really*? At the *Marriott*? – in *Miami*? – I mean Orlando? Are you sure?

Jean-Claude shrugged. 'Well, I'm only telling you what Jean-Luc told me himself. I'm sure he wasn't making all this up.'

'Of course not. I didn't mean ... I'm just so surprised. I ... I'd no idea the Marriott chain were customers of ours – of our American distributors, I should say. I'd have expected them to have reported ...'

The pregnant pause was taken by Jean-Claude as his cue to continue.

'Anyway, Henri, Monsieur Ducasse ordered a bottle of La Fayette–'

'*Château* La Fayette.'

'*Château* La Fayette ... the 96, still a bit on the young side but–'

'Not our greatest year.'

'No, but we're not ashamed of it.'

'Certainly not! ... And?'

'And ... well, it was ... OK. It was like – I mean, he knows our wines *very* well. Frankly, Jean-Luc thought that what he was drinking was a shade too light for *Château* La Fayette – Stéphane did too.'

'The son-in-law?'

'Son.'

'Whatever. The two of them are *experts* on La Fayette, I presume.'

'The Ducasses are good customers – have been for as long as I can remember. They buy at wholesale prices and–'

'*What*?'

'They provide us with an excellent service, Henri – always have done. Maybe their orders aren't big enough to attract *your* attention, but they're regular and loyal, vintage after vintage–'

'Oh, spare me the trip down memory lane, *please*. Anyway, the North American market for La Fayette is growing so strongly, Bourjois, that soon these bloody printers won't be able to afford it, whether at wholesale prices or otherwise.' Henri was on the point of launching himself into another one of his bouts of marketing hyperbole when he recalled the matter in hand.

'So,' he sighed, 'the whatsits – the Ducasses – thought their bottle of 96 La Fayette wasn't up to standard, and old Jean-Luc thought he was drinking Maréchal. That's what you're trying to tell me, isn't it?'

Jean-Claude nodded. 'Exactly.'

'But the bottle didn't have a Maréchal – or General – label on it, did it? ... *Did it*? I mean, it wasn't as though the hotel was trying to palm off a bottle of our second wine for–'

'Well–'

'There was a *Château* La Fayette label on the bottle.'

'Yes, but–'

'These yokels come across a bottle of our first wine which doesn't meet their "exacting" standards. In all probability, the hotel had badly stored it – too hot – too cold. Damn it – God only knows how they care for wine in Florida!' He shrugged in exasperation. 'I can't believe the oiks assumed there was a bloody false label on the bottle just because they thought the wine tasted more like Maréchal. A false label! I've never heard of anything so ridiculous. And as soon as old Ducasse gets back to France, he comes running to you with this cock and bull story. Jesus! – it's probably defamatory! – *actionable*! I hope the bastard hasn't been bad-mouthing our wine all around Bordeaux' – Henri gasped – 'or to the management at the Marriott!' He pointed a finger at Jean-Claude. 'I bet he's after free cases. Well, if your chum thinks he can get away with slander and keep our printing business–'

'Henri! Just wait a minute, will you? I haven't finished.'

Glaring open-mouthed, Henri was so outraged at being interrupted that by the time he'd thought of something suitably cutting to say, Jean-Claude was already completing his narrative.

'It's true the label on the bottle was a Château La Fayette label, but it wasn't one of ours.'

Henri closed his eyes and shook his head from side to side. 'What do you mean, "it wasn't one of ours"?'

'It *looked* like one of ours – the labels Ducasse prints for us, but' – Henri groaned – '... but ...'

'But *what*? This is getting more farcical by the–'

'The paper wasn't the same – very close but different. Jean-Luc only had to feel it and ...'

Henri glared at Bourjois maniacally, yet when he spoke, his voice was remarkably quiet. 'It wasn't the same paper?'

'No, it wasn't the paper Jean-Luc uses.'

'A rogue batch, perhaps. He can't check every roll of bloody paper he uses at his print works.'

'He seemed pretty sure.'

Henri stared pensively at a bookcase behind Jean-Claude. 'But the man can't be *absolutely* sure, can he? You have to agree that it's not beyond the bounds of credibility that his supplier could have cocked up and ... Why are you shaking your head?'

'It's not just the paper. He thought there was something fishy about the printing inks too, particularly the shade of red used for the vintage.'

'Oh, come *on*! There must be a dozen innocent explanations for something like that – storage in bright sunlight, dampness ... some glitch at the print works. One doesn't have to resort to the realms of conspiracy theories and counterfeiting and–' Henri pulled himself up short and frowned. 'Has he got this bottle with the mysterious label? Have you seen it? Surely, he didn't ask the hotel for the bottle and bring it back … did he?'

'No, I haven't seen it – the label. Jean-Luc only phoned me yesterday morning. He only got back from the States a few days ago. He thought we'd gone to another printer–'

'Ah! So, originally, he didn't think the label was "counterfeit". Maybe – just maybe – this yarn of his is a smokescreen – a pre-emptive strike – for some lousy labels he's delivered to us and which we're about to discover.'

'I really don't think so, Henri. The man's as honest–'

'Wait a minute! You said you hadn't seen the label, but you haven't answered my question about the bottle. Has he got it?'

'Er … I'm not sure.'

'What do you mean you're "not sure"?'

'I don't know – if he's got the bottle. He *has* got the label though.'

Henri's expression froze. For a few seconds there was silence. Then he rose from his chair. 'I think we ought to see it, don't you? – as soon as possible.'

'Yes.'

'You could pop over now and get it.'

'To Pauillac? – *now*?'

'Pauillac?'

'That's where Ducasse is – Pauillac.'

'Ah.'

'Wouldn't be any point though.'

'Why?'

'He's sent the label for analysis – a laboratory in Bordeaux.'

'He's–? A *laboratory*! … What the devil–?'

'Why do you look so horrified, Henri? I take it that if there *is* something criminal going on in America, you'd want to know about it?'

'What's *that* supposed to mean, Bourjois? Come to think of it, you started this fairy story with some cryptic comment about whether I'd seen our distributors affixing false labels. If you're–'

'I trust Jean-Luc Ducasse – one hundred percent.'

'He'd no right to send a label for analysis with some scandalous lies about our wine being … being … Fucking hell, it could be all round Bordeaux already! It's outrageous!'

'He hasn't told the lab guy anything, for God's sake. He just told him we were dual sourcing some labels and that he wanted to know whether his competitor was cutting corners on quality … that kind of thing.'

'Oh.'

Neither man spoke for some time.

Finally, after a heavy sigh, Henri said: 'All right, Inspector Bourjois, the Americans *are* labelling Maréchal as the *grand cru*. They must have been careless with the printing. It shouldn't have happened. It's incredible that Ducasse – of all people – should have spotted the fucking cockup. What are you going to do about it, Bourjois – bearing in mind that if this gets out, you'll be implicated?'

Jean-Claude could feel his brow burning. He'd been hoping against hope that there'd be an innocent explanation, but the nightmare had come true after all. 'I – I don't know. I ... How the hell did you think you could ever get away with this? How–?'

'Don't waste my time with a lot of sanctimonious crap, Bourjois. You know as well as I do that Maréchal knocks the spots off many *grands crus* – including some that retail in the States for three, four, or even ten times the price. Jesus! – most Yanks couldn't spot the difference between Maréchal and Lafite. False label or no sodding false label, the punter is getting good wine at a good price. So, where's the harm? We're just making more money to help pay for all the improvements you're always demanding.'

'Fraud's a serious crime, Henri. Some expert always spots it in the end. If Ducasse–'

'Ducasse isn't going to do *anything*.'

'Oh?'

'No, because you're going to sort him out.'

'Am I? I'm *not* involved in–'

'Oh yes you *are*. You're the *maître de chai*. Everyone will assume you're involved. You try and prove you're not. So that's why you're going to go and see Ducasse and tell him that we've traced the problem to our U.S. distributor. The labels on a consignment had been damaged – bad handling, a flood at the warehouse – and they used their initiative to get some new labels printed locally. I'm sure you can think of something. And because you're such mates and a paragon of virtue – nay, a saint! – he's bound to believe you. You'll thank him for bringing the matter to our attention and give him a case of our 1990.'

'I've told you, Henri, I'm not getting involved in this. I'm going back to the *chais* now to clear my desk. I'll tell everyone we've had a fundamental disagreement on the style of wine you want to–'

'You'll do no such thing! Have you forgotten about that sodding factory of a house you live in, Bourjois, and how my demented bloody father provided the finance for it?'

Jean-Claude's heart was pounding: this was exactly what he'd feared. 'That's all legal,' he croaked. 'There are contracts. As long as I keep paying off–'

'"*Legal*"? I've been to my lawyers, Bourjois, and I can tell you that the guarantee to the bank and the fucking loan of two *million* francs – converted, I recall, to some three hundred *thousand* euros when we dumped the dear franc in 1999 – could be set aside on the grounds that the Old Man was already loopy with Alzheimer's when you conned him. I mean, what rational employer gives a minion that sort of financial assistance, hmm?'

'I didn't "con"–'

'And anyway, the guarantee can be terminated at any time by giving six months' notice to the bank. You've also regularly missed repayments under *our* loan. Doubtless, you've been giving priority to the bank's mortgage, thinking us Bondés a soft touch.'

'I can easily find another job – and sell Le Porge.'

'Crap! If you jump ship, Bourjois, every prospective employer will think you're a prima donna, or smell a rat. And that vile house of yours is a white elephant. So, you're going to do *exactly* as I tell you, otherwise you and your family are going to be out in the street, and your kid is going to be out of his expensive school – unless, that is, your wife is now selling her shitty paintings, or your father-in-law has finally reconciled himself to his precious daughter's shotgun marriage to an impecunious tick.'

CHAPTER 7

Despite her restricted visibility in the back of the car, Laura had rarely seen a landscape so beautiful. Of course, the cloudless sky and dazzling sunshine helped in the portrayal of Entre-Deux-Mers as a rural paradise, as did the hot, dry air rich with the scent of early summer flowers rushing in through the open windows. And whenever she focused on the back of Quincy's large head, it occurred to her that the wine she'd consumed during lunch at the Régent was probably playing an important supporting role too.

It was really quite incredible how Quincy had got in on the act! From a chance meeting in a restaurant and a foolish slip of the tongue over the whereabouts of her putative preferred location for a Bordeaux pied-à-terre, Quincy – of all people! – was now privy to her most confidential plans and sitting in the front passenger seat of Lampre's battered Clio acting as if *he* was the client. In fact, the two men were chatting away like a couple of old biddies, and yet, because of the roar of the air as they sped along the D10 towards Cadillac, she was barely able to catch a word.

Quincy had insisted on taking the front seat because, as he'd passionately pleaded, squeezing into the back with his long legs would have been tantamount to torture. In all the circumstances, Laura could hardly have objected. And then, only a few hundred metres from the exit to Allées de Tourny's vast underground car park, Quincy had launched into a tirade against air conditioning – a major cause of summer colds, stiff necks, asthma and many other ailments too numerous to mention – with the result that orders were given for the windows to be lowered. That was when Laura became excluded from any meaningful participation in his enthusiastic interrogation of Lampre about Château Belle-Mère. Occasionally, when Quincy thought he'd extracted a particularly pertinent nugget of information, he would half-turn and, with a huge grin, pass it on to her.

Laura's initial irritation over the apparent hijacking of her vineyard project had begun to dissipate about ten minutes into the trip – the time it had taken Lampre to get them across the Garonne to the limits of Bordeaux's south-eastern suburbs. And then the magic of the Premières Côtes de Bordeaux's landscape had begun to calm Laura's nerves, and, to her surprise, engender a sense of fun and adventure. Even Quincy – the old rogue! – was seen in a different light. After all, two heads were better than one, and she needed an objective opinion about Belle-Mère – would she ever be able to say that crazy name without smiling? In truth, when all was said and done, Quincy was immensely knowledgeable: he certainly knew a darn sight more about the whole Entre-Deux-Mers region – 'E2M' as he called it – than she did. And although she wanted her project to progress expeditiously, she wasn't going to be rushed; Lampre could be very persuasive.

Yes, Quincey might be eager to curry sexual favours – perish the thought! – but he was clearly a man who wouldn't allow her to make a bad bargain. Mind you, whatever its plus factors, it would to take one hell of a lot of persuading to get her to change her mind about the Premières Côtes: people back home would scoff; you might as well go and make Chardonnay in Oregon, they'd say. Oh well, it would do no harm to look, and she was certainly enjoying the trip.

Stretching languidly, Laura moved to the centre of the rear seat to get a better view forward through the windscreen, and then leaned back with her hands behind her head. Steep wooded hillsides to her left and the Garonne's broad floodplain shimmering in the afternoon heat to her right; vineyards everywhere, some clinging to the lower slopes of the precipitous escarpment which marked E2M's south-western boundary, others planted in the gently shelving meadows bordering the wide river; villages built from a golden stone clustering around medieval churches with crocketed spires; châteaux, farms and cottages engulfed in rambling roses, ivy and trailing geraniums. If nothing else, E2M was a lot prettier than most of the Médoc, but then, the vine thrives best in poor soils. Perhaps that was why no wine from the Premières Côtes had ever generated any reputation outside the region: the land was just too rich and fertile. What a pity – it was like the Garden of Eden.

Laura's two companions didn't hear her sigh. Nor were they remotely aware of her shaking head as she considered the possibility that the whole idea of getting involved in wine making was complete madness, at least in Bordeaux. That was probably what Jean-Claude would tell her tomorrow. And, notwithstanding all his problems with Henri – the lack of investment, the arguments – he'd never leave Margaux and the Médoc and accept exile, as he would see it, on the *other* side of the river – not just the other side, but to the *south* of Bordeaux! Of course, there was always the bottle which she'd brought from the States. Using it would be very much a last resort, but when needs must–

No! Think positive, Laura! Maybe Jean-Claude will know of a decent Médoc estate, a little cru *bourgeois – good pun! – with potential, not yet on the market, and with an owner who's thinking of selling. After all, he knows every* maître *for miles around, and they all like and trust him. But if he balks at the idea of leaving a top name like La Fayette to go just around the corner to some petit château, well, I'll just have to convince him – without using my secret weapon if at all possible – that it would be better for the two of us to cut our teeth in a comparatively unknown appellation with potential. That's basically Quincy's philosophy – if I understood him correctly at the Régent. In fact, he seemed surprisingly positive about the whole idea of me buying a Premières Côtes vineyard from the moment he prised out of me the real reason for my meeting with Lampre.*

*

Over coffee at the Régent, Quincy confessed he'd known Lampre for years – they were both members of the local Lions Club – and confirmed that 'Pierre' was very well-connected and had 'something of a reputation with the ladies', which Laura thought was a bit rich. He'd also heard of Château Belle-Mère, but only because its wines commonly appeared on the *cartes des vins* of what he called 'run-of-the-mill' cafés and brasseries in Bordeaux – not that there was anything wrong with having a portfolio of loyal customers in the local hospitality trade. Skimming through Lampre's particulars – he'd snatched them from Laura even before she'd had a chance to read them herself – he opined that Belle-Mère's owners had clearly spent a lot of money – or rather, other people's money – on a grandiose scheme of improvements, including a new *cuvier* with state-of-the-art, computer-controlled stainless-steel vats, and an air-conditioned *chai*, both buildings being extravagantly clad in local limestone.

'So, they've aimed for high-volume, low-value sales,' Laura said solemnly. 'Not really what I had in mind.'

'It would certainly be a challenge, old thing. But Pierre's right in one sense – the Premières Côtes are on an upturn. There really is some excellent wine being made there now. Frankly, I'm surprised you're not better informed. Perhaps you're becoming a bit of a wine snob. Perhaps you only have time for *grands crus* these days – and your faddy Australian stuff, of course.'

'That does it!' cried Laura, snatching Belle-Mère's particulars out of Quincy's hands. Within seconds she was phoning Lampre & Fils on her mobile.

'I'll go and freshen up,' Quincy whispered.

When he returned from the washroom, Laura was smiling smugly. 'There – all arranged,' she chirped. 'I'll be visiting Belle-Mère within the hour.'

'Well, we'd better be off then.'

'"We"?'

'You don't think I'd let you go alone, do you, with that sex maniac?'

'But–'

'Don't be silly, Laura. It's no bother.'

'What? I ... Your afternoon appointment?'

'Cancelled.'

'When?'

'Just now – when I paid the bill on the way back from the loo. Mobiles are so handy, aren't they? Come on! We don't want to keep Pierre waiting, do we?'

*

Laura was jolted from her trance as the little car swerved off the main road with a terrific squeal of tyres and a vicious screech of clumsy gear changing.

'Sorry!' Lampre roared, '– almost missed the damned turning.'

Chuckling, Quincy did his now customary half-turn. 'Isn't this *fun*, Laura? – Formula I with scenery! Wouldn't have missed it for anything.'

A picture-postcard village was fleetingly glimpsed before the Clio, with its engine screaming, started to climb a narrow road that wound its way up a steep hillside.

'Where the hell are we?' shouted Laura above the racket.

'Langoiran, of course!' retorted Quincy as if coping with a senile grandparent. 'Surely you've been here before?'

'There's the château!' cried Lampre, taking one hand off the steering wheel and pointing wildly upwards and to the right.

Laura leaned over and stared: perched dramatically on a thickly wooded bluff was a huge ruined castle. Her eyes bulged. 'Oh, my God!' she moaned. 'If that movie set for *King Arthur – Camelot* – whatever – is Belle-Mère, Quincy, I'm–'

'That's the Château de Langoiran, you buffoon!' he guffawed, turning to Lampre and playfully thumping his shoulder. 'She thought that was–!'

'Belle-Mère!' exploded Lampre, taking both hands off the wheel as he threw himself forward.

'Mind that cyclist!' screamed Laura.

After the victim had extricated himself from a muddy ditch and been placated with a contribution of thirty euros towards the cost of remedying the minor damage to his bicycle, Quincy excused himself and retreated to a neighbouring copse to deal with a call of nature. While he was indisposed, Laura politely but firmly reminded Lampre that *she* was the interested purchaser of Château Belle-Mère – not Quincy; the Englishman was only along for the ride. If she heard any mention of the name 'Bourjois' in any connection at any time, she'd personally report Lampre to his professional

81

association for misconduct – and to the *gendarmerie* for reckless and dangerous driving.

'Just kidding!' she added, spotting Quincy emerging from the undergrowth.

As he strode towards them with the look of contentment of a man relieved of a bursting bladder, Lampre said: 'I've known Quincy for years. Charming fellow, but I wouldn't trust him as far as I could throw him – too many fingers in too many pies. ... Don't worry, Laura, your secret is safe with me.'

At the top of the hill, a gently undulating plateau of vineyards and woodland stretched in a verdant swathe to the horizon. After five kilometres of empty road, a large garishly painted sign decorated with representations of giant wine bottles stated that Château Belle-Mère was the next turning to the left, and that '*dégustation*' and '*vente*' were daily attractions. Lampre attempted yet another ninety-degree turn and swung the car between two massive stone pillars, each supporting a highly ornamental wrought iron gate. It was fortunate they were wide open, but then a general air of rust and decrepitude gave every indication that they'd not been closed in years.

To one side of the entrance, and almost camouflaged by rampant ivy, stood a decidedly run-down gatekeeper's lodge. What could be discerned of its fanciful nineteenth-century architecture reminded Laura of a Swiss chalet.

'Lovely cottage,' Lampre fizzed. 'Perfect for a housekeeper, head gardener – even a *maître de chai*.'

'*Very* nice,' Quincy empathised.

'It's empty then?' asked Laura. 'It certainly looks it.'

'Er ... nearly.' Lampre waved an arm theatrically. 'Now, what about that for an avenue! What an entrance! Very regal!'

Laura couldn't deny that the long gravel drive flanked on both sides by parallel rows of tall Lombardy poplars was impressive; she was momentarily reminded of the approach to Château Margaux. 'Pierre, what do you mean about the gatehouse being "nearly empty"?'

'What? Oh nothing – all fairly informal. I'm sure she'll be prepared to move if her son isn't retained. Very honourable people, the Fontaines. Madame Fontaine was something of a celebrity just before the War ... and for a while afterwards, but ... well, that's another story. ... Look! Over there between the trees, you can just see the lake. See it? Jolly big – there are swans and plenty of fish. Excellent for climate control, large expanses of water – cool things down in the summer and help to minimize frosts in–'

'Hang on, Pierre,' Laura interjected. 'Who's this old woman living in the gatehouse?'

'Belle-Mère's Miss Haversham?' suggested Quincy wickedly.

Lampre swerved to avoid a peacock. 'Bloody birds! Every time I come here they try to commit suicide. ... Er, "old woman"? ... Oh, you mean Madame Fontaine, the ex-owner's mother.'

'"Ex-owner"? *Owner*, surely?'

'No, *ex*-owner. Charles Fontaine – he's the manager-cum-*maître de chai* now. Nice chap.'

Before Laura could seek further clarification, the cool shade of the avenue was replaced by a dazzling blast of heat and light as the car drove onto an impressive expanse of finely raked gravel that would have done admirable service as a regimental parade ground.

'Bloody hell!' snorted Quincy, thrusting his head out of the window. 'Now that's what I call a château.'

Slamming on his much-abused brakes, Lampre's car skidded a few feet across the gravel. He bounded out: his safety belt had remained redundant throughout the trip from Bordeaux.

'Here we are, Laura, Château Belle-Mère. Now isn't that the loveliest house you've ever seen? Irresistible, isn't it?'

Relieved that they'd reached their destination in one piece, Laura extricated herself from the Clio's cramped rear quarters and came to stand by her companions. Lampre silenced himself for a few seconds: the house was its own best salesman.

He's right, Laura thought. *It is the loveliest house I've ever seen. ... So, what's the catch? There has to be a catch.*

'Well, Laura,' Quincy said slowly, 'I have to say that if you're not interested in this place, I might make an offer myself.'

There's the catch! Jesus, I'm thinking like a serious purchaser already!

Quincy held up his hands. 'Just kidding, you two. I've already got one great barn of a country house back in England. I certainly don't want another – not even a gem like this.'

The heavenly tranquillity of Belle-Mère's east front was rudely shattered by a tremendous grating of bolts. All eyes focused on the monumental double doors at the centre of the facade, a textbook example of mid-eighteenth-century symmetry and restrained neoclassicism built from the finest local limestone. Before the doors were fully open, two black Labradors shot out, barking furiously as they bounded down the steps towards the visitors. Behind them came a raucous shriek – in English.

'*Pum*phrey an' '*um*phrey! – *be*-'ave!'

It was a woman's voice which bore all the hallmarks of an upbringing in London's East End. Simultaneously, Laura and Quincy, who'd instinctively moved closer together for their mutual defence, shot fearful glances towards the dogs; Lampre's admonitions that they were harmless barely registered. But as the Labradors approached, their pace slowed, the barking ceased, and wagging tails became the order of the day. Then they performed a brief tour of inspection, whereupon, reassured that the newcomers were friendly, Humphrey and Pumphrey rolled onto their backs and stuck eight legs into the air.

'Madame Pronk,' Lampre announced, nodding towards the woman stomping noisily towards them across the gravel. 'Her French isn't too good,' he added between smiling clenched teeth. He was about to take a step forward when Laura gripped his arm.

'But that's ... It can't be! Quincy, tell me it isn't her – *please.*'

'I'm afraid, my dear, that unless she has an ugly twin sister, it is. Brace yourself.'

Madame Pronk was almost upon them. With milky-white skin and dyed-black bobbed hair, she was of medium height and slim, but big busted. Notwithstanding the scorching heat, she was incongruously clad in a black ankle-length sleeveless smock, and sported a pair of black Doc Martens. Nonetheless, she appeared remarkably fresh and cool. To be fair, she didn't look her fifty-two years.

Waving, Lampre shouted gaily: 'Hello, Suzanne!' Lowering his voice, he added: 'I don't understand. You know the Pronks already?'

'"*Pronks*"?' muttered Laura and Quincy simultaneously.

'Pierre,' Quincy croaked, 'this ... *creature–*'

'I just knew there'd be a catch,' Laura hissed, 'but, Jesus, this has to be some kinda–!'

'Welcome to Belle-Mère, folks. Pierre, darlin', 'ow lovely to see you again!' Madame Pronk's French was indeed execrable.

'Lovely to see you too, Suzanne.'

Lampre and Madame Pronk kissed each other's cheeks. Next in line, Laura held out her hand. She decided to speak in English.

'Hello. We've met before, I think. It *is* Susan–?'

'Well, I never!' blasted Madame Pronk as she bypassed Laura and planted herself in front of Quincy. 'Poor old Pierre must be losin' 'is marbles. When 'e told me 'e was bringin' a world-famous wine expert, I was sure 'e mentioned some female – Lorna Appledung or somethin'. Well, I said to Pronkie – Eric – me 'ubby – you'll meet 'im later – 'e'll answer any technical questions you might 'ave about the soil, the *cuvier* – all that kind of malarkey.' She grimaced with an expression of suicidal apathy. 'Pronkie'll probably bore the pants off you. That's why I normally keep 'im under lock and key unless it's really necessary to wheel 'im out from 'is glory 'ole.

'Anyway, I says to Pronkie, "She can't be *that* famous, this Appletree dame, or I'd 'ave 'eard of her." But *you*! – the Numero Uno! What a thrill! You've always been my favourite. And for a bloke your age, you're really quite hunky – quite sexy! Oops, there I go again. I'll be getting Pierre jealous' – she flashed a smile at Laura – '... and your lady friend, perhaps, if I don't watch me Ps and Qs.' Madame Pronk slapped one of her wrists. 'But I've got a little bone to pick with you, Hugh,' she mewed – 'Hugh' was pronounced very grandly – putting an arm through Quincy's and steering him towards the house, the dogs following obediently.

'I am *not*–'

'You're a very, *very* naughty boy,' she scolded, 'for not puttin' me other place in your little *Pocket Wine Book* thing – very naughty indeed. And after all these years and all them free samples I've sent you. I mean, you've got some of our neighbours in, and frankly, Hugh, their stuff tastes like shit.' She tilted her head upwards with the intention of subjecting Quincy to an expression of justifiable outrage, but he was staring down at her through a mask of bewilderment.

'I – I ... Your *other* place?'

'Oh *'onestly*, Hugh! Our château at – *near* St-Emilion ... Château Barrage. *You* know? Don't play games, darlin'.'

'Madame ... *Pronk*–'

'Hugh!' she cried, grinding to a halt. 'If we're going to be friends, darlin', don't ever call me that. I'm *Sue*, OK? – Sue Olivier. Olivier's me maiden name. Posh, isn't it? – like Laurence Olivier – no relation, mind you. Always use it professionally. Me 'usband's the Pronk – a right Pronk, if you get me drift. Belgian ... they're in fertilizers, the Pronks. Bloody loaded the lot of 'em – except soddin' Eric, of course. Disin'erited 'im when he married me, see.'

'Suzanne!' shouted Lampre.

Sue Pronk, née Olivier, tutted and turned her head. 'Shit! Why are those two ninnies still standin' by the car?' She nudged Quincy in the ribs. 'Oh! – is the girl with the old letch? I thought she was your ... Are you married, Hugh, darlin'? Would you fancy–?'

'Suzanne!' roared Lampre. Moving a few steps towards Sue and Quincy, he beckoned the former; Laura remained rooted to the spot, with hands on hips.

Quincy removed his companion's hand from his arm. 'I think ... *Sue*, that you'd better go and have a word with your *immobilier*. I'm afraid you've made a very serious mistake. The "girl", as you describe her, is the renowned transatlantic wine writer to whom "the old letch" was referring.

It is she, dear lady, and not I, who wishes to purchase a vineyard. And I hate to disappoint you, but the name "Hugh" does *not* appear on my birth certificate. Nor have I at any time changed my name by deed poll or otherwise to "Hugh". I suspect you are confusing me with someone else. Our international television celebrity looks a bit miffed, doesn't she? Ah, here's poor Pierre.'

'Suzanne, *chérie*, there's some confusion, I think. The young lady–'

'You stupid old goat! This bloke's just told me. If you did yer job properly and didn't spend 'alf your time chattin' up the talent ... Oh never mind, but if you've loused up another potential sale with them wanderin' 'ands, I'll ... Christ! I thought I recognised 'er. It's that ... Shit! I only met her a few weeks ago. She's that Jane ... Janet ... *Robson*!'

Quincy sighed. 'Jan*cis* Robin*son* – not *Janet*. ... Oh, for God's sake!'

Sue shot Quincy a withering look. 'Whatever. Don't budge, you two. I'll go and butter up our star.' She began to retrace her steps. 'I know you though,' she snarled, looking back over her shoulder at Quincy. 'In fact, I've seen you somewhere recently too.' But before either he or Lampre could enlighten her, Ms Olivier scampered away towards the solitary prospective purchaser with outstretched arms and a shrill screech of 'Janice, *darlin'*! Sor-*ry*! Usual French cock up!'

'"Janice"?' queried Lampre. 'Who – or what – is "Janice"?'

Quincy groaned and shook his head. 'Don't ask. I suspect, however, dear friend, that we will soon discover that we've had a wasted trip.'

*

Although Sue Olivier was wholly mercenary, it could not be disputed that she was an enthusiastic saleswoman. Indeed, she was one of that special breed who, given sufficient time and a little training, could sell almost anything to anyone. True to her class, however, Sue had never possessed the least interest in any of the products she'd sold over the years, including beverage vending machines, fashion accessories, and wine. And although she'd always enjoyed making money, it was the act of selling per se which gave her a thrill: whenever she closed a deal – be it large or small – she'd experience an extraordinary flow of adrenalin. In brief, she was addicted to selling; everything else in life was subsidiary. Yet, back in England some twenty-five years earlier, this addiction had come close to ruining her.

Abandoned by her unmarried mother at an early age and brought up by grudging relatives on a grim Dagenham council estate, Sue had left her mediocre school without any qualifications. But a ruthless determination to improve her lot in life led her through a succession of better-paid jobs until, in her mid-twenties, she'd saved enough to buy her own home and a direct-marketing fashion accessories franchise. Alas, operating under a highly regulated and restrictive agreement with her franchisor, First Lady – a large and aggressive American corporation – Sue had been unable to resist the temptation to seek and accept the occasional order from outside Essex, her allotted exclusive territory. Nor had she been reluctant to source 'identical' merchandise from counterfeiters in the Far East. Fellow franchisees in East Anglia and Greater London called foul, whereupon the awesome might of the English legal system was galvanized to punish Sue's wickedness.

First Lady engaged a prestigious firm of lawyers, a vitriolic war of words commenced, and writs for breach of contract, breach of copyright, trade mark infringement and passing off were served. During the preliminary skirmishes, Sue's solicitors were frenetically proactive and smugly confident, but their attitude changed when the third successive invoice for an amount in excess of ten thousand pounds remained unpaid. Sue's savings were almost exhausted, and although she'd temporarily fixed herself up with a telemarketing job for a motor insurance company, her income was barely sufficient to pay the mortgage. The solicitors terminated their retainer and sued for their unpaid fees. Scenting blood, the Americans pressed home and obtained judgment by default; the costs awarded to them greatly exceeded the damages Sue was required to pay.

Although she was now broke, First Lady started bankruptcy proceedings, solely for the dubious gratification of witnessing their former franchisee's public humiliation. On the eve of her first appearance in the Bankruptcy Court, Sue packed a small suitcase, removed a floorboard in her Basildon semi-detached, extracted a metal cashbox, and then drove to Gatwick Airport. For no particular reason, she took a commuter flight to Brussels. Being late evening by the time she landed, there were only a few planes scheduled for departure before the airport shut down for the night. A flight to Kinshasa caught her attention; she'd no idea where it was, but 'Kinshasa' sounded exotic.

The next morning, Sue found herself trying to explain to three immigration officers why she'd come to their country; it was still called Zaïre in those days, a name far more romantic than the misleading 'Democratic Republic of Congo'. Life in Belgium's former colony proved to be cheap: by noon, she was installed in one of the capital's better hotels; while lunching alfresco beside its swimming pool, she swiftly deduced that her fellow guests were mainly local bigwigs and Belgian businessmen. After a welcome siesta in her room, she awoke just in time to witness her first tropical sunset, and was intrigued by its rapidity. But as darkness fell, an intense feeling of loneliness overwhelmed her; for the first time since her miserable Dagenham childhood, she sobbed.

Sue helped herself to a Scotch from the minibar to steady her nerves. She had another, told herself something would turn up, and realised she was starving. Half an hour later she was sat in the hotel's bar, staring at a menu in French. She asked a good-looking European in his early thirties sitting alone at a neighbouring table if he could help translate; he was more than happy to oblige. It transpired he was a Belgian mining engineer returning home to Antwerp after a tour of duty upcountry. Improvising desperately, Sue said she worked for a British vending machine manufacturer which was investigating new export markets. After a few questions about whom she was seeing in various government ministries, he tactfully changed the subject and invited her to join him for dinner. She was happy to accept. When he crept out of her room around five the next morning, he left approximately a hundred pounds in local currency on the dressing table. For over an hour after discovering the money, she seethed with outrage, disgust and shame.

Two nights later, Sue dined at the hotel with an American, who, having spent most of the meal describing his perfect wife and two perfect children and their perfect home back in Salt Lake City, asked – as she partook of coffee and *petits fours* – how much she charged. 'Two hundred dollars,' she replied without hesitation. He raised his eyebrows. 'Fine,' he snapped.

After a fortnight, the manager asked to see Sue in his office. Three days later, with his assistance, she moved to the *Villa Tintin*, a tastefully furnished house with four domestic staff in Gombe, one of the city's best suburbs and home to most of the European population. Within a week, she was receiving French lessons from a visiting Swiss professor of chemistry at the Université de Kinshasa. He was a good teacher, but Sue would speak French for the rest of her life with a bizarre Essex-Swiss-African accent.

Eric Herman Pronk had a bright future ahead of him when he first met Sue in 1979; he also had a heart of gold. Although the youngest of three sons, Eric was destined to succeed his father at the helm of the Ghent-based Pronk fertilizer empire, his brothers having opted for careers in the law and ballet. At thirty-two, the only blot on the landscape was Eric's childless marriage to a very junior member of the Belgian royal family; Astrid was three years his junior and had married Eric for his money and excellent prospects of acquiring much more. A vast intellectual gulf separated them: Eric had a clutch of degrees, played the flute, and rarely travelled without his treasured box of watercolours; Astrid had been educated at a Swiss establishment where she'd excelled in flower arranging, deportment and the art of table laying. Her main interests were entertaining and being entertained.

Eric's work frequently took him to the Pronk fertilizer plant in Zaïre, trips which greatly facilitated Astrid's affairs. Within six months of their marriage, Eric found another man's underwear in his dressing room – duly washed and pressed by the maid. Astrid broke down and begged forgiveness, although it really was all his fault – leaving her alone so often and for so long. Her tears brought forth absolution, just as they always would do. And then an alcoholic night on the town in Kinshasa caused Eric to expose the failure of his two-year marriage to the works manager. Within the hour, he was pressing the *Villa Tintin*'s doorbell.

Eric sobbed so much after sex with Sue that she felt obliged to ascertain the cause of his misery. She then recounted her own disasters by way of consoling him. Forthwith, he promised to settle her debts in England, but she had no desire to rake up the ashes of the past: 'Sue Olivier' was dead and buried; as 'Louise La Blanche', she had a house with servants, a stunning client list and – to be blunt – a lot of fun. England could go to hell. Eric, however, didn't give up: he tried to frighten Sue into a sense of reality by warning her of Zaïre's political instability and the dangers of revolution and war; she risked being beaten and raped by a sadistic client – possibly someone in power. So far, she'd been lucky – very lucky – but he doubted that it would last much longer. Sue scoffed.

Five months later, Sue's landlord increased her rent by fifty per cent. She threatened to go elsewhere, but he pointed out she'd signed a five-year lease with no right to terminate. Then the hotel manager increased his 'referral fee' – also by fifty per cent. For some weeks, Sue ignored the increases. Then one night she awoke to find three Congolese in her bedroom, armed with a terrifying assortment of guns and knives. She had the sense not to resist while a machete was held to her throat and told what would happen if she didn't comply immediately with the new financial arrangements. After they'd left, she went downstairs to check on her housekeeper. The kitchen's back door was wide open; while closing it, she spied what looked like a football lying on the path outside. Tentatively, she switched on the garden lights. Her screams awoke the neighbours: the 'football' was the housekeeper's severed head.

It took Eric Pronk three days and much money to bribe the right people to procure Sue's release from police headquarters where she was being held on suspicion of murder. It took many more days and much more cash to get her on a plane for Europe. Somewhere over the Sahara, Eric proposed; Sue accepted readily. Within days, they were residing in a rented Ghent apartment. Astrid, however, refused to grant Eric a divorce, despite their defunct marriage and his offer of a generous financial package: the shame of being 'dumped for an English tart' would destroy her life, she claimed; there was also the Belgian Royal Family's standing to consider. Eric's father pulled no punches: a divorce would result in excommunication, disinheritance, and dismissal from the company. When Eric's elder brother, Léopold – the lawyer – turned up at the apartment and attempted to buy Sue off, Eric's self-control finally evaporated. After beating up Léopold, he swiftly instructed his lawyers to file a divorce petition, citing his wife's adultery. It was the only unchivalrous act of Eric's life; he would live to regret it.

Eric and Sue were married in a civil ceremony at Branne, a dull town on the Dordogne, five kilometres south of St-Emilion. Château Barrage, a fifteen-minute drive eastwards along the river, had become Eric and Sue's refuge shortly after the Pronk family declared war. It was the home of Eric's younger brother, Philippe, who, upon learning of the 'scandal', had rallied to Eric's side with dramatic declarations of filial loyalty and offers of assistance. Philippe had himself been banished when he'd first defied their father and opted for a dancing career. He promptly compounded his disgrace by abandoning ballet to 'marry' a dilettante twenty years his senior, Daniel Bendix-Cohn, whose father headed a prestigious Paris-based merchant bank. A defrocked Swedish rabbi conducted the televised 'marriage' in Barrage's former chapel; the Entre-Deux-Mers estate was the banker's gift to satisfy Daniel's latest whim of launching himself into the glamorous world of wine.

Although Daniel and Philippe had the very best intentions of turbocharging the nondescript red, white and rosé wines of Château Bendix-Cohn-Pronk – as Barrage had been renamed – the dilapidated house's refurbishment was their immediate priority. In any event, as neither of them had any technical knowledge of wine production, they were more than happy to delegate everything on that front to the incumbent *maître de chai*, a middle-aged gentleman of Neanderthal appearance brimming with earthy self-confidence.

Five years later, after Daniel had lost all interest in both wine production and his partner, Philippe found himself the absolute owner of the château's holding company, thanks to an apparently generous deed of gift. He soon painfully gleaned that the company was almost insolvent: there was no cash at the bank, the wine business was unprofitable, and Daniel had been kept afloat by 'loans' from his father. The *maître de chai* promptly abandoned the sinking ship, as well he might: much of the expenditure sanctioned for improvements to the wine production facilities had been channelled into bogus enterprises controlled by himself. To cap it all, the amount of money expended on the château's refurbishment far exceeded its market value.

At first, this depressing environment in which Eric and Sue sought sanctuary, seemed like a classic case of 'out of the frying pan, into the fire'. Furthermore, after only a few days in residence, Philippe began to doubt his sanity: how on earth could he have forgotten that his brother was a crushing bore? As for the Briton, well, she was horribly common – and, to boot, homophobic. On the second morning at breakfast, Sue said: 'You know, Phil, I just can't get over 'ow a big, strappin' lad like you can be a fairy.' She had a stock of similar gems.

Philippe could never have imagined that this hopelessly mismatched couple of drudges would be his salvation. Even before they'd finished unpacking, Eric was nosing around the *cuvier* ascertaining what all the equipment did and firing questions at the disgraced *maître de chai*'s mediocre successor. Meanwhile, surrounded by a mountain of unanswered mail from irate creditors and customers, Philippe was trying to keep Sue out of his office; she had a very irritating habit of questioning everything he did. He started cursing when she picked up the phone and, in execrable French, took it upon herself to offer substantial discounts to a customer who was threatening to cancel a large order due to alleged consumer disinterest in the estate's latest vintage. With Philippe pacing the room and wringing his hands, she went on to announce that 'the winery' had been taken over by 'an international conglomerate', she was the new 'CEO', work had already started to upgrade 'the product', and 'the enterprise' would soon be trading under 'a new brand'. During the ensuing fracas, very frank words were exchanged, but when Philippe subsequently retired to his bedroom to sulk, he was forced to admit that much of what Sue had said about marketing his wine made sense. Within weeks, and to their mutual relief, Eric bought him out – ironically with a loan from Banque Bendix-Cohn.

Château Barrage was resurrected. After a few years, it was booming as a supplier of decent, reasonably priced wines to almost every supermarket and budget eatery in France. There was, however, no melting of the ice between Ghent and Branne, albeit Eric's kin were consoled by his failure to sire any children, a state of affairs which suited Sue perfectly but which caused Eric much well-camouflaged sadness. The pride and arrogance of the Belgian Pronks led them to conclude presumptuously – yet, in the event, correctly – that Sue couldn't have children. Eric once had the temerity to suggest adoption; Sue's reaction, however, was so terrifying he never raised the subject again.

Had Sue been content with Château Barrage's success, she and Eric could have enjoyed a fairly prosperous lifestyle. Alas, when nearby Belle-Mère came on the market, she couldn't resist the challenge. Eric, being congenitally cautious, was unenthusiastic; he capitulated, as usual, after weeks of incessant bickering. Without doubt, Belle-Mère had considerable potential: the bankrupt owner, Charles Fontaine, a confirmed bachelor in his early fifties, had already done much to improve quality. For years the estate had produced pleasant dry white wines for drinking young, but on inheriting the estate when his father died, Fontaine resolved to transform Belle-Mère into a Premières Côtes showpiece for white, red and rosé wines. Rashly, his bank provided the necessary funds for the replanting, re-equipping and retraining of the château's loyal workers.

Although wines of good quality were being produced after only a few years – just as Fontaine had promised – there was one big problem: he hadn't the slightest idea about marketing. Almost the entire production of Belle-Mère's whites had long been sold to the same portfolio of restaurants and brasseries in and around Bordeaux. Now, he expected these same loyal customers to place smaller orders for red, white *and* rosé wines – and, furthermore, at higher prices. Unsurprisingly, they weren't willing to do his job of promoting these new products to their own customers – customers, moreover, who'd acquired an entrenched brand image of Belle-Mère being synonymous with decent white plonk. So, Fontaine found himself in a new and fiercely competitive market place without the skills or financial resources to exploit it. There was a cash flow crisis, the bank panicked, receivers were appointed, and Fontaine had a nervous breakdown.

The Pronks bought Belle-Mère at a rock-bottom price. In a sense, they got Fontaine thrown in as part of the bargain: desperate not to be exiled from the only home he'd ever known, or from his babies – the three promising new wines he'd sired – he offered his services as *maître de chai* on condition that he and his aged mother could remain in their home. More than willing to oblige, Sue thought she was being generous by putting the long-abandoned gatehouse at the Fontaines' disposal. As this was rent free, she'd no qualms in offering Fontaine a derisory salary. It was an insult, but in his weak and shell-shocked position, he'd made no protests.

Now, after three years of suffering her inimitable management style, and having been reduced to a state akin to feudal servitude, Fontaine had come to hate Sue. Indeed, he was secretly delighted that the Pronks' investment in Belle-Mère had been a failure: it was one thing selling Barrage's humble offerings to supermarket chains, but quite another matter finding a niche for a 'rising star' in the more discerning marketplace which had almost destroyed Fontaine himself. Sue's fundamental problem was that wine per se simply didn't interest her; she couldn't understand what all the fuss was about. If you drank a bottle of Barrage, you got pissed – good and proper for around eight euros; a bottle of Latour, Margaux or Lafite had the same effect but at a ludicrous price. And she'd drunk them all at some of the posh do's she'd been to, and, frankly, she preferred Barrage. She said so – bluntly; she called a spade a spade. So, when Sue cornered quality wine merchants at trade fairs and claimed that Belle-Mère's 'products' were the best wines ever produced in Bordeaux, she upset many fellow viticulturists – and made many more laugh and scoff. Stung by her lack of success, she'd finally attempted to emulate her achievements at Barrage: she increased volumes, thereby lowering quality, and attempted to 'flog' – as she was prone to say – two competing brands to her faithful Barrage customers. Eric warned her: he said it was like the old British Motor Corporation marketing an Austin Mini and a Morris Mini. She retorted that Rolls-Royce hadn't done too badly selling what was basically the same car under the Rolls-Royce and Bentley brands.

With a confused message being given to the trade, the ambiguous Belle-Mère brand suffered most. It was fortuitous, therefore, that from the outset Eric had insisted on Belle-Mère being conducted through a separate company with its creditors having no security over Barrage's assets. Accordingly, when receivership finally materialized, the Pronks could walk away from Belle-Mère without too much fallout affecting the faithful milch cow at Branne. Nevertheless, Sue was determined to prove a point: in her opinion, the bank had acted precipitously when foreclosing. If they'd only been prepared to extend the company's overdraft and give her time to put Belle-Mère on the market, everyone could have been happy. That was bad enough, but the injustice had been compounded by the accountants' valuation of the business as a going concern: it was far too conservative. If Belle-Mère were sold at such a discount, the bank's loans wouldn't even be cleared, there'd be an insolvent winding up, and the capital which the Pronks themselves had invested would also be lost. She might not be able to distinguish a St-Emilion from a St-Julien, but she knew that Entre-Deux-Mers was on an upward swing.

Despite the debacle, when the receivers' accountants came to Belle-Mère with the first prospective purchaser, they'd been impressed by Sue's proactive endeavours to dispose of it as a going concern – so much so, that they'd been content for her to handle all subsequent 'site visits' without the need for them to motor out from their comfortable Bordeaux offices. She had, therefore, been given a lifeline and an exciting marketing opportunity. Time, however, was now running out. The bank was getting restless: more than nine months had passed since the receivers' appointment, yet a realistic offer still hadn't materialised. Consequently, Sue was prepared to do almost anything to convince Laura Appleton – whoever she might be – that Château Belle-Mère was exactly what she was looking for.

CHAPTER 8

'You've got to see me *source* first,' Sue fizzed as she grabbed Laura's arm and attempted to steer her towards a gravel path which led into woodland.

'"Sauce"?' queried Laura as she tried to extricate herself from Sue's vice-like grip; she'd never liked tactile women. '"*Sauce*"?'

Sue seemed not to hear and turned her head. 'Come on, you two! You're like a couple of old codgers. You've got to see me *source* first, Quincy. It's terrific. Chop-chop! Last one to the *source* is a sissy!'

Quincy turned to Pierre Lampre for enlightenment.

'Oh, God!' the estate agent cursed between a forced smile. 'Not again! Has the woman no imagination?'

'Where's the vampire taking us, Pierre? – not to the kitchen, surely?'

'I wish!' snorted Lampre. 'You'll see soon enough, my friend. I don't want to spoil the show.'

Up ahead, Sue was setting a fierce pace as she embarked on her now standard itinerary for prospective purchasers; there was much to see and not a moment to spare. Somehow, she'd reattached herself to Laura's elbow.

'"Sauce"?' repeated Laura for the third time, as they entered the wood's welcome shade and relative coolness.

'Oh, you'll love it, Laura – very 'istoric – really ancient. I know 'ow much you Yanks love that kind of stuff. Never stops – summer, winter – just keeps gurglin' away. And such a romantic location – like a grotto – with Greek statues and everythin'. There's a sort of temple too – you know, one of them whatsits ... a placebo.'

'"Placebo"?'

'That's what Pronkie calls it, a placebo.' Noticing the look of total bewilderment on Laura's face, Sue added: 'I suppose all these 'istorical and architectural things are a bit double Dutch to you, darlin'.'

Laura sighed. She prayed that Quincy and Pierre would stop gossiping and catch up with them. She tried to reduce her pace, but Sue's momentum was a force to be reckoned with.

A few minutes later, acting as if she was undergoing a religious experience, Sue stood before the trio of perspiring visitors. Behind her, at the mossy centre of a stone wall built long ago into the hillside, water trickled from the mouth of what its sculptor had probably intended to be a lion's head. The representation, however, was somewhat naive, and the ravages of time had not improved matters. The water filled a dark, foul-smelling and roughly circular pool about four metres in diameter; on one side, four fluted but dilapidated Ionic columns supported a badly cracked cupola. The entire structure was covered in mildew, as were the 'Greek statues' which decorated it – in reality, two crumbling busts of Montesquieu and Montaigne. Three steps descended to the pool, where a row of slimy stepping stones led to the 'lion's head'.

Sue turned and stretched out her milky-white arms towards the miniscule cascade. 'The *source*,' she intoned. Behind her, someone sniggered. She guessed correctly that Dubloon was responsible, but when she spun round, everyone had a face seemingly devoid of emotion. 'Yeah,' she said, nodding her head, 'I was struck dumb too the first time I saw it. Terrific, ain't it?'

'I love your gazebo,' Quincy boomed, pinching Laura's elbow furtively. 'Ionic, isn't it?'

It was Sue's turn to be baffled, but she'd had a lifetime's experience of people talking over her head. She kept smiling and followed his gaze. 'Oh, you mean our little temple? ... Ironic? Do you really think so? ... Anyway, who's first for a refreshin' glass of pure Belle-Mère haitch-two-hoh, hmm? You see, we're not just famous for our wines, Laura – *oh* no!' All eyes followed Sue as she sprinted to the gazebo, picked up an old cracked glass secreted behind one of the busts, and descended the steps.

'Mind you don't slip on those stones,' Quincy warned with exaggerated concern. 'We wouldn't want you to have an accident, would we, boys and girls?'

Before Laura could think of an excuse to escape the horror of drinking the spring water, Sue had returned safely and was pushing the glass into her hand.

'There you are, Laura, darlin'. Get that down yer 'atch. You must be parched.'

'I – I–'

'Go *on*! It's not poisoned. I don't know, you Americans! Everythin's got to be sterile, pre-packed, and guaranteed one hundred per cent bacteria-free before you'll touch it. Old Lampre here's drunk enough of this stuff to float a battleship ... *sink* a battleship? – whatever – 'aven't you, Pierre? You love it, don't you?'

Lampre nodded unenthusiastically.

'Really?' said Quincy, wide-eyed. 'That would explain a lot of things. It's an aphrodisiac then, Sue?' Before she could frame a reply, he'd snatched the glass from Laura's hand, and, turning a blind eye to the ingrained lip marks around its rim, drained the contents in one gulp. With an aroma of rotten eggs, the lukewarm liquid reminded him of the allegedly medicinal waters of Buxton, Vichy, Baden-Baden and other spas which he'd had the misfortune to sample over the years. He pulled a face as if he'd just downed a tumbler of bathtub gin, doubled up, and then jumped into the air. 'Bloody *hell*!' he roared. 'Don't drink that stuff, Laura, my dear. I can feel it doing extraordinary things down in my nether regions already. You'd be throwing caution to the wind and panting for my exquisitely muscular body before you could say–'

'OK, everyone,' Sue shrieked, '– back to the 'ouse! Tempest fudge it!' She'd had enough: this wasn't how things normally turned out on her prospective-purchaser tours. Dubloon was taking the piss; she was going off him very quickly. Not that she'd ever really been on him: from the outset, she'd thought he was one of those creeps who hover around department stores' lingerie displays and sniff ladies' underwear when they think nobody's looking.

The tour of the house was conducted at an equally breakneck speed and without any offer of refreshments. Had it not been for Quincy's enervating cocktail of wicked humour and unbridled enthusiasm for the building, Laura, who was feeling both exhausted and dehydrated, might have degenerated into a wholly negative state of mind and asked to be taken back to Bordeaux. She certainly had to agree that the château itself had potential; indeed, 'potential' was a word which was hardly off Quincy's lips that afternoon. True, it had seen better days: ever since Charles Fontaine had taken the decision to upgrade the estate's wines, little had been spent on the house. There was a general air of fadedness, with peeling paint and plaster, rotting window frames, and numerous damp patches. Sue made light of it all, of course, drawing everyone's attention to the splendid furnishings – a veritable mountain of fine antiques collected by many generations of Fontaines. With a relatively small outlay, she opined, the house could become 'a real palace'. To her intense relief, both Lampre and Quincy wholeheartedly concurred. Quincy, in fact, could hardly control himself as he poured out suggestions on colour schemes, rearrangements of pictures and furniture, the restoration of period wall coverings, and so forth. Sue even began to consider the possibility that 'Quince' wasn't such an idiot after all.

Finally, to complete the tour of the house, the fatigued visitors trudged behind Sue into Belle-Mère's splendid dining room. It was dominated by a monumental yet filthy chandelier and more than a dozen gilt-framed full-length portraits of eighteenth- and nineteenth-century Fontaines. Interrupting Sue's discourse on the indications of hereditary insanity revealed in the portraits, Laura said frostily:

'In view of the château's size, there seems something almost perverse about the exile of Monsieur Fontaine and his aged mother to the gatehouse's cramped quarters, particularly as no one lives here permanently.'

Sue's eyes bulged. After a moment's hesitation, and trying to smile, she said: 'The point is, Laura, if you give an inch to them sort, they'll take a mile. I couldn't possibly 'ave Fontaine and that old biddy in the 'ouse – they'd act as if they still owned the bleedin' place! And there's no point me and Pronkie livin' here, seein' 'ow we've such a super château at Branne – you'll have to come and visit while you're over from ... Mind you, if you buy Belle-Mère, we'll be neighbours, so 'opefully we'll be seein' a lot of each other. Château Barrage is *fabulous* – not like this place at all. I mean, we've got all mod cons there thanks to ... Well, Pronkie's brother – you'll know 'im, Laura, being American an' all – the Philippe Pronk of the Albuquerque Ballet. He's even done stuff in front of your President Thingy. I think 'is last show was ... um ... *Annie Get Your Gun.* Apparently, all the cast were blokes – includin' Annie – and they danced to recordin's of rattlesnakes. It got rave reviews everywhere.'

Quincy was nodding vigorously. 'Sheer genius! I saw a touring company performance at Covent Garden with Nijinsky a few months back. Took my breath away.' Laura turned, looked out of one of the French windows and battled to stifle a fit of giggles.

'Nijinsky?' Sue looked and sounded incredulous. 'Bloody 'ell! That 'orse must be ancient by now. When did it win the Grand National? ... Mind you, I suppose they'd prefer an old nag on stage to a frisky stallion. It must be ever so difficult 'avin' real live animals with a load of blokes in tights prancin' around, but then I suppose you can't do Westerns without the odd 'orse or two.'

During the brief silence that followed, Quincy wondered whether Ms Olivier was pulling *his* leg.

'Anyway,' she continued in a businesslike tone, 'before we bought Barrage from Philippe, 'e'd spent loads of dosh tartin' the place up – completely gutted and refurbished it was. Every bedroom 'as its own facilities with a jacuzzi and everythin' – marble everywhere. Fantastic swimmin' pools – indoor and out. So, there really wasn't any incentive for us to move *here*. Actually, we did 'ave plans to turn this place into an 'otel ... one of them *Relais Châteaux* jobs–'

'Like Cordeillan-Bages at Pauillac!' bellowed Quincy. 'They produce their own wine too, although dear Hugh Johnson once branded it "rather lean".'

Sue looked as though she'd lost her thread. 'Quite. Anyway, Fontaine 'ad made such a mess on the wine front, we 'ad to sort that out first.'

She absent-mindedly ran a finger through the thick layer of dust covering the long dining table. 'Pronkie stays 'ere sometimes when 'e's got "technical stuff" to sort out with Fontaine. You saw 'is room – the one with all them books and stuff everywhere. Pronkie's always got 'is head in some thick old volume, or playin' that bloody flute of 'is, or paintin' them bleedin' flowers like he's Dick van Dyke or somethin'.

'*Anyway*, naturally we've done a bit of entertainin' at Belle-Mère – lunches, dinners and stuff for customers. We've put up quite a few VIPs, I can tell you. Well, Laura, you can imagine 'ow a place like this impresses the trade, especially a meal in this *fabulous* room. You can get at least twenty people round this table, you know – comfortable, not all bunched up. And we've got such lovely bone china and crystal – *and* silver. The Fontaines must 'ave spent a bleedin' fortune over the years. Nothin' but the best for them, of course. Per'aps if they'd ploughed a bit more cash back into the business rather than indulgin' themselves with fripperies, well, who knows ...'

Laura had moved back from the French windows and sighed impatiently. 'Perhaps we could go and see the *cuvier* now?'

'That would be nice,' Quincy agreed, glancing at his watch.

Sue forced an expansive smile. 'Of course! Just on the point of takin' you. *Very* impressive. State of the art – computers, flashin' lights – like NASA Mission Control in there. You'll feel very much at 'ome, Laura. Mind you, if you ask me, if you've seen one *cuvier*, you've seen 'em all. Oh, and a word to the wise – don't let Pronkie blind you with science. He'll drone on for ever about "malolactic fermentation" and "bladder presses"' – she pulled a face as if about to vomit – 'given 'alf the chance – 'im and that Fontaine! Thick as thieves them two.' She moved closer to Laura and Quincy. 'I wouldn't bother askin' Fontaine anythin' if I was you though,' she said softly. 'A bit funny in the 'ead. Gets very nervous under any pressure – 'ad a breakdown when 'e went bust, see. Never quite recovered. Still on medication. ... Quite good at his job though – at least, 'e 'as been under Pronkie's careful supervision.'

'I'm sure,' Quincy empathised gravely. 'Anyway, I believe Laura would bring in her own *maître de chai*, a very talented chap who'd want to run his own show.'

Sue raised her over-plucked eyebrows. 'Oh? Anyone I know?'

Laura scowled at Quincy. 'I very much doubt it, Sue. He's in a different league altogether – *very* different.'

Sue knew it was a put-down. It was no more than she'd have expected from this stuck-up American cow.

On their way over to the *cuvier*, Sue decided to try a different tack and reattached herself to Quincy. Thanks to his unequivocal approval of the house and imaginative suggestions for its transformation into a prestigious residence, he'd wholly rehabilitated himself. Moreover, despite Laura's obvious determination to prove that she was her own woman, there was no doubt that he had some influence over her: she seemed quite excited by all his plans for Belle-Mère. And maybe – just maybe – despite his repeated assurances to the contrary, the guy might be interested in the château for himself; she really couldn't afford to leave any stone unturned. Anyway, whichever of them acquired Belle-Mère, having a world-famous wine critic on her doorstep could do wonders for Barrage: favours would be owed – she'd make sure of that.

In the golden glow of the late afternoon sunshine, Sue had to admit that, notwithstanding his age, Quincy was a fine figure of a man. And such a glorious tan! She wondered where he'd acquired it. It was just a pity about his posh, fruity voice, but she could put up with that. Mind you, all that stuff about curtains, colour schemes and dadoes probably meant he was gay. On the other hand, she'd noticed that he couldn't keep his eyes off Laura's breasts. ... Very confusing!

The plan came to her in a flash.

'I've just 'ad a brilliant idea, Quince! Why don't you and Laura stay for dinner?'

A few paces behind, Lampre had taken the opportunity of Sue's transfer of loyalties to have a quick word with Laura. 'Don't take any notice of what that woman says about Charles Fontaine,' he whispered. 'The man's perfectly sane. Naturally, he's worried about his future – and his mother. If you buy this place – and believe me, Laura, I think you could make a real success of it – promise me you won't get rid of him. I'm sure Jean-Claude – I mean your *friend* – could work well with him.'

Laura was surprised by Lampre's earnestness. 'I really can't promise anything at this stage, Pierre. I've not even met Fontaine yet. And I'd need to talk to ... my "friend". I'm sorry, but –'

Having reached the *cuvier*'s main entrance, Sue and Quincy had turned to face the others. They were both grinning in a manner which Laura found slightly disconcerting. 'Oh, God,' she moaned, 'now what?'

Lampre managed some final words through a forced smile. 'Have an open mind, Laura. Just give Charles a chance. If anyone's mad around here it's not him. Pronk–'

'Here we are,' Sue announced, opening the door to the *cuvier*, '– Mission Control!'

99

There was no mention of dinner.

During their respective careers, Laura and Quincy had visited countless wineries across the globe. Nevertheless, because of their passion for the end product, it was almost unheard of for either of them not to display a genuine interest when visiting any structure housing vats and presses oozing the unmistakable odour of grape alcohol. They were not disappointed by Belle-Mère's *cuvier*. Sue watched with a wry smile as the two gurus' faces adopted expressions worthy of a couple of urchins let loose in a sweet shop.

Summoned by raucous shrieks of 'Pronkie!' and 'Visitors!', Eric Pronk reluctantly turned away from a vast console of buttons, switches, dials and coloured lights. Dressed in accordance with his wife's express standing instructions for what she called 'Open Days', he looked like a cross between a mad scientist and a hospital consultant doing his rounds. Beneath a starched white laboratory coat could be discerned a blue and white striped shirt, a red Paisley silk tie, perfectly pressed grey flannel trousers, and a pair of dazzlingly polished black brogues. He gave every appearance of an actor playing a part – as indeed he was: his usual everyday attire could have been politely described as 'rustic'. His wife was not so diplomatic: she invariably said he looked like a tramp.

Eric appeared much older than Sue. He'd once been quite a handsome man, but now his face was drawn and haggard, almost all his hair had gone, and fat bulged in the usual wrong places, a problem compounded by the lab coat, which was a size too small for him. After shaking the visitors' hands and nervously saying a simple 'Hello' to each of them – including Lampre whom he'd met many times – Eric began an earnest performance in his starring role as Belle-Mère's Technical Director. In a soft but clear voice, facts and figures flowed in perfect English with accomplished ease; he'd certainly learned his script well.

Within a minute, Sue had retreated to the door with Lampre. 'Well,' she yelled across the *cuvier*, 'there's no point me 'angin' about. It's all gobbledegook to yours truly. Anyway, me and Pierre 'ave some important business to discuss. Now don't overdo it, Pronkie, with the mumbo-jumbo – you're not lecturin' a couple of amateurs. See yer later!' Then the two of them disappeared into the sunlight.

Eric glowed red with embarrassment. 'Yes ... right ... well. ... So, as you probably know, Miss Appleton, and ... er, Mr Dubloon–'

'*Laura*, please.'

'And I'm Quincy. May we call you Eric, Monsieur Pronk?'

The host managed a slight smile. 'With pleasure – of course. ... Um, yes ... well, as you know, Belle-Mère is traditionally a white wine producer.

100

We – that is, Monsieur Fontaine – only recommenced producing red wine a few years ago after a lapse of almost a century, which explains why the average age of our Merlot and Cabernet Sauvignon vines is only eight years.'

'So, the reds are still fairly light then?' asked Laura pensively.

'Frankly, yes – but tasty.'

'And what's your blend, Eric?' enquired Quincy.

'Seventy per cent Merlot and thirty per cent Cabernet Sauvignon – about sixteen hectares in total, with a density of about five thousand vines per hectare. Average yields over the last two years have been about fifty-seven hectolitres per hectare, making our total annual production around nine hundred hectolitres.

'Nine hundred and twelve, to be precise,' Laura snapped, '– I've done the math – around a hundred and twenty-one thousand six hundred bottles.'

'That's my girl!' quipped Quincy. 'Mind you, Eric, we sensible British say "maths".'

Eric looked impressed. 'A hundred and twenty-one thousand six hundred exactly.'

'That's a lot of bottles from sixteen hectares,' Laura added with a note of concern.

Quincy wagged a finger at her. 'This isn't Château Margaux, Laura.'

'OK, but we all know that the best Bordeaux vineyards produce a maximum of *fifty* hectolitres per hectare.'

Eric held up his hands and sighed. 'We should be more selective with the crop, reduce volumes, and improve the quality. That's what Charles – Monsieur Fontaine – says all the time. He's right – *you're* right, Laura. It's what he was doing before we took over. He was getting around forty-five hectolitres per hectare, but ... well, Sue ... *we* couldn't afford to be so discerning.'

They were standing in front of a towering stainless-steel vat, one of a dozen in the *cuvier*. 'State of the art,' Eric said, patting it paternally. 'Frankly, it's better kit than we've got at Barrage. Charles chose wisely – electronically temperature-controlled, of course ... fully computerised.'

'How long does fermentation last in these beauties?' asked Quincy.

'About seventeen to twenty-one days at around thirty degrees centigrade. To be honest, I'd prefer three to four weeks but ... time is money.'

'And for how long do you age the red wine before bottling, Eric?' asked Laura.

'Twelve months. Ideally, we should aim for fifteen to twenty months, but again–'

'Time is money,' Quincy repeated.

'Precisely.'

'And how often do you replace the casks, new oak being better than–'

'Only twenty per cent are replaced each year, Laura. Before we arrived, Charles was achieving fifty per cent new oak per annum. We had to cut costs.' Laura and Quincy exchanged glances.

'The sooner I see some accounts the better,' Laura said. 'What about the whites?'

'About nineteen hectares, with an average age of thirty years – thirty-five per cent Sémillon and sixty-five per cent Sauvignon. The density is five thousand five hundred vines per hectare, average yields are about fifty-five hectolitres, and our annual production is around a hundred and thirty-nine thousand bottles. Again, we ferment for about ten to fifteen days in these stainless-steel vats, and then the wine is aged for nine months in oak barrels before bottling.'

'Just nine months,' Laura murmured. She tutted – and immediately wished she hadn't.

'I'd prefer twelve, of course,' Eric bleated.

'And how many of the barrels are new each year?'

'Same as the red, Laura, I'm afraid.' Silently, Eric thanked God that Sue wasn't around to hear all these apologies. Then, remembering that Lampre had disappeared too, he tensed. At this very moment they were probably ... He had to concentrate: Laura was asking a question about harvesting and the merits of picking by hand.

'We use machines at Barrage,' Eric replied, 'but then, let's face it, whatever Sue might say, we're just producing good, run-of-the-mill plonk, so hand-picking would be pointless. Charles was still hand-picking when we arrived. It almost broke his heart when we brought in the machines after a couple of years. Luckily, he'd planted the rows sufficiently far apart to permit machine-picking. It affected quality of course, but then, as Sue ... Well, it's not fair to blame her. I was a party to the decision – our sales figures were lousy. We couldn't go on acting like we were some Médoc *grand cru*.'

There was a brief tour of the *chai* – a fine modern building faced in stone and as clean and tidy inside as the *cuvier*. But, unlike grand estates' *chais*, the visitors couldn't feast their eyes on rows of bright new oak casks, or enjoy their heavenly fresh aroma: many of Belle-Mère's casks were almost black with age. The sight had a depressing effect on Laura: she imagined the cost of replacing them all with Tronçais oak from the Allier in central France, the most prized of all oaks for barrels; Jean-Claude wouldn't settle for anything less.

When they finally emerged from the *chai*'s refreshing coolness into the seething heat and dazzling light, Laura felt as though she'd walked into a furnace. The thirst which had been building up all afternoon finally became unbearable. She grabbed Eric's arm more tightly than she'd intended, almost causing him to stumble. Beneath the bleached cotton of his lab coat, she felt him flinch.

'Oh, I'm so sorry, Eric. I just wanted to ask you for a glass of water. I'm parched.'

'Me too,' croaked Quincy. 'Got a mouth like the bottom of a bloody bird cage.'

Eric looked horrified. 'Of course! I'm *so* sorry. Please forgive me. I should have offered … Didn't Sue–?' But before he could finish, the courtyard reverberated to the sound of the now familiar raucous shriek.

'Pronkie! It's almost *six* o'clock! I've been waitin' under the chestnut for ages!' With a face like thunder, Sue bounced towards them, the incongruous black garments flapping around her. 'You poor souls,' she lamented, pushing herself between the two visitors and grabbing each of them by the arm. 'I bet 'e's bored the pants off you, 'asn't 'e?'

Laura smiled. 'Actually–'

'Did you 'ave the pros and cons of bladder presses? That's normally one of 'is favourites. Bor-*ring*! Anyway, enough technical mumbo-jumbo! Time for drinkies and nibbles. Time to test the product, and I know you're going to *love* it – *them*, I should say, seein' 'ow we do all three colours. We like to do the tastin' bit alfresco – or do I mean al dente? … whatever – weather permittin' of course – in the shade of our wonderful 'istorical chestnut tree – on the *west* lawn. You'll love it, Laura, and such a view! *Fab-u-lous*! At least two 'undred years old – older than your country, I should think. Fancy!'

'The lawn or the view?' queried Quincy solemnly.

Sue's pitch floundered. 'What? … No, *silly*, the chestnut! Mind you … Oh,' – she smacked Quincy's wrist – 'you're 'avin' me on, you naughty tease!'

Eric stood in the courtyard watching the three rapidly receding backs. 'I should have left her in Kinshasa,' he murmured. He wished he could hide until it was all over, but he knew the form: after the *Source*, the House and the *Cuvier*, Phase Four of every tour was 'Drinkies' and a bowl of plain crisps under that bloody chestnut. What was so special about it anyway? Why not the terrace on the south front? Or around–?

'Pronkie! If you're not under that soddin' chestnut in two minutes – minus that lab coat – you'll be sent to bed without no supper. So, get yer bleedin' arse into gear!'

*

Towering over a wrought-iron round table and six matching chairs – once painted brilliant white but now chipped, peeling and rusty – the mighty chestnut stood on an extensive rectangular lawn which sloped gently westwards. In need of a good mow, the grass was bordered on three sides by badly maintained rose beds, which, nevertheless, supported a mass of hybrid teas and floribundas in full bloom. Some twenty metres from the chestnut, and separated from the fourth side of the lawn by a stone terrace, stood Château Belle-Mère's harmonious west front. The scent of the roses, the call of a cuckoo, and the distant bells of an unseen church were all contributing to Laura's sense of contentment on this beautiful summer's evening. Even Sue's constant babbling couldn't detract from the stunning beauty of the view across the rolling countryside of the Premières Côtes. It was nothing short of perfection: she could imagine herself being magically sucked into one of those torpid bucolic scenes painted by Monet or Cézanne. And now that she could at last sit down after more than two hours of tramping around Belle-Mère, the prospect of sampling its humble offerings didn't seem quite so unpleasant. If only Sue could be made to disappear; she was presently in full flow lecturing Quincy on the horrors of French labour laws.

As Eric poured white wine into four nondescript, standard glasses in accordance with his spouse's barked instructions, it suddenly occurred to Laura that Lampre was missing. Turning to Sue, she asked: 'Where's Pierre? Oh, and I'd still love that glass of water, Eric – sparkling if you've got it.'

Eric tutted. 'Sorry! Yes, of course. I'll just pop to the kitchen.' He put the wine bottle down beside the glasses he'd just filled, took one step towards the house, stopped, and then turned back. He looked almost happy. 'Lampre? He's gone ... I think. At least, his car's gone.'

'*Gone?* He can't have. I – we–'

'Pierre's 'ad to pop down to Langon for a while,' Sue trumpeted, halting her conversation with Quincy; she'd rapidly moved on from maximum hours and minimum wages to the possibility of a free feature on Château Barrage in *Wine Wisdom*. 'Got a call from 'is wife while you was in the *cuvier*. Seems her sister's 'ad a nasty fall at her 'ouse there. Expect 'e'll be back soon. Langon's only– Pronkie! Where the 'ell are you goin'?'

Eric had almost reached the house. 'I–'

'Get back here now and dish out the effin' glasses, for God's sake. We're all gaggin' for a–'

'Miss Appleton – *Laura*,' he shouted across the lawn, 'would like some water, Sue. I dare say we could *all* do–'

'*Water?*' Sue looked mortified. '*Water*, Laura? You mean you're not goin' to test the products? You can't be serious? You've got to test–'

Laura forced a laugh. 'Of course I'm going to ... *taste* your wines. I just need some water as well. I think we're all in danger of dehydrating in this heat, Sue.'

'Phew! For one minute, Laura, you 'ad me worried – Quince too by the look of things.'

Laura stared hard at Quincy. '"Quince"?' she mouthed. He hunched his shoulders and grinned.

Believing he now had the necessary authorisation, Eric continued towards the house, but almost immediately there was another burst of verbal machine-gun fire.

'I told you to get back 'ere! What the 'ell's *this* for, you idiot?' Sue grabbed a dainty silver handbell off the table and began ringing it furiously. 'Let them bleedin' tossers earn their money for once. They get paid enough.'

For a moment, Eric stood his ground. Then he began to retrace his steps. 'Joelle's sick, Sue. I sent her home. She looked terrible. There's only Jeanne here and she's busy preparing ... preparing ...'

Both Laura and Quincy felt the air temperature rise.

'You sent Jeanne 'ome?' hissed Sue incredulously, '– without consultin' *me?*'

Eric appeared to be on the point of saying something, but finally managed a mere nod. Quincy cleared his throat; Laura wanted to jump up and put her arms around the cringing husband.

Sue flashed one of her why-do-I-bother smiles. 'Oh well! Never mind! *C'est la vie*! So much for clear lines of managerial responsibility.' She started ringing the bell again as if everyone's life depended on it. 'Jeanne! *Jeanne*! JEANNE!'

By the time the next crisis began simmering, Belle-Mère's white wine had been thoroughly 'tested', and Quincy had devoured most of the flavourless soggy crisps lurking in an orange plastic bowl. The 'product' was 'quite pleasant' – Laura's phrase – with 'a subtle hint of ripe melons'. Quincy had used his favourite word of the afternoon, 'potential', more than once. Sue had knocked back her glass in one highly audible gulp and pronounced the contents 'fabulous'. Eric had said nothing: he kept looking at the house with increasing anxiety as 'Jeanne' failed to materialize.

After another bout of hysteria with the bell, Sue ordered Eric to pour the rosé; like its white cousin, it stood in a terracotta wine cooler of the type sold in their millions by IKEA to first-time home builders.

'Now *this*,' Sue gushed as she held up her glass to a beam of sunlight filtering through the towering chestnut's dense canopy, 'is somethin' *really* special. *Fabulous*, isn't it?'

Quincy nodded. 'Fabulous.' He thrust a huge hand into the plastic bowl, which had gravitated to his side of the table, seized the last crisp and devoured it. 'Yum ... *yum*.' Finally, he stuck his nose into the glass and inhaled deeply. 'Fabulous,' he repeated.

Laura cringed: he was going to say something embarrassingly sarcastic.

'I don't know about you, Laura,' he began slowly, 'but I'm sure I can detect a hint of ... No, it can't be!'

Sue was on the edge of her seat. 'What? ... *What*?'

Laura wanted to hit him. It wasn't fair on poor Eric.

'Well, if I'm not mistaken, there's just a tantalizing *soupçon* of – what does Robert Parker call it? ... Um–?'

'Oh, God!' croaked Eric, springing from his seat, '– that's done it!' He was again staring towards the house; everyone around the table followed his gaze. It was a vision: a tall, slender middle-aged man was moving regally towards them in a dazzling aura of reflected sunlight. With his silver hair, Laura's initial reaction was that Lampre had returned.

'Jesus effing Christ!' hissed Sue. 'It's 'is bleedin' lordship. Who the 'ell does 'e think he is today – the soddin' butler?'

Eric shot a terrified glance at his wife. 'I'll handle this, Sue. We've got guests.'

'The 'ell you will! I told you to keep 'im out of the way. I warned you that if 'e pulled another stunt like–' She leaned across the table and signalled to the guests to huddle together. 'It's Fontaine,' she whispered. 'I'm *so* sorry. The twat can't bear to be left out of *nothin'*. Just 'umour 'im, OK? Don't worry,' she added ominously, 'violence ain't his scene ... usually.'

There was a moment's silence as the motley group under the spreading chestnut focused on the approaching spectacle and digested its details. The dazzling flashes of light turned out to be reflections from the impressive volume of silver and cut crystal which Charles Fontaine was bearing: on a huge salver stood not only a magnificent silver wine cooler containing several bottles, but also at least a dozen impressive wine glasses and two silver platters. Appearing completely at ease with the undoubted weight of his burden, Fontaine scanned the assembly with humorous sparkling blue eyes set in a face which radiated an almost hypnotic charm. His clothes were classic, casual and well-worn – a Façonnable polo shirt in British Racing Green, and beige light-cotton Burberry trousers. On his feet he sported black silk socks and a pair of black Bally loafers.

Style and breeding, Laura said to herself; so, too, did Quincy.

Thankfully, Sue's thoughts went unspoken. Instead, she muttered murderously: 'Jesus, the bleedin' Crown Jewels! I 'ope we're insured. If he drops that lot ...'

Eric finally took a step forward. 'My, my, *my*, Charles, let me help you. You're spoiling us with such munificence.'

'That's very kind of you, Eric,' Fontaine drawled, 'but I'm fine, thank you. ... Good evening, everyone,' he added, switching to English.

'Good evening!' the guests chorused.

'I'll just put this down and then ... There we are.' He stood back, straightened himself, and looked around the table, smiling broadly.

'Fontaine–' Sue began.

'And a very good evening to you too, Madame Pronk – sorry ... *Olivier* – I mean *Ms* Olivier. Now, don't worry – everything's under control. I thought you'd be rushed off your feet – what with our visitors, being short-staffed, and Jeanne's extra-culinary workload. ... So, I thought you'd appreciate another pair of hands.'

For the first time that day, and despite the heat and all her exertions, Sue's skin finally turned red. 'I – I ... You – you ...' She glowered at her husband. 'Pronkie?' she croaked despairingly. Palms upwards, he held out his hands in a gesture of innocence.

'Miss Laura Appleton and Mr Quincy Dubloon,' Fontaine said warmly with a slight bow of his head, offering his hand first to Laura. 'How do you do? Such an honour – such a thrill!'

'It's a pleasure to meet you, Monsieur Fontaine,' Quincy replied.

'A *great* pleasure,' Laura added. 'Eric's been telling us all about your admirable efforts to transform and upgrade your family's old estate.'

'Oh! Eric's *too* kind! ... Please, *do* sit down.' Fontaine started to remove items from the salver and distribute them around the table. 'I myself,' he said rather grandly, 'would have welcomed you to Belle-Mère upon your arrival ... if I'd known. ... It was only when I visited the *cuvier* this afternoon upon my return from an unscheduled trip to the' – he glanced momentarily at Sue – '... *supermarket* in Langon, that I realised we had such eminent visitors. Naturally, I recognised two of the world's most illustrious wine experts immediately, but ... well, I'm sure you'll understand that I did not wish to interrupt your discussions with Eric, which, I assumed, were confidential.'

Laura felt herself blush. 'Oh ... well ... I–'

'Bang on, Fontaine!' snapped Sue. 'Our discussions *are* confidential, so if you wouldn't mind–'

'However,' Fontaine continued, 'I thought that as you were staying to taste some of our wines,' – he flashed a glance at the open bottle of rosé and emitted a faint sigh – 'I'd come and introduce myself and–'

'I 'ope you ain't brought none of that *old* stuff,' Sue snarled, scanning the salver intently, 'because if you 'ave–'

'I thought I'd come and introduce myself and bring you some water – sparkling and flat – and fresh bread which dear Jeanne, our housekeeper–'

'"*Our*"?' snorted Sue.

'– baked this afternoon. She's *such* a treasure. Water and bread are so useful for refreshing and cleansing the palate when one's tasting, I think.'

'Absolutely,' said Laura.

Quincy nodded wholeheartedly. 'I say,' he chirped, 'did "dear *Jeanne*" also bake these little savoury pastries?' He popped one in his mouth. 'Scrumptious!'

'*I* didn't ask Jeanne to bake no–' Sue interrupted herself. 'Just a minute, mate! I thought she was rushed off 'er big bleedin' kipper feet because of that pea brain Joelle skivin' off again.'

Fontaine smiled condescendingly. 'Don't worry, Ms Olivier. Jeanne, I assure you, is not behind schedule, but I have a small confession to make.' Quincy's' huge hand froze over the plate of pastries. 'I made them myself. I hope you don't mind.'

The previous year's vintage of the Belle-Mère rosé, which had only been a few months in bottle, was not pleasant even when drunk out of the Napoléon III crystal glasses delicately engraved with bunches of grapes that Fontaine had insisted they use. Laura and Quincy were polite, but their lack of enthusiasm couldn't be disguised. It was 'a new product line' Sue advised defensively, which, after only two years 'off the drawing board', was still being 'perfected'. She thought the bottle might be corked and suggested opening another, but the guests were more interested in Fontaine's Louis-Philippe silver wine cooler and pretended not to hear her.

Shortly after seven o'clock, they moved on to the red – and fresh antique glasses. There was a long, pregnant pause as everyone sniffed and slurped, and then Quincy broke the silence with a booming 'Jolly good!' Laura had to agree: the wine was much better than she'd anticipated. And retailing at just six euros a bottle, it was an absurd bargain. In consequence, Sue stopped sulking about the rosé and relaxed a little, notwithstanding the 'we-can-do-a-lot-better' negative marketing from the Technical Director and *maître de chai*.

Twenty minutes later, Sue's mobile rang to the tune of *Colonel Bogey*: it was Lampre. For about thirty seconds, she kept repeating 'Oh dear!', 'Poor thing!' and 'Oh 'ow awful!'. Then, abruptly terminating the call, she said: 'The good news, everyone, is that Pierre's sister-in-law is OK – she's only broken a leg. But the bad news is that 'e's stuck at the 'ospital in Langon waitin' for 'is wife to arrive. Apparently, the old bird's only just left some bleedin' hotel near Pau where she's been on a course all day learnin' 'ow to cook foie gras – of all things! – and 'e don't know when 'e'll be able to come back to take you two into Bordeaux. What a carve up!'

The news was digested during a brief silence.

'I know!' continued Sue suddenly, causing Quincy to spill wine down his shirt front. 'Seein' 'ow you two probably ain't got nothin' better to do, why don't you stay for dinner? What d'you say?'

As Laura's mouth fell open, she stared beseechingly at Quincy, simultaneously racking her brain to think of a credible excuse to escape. 'I – I – *we* ... Quincy, don't you have to–?'

'What a capital idea!' he roared through a mouthful of crumbs. 'Every cloud has a silver lining, I always say. I've got *nothing* on tonight – completely at a loose end. It would give us a great opportunity, Laura, to chat to Charles and get his perspective on Belle-Mère and its potential.' He glanced at his watch. 'And as we've still got another hour or two of daylight, we could take a gander at some of the vines.' He waved a huge arm towards the surrounding vineyards. 'We really ought to see a bit of the *terroir*, old thing. You haven't got a date or anything tonight, have you, Laura?'

She opened her mouth, but Sue beat her to it. 'Fabulous, Quince! Just one teeny-weeny problem, though. Charles – *Fontaine* – can't ... um ... His mother–'

'What I think Ms Olivier is trying to say, is that I always dine with dear Mama. In any event, Laura, as a prospective purchaser – and, dare I say, as my possible future employer – well ...'

'Quite! barked Sue. 'It's unthinkable – '*im* – a mere employee – eatin' with *us*.'

Laura glimpsed the stoic expression on Fontaine's noble face and resolved to stay, although now that Quincy had pulled the rug from under her feet, perhaps there was no option. She breathed deeply and then projected the broadest smile she could manage. 'I'd be delighted to stay. Thank you, Eric and Sue.'

'Smashin'!' screeched the hostess, rubbing her hands together.

'Wonderful,' mumbled Eric, staring at his glass.

'But on one condition,' Laura continued – the smile on Sue's face froze – '... that Charles dines with us.' She put a hand on his arm. 'Please, Charles, can't you make an exception just for once? This is very important for me. There are so many things I'd like to discuss with you – and Eric – about the estate. ... *Please*.'

'My mother,' Fontaine began slowly while staring at Sue, 'well ... she–'

'Couldn't Madame Fontaine join us too?' asked Quincy brightly. 'Or is she an invalid, or–?'

'Yes!' barked Sue. 'She's ... well, you know, at her age she's–'

'My mother, Quincy, walks two kilometres every morning – *unaided* – plays at least one Beethoven sonata on the piano before lunch, and currently spends her afternoons writing a biography of the fourth Duc de Deauville, to whom she is related through her mother's family.'

'The "Duke de Deauville"!' mocked Sue. 'Well, with all that blue blood in her veins, she won't want to drag 'erself away from "the gatehouse" and eat with us riff-raff.'

Quincy pretended not to hear, and, as Fontaine rose stiffly from his chair, said excitedly: 'The *fourth* Duc de Deauville? The explorer who discovered the long-lost city of Xata Chonkabak in the Peruvian Andes?' Fontaine nodded. 'How *marvellous*! I'd love to meet her. Oh *please*, Charles, *do* try to persuade her to join us for dinner – *please*.'

'Well, I ... I know she'd very much like to meet Laura and yourself. She took out a subscription to *Wine Wisdom* when it was first published and hasn't missed an issue since. And she loved your series on television, Laura, the *Temples du Vin* one – we *both* did! By the way, the last time I was in Los Angeles – must have been ... ooh ... 1993, I suppose – I had a glorious meal at La Maison Blanche. Your father – what a genius! – was kind enough to give me a tour of the kitchens – my cousin too, who was dining with me. He was our consul in Los Angeles at the time and ...'

While Fontaine tried to recollect the delicacies he and the consul had been served, Sue shook her head from side to side as she scowled at Eric, who, however, continued to stare into his glass. Yet again she'd been eclipsed – made to feel like a guest in her own home. ... OK, not 'home', but – what the hell! – like some dim secretary. He'd be sorry – they'd *both* be sorry, Fontaine and Pronkie – very, *very* sorry indeed.

Sue jumped up from her seat with such force that it fell backwards and partly embedded itself in the lawn. 'Right! Fine! OK!' She flung her mobile across the table towards Fontaine. 'Enough trips down memory lane, mate. Let's get this show on the road. So glad you're stayin' for dinner, Laura – Quince. Fontaine, you'd better phone your old mum down at the gatehouse and tell her to put her spinnin' wheel away and get into her glad rags. Then tell Jeanne to set two extra places for dinner. Then–'

'*Two?*' queried Fontaine with a hint of mischief. 'Don't you mean *four?*'

Sue scowled. 'Four? I 'ope you're not goin' to tell me that the Duke and Duchess of – of' – she waved a hand dismissively – '… wherever – are payin' you a state visit down there, are you?'

'Of course not. They're dead. I'm referring to our two illustrious guests, or maybe–'

'The guests!' Sue shot round the table and tugged them from their seats. 'Of course! – *four* places! Come on, you two – chop-chop! – to the vineyards! And you, Pronkie – we need you to explain what's what. I can never tell the difference between a Sauvignon and a Sémillon – can you, Laura? I thought a grape was a bleedin' grape until I came to France.'

Halfway across the lawn, Sue stopped abruptly, turned around and glowered at Fontaine, who was just about to lift his great silver salver and walk back to the house. 'As for *you*, mate, put a tie on for dinner. This ain't a bleedin' golf club!'

It was an enigmatic remark which puzzled the visitors, but Laura, at least, had no time to analyse it, for Sue gripped her arm tightly and cooed: 'Well, well, well – la Maison Blanche! So, your dad's a chef at the White House! I bet he could tell a few stories!'

CHAPTER 9

With his hands in his pockets, Henri de Bondé stood at one of the study windows and watched Jean-Claude's car pull away from La Fayette's main gate.

'Enjoy your weekend with the fat fag, you sad little man,' he sneered.

Tiquetorte had phoned a short while earlier from his surgery with the customary graphic account of what he and Bourjois's wife had got up to that afternoon at the antique shop, adding towards the end of the conversation a tedious snippet of gossip about some celebrated Parisian art dealer staying the weekend at Le Porge. Both of them had heard of the Galerie Buffet, but it was not an establishment they themselves had ever visited – or would ever wish to visit. 'A disgustingly gross old queen' was how Sophie had described him, Tiquetorte reported, and then he proceeded to crack a joke about Buffet trying to have his wicked way with Bourjois. Henri had laughed dutifully, but when he'd finally managed to terminate the call – he was getting fed up with Geoffroy's constant gloating about the relationship with Sophie – the irritating, nagging thought occurred to him that what really lay behind the joke was an assumption that Buffet would inevitably find Bourjois attractive – at least in a rustic, labouring peasant kind of way. A certain type of woman, no doubt, found that look irresistible too. Henri pictured frustrated middle-class housewives spending their empty afternoons at the cinema in Bordeaux, staring rapturously at images of that Australian ... Thingy ... or was he American? ... Canadian–?

'Oh, for God's sake,' Henri muttered, 'stop wasting time.' As was so often the case, Bourjois was the cause – bloody, sodding Bourjois – the constant thorn in his side. The very sound of his name made him cringe. It always had – right from the moment they'd first met. Sensing his muscles tighten, he began to pace around the room. He tried to think of something else. ... Yes, his excursion to Geoffroy's Cap Ferret beach house for the weekend, what with Nancy and the children having gone to her parents' place on Ile de Ré – thank God! He'd drive over in the Mercedes convertible after a leisurely breakfast tomorrow morning and–

But it wasn't working: he could see Bourjois, aged five or six, standing at the château's front door with his tarty mother, both dressed in their Sunday best. She was reeking of cheap perfume; he was smiling ... so sweetly ... so saintly...

Henri had suffered the ignominy of opening the door, rather than one of the servants, thanks to 'La Vache Qui Rit' – 'the Laughing Cow'. That was his nickname for Great Aunt Hortense, his deceased paternal grandmother's sister, who'd been wheeled out of self-pitying widowhood on a decaying family estate near Barsac in order to assist Guy in performing his role as a single parent.

When the bell rang, La Vache had said with her fake sweetness: 'Go on, Henri. Don't wait for the major-domo. Open the door – it's a lovely surprise just for you.'

Picturing the postman with a huge package – the toy fort he'd been begging for – he'd raced to the door, but on the other side were merely those two peasants from the village. He promptly ordered them to the *chais*. Then La Vache was behind him, apologising and inviting the oiks in.

'This is Jean-Claude, your new playmate,' she said, smiling broadly. The 'new playmate' stuck out his hand, and, like a performing doll, enunciated theatrically: 'How do you do, Henri?' What he remembered most vividly was La Vache pushing himself forward with a fist in his back. 'Go on, Henri, be a gentleman,' she commanded. 'Shake Jean-Claude's hand. You wouldn't want me to tell your papa that you're a rude little boy, would you, dear?'

No, he certainly would not: there'd be one of those terrifying sessions in the study ... in this very room ... bending over this desk. Of course, she *did* tell the Old Man anyway; she couldn't help herself. She always said the same thing: 'I don't want to tell tales out of school, Guy, dear, but I think you really ought to know that Henri ...' and then she'd proceed to make some capital offence out of a trifling misdemeanour.

Sighing, Henri stopped again in front of the window. '"What a *lovely* little boy,"' he whined in a high-pitched voice, mimicking La Vache, '"– such *fine* features – just like his father." ... And the Old Man was just as bad. "What perfect manners Jean-Claude has – and so well-behaved. You could take a leaf or two out of his book, Henri. *He* doesn't have all these ridiculous tantrums. *He* doesn't shout and scream when he loses a game. *He* ..."'

The list of Jean-Claude's admirable qualities was endless – *endless*! ... And why had the Old Man been so set on forcing the two of them to play together? And La Vache? And Bourjois's parents? Why? It must have been obvious to all of them that he couldn't stomach the sight of the little git. After all, their sessions together almost inevitably ended in fisticuffs – often with something valuable getting broken. And, presumably, unless he was a masochist or simply mad, Bourjois must have detested being dragged up to the château for games with 'the young master', as the cretin's parents invariably referred to himself. In the end, it had been a relief to be sent to boarding school, just to get away from that precocious saint – a sodding saint who was growing faster than himself, who could run rings around him in any game, and beat him in any race – whatever the distance. And La Vache would rub salt into the wound with her mantra: 'Such sturdy, powerful legs, Jean-Claude has – not like Henri's matchsticks.' Christ, if she said that once, she must have said it a hundred times.

Henri managed a smile. It was amusing to think of the plans he'd made – usually when lying in bed and before dropping off – to kill Bourjois: they'd go skating on the frozen pond in winter and he'd dare him to skate over the thinnest ice in the centre; he'd drop one of the puppies from an upstairs window onto the roof of the conservatory and beg Bourjois to rescue it, while failing to warn him of the weak central support that Papa was always telling the major-domo to get replaced. Oh, there were scores of them! In the end, it had been so simple.

There'd been a typically unpleasant session of 'Cowboys and Indians' in the attic that had started with Henri being equipped with a battery of weapons, including a gun which fired rubber suction darts. Within half an hour, Jean-Claude had captured them all, and Henri was tied up in Jean-Claude's' tepee – an old clothes horse pushed into a V-shape on the floor and draped with a moth-eaten tapestry. After Henri's release, the two boys had returned in brooding silence along the labyrinthine corridors and down the many flights of stairs, with Jean-Claude a few steps ahead. When they reached the first-floor landing at the top of the grand staircase, something inside Henri snapped: Jean-Claude's back was a glorious target. He lunged and pushed with both hands. Down he went, rolling like a top – a thrilling sight! – until he reached the hall's polished chequerboard marble floor. His head hit it with an audible crack.

Henri couldn't be sure how long he'd stood on the landing, staring at the immobile body and savouring the delicious thought that at last he'd finally rid himself of his detested 'playmate'. But then he heard a groan, Jean-Claude's eyes opened, and a hand suddenly gripped Henri's shoulder. In terror, he swung round, and there stood La Vache shaking her head from side to side. 'Oh dear,' she whispered, 'better luck next time.' It was bizarre, but those were her exact words.

When his father returned that evening from a business trip to Paris, Henri feared he'd receive the beating of his life. Christophe Bourjois and Guy were closeted together in the study for over an hour, and when Monsieur Bourjois finally left, Henri received the dreaded summons.

The Old Man was sombre rather than angry. He said it was a miracle Jean-Claude hadn't died. The lad's father had come straight from the hospital: poor Jean-Claude had a couple of cracked ribs, a lot of bruising and concussion; he was being kept in for observation, but the doctors were hopeful there'd be no complications. Jean-Claude had even managed to tell Christophe that he and Henri had been playing tag and that he'd tripped running down the stairs.

'Was that what really happened?' the Old Man asked. 'Auntie says she heard the two of you running hysterically along the corridors before the accident.'

At first, Henri had been too stunned to answer. He'd thought it was a trap – some clever scheme by all of them to get him to confess. But he finally managed a nod and mumbled something about Jean-Claude tripping. And then Guy had started his usual sermon: Jean-Claude was such a good example to emulate; Henri could learn so much from him; God should be thanked for saving his precious life. ... On and on and on. Tomorrow, they'd go together and see dearest Jean-Claude in the hospital and take him some of his favourite *bonbons*. That was when Henri finally exploded.

'I don't want to play with that boy anymore!' he screamed. 'In fact, I never want to see him in our château again – or anywhere near it! I hate him! I can't bear the sight of him! I wish Jean-Claude *were* dead! Next time I'll make very sure–!'

Stroking his chin, Henri scanned the study. It was strange really that the Old Man hadn't flogged him. Instead, after what had seemed like an eternity of terrifying silence, he'd seized him by the arm and marched him up all those flights of stairs to the attic; the bastard never said a bloody word. He was locked in for the night: no food, no water, no bed – nothing; he'd even had to relieve himself in a corner. Dearest Papa, such a kind, honourable and generous man – 'a proper gentleman'! That's what everyone said. If only people had known what he was really like. ... Anyway, the threat worked and he got his way: Saint Jean-Claude never came to play again.

'I suppose he must hate me as much as I hate him,' Henri said aloud, pensively. 'Maybe more.'

It suddenly struck him as incredible that he'd never thought of this before. So, why hadn't Bourjois left, he wondered. Why hadn't he left years ago? He could have got a good job anywhere. Was it his beloved Guy who kept him at La Fayette? Was he trying to keep up some idiotic tradition – generation after generation in the *chais*? Or was it just a lack of initiative – institutionalised, like a criminal who'd spent most of his life in gaol?

Henri sighed. *All those discussions with Geoffroy and Alain de Carbon Blanc about getting Bourjois involved in our schemes for increasing revenue in the North American market – what a bloody waste of time! – just as I warned them. I told them there were plenty of dynamic* maîtres de chai *seeking jobs at prestigious vineyards, men – unlike Bourjois – with a taste for the good life, flexible men who'd be prepared to take calculated risks. Wimpy Geoffroy whined about it being a case of 'better the devil you know', but he hasn't suffered a lifetime of Bourjois. I should have given the git notice months ago, when he first started moaning about unlabelled bottles being shipped to the States. … Should I just give him notice now? – three months or something? Alain will know, being a lawyer. Would Bourjois be furious or relieved? … Furious, probably – about the connection between his family and La Fayette being severed. He'd certainly been terrified by my threat to terminate that outrageous guarantee the Old Man had given to the bank! And under the second mortgage of that vile Le Porge house to secure the Old Man's loan, the mortgagee can vary both the amount of the capital repayments and the interest rate in line with normal commercial practice. Bourjois has only repaid a fraction of the loan, and the interest rate is risible. Anyway, first things first – hold fire until he sorts out that bloody printer.*

Henri glanced at the mantelpiece clock: a few minutes after seven, which meant that bloody Sam Mayer should be out of his meeting in New York. Time to tell him of this bizarre coincidence – Ducasse getting a bottle of the falsely labelled Maréchal served to him at the Marriott in Orlando! Could the git have put the hotel's management on notice that something was wrong? … Surely not. In any event, would a mere wine waiter at a resort hotel give a fig about some French codger with lamentable English making obtuse technical comments about the label on a bottle of unpronounceable foreign wine?

Still, it couldn't be dismissed lightly. Mayer had slipped up: the labels had to be more than 'excellent copies' – they had to be perfect, and with modern digital colour reprography, there was no reason to accept second best. It was peculiar, though, that Ducasse had seen fit to submit the bloody label for analysis instead of bringing it straight to La Fayette. … Maybe he really was worried that he'd supplied it. … But hang on: even if that was his concern, the old coot was claiming that a bottle of Maréchal de La Fayette had been masquerading as *Château* La Fayette – or so Bourjois said. Was it possible …?

Henri suddenly felt very hot. Had Bourjois conned him? – that there was no label at all? – that there never had been a dubious bottle of wine? Had the bastard just been fishing – throwing bread on the water to see if

116

his gullible employer had something to hide? *Jesus Christ! I'm torturing myself with bloody stupid conspiracy theories.* He pulled the phone towards him and tapped out a New York number.

'*Good afternoon. Mayer Fine Wines. Mr Mayer's office. Barbara speaking. How may I help you, please?*'

'It's *Baron* de Bondé *again*,' Henri snapped. 'Is he back yet?'

'*Ah, Mr de Bondé.*' Barbara no longer sounded cheerful. '*Yes, I'll put you through. One moment, please.*'

CHAPTER 10

In Château Belle-Mère's grand but faded dining room, Sue sat at the head of the table with Quincy at her left hand and Laura at her right. Madame Fontaine sat between Quincy and her son; directly opposite her was Eric Pronk. Together, they barely occupied one third of the table, the fourteen empty chairs giving the room a somewhat melancholy appearance. Madame Fontaine, however, was doing her very best to provide entertainment – to the obvious annoyance of the official hostess, and despite her repeated efforts to steer the conversation back to the estate's 'fabulous' wines.

Frankly, the guests found it impossible not to give the elderly former chatelaine their undivided attention. She was a handsome woman of medium height with a svelte figure and a head of strong fashionably cut and styled silver hair. Her clothes, like those of her son, had been worn for many seasons, but were elegant without being ostentatious. She was, furthermore, one of those cosmopolitan characters who could effortlessly switch from one language to another – often in mid-sentence – and assumed that everyone around them could do likewise. And because of her background and eighty-five years, she had ingrained in her the manners, bearing and style of a generation and class that had grown up in a pre-war world where colonies, servants and dressing for dinner were taken for granted. Consequently, Sue regarded her as a wholly alien creature; along with her doting, foppish son, she'd been rightly exiled to the distant gatehouse.

'I do believe,' said Madame Fontaine with a hint of excitement in her resonant and confident voice, 'that the last time I sat at this table with an *American* lady was June – or possibly July – 1937.' She shook her head and turned to her son. 'Can that be right, Charles? Surely there must have been some *other* American ladies?'

'Plenty of American *gentlemen*, Mama,' Charles replied with a hint of innuendo. 'Actually–'

'Do you like the pâté?' interrupted Sue forcefully, looking from Laura to Quincy. 'It's local – 'ome-made. I think it goes smashin' with our fabulous white, don't you? Grab some more toast, Laura. Quince, you ain't got much pâté on yer plate. Come on, there's plenty of it.'

Laura's and Quincy's eyes met across the table: he winked; she winked back. The 'home-made' pâté had been served up as a single column straight from the tin, its surface moulded with telltale ridges and grooves.

It reminded Laura of a TV commercial for a brand of dog food, albeit she had to admit that, whatever its origins, the pâté was quite tasty.

'Mmm, it's *very* good,' Laura said, taking a slab of roughly cut and savagely toasted wholemeal bread.

'I'd *love* some more,' Quincy enthused. 'And who, Madame Fontaine, was the American lady of 1937 vintage?' Sue shot him a black look.

Madame Fontaine was delicately slicing some pâté from the small portion to which her son had helped her; she'd declined any of the toast. 'Ah yes, the *lady*.'

'Do I detect a note of disapproval?' asked Quincy mischievously.

Madame Fontaine rocked slightly from side to side and put down her knife and fork. 'Well, Monsieur Dubloon–'

'Oh *please*, Madame Fontaine, do call me Quincy.'

'With pleasure, *Quincy*.' She did not, however, reciprocate the offer of informality, but then, even her son addressed her as '*vous*'. 'Well ... Quincy, I was only nineteen at the time, but I must confess that the lady in question did *not* create a very good impression on me. Nor, I'm afraid, did her husband.'

'Another American?' asked Laura coolly.

'Oh *no*, my dear. Well, of course, that was half the problem. I think, Quincy, that you English were very wise to get rid of him – he would have made an awful king. His brother, on the other hand, was such a lovely man. You know, I remember going up to Paris for his State Visit the following year, 1938. ... Yes, it must have been May 1938 because I almost couldn't go. My younger brother, Serge, had nearly died of malaria in Sénégal that spring. He'd been visiting Uncle Georges who was aide-de-camp to the governor. ... Anyway, everyone, of course, wanted to see the new King George VI and Queen Elizabeth – we knew so little about them – and as we had family in the Quai d'Orsay who were organizing everything, my parents and I managed to get invited to one or two little functions. Oh, the pomp! – the colour! – all those soldiers in their dazzling uniforms! ... They were really quite small, you know, the King and Queen – but so majestic. ... He was *very* handsome. ...

'Well, the crowds were incredible and wildly enthusiastic. Everyone shouted "*Vive le Roi! Vive la Reine!*"– me too. ... I think the French still wished they had a royal family–'

'Oh, Mama!'

'No, Charles, they did – and still do. But that's another story. And then, back in 1938, Laura, we had Czechoslovakia, and Hitler, and Munich. Everyone knew war was coming, but we wanted to bury our heads in the sand. We wanted to believe in the silly Maginot Line. And yet, if there was going to be a replay of 1914, then England would have to help us. The Americans, Laura, were so isolationist and we knew they'd be only too happy to see our Empire – and the British Empire – destroyed. Such jealousy! … Like the Germans, really. … So, when the King and Queen came to Paris that year it was a wonderful boost to morale, you see.'

'Very interestin', I'm sure,' Sue snapped, scowling at both Fontaines. 'I think our glasses could do with a top up, Fon – *Charles*.'

Eric began to rise from his seat. 'Oh, sorry! I'll do–'

'Let – *Charles* – do – it,' ordered Sue through gritted teeth, motioning to her husband to sit down.

Fontaine was quickly on his feet. 'Of course! How remiss of me!'

His mother smiled at Laura – a smile which proclaimed *You see what we have to put up with?*

'I think I should open another bottle or two of white, Ms Olivier,' Charles added. 'I'll just go–'

'You know, Madame *Pronk*,' interceded Madame Fontaine with heavy emphasis on the 'Pronk', 'I suspect that the 1993 would be absolutely wonderful with this *heavenly* pâté, not quite so … dry.'

Sue raised her hands in despair. 'Oh no, love, they won't want none of that *old* stuff – before our time anyway. It's probably gone off. And the bottles'll be bloody filthy. We'll stick to–'

'I'd love to try the 93!' cried Laura. 'Wouldn't you, Quince?'

Quincy seemed to be in a trance. 'Er … what? … Oh yes – yes of course.' He turned to Madame Fontaine. 'You mean that the American lady who dined here – in this *very* room – in 1937 – was Mrs Simpson – old Wallis? I can't believe it!'

Madame Fontaine nodded. 'The very same.' She shot a glance at her son. 'Go on, Charles, Monsieur – *Quincy* and … Laura would like to try your 93 *blanc*.'

Sue sighed melodramatically. 'Yes, yes! Go on then. Never mind me. You lot won't like it, but then what do *I* know?'

As Charles left the room, Laura said: 'Jesus! I get it – the Duke and Duchess of Windsor – here at Belle-Mère. Wow! How come?'

Sue took a deep breath, but before she could change the subject, Madame Fontaine was once more in full flow. 'A long story, my dear, but as I remember it, early in June 1937 the Windsors got married at the Château de Candé in Touraine, the home of that awful self-made millionaire, Charles Bedaux – invented the "Bedaux System" … some nonsense to do with "time and motion" – whatever that might be. Ghastly little man – turned out to be a Nazi! In fact, I think he was tried for treason in America … during the War. Anyway, the Windsors were at Candé and decided to motor down to Biarritz one weekend, breaking their journey here. It was such a special occasion – historic, I suppose – that my wonderful parents permitted me to attend the dinner.'

Quincy's face was a picture of incredulity. 'Why did the Windsors stop here? I mean–'

'Dear Papa had served in Maréchal Foch's headquarters during the War – the Great War, that is – and had met the Prince of Wales, as he then was, on many occasions while the Prince was serving on the staff of the B.E.F.'s Commander-in-Chief. They'd got on very well and had remained on friendly terms.'

'"B.E.F.?"' queried Laura.

'The British Expeditionary Force,' explained Quincy.

While Madame Fontaine described her memories of the Windsors, Charles returned with the bottles of the 1993. To Sue's bewilderment, he procured fresh glasses.

'What struck me most about Windsor,' Madame Fontaine continued, 'were his hands – like a mechanic's. They were rough and scaly, and one thumbnail was disfigured. And one of his eyes was much lower than the other.' She then launched into a description of the Duchess's spotty complexion, but interrupted herself in mid flow. 'My dear Charles,' she extolled warmly, 'I don't know about you, but I think this is even better than when we last tasted the 93. ... When was that? ... Easter?'

Charles nodded and waited for the guests' opinions.

Sue contorted her face. 'Ugh! It's–'

'*Excellent!*' enthused Quincy, '– truly excellent!'

Laura was nodding in agreement. 'Wow! This is heady stuff – so full of fruit. I'm amazed. Please, I don't mean to be rude, but I *am* amazed you can produce a white wine with such excellent ageing properties. If this is what Belle-Mère is capable of, then ... well ...'

Eric put down his glass, stopped staring at the remains of the tinned pâté on his plate, and looked at Charles. 'Belle-Mère is capable of producing even *finer* wines, Laura, isn't it, Charles? If'– he stole a glance at his wife – '... if–'

A pragmatic businesswoman would have seized the opportunity: Sue had a vested interest in selling Belle-Mère in toto – that was her 'product', of course, not a particular vintage. But her blind spot with respect to the estate's pre-Pronk days became an insuperable problem when coupled with her severe inferiority complex. The little silver bell had accompanied her from the chestnut tree. Now she grabbed it and began shaking it furiously. Yells of 'Jeanne! Jeanne! *Jeanne!*' reverberated around the great room.

Ten minutes later, the diners were tucking into *confit de canard*, accompanied by boiled *haricots verts* and diced potatoes fried in duck fat. It was simple fare and, like the pâté, the duck legs had come out of a tin. Nevertheless, both Laura and Quincy enjoyed the food: it was the sort of dish they'd been savouring in and around Bordeaux ever since they'd first visited the city; if only subconsciously, it generated feelings of nostalgic contentment. Fontaine was instructed to serve the two most recent vintages of Belle-Mère *rouge* – one of them had already been tasted in the garden – which, though barely indistinguishable, were pleasant enough. While Quincy and Madame Fontaine continued analysing the Windsors' post-Abdication careers – with an occasional observation or criticism from Charles – Laura endeavoured to make conversation with her ostensible hosts. It was not an easy task: Sue appeared to be devoid of any interests beyond her business activities at Belle-Mère and Barrage; Eric kept his head down, albeit he did manage to convey a few more opinions on how Belle-Mère's wines could be improved and marketed, albeit as this implied criticism of what Sue and himself had been doing for the last few years, she felt bound to contradict him. Such contradictions, moreover, were increasing in both volume and vehemence with each gulp of the very wine that had defied her marketing strategies.

After more incessant bell-ringing, a hot and sweaty Jeanne finally materialised giving every impression of having sampled more vintages than the diners. Her cacophonous removal of the main-course dishes was followed by violent deposits of a large glass bowl of lettuce – awash in an oddly creamy vinaigrette – and a rustic wooden board sporting three vast blocks of seemingly identical hard cheeses. As Eric offered the weighty cheeseboard to Laura, she tried one further attempt to switch the conversation away from business.

'And how did you two meet?' she asked, looking from one Pronk to the other. Across the table, Madame Fontaine, who'd been enchanting Quincy with gossip about the late Princess Grace of Monaco and the Monégasque royal family in general, ground to an abrupt halt. For a few seconds, a deathly silence reigned.

'Someone seen a ghost?' asked a bemused Quincy, who'd not heard Laura's question.

Sensing she'd made an awful gaff, Laura picked up the solitary cheese knife. 'I think I'll try a piece of each.'

'We met in Africa,' Eric said quietly. He paused. 'The Congo.'

The palms of Quincy's huge hands hit the table. 'Good Lord! What on earth were you doing in that awful hole! I was raised in Kenya – loved the place.'

Eric looked at his wife. 'I ... We–'

'You were both in fertilizers, weren't you?' said Madame Fontaine softly, as if jogging a poor memory.

Eric nodded with obvious relief. 'Yes ... fertilizers.'

'Pronks,' said Sue grandly, 'are the biggest fertilizers in Belgium. Everyone's 'eard of Pronks Fertilizers.'

Quincy nodded sagely. 'Ah yes. ... And did you work for Pronks in the Congo, Sue?'

'Um ... no. I was with–'

'ICI,' Eric snapped, '– the competition ... in those days.'

'Madame Pronk,' said Madame Fontaine with an apologetic smile, 'I know Charles will get cross with me,' – she patted his arm – 'but with these *delicious* cheeses I can thoroughly recommend our 1995 *rouge*, which, in my humble opinion, is drinking well at the moment.' She waved one hand dismissively. 'Oh, I know there are all these faddy people nowadays who keep telling us that one should drink white with cheese, but I'm a traditionalist, I'm proud to say. I'm sure Charles wouldn't mind popping down to the cellar and–'

'Fabulous!' cried Sue with a huge smile. 'Marvellous! If you wouldn't mind ... *Charles?*'

Fontaine's eyes were popping out of their sockets. 'My pleasure,' he finally managed.

Eric also rose from the table. 'I'd better come with you. I did a spot of stocktaking the other day and moved the 95s. You'll never find them.'

The Congo was forgotten – for the moment.

The 1995 Belle-Mère *rouge* was 'an admirable effort', as Quincy described it; even Sue managed a complimentary remark, much to everyone's surprise. Two bottles were consumed with ease as the diners demolished the unaesthetic yet remarkably appetising cheese blocks. Led as usual by Madame Fontaine, the conversation began to drift over Laura. She found herself focusing more and more on the room's features – paintings, furniture, ornaments, the floral details of the plasterwork in the cornices. For almost three hundred years, she reflected, diners had sat here and enjoyed themselves – eating, drinking, gossiping, arguing, plotting. ... Plotting? Why did that make her think of the Windsors? ... No matter, but their association with Belle-Mère could be a useful marketing angle if she turned the place into a hotel. Perhaps there were other celebrities who'd visited the château? Maybe the Windsors were just the tip of an iceberg?

A hotel? ... Where the hell did that notion come from? Absurd! I don't know anything about running hotels! ... On the other hand, I do know something about restaurants. But a high-class restaurant out in the sticks?

Who'd travel all the way to–? Lots of people of course! Some of the best restaurants in France are in the middle of nowhere – look at Michel Guérard with his three Michelin stars at Eugénie-les-Bains – a village that's about as interesting as watching grass grow. And with my Maison Blanche connections ... Maison Blanche? ... Maison Blanche! Would Dad be prepared to cross the Atlantic?

Things had been really tough for him since the divorce, Laura reflected. Even now, she still couldn't think of Mom and Mombrier – 'The Two Moms' as she'd come to call them – without cursing them – kicking Dad out of his own restaurants, thanks to their controlling interest. Christ, they'd been smart over the years! But the truth was that Dad had taken Mom for granted: he'd become so obsessed with food, his kitchen and his *brigade* that he'd failed to realize his 'best' friend was ... Well, that was all water under the bridge. What had also hurt was the fact that the Maison Blanche restaurants had prospered without Dad. He'd headed north to Seattle to make a fresh start, where Appleton's was now doing OK, but ... well, his heart wasn't really in it. He'd begged her to join him, but she didn't want to be a 'Mom-substitute' – marketing, managing, front-of-house – that wasn't her at all. She was a wine guru, and she wanted her own vineyard.

'OK,' he'd said, 'buy a vineyard in Oregon – Washington – somewhere near Seattle.'

'Just one big problem,' she'd told him bluntly. 'Despite all the hype, America ain't Bordeaux – never will be – just like a Cadillac ain't a Rolls-Royce.'

Maybe she could persuade Dad to move to Europe. ... What was keeping him in the States? Surely not Appleton's by all accounts. He'd adore Belle-Mère, especially if it meant being with his beloved daughter. And with his expertise, a superb restaurant could be created. And what a setting! What a house! She'd need to see more properties, naturally, but unless there were some nasties dug up by the lawyers or accountants when they did their 'due diligence', she doubted there'd be anything better on the market in Bordeaux in her price range.

And what about her plans for Jean-Claude? ... Dad would definitely get on with him like a house on fire – they were very similar in many ways, very similar indeed. The Fontaine wines were good – much better than she'd care to let on to the Pronks – and with Jean-Claude's genius they could be enormously improved. Belle-Mère could become a Mecca for wine lovers and gourmets! But she still had to persuade him to leave La Fayette – and that bitch Sophie. Once and for all, he had to be made to see that their pathetic marriage had been dead for years. And why would he want to go on working for that creep Henri now that Guy was a senile old goat? Tomorrow she'd definitely bring out the big guns. It would be one hell of a gamble, but what alternative was there? And she'd phone Dad and float the idea of a life together in Europe. Hell, the house was big enough for them all! He could live in the gatehouse if he wanted, unless–

Laura focused on the Fontaines. She'd need to check the lease – or whatever it was they had; she wasn't a charity. They seemed nice enough but her own folks came first. And if Jean-Claude didn't want Charles poking his nose around the *cuvier*, then he'd have to go too – reasonable notice, of course. Or would they need him as a consultant for a season or two?

Tomorrow – a big day! So much to sort out! I'll need to see Lampre as well. Does he work Saturdays? Knowing the Bordelais– Lampre! Where the hell is he anyway? She glanced at her watch. *Christ, almost half ten!*

Across the table, Madame Fontaine was passionately decrying the substitution of the vile 'euro' for the glorious franc.

'I'm so sorry to interrupt,' Laura said, 'but Quincy and I really ought to be getting back to Bordeaux. I was wondering whether there was any update from Pierre.'

Sue snapped out of a trance, induced by the euro discourse 'Oh blimey! I'd quite forgotten about 'im.' She tried to look concerned. 'Maybe 'e's phoned and spoken with Jeanne.'

Procuring Jeanne took far more shouting and ringing of the silver bell than previously. When she did finally appear, her grubby apron had been replaced by a raincoat, which, by all appearances, had been in the service of its mistress for several decades.

'I'm off,' she grunted in French. 'My Jules is here to run me home. If you want coffee, you'll have to make it yourself.'

With a patronizing smile, Sue barked in English: 'I thought you was doin' *tarte-tatin*?' Eric translated.

'Burned,' growled Jeanne. It was one of the few English words she knew.

Sue glared at Eric. 'Christ! Right! Well, piss off then. See you at eight tomorrow morning. And I mean *eight* – not bleedin' ten past.'

Jeanne sniffed and turned towards the door.

'And Pierre?' prompted Laura.

Initially, Jeanne seemed unable to recall anyone by the name of Pierre Lampre, or even to comprehend the word *immobilier*. At one point during the interrogation, Madame Fontaine leaned towards Laura and whispered: 'We used to have such wonderful staff, including a superb young lady in the kitchen. She has her own restaurant in Paris now.'

125

Eventually, after a graphic description of Lampre and numerous references to sisters-in-law, accidents, fractured limbs and hospitals in Langon, the penny dropped. It transpired that Lampre had telephoned at some stage during dinner and had asked to speak with Madame Pronk, but Jeanne had told him she was 'tied up'. He'd said something about his wife's car breaking down on the road from Pau and having to go and collect her, so he wouldn't be able to take an American woman to Bordeaux for the night. In no uncertain terms, Jeanne had told him she didn't want to hear such filth and slammed the phone down.

When Jeanne finally clomped out of the dining room, Quincy's side of the table exploded with laughter; even Sue and Eric managed a chuckle. Laura, however, was not amused: she thought Lampre's conduct was wholly unprofessional.

'I'm glad you all think it's so funny,' she muttered, 'but we're looking at a possible major real estate transaction here! If this is how the guy treats important clients, no wonder he's got such shitty offices downtown. He should have phoned *me* with his lame excuses. He's got the goddam mobile number. Anyway, Quincy, how the hell do we get back to Bordeaux now?'

'For goodness' sake, old thing, calm down. It's not poor Pierre's fault that his bloody sister-in-law's broken her damned leg, or that his wife's car has conked out en route from Pau, is it? Be fair. Anyway, we're not marooned out in the deserts of New Mexico. This is France – civilization! We'll get a taxi.'

'You *won't*,' said Eric emphatically, '... not out here – not at this time of night.'

Sue tutted and patted Laura's hand. 'You're quite right, love – Lampre's 'opeless. Couldn't organize a piss-up in a brewery. The numpty should 'ave phoned earlier and told us all about this malarkey with the old dame. But don't worry, Pronkie'll run you both back, won't you, duck?'

Eric, looking as if he'd been asked to murder someone, began to stammer incoherently.

Grinning, Quincy said: 'Oh, we couldn't put Eric to all that trouble, could we, Laura?'

'Nonsense!' blasted Sue, '– no bleedin' trouble at all!'

'I – I – I think I'm rather over the – the limit ... dear. The police are awfully strict these days, especially on – on – on Friday nights.'

'You've only 'ad a few bleedin' glasses!'

'Sue, I've consumed over one and a half bottles of wine in the last four hours. I hardly think–'

'Eric's right, Ms Olivier,' Charles intoned earnestly. 'Alas, I find myself in the same position, otherwise I should most willingly volunteer my services to transport our dear guests back to town.'

Laura shook her head slowly from side to side. 'I don't believe this! I sure as hell don't want to end up wrapped around a street lamp, or get anyone booked on a drunk-driving rap, but–'

'So, Sue and Eric,' Quincy interjected, flashing a joyous smile, 'there appears to be only one solution. Laura and I will have to spend the night here.'

*

With his hands behind his broad neck, Quincy lay naked on the bed, racked by indecision. Just a few inches behind him, in the room on the other side of the wall, lay the woman he'd desired for so long. Oh, what he wouldn't do to climb into her bed! 'So near and yet so far,' he kept murmuring as the frustration mounted. The irony was that beyond the wall on the other side of his room, the rapacious and equally frustrated Sue Pronk was probably praying that even at this late stage he might still accept the oblique invitation to share her bed. On his way back from the bathroom before turning in – neither his room nor Laura's enjoyed en suite facilities – Sue's door had stood ajar. As he passed, she'd called his name. He paused for a couple of seconds, but then continued along the passage. On reaching his room, however, he heard his name again – louder this time. He looked back: Sue was standing outside her door, smiling seductively.

'Didn't you hear me?' she cooed.

'Sorry?'

'Just now ... as you passed. I called you.'

'Oh?'

'I just wanted to say goodnight.'

'Ah. Goodnight.

'Got everythin' you need?'

'Yes thanks.'

'Apart from pyjamas, of course.'

'I–'

'Oh, but you don't wear 'em. You said before.'

'Hmm.'

'Well, goodnight then.'

'Goodnight.'

'If you need anythin' – anythin' at all – don't 'esitate to ask. I'm a very light sleeper these days, what with all the worry and everythin' over this place. And Pronkie's room – don't forget – is next to 'is study on the ground floor, so there'd be no point runnin' to 'im for 'elp if one of Belle-Mère's spooks wakes you up in the middle of the night, would there, Quince?'

'"Spooks"?'

'Ghosts. You know, *fantômes*. All big 'ouses 'ave 'em.'

Quincy smiled indulgently. 'Goodnight, Sue.'

So, there was Quincy's dilemma. He really couldn't help smiling. Life was truly remarkable – bizarre! Frankly, he had a strong suspicion that this unscheduled stopover had been engineered by the vampire next door and Lampre – the old rascal! And in view of a comment Laura had whispered in his ear while ascending to their quarters for the night, the same thought had been exercising her mind. Indeed, her attitude suggested that she thought he himself had something to do with it. How delicious!

'Château Belle-Mère,' he chuckled softly. It was such a ludicrous name, and yet oddly charming. He had to admit that, with the right expertise and much hard work, the estate had potential – a hell of a lot. He focused on the curtains gently swaying before his open window and wondered whether there might be some merit in considering the possibility of investing in Laura's project. After all, the receivers were offering the property at a reasonable price: not only were there good vineyards, but also a fine house furnished with some superb antiques. In fact, he doubted that they appreciated the true value of the château's contents, but that was their problem.

The Pronks, he remembered, had also mentioned the possibility of a hotel, and that seemed an option most worthy of consideration. Belle-Mère couldn't be more than a twenty-minute drive from the A62, the *Autoroute Des Deux Mers* – the Atlantic-Mediterranean trunk route – which could prove a superb feeder for the right class of tourist. And if they could get the place into the Relais & Châteaux chain, the capital value of their investment would soar in just a few years!

As Quincy's mind raced, he recalled the gossip about Laura's father – how he'd been pushed out of his own restaurants in the States by his ex-wife and their scheming sommelier. What had happened to Bryan Appleton? Could he be brought on board – provided he hadn't lost his marbles? Perhaps Belle-Mère could become a 'Temple of Wine' and a 'Temple of Gastronomy'! With his excitement mounting, Quincy raised himself off the bed and began to pace up and down the room. The combination of *two* leading wine experts – one on each side of the Atlantic! – plus Laura's marketing power as a media personality, his own pre-eminent wine publications, an American culinary icon, an architectural gem, heavenly countryside–

Bloody hell! Americans – the real big spenders – would be queuing up to stay at Belle-Mère, and they'd love all that stuff about the Windsors! There'd be a Windsor Suite ... and a Cartier Suite – the Windsors spent half their lives shopping at Cartier! ... He could sell Woopston Parva for a couple of million pounds – and the apartment in Bordeaux for at least half a million euros – and have his own apartment at Belle-Mère. Or, depending on the Fontaines' rights, if any, he could take the gatehouse. ... No, he'd prefer a suitable set of rooms in the main house if possible. ... Or he could build a new house for himself in the grounds. ... For himself? Surely, the intimacy of their working relationship would almost inevitably lead Laura to ... Well, she'd be so grateful for all his financial support, the backing of his publications – not only for the wine, but also for the hotel and its restaurant – that she'd see him in a new light. She'd discover the *real* Quincy Dubloon – the kind, caring, passionate man who could satisfy *all* her desires.

Staring into the mirror above the fireplace, he whispered: 'Let's face it, there's no woman I can't satisfy. I'll make Laura realize youth isn't everything. I'll do things to her she wouldn't even believe possible. ... And I don't think she's into kids.' The only reason why she'd rejected him for all these years was just a matter of blindness caused by the brainwashing of the almighty American image machine. People like Laura had suffered a lifetime of conditioning to seek sexual fulfilment – and maybe romance – with cool, laidback pretty-boy characters like Tom Cruise, Leonardo DiCaprio, Brad Pitt and ... well, he didn't go much to the cinema these days. He saw himself in the Errol Flynn/Gary Cooper/Clark Gable mould. No! – far too old – the Harrison Ford/Harvey Keitel mould? No, no, no! Still too old! ... Mel Gibson?

Anyhow, Laura had to have her eyes opened – and he *could* open them. It might take time and a little financial web spun around her, but it would be worth it. And when they were finally opened, Laura would desire him as much as he desired her, perhaps even more. Come on, it would be more than desire! She would *love* him. Dare he hope that his most fervent wish might come true at last? Would his decades of loneliness finally come to an end, here at Belle-Mère? Would she agree to–?

The bedroom door opened and Sue stepped in – grinning. 'I 'eard them floorboards creakin',' she whispered. 'I knew you was restless.' She threw off her dressing gown. 'Jesus Christ, Quince, you're in great shape for a man your age!'

CHAPTER 11

Sophie Bourjois smiled sweetly at her guest. 'Would you like another piece of gâteau, Dominique?'

Through a mouth stuffed full of *pruneaux* and pastry, Dominique Buffet managed something which sounded like 'Absolutely, darling!' In the process, he sprayed some blobs of masticated food across the table; a few landed in Jean-Claude's glass of Barsac. He stared at them pointedly and wondered whether he should make a show of fishing them out, but the gesture would probably be lost on Buffet, and there was no point in upsetting Sophie. In any event, he didn't want any more wine, even though it was a magnificent Barsac-Sauternes, the 1986 of Château Climens. As he'd repeatedly told Sophie over the years, Sauternes were not really 'pudding wines': just because they were sweet didn't make them an ideal accompaniment for all sugary confections. They could be heavenly with foie gras, for example, or even as an aperitif. As usual, however, Sophie had insisted on Sauternes with tonight's pudding course, and both she and the odious Buffet were knocking it back with gusto, even though at the outset she'd thought that a Barsac was some kind of poor man's substitute. Which reminded him: he'd better refill their glasses. Then he'd undertake another check on Alexandre upstairs. No doubt, the lad would still be sleeping soundly, but any escape – however brief – from this ghastly dinner was essential.

Gobbling more gâteau, Buffet said: 'But, darling, are you absolutely sure you can finish the entire *Orifices* by September? I mean, if we're going to hold your show during the second week of October, one must definitely have all the canvasses ready for crating and shipment before mid-September so we can organize the catalogue and the hanging in the gallery without any last-minute crises before the vernissage. I mean, there'll be some *ever* so important VIPs invited. I have to check dates and everything, but I'm sure dearest Sean Kunstmann will come over and buy at least one of the *Orifices* – maybe more ... who knows?'

Sophie's eyes bulged. 'Sean Kunstmann! Oh, my God! Do you honestly think so? How marvellous! I just can't believe it.' She looked up at her husband, who was pouring her some more wine. 'Jean-Claude, can you imagine Sean Kunstmann buying one of your wife's paintings? Can you? Isn't it incredible?'

Jean-Claude flashed a smile. He knew that Kunstmann was an American movie star, but that was the extent of his knowledge. 'Great,' he said.

'"Great",' Sophie mimicked, rolling her eyes at Buffet. '"*Great*"! He probably hasn't a clue who we're talking about. Never goes to the cinema, would you believe?'

Buffet gasped melodramatically. 'Oh, you poor sweetie! How dreadful! I couldn't live without the movies.' He was staring intently at Jean-Claude as he refilled his glass. 'You know, in the right light you bear a certain resemblance to Sean. I think it's those full lips and that Roman nose of yours. Of course, with a nose like that, I bet you've–'

'Dominique! Behave yourself. He *is* my husband, you know.'

'Oh, I *do*, darling, and believe you me, if he was a free agent I'd have made a pass at him as soon as I walked through your front door. If you're a fair representative of the local talent, Jean-Claude, I've got a great day in store on the beach tomorrow. I suppose it's all that toiling in the vineyards, fresh air and sun.'

Red with embarrassment, Jean-Claude replaced the bottle in the ice bucket on the side table and began to move towards the door. 'I'll just go and take another look at Alexandre,' he mumbled.

'Oh, for Christ's sake, honey,' Buffet pleaded, 'stop running away every five minutes. You're beginning to give me a complex. I'm sure the divine little fellow's perfectly all right. He's not a baby, is he? Anyway, whenever you leave the room, it's like a light going out.' Sophie began to giggle: she was ecstatically happy and verging on paralytic.

Jean-Claude hesitated for a moment. He desperately wanted to escape, and yet, it was difficult to lose his temper with someone who was bombarding him with the most bizarre compliments.

'I bet you look gorgeous in denim,' Buffet snapped. Turning to Sophie he added: 'He does, doesn't he? Tight jeans! They must turn you *wild* with desire, darling.'

For the first time since the start of the meal, Sophie looked discomforted. She hesitated. 'Well ...'

Buffet might have appeared fatuous but his senses were, nevertheless, fine-tuned to the nuances of human relationships. All evening, and despite his babbling, he'd been receiving and noting signals indicating an absence of desire between the married couple. Now, as a result of Sophie's hesitation and obvious embarrassment, he felt he had the final piece of damning evidence. Jean-Claude would certainly have been surprised to learn that Buffet experienced no pleasure from this conclusion. Instead, a brief yet undoubted feeling of sadness rippled through his body. He told himself to move on rapidly.

'Clad in delicious denim, dearest Sean makes me tremble at the knees. That scene in *Abattoir Cats*, the one where he has a big fight with the Mafia henchmen and ends up in the East River and everyone thinks he's snuffed it after that halo of bullets, but then he climbs up onto a landing stage in the early morning sun, all dripping wet and his jeans hugging his groin ... I mean, just for a few seconds you could see everything – and I mean *everything*. I thought I was going to have a fucking orgasm – in the Gaumont on the Champs-Élysées!'

Buffet's laughter, which sounded like a squealing pig, set Sophie off with overenthusiastic gusto. Jean-Claude, who'd dutifully regained his seat, managed a polite but forced smile. Buffet patted his hand. 'Are you going to come with us to the beach tomorrow, honey? I do hope so. You look like a man who could do with a bit of relaxation – sun, sea, sand and–'

'"*Relaxation*"?' barked Sophie. 'You must be joking. My husband doesn't know the meaning of the word.' She glared at him. 'I assume you'll be working at La Fayette tomorrow as usual – catching up on all your "paperwork", or whatever it is you do on a Saturday, won't you, Jean-Claude?'

Buffet groaned. 'Shit! How tedious!' Wagging a chubby finger at Jean-Claude, he added: 'You know what they say about "all work and no play", darling.'

'Exactly,' agreed Sophie. 'I can't remember when we last had a family holiday, let alone the two of us just slipping away for a weekend break – Paris, Saint-Tropez – anywhere for God's sake. But no, there's always some crisis or disaster at that bloody vineyard. Frankly, Dominique, it's a miracle they ever produce any wine at all, what with the frosts, the storms, the floods, the droughts, the pests, the mould. The list's *endless* – positively biblical. I mean, have you ever heard anyone say "The rains came late in Chianti this year."? I think these wine people make it all up to justify the ludicrous prices they charge. After all, if it's so bloody difficult to grow grapes here, as they try to make out, how come they've been churning out the world's finest wines for centuries, hmm?'

Jean-Claude could feel his shackles rising, but he didn't want an argument, particularly in view of Sophie's inebriation, a state of affairs evinced by the customary increase in the volume of her voice. Her attack on his vocation was facile – undoubtedly intended to amuse their guest – but her jibes about holidays were a dishonourable slur on his paternal and husbandly responsibilities. Before he could respond, however, Buffet came to his defence.

'*Le pauvre*,' he cooed. 'Isn't she a nasty-wasty little bitch, darling? We don't like her anymore, do we?' Jean-Claude stared at the tablecloth while his hand was patted again. 'I suppose,' Buffet continued, 'it's just possible that these gorgeous wines – like the La Fayette we've guzzled tonight – are *so* fantastic, Sophie, precisely because hunky Jean-Claude here and his counterparts work their gorgeous butts off all year round. Mind you, chuck, one can overdo this dedication-to-duty mania. I mean, the little lady and the sprog need your TLC too. Christ, I wish you had some for me!'

Buffet swung to face Sophie. 'Did I tell you, darling, that Gustave and me finally split up last week? What a scene in the gallery! He smashed three vases of white lilies. I've never seen the Marquise de Boulogne move so fast in all my life – eighty if she's a day. One minute she was almost wetting herself with excitement in front of a painting by this Bosnian youth I discovered last year, Osman,' – he licked his lips – 'this grotesque representation of Milösevic's entrails, and then she's like a bat out of hell, racing her wheelchair into the disabled persons' restroom to take cover while Gustave had his breakdown. It took over an hour to coax her out again. In the end, we bribed her with a bottle of Veuve Clicquot, some caviar and the taxi fare back to her apartment in Avenue Montaigne.'

When Sophie's hysterical giggling subsided, Jean-Claude said: 'It's a very demanding job, Sophie, being a *maître de chai*. However, in the last twelve months I've tried on several occasions to organize a trip away together, but you always had some commitment or other – a vernissage, a party, an auction with Cathérine, a–'

'What the–?'

'In January – or was it early February? – I suggested a long weekend in Paris. I even got some brochures and–'

'Oh *that*,' Sophie snorted contemptuously. 'If I remember correctly, you had in mind some two-star dump out at La Défense' – Buffet grimaced theatrically – 'full of grotesque British package holidaymakers, no doubt, plus a show at the Moulin Rouge and a trip on a *bateau mouche*. Did you honestly think I was going to change any plans to indulge in that sort of tacky excursion?'

'Oh, I don't know,' Buffet chirped with fluttering eyelids, 'it sounds dead romantic to me.'

But Sophie was not amused. '*Really*? A two-star hotel – "romantic"? How would *you* know? I doubt you've ever passed the portals of anything less than a five-star *palace* for as long as you'd care to remember, and that in Paris you haven't the slightest knowledge of any hotels other than the Ritz, the George V and the Crillon.'

'Wicked, *wicked* girl! That's a monstrous lie. You're making me out to be a horrid snob. I'll have you know that from time to time I've endeavoured to procure the favours of a spot of rough trade with the promise of a humble bed for the night at the Plaza Athénée, the Bristol, or even' – Buffet lowered his head – 'the Prince de Galles.'

'Game, set and match!'

Jean-Claude told himself to remain silent. A dam, however, had burst within him. 'Despite appearances,' he began softly, but the sentence remained unfinished. 'Some more Barsac, Dominique?' he asked, rising from his seat. 'A *digestif*? ... coffee?'

'Never touch spirits anymore, honey, and I only take coffee at breakfast and lunch. Wine, on the other hand, I can never resist. Go on then, top me up with your delicious Climens.'

Like a delayed-action bomb, Sophie hissed: '"Despite appearances" *what*?'

Jean-Claude simply shrugged his shoulders and proceeded to refill Buffet's glass; Buffet noticed his host's shaking hand.

'"Despite appearances" *what*?'

'Nothing.'

'Come on, out with it, and if you don't mind, Jean-Claude, could *I* have some more wine too?'

He held up the empty bottle. 'Sorry. I didn't think. ... Sorry.'

Buffet pushed his glass towards Sophie. 'Now, now! No tantrums or you'll get sent to bed with a smacked botty. You can have mine.'

Sophie pushed it back, almost knocking the glass over. 'No thanks. We've got *bottles* of the stuff, for Christ's sake! He'll open another one. Jean-Claude–'

'We don't have another 86 Climens, Sophie. That was the last.'

'Please don't open more wine on my account, you two.'

For an instant, Sophie glared at Buffet: obviously, he was taking sides. It really was pathetic how this fat, middle-aged, balding fag was flirting with her husband. 'I'm still waiting, Jean-Claude,' she snarled. '"*Despite appearances*"–?'

'Put a sock in it, Sophie!' Buffet screeched. 'Talk about a bitch with a bone! Jean-Claude, sweetie, if you don't tell her what you were going to say, the poor cow will go on and on all night.'

Jean-Claude managed a smile. 'Well,' he sighed, 'I was only going to say that ... um–'

'Yes, yes – go on!' urged Buffet with fake excitement.

'Well, that despite appearances – like, this house and everything – our financial resources are limited. I mean, we don't have the money to stay at places like the Ritz or–'

'That's *enough*! One doesn't–'

'Jesus! – you're making out that I'm some kind of miser, Sophie. Be fair. On my salary and what you make from your paintings, we can barely afford to keep up–'

'*Enough!*' Sophie's eyes burned with a murderous expression. Yet, even in her befuddled state she had the sense to realize that a row in front of Buffet could prove disastrous. Willing herself to be calm, she turned to him and smiled. 'I'm *so* sorry, Dominique. Of course, we Parisians tend to forget how country folk can be so–'

'Frank?' he suggested with a giggle, vainly attempting to lighten the atmosphere. 'And by the way, Sophie, "despite appearances" I was raised on a ramshackle dairy farm in Touraine.'

She managed to keep smiling. '*Really*? How ... *charming*! ... What I was going to say was ... "canny". With your rural childhood, Dominique, you'll know exactly what I mean. Country folk are always pleading poverty and moaning about the price of turnips, the cost of fertilizer, or the inadequate subsidies from Brussels. They drive around in tatty Citroën vans, wear clothes that would be rejected by any self-respecting Somalian refugee, and – and ... well, believe you me, most of them are bloody loaded.'

Nodding his head vigorously and pretending to empathize, Buffet said: 'I always say you should never judge a book by its cover. You don't drive a Citroën van, do you, Jean-Claude?'

'Of course he bloody doesn't!'

'Well then, he can't be one of those "canny" farmer types.' Buffet smiled broadly at Jean-Claude, leaned towards him, and let the fingers of one hand gently slide down his shirtsleeve. 'Gorgeous fabric, darling,' he purred. 'If I'm not mistaken it's one of Armani's little numbers from this season's collection. Can't see any refugee – Somalian or otherwise – turning their nose up at *this*. I bet you've got a wardrobe full of the most exquisite things, haven't you, honey?'

Jean-Claude didn't know what to say.

Fearing another admission of straightened circumstances, Sophie snapped: 'Actually, he's got some *very* nice clothes. Of course, I choose *everything* for him, otherwise he'd certainly look like one of those "canny farmers". Before I met him–'

'He was dressed head to toe in denim! I just knew it. No wonder you fell for the gorgeous hunk.'

Jean-Claude pushed his chair back. 'Please excuse me but I really must go and check on Alexandre. He was complaining of a tummy ache earlier on.' As he reached the dining room door, Buffet said:

'Look, joking aside, Jean-Claude, if – and I mean *if*, because it's really none of my business – but if by any chance you *have* got financial worries, I can almost guarantee that, come October, you should be receiving a healthy injection of funds.'

Jean-Claude had turned around; his brow was furrowed. 'Sorry? I don't understand.'

It was Buffet's turn to look bemused. 'Oh *really*, honey! Tut, tut! What the hell do you think we've been talking about all evening?' Jean-Claude continued to look blank; Buffet turned to Sophie for support. 'Honestly, what *is* he like? Talk about head in the clouds! – or should I say "vines"?'

Sophie kept smiling, albeit she, too, was puzzled. Surely, he wasn't about to offer them a loan? Frankly, finance had never been one of her strong points. Only that afternoon, Geoffroy had mentioned something at Cathérine's shop about her charging too little for her paintings. He said it made her look 'cheap and undistinguished'. He'd recently received a catalogue from a Paris gallery – it had been addressed to his wife, he insisted – and from what he could see, 'paintings no better than yours' were being sold at ten times – or even *twenty* times – her prices. She'd opined that the painters were probably famous. With wounding tactlessness, Geoffroy had replied:

'Well, if they can flog their rubbish for seventy-five *thousand* euros plus, I'm sure you can sell yours for a damned sight more than a lousy three thou' a throw.'

In fact, now that she thought about it, this conversation had flowed from her references to Buffet coming down to Le Porge to see her *Orifices*. Geoffroy had made some tasteless remarks, and had then warned her not to be bamboozled by 'some Parisian queer generous with flamboyant praise but mean with the cash'. She'd said that chance would be a fine thing, and seriously doubted that Buffet would have the slightest interest in the paintings once he saw them in the flesh. Well, she'd been wrong about that – thank God! Dominique's enthusiasm had gone beyond her wildest dreams, but so far, she'd not had the courage or inclination to raise the tiresome issue of money, and no specifics had been forthcoming from him, just a barrage of incomprehensible stuff about commissions. In truth, to get exhibited in his gallery, she'd be happy to do almost anything – even pay for the privilege. Not that she had any money, of course. ... Maybe Papa could be persuaded–

Concentrate! Damn all that bloody wine! – champagne, white, red, Sauternes ... Barsac? – whatever. And how come old Buffet's as sober as a judge after all that lot? What's he talking about anyway?... Oh, not commissions again? ... sliding scales? God! It's all so complicated. And what's it got to do with Jean-Claude anyway? Who's the bloody artist?

Buffet was smiling at her. 'Lost your tongue, darling? You *are* happy with my fees, aren't you? I'm not sure Jean-Claude is though. Look at his puzzled little face – so sweet.'

'No, no,' Jean-Claude croaked. 'I mean ... I'm sure they're fine. I really don't know anything about–'

'Of course he's happy with them, Dominique,' Sophie interrupted. She paused and absent-mindedly flicked some crumbs from the tablecloth. 'So ... it's ... *ten* per cent of the *first* sale–?'

'No, no, *no!*' groaned Buffet. 'Come on, Dolly Daydream, let's put Mr Thinking Cap on, shall we? It's twenty-five per cent of the first hundred thousand, twenty per cent of the second, and fifteen per cent of everything over three hundred. So, darling, if, for example, we sold some pickies for four hundred thousand euros, I'd get twenty-five thousand, plus twenty thousand, plus thirty thousand, making seventy-five thousand euros in total. ... Is that right? ... And *you*, dearest Sophie, would walk off with three hundred and twenty-five thousand euros. Got it or do you want me to draw you a diagram?'

There was silence.

Finally, Buffet cupped his hands around his mouth. 'Hello! Anybody there? Are you reading me? Over and out!'

Jean-Claude shifted nervously by the door. 'Do you honestly think you'll be able to sell *any* of the *Orifices?*'

Buffet sat bolt upright. 'Good God! Ye of little faith! I'll be *very* disappointed if we don't flog at least half the shitty things.'

Sophie seemed to be in a trance. 'Ah ... right ... at least half. Um ... how much – I mean what sort of figure ...? What *should* we ask for them, Dominique?'

Buffet flung his podgy arms in the air. 'Good question, darling. Don't know about you, but I had in mind forty thousand for the really yucky ones – maybe fifty thousand. Actually, there's one disgustingly rich bitch in Hollywood I know who'd probably gobble up the male arsehole – especially as it's so hairy. ... Did you pose for that Jean-Claude? Oops! Sorry, darlings! You can slap my wrist if you want. ... Now, where was I?... Oh yes. Well, he'd probably be happy to go up to a hundred thousand *dollars* for it. And then there are all the bestiality pervs – especially in New York. Frankly, Sophie, the sooner we get your stuff on the Internet, the better.' Buffet rubbed his chin. 'I wonder if I could get Cathérine to the vernissage.'

Sophie tried to focus on something. 'Cathérine? ... Cathérine *who*?'

'Cathérine de la Rochefouquet, silly – our Minister of Culture.'

Jean-Claude moved a step closer to the table and cleared his throat. 'Forty ... *fifty* ... thousand? You mean for the *entire* collection? I–'

'Don't be daft! Dear God, why do I always fall for the innocent, naive types? *Each*, of course, darling – *each*!'

It was when Sophie mumbled 'each' for the fourth time that her eyes momentarily met her husband's. As they did so, there was a mutual realization that something of momentous importance had just occurred – that their lives had irrevocably changed. Dominique willed himself to keep smiling. Even though he was a good actor, it was both a difficult and an unpleasant task, for it was slowly dawning on him that in all probability he'd just driven the final nail into a coffin – his hosts' marriage.

CHAPTER 12

The next morning, there were just Jean-Claude, Alexandre and Richelieu – the Dalmatian – down for breakfast, but then Sophie rarely surfaced before ten o'clock. As for the weekend guest, he'd stated before turning in that Sophie's civilized behaviour in this respect suited him admirably. Consequently, when father and son joined each other for coffee and fresh bread around half past seven, they only had the housekeeper, Denise Épine, for human company.

'Housekeeper' was the grand title which Sophie had decreed for Madame Épine, a buxom widow in her late fifties. Six mornings a week, she came from the village on a vintage *mobilette* armed with a baguette and local gossip. She was punctual if nothing else, always arriving at seven on the dot whatever the weather, and departing four hours later precisely at eleven. Due to myopia and an inexplicable stubbornness to replace the spectacles she'd worn for the last twenty years, the cleaning performed between these hours left much to be desired. However, as cleaners were a rare commodity in the Le Porge neighbourhood, she enjoyed security of tenure. On the other hand, her early morning arrival ensured that Jean-Claude – 'Monsieur Bourjois' as Sophie required her to address him – got 'a proper breakfast', albeit this was not much consolation: he would have preferred to begin his day in peace without 'Denise' – as Sophie required him to address her – fussing like an overprotective mother hen; a cup of coffee and a croissant at his desk at La Fayette would have been ideal.

In fact, on her employment's commencement – following a gruelling series of interviews by Sophie – there'd been no question of Denise starting at cockcrow. Nonetheless, having quickly taken a shine to Jean-Claude, she'd unilaterally altered her hours to provide him with the sort of meal she believed 'a working man' needed at the start of a long day. He'd pleaded with her, but she'd said that as an incurable insomniac – one of the many ailments from which she constantly suffered – letting her prepare his coffee at seven a.m. would be doing her a good turn.

Alexandre – 'Monsieur Alexandre' as Sophie required the housekeeper to address him – did not like Denise, but then, during term time he only had to suffer her on Saturday mornings and very briefly on Mondays, when, just after seven, one of his parents – usually Jean-Claude – would drive him back to his Bordeaux boarding school; mercifully, Denise had Sundays off. Thanks to her, it was a widely held belief in Le Porge that

Alexandre was not a normal ten-year-old boy. Youngsters – almost exclusively offspring of 'canny country folk' – called him 'a sissy', or worse, albeit their negative attitudes were not based on much in the way of empirical evidence: Alexandre had never fraternized with any of them; apart from brief glimpses of him sitting rigid and expressionless in a parental car, he was rarely seen outside the Bourjois residence. Nonetheless, they overheard their parents discussing Denise's reports of the 'goings-on' up at 'the Airport'– their nickname for her place of work: when first built, some local wag had said it reminded him of Bordeaux Airport's terminal building. Fresh instalments of 'Airport Life' were communicated to village residents whenever they bumped into Denise. This was a daily inevitability, for she was a fixture in all of Le Porge's established meeting places, including the *boulangerie*, the post office, the *mairie* – from which a great swathe of the surrounding countryside was administered – the church, the doctor's surgery and the café. Indeed, a resident could say *au revoir* to Denise at the post office and walk to the *boulangerie*, only to find her already ensconced and repeating what she'd just broadcast in front of the postmistress. Her *mobilette* had a lot to answer for.

Consequently, Le Porge's citizens had come to believe what Denise believed, namely, that Jean-Claude was a saint married to an amoral vampire – a vampire, moreover, who'd begotten the Devil's child. Take, for example, her discourse yesterday at the *mairie* after she'd finished giving the Airport a final 'once-over' in anticipation of Monsieur Buffet's much heralded weekend stay. Friday morning was one of the occasions when Monsieur le Maire's part-time secretary, Geneviève, put in an appearance; Denise popped in, offering – without conviction – to help out at the commune's *Fête Nationale* fireworks display on 14 July. Luckily for both ladies, Geneviève's boss was down at Le Porge Océan having a site meeting with representatives of La Maison de la Forêt about resurfacing the coastal cycleway, one of Le Porge's proudest tourist attractions. Halfway through her second cup of coffee in the mayor's office, Denise was in full flow, using first names as usual.

'You won't believe all the stuff Sophie's done to make the Airport comfy for her VIP guest, Geneviève. He's ever so important, you know, and she's so lucky to get him down here. She says his Paris gallery is one of the most famous in the world. All the best painters get exhibited there. Any more of those biscuits, dear? … Anyway, this Monsieur Buffet must be ever so posh – all those exotic soaps, creams, shampoos and things Sophie's laid out for him in the bathroom! Apparently, he's *very* particular about his skin, very particular indeed – and thanks to Clinique, he's fifty-eight but only looks fifty. Isn't that wonderful?'

'Sounds a right poof to me.'

'Oh, Geneviève, don't be so narrow-minded! Sophie's got lots of friends like him. Well, they're artists, aren't they? You can't expect folk like that to be normal, can you? And if she wants to make her way in the world and sell those paintings of hers, she can't be too fussy, can she? And between you, me and the gatepost, Geneviève, they really do need the money. Jean-Claude works so very hard, and he's got an excellent job, but, as I've said before, dear, I honestly don't think he gets paid that much. And as far as I'm aware, Sophie hasn't sold even *one* of her paintings for ages. … Of course, they're very unusual.'

'Pornographic by all accounts.'

'That's a nasty word, Geneviève. The likes of me and you can't be expected to understand these things. Mind you, it's probably just as well Sophie doesn't allow Alexandre to go into her studio. The poor lad would probably have nightmares if he saw all those pictures of … well, you know.'

'Oh, come on, Denise! I remember you saying he reads sex books. That kid probably knows more about women's fannies and blokes'–'

'I never did! I said he reads the *Larousse Médical*. As you'd expect, it contains some *very* explicit photographs. Sophie says she's very much against censorship, and the sooner children get to know how their bodies function and everything, the better. Anyway, Sophie's hoping that this Buffet will like her paintings and put them on show in his gallery. She says that if that happens, she's almost bound to sell some. I bet Jean-Claude's got his fingers crossed, because he looks so worried these days. At breakfast I often see him staring at all these invoices, bank statements, Sophie's credit card statements – they're the worst – just shaking his head.'

'*Le pauvre!*'

'Exactly. And Alexandre's school fees are going up again next term. They make such huge sacrifices to give that lad a good education. Mind you, if Jean-Claude had had his way, Alexandre would never have gone to that place in Bordeaux. He always said they couldn't afford it – the uniform alone costs a small fortune.'

'*Uniform*! I thought only the stupid English went in for that nonsense. It's no wonder they haven't a clue what to wear when they grow up.'

'Oh no, dear, you're wrong there. Alexandre says uniforms are very "democratic" – they put everyone on the same level and stop the kids showing off and making poor kids feel inferior.'

'Christ! He's not a communist, is he?'

'Don't be ridiculous. … *And* he thinks – how did he put it? … "The youth of today are slaves to fashion. Therefore, not having to waste so much time thinking about what to wear each day liberates the mind for more creative pursuits" – something like that. He's ever so clever.'

'Sounds a right prat to me. How old is he again?'

'Ten.'

'Bloody hell! ... Is he still giving you tips on how to do your work better?'

'To be honest, Geneviève, I don't really see him all that much – not even during the holidays. Like last Saturday – apart from breakfast, he spent all the time in his study with his books and stuff. Mind you–'

'"*Study*"? He's got a "*study*"?'

'It's his bedroom really, but he calls it a study. As I was about to say, he gave me some very useful tips on how to make coffee a few weeks back.'

'The cheeky little bugger! What does *he* know about it? Talk about teaching your grandmother to suck eggs.'

'Oh no, Geneviève, he's quite the expert. In fact, he prepares Sunday breakfast now for all three of them. He said it was "invaluable to know the lot of a servant so that when one grows up one will know how to deal with them." One of his friends at school told him that – a duke's son.'

'A *duke*! So much for the bloody Revolution.'

'Anyway, he'd got to reading the coffee packets and told me I should warm the pot first with boiling water, and then pour just a *little* water on the grounds – but it mustn't be boiling because it damages the flavour – then let them swell for ten seconds, and then pour the rest of the water into the pot. They've got one of them cafetière things, by the way. Apparently, you only pour boiling water on tea, Alexandre says. For coffee, it must be just off the boil.'

'I couldn't cope with a kid like that.'

'No, I don't suppose you could. Jean-Claude's ever so patient with him, but then I've never seen Jean-Claude get cross or lose his temper with anyone. Take the other Monday morning, when he was rushing a bit because he'd thought Sophie was going to take Alexandre back to school because she and that Cathérine – the snooty antique dealer woman – were going to an auction in Biarritz, and then discovered she'd changed her mind because she wanted to spend the day rearranging her studio so it wouldn't look quite so untidy for Monsieur Buffet's visit. Well, Jean-Claude was slurping his coffee a bit, being in a hurry an' all, and then put his knife in one of them crystal jam pots they've got instead of using the silver spoon. The next thing I know, Alexandre's got his fingers stuck in his ears saying, "I say, Papa, what a frightful commotion! My chum Bruno says that you can always tell a chap's background by his table manners." Just like a little lord he sounded.'

'The bastard!'

'Geneviève, *please*. The poor boy was only repeating the sort of thing he probably hears all day long at that school.'

'Jean-Claude should have given him a bloody good thrashing.'

'Honestly, Geneviève! Anyway, Jean-Claude couldn't even if he'd wanted to – Sophie doesn't believe in that kind of thing. ... Well, Jean-Claude was so calm. He put down his cup, looked his son square in the eyes and said, "Alexandre, you will remember, I'm sure, that the Bible tells us that it is Man who makes manners and not manners that make a man."'

'Good for him! I bet that put the little devil in his place.'

'As a matter of fact, Alexandre then said something like, "Papa, your biblical misquotation is most illuminating. However, I believe this may be an appropriate moment to inform you that I have become an atheist." What a way with words that lad has! He wouldn't last five minutes in a state school.'

'And?'

'And what?'

'What did Jean-Claude say to that atheist crap?'

'He told Alexandre he'd ten seconds to get in the car.'

*

Jean-Claude tried to stop thinking about the implications of last night's bombshell. It wasn't easy; he'd been awake for most of the night listing and evaluating them. At his side, Sophie had slept like a baby; she'd not even stirred when he'd got up. But then, she'd had a lot to drink – before, during and after dinner – especially after dinner when the import of Buffet's financial predictions had sunk in and she'd ordered more champagne. Finishing his coffee, Jean-Claude stared at his uneaten croissant – 'a special weekend treat' as Denise had called it. He wasn't hungry. In fact, he felt quite queasy; the croissant's buttery odour wasn't helping. He pushed the plate away.

'Alexandre, would you like another croissant?' The boy didn't look up from his book and appeared not to hear. His empty plate, together with the surrounding area of tablecloth, were immaculate. Jean-Claude shook his head: it never ceased to amaze him how Alexandre could eat a croissant without creating any mess at all. Frankly, it was unnatural.

Moaning about an aching back, Denise clattered into the kitchen with another tray of dirty crockery from the dining room in an aggressive attempt to eliminate the evidence of Buffet's *grande* fête. She began attacking the dishwasher; Alexandre raised his head.

'Does she *have* to make so much noise?' he hissed. 'And I hope she realizes that's Mama's best Limoges.'

For a few seconds, Jean-Claude felt mildly irritated. Why hadn't Alexandre said '*our* best Limoges'? ... or 'your and Mama's best Limoges'? ... or even plain 'your best Limoges'? Then he scolded himself for being ludicrously oversensitive. He really had to stop reading so much into a ten-year-old's throwaway comments.

'Alexandre, would you like my croissant? ... What are you reading by the way?'

Alexandre put his book down and sighed. 'No thank you, Papa. One must be careful about cholesterol. With respect to my book, I am *trying* to read *Le Misanthrope*.'

'Ah.'

'By Molière.'

'Yes ... of course.' Jean-Claude knew who Molière was; he dimly recollected studying this particular play at school. He'd hated Molière. In truth, he'd hated all arts subjects; only science, handicrafts and sport had interested him. 'Are you sure you don't want another croissant?'

'Quite sure, thank you.'

Jean-Claude didn't look forward to breakfasts with Alexandre, and because this made him feel ashamed of himself, he was even tenser during these ordeals than on the mornings when he only had to cope with Denise.

'I intend to secure a part in next term's performance,' Alexandre announced.

'Ah.'

'I should love to play the role of the leading character, Alceste. I suspect, however, that it might be just a little too demanding for me at this stage in my scholastic career.'

'Possibly.'

'Be that as it may, Papa, I do find so much of Alceste's philosophy extraordinarily apposite to my own experiences of life.'

Denise had thundered back into the kitchen with yet another tray of debris. 'Eat up, you two!' she bellowed. 'Got to keep your strengths up.' As she bent over the beleaguered dishwasher and presented her extensive posterior to father and son, Jean-Claude picked up his croissant and threw it into the dog's basket. Richelieu devoured it in seconds.

Looking from his father to the dog, Alexandre sat expressionless for a few moments. 'Take, for example,' he continued, 'Alceste's profound dictum, "*C'est n'estimer rien qu'estimer tout le monde*", which, I suppose, one could translate into modern French as "To admire all is to admire nothing." What Molière is indubitably trying to say here, is that only a fool or a knave goes around asserting that he loves or admires everything and everyone he sets eyes on.'

'Ah.'

'That's very true, don't you think, Papa?'

'Probably.'

'"*Probably*"? ... Well, Molière was criticizing the excessively flamboyant manners of Louis XIV's court at Versailles, of course, but' – Alexandre glanced disdainfully in the direction of Denise's rear quarters as she attempted to rearrange the dishwasher's contents to accommodate a large serving plate – 'I suspect that if Molière were alive today and familiar with our modest household, he might have written those lines with a humbler personage in mind. And, furthermore, had he met Mama's guest, I venture to suggest that Molière would have been of the opinion that Monsieur Dominique Buffet would have fitted in very well at the Sun King's Versailles. Frankly, Papa, I have never met a fellow who is so extravagant with his compliments. I assume he greatly admired Mama's paintings. ... Is he going to exhibit them in his gallery?'

Denise suddenly suspended her attack on the dishwasher.

Jean-Claude cleared his throat and rose from the table. 'Er ... I really must be going. Um ... yes – I mean, yes, he *did* like Mama's paintings – a lot. And yes, he *is* going to exhibit them in his gallery.'

'How wonderful!' cried Denise, returning to an upright position and giving her back to the dishwasher. 'I knew someone would like them sooner or later. I always told her–'

'Thank you, Denise,' Alexandre interrupted. 'I should be most grateful if you could go upstairs to my study forthwith and make the bed. I wish to commence my weekend assignments at eight a.m., and, as you know, I prefer to work in a *tidy* room.'

Denise and Jean-Claude exchanged meaningful glances.

'Goodness me, Monsieur Alexandre,' she said, closing the dishwasher violently, 'you *are* a well-organized little boy – *quite* unique.'

'Unique, Denise, is an absolute. I may – or may not be – "unique". I cannot, however, be "*quite* unique".' Before either adult could digest Alexandre's lecture, let alone respond, he asked: 'Papa, does this mean we're going to live in Paris like Grandpapa and Grandmama?'

Denise stopped dead in her tracks.

In view of the expression of bewilderment on his father's face, Alexandre felt bound to elucidate. 'Mama said that if Monsieur Buffet exhibited her paintings, it was very likely she would – and I quote – "make a killing", and that in a year or two she would be making enough money "to buy our freedom" and "earn our passage back to civilization". Upon enquiry, she informed me that that meant Paris. My friend Bruno says there are some extremely smart schools in Paris and that he'll probably be going to one of them next year. His papa is the Duc de Dieppe, you know. I do hope we won't be separated.'

Jean-Claude suddenly felt very hot. One of the awful scenarios he'd considered in the early hours seemed to be coming true. Both Alexandre and Denise were watching him intently and waiting for a response. He knew what they were thinking – that Sophie had never mentioned to him the possibility of anyone moving to Paris. The silence was unendurable; his head seemed to be close to exploding. He wanted to run to the car and get away from all of them, as far away as possible. As if reading his mind, Denise came to the rescue.

'Well, Monsieur Alexandre, I'm sure your mummy and daddy will have a lot to talk about once Monsieur Buffet has returned to Paris and they've had a chance to discuss things in peace. But as we grown-ups say, "Don't count your chickens until they're hatched." Anyway, Daddy's got a *very* important job here. I don't think Mummy would expect him to give it up and go gadding off to Paris.'

'As a matter of fact, Denise,' Alexandre said with a sigh, 'it never crossed my mind for one moment that Papa would come with Mama and me to Paris. I dare say we would spend the occasional weekend and holiday here – when we we're not at Grandpapa's château in Normandy, of course. ... Bruno says older houses are so much nicer than modern ones. I suspect that when Mama's rich, she'll sell this house and buy a château. Maybe she could even buy Papa a vineyard of his own.'

For ten seconds or so, the only sound in the kitchen was the dishwasher's soporific whooshing. Alexandre appeared to be in a trance. Then he looked at his watch. 'Denise, my study – *please*.'

*

It was a miracle Jean-Claude didn't have an accident driving to La Fayette, such was his lack of concentration on the road ahead. All he could think about were Sophie and Alexandre. Would they really leave him for Paris? And if so, would the Le Porge house be sold? ... But Denise was right about counting chickens: *Les Orifices* might not sell; Buffet could be wrong – his track record couldn't be a hundred per cent, surely? Despite all his big talk, what sort of nutter would pay forty thousand euros – or even more! – for one of Sophie's vile daubs. And how would all this madness affect his own plans – resigning from La Fayette and emigrating to Australia or America?

Jean-Claude had covered more than half the distance to Margaux before realizing he'd made no inquiries about how Alexandre was going to spend the afternoon. There was no way Sophie would take him down to the coast: he detested sun, sand and sea – and he'd wreck the plans which she'd made for Buffet to savour Le Porge's gay beach. Christ – there was no way Alexandre should get an eyeful of that sort of thing! On the other hand, it would be irresponsible to leave him alone all afternoon in the house, even if he did insist – as he usually did – that he was more than capable of looking after himself, and that he was perfectly content to read his books, do his homework, and finish his three-dimensional jigsaw of Notre-Dame de Paris – or whatever it was he was currently working on.

Why can't he like football? It would be great fun going to matches together in Bordeaux and supporting the Girondins, just like Dad and me did. ... Or cycling! We could go cycling in the forests. After all, people come from all over Europe to cycle here. There are hundreds of kilometres of cycle tracks along the coast. You can cycle almost to Biarritz – apart from a few minutes on the ferry from Cap Ferret to Arcachon. But Alexandre doesn't like cycling either. Why? ... Surely, he has to do some kind of sport at school? ... What? ... Why don't I know? ... Maybe I'm a lousy parent. Sophie said as much to Buffet over dinner. All that stuff about us never going on family holidays! When has Sophie ever expressed any interest in going on 'a family holiday'? Alexandre certainly hasn't ... has he? ... Of course not! He can hardly bear to leave his bedroom – sorry! – 'study'.

Still, I really ought to go back and ensure he isn't abandoned by those two. What if Buffet brings one of his conquests to the house? Sophie's hardly likely to tell him to behave, is she? – not with her 'ticket to freedom' at stake. Jesus! Could she really have said all that stuff to Alexandre? Is she so desperate to return to Paris? But he wouldn't make up something like that, would he? He might be ... different, but he's certainly not a liar. No, he's honest, obedient and trustworthy – and hardworking – and intelligent – very intelligent – too bloody clever for his own good sometimes! But he'll grow out of it – this supercilious, snotty, bookworm nonsense. It's just a phase – all kids have phases. In a few years, he'll probably rebel – grow his hair, become a Marxist, refuse to wear that daft uniform, get threatened with expulsion, do drugs and stay out all night with the surfing crowd down at the Ocean!

Jean-Claude smiled: Alexandre was a good kid really; he'd turn the car around and go back. To hell with La Fayette! The two of them could go into Bordeaux and visit some of those museums the lad was always talking about, have some lunch, and then–

Lunch! Laura!

Groaning and cursing, he pressed his foot on the accelerator. He couldn't put her off a second time. In any event, he had to find out about this bottle she'd brought over from the States. If Laura had suspicions about Maréchal being passed off as his first wine, he needed to know – and to ensure she didn't start blabbing her mouth off. Americans could be so indiscreet – and mercenary. All these 'big decisions' she'd talked about on the phone yesterday morning. He wouldn't be at all surprised if she was planning a new TV series on wine fraud – there was enough of it about. And she must have acquired a lot of inside knowledge over the years. Some while back, didn't she say something about growers in several countries offering big cash payments in return for her plugging their wines? And she'd also advised him to steer a wide birth around certain writers and critics whom she believed had allowed themselves to be corrupted.

No, I've got to see Laura – and alone. Poor Alexandre, but knowing him, he'll be happier at home with his books. Mid-morning, I'll phone Sophie and make sure she understands the ground rules. Buffet's a guest in our house – the home of an impressionable ten-year-old. It's not a knocking shop, so the guy can't bring anyone back. I should be home by four – don't mention lunch with Laura! – so Alexandre won't be alone for more than a few hours.

CHAPTER 13

While Jean-Claude was driving to Margaux, Laura and Quincy were taking separate pre-breakfast walks through Château Belle-Mère's grounds. It was a cloudless morning without a breath of wind, and the rolling landscape of Entre-Deux-Mers couldn't have looked lovelier. Their paths finally crossed down by the lake.

'Sleep well?' they asked each other simultaneously.

'Like a log,' Laura said, 'until about six.'

'Me too.'

During his walk, Quincy had convinced himself that Laura must have heard something during the night which would have led her to conclude that he and Sue had sex. To his amazement and delight, she'd known exactly how to arouse him; it was as though she possessed some kind of sixth sense. He'd been reliving the adventure with deeply conflicting emotions – excitement and acute embarrassment. Laura would now see him as a complete hypocrite – at best – or a sad, frustrated middle-aged man at worst. In either case, they were hardly emotions that would assist in facilitating any kind of partnership between them. He'd been dreading meeting her.

As they stood together, watching three white swans glide across the lake, Quincy sneaked another glance at Laura's face. Unless he was deluding himself with wishful thinking, she appeared remarkably serene.

'Absolutely enchanting,' she purred, turning to meet his gaze.

'Um ... what is?'

'The swans, of course.'

'Ah yes, the swans. ... Breakfast is at nine, apparently. I popped into the kitchen earlier on and–'

'Me too. Not exactly welcoming is she, that Jeanne?'

'No.'

'Grouching about having to lay out breakfast under the chestnut tree when I saw her. "Her Majesty's orders," she said.'

'"Her Majesty"?'

'Sue presumably.'

'Ah.'

'Quincy, are you sure you slept like a log last night? You look and sound kinda distracted. What's up?'

'Me? Distracted?'

'Yeah, even sort of guilty, like a teenager who's taken his dad's BMW out to impress his girl and now has to tell him it's wrapped around a streetlamp.' Laura's expression became serious. 'It's not Lampre, is it? He *is* coming to collect us this morning – *soon*? I've got an appointment at ... at–'

'No, of course not. He'll be here between nine-thirty and ten. He called when I was getting my orders from Sergeant-Major Jeanne.'

'Jesus, he's cutting it fine! It won't give me much time to change and get to Margaux by noon.'

'Margaux? You're tasting *today*? – on a Saturday? – at Margaux? I'd hoped ... well, I thought ...'

'What?' Laura glanced at her watch. 'Almost eight forty-five. Come on, let's get back to the house. I can't imagine why we have to hang around until nine. We don't have to wait for the dreaded Sue, do we? Have you seen her this morning?'

'No – no I haven't – seen Sue, that is. The Sergeant-Major told me she was in her office pulling papers out of filing cabinets and generally making a mess – a mess which she'd then have to clear up, et cetera, et cetera. I suspect, Laura, that Mrs Pronk is procuring copies of Belle-Mère's accounts for you to study over the weekend. Mr Pronk, by the way, seems to have done a bunk and returned to the illustrious Château Barrage.'

By the time they reached the chestnut tree, Quincy had concluded that there was nothing abnormal about Laura's behaviour: she was either ignorant of his night of passion or simply didn't give a damn. The former was almost incredible, but all things considered, more probable than the latter. Under the tree, the table appeared to have been laid by an undomesticated lumberjack: in addition to the haphazardly-arranged chipped earthenware crockery and picnic-like stainless-steel cutlery, there were two very long baguettes, a brick of butter, and a glass bowl containing some kind of jam.

Quincy licked his lips. 'Yum, yum! One might be excused for thinking that this lot fell from the sky. All we need now is the coffee.' He looked up into the tree expectantly.

Coffee, milk and a few portion-control wrapped sugar lumps arrived a few minutes later, coupled with a stern reminder from Jeanne that she'd told them breakfast would be ready at nine and not eight-fifty, and that they'd better not go making complaints about being kept waiting to 'Her Majesty': Belle-Mère wasn't a hotel.

Not yet, Laura mused.

After his third chunk of baguette, Quincy said: 'You know, Laura, I think this place would make a marvellous hotel.' During the next five minutes, Laura heard a very persuasive case.

'You've clearly thought a lot about this, Quincy. You must have been awake half the night. I thought something was afoot down by the lake. But I don't know anything about running hotels – nor do you for that matter. I just want a vineyard, for Christ's sake – as if that wasn't enough! Anyway, converting Belle-Mère into a luxury hotel would cost a fortune. Confidentially, Quince – and I mean *confidentially* – I'd need a loan just to *buy* the place and get the wine production side up to scratch. A hotel's impossible. And a fine hotel needs a fine restaurant.'

'Naturally.'

'And such a restaurant needs a genius in the kitchen – and I sure as hell know what I'm talking about! And when the chef ain't the owner, *boy*, have you got problems! Why? – because the owner becomes his slave – "I want this, I want that, I want more money, I want more staff, I want a piece of the action. And if I don't get what I want, I'm off – and you can say goodbye to your Michelin star, goodwill and clients."'

They ate in silence for a while, both secretly hoping that Sue wouldn't materialize.

Finally, Quincy said: 'There's your father, Laura.'

She choked on her jam-coated bread and gulped a mouthful of coffee. '*Dad*? You must be joking!'

'Why?'

'Why? *Why*? Because for one thing, he's already got a restaurant – in Seattle. Haven't you heard?'

Quincy effortlessly demolished Laura's arguments that Bryan would never leave Seattle. What he said proved very reassuring: he recited most of the points which she herself had identified while lying in bed some nine hours earlier.

'Well, I don't know,' Laura sighed. 'Dad can be very stubborn. But honestly, Quince, so what? It's academic. Even if I wanted a hotel – and I don't – I couldn't afford one. *Point final.*' She looked at her watch – almost nine twenty-five. 'I wonder if Lampre has turned up yet. Have you heard a car?' She breathed deeply in preparation for another tirade against the elusive estate agent.

Quincy watched her chest expand. 'Let's be partners,' he blurted.

'Excuse me?'

'Partners – in Belle-Mère – a joint venture – maybe with Bryan. I could invest a few million – *pounds* that is – and if Bryan were to sell up in Seattle, why, we probably wouldn't have to borrow one bloody euro. Come on, Laura, what about it? I need a new challenge too – I'm bloody bored. Don't you think I'd be rather good at playing the "*Mein Host*" role?' He smiled with almost juvenile enthusiasm.

It took Laura a few seconds to regain her powers of speech. She was about to agree with his final remark when the garden exploded.

'Quince! Laura! So sorry I'm late! Pumphrey an' 'umphrey, you little buggers – *be-'ave!*'

In the final seconds before the canine duo set about the guests with frantic attempts to lick their faces in fraternal greetings, Laura managed to hiss: 'For God's sake don't tell that cow about any partnership. She'd wham up the price before you could say "ironic placebo."'

Sue poured herself half a cup of lukewarm coffee: she wasn't 'a breakfast person'. In any event, she had to dash to Barrage, where a party of Chinese wine merchants on a buying trip were expected around eleven. 'They're lookin' for a new supplier of French vino for a chain of state-owned 'otels,' she explained brightly. 'They was right in the middle of their negotiations yesterday with their usual people – one of them poncey places in St-Emilion – when, during lunch, the owner's wife, this snooty Castelnau dame – I've met her, actually, at one of me Lions' dinners – always in twinset and pearls actin' like butter wouldn't melt in her bleedin' mouth. ... Well, seems she 'ad too much of the old vino at lunch and got into a slangin' match with the Chink 'ead 'oncho over 'uman rights or some rubbish. Anyway, the Chinks surfed the net overnight, saw me super Barrage website – it's so cool! – you should take a butcher's – and there was an email waitin' for me this mornin' askin' for a site meetin' and a product samplin' ASAP. Sent Pronkie over first thing to get the ball rollin'.'

While talking, Sue had handed Laura a folder of accounts and a standard confidentiality agreement in duplicate from the receivers, but she barely acknowledged Quincy's existence. In a sense, he was relieved: fluttering eyelashes or any tactile gesture indicating the possibility of some form of intimacy between them would have been acutely embarrassing. And yet, to be totally ignored after all their hours of carnal delights made him feel strangely discontented.

As Sue accelerated away from the table with the faithful Labradors, she shouted over her shoulder: 'If you need any more info, Laura, don't 'esitate to give me a buzz – any time – day or night. Old Lampre should show up any minute. By-eee!'

The prediction proved correct: just before ten, Quincy and Laura were once again squeezed into the *immobilier*'s little car, hurtling towards Bordeaux in a manner which reminded Quincy of yuletide police advertising campaigns against drinking and driving. Lampre was not in a talkative mood, explaining that he was exceedingly tired after a dreadful night of having to cope with a very difficult hospitalised sister-in-law, a hysterical wife marooned in Pau – thanks to her insistence on driving a British Mini of 1980s vintage – and operating a shuttle service between the hospital in Langon and his sister-in-law's house. He'd only got to bed around four. When he finally asked about Laura's views on Belle-Mère, she didn't bubble with enthusiasm. On the contrary, she recited an extensive list of defects, problems and concerns; Quincy contributed much sympathetic nodding. Lampre, however, having decades of experience of dealing with prospective purchasers, was not fooled: his spirits lifted, albeit he was intrigued by the supporting role which Dubloon was playing in Laura's performance.

As they approached Bordeaux along the opposite bank of the Garonne, the city presented a glorious vista across the wide river: the homogenous neoclassical facades of the eighteenth-century terraces lining the celebrated Port de la Lune's quays; the soaring spires, towers and turrets of numerous medieval churches; the grand gateways through the old city walls; the Bourse, which many tourists assumed was yet another extravagant royal palace of the *ancien régime*; and, still moored adjacent to it, the great white liner which Laura had admired yesterday morning.

Gradually, as he scanned this stunning panorama, Quincy became aware of a bizarre sensation flowing through his body: it was like some magical force energizing and rejuvenating him. His thoughts on Belle-Mère's future evaporated. He glanced over his shoulder: Laura was also staring across the river, her dreamy face suffused in a sensuous golden aura. Perhaps it was a reflection of the morning sunlight off the stone buildings on the opposite bank. In any event, never had she looked more beautiful.

With Lampre zigzagging wildly through the traffic heading for the Pont de Pierre, Laura's right hand clutched the back of Quincy's seat; he tapped it gently. 'Laura, do you know how Victor Hugo once described Bordeaux?' Without averting her gaze, she slowly shook her head. '"Take Versailles, add it to Antwerp, and you have Bordeaux."'

'I don't think he was trying to be complimentary,' Lampre snorted.

'Maybe not,' sighed Quincy, 'but I happen to like Versailles – and, for that matter, Antwerp.'

'I've never been to Antwerp,' Laura murmured. 'If it's anything like this though, I'd better go and take a look.'

'You should – the city of Rubens, Van Dyk–'

'They don't have vineyards around Antwerp,' Lampre advised earnestly. 'And you know what Belgians are like. I mean, what can you expect from a country which is just a rather wide border crossing between France and Holland? No wonder they're schizophrenic.'

Quincy didn't want any unpleasantness to spoil his poetic mood. 'I don't know who it was,' he continued, 'but somebody once said, "Because of their need for harmonious stability combined with prestige, architecture is the art form best suited to the temperament of the Bordelais.'"

Laura nodded. 'Yeah, I can buy that.'

'Do *you* know who said that, Pierre?' asked Quincy.

'Sounds just like the sort of thing *you'd* come up with, if you ask me.'

'No, no! I assure you I read it somewhere.'

While Lampre overtook everything on the Pont de Pierre, Quincy ruminated on the words 'harmonious stability' and 'prestige'; so, too, did Laura. In fact, she kept silently repeating them as she pictured herself and Jean-Claude standing together arm-in-arm in front of Belle-Mère's stunning main entrance. Could she change the name – with the consent of the appropriate regulatory authorities of course – to Belle-Mère-Appleton? After all, if the Rothschilds could do it at Mouton and Lafite, the Bartons at Léoville, and the Browns at Cantenac, why not the Appletons at Belle-Mère? Why not indeed?

Quincy, on the other hand, was wondering whether any kind of title came with the property: in England one could buy manorial lordships; did such things exist in France? He'd have to make discreet enquiries of Charles Fontaine. ... Good Lord! He was getting carried away! Be sensible! ... But the name could be changed, of course – Belle-Mère indeed! They'd be the butt of endless music hall jokes; Parker and Johnson would have a field day, constantly ribbing him. No, Château Appleton-Dubloon would be much better – Dubloon-Appleton even better! Who'd be investing more money anyway?

As agreed, Lampre dropped off his passengers at the entrance to the Allées de Tourny underground car park. He promised to phone Laura on Monday morning to see how she'd got on with her perusal of the Belle-Mère accounts, and 'to discuss financial matters generally', by which Laura took him to mean introducing her to some bankers to procure 'the small loan' he'd mentioned at his office. Deposited without injury in front of Le Noailles, Laura and Quincy stood in uncomfortable silence wondering what the other would say about the issues they'd discussed over breakfast.

Quincy cleared his throat. 'I don't suppose you've got time for a coffee, Laura – here or at the apartment?'

She shook her head. 'Sorry. Love to, but I desperately need to change and then get to Margaux by twelve.'

'Oh yes. Margaux. Of course.' Quincy looked slightly crestfallen. He prayed for a miracle and hoped that, like yesterday, he'd be able to tag along to whichever châteaux she was visiting. After all, no proprietor or *maître de chai* would slam the door in *his* face! And although he was invited to lunch in Pomerol at one of the new boutique châteaux producing ludicrously overpriced wines from a few hectares of vines, he could easily – and happily – make some excuse.

'We do need to talk, Laura. I *am* serious about a joint venture, you know. Did you manage to give it any thought in the car? You were very quiet.'

'Me? I thought you were the quiet one.' Laura shot a glance at her watch. 'Must fly, Quincy. Look, I need time to think. I'll call later today. Maybe we could run through the accounts together tomorrow.'

Quincy's heart sank: Sunday, the Bordelais day of rest when everything apart from the *boulangeries* and a few bars and restaurants were shut and everyone headed for the coast, weather permitting. He had an invitation to someone's beach house somewhere, but that was another commitment he could wriggle out of. He'd make one final attempt to secure a Saturday encounter.

'What about dinner tonight – or even a late lunch after your tastings at Margaux? The Lion d'Or at Arcins is just down the road and supposed to be very good.'

Laura could have made dinner – albeit by chucking an open-air concert of twentieth-century chamber music in Notre-Dame's cloisters sponsored by Haut Brion – but she wanted Quincy to stew a little: best not to appear too keen.

'Sorry, I'm with the Haut Brion crowd tonight,' she said vaguely.

'Really?'

'A charity gala at Notre-Dame. Aren't you invited?'

Quincy tried to conceal his pique. 'No ... no I'm not. How very ... grand.' It occurred to him that he sounded jealous. 'Right then! I suppose it'll have to be tomorrow. I'll await your call.' He fumbled in his pockets for one of his cards. 'Here. If I'm not at home, you can get me on my mobile.'

To his surprise, Laura air kissed his cheeks, something she'd never done before. 'Fine! Have a nice day!'

'You too.'

Quincy walked slowly to his empty apartment just five minutes away in Cours de Tournon. By the time he reached the building's front door, he'd managed to pull himself together: Laura had not rejected his Belle-Mère proposals, and she *did* want to go through the accounts with him tomorrow. In the meantime, he could make some enquiries about disposing of that barn of a manor house in Wiltshire. To be honest, he'd never really liked Woopston Parva. He'd phone the estate agents in Chippenham and sound them out – *now*. And then he'd better get ready for that tedious lunch in Pomerol.

In his elegant sitting room, Quincy sat down at his desk and scanned the telephone. There were five recorded messages: his secretary in London gave a masterfully succinct report of Friday's highlights at *Wine Wisdom's* offices; the Pomerol château owner reminded him to bring a swimming costume if he wanted to make use of his pool; and Henri de Bondé had called three times in the last hour moaning about him not answering his mobile, and ordering him to phone urgently.

*

At Belle-Mère, Jeanne was even more bad-tempered than usual, thanks to the duties piled on her shoulders by the dinner guests' unscheduled stopovers; beds had to be stripped and remade for a start. That was bad enough, but with all her years of experience in domestic service, there was one thing she really knew about – stains. The Englishman's sheets told a story – a very messy story – and judging by the lingering odours of Rive Gauche, it was one which involved Madame Pronk – again; the washing machine would have to be put on boil wash. It was when she bent down to examine the mattress that she spotted one of her pet hates lying under the bedside table – a mobile phone; the Englishman had left more than one unpleasant visiting card, she fumed. Hesitantly, and with a sneer of disgust as if touching something that might either explode or infect her with leprosy, she placed the offending article in a pocket of her shabby housecoat. By the time she'd retraced her steps to the ground floor to load the washing machine, she'd forgotten all about it.

*

Such was her state of euphoria, Laura could have jogged to the Hôtel Continental from Allées de Tourny. With Quince backing her, how could Jean-Claude fail to be won over to the Belle-Mère cause? And loveable old Charles Fontaine could well be a sort of Guy de Bondé substitute for him. So, now – thank God! – it seemed very unlikely that she'd have to stoop to blackmail tactics with her mysterious bottle of wine. Pausing briefly in front of the mirror before showering for the second time that morning, Laura felt a sense of pride in her trim naked body; her exceedingly expensive health club in New York had certainly paid dividends. If only she could find a way of exposing it to Jean-Claude without making herself look cheap or brazen. As she stepped into the shower, she said aloud and matter-of-factly: 'I wonder if I'll have to sleep with Quince to procure his investment?'

156

CHAPTER 14

La Fayette's tasting room was the only part of the working château on which Henri de Bondé had no qualms about spending money; he'd even engaged a prestigious firm of interior designers to completely refurbish it. As a result, considerable quantities of Carrera marble had been employed for both the floors and work surfaces, while various *antiquaires* had supplied suitably impressive chandeliers, candelabra and *armoires*; adding colour, the walls hosted more than a dozen still-life paintings that featured a bunch of grapes, a bottle, a decanter or a glass of wine somewhere on the canvas. The numerous marble sinks – for spitting tasted wine as well as for washing the crystal ware – had been designed by Philippe Starck, no less. It was all a far cry from Jean-Claude's office in the *chais*.

Paradoxically, the tasting room was used infrequently: the days had long passed since Guy de Bondé had been happy to welcome almost anyone who might happen to beat a path to his gate while touring the Médoc's long-established wine routes. For him, it had not been a matter of marketing or publicity; indeed, in common with many Margaux and Haut Médoc *grand cru* vineyards, La Fayette had never succumbed to advertising itself at the roadside with representations of giant wine bottles emblazoned 'Dégustation', 'Vente' or 'Accueil Visiteurs'. That sort of thing was best left to the commune cooperatives and humble vineyards on the one hand, and prestigious estates owned by insurance companies and parvenus on the other.

No, for Guy it had been a matter of simple pride in his wine, coupled with respect for someone who'd had the courage to surmount the obstacles which tended to intimidate most members of the public and persuade them to drive on – the very absence of public notices, the tall wrought-iron gates, the long gravel drive. In many cases, such visitors would either nervously ring the bell at the château's main entrance, or peer into one of the *chais* and ask politely to taste the wine. Guy didn't fret if no sale resulted; sometimes it was only too obvious that the price was beyond their budget. In any event, as about half the château's production was sold wholesale in the spring following the harvest, and the bulk of the remainder by the time it was bottled, there were often no stocks available.

Henri thought his father's behaviour was idiotic: he'd no patience for time-wasters. Once in de facto control, therefore, Henri *did* have notices erected at the entrances to his father's property. Translated, they read:

'Château La Fayette is **<u>NOT</u>** open to the public', and 'Visits by appointment only'. Henri reserved his worst tantrums for those 'peasants' who had the effrontery to ignore these notices – mainly, but not exclusively, foreign tourists professing an inexcusable ignorance of French. Naturally enough, the worst culprits were Americans and Britons. Although supplemental notices in English, German, Dutch and Spanish had rendered most of the subsequent proffered excuses void, there'd been little reduction in the number of trespassers.

Consequently, the deluxe tasting room was almost exclusively used to 'entertain' significant trade and private customers – actual or potential – plus representatives of 'the media' who, as far as Henri was concerned, included people like Laura Appleton. Without exception, Henri disliked wine writers and critics. There were three principal reasons: first, he had yet to meet any who were not snobbish, middle-class pen-pushers who thought they were superior beings because they constantly mixed with aristocrats like himself; secondly, left to their own devices, they never wrote or said exactly what he wanted them to write or say about his wine; and thirdly, Henri found the very concept of earning one's living through criticism of the endeavours of others – whether literary, artistic or producing fine wines – so ungentlemanly as to be beneath contempt. He had no problems with one of his Rothschild neighbours telling him over a *coupe de champagne* during an entr'acte at the Grand Théâtre that he preferred the 90 La Fayette to the 89. It was quite a different matter, however, when some towny who couldn't grow a single vine to save his or her miserable life – let alone produce a bottle of wine – did the same thing through the medium of a thousand-word article in some rag after having raided a thesaurus for every ludicrously inappropriate epithet under the sun.

Nevertheless, for obvious commercial reasons, Henri had to entertain such excuses for human beings and be civil to them; in truth, he did an outstandingly good job of concealing his true feelings. Laura Appleton, for example, erroneously believed that Henri had long ago forgiven her negative reaction to his quasi-bribe to get himself substituted in place of Bourjois as her guide to La Fayette in the *Temples of Wine* series. And yet whenever their paths crossed, particularly in the States these days, he was always so polite and charming. Of some relevance in this connection, was the role Laura had played in procuring the appearance of La Fayette's wines on the *cartes des vins* of the Maison Blanche restaurants following her *stage* under Bourjois's tutelage. And there was Henri's presumption, notwithstanding their change of ownership and the current open secret of a frosty relationship with both her mother and 'Uncle' Daniel, that Laura herself had ensured a continuation of the status quo ante.

Thus, when Henri discovered that Laura was about to pay his château a visit this very Saturday morning, he was engulfed by a turbulent flow of conflicting emotions. The chain reaction was triggered as he cheerfully passed the tasting room at around eleven-thirty to collect his Mercedes SLK convertible from the garage – his preferred vehicle for fine weather – and, through a window, spied Bourjois polishing glasses. Henri had yet to make any final decision on his future – he wanted to consult Tiquetorte and Carbon Blanc – and had no desire to engage this most troublesome of employees in conversation on such a heavenly morning, thereby delaying his departure for Cap Ferret. But it was a standing rule that Bourjois should give him prior written notice of tastings to permit himself to decide whether an invitee's status required his presence, and, furthermore, to dictate the quantity and quality of the food to be provided. In any event, as a tasting on a Saturday morning was unusual, Henri felt bound to investigate. Consequently, with exaggerated irritation, he stormed into the tasting room and fired from the hip.

Jean-Claude was startled by Henri's sudden appearance, a reaction which caused his employer to conclude immediately that he'd caught him in flagrante delicto. His confession that Laura Appleton's arrival was imminent made Henri temporarily schizophrenic. Despising her as he did, and bearing in mind she was not a trade customer, he would have been more than happy to allow Bourjois to conduct a *dégustation*: he'd much rather enjoy the delights on offer at Tiquetorte's ocean villa than suffer the inane chatter of another tedious American. After all, she and Bourjois appeared to be on very friendly terms. Indeed, over the years it had not escaped his notice that Appleton was like a bitch on heat whenever Bourjois was in her vicinity.

However, the point was that a tasting had been arranged with one of America's most influential wine writers, and he knew nothing about it. Indeed, Bourjois's behaviour was such a flagrant breach of established procedure that he must have acted maliciously. The conspiracy theories of the night before raised their ugly heads once more. Could Appleton's surprise appearance have something to do with the Great Label Mystery? Was the plot thickening? Which reminded him: had Bourjois spoken to that bloody printer yet?

Jean-Claude was already in a state of nervous exhaustion, thanks to the overnight developments at Le Porge, coupled with worries about his relationship with Alexandre, Sophie's scolding down the phone a few moments ago when he'd dared to suggest that she didn't know how to handle Buffet – 'If you're so bothered about Alexandre's well-being, why the hell don't you come home and look after him?' – and his torment over

Laura's mysterious bottle of La Fayette. In consequence, it only took a few sparks to light his very short fuse. Deep within Jean-Claude's head, a roaring like rollers crashing on a rocky shore began to drown out much of Henri's vituperative haranguing.

'... no one's bloody irreplaceable, Bourjois, not even you. ... sick and tired ... acting like *you* own this place. ... You're nothing but a damned paid employee! Just because my demented father used to think the sun shone out of your arse for all those years ... doesn't cut any ice. ... I should have been told. ... It's a bloody disgrace! God only knows what rubbish you'll give her to eat! ... not even any fresh bread! ... You look like something the cat's brought in – scruffy jeans – dressed for the bloody beach! What sort of impression ...? Don't be so damned impertinent! Who the hell do you think you are? ... I happen to be going to Cap Ferret ... none of your fucking business! ... always were a cocky bastard – from the very first moment when you and your tarty mother turned up–'

Henri was now standing so close that Jean-Claude's face was being splattered with saliva. As the pain in his head became unbearable, he felt his right fist hit something soft. He knew it was Henri's stomach, and yet he watched in disbelief as the guy, screaming like a child and doubled-up in agony, flew backwards into a table, causing bottles and glasses to fly in all directions.

The sound of smashing glass gave way to the rumbling of a solitary bottle rolling backwards and forwards somewhere. An antique *armoire* had finally arrested Henri's retreat; he was sat on the floor with his back against it. Groaning, and with one arm over his stomach, he rocked to and fro; red wine was trickling onto him from a neighbouring table. Instinctively, Jean-Claude felt he should say something by way of an apology and proffer some kind of help, but he neither spoke nor moved; he just stared at his victim.

Henri was not badly injured: he'd been winded and humiliated; later, some bruising would develop. But then he noticed the red stains on his sherbet-yellow polo shirt. 'Oh, my God! I'm bleeding. I'm *bleeding*! You've ruptured something! Oh, my God!'

'It's wine, you bloody idiot.'

Jean-Claude still hadn't moved by the time Henri finished verifying the stains' source. Then, clutching his stomach, he surveyed the tasting room. 'Jesus Christ, what a fucking mess! And one of the doors of this *armoire* has cracked. Seven thousand euros this bloody thing cost.' He shook his head from side to side. 'You're finished here, Bourjois – *finished.*'

Jean-Claude snorted. '*You* can't run this place, Henri. You're not thinking straight. You need a *maître de chai*. They don't grow at the side of the road.' He hardly recognised his own voice: his mouth was so dry he could barely enunciate. He tried to lick his lips.

'How graphically put, Bourjois! But as I said before, nobody's irreplaceable – not even you. I want you out of here – today! – *now*! Your deputy – what's-his-name – can handle things until I find a permanent replacement. We'll cope, don't you worry. Get over to the *chais* and start clearing your desk! I'll come with you to make sure you don't walk off with anything.'

Henri began limping towards the door, but Jean-Claude stood his ground. 'You can't just throw me out. I mean ... I've got rights – three ... *six* months' notice – compensation. The law–'

'Don't start quoting the fucking law at *me*! "*Rights*"? *You*? Look at this place – look at *me*! Christ, if this doesn't justify summary dismissal– There's enough evidence here, Bourjois, to have you charged with assault and battery, malicious damage–'

'You wouldn't dare. I – I ... I know too much.'

Henri cocked his head on one side. 'Bourjois, I'll let you in on a little secret. If you'd been prepared to play ball with us, you could have had a cut of the action. There's so much money to be made out of this game – so many opportunities to play around with labels, vintages, first wines, second wines. Château Margaux even watered down its wines in the early nineteenth century. Not very subtle, was it? No wonder they got caught with their pants down. Mind you, if they did it today most of these self-appointed "wine experts" wouldn't dare voice any concerns. They'd still lavish praise on the stuff as though their lives depended on it. Those geeks come here, slurp some three-month-old murky liquid that tastes like battery acid – like all Médoc vintages at three months – wax lyrical about "blackcurrants and tobacco", "toasted oak and chocolate", and then miraculously predict that in ten years it will have matured into the finest wine one's ever produced! What a fucking farce! Next year, they come back, taste an equally disgusting brew, and declaim it smells like rotten turnips and wet dogs and is only fit for disinfecting the drains. That's the fraud, Bourjois – the *real* fraud.

'I thought that once the awesome reality of your position had sunk in, you might have lost your saintly persona. Far from it! Your reaction to General Lafayette and all this Florida business – Jesus! ... Mind you, I'm beginning to think that's a little ruse of your own. Anyhow, a leopard can't change its spots. I told my partners at the outset that *you'd* never change, but *they* knew better. Well, Bourjois, you've fucked up right and proper now. No wonder your bloody wife–'

Henri realized he'd gone too far: the expression on Bourjois's face was murderous. He glanced nervously at the door; it was only a couple of metres away. 'Go and clear your desk, Bourjois. Don't make things–'

'What about my wife?'

Henri started for the door, but Jean-Claude beat him to it. 'Oh no, you're not going anywhere, mate.'

Henri took a step back. 'Now don't do anything you'll regret. You've done enough damage for one day.'

'*Really?* Come on, what about my wife?'

Henri's eyes darted around the room in search of a weapon. 'Nothing. For God's sake, Jean-Claude–'

'"*Jean-Claude*"? My, *my*! We are a frightened little mouse, aren't we? You always were a coward – a miserable back-stabber. Or should I say "back-pusher"?'

Henri blinked nervously. He saw Bourjois as a child lying prostrate at the bottom of La Fayette's grand staircase. 'Look, I – I ... I only meant that ... I was only suggesting that your wife has to ... to work so hard – at her painting because, because ...'

'"*Because*"?'

'Because you're just a bloody *maître de chai*, of course, and – and you're clearly living beyond your means ... that's all. One hears things. ... *You* know?'

Jean-Claude felt wrong-footed. '"*Things*"?' What "*things*"?'

Henri detected what appeared to be a weakness. 'Just ... things.'

Before his eyes, Jean-Claude could see all the myriad invoices Sophie was constantly depositing around the house. They turned up in fruit bowls and down the back of chairs – records of purchases for which he'd neither need nor desire, be they Oriental silk cushions, handcrafted Scandinavian Hi-Fi equipment, or coffee-table books on sub-Saharan wood carvings. Of course, if Buffet's predictions proved correct, Sophie would soon be able to buy Bang & Olufsen lock, stock and barrel. ... *If.*

Jean-Claude wiped his brow. 'What we spend our money on is *our* business, OK?'

'Of course. Point taken.'

The noise of a car being driven across the cobbled courtyard with its sound system blaring, made both men glance anxiously out of the window.

'Oh my God, Henri, it's Laura!'

'Bugger! I'd completely forgotten. She can't see me like *this* – or come in *here*, for Christ's sake! What the hell do we do, Bourjois? You got us into this shitty hole!'

'Stop shouting! She'll hear you. Quick – against the wall!'

They took up positions on either side of one the windows and watched Laura kill the music and get out of her hired car. She looked towards the first-year *chai* that housed Jean-Claude's office, and then focused on the tasting room. She hesitated. 'Jean-Claude! It's *me-ee!*'

'You'll have to go out, Bourjois,' Henri whispered. 'You'll have to. Oh, my God, if she gets a whiff of what's been going on in here, she'll crucify me. She'll blab. You know these Americans – even the sodding CIA can't keep a secret these days. Get out there and organize a tasting in your office – or the *chais*. Yanks like all that rustic charm crap. Go on! Quick!'

Laura started to walk towards the first-year *chai*, assuming that her host was likely to be secreted in his beloved office. 'Jean-*Clau-aude!*'

'What's it worth, Henri?'

'Sorry?'

'You heard. You're right. She could do a lot of damage over in the States with a few well-chosen words – especially if I'm off the payroll today. Maybe she'll write that our latest vintage smells like rotten turnips and wet dogs and is only fit to disinfect sewers.'

Henri's sneer slowly turned into a wry smile. 'Well, well, well. Perhaps I've misjudged you after all.'

A deal was swiftly reached: Jean-Claude wanted the world to think he'd be leaving La Fayette through his own choice; Henri conceded that summary dismissal would raise eyebrows throughout the industry and generate the sort of rumours La Fayette could well do without, particularly with someone like Laura Appleton hanging around Bordeaux. Accordingly, they agreed to act out a charade: it would be business as usual to the outside world, but Jean-Claude would immediately seek a new job. Once secured, Henri would appear magnanimous and release him from his obligations to work out the six months' contractual notice. However, in the unlikely event that he didn't find suitable employment within three months, he'd go anyway: they'd say he was taking sick leave – stress, exhaustion – they'd work out the details if that bridge ever had to be crossed. But to eliminate any double-crossing, Jean-Claude wanted Henri to present him with a bonus cheque in front of Laura – and mention a new contract.

Jean-Claude almost collided with Laura in the first-year *chai's* doorway. Her face lit up.

'Oh, Jean-Claude! I was beginning to think you'd done a bunk!'

'I'm *so* sorry, Laura. I didn't hear your car.'

They kissed each other's cheeks. She made a critical comment about the smell of cigarettes on his breath. He apologized for being a bit disorganized, claiming Henri had detained him up at the house.

Laura grimaced. 'Ugh! Bad news?'

'No, not really. ... Um ... Do you mind if we conduct the tasting here? It's just that, what with Henri droning on, I haven't had a chance to get things set up in the tasting room. It's a bit cosier – more *convenient* I mean ... getting the wine straight from the *barriques* ... and everything.'

'Suits me fine.' Laura looked towards the house. 'Is Henri–?'

'He's off to Cap Ferret shortly. He'll come and say "hello" before he leaves. His wife and kids have gone to her family's place on Ile de Ré.' Jean-Claude glanced at Laura's Louis Vuitton shoulder bag and thought of the mystery wine bottle. 'So ... so, we'll be completely alone.'

When Henri finally made his appearance, Laura was standing by a table in the first-year *chai* tasting the young wine from last autumn's harvest. As he approached through the cool gloom with a proprietorial swagger, Jean-Claude noticed that the calculated 'I-just-threw-any-old-thing-on' image of an hour ago had been replaced by a coordinated Burberry outfit of beige slacks, checked short-sleeved shirt and matching canvas shoes. Unhesitatingly embracing Laura, Henri gushed greetings like water from a burst main.

'I'm sure Jean-Claude is looking after you *admirably*, although I must apologize for neither of us being on hand to welcome you when you arrived, but we were having one of our frequent technical sessions, and you know how the dear boy gets carried away, bless him. I would stay and participate in the tasting – ah, I see you're already swirling between your expert digits another one of Jean-Claude's embryonic miracles. Even if I say so myself, Miss Appleton, given time, I think a certain Mr Parker might award this little beauty a ninety-plus score.'

Laura glared at Jean-Claude. 'Really? Robert's already been and–?'

'Tut, tut! I've said too much as it is, Miss Appleton. Anyway, I *would* stay, but I know how much you admire Jean-Claude – don't we all? Alas, I have to dash to the airport. Someone from Buckingham Palace is coming down for the weekend – very hush-hush. Taking him to our place at Cap Ferret for a spot of sailing. With all these economies forced on the poor old House of Windsor, the Queen is investigating the possibility of cutting out the middle men – like Berry Brothers – and buying directly from the producer.'

Laura's eyes boggled: this was news to her.

'Anyway, wonderful to meet you again, Miss Appleton, but must fly. Oh, how's your father, by the way? I saw Mrs Appleton – I mean Mrs Mombrier – in Los Angeles a few weeks ago. Never seems to age. Marvellous! Mind you, Mombrier looked a lot older. Still going strong on the sommelier front though, and what a super selection of *our* wines on the *carte*. Marvellous!

'Oh, Bour– Um, Jean-Claude, before I go, here's the – do excuse me, Miss Appleton, talking shop for just a second – here's your bonus cheque.' Henri lowered his voice slightly. 'That's the right amount, isn't it – five thousand?'

Jean-Claude smiled and nodded. 'Yes. Thanks.'

'Well, you deserve every euro of it, old boy. Oh, and I've chased Carbon Blanc, and he's promised to let us have your new *five*-year *fixed*-term contract on Monday morning.' Henri turned to Laura. 'Can't afford to let him get away, Miss Appleton. Unique is our Jean-Claude. Irreplaceable!'

The smile on Laura's lips froze as her brain went into overdrive.

After Henri's footsteps had died away, Laura said: 'Well, what a performance! Typical Henri. The Bondés don't have a villa at Cap Ferret, do they? And Buckingham Palace? – my fanny! – all bullshit and spin! Does he honestly think anyone would fall for that crap? … Oh, by the way,' she added casually, 'well done about the bonus. But since when has Scrooge been handing out bonuses? And for what? I mean, I'm sure you deserve a bonus. I'm just surprised that–'

'The bonus is for … well, thanks to increased sales in America, profits are up, and … and I thought I was due some of the credit. I had it out with Henri this morning. As for the Queen of England stuff, frankly, Laura, nothing would surprise me when it comes to Henri's marketing activities. … And the place at Cap Ferret is the family doctor's villa, but all these Bordelais toffs are related.'

Laura began agitating her glass again, using the distinctive technique she'd learned at Bordeaux University, where her mentor, Professor Dubourdieu, had decried the classic 'swirling technique' and insisted on his students using the 'shaking technique' – rapidly but carefully shaking the glass to produce a 'choppy sea' effect, thereby greatly speeding up the wine's aeration and the consequent release of its aromas and flavours. It's an acquired skill; the novice is likely to end up splashing wine everywhere. Jean-Claude was a traditionalist and a minimalist – the briefest of swirls, a sniff, a quick gulp, a rapid sucking-cum-splooshing action, and spit. Laura, however, was meticulous. She would always take a good mouthful of the wine, roll it around her mouth languidly, and then suck in air between her lips to volatilize it. After a few seconds of apparent meditation, she'd spit it out in the receptacle provided. This was the procedure she now followed.

Nodding contentedly, Laura said: 'Well, whatever Parker may – or may not – say about this six-month-old brew, given time it *is* going to be a great wine, Jean-Claude – one of the best of the vintage I've tasted so far.

Well done!' In the same breath, and before he could acknowledge her praise, she added: 'And a new contract? What's that all about?'

Jean-Claude pretended to examine a neighbouring *barrique* for any weeping between the staves. 'Nothing. Just tidying up loose ends. You know what lawyers are like.' He shrugged his shoulders.

Laura began making notes about the wine on a printed tasting card of her own design. She tried to concentrate, but the bombshell of a Monday deadline to get Jean-Claude committed to Project Belle-Mère had unnerved her. 'How did your dinner go last night with the guy from Paris?' she asked nonchalantly, glancing at the bottle in her shoulder bag. 'Was it as awful as you thought it would be?'

'Er, no – not really.'

Laura bristled: it was like getting blood out of a stone. 'So did he like the *Orifices*?' She started chuckling, but Jean-Claude remained unsmiling.

'Seemed to.'

'So, he's going to *exhibit* them?' she asked incredulously, looking up from her notebook.

'Apparently.'

'Jesus! You're kidding?'

'No. Do you want to taste the 2000 Maréchal now?' It was the question he'd been dreading to ask. 'I'm quite proud of it, actually.'

Laura nodded on autopilot. 'Sure. ... So, if this Buffet guy is hooked, Sophie could be making big bucks soon, yeah?' She was rapidly attempting to evaluate yet another unforeseen development and how it might also affect her plans and strategy.

'I suppose. To be honest, I haven't really given it much thought.'

Laura watched Jean-Claude walk over to a row of *barriques* on the other side of the *chai* to procure some Maréchal. *Not given it much thought! Christ! – he can be infuriatingly laid-back. It really will be a hands-on exercise to steer him in the right direction.*

Some minutes later, Laura held a glass of the cloudy young second wine.

'As with the 2000 La Fayette,' Jean-Claude opined, 'I think it's better than the 99.'

Laura detected a distinct note of nervousness in his voice.

'I'm sure 2000,' he continued, 'is going to be a great vintage for Bordeaux – as good as 1990 – if not better.'

The ritual of studious observation, sniffing, glass-shaking, gulping, sucking and spitting followed in silence. Despite the relative coolness of the *chai*, Jean-Claude could feel perspiration trickling down his back; he was following Laura's every move as if his life depended on it.

'As one would expect,' Laura intoned, 'it's lighter than the 2000 first wine, and it doesn't have that super aroma of blackcurrants. ... And yes, there are some rough edges, but they'll soften up in a year or two. Nice vanilla nuance lurking there. Oh, for heaven's sake, Jean-Claude, don't look so worried! You knew I'd love it. It'll compete strongly with many top-flight first wines I can think of.'

After another couple of mouthfuls and some note-taking, Laura asked to taste the recently bottled offerings of 1999 in order to evaluate their progress since her last *dégustation* at La Fayette. A few minutes later, and with what she thought was a distinct lack of enthusiasm, Jean-Claude returned with some bottles from his office.

'The 1999's are not as bad as I'd feared, Laura,' he said. 'I mean, there was so much rain here around vintage time, so we had all the usual problems of getting rid of water in the juice. Sure, we limited the crop and picked at the optimum moment ... and we used some of the new concentration methods. ... Give them five to ten years and hopefully–'

'Cut the crap, Jean-Claude, before your false modesty makes me throw up. Just pour the goddam stuff!'

After the *dégustation* was complete and Laura had exhausted her superlatives, Jean-Claude's tension was at breaking point: the game of cat and mouse had gone on long enough. As hard as he tried, he couldn't stop himself staring at Laura's shoulder bag; it was propped against a leg of the table. If she wasn't going to put him out of his misery, he'd have to take the initiative; he really couldn't stand any more gossip about lunch at the Régent yesterday with Quincy Dubloon, and some nonsense about him losing his trousers at a meeting with Alain Juppé. Frankly, he'd completely lost the thread.

'Sorry to interrupt, Laura, but I've booked a table at Lamarque for half past one and it's already quarter past. This bottle of wine you mentioned on the phone yesterday, if you've brought it, do you want me to taste it or not?'

Laura was taken aback by Jean-Claude's abruptness, and it suddenly occurred to her that he might not be as naive as she'd imagined – that, thanks to what she now realised was probably a foolish joke about the bottle, he feared he was about to be accused of being mixed up in something unsavoury. She should have kept her big mouth shut! She'd only intended to sow a few seeds of doubt in his innocent mind in order to make him consider the possibility of something fraudulent occurring at La Fayette, and that he could be implicated – guilt by association. Now was the time to galvanize all her diplomatic skills.

'Oh *that*,' Laura replied dismissively. 'Sorry! I'd forgotten all about my crazy bottle of wine. Where's your corkscrew?' With impressive expedition and skill, she opened the bottle, poured two glasses, and handed one to Jean-Claude with what she hoped would be accepted as a genuinely warm smile. She held up the bottle for him. 'There you are, the 1999 Château La Fayette that's done a round trip across the Atlantic. A first for both of us, I should think.'

Jean-Claude didn't even have to drink it: one whiff of its bouquet and he knew exactly what it was – 1999 Maréchal. As he took a very reluctant mouthful, he reached across the table and picked up the bottle. Just for a second, he considered dropping it, but then Laura said 'May I?' and took it from him. She placed it on the table beside the other bottles of 99 La Fayette; in the *chai*'s subdued lighting, everything about them looked identical.

Laura regarded him quizzically. 'So? Cat got your tongue? What's the verdict?' She bit her lip: both questions sounded accusatorial.

Jean-Claude wanted to get out into the light and fresh air, to drive to the Ocean, to strip naked and swim and swim and swim. ... She wanted him to say it was Maréchal; she knew what he knew. He shrugged his shoulders. 'Where did you get this? Maybe a bad barrel, something wrong with the bottling machine – we've had big problems this year ... remember? I told you. ... Or storage somewhere along the line – Christ only knows how long these containers are left in the sun at the docks. Henri will be furious when he finds out. Perhaps an entire consignment has been affected. We'll need to trace it. ... Where *did* you get this bottle?' In the following brief silence, he felt idiotic: never had he said such patent rubbish. Now she'd pounce – and with good cause. *Quick! Smile, burst out laughing, and make some joke about how clever she's been in having a bottle of Maréchal – or General – rebottled and then recorked and sealed. Now, before–*

'Planters Inn, Charleston ... South Carolina,' Laura said casually, even though she was stunned by Jean-Claude's blatant lying. 'I was one of the guests of the Charleston Wine Society's Annual Dinner a fortnight back. They wanted to serve the rack of lamb with one of my all-time favourites, the 1982 La Fayette, but the Planters' suppliers sent 1999 by mistake. The Society's President was so apologetic – we got Palmer 1990 with the lamb, by the way – but I said I'd love to taste the 99 La Fayette in any case. I don't think the president liked it at all, I'm afraid to say. Anyway, I thought you should know, Jean-Claude – hence this bottle.'

'Well, I'm in your debt, Laura. I'll pop it in the wine fridge immediately with a vacuum stopper and bring it to Henri's attention first thing on Monday morning.' He opened the table drawer for the necessary apparatus, saying: 'I don't know about you, but I'm starving. Do you need to powder your nose or anything before we drive down to Lamarque?'

Laura watched in fascination as he fumbled for the vacuum pump and rubber stopper. 'No, I'm fine, thanks. What about you?'

'Hmm?'

'Do you need to "powder *your* nose"?'

For the first time since her arrival, Jean-Claude managed to laugh. 'To be honest, Laura, I'm bursting.'

She laughed too. 'Well, I'll do this while you go to the john.' He didn't protest as she took the equipment from him: not only was he anxious to relieve himself, but also to have a few minutes alone to gather his wits; it had been a morning of total lunacy on all fronts.

Feasting her eyes on his broad back and denim-clad buttocks, Laura watched Jean-Claude walk briskly towards the far door. Down the corridor, in the minimalist staff lavatory, he vomited his stomach's meagre contents and then urinated. Lunch at Port de Lamarque was the last thing he wanted, and he tried desperately to come up with a credible excuse to get out of it. By the time he returned to the *chai*, he'd settled on a call from Sophie while he was in the washroom telling him to get back to Le Porge: he had to look after Alexandre while she took Buffet to the beach. It was only half a lie – not really a lie at all. Approaching Laura down the long rows of barrels, he felt the bile rising once more and tried not to think of the taste of vomit in his mouth, but then the thought occurred to him that Laura would detect the smell on his breath. His heart raced even faster.

'Jean-Claude, I've been thinking. Would you mind terribly if we didn't go to Lamarque?'

A ray of sunshine, Jean-Claude thought, appearing through the storm clouds. He was speechless.

'It's just that ... well, the more I think about it, what I need to discuss with you is *so* important – and *so* confidential – I really wouldn't want anyone to hear one word. Frankly, we have to be alone – just the two of us somewhere. You could cancel the reservation, couldn't you? I mean, it's not as though it's a fancy place or anything.'

He nodded. 'No problem.' Saved! Another postponement! Presumably, his obvious lies about the wine had thrown her. God only knew what she had in mind to do about it – probably some nasty piece of investigative journalism. The way he felt at the moment, he didn't care. At least he'd have a day or two to muster his thoughts and excuses. He just wanted to get away, go home and–

'Great! I knew you'd agree. Now, don't get mad, but I kind of thought you'd understand, so, just on the off chance, I got the Continental to loan

169

me a cool box, and on the way up I bought some ham, cheese, fruit, bread and Badoit. All you have to do is supply the wine' – she looked around her mischievously – '… which, I guess, shouldn't be a problem, and we're all set for our picnic. I thought the old fort down by the river – Fort Médoc – would be perfect. How does that grab you?'

Jean-Claude was paralysed.

Laura took a step forward, seized both his hands, and held them tightly. 'Great! That's settled then. There are going to be some big changes in your life, honey – for the better – believe me! But first, you have to tell me all about the gun Henri's holding to your head. … OK?' She felt his body tremble and knew she'd struck gold. Her gamble had paid off.

*

Kilometre after kilometre through the dense forests of ubiquitous conifers, the narrow empty road ran straight as an arrow, enabling Henri to put the Mercedes through its paces as he sped furiously south-westwards across the Médoc peninsula. He was following his standard direct route to Cap Ferret through Castelnau-de-Médoc, Ste-Hélène and Le Porge. For the most part, they were little-used 'D' roads, which was just as well, for he needed to vent his anger and frustration: never in his life had he suffered such a humiliation, and it was going to be extremely difficult recounting the morning's events to Tiquetorte and Carbon Blanc without even more embarrassment. For damage limitation purposes, he'd muster plenty of credible exaggeration and embroidery – and a few lies, naturally. Sparks would probably fly when they learned he'd already set in motion Bourjois's departure, but in view of the injuries he'd visibly incurred, coupled with colourful details of Bourjois's violence, they'd surely accept that the thug couldn't be kept on. He would not, however, mention the frantic horse-trading while Laura Appleton wandered around the *chais* in search of Bourjois – and certainly not the five-thousand-euro 'bonus'! In any event, that was being paid from his own personal account; he'd get that back if it was the last thing he did.

Henri began to feel better when he accelerated the Mercedes to 200 KPH on the perfectly straight ten-kilometre stretch of the D5 between Saumos and Le Porge. On balance, things had worked out rather well. It was a bitter pill to swallow, but he'd overreacted to Bourjois's announcement of Appleton's visit. And sacking him on the spot would have been a big mistake. Nevertheless, in three months at most, Bourjois – the cross he'd had to bear for most of his life – would be gone. They could recruit that young chap, Patrick Audinette, from Château Bon Mot at St-Estèphe: top of his class in the Oenology Faculty at Bordeaux University, excellent training at a prestigious Pessac-Léognan *grand cru*, and a promising start at

170

Bon Mot by all accounts. But the gossip was that both the *maître* and the owner had been rubbed up the wrong way by his new-fangled ideas and over-zealous interest in marketing. Nor had his superiors been amused by the young man's acquisition of a BMW 3 series convertible, a swanky apartment overlooking Bordeaux's prestigious Parc Bordelais, and a wardrobe of avant-garde Italian designer outfits. They'd found him with his hands in the till, so to speak: he'd helped himself to some cases of Bon Mot and sold them – so the rumours went – to shady acquaintances who shared his penchant for Bordeaux's risqué nightspots. He was now on 'garden leave' and anxious for lucrative employment. His father, a bank manager and client of Carbon Blanc's law firm, had brought the chap's 'admirable qualities' to Alain's attention only a few days ago, coupled with a request for him to look out for any suitable openings which might come to his notice. Alain had mentioned Audinette on the phone last night when Henri had sounded him out on the possibility of getting rid of Bourjois. Indeed, an interview had been set up for this very afternoon at Cap Ferret around four. What had been a rather speculative possibility now appeared to be most fortuitous.

In view of his determination to exercise the powers under Bourjois's mortgage deed to procure a realistic and commercial arrangement, Henri decided to make a brief detour at Le Porge: he wanted to ascertain that the hideous Bourjois homestead was being properly maintained. For all he knew, Bourjois could be so strapped for cash that the place was going to rack and ruin; bearing in mind Le Porge Océan's proximity, there might be a bloody campsite in the garden – even caravans! He pressed down on the accelerator.

*

Alexandre had not ridden his bicycle for a very long time. In fact, he couldn't remember when he'd last ridden it. The wretched contraption lay propped against the back wall of the double garage – dusty, rusty and rather forlorn. Reluctantly, he walked towards it.

'It really is in*tolerable*,' he muttered. 'One would think I were some kind of servant.' He stared at the grimy saddle and wondered whether he'd just used the subjunctive tense incorrectly. He pulled out a handkerchief and did his best to remove the worst of the filth. Then he took a step back and surveyed the machine. It was too small: he'd received it for his eighth birthday; now he was ten. It was an insult to expect him to cycle into the village on it. What on earth would the oiks say if they saw him?

Alexandre sighed again as he started to pump up the flat tyres. 'Intolerable – absolutely intolerable.' Still, he reflected, if he wanted to go to Paris and escape the horrors of living somewhere as plebeian as

Le Porge, he'd better 'get his skates on' as Mama had so colloquially put it, and get that dreadful man's newspaper.

Alas, Dominique Buffet couldn't start his day without newspapers, a distressing fact which Sophie had discovered when he finally materialized from his quarters shortly after noon. He had arisen an hour earlier, but his bathing couldn't be rushed, and then he'd had to be absolutely sure he wore the right outfit. He'd experimented with three pairs of shorts and four tops before settling on matching multicoloured floral Bermudas and a very loose-fitting short-sleeved shirt. In the meantime, Denise had left to broadcast around Le Porge the latest 'Airport goings-on', leaving a nervous Sophie to cope with Buffet's breakfast. She hovered for over an hour between the kitchen and the guest suite's door, popping croissants in and out of a warm oven, making fresh coffee and trying to decide whether the sounds of gurgling water, creaking wardrobes and the occasional verse of *New York! New York!* gave any meaningful indication as to when Dominique might make an appearance.

When he did finally emerge and was asked what he would like for breakfast, Sophie was blasted with a cry of 'Brunch, darling!'. Brunch, it transpired, meant grapefruit juice – he'd recently got bored with oranges – bacon, eggs, an assortment of cheeses, croissants, a peach or two, and plenty of *café au lait*. Then they could go straight to the beach.

Through a forced smile, Sophie said: 'Fine! – of course! – no problem!'

Waddling with her into the kitchen, Buffet asked: 'Where are the papers? Must keep up with the gossip, darling.'

'The *Sud-Ouest* is on the hall table, I think.'

'And the others?'

There were no others; Sophie felt so utterly provincial.

Buffet was prepared to compromise. 'I'll make do with *Le Figaro*. I just *have* to read the art critic's column – he's reviewing some dreadful English woman's exhibition at the Galerie Down Town in Rue de Seine. The hag spent twenty years in the Dordogne painting pedestrian neo-impressionistic representations of her vegetable garden before seeing the light and doing bizarre things with baked dung. I turned her down – dung's not my thing at all.'

When Sophie burst into Alexandre's 'study', he was taking a well-earned break from *Le Misanthrope*. He stood in front of his sound system conducting the Toulouse Chamber Orchestra in a performance of François Couperin's *L'Apothéose de Lully*, which, although written after Molière's death, was the only CD in his still limited collection that could possibly assist in conjuring up the atmosphere of Louis XIV's Versailles.

'I say, Mama,' Alexandre protested, 'I think a polite knock would be in order before entering a chap's sanctum.'

'If you want to leave this dump and go to Paris,' Sophie snarled, 'you'd better turn off that racket and get down to the village – *now*. Tante Dominique wants the bloody *Figaro*, and I have to prepare a sodding state banquet for her.'

And thus it was that Alexandre wheeled his diminutive bicycle down the gravel drive, opened the gates, and looked up and down the road. Nothing, thank goodness, but then it was rarely used except by the forestry people. He pushed off northwards, cycling inexpertly, the machine screeching protests against its lack of maintenance. Being a stickler for rules and regulations, and despite having the road to himself, he cycled as close as was safely possible to the right side's edge; in any event, the highway was barely wide enough for two-way traffic. His apparent wisdom, however, exposed him to another danger: the road, like most of those through the forests of the Landes, was bordered by deep drainage dykes – part of a massive network which, over several centuries, had transformed Europe's last great wilderness from a nigh impenetrable marshy plain; the sparse population had needed two-metre-high wooden stilts to get about.

With their dark, brackish waters, Alexandre had always feared both the dykes and the larger canals into which they fed. This might explain why, as he thought of life in Paris, his bicycle began to drift towards the centre of the road and away from the precipitous trench. He imagined a new school where he wouldn't have to put up with facile remarks about his father being 'a servant', 'a peasant' or 'a serf'. The worst detractor had been vile Benoît de Bondé, who'd told everyone that Papa was *his* papa's servant! Then, when Benoît transferred to a boarding school near La Rochelle, he'd declaimed that his father didn't want him educated alongside 'a servant's boy' – a servant, moreover, who could only afford to send his son to a private school because his father-in-law – Mama's papa – was 'a rich Jewish tailor'. Such a nasty pack of lies! Naturally, he didn't tell his parents, but he did take a newspaper cutting to school about Grandpapa Charpentier which described him as 'a millionaire industrialist'. Alexandre's 'dossier' also included a photograph of Grandpapa's and Grandmama's wedding in Rouen Cathedral: even the dimmest schoolboy knew that Jews didn't get married in cathedrals! But when all was said and done – and it was a ghastly thing to have to admit – Papa was a sort of servant. Nevertheless, after Benoît had departed for La Rochelle, he'd told anyone who would listen that his father was not just a *maître de chai* but also both a director of the La Fayette company *and* a shareholder.

'Paris,' Alexandre murmured to himself dreamily. *I do hope we'll have an apartment in the Seizième Arrondissement. I'll be able to attend the Comédie Française and see Molière performed as it should be. I'll go to the Opéra, organ recitals at Notre-Dame – so many things.* 'Paris!' he cried with uncommon exuberance, applying extra pressure to the pedals.

The sounds of a vehicle brought him back to reality, and, concentrating on the road ahead, he saw a sleek shiny object racing towards him. 'My Goodness! In all probability that bounder's breaking the speed limit.' He swerved away from the centre of the road and veered dangerously towards the right-hand dyke. With a shriek of abject terror, he overcompensated and swung back to the middle of the road.

At that moment, luxuriating in his powerful Mercedes, it suddenly occurred to Henri de Bondé that, with his impromptu detour via the Bourjoises', he'd better phone Geoffroy and let him know he'd be running a little behind schedule. He started to tap out the number on the car phone just as the distant apparition ahead began its erratic zigzagging. 'What the–?' he yelled, pounding the horn. 'Get over to your own side, you fucking prat! ... Jesus! A kid! **Get** *over*!'

The frenetic blasts of the speeding car's horn only made matters worse: Alexandre's confusion and terror increased with each one; his actions became uncoordinated and irrational. He could have stopped pedalling, but there was a vitally important and urgent mission to procure a newspaper. He could have slammed on the brakes, but he had vivid recollections of an accident caused by doing just that, and being thrown over the handlebars: he'd end up in the deep, dark dyke, or under the wheels of the maniac rushing towards him. He just needed to get control and–

In those final seconds, perhaps Alexandre put too much pressure on the pedals, but as the chain detached, the machine lurched violently to the left.

At the last moment, with the horn screaming pointlessly, Henri slammed on the brakes with all his might. The Mercedes spun wildly. His life flashed before him.

*

With its engine still running, the car was pointing in the wrong direction. Tears formed in Henri's eyes – tears of exquisite joy. He switched off the engine, opened the door, and deeply inhaled the pine-scented air.

'It's all right,' he sighed. 'Thank you, dear God. Thank you!' Wincing with pain – due to Jean-Claude's punch – he got out and walked shakily around the car. 'Not a scratch!' he cried incredulously. 'Not a dent!' With a snort, he added: 'Didn't even hit him then.'

174

After a further examination of the Mercedes, it occurred to Henri that he ought to investigate the fate of the delinquent cyclist. But neither a child nor a bicycle was anywhere in sight. Perhaps he'd scarpered into the forest – terrified that he'd caused an accident. Henri walked back towards Le Porge for about thirty metres, to where the skid marks began. He scanned the dykes on both sides and the neighbouring forest. Nothing. But a few metres from where he stood, the water of the right-hand dyke appeared to have been disturbed: some mud was oozing up to the surface.

'Maybe I imagined the whole bloody thing,' he mumbled as he began to walk back to the car. 'Or maybe when Bourjois attacked me and I hit that *armoire*– Christ! I could be concussed and – and–!'

Suddenly, as he relived his beating in the tasting room, Henri had a nightmarish vision. Panic-stricken, he spun round and stared at the oozing, spreading mud in the fetid water. 'Oh, my God! No! I – I ... It wasn't my fault! He–!'

Out of the corner of his eye, he saw something move on the top of the bank. Then a small, hunched figure scuttled away into the dense, dark forest. '*Bastard*! You could have killed me, you sodding little oik! You almost wrecked a very, *very*, **very** expensive car! If I get my hands on you, I'll – I'll ...!

It took a few minutes for Henri to calm down and convince himself that he'd done absolutely nothing wrong and hadn't suffered anything remotely akin to shock or terror. On balance, however, it might be wise to check on Bourjois's dwelling another day. He just wanted to get to Cap Ferret, have a drink, and take something for his aching bruises. What a hell of a morning!

*

While Sophie busied herself in the kitchen, Buffet sat on the terrace and flicked disinterestedly through the provincial *Sud-Ouest*. His insatiable desire for a copy of *Le Figaro* evaporated, however, when his mobile rang and he found himself getting a blow-by-blow account of the dung exhibition from an ex-boyfriend who had the *Figaro*'s review in front of him. Even Sophie could hear the squeals of laughter from her hot, smoky kitchen. By the time brunch was finally served, Buffet had finished with Paris and was talking shop to a temperamental and insomniac artist in Rio; he mouthed words of apology to Sophie while helping himself to bacon and eggs. In fact, throughout the meal there was an endless succession of calls.

At one point, Sophie did think of Alexandre and the need to feed him, but at that very moment her mobile began ringing. It was Cathérine: had Buffet been hooked by *Les Orifices* or not? Sophie gushed excitedly: she wanted to raise her head high and make the mercenary *antiquaire* die with envy. When Cathérine finally said she had to go, claiming a very important lunch appointment with an American dealer, Sophie had a terrible shock: Buffet had been abandoned for more than twenty minutes! She dashed back to the terrace only to find him still jabbering like a demented hag, with her tastefully laid brunch table now looking as if it had been hit by a cruise missile. Glancing at her, Buffet mouthed more apologies and a plea for fresh coffee.

Around one-thirty, Buffet slammed the mobile down and cried: 'Enough! I'm switching that motherfucker off. The crap I have to listen to from those queens!' He glanced at his watch and screamed. 'Shit! We're missing all the action down on the beach. Come on! No time to lose. The things I've heard about Le Porge in Paris!' Sophie began to clear the table; he slapped one of her wrists. 'Bad girl! Leave it for that Mrs Mop of yours. To the beach!'

Racing upstairs to get her things, Sophie imagined Jean-Claude's reaction when he got back from La Fayette and discovered the state of the terrace. Should she ask Alexandre to clear up the mess? Fleetingly, it occurred to her that he'd not materialized for 'brunch'. Nor, come to think of it, had she seen that damned paper – not that Buffet had mentioned it since the bloody mobile had begun ringing. Alexandre must have brought him the *Figaro* while she was preparing that mountain of greasy food, or while she was talking to Cathérine. And knowing Alexandre, he'd probably made a snack for lunch and retreated to his 'study'.

Just as Sophie burst into the precious 'sanctum' – without the customary formalities – down in the hall, Buffet began squealing for her to hurry up. She'd intended to say that Papa would be home soon, that she and Monsieur Buffet would be back between five and six – at the very latest – and that if he hadn't had any lunch, there were loads of leftovers in the fridge from their guest's two feasts. But as the room was empty, she just assumed the lad was in his hallowed en suite bathroom. With Buffet now screaming her name, she spun on her heels. 'Bye-bye, darling. See you later. Be good!'

CHAPTER 15

Situated on the left bank of the Gironde estuary a few kilometres north of Margaux, Fort Médoc was built in the seventeenth century to protect Bordeaux from naval attack. Due to advances in weaponry technology, however, it had become almost redundant by the end of the nineteenth century and was abandoned by the French military. Decay set in, a process exacerbated during the Second World War, when the Germans cannibalised much of what remained of its structure; the troops billeted in some of the neighbouring châteaux did a good job of desecrating them too. Although substantially restored by local amateurs, the fort has not become a major tourist attraction: visitors to the Médoc seek celebrated vineyards and their châteaux, not the remains of military installations. Consequently, on this glorious Saturday afternoon in early June, Laura and Jean-Claude had the place very much to themselves for their picnic lunch; even the ticket lady had disappeared from her usual place within the entrance archway. Jean-Claude had barely spoken during the ten-minute drive from La Fayette, but then there'd been little opportunity: Laura, at the wheel of her rented car, had talked almost continuously about Belle-Mère. Unsurprisingly, he'd paid scant attention: all he could think about was her bizarre remark about Henri 'holding a gun' to his head – a remark which had still to be explained. So, by the time they reached the fort, he'd got the impression that Dubloon and herself had merely gone to Belle-Mère for a tasting.

Scattered around the fort's former parade ground – now a vast lawn – were various rustic picnic tables. Despite the absence of other visitors, Laura selected the most isolated and marched towards it with Jean-Claude in tow. To his bemusement, she continued cracking jokes about someone called 'Sue Pronk' while laying out the food and he opened the wine. Finally, she said '*bon appétit*' and he replied with a courteous '*merci pareillement*'. Then he raised his glass and said '*santé*' with a forced smile.

Laura stared at him through her sunglasses. 'To us,' she toasted.

In silence, they helped themselves to bread, cheese and ham, while above the fort's towering riverside embankments, the superstructure of the white cruise liner that had been moored that morning adjacent to Bordeaux's Bourse glided silently by on its return journey to the sea. Her name, *RENAISSANCE*, stood out aft of the bridge. Laura felt it was a good omen; it was time to lay her cards on the table.

'They've done a lot of work on this place since I was last here,' she said, looking around. 'That building over there – the one that looks like a chapel – was just a pile of stones from what I can remember.'

Jean-Claude nodded.

'It was one of those outings you would invite me to during my *stage* – picnics, barbecues, beach parties. You said you didn't want me moping around Bordeaux at weekends and getting into bad company. ... Remember?'

Flicking a fly away from the ham, Jean-Claude tried to smile. 'Did I?'

'Yes, you *did*. But the joke was that Sophie was always trying to fix me up with some weirdo or other.'

'Surely not?'

'Of course she did. Trust you not to notice! That time we came here, it was some antique dealer – can't remember his name. He had teeth like a rabbit and desperately needed an underarm deodorant. After lunch, Sophie "suggested" he should take me for a walk along the river and point out "the landmarks". Well, as soon as we were alone, the creep got very fresh. And then when he realised I wasn't interested, he became quite aggressive.'

Jean-Claude stopped eating and looked genuinely shocked. 'You're kidding? I mean, I'd no idea. If I *had* known ... well, I assure you, Laura, I would have given him–'

'Oh, I can imagine what you would have done. You were always so protective – like a father – I mean big brother!'

Jean-Claude shifted uncomfortably. 'Well, you were an attractive young American in a foreign country and ... and I felt sort of responsible for you.'

Laura took a sip of wine. 'I know you did, which, I suppose, was why I could never say anything about what Sophie was up to. And, of course, in a way you were my boss. I suppose she felt kind of threatened. I mean, you guys had only just got married and–'

'"What Sophie was *up to*"? What do you mean?'

Laura tossed her head back. 'Oh, it was so long ago. I should never have mentioned it. Sorry! But seeing this place again–'

'Is this "the important matter" you wanted to talk about?' Jean-Claude's tone was defensively business-like.

Laura managed a good impression of choking on a piece of Pyrenean *brebis* cheese. 'No – of course – not!'

Jean-Claude passed her a bottle of Badoit and told her to take a good mouthful. 'So?' he prompted, once the choking had subsided.

'Well, Sophie used to tell everyone I was a nymphomaniac – that I'd drop my panties for any guy. Christ, don't look so shocked! Come on,

Jean-Claude, she said as much in your goddam cellar in Margaux – remember?'

Jean-Claude was reeling with confusion: this conversation was the last thing he'd expected during their surprise picnic.

'And,' she added refilling their glasses, 'those "escorts" told me so – well, two of them did – maybe three – when I failed to respond to their ham-fisted advances.'

Slowly shaking his head, Jean-Claude began to remember some of the strange things Sophie used to say about Laura at the time, including a few vague recollections of obliquely critical remarks. Abruptly, he pictured Sophie lying on a beach with a naked Buffet surrounded by a gaggle of sycophantic, flirting narcissi. She was acting like a pimp! To flog her sick paintings, she was prepared to procure pretty boys for his gratification. So, Laura's story shouldn't really surprise him. He wondered whether he knew Sophie at all. ... Was she fit to be a mother? ... Did he still love her? His brain seemed to explode. It was like being struck by lightning without any indication of an impending electrical storm.

Laura was cutting the fat off a large slice of *jambon de Paris*. Nonchalantly, without looking up, she asked: 'Why did you lie at La Fayette about the bottle of wine? We both knew it was Maréchal, and you knew that I knew you knew. Sorry, that sounds like a line from a Hope and Crosby *Road* film.'

The analogy washed over Jean-Claude. He'd been softened up by Laura's artillery barrage, and now that the frontal assault was upon him, he was incapable of offering any resistance. Like a scolded child, he lowered his head.

She pushed on relentlessly. 'Jean-Claude, you're one of the most straightforward guys I've ever met. I could never believe you'd knowingly do anything dishonest or dishonourable – Jesus, I think you'd rather die! Which is one of the reasons why I believe you'd make an admirable business partner.' She waved a hand dismissively. 'OK, I haven't been quite honest with you about my visit to Belle-Mère yesterday.'

Jean-Claude finally looked up. He wiped his furrowed brow with a paper napkin, and, with trembling fingers, undid another couple of his shirt buttons.

Although excited by the sight of the curly black hair revealed below his Adam's apple, Laura added calmly: 'What I mean is that for years I've wanted my own vineyard – here in Bordeaux. I've been to every wine-producing region of the world – God knows I've seen some beautiful places! – but Bordeaux is incomparable. The scenery, the climate, the architecture, the food, the people – oh, I don't mean the Henri de Bondés of

179

this world, but the ordinary folk with their love of life, sense of fun, and a passion for quality. Anyway, I think I might have found the right place. Obviously, you need to see it, and I still have to study the accounts and stuff, but I think it's got great potential. Yeah, I know the Premières Côtes can't rank with Margaux, and for you it might look like demotion, but I honestly believe we could make excellent wines at Belle-Mère – as good as La Fayette's – given time, of course – great whites too. And it's such a fabulous château – the house I mean. Dubloon agrees. In fact, he loves the place so much that he's very keen to come in with us – even to put up some of the capital. And *big* money – several million – *pounds*!'

Laura realized she was getting carried away by her own enthusiasm, and was diverging from her carefully crafted script. She had to sound hard-headed, practical and commercial, and not gush like some naive amateur.

'The point is, Jean-Claude, I've always thought of you as an obvious partner in my venture – no one could be a better *maître de chai*. You're rightly admired and respected – and not just here in Bordeaux, but across the world. And yes, I know you have a very long family attachment to La Fayette – and the Médoc – but where is La Fayette going? On the quality front, nowhere. It can't, because Henri won't invest – except in hype, spin and marketing. You're on a plateau and you know it – in a kind of rut really. And you hate the guy – don't pretend – and he hates you. Jesus, what a working environment!

'OK, you could go to any number of great vineyards here – or abroad – but you're still going to be a mere lousy employee at some guy's beck and call. And where's the challenge at some premier division joint that's already at the top? You'll just have the worry of keeping it there. I'm talking about a *real* challenge – the creation of a new gem – and not just working as a paid hack, but in *partnership* with a share of the profits, a say in the management – everything – a stockholder – a director.'

Laura continued in this vein for some minutes as visions flashed with stroboscopic speed in Jean-Claude's fevered brain: a fine office with himself chairing board meetings; the President of the Republic presenting him with a gold *tastevin* at the Élysée Palace; *Sud-Ouest*'s front page headlined **LA FAYETTE LABEL FRAUD – EMPLOYEE CHARGED**; wandering alone through empty rooms at the Le Porge house. Desperately, he tried to concentrate on Laura's endless jabbering.

'But you can't blame me for being puzzled,' she purred, smiling sweetly. 'I felt sure it had to be some labelling blunder. It should never happen, of course, but even the biggest and most reputable corporations make mistakes from time to time. I tried to joke about it on the phone yesterday morning, but when you reacted so oddly today, I was – well, to be frank – stunned. It made no sense – *you* pretending that the wine was your *first* wine – particularly to me – which is why I believe, knowing that you couldn't possibly be involved in anything remotely dubious, that Henri has got some stick to beat you with. Jean-Claude, honey, we can't begin our partnership with some crazy misunderstanding between us, can we?'

Jean-Claude just stared at Laura, as though he was looking straight through her.

'Do you know what I think, honey?' You knew that bottle was Maréchal before you even sniffed the wine in your glass. I could see it written right across your face. You've known – or at least suspected – for some time that Henri's been up to no good, haven't you? – that something weird has been going on with the labelling at La Fayette?'

Jean-Claude rose from the wooden bench and, with trembling hands, lit a cigarette. He turned to face the river and stared hard in the direction of distant Blaye. 'You're wrong about one thing, Laura,' he said in a voice charged with emotion. 'I hadn't the slightest idea about this labelling scam – if it is a scam – until two days ago.' He could hear a cuckoo somewhere in the woods; a small freighter moved languidly across his field of vision on the ebb tide.

Laura came to stand beside him and put an arm around his waist. 'I think you'd better tell me everything,' she said softly.

In view of Laura's extraordinary business proposition, Jean-Claude decided to be economical with the truth: something told him that his employment prospects at Belle-Mère wouldn't be enhanced by painting a picture of La Fayette as an enterprise riddled with fraud. So, he just mentioned Jean-Luc Ducasse's account of what had happened in Orlando, Henri's initial protestations of innocence yesterday, and his undertaking to make immediate enquiries of the New York distributors; he certainly kept quiet about that morning's fracas in the tasting room.

Earnestly, Laura asked: 'And what did these distributor guys say? Oh, do you want any more ham or cheese? ... a peach?'

'Er ... no – no thanks.' Jean-Claude watched Laura begin to pack the plates and cutlery in the cool box. She looked around for a litterbin to dispose of the uneaten food. It seemed such a waste, he reflected, but he couldn't eat another thing.

'I think I saw something for the trash when we came in,' Laura said, dividing the last of the wine between them. 'Oops! Sorry, a little sediment. I'll never make a good sommelier! ... So?'

'Hmm?'

'Did Henri say whether he'd spoken to the distributors? What are they called by the way?'

'Er ... Mayer Fine Wines – a Sam Meyer is the boss.'

'Never heard of them – or him.'

'It's a newish outfit, apparently.'

Laura nodded. 'And?' Jean-Claude looked blank. 'Did Henri speak to them – the distributors?'

'Um ... I don't know. He didn't say.'

'Didn't you ask him this morning?'

'I forgot.'

'You *forgot*?'

'There wasn't time. We were still ... we were still on the technical stuff when you arrived. And Henri was terrified you'd be in a foul mood for the *dégustation* if I kept you waiting.'

'And the printer? Have you chased him for his lab report?'

'He wasn't in yesterday afternoon.'

Laura studied the last few drops of wine in her glass. 'So why *did* you pretend that my Maréchal was a defective La Fayette?'

Jean-Claude reached for another cigarette. 'How did you expect me to react when you seemed to be playing some kind of game with me? And in view of what I'd only just discovered myself and your knowledge of our wines, it certainly occurred to me that you suspected that bloody bottle was incorrectly labelled. So, Laura, as we stood there in the *chai* going through your little charade of a *dégustation*, you won't be surprised to learn that it crossed my mind that you thought you'd got a juicy story – a sensational fraud – and that I was mixed up in it. I wondered–'

'That never occurred to me – I swear!'

'I wondered why you hadn't phoned me straight away from the States. You could have told me the whole story yesterday morning – or when you got to La Fayette today. Maybe–'

'Come on, Jean-Claude, if I'd suspected you of anything shady, would I be offering you a partnership at Belle-Mère – or wherever I invest? Try and see it from my angle. How the hell do you tell a great *maître de chai* – a dear friend – that you suspect his wine is being marketed fraudulently? OK, trying to be kinda light-hearted about it was a mistake – I see that now. Hey, for all I knew, you could have tasted the wine, burst out laughing and said, "Oh, Laura, you needn't have bothered humping this all the way across the Atlantic. We discovered a month back that the label-machine operator fouled up and incorrectly labelled a dozen cases of Maréchal. Our distributors spotted the error after a few bottles had been sent out. There's been a recall, lots of red faces, and an offer of compensation to aggrieved customers." Imagine, then, my shock when you said we were tasting a bad bottle of Château La Fayette! I think we're quits, pal.'

182

Out of the corner of his eye, Jean-Claude noticed a man in his twenties playing football with a little boy near the restored neoclassical officers' quarters. An attractive young woman sitting on a tartan rug was watching them appreciatively; judging by the lad's shrieks of 'Mummy!' and 'Daddy!', the family was British. As images of Alexandre alone in his 'study' exploded, Jean-Claude glanced at his watch: it was almost half past three! He should get back – at least call and ensure Alexandre was OK. Of course, he tended to ignore phones. ... Another joyous shriek of 'Daddy!' brought him back to the idyllic scene of merry footballers. 'Tell me more about Belle-Mère, Laura.'

*

The British family had long gone, the last bottle of Badoit had been drunk, and Jean-Claude had been visibly transformed. 'What do you think I should do now?' he asked.

It was exactly the question Laura had been hoping for. 'First, you've got to see Belle-Mère. What about tomorrow? I'm sure I can arrange it. I'm supposed to be going through the accounts with Quincy, but I can easily reschedule that.'

Jean-Claude nodded. 'Sure ... tomorrow. I can't see any problems. I sometimes visit Tante Colette in Bordeaux on Sundays – alone. No need to upset Sophie at this stage.'

'Quite. Secondly, don't cash Henri's cheque – sounds fishy to me. I don't buy this bonus thing. If you ask me, he's trying to implicate you in his fraud. Let me see it.'

'*If* there is fraud,' Jean-Claude corrected, searching in his trouser pockets.

'Oh, come on! ... Look, on Friday you virtually accuse him of fraud, and the next day Scrooge is giving you a "bonus". I bet if you threatened to make trouble now, he'd threaten to tell the cops that the bonus was actually your share of the scam.'

'*Really*? I hadn't thought of that.' Jean-Claude unfolded the cheque and handed it to Laura.

'Aha! Just I suspected. It's not drawn on a company account – it's a *personal* cheque.'

'Oh?'

'Doesn't that strike you as rather odd?'.

'Er ... I suppose so. Yes.'

'Like I said, don't cash it.'

'What do I tell him? He's bound to ask–'

'Hang on! I'm just coming to that.'

'Yes, ma'am.'

'Thirdly,' Laura continued, smiling as she handed the cheque back, 'there's this printer guy. Tricky.'

'Why?'

'Because should there ever be a fraud investigation–'

'*If* there is fraud.'

'OK, OK! ... Anyway, he might tell the authorities that he'd told you all about his concerns, and then they'd ask *you* what action you'd taken.'

Jean-Claude shrugged. 'I'd just say that I'd informed my employer, and that he'd given me some explanation like the one suggested yesterday – American replacements for labels damaged in transit, or whatever.'

Laura pulled a face. 'If you were the examining magistrate, would *you* believe that?'

'Well, what else can I do?'

'I say you should quit La Fayette immediately. Tell Henri first thing Monday morning that you've been unhappy for some time about the way the château's been run, that you feel your reputation is suffering from the lack of investment, that whatever may be the explanation for the mysterious label from Orlando – labelling – or relabelling – by overseas distributors without the château's consent, it's unacceptable and clearly indicates a hands-off managerial style with which you're uncomfortable. Tell him you've been looking around for a new position, that you've received an offer which it would be madness to refuse, that your new employers want you to start like yesterday, and that it would be inappropriate, therefore, for you to accept the bonus cheque. So, you give it back to him – or rip it up – whatever.'

Jean-Claude sighed. 'You make it all sound so easy, but ... well, I can't just walk out after all these years and leave the place in the lurch. And leaving without notice would shock everyone in Bordeaux – it's just not done, and they'd smell a rat. Anyway, Henri wouldn't stand for it. Perhaps he could get a court order to stop me from working at–'

'Crap! For a start, this is one of the quietest periods for a *maître de chai*. The *vendange* doesn't begin for another three months, and the *assemblage* for last year's harvest is all done. You've got a deputy and – and ... Henri will dress things up just fine with a low-key announcement about an offer you couldn't refuse – a mutually amicable arrangement – wishing you every success for the future and–'

'But, Laura, I *haven't* been made an offer – not formally. It might take you months to buy Belle-Mère – or some other place if that falls through. I haven't got a new job to go to on Monday. And I have a wife and a child, bills to pay, a mortgage. ... I need a regular income. I can't just up and leave – even if Henri was prepared to let me go.'

Laura was smiling broadly. 'No problem! I can hire you now – as my consultant – on a six-month contract, if you like – at your current salary. And for Christ's sake, Jean-Claude, we both know that you could get a job tomorrow at half a dozen premier league vineyards around the world. OK, Henri may kick up a fuss, but I bet anything you like that he can't legally force you to work out your notice at La Fayette. Whether he could stop you working for another vineyard during the notice you should have given – what is it? – three months? ... six?'

Jean-Claude looked vague. 'I'm not sure.'

'Jesus! Anyway, when you tell Henri you'll be coming to work for *me* – *with* me – he'll probably piss his pants with worry that if he doesn't let you go on *your* terms, I'll screw him real bad in the States.'

Jean-Claude finally noticed that they'd been enveloped by the shade of a neighbouring sycamore. 'Oh, my God, Laura, it's nearly quarter to six! I've got to dash. I'll never get home now before Sophie gets back from the beach. Christ! – she's probably back already. I made such a fuss about her leaving Alexandre alone all afternoon and – and ... God only knows how she'll react to the idea of us working together – me leaving La Fayette and starting from scratch in Entre-Deux-Mers. ... Belle-Mère's a hell of a trek from Le Porge, and you know how much Sophie is wedded to that barn of a house of ours.'

'Well, you could all live at Belle-Mère. I suspect Sophie would rather enjoy being a chatelaine in a grand house. It truly is–'

'I'm locking up in five minutes!' a female voice bellowed. Far across the great lawn in the gatehouse archway, stood the custodian with her hands on her hips.

While Laura grabbed her carrier bag of refuse, Jean-Claude picked up the cool box. As they strode side by side across the grass, he said: 'I don't know how big Belle-Mère is, Laura, but Sophie and me can't afford to buy a château for a home. There's a huge mortgage on Le Porge – very little equity – and ... well, I have no savings. To be honest, I haven't got any money to put into this business venture.'

'Have I asked you to? Your investment will be your genius and reputation. That's worth more than its weight in gold. And the house comes with the job, honey.'

The custodian was standing in the barrel-vaulted tunnel which led under the massive ramparts to the fort's entrance arch and drawbridge. '*Merci et bonsoir,*' she said with a smile.

Jean-Claude reached in his pocket for some coins. 'I'm so sorry but you weren't around when we arrived at lunchtime. We owe you some money.'

Laura couldn't help smiling: the man was a paragon of integrity.

'Oh, I've cashed up and everything,' the custodian replied. 'I'll let you off this time!'

On the brief drive back to La Fayette, Jean-Claude asked: 'If the plan is for Sophie and me to live in the château, what about you? I thought you said you were planning to base yourself in Bordeaux.'

'Details, Jean-Claude. It's a huge place. It's got wings – east, west, north, south! – old stables, a gatehouse – lots of places that could be converted into an apartment for me.' She decided, however, not mention Dubloon's tentative plans to move onto the site as well: it might sound like a commune.

'*And* a hotel? *And* a restaurant?'

'Possibilities. There's a hell of a lot of land. You have to see the place.'

When Laura pulled up at the entrance to La Fayette's *chais*, she released her safety belt and was about to open her door, when Jean-Claude leaned across and kissed her on the cheek.

'Don't bother getting out, Laura. See you tomorrow. Eleven o'clock outside the Continental.' Before she had time to react, he was slamming the passenger door shut. He bent down to the level of the open window. 'OK?'

She nodded. 'Fine. Any problems, I'll phone.'

'Call me on the mobile. Sophie–'

'Sure.'

'And thanks for your confidence in me. ... Well, thanks for *everything*.' Then, already gripping his car keys, he sprinted through the archway into the cobbled courtyard.

Just a peck on the cheek, Laura lamented. Picturing her scheduled evening of contemporary chamber music in Notre-Dame's cloisters with the cream of Bordeaux society, she shot away from Château La Fayette with obscene oaths drowned by screaming tyres.

CHAPTER 16

As Jean-Claude sped home, it was unsurprising in view of the day's extraordinary developments that he gave little thought to the several hours of solitude which, he presumed, had been Alexandre's afternoon treat. If Sophie was belligerent, he'd simply say there'd been a crisis at La Fayette – the discovery of some bug attacking the vines would do. And if she went over the top, he could knock the wind out of her sails with a dramatic announcement: Laura Appleton was offering him part-ownership of a both a vineyard and a grand château – a château, moreover, where some king of England had been wined and dined; Sophie wouldn't be the only member of the Bourjois household whose career was taking off! And she wouldn't dare make a scene about Laura in front of Buffet; on the contrary, she'd probably be thrilled by the good impression it would make.

But an announcement in Buffet's presence was certainly not Jean-Claude's preferred option: apart from any other considerations, he'd look a complete idiot when it emerged that he hadn't even seen Belle-Mère! No, the timing and nature of any disclosure about Laura's plans had to be very carefully thought through – very carefully indeed – and not just to Sophie: if things worked out on the Laura front, there was Henri to reckon with too; for a start, there was that bloody cheque burning a hole in his pocket!

These, then, were the considerations which exercised Jean-Claude's mind for most of the journey to Le Porge, together with some speculation over what Sophie's true feelings might be if faced with the prospect of Laura living and working in intimate proximity at Belle-Mère. He was still worrying away when, at a few minutes before seven, he raced his car up the gravel drive to the house and made a beeline for the detached double garage. As he braked violently to a halt in front of one of the closed doors, he was both shocked and oddly thrilled by the realization that Sophie's car was nowhere to be seen. Surely, she and Buffet couldn't still be at the beach, could they? On reflection, however, it wouldn't surprise him. But the sardonic smile was quickly wiped off his face as he thought of Alexandre and how indifferent both Sophie and himself had been to the abandonment of a ten-year-old child for so many hours, even if the boy preferred his own company. And yet ... well, bearing in mind Alexandre's hermit-like existence up in his ivory tower of a study-bedroom, there was the distinct possibility that he'd be wholly unable to contradict any claim by his father that he'd returned one, or two – even three! – hours ago.

Striding towards the front door, Jean-Claude's self-confidence evaporated. What if Sophie had already returned and then gone out again – to the *boulangerie* in Le Porge to procure extra rations for Buffet? Or maybe her car was *in* the garage? It was very unlikely, of course, as she invariably parked it at the front door. Nevertheless, to be absolutely sure, he'd better check. He dashed back, only to find the garage empty; he was still in with a chance.

Once in the house, Jean-Claude stopped himself just in time from shouting 'Alexandre! I'm home!' as Richelieu emerged from the kitchen and added more scratches to the front door in a plea to be let out. 'Poor dog,' he empathized, 'you must be bursting! Off you go. I'll take you for a long walk later.' At the foot of the stairs, he stood still for a few seconds, breathing deeply and listening for any sounds of life; there were none. *Jesus! – what should I say to the lad? … Something like, um … 'Oh, Alexandre, you're not still learning your Molière, are you? I did shout up the stairs when I got back from Margaux. I've been out in the garden ever since, doing a spot of weeding. Aren't you hungry? Goodness knows where Mama and Monsieur Buffet have got to!' … Yes, that should do fine.*

When he reached Alexandre's door, Jean-Claude knocked as usual; there was no answer. He knocked again and called his son's name. Silence – which indicated that the lad was in his bathroom, for he'd reached that stage in childhood when manifestations of nudity and bodily functions at the level of the parental interface became matters of acute embarrassment. Tentatively, he opened the door. Sure enough, the room was empty and the door to the communicating bathroom was shut. Although he knew that Alexandre loathed any disturbance while 'inconvenienced', Sophie could return at any moment, and he had to establish his alibi without delay.

'It's just me, son!' he said brightly, bending over Alexandre's desk and noting the open text of *Le Misanthrope* and a voluminous tome on the architecture of Versailles. 'Didn't want to disturb you when I got back from La Fayette. I shouted up the stairs, but I suppose you didn't hear me. I've been working in the garden round the side–'

The performance was interrupted by the sounds of two car doors banging rapidly in succession, followed by animated voices and hysterical laughter reminiscent of parakeets. Jean-Claude sighed melodramatically. 'At last, Alexandre! Maybe we'll get something to eat soon. I don't know about you, but I could eat a horse.' Striding across the room into the corridor, he slammed the door shut behind him and raced to the landing.

Attired in stunningly colourful *pareos* and designer sandals procured from a beach peddler, Sophie and Buffet stood at the foot of the stairs, prattling and giggling. They were both as red as boiled lobsters: their

188

expensive sun creams had been unable to withstand lengthy periods of wallowing at the water's edge with their new friends, whose addiction to Le Porge's delights since early spring had blessed them with such deep tans that fears of burning had long since ceased to figure in their thoughts – only wrinkling, for which they all had potions and lotions aplenty.

'Hello, you two!' chirped Jean-Claude with exaggerated merriment. 'Enjoy your afternoon? … You look rather … red.' They seemed not to hear him.

'But, darling,' Buffet fizzed, 'if I'd known, I could have brought the most *bizarre* outfits!'

'Well, I still think you'll look great as an American tourist in Bermuda shorts. We'll just give you a camera and one of Jean-Claude's baseball caps. Look, we'll have to get our skates on if we're going to make the formal dinner at nine. We need to leave here around eight-fifteen – eight-twenty at the latest.'

Jean-Claude was halfway down the stairs when Buffet spotted him.

'*Darling*! We've missed you *terribly*, but oh what a *divine* afternoon we've had! Such *hunks*! And the action in the dunes! Mind you, for all their perfect bodies, none of them queens were as gorgeous as you. Oops, what am I like? It's the excitement! Party time! To the shower! Who wants to scrub my back? … Anyone? … No one? Suit yourselves, darlings. Bye for now!' He burst into *YMCA* in a surprisingly rich bass voice and headed for the guest suite.

'You've got *thirty* minutes, Dominique,' Sophie yelled as she turned and began to run up the stairs.

'"*Party*"?' queried Jean-Claude as she passed him. 'What party?'

'Oh, you *were* invited, but I said you wouldn't want to go. Anyway, you have to babysit – so to speak.'

When Jean-Claude caught up with Sophie in their bedroom, she was already ransacking a wardrobe for a sari she'd bought during a premarital trip to India; she'd worn it several times to costume parties over the years.

'God! I hope it doesn't need ironing. … Where the hell is it? The last time– Ah, here it is.'

'Sophie, what's all this about a party?'

She was holding up the sari and shaking her head. 'It'll have to do, I suppose. Hell! – there's a wine stain! … Oh, never mind, nobody'll see it in subdued lighting. Now where's that ankle bracelet?'

'Sophie!'

She tutted. 'Please, I haven't got time to … One of the boys on the beach – the one who wasn't gay as it turns out – he just wanted to *meet* Dominique – he paints.' Sophie stripped and moved into the bathroom;

189

Jean-Claude followed. 'His father's the Marquis de Forgeron. You'll know him – Château Forgeron?' Jean-Claude nodded. 'They're having their own *Fête de la Fleur* tonight – not at the château but at their Cap Ferret place. Anyone who's *anyone* will be there! Seems the marquis is a bit unconventional according to Dakota.' She leaned into the shower cubicle and turned on the water.

'Dakota?'

'Dakota's the one who asked us ... to the party. He's Forgeron's son – by the third wife ... some American cosmetics heiress, I think.' Then she was under the water.

While Sophie showered, Jean-Claude sat on the bed, his thoughts flitting between Laura's Belle-Mère proposition and Sophie's party. He certainly wouldn't have wanted to attend a bloody costume party with a load of Bordelais socialites looking down their noses at him. Christ! – not *any* old costume party, but one hosted by a man who'd scandalized the Médoc with his licentious behaviour and reckless extravagance! Buffet would certainly be in his element. However, the point was that he resented Sophie's presumption – making decisions on his behalf – he wasn't a child! He even felt like destroying her equilibrium by detonating the Laura bombshell. But no, that *would* be childish. Better to wait until tomorrow when Buffet was safely on his way back to Paris.

Sighing, Jean-Claude experienced rapid flashbacks to the *Fêtes de la Fleur* he'd attended before Guy had become incapacitated – the great dinners organized by the growers in mid-June to celebrate the flowering of the vines, a delicate time when, to avoid damage to the flowers and the loss of pollen, all work around them should cease. '*Vigne en fleur*,' he recited under his breath, '*ne veut voir ni vigneron ni seigneur*.' Such fond memories ...

Held at a different château each year, the *fête* is a matter of great pride for the host. Unlike some proprietors, Guy de Bondé had always insisted that his senior employees should accompany him – including the *maître de chai* – rather than his limited allotment of tickets being offered only to family, important customers, and professional advisers. And then, when Guy appointed Jean-Claude assistant *maître de chai*, he'd added him to the guest list. It was extraordinary how he always managed to put both father and son at their ease in such august company – even introducing them to everyone, occasionally raising eyebrows in the process. The 1990 *Fête de la Fleur*, at Château Prieuré Lichine, just down the road from Margaux, was the most dazzling he'd ever attended. There were royal blue carpets covered in rose petals, Régis Dho designed the hundreds of Limoges plates in blue and gold, and Birgit Nielsen dressed as a Martian materialized from a flying saucer on the château's helipad. Naturally, the traditionalists and snobs like Henri had scoffed, but then their sort had always looked down on the Lichine family: for a start, they weren't of French origin; that could be forgiven, but their humble Russian background could not.

Sighing and shaking his head, Jean-Claude ruminated on his invitations ceasing, like so many other things, with Henri's assumption of the mantle of power at La Fayette. Well, no doubt the Premières Côtes had its own *fêtes*. They wouldn't be as grand as the Médoc's, but Laura's and Quincy Dubloon's attendance would certainly enhance their standing! And from her description, Belle-Mère's impressive château would make an admirable venue! He chuckled: he was already thinking like a loyal Belle-Mère executive!

'Care to share the joke?' snapped Sophie, slipping into her sari. 'You were daydreaming – about wine, no doubt.'

'Er … no – yes. I mean … I was just thinking of the *Fêtes de la Fleur* we used to go to.'

'Christ, I can't think of anything less amusing!' Sophie didn't like to be reminded of the humiliation. She'd never been able to decide what had been worse: she, a multimillionaire's daughter, being snubbed by titled – yet often impecunious – vineyard owners' wives bedecked with the mandatory strings of pearls, all constantly searching the assembled throng for someone higher up the Bordeaux social register to talk to; or vile Henri de Bondé phoning her three or four years ago – or whenever it was – to explain why he needed to entertain 'VIPs' at the *Fêtes* and not employees and their spouses. She could have killed him; she'd cried for hours. Jean-Claude had said she was overreacting; she could have killed him too.

'Actually,' Jean-Claude continued, 'you would have loved the 1990 *Fête* at–'

'I haven't got time for tedious reminiscences now. … By the way, you'll have to prepare supper. You don't mind, do you?'

'Well–'

'There's a bloody mountain of leftovers in the fridge from last night, for God's sake! Alexandre loves cold cuts and cheeses, anyway. I suppose I ought to go and wish him good night. Jesus! – where's that sodding lipstick?' She began ransacking drawers. 'Here it is! That blasted cleaner …'

Jean-Claude trailed behind Sophie into the corridor. She turned left towards the landing, changed her mind, and almost collided with him.

'Christ! You're like a bloody shadow!' She sped down the corridor and burst into Alexandre's room without knocking.

From the ground floor, Buffet squealed: 'I'm ready! Come out, come out wherever you are!'

Jean-Claude peeked down the stairs. Buffet was preening himself in front of the hall mirror, looking every inch an obese, middle-aged, sunburnt American tourist – minus baseball cap and camera. There was no way he was getting *his* camera – not in a million years!

'Good night, Alexandre,' Sophie cooed. 'See you in the morning.'

Jean-Claude looked up to witness the spectacle of his wife trying to trot in a sari; she looked cross.

'That boy,' she gasped as she reached the landing, 'is spending an unhealthy amount of time in the loo. You'll have to speak to him.' Jean-Claude looked blank. 'Man to man,' she added in a manner suggesting that the very idea of such a conversation was ludicrous.

Jean-Claude blushed. 'Ah.'

Within five minutes, the partygoers had departed – Buffet sporting suitable headgear but without a camera. Half an hour later, Jean-Claude had arranged a very impressive display of smoked duck, Bayonne ham and half a dozen cheeses on the kitchen table. He'd toasted some bread for the foie gras – one of Alexandre's favourites – and made a green salad with a dressing from one of Tante Colette's excellent recipes. He stood back and admired the spread, wondering whether he should light some candles and add a bowl of flowers – the sort of refinements Alexandre appeared to appreciate. But would they really be appropriate for a 'man-to-man' discussion? … On reflection, was suppertime a suitable occasion for that kind of thing anyway? He rearranged the cheeses and concluded that it was not. On the other hand, it might be useful – particularly with Sophie out of the house – to raise – hypothetically, of course – the possibility of a move from Le Porge to one's own château in the rolling countryside of Entre-Deux-Mers. Wouldn't Alexandre prefer that to accommodation in a claustrophobic Paris apartment, where, no doubt, Monsieur Buffet and others of his ilk would constantly be entertained?

Jean-Claude decided to add candles and flowers to his table after all.

Shortly after nine, and with the candles glowing cosily and having fed Richelieu, Jean-Claude went in search of his son, only to find the study unlit in the fading twilight – and the bathroom door still shut. 'Alexandre! Supper's on the table!'

Five minutes later, Jean-Claude ascended the stairs once more, this time with a hint of uneasiness. He knocked on the bathroom door; the lack of response was troubling; he resolved to open it.

*

Having searched the house, Jean-Claude scoured the garden. With mounting panic, he repeated his searches as darkness fell. By quarter past ten he was frantic. Could Alexandre have run away? Should he phone the *gendarmerie*? – Sophie? But what if Alexandre returned with his tail between his legs while she was driving back from Cap Ferret? She'd kill them both! And anyway, how far could he have got since Sophie said goodnight to him? … As far as Le Porge? He could take the bus from there to Bordeaux, but didn't the last one leave around six-thirty? The poor kid was probably trying to make a point – seeking attention – a protest against his abandonment. He couldn't blame him.

Jean-Claude dashed out of the house, leaving the lights blazing and the doors unlocked. But just as he was about to drive off, he suddenly realised that he hadn't checked the garage. That was when the thought finally occurred to him that Alexandre might have taken his old bike. And he felt something akin to relief upon discovering that it was indeed missing. At last, he had a clue – one which seemed to confirm the running-away-protest theory. He pictured Alexandre down at Le Porge: he'd be sitting on the steps in front of the church, wondering how long it would take his parents to discover him. Someone had probably already taken pity on him. Jesus! He'd be taken to Denise! It would be her juiciest piece of gossip for years! Did she have his mobile number? Could she already have phoned Sophie?

'It'll all be *my* bloody fault!' he cried. 'He'll have blabbed – that I was out all day! Christ! – why couldn't the little bugger have delayed his tantrum until Buffet pissed off back to Paris?' But there was still a chance he could get to him first. Gravel flew in all directions as the little car shot off.

CHAPTER 17

At Cap Ferret, Sophie was not enjoying the Marquis de Forgeron's *Fête de la Fleur*. She couldn't fault the venue – a vast split-level ultra-modern villa redolent of Beverly Hills – or the refreshments, a gargantuan spread of the most extravagant fare served by an army of beautiful young waiters kitted out as gladiators. And in any other circumstances, she would have been enchanted by dining on an elevated terrace under the stars in balmy air rich with the scent of pine and jasmine – a terrace, moreover, that overlooked an illuminated swimming pool amid a garden of subtropical appearance in which over a thousand candles flickered magically. Yet the beauty of the scene barely registered, for sitting at her large circular table – one of a dozen on the terrace – were not only Geoffroy de Tiquetorte and his wife, Cassandre, but also the latter's 'partner' – as Cassandre had pointedly introduced her – Pandore. It was all horribly embarrassing.

Sophie had experienced a foreboding of the shape of things to come when two beefy bouncer types dressed as centurions had stopped her car at the villa's gates: despite both her name and Dominique's being on the guest list – albeit in manuscript at the very bottom – and producing their driving licences, they'd been most reluctant to admit them. If that wasn't bad enough, the centurions flanking the villa's front door accused them of being gatecrashers. Just as voices began to get raised, Dakota de Forgeron materialized in the guise of 'Narcissus'. Sporting a great deal of eye make-up, he wore a skimpy tunic and much gold jewellery. A painfully thin 'slave girl' was in tow, clad in sacking which had been expertly shredded to reveal her diminutive breasts.

'It's OK, Pierre,' Dakota said to one of the centurions, 'I know these two.' He put his hands on his hips and stared in horror at the new arrivals. 'Shit! Did I forget to tell you it was a Greco-Roman party?'

The slave girl burst into a fit of giggles. 'He's surreal,' she purred.

Kissing Dakota's cheeks, Dominique cried: 'He's a bleeding bastard, darling! I think you should bend over and take what you deserve – a bloody good–!'

Dominique squealed with delight as Dakota swiftly turned his back, raised his arms in the air and touched his toes, revealing shapely naked buttocks. But before Dominique could aim his first slap, Dakota was already upright and grinning in the direction of the front door.

'Hi, Dr de Tiquetorte! – Madame de Tiquetorte!'

Sophie spun round. The expressions on the faces of the two secret lovers were pure silent-film melodrama – the Guilty Parties. They stood frozen to the spot as Cassandre offered her cheeks to Dakota.

'Divine butt, dear boy!' she boomed. 'I'm glad to see your father's parties are continuing to live up to their reputation. I wouldn't miss one for the world. Even the purgatory of putting up with Geoffroy for the evening is a price worth paying.' She glanced fleetingly from Sophie to her husband as they finally greeted each other with hesitant formality.

'Good evening, Madame Bourjois.'

'Good evening, Dr de Tiquetorte.'

Cassandre snorted like a horse and prodded Dominique in the ribs. 'I know you, don't I?'

'This is Dominique Buffet,' Dakota enthused, 'the famous Paris art dealer – the Galerie Buffet guy.'

Cassandre took a step back and looked him up and down. 'My God! I can't believe it! Dominique, you old rogue! How's the art racket? Still flogging crap to cretins with more money than sense? Jesus, *you've* put on weight! No wonder I didn't recognise you. What the hell are you supposed to be anyway? – a gatecrasher?'

Dominique cocked his head on one side. 'And a very good evening to you too, Cassandre. Long time no see!' He sniffed the air violently. 'I thought so – the unmistakable scent of *Eau de Lesbos*, rich with the tang of long-haired bitches. Still breeding Labradors, are we? And this incredible hulk,' he added, turning to an Amazon dressed as a female warrior from the uncivilized world, 'must be your latest kennel maid. Or is it dearest Gérard Depardieu in drag as Astérix's mother-in-law?'

'Bad vibrations,' the slave girl mumbled. 'I need cool waves. Lapis lazuli, lapis lazuli, lapis lazuli–'

'Quite, dear,' sighed Cassandre wearily. 'Pandore, *mon amour*, the fat faggot is Dominique-the-human-vacuum-cleaner-Buffet – eats his own weight daily. Dominique, meet Pandore, my *partner*.'

Geoffroy rolled his eyes and groaned belligerently as Pandore stepped forward with a mischievous smile and a vicious handshake. 'Hi! I guess you're supposed to be a Yankee tourist doing the Coliseum or the Parthenon. Subtle but cheap.'

'That's my fault,' Dakota admitted. 'Seems I forgot to tell these guys about the theme. Must have smoked too many spliffs on the beach this afternoon!'

'Oh, I *see*,' Cassandre blasted, winking at Dominique, '– new recruits! How thrilling! I suppose all *this*' – she swung an arm in a semicircle – 'must seem terribly provincial to you two Parisians.' She looked from him to Sophie, as if noticing her for the first time.

'Oh, I'm not – that is I *am*, but ...' Sophie dried up; everyone was staring at her expectantly. 'Um ... what I mean is ... um ...'

'Dominique,' Dakota interjected, 'one of the staff didn't turn up – our butler chap back at St-Julien – upset stomach or something. He's sort of ... well–'

'Short and fat?' prompted Pandore.

'I can see you two are going to be great friends,' Dakota continued. 'OK, let's just say his toga would probably fit you.'

While Dominique gushed with gratitude, Dakota looked apologetically at Sophie. 'Sorry, but I'm not sure there's a spare costume for *you*. Maybe the housekeeper could rustle up something with a sheet and safety pins.'

'A shroud?' suggested Pandore.

'Cow!' hissed Dominique.

'Just kidding,' Pandore snapped, pushing herself between Geoffroy and Sophie. 'Actually, *chérie*, you're just beautiful the way you are – fabulous sari!' She put a muscular arm around Sophie's shoulders. 'Get it in India?' Sophie nodded. 'Well, you can be an exotic oriental princess captured by Alexander the Great, can't she, everyone? Didn't he go to India?'

Geoffroy, posing in a tacky, rented Caesar costume made from shiny man-made fabrics, said: 'Of course he did. Everyone knows that. He even sailed down the Indus, as a matter of fact.'

Pandore pulled a face. 'Ah, the all-knowing polyester Caesar speaks. Thought you'd lost your tongue, Nero ... or are you Caligula?'

'Actually–'

'I'm sure,' Cassandre interrupted, 'she'll make a most extraordinary impression as a personage of breeding from the Indian subcontinent – even with her sunburn. One really should take more care of one's skin, my dear. I don't think we've been *properly* introduced.' Regally, Cassandre stood her ground beside Dominique.

The temperature in the hall seemed to drop a few degrees.

'She's Dominique's latest fag hag, of course!' roared Pandore, giving Sophie a playful punch in her midriff. 'Aren't you, *chérie*?'

'Don't be so bloody vulgar!' hissed Geoffroy. 'My God, you people have one-track minds. This is *Madame* Sophie Bourjois, the ... the famous painter. Monsieur Buffet is her weekend houseguest at–'

'"You *people*"?' sneered Pandore. 'What *can* he mean?'

'You're very well informed, Geoffroy,' his wife observed. She held out her hand to Sophie. 'How do you do, *Madame* . . .?'

'Oh, *do* call me Sophie.'

'I'm going to the terrace for a drink,' the slave girl said to no one in particular. 'Lapis lazuli, lapis lazuli, lapis lazuli ...'

As though auditioning for a toothpaste advertisement, Dakota's smile returned with a vengeance. 'Yeah! Great idea! Let's go through. Papa's holding court there.'

'What about my costume?' shrieked Dominique.

'Sorry! It'll be in one of the guestrooms – where the staff have been changing. Follow me.'

'To the ends of the earth, darling boy!'

Scanning the other guests, Dakota said: 'Tic-Tac will take you to the terrace, OK?'

Cassandre grimaced. 'Who or *what*, may I ask, is "Tic-Tac"?'

As Dakota steered an ecstatic Dominique to an adjacent door, he pointed at the slave girl. 'She is, of course. Sorry! Thought I'd introduced her.'

'I hope she's got a frigging map and compass,' Pandore snarled. 'Look at her. Turn that airhead round twice and she'd be lost. And I've seen better tits on schoolboys.'

'Oh, for God's sake,' fumed Geoffroy striding away, 'I know this house like the back of my bloody hand!'

With Tic-Tac following hesitantly in his wake, Sophie watched them recede in horror as Cassandre and Pandore positioned themselves on either side of her and took an arm each. She felt like a captain who, having been set adrift in mid-ocean by a mutinous crew, observes his ship disappear over the horizon.

'So ... *Sophie*, how do you know old Geoffroy?' asked Cassandre.

Simultaneously, Pandore whispered in Sophie's ear: 'Don't worry about the Ice Maiden. You stick with me, doll, and you'll have an evening you'll never forget.'

Notwithstanding her adultery with Geoffroy and somewhat unconventional art, Sophie possessed an essentially puritanical soul. In consequence, the ambience of latent and ambivalent sexuality pervading Forgeron's *Fête de la Fleur* made her feel decidedly uncomfortable. Her negative feelings were compounded not only by Pandore's unwelcome attentions, but also by a rapidly crystallizing impression that the intellects of all those present had been prematurely arrested around the age of fifteen. Matters were not helped by Sophie's age: apart from Geoffroy, Dakota and Tic-Tac, she was the youngest guest at the party. In a sense, this was hardly surprising, for the host, Vincent de Forgeron – now in his late fifties but looking much older due to decades of assorted drug addictions, heavy smoking and debauchery – reserved this *soirée* for the survivors of the extensive coterie of beau monde acolytes that had orbited around him thirty years earlier. Once a year they endeavoured to rekindle the flames which had fired their frenetically and calculatedly self-indulgent adolescence by attending the annual *Fête*.

In truth, many of the attendees loathed Vincent: they couldn't rationalise how he'd achieved such phenomenal financial success despite being a full-time playboy who invariably communicated with his minions by terse emails from one or other of the overseas hotels in which he resided for most of the year. Furthermore, they'd been shocked by his mixed-race unions: he'd divorced his first wife – a sixteen-year-old Indonesian prostitute – in order to marry an 'exotic dancer', aged seventeen, from São Paolo; several spouses from humble origins and tropical countries had followed. Dakota, however, was the product of a rare coupling with a white woman, a 'hostess' at one of Manhattan's most risqué nightclubs. There'd been no marriage, but rather several years of intermittent and turbulent cohabitation, including some sojourns at Château Forgeron, from which the commune of St-Julien had still to recover fully. In due course, Dakota had been the subject of formal custody proceedings and given a conventional and expensive education at a prestigious New England military academy. His tales about his mother's background were legendary; hence Sophie's references to 'a cosmetics heiress'.

Vincent credited his business acumen to no more than an ability to see the wood for the trees – that, like Mercedes-Benz, one should not put all one's eggs in one basket, but have a range of products to suit all pockets and tastes. Consequently, within five years of inheriting Château Forgeron after his father's death, Vincent had been producing no less than four wines: the 'luxury brand' first wine, Château Forgeron – a star performer in almost every vintage; Marquis de Forgeron, the fine second wine – and often worthy of *grand cru* status itself; pleasantly fruity F de Forgeron – a decent Médoc for drinking within two to three years of the vintage; and Forgeron Cub – a blended non-vintage Bordeaux for easy and immediate slurping.

Traditionalists had been horrified by the name of a Médoc *grand cru* being associated with supermarket plonk, and by the drab, functional industrial unit constructed on Pauillac's outskirts for Cub's production; they'd confidently predicted disaster. But a sexy advertising campaign aimed at younger consumers got the Cub brand off to a flying start on both sides of the Atlantic. And when the first generation of Cub drinkers matured, they tended to remain loyal, moving on up the Forgeron range. It had been a winning formula: Cub now outsold all other Forgeron wines in both volume and value, the handsome profits funding a continuous programme of investment and improvements. Paradoxically, Château Forgeron itself had graduated to the dizzy heights of Bordeaux's Premier Division, thereby swelling the envy – and, in some cases, even hatred – of Vincent's competitors. But while they wrung their hands and worried about cash flow and the weather, he amused himself in distant parts of the globe.

Quincy Dubloon had studiously followed his former friend's life since Cambridge. And although Quincy had himself achieved a certain degree of notoriety and fortune – albeit on quite a different level – these matters of commonality had not served to restore any kind of relationship between them. In any event, Vincent avoided conventional wine industry gatherings and critics, and rarely read anything except his own company's accounts and the one-page 'Executive Summary' reports emailed to him weekly from St-Julien. Indeed, it was only through the latter that Vincent had been kept aware of the maintenance of *Wine Wisdom*'s perennial aloofness towards all his wines – an editorial policy which actually didn't bother him in the least: like all similar publications, he reasoned, *Wine Wisdom* was bought and read by wine buffs – *amateurs* – who constituted a fraction of one per cent of wine consumers.

During their youth, Vincent and Cassandre de Tiquetorte – née Dumonnet – had been neighbours in St-Julien, where her family had owned a substantial vineyard. Being like-minded spirits, they'd become very good friends. Indeed, their mutual fascination with things sexual led them to lose their virginities with each other; Vincent had been sixteen – Cassandre a mere fourteen. Twenty-one years later, Cassandre was still unmarried and childless: there had been boyfriends – and even one engagement – but sooner or later she'd always drift back into a relationship with a butch female. Monsieur and Madame Dumonnet despaired: Cassandre was their last hope, for their other children had also been disappointments – not through unconventional relationships, but because none of them had married into titled families. Yes, the Dummonets had all the trappings of the *aristocratie Bordelaise* – vineyard, château and wealth, thanks to their respective ancestors having prospered in the Gironde for over a century as lawyers, doctors and bankers – but the jewel in the crown, that vital '*de*' before their surname, had eluded them. Alas, with thirty-five-year-old Cassandre now living in a Paris attic with a sculptress whose meagre income was supplemented by nocturnal mud wrestling, all seemed lost.

Then, one day, Madame Dumonnet rashly unburdened herself to her Bordeaux manicurist, who promptly breached the confidence to her next client, a twenty-two-year-old medical student at Bordeaux University – Geoffroy de Tiquetorte. Geoffroy was the youngest of four impecunious brothers whose father had borrowed heavily to invest in bogus Algerian tourist developments using the de Tiquetortes' three vineyards as security; he'd lost everything. Within days of becoming aware of Madame Dumonnet's 'problem', Geoffroy was having lunch with her at Le Noailles; twenty-four hours later, he was at St-Julien thrashing out the details of a financial package with her pessimistic husband. But having been cut off without a franc by her thoroughly alienated parents, Cassandre finally had the good sense to realise that she was getting too old to live on the breadline. So, she stunned her family by agreeing to marry young Geoffroy, but only in return for a generous annuity for life and a transfer into her own name of the Dumonnets' country estate near Périgueux. For his part, Geoffroy 'requested' an identical annuity and the Dumonnets' superb townhouse in Rue d'Aviau.

Cassandre's parents demanded their own conditions in the prenuptial trust deed: should the spouses ever separate or divorce, the annuities would cease; should they produce a son and heir, they'd each receive a million francs; bonuses of ten thousand francs were payable whenever they jointly attended a 'public function' – not exceeding ten in any year – of which prior notice had to be given to the Dumonnets' lawyers to permit verification. A schedule to the deed contained a non-exhaustive list of 'public functions'; Cassandre demanded the inclusion of Vincent's *Fête de la Fleur* because she knew Geoffroy would detest it. Accordingly, his presence at Vincent's party this June evening was solely for the most mercenary of purposes, a fact known by Vincent – he'd given Cassandre invaluable advice on the marriage once she'd resolved to go through with it – and an obese, balding, middle-aged gentleman dressed just like Geoffroy in a dowdy Caeser costume. He was a partner in the late Dumonnets' law firm and a trustee of the prenuptial trust.

Geoffroy had been in a foul mood long before his arrival at the hated *Fête*. For a start, an oddly neurotic Henri de Bondé had arrived at Cap Ferret, late for lunch, announcing the termination of Bourjois's employment, which he'd tried to justify with all the fervour of a religious fanatic. And in the middle of all that hysteria, it transpired that half-witted Alain de Carbon Blanc had forgotten to tell him about some blasted job interview he'd arranged with a candidate for Bourjois's job – and on a Saturday afternoon to boot! – and at *his* damned beach house! To cap it all, Cassandre turned up around seven in her filthy Land Rover with the revolting Pandore, and promptly announced that her 'partner' would be accompanying them to the party – something she'd never done before.

But to walk through the front door of Forgeron's den of vice to be confronted by both Sophie Bourjois and her sodomite friend – not to

200

mention the buttocks of Forgeron's illegitimate spawn – was beyond the pale. Rarely had he felt more determined to extricate himself from an arrangement that had become an intolerable embarrassment. Twenty years ago, it had seemed like a stroke of genius – a lucrative marriage of convenience contracted to banish the spectre of poverty hanging over him. He'd even believed that, given time, Cassandre would see the error of her deviant ways and be a true wife. Alas, it had taken him a long time to grasp that the financial inducements to having children were of no relevance to her, and that she'd rather die than have sex with him; trying to force her had been a big mistake.

But his 'extravagance' – as Cassandre was apt to describe his love of the finer things in life – had quickly locked him into the prenuptial agreement, with the result that, in the absence of alternative means, he couldn't afford to forego its financial benefits without risking bankruptcy. Over the years, he'd tried hard to generate sufficient wealth to render his marriage superfluous, but despite his medical entrepreneurialism and investments in Henri de Bondé's ventures, he'd remained gallingly dependent on Dumonnet money.

Thus, when Geoffroy emerged onto Vincent's terrace and snatched a *coupe de champagne* from a passing waiter's silver tray, he experienced a feeling of such despair that he resolved to bring his humiliation to an immediate end. He glared at the host reclining on an Empire chaise longue – 'holding court' to use his son's apt words. To hell with the bloody party – he'd leave! This time he'd do it for sure. He'd march up to that pervert of a lawyer hovering over there, and spell it out to him. So what if he forfeited the annuity? He could economize – he *could*! The Cap Ferret villa would go for a start – once the summer season was over, of course – *and* the expensive consulting rooms on Allées de Tourny; there were plenty of cheaper alternatives close by. And – and …

Sophie was trying to catch his attention. Looking completely miserable, she was cornered by the elephantine Pandore while Cassandre gossiped animatedly amongst a semicircle of guests that had been granted an audience with an imperious Forgeron. But what made the greater impression on Geoffroy was the expression of childlike innocence on Sophie's beautiful face. He was not a poetic man, yet among this motley band of degenerates, Sophie looked like an exquisite, delicate flower – an orchid, perhaps – desperately attempting to survive at the centre of a patch of ugly and uncontrollably rapacious weeds. He should do the decent thing and rescue her. In any event, he was intrigued by Sophie's presence, and ought to explain a few things himself: during their sex yesterday lunchtime he'd mentioned neither a weekend party nor, more importantly, attending one with the much-lampooned Cassandre.

He smiled warmly at Sophie; she pursed her lips, and he beat a course to her side.

Pandore was in full flow, recounting in a booming voice the joys of Labrador breeding. Geoffroy took hold of Sophie's arm, and, without looking at Pandore, said: 'Please excuse us one moment. I just want to give Madame Bourjois the results of some tests which I know she's been anxiously awaiting.' He led her away from a gawping Pandore towards the empty tables where dinner would be consumed in due course. Within minutes, Sophie was empathizing as she digested Geoffroy's fictional account of his wife's 'drug addiction'.

'So, at *this* kind of party,' he concluded, 'there's always the risk of her shooting up – *and* drinking too much. I can't afford to let her out of my sight for one moment. It's happened before at Forgeron's *Fêtes de la Fleur*. Well, bearing in mind that he and most of the guests are junkies, it's hardly surprising, is it? On one occasion, Cassandre nearly died.'

'No!'

'I'm afraid so. ... Look, I didn't tell you about the party, Sophie, because I feared you'd get some foolish ideas into your head about me accompanying Cassandre to such a peculiar event. And I didn't want to mention Cassandre's addiction for ... well, for obvious reasons.'

Overflowing with sympathy, Sophie told him she understood. Then she proceeded to summarize what had happened on the beach that afternoon, and how she and Buffet had come to be invited.

Tactlessly, Geoffroy said: 'I suppose "*Dakota*"– what a vile name! – couldn't invite that Buffet idiot without inviting you as well. And I suppose Buffet has led the brat to believe that if he gives him what he wants, he'll exhibit his paintings. ... I don't suppose that pederast was interested in your stuff, was he?'

'I don't follow,' she said, sounding both a little hurt and touchingly angelic. 'Actually–'

'Oh, come on, Sophie, you can't be *that* naive! Don't be taken in by that halfwit, er ... Bric-à-Brac.'

'Tic-Tac.'

'Whatever. Take a good look around – perverts the lot of 'em! Christ, darling, we're the only straight people here! And knowing something about Forgeron, I bet he'd be quite content for his son to offer Buffet sexual favours. And if that didn't work, then he'd no doubt *pay* the old fruit to get the brat's daubs exhibited. Ah, talk of the devil – or should I say "devils"?'

Through a timely gap in the throng, Sophie caught sight of Dakota whispering into Dominique's ear. They started laughing, and, after coyly combing the terrace, spotted both her and Tiquetorte staring at them. With all-too-obvious embarrassment, they smiled and waved.

'See what I mean?' sneered Geoffroy, '– thick as thieves!'

Sophie sighed: despite her own moral convictions, she'd long ago learned not to voice opinions in public which might be interpreted as reactionary. After all, she moved mainly in artistic and Bohemian circles, and, in consequence, had to be very careful not to give offence to highly sensitive aesthetes. As a corollary, she invariably felt uncomfortable when politically incorrect utterances were voiced in her presence: those quick to judge others might reach a verdict of guilt by association in view of her proximity to, or friendship with, the intolerant party. But here, in their relatively private corner of the terrace, and with only the ubiquitous sounds of chill-out music playing from concealed mini-speakers for company, Sophie grasped that she and Geoffroy were indeed the persecuted minority and, as such, needed to stick together.

'You might be right,' she said nodding, although she couldn't help wondering whether Geoffroy had overlooked the role she herself had played in bringing Dominique and Dakota together in the first place. 'Do you know, Forgeron barely acknowledged my existence when we were introduced? And that Dakota person couldn't even remember my name! Buffet had to prompt him! And I didn't like at all the smile on Forgeron's face when Buffet said my husband was "a gorgeous genius"' – she mimicked him camply – 'who made "the most fabulous wines" at … "Where is it, darling?". I could have killed him – Buffet, I mean. Why did he have to bring up Jean-Claude?'

'Indeed.'

'And when I said "Château La Fayette", that clapped-out bloody marquis turned away, looked at your wife with a silly grin on his face, and said, "Oh yeah, that rings a few bells." Then he acted as if I didn't exist.'

'Typical! I haven't even bothered to greet him. I wasn't going to join the queue of sycophants lined up before that reclining degenerate.'

'I don't blame you.'

Geoffroy looked at his watch. 'Christ! No wonder I'm bloody starving – it's almost quarter to ten!'

'Me too! I've hardly eaten a thing all day – haven't had the chance, what with running around like a headless chicken to keep Buffet fed and watered.'

'I can imagine. … What in Christ's name is that bloody awful music? Anyone would think we were at an Arab funeral.'

As Sophie tried to think of a suitable reply, Geoffroy nodded in the direction of two huge black men posing as Nubian slaves, who were moving solemnly towards a colossal bronze gong that stood on a platform behind Forgeron's chaise longue. 'At last!' he snorted. 'Looks like battle is about to commence. We'd better move over to the food before that rabble scoff the lot.'

'It's *Buddha Bar*,' Sophie mumbled.

'What?'

'The music.'

'Never heard of them. ... How do *you* know anyway? – not *your* kind of thing, surely?'

Sophie watched one of the 'Nubians' exchange a few words with Forgeron and thought of the complete collection of *Buddha Bar* CDs in her studio. 'God, no! Jean-Claude is into that sort of stuff.'

'That figures!' Geoffroy wondered if Bourjois had told Sophie yet that his career at La Fayette was finished. 'I really don't know how you cope,' he added. 'You should leave him.'

The 'Nubians', now in position on either side of the gong, slowly raised their drumsticks with great solemnity, while Forgeron, dressed in a bespoke outfit which proclaimed him to be the only true Caesar at the party, lifted a hand clutching a purple silk scarf. Thanks to much shushing and the *Buddha Bar* master switch being thrown, silence fell upon the terrace.

'Maybe I *will* leave him,' Sophie whispered, '– at least, that is, if Buffet keeps his promise. You see, Geoffroy, you were wrong about one thing – he *is* going to exhibit *Les Orifices*. In fact, he's convinced he can sell the lot for hundreds of thousands.'

Geoffroy stared at the Nubian tableau for a few seconds. 'I'm going to divorce Cassandre,' he murmured. The words inexplicably electrified and emboldened him. 'I love you, Sophie. I think we should get married.'

Sophie dropped her champagne flute a fraction of a second before Forgeron let go of his scarf. Everyone instantly turned away from the gong spectacle and stared towards the source of the shattering glass, while the 'Nubians', thrown by the crack of cut crystal smashing on marble, attacked the gong asynchronously. The effect was rather comical, but the guests' laughter was not what the host had intended. Sophie, however, was oblivious to everything, including Vincent's murderous stare in her direction.

Once Geoffroy and Sophie had helped themselves to their first course and escaped from the sort of unseemly melee which, irrespective of social backgrounds, generally materializes at buffets, they returned to the far end of the terrace and sat down at an empty table. Within seconds, an unsolicited waiter served them some Forgeron Cub *blanc* and Badoit. As soon as he was out of earshot, Sophie said:

'Now, what on earth was all that divorce and marriage stuff about, Geoffroy?' Her tone, however, was not unfriendly.

He raised his glass. 'To us, darling!'

'Geoffroy, *please*!'

'Come on! It's a toast.'

'People are looking.'

'They're not.'

'They– Oh, God! What the hell …?'

The moment for a romantic toast had passed: making for their table and balancing overloaded plates, were two middle-aged men dressed in grey suits, white shirts, striped ties and heavy black brogues. They smiled sheepishly at Sophie and Geoffroy as they reached the table.

Standing to attention, the thinner of the two said: '*Bonsoir. Est-ce que cette table est libre? Pouvons-nous manger ici avec vous?*' The accent was unmistakably English.

Geoffroy groaned. 'Trust our luck!' he muttered.

'*Oui, oui! – mais bien sûr,*' Sophie said, smiling. She prayed the Britons would sit on the far side of the large round table, but they deposited their plates at the next two seats to her right.

'I'm Philip,' the thinner man said, continuing in French as he sat down beside Sophie, '– Philip Rimmer. And this' – he prodded his portly companion in the ribs – 'is David Warbler.'

'Hello,' said David in English.

'Tut, tut, tut!' scolded Philip.

'Sorry. … *Bonsoir.*'

Following further formal introductions, it transpired that Philip and David – the very same Philip and David whom Laura had witnessed at the Café Comédie yesterday morning – were directors of Château Forgeron's British distributors, Larboard & Chitterling, a most prestigious firm of London wine merchants with an impeccable pedigree. With Philip masticating a mouthful of smoked salmon, David straightened his tie and said:

'I suppose you're wondering why we're not in fancy dress?'

'Aren't you?' sneered Geoffroy. 'I thought you were a couple of accountants from distant Londinium. Where are your abacuses?'

David appeared not to understand and glanced at Philip for assistance. Philip laughed as politely as he could manage with a mouth stuffed with food. 'Oh, *very* good – very *Gallic*! "A couple of accountants", David! *Très drôle!*'

Sophie was hardly listening: in addition to the excitement generated by Geoffroy's extraordinary announcements, she was searching the terrace for Dominique and Dakota; she'd lost sight of them during the stampede to the food and hadn't seen since. Her mind was running riot with the possibility that Dakota was in the process of ousting her from the October slot at the Galerie Buffet – the scheming little queen! God only knew what he was letting that pile of blubber do to him behind some locked door or other.

David was warming to his theme. 'Well, we were invited *ages* ago, weren't we, Philip? ... around Easter, I think. But there was never any mention of fancy dress – *never*. The invitation cards definitely state "lounge suits". To be absolutely honest with you, Sophie and ... er, Geoffrey–'

'Geof*froy*.'

'Sorry! ... Geof*froy*.' Having emphasised the second syllable ludicrously, David paused theatrically. 'Anyway, to be honest, we were both stunned – to be invited, I mean. As far as we know, the Marquis has never been to our offices for *years* – we'd never even met him until tonight.' David lowered his voice. 'Naturally, we'd heard he was a *soupçon* ... eccentric – brilliant businessman, of course.'

'Brilliant!' agreed Philip.

'Of course,' muttered Geoffroy.

'One would have thought,' added Philip, 'that he'd be frightfully *en colère* – *absolument fou* – seeing us dressed like *this*. But the dear chap seemed positively delighted, didn't he, David?'

'*Absolument*! He was frightfully apologetic, wasn't he, Philip? Mix up at the printers or something.'

Philip nodded and gobbled another pile of smoked salmon. 'I gather,' he managed to say, 'that there's a sort of Roman theme.' He shot a sideways glance at Sophie. 'I suppose no one told you either.'

Sophie was distracted by the spectre of Dominique waddling towards their table with Dakota a few paces behind. 'Sorry?'

'He said you didn't know about the theme,' David explained slowly and loudly, as if interpreting Philip's French.'

'No, I ...' Sophie pursed her lips: the conspirators were both grinning at her impishly as they approached. 'No ... no I didn't.'

'So, you came in your national costume,' David continued. 'How lovely! Wonderful country, India. Do you know Simla?'

Geoffroy was following Sophie's gaze. 'Ah, here come the pederasts.'

Philip and David looked at each other and mumbled 'Oh dear!' simultaneously. Under his breath, David added: 'Maybe it was a blessing in disguise that the *memsahibs* weren't invited after all.'

Dominique, who was carrying two plates of starters for himself, had to decide whether to sit next to stuffy Tiquetorte or a middle-aged man in a grey suit, or strike out for the empty side of the table. He chose Tiquetorte: in a foppish, aristocratic kind of way, he was quite handsome. Dakota dutifully sat next to Dominique, and, to the surprise of both Sophie and Geoffroy, not only remembered the Englishmen's full names but also ensured that they'd been introduced to everyone.

Giggling, Dominique said: 'Bet you anything Phil and Dave's clothes are all held together by metres of Velcro. Any second, they're going to rip them off to reveal pierced nipples and leather posing pouches and dance wildly on the table like John Travolta in *Saturday Night Fever*.'

Completely expressionless, Philip said: 'Spoil sport. You've seen our act before, haven't you?'

Banging the table, Dominique burst out laughing and put a fat arm around Dakota's and Geoffroy's shoulders. '*See*! The English *do* have a sense of humour after all. What a great sandwich – me – a delicious slice of ham – between two divine hunks! Yummy!'

Geoffroy, detaching the offending limb, snarled: 'If you don't mind, Buffet?'

'Oh dear, oh dear! The lady doth protest too much, me thinks. By the way, darling, the name's Dominique and–' He blasted the table with a wild scream. 'Mary, Mother of Christ! Quick – under the table, Sophie. That dyke who's got the hots for you is heading this way with her jolly chum, Madame Cassandre de Tiquetorte. Oh, Geoffroy, darling, does she still like mud wrestling?'

With a mountainous portion of fresh Arcachon Coquilles St. Jacques, Pandore marched towards the table as if storming the Bastille. 'So, this is where you're all hiding!' she roared through a huge smile directed exclusively at Sophie. Scowling at Tiquetorte, she snapped: 'I'd like to sit next to Sophie if you don't mind, Geoffroy. I *strongly* advise you,' she added, just as Cassandre reached the table with a minimalist salad of *mâche*, cherry tomatoes and quails, 'to sit with your *wife*.'

'And I *strongly* advise you to piss off.'

Philip rose from his seat. 'Come on, David, I think we should investigate the main courses.'

As David sadly eyed his unfinished smoked salmon, Pandore cuffed Buffet on the back of the head. 'Bugger me! Your English minders are a bit long in the tooth, Tante Dominique.'

Cassandre lowered herself wearily into the chair next to Dakota. 'Please don't be vulgar, Pandore, dear. And stop teasing Dominique. Now be a good girl and come and sit next to me.'

Sophie feared a riot, but with a conspiratorial wink at her across the table, Pandore dutifully threw herself into a groaning chair. Geoffroy immediately pressed his right knee against Sophie's left, and she experienced a surge of maternal protectiveness. She had to admire his sangfroid in the face of such humiliation before all these people. And the torture he was prepared to endure solely to protect his dreadful spouse from her own self-destructive foolishness was truly inspirational. Out of the blue, she was struck by the thought that marrying Geoffroy might not only be an option for the termination of her own marital slavery, but also a great kindness – an honourable mission to rescue him from what must be a living hell. She tried to imagine herself at a dinner party attempting to cope with Jean-Claude flirting with a gay partner, and shuddered. Geoffroy promptly removed his knee and shot her a perplexed look. Her knee immediately went in search of his as she said brightly:

'I was just thinking of my husband, Dr de Tiquetorte, and how pleased he'll be when I pass on to him the test results which you've just given me. Such wonderful good fortune bumping into you this evening.'

Pandore choked. 'Christ! You're not up the bloody duff, are you, *chérie*?'

Dominique was accurately reading all the signals. Poor Jean-Claude, he thought sadly, tucking into his lobster. It was bizarre that Sophie could prefer Tiquetorte – a pompous bigot – for sweet, cuddly Jean-Claude. What on earth could that toff offer her? More money perhaps, although from what he'd been able to glean from Cassandre, he was certainly no millionaire. Was it the name? Well, Sophie didn't seem the type who was easily impressed by such things as a '*de*', but then one never knew. And he certainly didn't seem to be a bundle of laughs. Or was she just another bored woman a few years off forty, looking for a bit of excitement? Whatever the truth, there was no doubt that Sophie was cold-shouldering him for some reason – and after promising her a show for those pissing awful paintings! Artists! What a temperamental bunch of wankers! Still, they paid the bills, thank God. The money some twats were prepared to pay for crap never ceased to amaze and delight him!

Philip and David returned with generous portions of *ris de veau* and apprehensive expressions as though they were expecting a *crime passionel* to have been committed during their absence.

'You haven't seen a slave girl on your travels, have you?' asked Dakota in English.

Philip raised his eyebrows and found himself incapable of framing a reply.

Seemingly unphased, David said: 'Um … no. … I don't think so. … Actually, slavery's illegal, isn't it? Mind you, I did read an article in the *Daily Telegraph* recently–'

'No, no, David,' Dakota interrupted with a chuckle, '– *here* – at the party!'

'"*The Daily Telegraph*",' Pandore mimicked. 'Jolly good show, old boy!'

Cassandre scowled; Geoffroy snorted.

'*Here*? Oh, I *see*! A slave girl – fancy dress and all that. Sorry!'

'"Sor*reee*"!' Pandore's impersonation was very good.

'My girlfriend,' Dakota explained, 'Tic-Tac.'

'So, you're an *artist*!' intoned Cassandre incredulously, looking across the table at Sophie, who was waiting for Geoffroy to finish his plate of assorted seafood in the hope that they could return to the buffet together. 'Like dear Dakota here,' she added. 'What do you paint exactly?'

Chewing a healthy chunk of offal, Philip said: 'If I'm not mistaken, a slave girl is heading this way as we speak.' He spotted the exposed breasts. 'Oh my giddy aunt!'

'She paints fannies and arseholes!' trumpeted Dominique. 'Right up your street, Cassandre.'

Pandore clenched her fists. 'Far out! Guys' or gals'?'

'Both!' cried Dominique licking his lips. 'In fact, I've already got you two dykes down on the guest list for Sophie's exhibition at my gallery in October.' Sophie gasped. 'Hope you can make it.'

'Where the hell have you been, *bébé*?' asked Dakota as Tic-Tac reached the table. 'I was kinda worried.'

There were two empty seats separating David from Pandore. Tic-Tac scowled at Pandore and opted to sit next to David. He and Philip half rose, crowing '*Bonsoir*'.

'Hi.' Tic-Tac's eyes narrowed as she looked the English up and down. 'I went to our room to get my hay fever pills, and while I was there' – she glanced at Pandore – 'I got locked in. It took ages to attract someone's attention.'

Geoffroy leaned towards Sophie. 'It was probably our fat friend,' he whispered in her ear, '– in order to get her out of the way while he touched up the boy.'

'More tests results, Geoffroy?' queried Cassandre.

'That's right, my love.'

Grinning broadly, Dakota came around the table and smothered Tic-Tac in kisses; Pandore pretended to vomit. 'Now don't get paranoid, *bébé*. I told you – Papa always plays practical jokes at the *Fête*. It's a tradition.'

'The servants get a list,' Cassandre added. 'You're lucky you only got locked in a room, my dear. I mean, look at *these* two.' She stared at the Englishmen, who appeared to be wholly mesmerized by their plates of *ris de veau*. '*They* must feel positively ridiculous.'

'Sorry,' said Philip, 'I think I've lost the thread. French a bit rusty, I'm afraid.'

Dominique shook his head. 'Crap! Your French is bloody brilliant – for an Englishman. No, no! Just kidding! Better than my English for sure.'

Philip glowed with pride. 'That's very kind of you, er …'

'Dominique.'

'Dominique. Very kind indeed.'

'"Very kind in … *deeeed-d-d*",' Pandore mimicked.

David looked hard at her; a mischievous smile slowly formed. 'Got it! Now I know who you remind me of, madame – Edward Heath – *Sir* Edward Heath, I should say. Remember him – the prime minister who took Britain into the Common Market? The same mouth, the same eyes – the same *hairstyle* even. You're the spitting image! And the way you said "indeed" … well, it's uncanny. Frankly–'

'David,' Philip hissed, 'that's enough!'

Pandore was endeavouring to look incandescent. 'You'll regret you said that, my little chubby Englishman. Once dinner is over, you're going to have to dance with me – or take a swim.'

'I'd take a swim if I were you,' Cassandre advised.

'I suppose the military two-step is your dance,' David said raising his glass.

Philip sighed. 'Easy on the *vin rouge*, David.'

'So, how does it feel to be the victims of a practical joke?' sneered Geoffroy, rising from his seat; Sophie looked up at him expectantly. 'Ready for the next course, Madame Bourjois?' Sophie nodded and he pulled the chair back for her.

Cassandre tutted. 'For Christ's sake, Geoffroy, call her "Sophie". That's how you usually address her, isn't it – at least in bed?'

'I'll come with you,' Dakota said swiftly. 'I need to get some food for Tic-Tac. What would you like, *bébé*?'

'Can't she get her own bloody food?' mocked Pandore.

'Practical joke?' responded Philip finally.

Dakota groaned. 'Yeah, like Tic-Tac. ... Look, I'm really sorry, guys – so embarrassing. Your invitations and all that crap about lounge suits. Well, every year Papa invites two ... um, how can I put it?'

'Boring old farts?' suggested Pandore.

'Well, two foreign pillars of society, and ... and ...'

'Say no more, dear boy,' said Philip. 'We get the picture. Mind you, I seriously doubt that *we* could be described as "pillars of society".'

'Charming!' sniggered David.

'But if you survive the course,' Cassandre said, 'you win a prize, and they're usually very nice prizes.'

'"Survive the course"?' queried David. 'I'm not sure I like the sound of that.'

During the next hour or so, the table of nine settled into a fairly comfortable routine of eating, drinking and conversation. Although nothing contentious or profound was said, no one was bored or fractious – no one, that is, except Geoffroy. Having stunned himself by proposing marriage to Sophie, he really needed some peaceful contemplation to ascertain whether this was a sensible idea or not. But trying to think clearly was proving impossible, what with the constant hubbub of inane chatter going on around him, coupled with the incessant wailing of the mind-numbingly awful 'music'. And to make matters worse, everyone was talking about 'Art'. Apart from a few brief interludes when he'd returned to the buffet to sample another delicacy, Philip had monopolized Sophie for at least half an hour with a monologue on British post-war painters; he claimed to own 'quite a reasonable collection'. Sophie was obligingly enthusiastic, albeit Geoffroy suspected that she was only being polite. In any event, the names batted around by the two of them – 'Hockney', 'Bacon', 'Hoyland' – meant absolutely nothing to him. To be fair to Sophie, she did make several efforts to involve her lover in the conversation, but because his lamentable ignorance of the subject was so glaringly obvious, she only managed to make him feel even more uncomfortable.

On his other side, adding fuel to the fire, were chichi Buffet and his catamite. They, too, were ignoring him, which, in truth, was a relief: they were droning on and on about Dakota's 'style', 'visions', 'ambitions' and 'hopes'. On the other hand, he overheard statements evincing that there was no question of Buffet handling the brat's work: he'd yet to produce sufficient canvases to merit any kind of exhibition; moreover, his current interest in 'soft focus quasi-photographic realism' – whatever that might be – was not at all the sort of thing Buffet dealt in. Lacking an opportunity, Geoffroy had yet to relay this information to Sophie. In any event, to avoid rendering his isolation absolute by effecting a rapprochement between her and Buffet, he thought it better to postpone any disclosure.

Meanwhile, Cassandre and Pandore were oddly businesslike as they discussed arrangements for entering several of their Labradors in shows around the country. And after a hesitant start, Tic-Tac and David were chatting thirteen to the dozen, although with all the background noise Geoffroy wasn't sure of the subject matter. However, the words 'Normandie', 'Queen Elizabeth' and 'liberté' had cropped up several times, so he assumed they were having some boring historical discussion, with David lecturing the halfwit about how England once ruled France, and the halfwit telling David that it was about time England had a 1789-style revolution and executed the entire dysfunctional Royal Family, along with the aristocracy. She looked like a communist, Geoffroy concluded – the sort who liked to preach revolution at decadent parties, such as this, and who, thanks to millionaire parents and 'partners' – to use that dreadful contemporary term – had never done a day's work in their pathetic lives, and never would do.

Reaching the end of his tether, Geoffroy drained his glass and signalled to a hovering wine waiter.

'Yes, sir. Red or white, sir?'

'Red of course! Can't you see I've got a plate of cheese in front of me?'

'Yes indeed, sir, but many people prefer white with cheese these days, especially with the softer cheeses, such as–'

'Don't lecture *me*, sonny!'

'Sorry, sir.'

'I don't give a damn about what "*people*" do! Just do your bloody job and pour me a glass of *red* wine.' Conversation around the table had fizzled out, and Geoffroy realised that everyone was looking at him. 'The most damnable thing,' he said, trying to control himself, '– bloody waiter trying to tell me what to drink – *me*!'

'I assure you, sir–'

'My family, sonny, owned some of the finest vineyards in Pauillac for over three hundred bloody years and–'

'"*Owned*" being the operative word,' Cassandre snapped.

Momentarily, the corners of Geoffroy's mouth scowled downwards. 'I mean,' he pressed on rapidly, 'no one in Bordeaux drinks *white* wine with *cheese*.' He laughed nervously. 'Do they?'

'Oh, *what* are you like, you Bordeaux folk?' chided Dominique. 'Such a lot of fussy queens I never did meet!' He grabbed a piece of Reblochon from Geoffroy's plate, took a swig from his own glass of white, and then repeated the process with a gulp from Dakota's glass of red. He burped explosively – much to Dakota's and Pandore's amusement – and announced that he preferred the white.

For a few seconds, Geoffroy remained speechless. He just stared at Buffet, who, gargling with a mouthful of Badoit, was continuing his party tricks.

Philip said – loudly in French – as the dejected waiter passed him: 'Actually, Geoffroy, I've always been slightly mystified by the rigidity of the Bordelais in insisting on *red* wine with cheese.'

'Oh?' he snarled.

'In my humble opinion,' Philip continued in French, 'great red wines are positively massacred by powerful cheeses. The only survivors are acidic or sweet whites.'

Geoffroy snorted. 'Well, being *English* you'd be an *expert*. I mean *England* is world-famous for its cheeses – and wines, isn't it? The names just slip off the tongue, don't they, everyone?'

Taking a cigarillo out of a silver case, Cassandre said: 'For God's sake, Geoffroy, be a dear and lighten up.'

Sophie smiled nervously at her lover; she knew it was a very difficult evening for him. She wasn't exactly sure what Cassandre was smoking, but she suspected it wasn't an ordinary cigar. 'Well, I love English Cheddar,' she said, tapping Philip's hand, 'but I agree with Geoffroy – red wine for me every time with cheese – and especially with Cheddar.'

'Oh yes,' David agreed, with the sort of exaggerated hand gestures brought on by inebriation. 'With a fine claret you can't beat traditional English cheeses – Lancashire, Wensleydale, Double Gloucester–'

'I could just eat a great lump of Stilton!' enthused Dominique.

'Me too!' cried Dakota.

'I prefer that Welsh one,' Tic-Tac mumbled with a tone almost amounting to merriment. 'What's it called?'

'Caerphilly?' prompted David.

'That's it!'

'So much for patriotism!' roared Pandore playfully as she thumped Tic-Tac in the ribs.

Cassandre blew a cloud of smoke into the air. 'I really don't know what you're all talking about. Frankly, I'd no idea one could buy such things as *English* cheeses in Bordeaux.'

Sophie was about to say that her dear little cheese man in Rue Montesquieu had rather a nice selection, when Geoffroy snapped: 'Who the hell cares, anyway? Their cheeses will be full of mad cow disease.'

David groaned theatrically; Philip began laughing – or rather braying. 'My dear chap, you can't believe such nonsense, surely?'

Geoffroy knew he was on very shaky ground and waived an arm dismissively. 'Anyway, your friend here has admitted that *red* Bordeaux is best with those English cheeses he mentioned.'

Philip continued to smile pleasantly. 'Absolutely! I, too, love claret with cheddar. But what *I* said was that *fine* red wines and *powerful* cheeses don't mix.'

'Exactly,' Dakota agreed nodding. 'That's what Philip said all right. Spot on if you ask me.'

'Ah, the Boy Wonder agrees,' Geoffroy mocked. 'What a surprise, but then you're not a Bordelais either, are you?'

Dominique puffed up his ample chest. 'Why don't you pick on someone your own size – and age – darling? And what's the big deal about being Bordelais? Anyway, who around this table, apart from you and old Cassandre, are actually from bloody Bordeaux?'

'Well,' said Cassandre, 'I don't normally rush to my husband's defence, but as a Bordelaise I think all Geoffroy is saying is that here in our region we have a tradition of drinking red wine with cheese. It's something we've been brought up with, and we like it. The Germans drink beer with everything, the English love tea with fish and chips – or so I've heard – and the Americans are never happier than when they've got a can of Coca-Cola in their hands. *Chacun à son goût.*'

And that seemed to be that: Cassandre had had the last word; Dominique left to get some more pudding; Dakota and Tic-Tac decided to go and dance down by the pool, where some brave souls had initiated proceedings; Pandore moved into Tic-Tac's empty chair.

'You and the airhead seem to be getting on like a house on fire,' she said to David as he finished the last of the cheese and grapes on his plate.

'Airhead?'

'The bimbo, that Tic-Tac.'

'Ah.'

'Fancy her, do you?'

'My dear Pandore, I'm a happily married slave with a dear spouse in leafy Surrey. In any event, sweet Tic-Tac's far from being any of the nasty things you called her. *Au contraire*, she's a–'

'A communist, if you ask me,' Geoffroy grunted from across the table. 'Looks the sort.' Sophie turned her head sharply and stared hard at him.

'You need help, mate,' Pandore said.

'Well,' David continued, 'I really wouldn't know about that. All I can say is that she's a very intelligent and interesting young woman. She's studying naval architecture at university. ... I think she said Hamburg ... or was it Bremen? – no matter. Speaks fluent German, of course.'

'Ships are one of David's hobbies,' Philip explained.

'Quite so,' David admitted. 'Well, dear Tic-Tac–'

'"*Dear* Tic-Tac"?' scoffed Pandore.

'Dear Tic-Tac has written a fascinating thesis on the little-known design defects of some of the greatest transatlantic liners – all sorts of nasty engineering problems which the shipping lines hushed up at the time.'

'How *interesting*,' Cassandre murmured, pulling a bored face at Geoffroy, who responded similarly while secretly experiencing amazement at Tic-Tac's hidden talents.

'Absolutely,' David went on. 'The things I've learned this evening about the *Queen Mary* – and the *Queen Elizabeth* – and the *Normandie* – and the dear old *Liberté* – just fascinating!'

Geoffroy fumed inwardly.

'Steady on, old boy,' Philip said. 'Perhaps now's the time for that dance you've been promised by Pandore.'

She slapped David on the back. 'Oh yeah! Come on, Englishman!'

'Well – I … This pop music stuff really isn't–' She dragged him to his feet.

'If you're not back in fifteen minutes,' Philip sniggered, 'I'll text London to advertise your job in *Wine Wisdom*.'

Pandore and David almost collided with Dominique, who was returning with two plates of assorted *tartes* and *gâteaux*. 'Come and sit in Dakota's seat, Cassandre. You and me can have a good gossip at last about the old crowd in Paris and everything.'

Geoffroy groaned. 'Christ! Let's dance, Sophie.' He rose and offered her his arm.

'"*Dance*"!' exploded Dominique. '*You*? I wouldn't have thought Techno was quite your thing, darling.'

Sophie stood up and looked at Casandre nervously.

'Oh, go ahead, my dear. Be careful though – he's got two left feet.'

'Please excuse us,' Sophie said to Philip politely.

'You carry on.' He paused. 'I hope David took his pills tonight.'

'Pills?' Sophie looked concerned. 'What's wrong with him?'

'His heart. Please don't let Pandore wear him out, will you?'

Standing at the terrace rail a short while later, Philip spotted his colleague and the mighty Pandore in the thick of the scrum to one side of the illuminated pool. Everyone was gyrating robotically, except David: he was managing a rather sedate twist-like motion, the only 'modern' dance movement known to him. Thankfully, he – or Pandore – had removed his suit jacket. Philip hoped it was in a safe place: one never knew who was present at parties. Out of the corner of his eye, he saw Sophie and Geoffroy join the dancers, albeit the obnoxious Frenchman appeared even more rhythmically challenged than David. After only a few minutes, they left the dance floor and went to stand at one corner of the pool. Philip's eyes returned to David and Pandore. He'd just resolved to go down himself and rescue the poor chap, when, to his relief, she led him to one of the tables on the other side of the pool, where they sat down laughing. As Philip waved from his lookout, he noticed Sophie and Geoffroy walking away from the throng along a meandering gravel path.

CHAPTER 18

Due to his forced attendances of Forgeron's *Fêtes de la Fleur* over the years, Geoffroy had become well acquainted with the layout of the host's Cap Ferret villa and its garden. Indeed, it had become his custom to escape the bedlam and, accompanied by a suitable female partner, make temporary use of the guest cottage situated in the pines just a few minutes' walk along the path to the beach. Tonight was not going to be an exception. Luckily, although some guests were staying there, they'd left the doors unlocked and the lights burning – just as he'd anticipated. Despite her initial reluctance to invade someone else's privacy, Sophie was persuaded to join him on the living room sofa. It was here that he earnestly confirmed his desire to divorce Cassandre; her relationship with Pandore would be sufficient grounds. Yet, as he spoke, the thought occurred to Sophie that, in the light of various remarks by Dominique during the course of the evening, Cassandre's lesbian tendencies must have been evident for many years. It was odd, therefore, that Geoffroy had not sought a divorce long ago, especially as there were no children – at least, not as far as she was aware.

Placing an arm around Sophie's shoulders, Geoffroy went on to say that after several months of intimacy, he was convinced they'd make a perfect match, and that as her marriage was undeniably dead, divorcing Jean-Claude would make complete sense. Nevertheless, he didn't want to rush her into anything. Above all, in view of the mistake she'd made in marrying Jean-Claude – a rash decision which, amongst other things, had alienated her beloved parents – it was vitally important that they should approve of himself from the outset. In fact, it was his firm desire to effect a rapprochement between Sophie and her parents – a dear couple, no doubt, who, one had to remember, were not getting any younger, and who deserved to see more of both their daughter and grandson. And talking of Alexandre, he was another person whose best interests had to be considered carefully: before any irrevocable decision was taken, the boy and himself should meet in order to ensure that they could be friends – no, more than friends – like father and son.

'Well,' said Sophie admitting to herself that everything Geoffroy had said made perfect sense, 'I'm sure you and Alexandre will get on like a house on fire – you've much in common. But you're right, of course. You should meet him as soon as possible. Maybe you could come over to the studio one day ... once his school breaks up for the summer vacation ... in a fortnight, I think. ... You could pretend to be a client or something.'

Geoffroy nodded slowly. 'Possibly. We need to think about it.' He sighed and looked deep into her eyes. 'I can't promise you a fortune, Sophie. I'm not a rich man – oh, I make a comfortable living, of course, and I've two nice houses but–'

'Oh please, Geoffroy, I'm not a fortune seeker!'

'No, no! Of course not! I didn't mean – that is ... I–'

'So, Cassandre has no interest in Rue d'Aviau then?'

Surprised by the question, Geoffroy briefly hesitated. 'Er, no. I gave her the house near Périgueux in return for her relinquishing any claims to Rue d'Aviau.'

'Oh, I see.' It was Sophie's turn to pause for a few seconds, nodding slowly. 'Anyway,' she continued, flashing a smile, 'I could be a rich woman myself soon, Dr de Tiquetorte.'

'Oh?'

'I told you just before that bloody gong fiasco. Weren't you listening – Buffet's proposed prices for *Les Orifices* and all that? I don't know, but I always find talking about money so embarrassing. ... I suppose I shouldn't count my chickens until they hatch but ... well, having told everyone over dinner that the show's still on, he wouldn't dare go back on his word, would he?'

Geoffroy tried hard not to look excited. 'No, I suppose not. By the way, what were those prices you mentioned? Figures! You know me, in one ear and out the other.' She told him again, and, with his estimation of her marriageability reinforced, he kissed her lustily. 'Congratulations, Sophie! Wonderful! It's ... it's what you deserve, I'm sure. Fame at last!'

'The only cloud on the horizon now is Dakota. I do hope Buffet doesn't dump me for him at the last minute!'

Geoffroy slapped his forehead. 'Sorry! Silly me! Forgot to tell you! Buffet will definitely *not* be exhibiting that little tick's works. Apparently, he doesn't like the kid's style or something. I heard them chatting at dinner.'

'Oh, Geoffroy! Why the hell didn't you tell me before, you chump?

But Sophie was so relieved that she flung her arms around his neck and kissed him with all the passion she could muster. Within seconds they were tearing at each other's clothes.

*

When Jean-Claude phoned Denise on his mobile from outside Le Porge's church, it was immediately obvious that she'd been happily watching television – not comforting a runaway child. He pretended that he was at home and had merely phoned to ask her to bring an extra baguette on Monday morning just in case Monsieur Buffet stayed over on Sunday night. Then he dashed back, praying for a miracle, but there was just a subdued Richelieu to greet him. Finally, he plucked up sufficient courage to phone Sophie and inform her of Alexandre's disappearance – only to discover her mobile ringing furiously in the bedroom, where she'd dumped it with her beach things. Directory Enquiries were uncooperative: if there was a Forgeron at Cap Ferret, he was ex-directory. So, Jean-Claude telephoned Château Forgeron itself and eventually procured the Cap Ferret number from a bilious major-domo, who, in a fit of indiscretion, doubted the caller would get any sense from anyone at the villa. The prediction proved correct: on each of his six calls, he found himself talking to someone who, for some extraordinary reason, thought he was playing a practical joke. In the end, he jumped back into the car. Within forty minutes he was being interrogated by a group of suspicious centurions.

Out on the terrace, Cassandre was enthusiastically describing for Dominique's benefit the demise of Pandore's predecessor.

'... a *Bretonne*, darling, whose two passions were bricklaying and motorbikes. She came off her Harley-Davidson on a nasty bend between Périgueux and Brantôme and–'

Dominique let out a shriek and grabbed Cassandre's arm. 'Jesus Christ! Jean-Claude's over there with that gorgeous centurion I fancy. What the hell's he doing here?'

Cassandre turned her head. 'Hmm. Don't know about the centurion, but the other one's rather dishy. Who is he?'

'*Jean-Claude*. Oh, he's spotted me! Coo-eee! ... He's Sophie's husband and–'

'Oh, my God!' they chorused, staring in horror at the empty seats formerly occupied by Sophie and Tiquetorte.

Once Dominique had vouched for him and the centurion had retreated, Jean-Claude endeavoured to explain his presence, while Dominique gasped, groaned and patted the frantic father's hand. Meanwhile, just a few seats away, Philip was joined by Comte Bertrand d'Expiremont, the owner of an excellent Moulis *cru bourgeois* – another wine in Larboard & Chitterling's stable. Dressed in drag and claiming to be Cleopatra, Expiremont promptly confessed a lifelong desire for a sex change. Acutely embarrassed, Philip tuned in to the neighbouring conversation between Dominique and the new arrival.

Pushing aside a half-consumed mountain of meringues, Dominique tried to rise. 'I think you should stay here, Jean-Claude, while I go in search of Sophie. Then we can all go home together. I think we'll have to inform the police, don't you?'

Philip leaned over. 'Sorry to butt in, Dominique, but do I gather there's a spot of bother? If you're looking for Sophie–?'

'Yes, I am,' cried Jean-Claude, '– *desperately*!'

'Oh right. Well … um, about twenty minutes ago I saw her walking in the garden with that chap Geoffroy – the gentleman who was sitting next to her during dinner.'

'Oh *fuck*!' shrieked Dominique, slumping back into his chair.

'*Perfide Albion*!' muttered Cassandre.

Within seconds, Philip was pointing out the path.

As Jean-Claude sped off, Dominique grabbed Cassandre's arm. 'We'd better go after him,' he wailed. 'God only knows what he might do – even murder your husband!'

'*Really*? I wouldn't miss that for the world! Chop-chop! There's no time to lose!'

When Jean-Claude peered through the guest cottage's open French windows into a softly-lit living room, he was confronted by the back of a naked man having sex with someone lying on the floor. Then he recognised Sophie's grunts, groans and cries of 'Oh *yes*!' Dominique and Cassandre, though still some fifty metres back along the path, heard Jean-Claude's roar of rage and Sophie's screams. When they reached the French windows, their pounding hearts beat even faster: Geoffroy – wailing 'My teeth! My teeth!' – was lying in a corner next to a devastated television set with blood pouring from his mouth; Jean-Claude was violently shaking a hysterically sobbing Sophie.

'Our son's missing,' he yelled, 'and you're fucking this bastard!' He snatched her sari off the sofa. 'Get this fucking thing on *now*!'

Frozen to the spot, Dominique watched with fascinated horror, but Cassandre started laughing. 'Oh *yes*!' she gloated. 'This is just *wonderful* – better than anything Vincent could have organized! The best party *ever*!'

Geoffroy began to crawl around the floor on all fours. 'My teeth! My bloody front teeth! Cassandre, help me! *Help* me!' But she just shook her head contemptuously and laughed even louder.

Dominique finally took a step forward. 'Let me help Sophie with the sari, Jean-Claude,' he pleaded. 'I–'

'Don't touch her, you fucking pimp! Did you get some weird kick out of fixing her up with this piece of shit? Jean-Claude lunged; Dominique screamed and fled out the French windows.

Fumbling with the sari, Sophie shrieked: 'Don't hurt him! My exhibition! You're ruining *everything*!'

'And *you*!' roared Jean-Claude, turning to Cassandre, '– shut the fuck up!'

But Geoffroy's announcement between choking sobs that he'd found one of his front teeth, made Cassandre laugh hysterically, whereupon Dominique rushed back into the room and dragged her outside. 'I always tell myself never to get involved in domestic tiffs,' he hissed, 'but here I am again being wrongly abused. Somehow I don't think Jean-Claude will be giving me a lift home, do you, darling?' Cassandre just continued laughing her head off.

When Sophie finally managed to get into the sari, Jean-Claude frogmarched her outside, leaving Geoffroy – still naked – blubbing about his devastated teeth and the impossibility of allowing a living soul to see him in this state.

'Please let me come with you,' Dominique pleaded as the Bourjoises passed him. 'You've got it all wrong, Jean-Claude. Cassandre and me had nothing to do with this. We can't stand that Geoffroy git. We–'

Giving him an almighty shove, coupled with another blast of 'Fuck off!', Dominique fell backwards into the shrubbery, crushing an oleander.

The sight of a tall, dark, handsome man almost dragging an extremely agitated woman in a sari – *the* woman in a sari who'd fouled up the great gong-banging ceremony – surprised few of the guests who witnessed it: the general assumption was that yet more scheduled entertainment was being acted out for their benefit. After all, ten minutes earlier, Expiremont had pushed a fully clothed Philip into the swimming pool; he'd been rushing to David's side after a distraught centurion had deliberately misinformed him that his friend had suffered a heart attack. Back on terra firma, however, Forgeron presented both Englishmen with a magnum bottle of 1982 Château Latour for their sportsmanship, which, true to form, they graciously accepted.

Yet, Forgeron was not amused by the spectacle of the sari-clad woman being frogmarched through his party by an apparently outraged partner. Thanks to Cassandre, he knew all about Geoffroy's predilections – in particular, that at almost every *Fête de la Fleur* he lured a victim to the guesthouse. In truth, for the previous five years, his exploits had been secretly videoed and a copy given to Cassandre for her amusement. This year, it had been Forgeron's plan to screen the video as the pièce de résistance of the night's proceedings. Now he was wondering whether the screening would have to be dropped – even whether he should intervene in the fracas. But before he could reach a decision on the latter, the fleeing couple had already reached the upper terrace.

*

Overwhelmed by shock, humiliation, embarrassment and grief, Sophie behaved robotically and did exactly what Jean-Claude told her. With only a lame protest that they couldn't abandon Buffet, she got into the car. She was still closing the door when he put his foot down and the ageing Peugeot sped away from the villa in a storm of flying gravel.

For a few minutes neither of them said a word. Finally, after blowing her nose on a tissue she'd found in the door pocket, Sophie said: 'What did you mean – about Alexandre – gone? *Gone? Gone where? When?* You haven't … you haven't upset him, have you? – *done* anything?'

Jean-Claude stared fixedly ahead. 'What the *hell* do you mean? Of course I haven't! – or "done" *anything*! *I'm* not the one who's filled his head with ideas about going off to Paris to live – buying your "ticket to freedom" – isn't that what you told him? Us living separate lives – me here, and you and Alexandre in Paris with your "sophisticated" friends. Well, if that bunch tonight are a representative sample – Jesus! I can't believe that you and that – that *fucking* doctor – Henri's best friend – *him* – of *all* people – that *you*–!'

'Well, thanks to *you*, nobody will be going to Paris now. And for God's sake stop bloody swearing! I've never heard you use that word before! And don't change the subject! It's Alexandre, for Christ's sake – my baby – we should be talking about.' She began to weep. 'We've got to find him! Where've you looked? When did you last see him? I just don't understand it. Alexandre would never run away – *never*! Oh, God, something awful must have happened! I'm being punished for my sins! *Please*, God, *please* don't let any harm come to him!'

After blowing her nose again, Sophie repeated her questions and Jean-Claude wearily told her of his searches of the house and grounds, his discovery of the missing bike, and his frantic drives around Le Porge. Talking seemed to calm him.

'But *when* did you last see him?' she croaked, '– before or after supper?'

Ignoring her, Jean-Claude snapped: 'Was he all right this morning? Did he do or say anything which seemed odd or unusual?' He finally shot her a glance. 'Christ! – you don't think Buffet might have done something? Did you leave him alone with him?' He began shaking his head and groaning. 'Maybe the guy's a … Oh, Sophie, if that bastard has tried any funny business – if he's laid one finger on our boy, I'll – I'll … You brought that pervert into our house! You–!'

'Stop it! What the hell are you talking about? You're jumping to all sorts of vile conclusions. You don't know anything. Buffet isn't … he isn't–'

'You don't *know*!'

'And nor do you!'

All of a sudden, Sophie remembered Buffet's request for *Le Figaro*, Alexandre's reluctance to cycle into Le Porge, and … and … Had she seen him since? … Had she? She couldn't remember! After a few moments, she said: 'We've got to stop arguing. We have to think calmly. Maybe he went to Denise's – or a friend's house.'

'You know perfectly well that he doesn't have any friends in Le Porge. And he hates Denise. Anyway, I phoned her. He's not there.'

'Jesus! Now it'll be all round–'

He cut her short and explained his subterfuge, but she didn't seem to follow.

'When *did* you last see him, Jean-Claude? I keep asking you, but you don't answer. … Come on – *tell* me!'

Hesitantly, he began his confession: he hadn't, in fact, seen Alexandre since his departure for La Fayette after breakfast, albeit the lad could have been in the house at some time after his return, as he'd assumed. His voice, however, became a blur: Sophie's thoughts kept returning to the undoubted destruction of her relationship with Buffet. And yet, every time she experienced a flashback to that scene in the guesthouse when Jean-Claude laid into Geoffroy like a prizefighter, she was shocked by the realisation that the brutality and unprecedented obscenities aroused her. By contrast, Geoffroy had behaved like a complete wimp. In truth, he'd behaved like a reactionary, homophobic prig all evening. But then, to be fair, he'd been worrying about Cassandre and her 'problem'.

Would he ever meet Alexandre now? … Oh, Alexandre was too sensible to do anything silly! He had to be safe and sound – somewhere. … But did she really want him to meet Geoffroy? … Why had he stayed married to a lesbian for twenty years? … To her shame, she tried to picture him without his front teeth, and wondered what he'd look like with false ones.

When they were only a few kilometres from home, Jean-Claude said: 'What puzzles me is the missing bike. He hates that bike – always has done. What would make him use it now?'

Experiencing another playback of Jean-Claude's powerful punch to Geoffroy's chin, Sophie thoughtlessly responded: 'Well, he used it this morning because I sent him to Le Porge to get the *Figaro* for Dominique.'

From that starting point, a determined line of questioning inexorably brought two equally incredulous parents to the startling conclusion that Sophie hadn't seen Alexandre since she'd instructed him to fetch the newspaper! Recriminations flew as the horror of the situation sank in. They didn't even know if Buffet had ever received his damned paper, though Sophie felt sure he had because there'd been no indication that he hadn't – and Buffet was not slow in coming forward. But *he* was back at Cap Ferret and God only knew how he felt about being liberally insulted, assaulted and abandoned. Sophie couldn't restrain herself from firing a barrage of criticism of Jean-Claude's treatment of their guest, but that merely served to rekindle the flames of his anger and to provoke a graphic reminder of precisely what had caused Buffet's abandonment.

As they roared down the final stretch of road, Jean-Claude said anxiously: 'How do you think the police will react when we tell them that although neither of us had seen Alexandre since before midday, we did nothing until after nine p.m.?'

Stunned by the question, Sophie was speechless. In the silence, Jean-Claude pictured the bottles of wine in his office at La Fayette. A police investigation! They'd start with Alexandre's disappearance, probe and investigate, find out about the party at Cap Ferret, talk to Tiquetorte, make enquiries at La Fayette, and interrogate his colleagues. Lots of little jigsaw pieces. They'd start putting them together and–

'Jean-Claude! Are you listening? I said we can't tell the police.'

'What?'

'We can't tell them about all this.'

'All *what*?'

'For Christ's sake – about not seeing Alexandre all day, of course!'

'Don't be stupid! Lying will only make matters worse. Someone might have seen him at the very moment when we're claiming he was at home. And, when found, Alexandre could – almost certainly would – contradict us. Then the police would make fresh enquiries into why we'd lied!'

They were still arguing about when to notify the police and what to say to them as Jean-Claude brought the car to a screeching halt at their front door. They both jumped out.

'Maybe he's back,' Sophie wailed, '– or did *you* leave all the lights on?

'Yes, and the door unlocked.'

'Jesus, I hope we haven't been burgled! I mean–'

Jean-Claude seized her by the arms as she was about to open the door. 'Money and possessions! That's all you ever bloody think about. They're all you've *ever* thought about. I just don't understand you. Our little boy has disappeared and–'

He broke off as the door began to open; Sophie cried out in horror. A filthy urchin covered in scratches and bruises and dressed in rags appeared before them clutching a huge half-eaten sandwich.

'Alexandre!'

'Darling!'

Despite the boy's protests about his bruises, he was attacked from both sides by hugs and kisses, followed by a bombardment of questions, protestations of love, admissions of terror, and confessions of parental deficiencies. Alexandre, however, appeared wholly bemused and said nothing.

'God only knows what's happened to him,' Jean-Claude whispered. 'We'll have to examine him. If ... if anyone's *done* anything to him, I'll – I'll–'

'He's in shock. Let's get these filthy clothes off him and bathe him. Go and run the bath, Jean-Claude, and I'll get the first aid box. Come on, Alexandre, everything's all right, darling. You're safe now.'

Jean-Claude lifted the boy into his arms and moved towards the stairs. 'Do you think we should send for a doctor?'

Sophie hesitated. 'No – not just yet.'

Jean-Claude concurred, albeit with a hint of unconvincing reluctance.

Halfway up the stairs, Alexandre said: 'I wondered where you both were when I got back. I suppose it was your night off, Dubois.' Wholly confused, Jean-Claude was still thinking of a response when Alexandre added: 'I really don't think you and Madame Dubois should have rows here, you know. If you must have rows, you should do so in the servants' quarters and not in the Royal Apartments.'

When Sophie entered the bathroom with the first aid box, Jean-Claude murmured that Alexandre was obviously hallucinating, and, judging by all the bruises, had had a very serious knock to his head; he feared concussion. 'I think he should have an X-ray – a brain scan – whatever, as soon as possible.'

Sophie, on the other hand, expressed her own concerns about how they could explain this ghastly state of affairs to *anyone*. She suggested they should wait and see how he was in the morning; Jean-Claude didn't object. As they bathed him, Alexandre was again asked what had befallen him, but he merely shook his head. Then, after the shampoo had been rinsed from his hair, he said boldly:

'You're not Le Grand Condé's spies, are you?'

His parents looked at each other and sighed. 'No, of course we're not,' they chorused.

'You *are* loyal servants of the King?' he asked earnestly.

They nodded.

Whispering to Sophie, Jean-Claude asked: 'Who's "Le Grand Condé"? – rings a bell.'

'Wasn't he a royal prince and one of Louis XIV's generals?'

'What are you two whispering about?'

'Oh, just reminding Papa about Le Grand Condé, darling.'

'Louis II de Bourbon, fourth Prince de Condé,' Alexandre declaimed, 'is the King's most trusted general, but during the civil wars of the Frondes he was always changing sides. Cardinal Mazarin had him imprisoned, you know. Then Condé went and joined the Spaniards and was condemned to death for treason. Terribly arrogant chap with unrestrained temper and limitless pride – in himself, his race and his house. I said he couldn't be trusted, but the King wouldn't listen to me.'

Sophie and Jean-Claude exchanged worried looks. 'We'd better get him to bed,' Sophie said. 'Come on, Alexandre, out of the bath and let's get dry and warm.'

As Sophie rubbed him gently with the towel, Alexandre said: 'Anyway, this morning – or yesterday – or … well, whenever – I was entrusted with a vitally important mission to procure secret papers from Paris.'

'I think he means Le Figaro,' Sophie murmured.

'And having saddled my trusty steed I set off on the turnpike to the capital. I had not gone far through the Bois de Boulogne when I espied far off a silver steed galloping towards me in the centre of the highway. At first, I thought nothing of it, believing, not unreasonably I think, that the fellow would move to his side of the turnpike and pass me on the left as is customary – and indeed required by Royal Decree.'

Jean-Claude picked up Alexandre and cradled the boy in his strong arms. 'Come on, young fellow, you've had an exciting day by all accounts. You can tell us the rest of your adventures in the morning.' As an aside to Sophie, he added softly: 'From what I can see, I don't think anyone's … I mean, there's no sign of any … *interference*. He'll be OK.'

Once safely tucked up in bed, Alexandre said: 'The fellow came straight for me, Dubois. He was clearly trying to force me off the turnpike and into the dyke. Had I not reined my mount violently to the right at the last moment, well, I fear there would have been a most terrible accident. As it was, the poor beast flew into perilous waters, but I was thrown clear over its head and across the dyke into the forest.

'I suspect I may have collided with a tree and been knocked unconscious. Be that as it may, when I finally came round, I feared for my life in view of the murderous attack upon me by that treacherous knave. He and his men, no doubt, were combing the forest for me. And so, I crawled deeper into the Bois and sought to conceal myself until nightfall. I wandered for many a long hour hoping to come across a woodman's crude cottage and procure both sustenance and directions to the Palace, but not a living soul crossed my path. And then, just when I began to fear that the Almighty had forsaken me, I did espy a dim light through the trees. With fresh hope in my heart, I fought my way through the thick undergrowth, and, thanking God for his mercy, finally found myself at the perimeter walls of the great park with the Palace grandly illuminated in the distance as if for one of His Majesty's *Grandes Fêtes*. I must say, Dubois, I was singularly disappointed by the absence of both the Court and the servants upon my return, for I had sorely wished to communicate Le Grand Condé's crime forthwith to His Majesty.'

And with that, Alexandre closed his eyes and appeared to fall asleep.

'I'd better stay with him,' Sophie whispered. 'Could you fetch the old camp bed? I think it's in the store room.'

Jean-Claude nodded. '*I'll* stay with him, if you like.'

Sophie shook her head. 'No ... no thanks.'

Jean-Claude was about to leave the room when both he and Sophie were startled by Alexandre's voice.

'It *was* him, you know!' he exclaimed pushing himself up. 'I saw him as his silver steed thundered by. I'd observed him not long ago, you see ... at the Sorbonne ... collecting his evil son. I will never forget Le Grand Condé's face. I must tell my father, the King, for I fear that he is in mortal danger!'

*

Jean-Claude was awakened from a terrible nightmare by his own cry. The visions of unspeakable horrors involving both his wife and son were so vile that he began to sob. The corridor light came on, and Sophie appeared in the doorway.

'Are you all right? ... My God, you're crying.' It was the first time she'd ever seen him shed tears. She came and sat on the bed. 'Want to talk about it?' He shook his head. 'That bad, eh? Sighing, she stood up and made to return to Alexandre's room.

'What time is it, Sophie?'

She peered at the alarm clock on the bedside table. 'Er ... just after four-thirty.'

'Thanks.' He wiped away the tears with the back of his hand. 'Is Alexandre OK?'

'Fast asleep. He woke up once – shortly after you went to bed – complaining of a nasty headache. I gave him paracetamol and he quickly nodded off again. ... I'm going to take him into Bordeaux in the morning for a complete check-up. His health is more important than anything – certainly more than our selfish sensitivities.'

Jean-Claude nodded. 'Good.' As Sophie moved towards the door, he asked: 'Do you love him?' She spun round.

'Alexandre? Of course I do! What a bloody silly–!'

'No, no – not Alexandre … *him* … that–'

'Oh, the *doctor*.' She leaned against the doorframe. 'I've been asking myself the same question for hours. … No – no, I don't love him, Jean-Claude.'

He began shaking his head. 'Then *why*, for God's sake?'

An incredulous expression appeared on Sophie's face 'Why? Why do you think? For sex – fun – a laugh – to feel desired – for excitement. Remember any of those things, Jean-Claude?'

Staring at his hands, he said meekly: 'Have there … been … others?'

Sophie snorted. 'I *wish*!' After a few seconds she said softly: 'I don't know why I said that. … No, there haven't been "others". I've never even consciously looked for anyone else. It was Cathérine who introduced me to Geoffroy – months ago – as a possible client.'

'Cathérine? *Months* ago? You mean tonight wasn't the first …?'

Returning to the bed, Sophie sat down and recounted the whole story; Jean-Claude remained silent throughout. Finally, she stood up, saying: 'I must check on Alexandre.'

'You'd better come back once you've done that. Tiquetorte's a crook, Sophie. I was going to tell you everything on Thursday night, but – damn that Cathérine!'

At first, Sophie couldn't help wondering whether Jean-Claude's bizarre tale about Henri de Bondé's involvement in fraudulent practices was an extraordinary fabrication intended to ensure Geoffroy's alienation, or, alternatively, that it was a desperate attempt by a shell-shocked husband to win his wife's sympathy and save their marriage. She was also cynical about his assertions that Geoffroy was not just the de Bondés' family doctor, but also one of Henri's oldest friends – indeed, a shareholder in La Fayette; that it had been common knowledge throughout the Médoc that the Dummonets' had, in effect, paid Geoffroy to marry Cassandre. But as dawn broke and the detail built up to form a clearer picture, she came to the conclusion that Jean-Claude was telling the truth; after all, she'd never known him to lie about anything. And the realisation that she'd probably been used by Geoffroy and his unsavoury colleagues as an unwitting pawn in some nebulous criminal conspiracy, made her feel as if it was she, and not Geoffroy, who'd been punched senseless by Jean-Claude. The doctor's apparent fascination with her reports of domestic trivia was now seen in a very different light. She pondered telling Jean-Claude that Geoffroy had proposed to her, but finally vetoed the notion: he'd ask what her response had been.

'Do you want a divorce?' Jean-Claude asked abruptly.

She'd anticipated this question, but the blunt words threw her. 'Do *you*? I mean, I'm the adulterous party.'

'I don't know. ... Our marriage hasn't exactly been a bed of roses of late, has it?'

'No, it certainly hasn't.'

With a lump in his throat, Jean-Claude hunched his shoulders. 'You've never really been happy in Bordeaux, have you? To be honest, I'm amazed you've stuck it out for so long.'

'Me too.'

'What with all the nightmares at La Fayette, I was going to try and convince you to go abroad with me – California, Australia–'

'Really? Good God!'

'You would have refused then?'

'Oh, Jean-Claude, can you honestly imagine Alexandre in Napa Valley, or coping with the outdoor life of Australia? ... Can you?'

They both smiled wanly.

'No, I can't,' Jean-Claude admitted sadly. He thought of Laura's plans for Belle-Mère and wondered whether he should mention them now. Then he recalled Sophie's behaviour the night she found the two of them in the cellar at the old Margaux house.

'So, what next?' she asked. 'I suppose we ought to put the house on the market for a start.'

Jean-Claude felt his stomach heaving. 'Oh ... right ... OK – if that's what you want.'

'Well, if you're going abroad–'

'I didn't say that – it's just an option, a possibility.'

'But you're worried about this fraud and your possible implication. ... Jesus! How the hell did we get into such a bloody mess?' Tears followed a half-hearted laugh.

Jean-Claude put an arm around Sophie's shoulders and hugged her tightly. 'I'm so sorry,' he murmured. 'I tried. I wanted you to be happy. I wanted you to have this house, but I couldn't pretend to be anything other than a *maître de chai*. I didn't know the cream of Bordelais society and I–'

'Oh, fuck Bordeaux and the Bordelais! Fuck them all! ... Sorry, Jean-Claude ... sorry. ... Vulgarity seems to have infected both of us this weekend. ... Where's a handkerchief?' After wiping her nose and drying her eyes, she said: 'It's not your fault. Don't get me wrong, but I didn't come from a family of good, honest country folk like you.'

'"Canny" was what you said to Buffet.'

'Oh, shut up, you silly boy! You know what I mean. The snobbery here, with its rigid class structure, obsession with titles and rank, petty jealousies, contempt for the outside world – it's stifling. I'll say one thing for the Bordelais though – they're consistent. You can't buy your way in

– it's a family coat of arms or nothing. That's why *we're* nothing here, darling. That's why people like Henri treat you – *us* – like dirt. We'll *always* be nothing. I'm sorry, but it's true and you know it.'

'Guy wasn't like that.'

'Guy was the exception that proved the rule. Maybe you can put up with it, but I can't – and you damn well shouldn't.'

'I'm not going to.'

'Good for you. So, you *will* go abroad then?'

'No. I'm staying put. Jesus Christ, Sophie – you're the one obsessed with the titled fops. There are thousands of vineyards owned by ordinary folk.'

'Don't get mad with me, Jean-Claude, but you know as well as I do that as long as you're a mere *employee* in the Bordeaux wine business – even a respected *maître de chai* – you're stuck. Even bloody antique dealers look down on you! Yet, everyone at *your* level and below feels uncomfortable because we live in this "swanky" house – they think you've betrayed your class. Hell, Jean-Claude, we don't have *any* real friends at all!'

'So, if I *owned* a vineyard, you'd be happy to stay in Bordeaux?'

'That sounds sort of below the belt.'

'It's not meant to be.'

'Anyway, it's academic – hypothetical.'

'No ... no it's not, Sophie. There's something else I haven't been honest with you about. I didn't explain why I was so late back from La Fayette yesterday.'

Taking a deep breath, Jean-Claude began to tell Sophie all about Château Belle-Mère.

CHAPTER 19

That Sunday morning, events began to move rapidly. Just after eight, Sophie and Jean-Claude were awoken from a deep sleep. With the front door bell ringing furiously, they found themselves lying in each other's arms on top of their bed. They bolted down the stairs to discover a visibly anxious Dominique and an equally concerned Dakota standing on the doorstep, still dressed in their party costumes. They'd not been able to sleep at all, they claimed, such was their worry about Alexandre. Had he been found?

Information was exchanged over a simple breakfast, efficiently organized by the two visitors no less, and by the time a third pot of coffee was under preparation, the world seemed a better place from everyone's point of view: Alexandre was safe – 'he'd simply gone for a walk in the forest before supper and got lost'; Jean-Claude apologized to 'Dominique' for his appalling insults and erroneous allegations; Dominique was understanding personified and confirmed that Sophie's exhibition was still on; and Dakota disclosed that, at around two in the morning, Tiquetorte had been led from the villa with his head covered by a blanket and driven away in a private ambulance to Bordeaux's dental hospital.

An itinerary was quickly agreed. Dakota would return to Cap Ferret with the keys to Sophie's abandoned car. He'd drive it over immediately, followed by one of the Forgeron staff. In the meantime, Dominique would pack. He'd be collected on Dakota's return, entertained for the day, and finally put back on the train to Paris. Sophie would drive Alexandre to a top Bordeaux clinic for a check-up, while Jean-Claude would attend what Sophie described as 'a vitally important meeting affecting the whole family's future', words which would stimulate wild speculation by Dominique and Dakota for the rest of the day.

The spouses drove into Bordeaux in separate cars. Alexandre appeared to have returned to the twenty-first century and to his normal precocious self. On the other hand, he'd no recollection of the events leading up to his accident from the moment he'd set off on the road to Le Porge. As soon as the clinic's admission procedures were completed, Jean-Claude drove round to the Continental. Laura was already awaiting him, dressed in a summer Escada Sport outfit that suggested she anticipated a day's sailing at Arcachon. In accordance with Sophie's express instructions, Jean-Claude made no mention of any of the untoward events of Saturday night.

Consequently, on the drive to Belle-Mère, they concentrated on the matter in hand, with an unusually talkative Jean-Claude bombarding Laura with queries.

When they arrived around noon, a thoroughly vibrant Sue flirted openly with a calculatedly cool Jean-Claude while subjecting him to the standard tour – as if she'd forgotten that Laura had been inducted only two days earlier. Consequently, because Laura had summarised Friday's farce on the drive over, she and Jean-Claude shared many stifled giggles and private jokes behind Sue's back. 'Pronkie' was also wheeled out – minus his lab coat – for a thorough grilling in the *cuvier*, but of the Fontaines there was neither sight nor sound.

Driving back to Bordeaux, Jean-Claude surprised Laura with a declaration that he'd immediately fallen in love with Belle-Mère. Obviously, Sophie and Alexandre would have to see the place before he could make any final decision, although in view of Buffet's plans for her career, she'd probably be spending much time in Paris from now on. Laura glowed inwardly, but her mind raced when, crossing the Pont de Pierre, he said he had a confession to make.

'To be honest, Laura, I've already told Sophie about Belle-Mère, including, of course, your involvement.' She panicked, but then he added with a chuckle: 'It may sound crazy, but Sophie seemed wholly unconcerned about … well, *every*thing. By all accounts, her jealousy has … evaporated.'

No jealousy could only mean one thing, Laura concluded: Jean-Claude's marriage was indeed dead.

*

That afternoon, Laura met with Quincy at his Cours de Tournon apartment to study Belle-Mère's accounts; Jean-Claude had declined her invitation to join them, claiming to be innumerate and that he had to get back to Le Porge. Notwithstanding Laura's assertions that Jean-Claude was rather shy and needed delicate handling, Quincy was mildly put out that she'd not even consulted him about the 'Belle-Mère jaunt'. On the other hand, he was delighted by the prospect of someone of Bourjois's calibre serving as *maître de chai*: Fontaine was good, but clearly not in the same league; Laura concurred that he should stay on for a while as a consultant. The two wine gurus moved on to examining the accounts. After several hours, they concluded that tomorrow – Monday – lawyers, accountants and estate agents in France, the States and England would be instructed to get the ball rolling. Doubtless, there'd be tough negotiations with Belle-Mère's receivers: they'd have to see sense and reduce the asking price.

It was early evening by the time Quincy declared: 'Let's call it a day, Laura. How about dinner at the Régent? – it seems to bring us good luck.'

'Fine. I'll just nip back to the Continental to change and phone Dad in Seattle. With the time difference, he should just be preparing lunch for himself at home.'

Quincy offered to reserve a table and to meet her in the hotel's reception at eight.

In her room at the Continental, Laura listened with dismay to Bryan's negative reaction to any involvement in the Belle-Mère project. '*Honey, I've just gone through one traumatic move. I'm too old to cross the Atlantic to start again, and I'm strapped for dough.*'

Laura begged and pleaded. 'The least you can do, Dad, is fly over and have a look at Belle-Mère.'

He said he'd think about it. Half an hour later, he called back with the answer she'd hoped for.

*

At opulent Château Barrage that evening, Sue was watching a DVD of *Love Story* in her very private sitting room when, just after ten o'clock, the phone rang. To her delight, it was Jean-Claude Bourjois: he might have been a tad distant and unresponsive to her charms at Belle-Mère, but she'd admired both his humility – a rare Bordelais characteristic – and his heavenly good looks. If only she'd been able to secure a *maître de chai* like him …

Politely in English, Jean-Claude said: '*My apologies for the late hour, but could I bring my wife and son over tomorrow afternoon to see Belle-Mère? I mentioned the possibility, remember?*' He didn't reveal that Sophie and himself were at Tante Colette's Bordeaux house: Alexandre was being kept in overnight at the clinic for observation, albeit the doctors had found nothing untoward and had confirmed that he should be discharged in the morning.

'I'll 'ave to rearrange one or two appointments,' Sue fibbed, 'but–'

'*We could make it some other time.*'

'No, no! I'd be delighted to see you – *all* of you – around three, if that's OK?'

'*Perfect! It won't be necessary for Monsieur Pronk to be present as Madame Bourjois isn't interested in technicalities – only the house and grounds.*'

'What a very sensible wife!' bubbled Sue, whereupon Jean-Claude laughed a most intoxicating laugh.

Sue had just put the phone down when it rang again. It was Quincy Dubloon, who, despite his breezy style and a joke about accountants, creativity, and works of numerical fiction, rapidly returned to the matter which had already been the subject of no less than six calls to her since noon yesterday – his missing mobile phone.

'*Has it been found yet?*' he bleated. '*I'm really **most** inconvenienced without it. Have you finally managed to get hold of that mad housekeeper, the formidable Jeanne?*'

The poor man was getting quite frantic, Sue noted. 'Quince, love, I've searched your room at Belle-Mère again – *and* the dinin' room, *and* the *cuvier, and* around the great chestnut. Nothin'. And no, I 'aven't spoken to Jeanne yet 'cause she went to Lacanau for the weekend – as I've already explained. Her daughter 'as a cabin there, and they ain't on the bleedin' phone. I'll speak to her first thing in the mornin', as promised.'

Quincy tutted. '*Look, old thing, would you mind if I came over tomorrow and searched for the mobile myself? It really is* terribly important. *Of course, if Jeanne has found it, I could collect it without further delay. Would eight-thirty in the morning be all right?*' He heard a melodramatic sigh.

'Feel free!'

They were saying their goodbyes when Sue interrupted herself. 'Oh, I've just thought. I've got Laura's *maître de chai* bloke comin' out tomorrow afternoon with his wife and kiddie for a butcher's. If Jeanne 'as found your mobile, I could give it to 'im and 'e could drop it off in Bordeaux, savin' you a trip. It'd be a shame not to see you, but–'

The force of Dubloon's interjection took Sue completely by surprise. '*In no circumstances should you give the phone to anyone!*' Realising his vehemence must have sounded excessive, he added quickly: '*Sorry, my dear, it's just that having lost it once, I can't take any risks of losing it again. In any event, I don't want to hang around the whole day waiting for the precious thing.*'

In a sense, Sue was pleased by his response: she wanted to see Quincy again – especially alone. But for a man who'd seemed so at ease with himself and laid back on Friday, the Case of the Missing Mobile certainly appeared to be generating a lot of unnecessary tension.

She restarted *Love Story*, but thoughts of Quincy and his pesky mobile made concentration difficult. In the end, she gave Jeanne another ring at home. As luck would have it, the scatterbrain had just got in, but from the tone of her voice, she wasn't pleased to be pestered by her employer. There was a litany of complaints: sunburn, traffic jams all the way back from Lacanau, and now supper to prepare for her gluttonous husband and his lazy, good-for-nothing sister. When Jeanne finally obeyed orders and focused on the issue of Monsieur Dubloon's mobile, she appeared incapable of following Sue's line of questioning, and pleaded ignorance. Matters were not helped by frequent shouts from the glutton demanding that his wife should 'stop gassing and get a bloody move on with supper!' Nonetheless, a concentrated bombardment of obscenities from Sue caused Jeanne to experience a dramatic recollection of finding 'one of them nasty things' under a bed – somewhere. But where, and what did she do with it?

Within an hour, having driven over from Barrage, Sue was in Belle-Mère's kitchen searching through the pockets of Jeanne's three drab and grubby housecoats, and wondering aloud why the woman needed three and why she never washed them. Finally, having extracted rubber bands, soiled paper tissues, an unwrapped boiled sweet, and a broken clothes peg, Sue struck gold and cradled the mobile in her hands. Her luck was in: although the level was clearly low, the battery was not yet exhausted. A flashing symbol indicated there was at least one voice message.

In fact, there were three – all from the previous day. She pressed the speaker button. One was timed 15:03: an English estate agent was returning Mr Dubloon's call; he'd try again on the Bordeaux apartment number. 'Pippa' had phoned at 13:36: an aunt had died in Stoke-on-Trent and she hoped that Mr Dubloon wouldn't mind if she took next Thursday off to go to the funeral. And 'Henri', a Frenchman who sounded both supercilious and irritated, had left a message at 09:16 – while Quincy had been breakfasting with Laura under the chestnut – complaining that 'the article' hadn't appeared as promised in *Wine Wisdom*'s latest edition, which really wasn't good enough in view of what 'Dubloon' was getting paid. It had better appear in the next issue 'or else'. 'Henri' concluded with a plea for 'Dubloon' to phone back *tout de suite* with confirmation.

Fearful that the battery was about to die, Sue hurriedly identified 'Henri's' number from the phone's memory and wrote it down on the pristine kitchen notepad which Jeanne was supposed to use for her shopping lists. She was just in time: the mobile began to bleep plaintively and the screen went blank. She was replacing it in the housecoat's pocket when the sound of a throat being cleared caused her to scream and drop the phone. She spun round to find Charles Fontaine standing in the doorway. Clothed in a silk Paisley dressing gown and holding a revolver in his right hand, he looked very pleased with himself. For once, Sue was speechless.

'Oh, it's only *you*, Madame *Pronk*,' he said lowering the gun. 'Sorry to startle you – sprinted up from the gatehouse. I heard a car, saw lights in the house, and thought we had burglars.' He stared pointedly at Jeanne's soiled uniforms, shot a glance at the mobile on the floor, and grunted. 'Well now, what have we got here? ... I think I should make some coffee, and then we can have a little chat. How does that grab you?'

*

Sunday proved to be a rather black day for the motley triumvirate of Geoffroy de Tiquetorte, Alain de Carbon Blanc and Henri de Bondé. At Geoffroy's villa, Henri finally surfaced around ten after a restless night during which he'd spent hours reliving the accident near the Bourjoises' house. The ministrations of his partner for the night, the nineteen-year-old daughter of transsexual wannabe Comte Bertrand d'Expiremont, had done nothing to soothe him. At dawn, during one of his brief moments of sleep, she'd departed and, in anticipation of Forgeron's customary gargantuan picnic breakfast on the beach, had returned to the ongoing party.

There were two surprises awaiting Henri: firstly, Geoffroy's bed had not been slept in; and secondly, the repulsive Pandore was downstairs in the kitchen preparing a vast breakfast for herself and a bowl of fresh fruit for Cassandre. Pandore's first announcement was depressing: rather than returning straight to Périgueux after breakfast as originally planned, she and Cassandre were going to spend the day at Cap Ferret. Her second was unbelievable: Geoffroy had been beaten up at the party by one of Henri's employees – 'some macho local kid' as she put it. The third announcement was horrifying: the doctor's aggressor had come to the party looking for his wife – 'a dishy little artist called Sophie' – because 'their boy had disappeared', only to find Sophie and Geoffroy 'shagging' in the guest cottage. Gleefully, Pandore revelled in lurid details of Geoffroy's injuries and ignominious departure from the party.

Retreating to his room, Henri sat on the bed for ages, desperately trying to comprehend the implications of Bourjois's discovery of Sophie's adultery. Geoffroy thought he'd been so clever screwing Sophie. Well, now he, too, had felt the force behind the maniac's fists. It served him right! God only knew what Bourjois would do next. *Christ – he'll think I put Geoffroy up to it! He'll come looking for me – armed!* Henri's body temperature suddenly seemed to rocket. *Bourjois only went to the party because 'their boy had disappeared'? ... Could it be that he was the idiot cyclist? Did he jump or swim across the dyke? Was he catapulted off the bike? Is he still wandering in the forest? ... concussed? ... bleeding to death? ... already dead? Are the police already dredging the dyke, combing the forest, and interviewing Le Porge's residents? Someone must have seen my Mercedes roar off down the road to ...* He pictured the long skid marks and a roped-off crime scene. *What if they discover a body? ... What if I'm implicated? Bourjois could reveal* everything!

Then something very odd occurred to Henri: if the little bugger had disappeared around lunchtime, how come Sophie went to Forgeron's bloody party? It just didn't make any sense. One thing, however, was certain: he didn't want Bourjois back at La Fayette – *ever*! Somehow, he'd have to get hold of the brute and tell him that, in view of all that had occurred at Forgeron's party, there should be a clean break immediately. He'd pay him three months' salary in lieu. A fellow employee would clear out his things and bring them to Le Porge. Galvanized into action at last, he grabbed his mobile and began phoning frantically: to Patrick Audinette, the malleable candidate to replace Bourjois – he was still in bed at his Bordeaux apartment after a night out at *La Factory* – ordering him to start work the following morning; to Jean-Claude's assistant, informing him of Bourjois's immediate departure due to 'deep personal reasons'; and to his wife on Île de Ré, reporting Bourjois's summary dismissal due to his homicidal attack on Tiquetorte, and a request for her and the children to remain on the island for their personal safety until the situation had settled down.

When Henri finally plucked up courage to phone Jean-Claude himself, there was no reply at Le Porge; nor did he answer his mobile. In fact, in his haste that morning to get Alexandre to hospital and to keep his appointment with Laura, he'd left it on the hall table. Henri was still trying to contact him when, at around twelve-thirty, there was a polite tap on his bedroom door. In walked Alain de Carbon Blanc, dressed like a naval officer in tropical kit, including white shirt, white knee-length shorts and socks, and white shoes.

'Ah, so this is where you're hiding,' he drawled, looking disinterestedly around the room. 'Good God, man, you're not even dressed! Just seen the lesbians downstairs, sunbathing bloody naked on the terrace, would you believe? Yuck! Got the in-laws round at my place. And my brother. And his blasted kids. Place is like the Champs-Élysées on New Year's Eve. Frightful! … What about poor Geoffroy? Talk about a bloody come-uppance! Well, I mean, he was asking for trouble, wasn't he? Mind you, the chances of Bourjois's missis being at that party of pervs *and* him turning up out of the blue, well, bloody incredible! Apparently, Bourjois Junior had disappeared, and Jean-Claude went loopy searching for him. Actually, between you, me and the proverbial gatepost, it wouldn't surprise me if Bourjois beat the kid – I mean, your boy said that Bourjois's boy was absolutely barmy, remember? Incredible they went to the same school! – well, for a while. Anyway, never trust the quiet ones, I always say. … Er, where was I?

'Oh yes. Did I tell you–? No, couldn't have – the dykes have only just found out. Seems they've become rather matey with some queer arty-farty bloke from Paris. … Apparently, he's taken a bit of a shine to that Forgeron lad. ... Is he the American bastard or the Brazilian one? ... Never mind, the point is ... um ... the point is that they're all mates *and* – you won't believe this! – they're all chummy now with the Bourjois clan! Well, common bonds ... art, perversion – drugs, I shouldn't wonder – all that kind of stuff. So, they – the Forgeron delinquent and his faggy friend – have been to the Bourjois homestead this morning and discovered that the boy is reunited with the anxious parents and – you'll never *ever* believe this! – far from Geoffroy buggering up their bloody marriage, seems Bourjois's thrashing of our friend has rekindled the old marital bonds – if that's the right analogy. Bloody marvellous, isn't it? Can't understand the middle classes at all. ...

'I say, you're a bit reticent this morning – or should I say "afternoon"? Cat got your tongue? ... You look bloody awful. Suppose that Expiremont popsy kept you up – so to speak! – all night. Some chaps have all the luck. Well, not Geoffroy, I suppose ... in the end. Do you think we ought to go and see him? ... I wonder if he can speak? Lost his front teeth, apparently. Bloody disgrace, if you ask me, bursting into someone's party uninvited and picking a fight, even if the chap was shagging his better half.'

Henri got up from the bed and walked to the open window.

'That's my boy!' chirped Alain. 'Come on, get dressed and I'll open a bottle of champagne. Wonder what sort of grub Geoffroy's got in the fridge.'

'So,' Henri said softly, 'Bourjois's boy is OK?'

'What? ... Oh – apparently – yes. Have a shower, Henri. I always say, that when a chap–'

'So, what happened to him?'

'Who?'

'Bourjois's boy.'

'Oh *him*. Well, the Wicked Witches out on the terrace can fill you in on all the dreary details, but *apparently* the miserable wretch went off for a walk in the forest last night and got lost – or some such nonsense. Sounds batty to me. I'm telling you, that weirdo Bourjois gave the kid one thick ear too many while his mother was out at that orgy thing, and he ran away. Bet the boy's abused. Probably covered in bruises ... broken ribs – God only knows! I remember this chap at school ...'

As Alain droned on, Henri's relief at hearing the news of Bourjois Junior's 'safe' return to the bosom of his family evaporated. Watching the pine trees around Tiquetorte's villa swaying in the Atlantic breeze, he wondered who was the boy on the bicycle? Had he got home safely ... or was he still out in the forest? He should watch the local TV news, but people like himself didn't watch such trivia. He'd arouse suspicions. Or he could tune in to a local radio station. Was there a radio in the villa? He'd have to be very discreet. If only he could have the bloody house to himself for half an hour.

Fortuitously, Cassandre and Pandore went down to the beach: they'd arranged to meet Dakota and Dominique for a picnic lunch; after eating too many oysters the night before, Tic-Tac was feeling a bit under the weather and had decided to spend the day in bed. Alain, however, had no intention of leaving and was too thick-witted to take on board any of Henri's hints. So, he took the opportunity to update Alain on the decisions he'd taken over Bourjois's future. Alain concurred wholeheartedly; in truth, he was somewhat alarmed about his own safety as the full implications of the maniac's savagery sunk in.

Cassandre and Pandore returned shortly before five, looking very happy.

'Are you two going to visit Geoffroy at the hospital this evening?' asked Cassandre brightly.'

'*I* can't,' Alain replied. 'Lumbered with my people. Driving back to town in the morning.'

Henri nodded. 'Probably.'

'Oh good,' Cassandre said. 'Could you tell the toothless wonder that I've decided to divorce him and tear up the contract – he'll know what I mean. Pandore and I have decided to tie the knot – even if we have to go to Holland or Sweden – one of those dotty liberal countries that recognises same-sex marriages – and to adopt an orphan. Apparently, there are loads on the market in Niger ... or Côte d'Ivoire – well, one of our ex-colonies anyway.'

When they were alone again, Alain rolled his eyes and said: 'Bloody hell, Henri, whatever next? And it's all the fault of that damned peasant, Bourjois. He deserves a jolly good thrashing if you ask me.'

*

Having been transferred from the Dental Hospital in mid-afternoon, Geoffroy was propped up in bed in the best suite of a very exclusive clinic tucked away in a quiet street leading off Cours Georges Clemenceau. Topped up with painkillers, he was trying to digest the import of Henri's report of the day's developments. His friend sat in a Barcelona chair studying an eighteenth-century engraving of the Bourse in a conscious attempt not to stare at the awful gap in Geoffroy's front teeth whenever he mumbled something.

'So, you're telling everyone you fell down the stairs at *your* villa? Is that wise, old boy? I mean, somebody at the party is almost bound to blab, don't you think?'

Geoffroy said nothing.

'Well, anyway,' Henri continued, 'I strongly advise against any kind of proceedings against Bourjois – whether civil or criminal. You're in shock – you're not thinking straight. It would be madness. And you've already told the staff here it was an accident. Of course, they can't possibly believe you. They must be experts on injuries, surely? And ... and ... well, I didn't want to tell you this, but ... um ... I'm afraid there's a video of what happened – Cassandre told us – Alain and me.'

Geoffroy tried to speak, but just moving his lips was agony.

'Yes, I know exactly how you must feel. I couldn't believe it either. Well, actually, on reflection, I can because it's the sort of thing one would expect from a deranged and debauched piece of shit like Forgeron. To be absolutely one hundred per cent honest, Forgeron has videoed your activities in the guest cottage at each *Fête de la Fleur* over the last four or five years. It's the Anglo-Saxon influence, if you ask me. He went to Oxford, you know ... or was it Cambridge? – one of them anyway. And all that low life in New York and San Francisco ... well, I ask you – a recipe for disaster!' Henri sighed with apparent sadness over the corruption of a blue-blooded Frenchman.

'So, for God's sake, Geoffroy, don't drag Bourjois into court.' Henri leaned forward and patted his hand. 'Don't worry, old chap, we'll get him. He'll live to regret what he did to you – what he's done to *all* of us. I promise.'

Geoffroy pointed to a notepad and pen on his bedside table. Henri passed it to him. With obvious pain, he laboriously wrote some words and then handed the pad back. In a shaky hand he'd written:

Must destroy him.
Ask Sophie to visit me.
Need money.
You must now implement next phase.

Henri stared long and hard at the words as if they were an impenetrable examination question. He shook his head slowly. 'Not sure about this Sophie thing. By all accounts the bloody woman has dumped you, and the deranged duo have been reconciled. Ah, you can shake your head, Geoffroy, but I have it on good authority.' After more head shaking and another note, Henri received Sophie's mobile number. He was more forthcoming about the 'next phase' request: with the new *maître de chai* in place, it would certainly be 'full steam ahead.' Then Henri asserted that duty called at La Fayette: he needed to burn the midnight oil preparing for the new broom's imminent arrival.

On the drive home, Henri continuously flicked between local radio stations, but there were still no reports of any missing child around Le Porge. Whoever had scampered away into the forest must have got home safely, thank God! When finally ensconced in his study at La Fayette, and having summoned the housekeeper, Marie-Thérèse, to make him a light supper, he tried phoning Jean-Claude again, but without success. Muttering obscenities, he just couldn't understand where the cretin could be on a Sunday night. Nor could he get through to Dubloon, whether on his mobile or the Cours de Tournon landline. By eleven-thirty, and having consumed most of a bottle of Pavillon Blanc de Château Margaux, Henri had sufficient Dutch courage to phone Sophie; if nothing else, she might be able to get a message to her thug of a husband not to turn up for work in the morning. But she didn't answer her mobile either! Where could all these miserable oiks be?

When Henri finally went up to bed, he felt completely shattered. It had been a very long day – indeed, a traumatic weekend from start to finish, thanks to you-know-who. Well, tomorrow he'd be out on his arse, and good riddance! For the first time in thirty years, he fell asleep contemplating various nasty methods for murdering Jean-Claude. He particularly enjoyed drowning him in a *barrique* of Château La Fayette – or would Maréchal have been more appropriate?

Forty miles away in a private nursing home – another institution in which Henri, Geoffroy and Alain were shareholders – Guy de Bondé dreamed again of sex with Jean-Claude's mother. At least, that was the woman he saw in his demented mind – not that he knew who she was. Nor, for that matter, would he have recognised Jean-Claude, or even his name if it had been spoken to him.

CHAPTER 20

When Algeria finally obtained its independence in 1962 after almost a decade of violent strife, 750,000 residents of French origin – the 'pieds-noirs' – abandoned the once glittering showpiece of the *Empire Français* and flooded into France, a country many hardly knew. A significant number arrived with only what they could carry, but those with foresight had been realizing assets for some years and transferring their capital from North Africa. Still, there hadn't been much demand for Algerian real estate during the years of conflict preceding independence, and even the most astute faced a significant decline in their living standards.

Bordeaux had long been an important port for the North African routes, the regular sailings being a constant reminder to its citizens of the chance of a better life overseas. In consequence, considerable numbers of Bordelais had been lured to Morocco and Algeria following the First Word War and the Wall Street Crash in 1929. But these pieds-noirs were not universally welcomed when they came 'home'. Take, for example, Nicolas Tari, who'd been a major landowner in Algeria with vineyards and orange groves around Oran. As early as 1947, he was the first pied-noir to make any significant investment in the Bordeaux wine trade when he bought Château Giscours, a Margaux *grand cru* that had been in decline for decades; there were even trees growing in the *chais*. Over the years, he restored Giscours to greatness, but for certain Bordelais the family remained '*étrangers aux idées bizarres et déconcertantes*', a prejudice compounded in 1979 when Nicolas's son founded Bordeaux's first polo club. Notwithstanding the wealth and background of its members, many Bordelais were critical of a distinguished estate being used as a sporting arena.

Hector Lebrun was also a pied-noir. He arrived in Bordeaux from Oran in the late spring of 1962 with his wife Mathilde and their two attractive daughters, Marie-Claude and Thérèse, aged twenty-three and nineteen respectively. Until they got their bearings, the Lebruns lived in a large but decrepit furnished apartment on Rue Vital-Carles, a fine thoroughfare connecting Cours de l'Intendance with St André's Cathedral. Within six months, however, Hector acquired Château Brèche-Dent, a *grand cru* vineyard at Soussans, a few kilometres north of Margaux. Although, like Château Giscours, it was in a chronic state of decay, the *terroir* was good, so he had high hopes. The following June, he attended the Médoc's *Fête de la Fleur*, accompanied by Mathilde and their daughters. It was the elder, Marie-Claude, who caught the attention of a thirty-one-year-old bachelor, Guy de Bondé of Château La Fayette, who, exceptionally, did his best to make the Lebruns welcome – as indeed did La Fayette's young *maître de chai*, Christophe Bourjois, and his wife, Joséphine. They all got on well together, albeit Joséphine, a railway porter's daughter raised humbly near Bordeaux's Gare St-Jean, felt way out of her depth, and, in consequence, drank too much wine to calm her nerves. Like most attendees, the Lebruns thought Guy rather gauche in bringing such humble individuals to the *Fête*. Nonetheless, Marie-Claude and her mother agreed that he was the most eligible bachelor they'd come across so far; he was certainly one of the best-looking men there. Indeed, as far as Marie-Claude was concerned, there was only one man who was even handsomer – Christophe Bourjois, but she wisely kept silent on the point.

Guy had found himself running La Fayette as a result of circumstances rather than design. Honouring a family tradition for the youngest son to enter the army, Guy had followed numerous forbears to St-Cyr, France's prestigious military academy. In due course, he was commissioned; in 1954, he was posted to Algeria, shortly after the outbreak of the troubles there. At that time, his father, Baron Eric de Bondé, divided his life between Margaux and politics: for many years, he'd served in the *Assemblée Nationale*; occasionally, he even held junior ministerial office. Guy's elder brother, Robert, being destined to inherit La Fayette, had been groomed to run the estate. But in 1959, he shocked his father by opting for a career behind the wheel of a racing car. As a result, strings were pulled to release Guy from both his commission and his dangerous military service. Just a few months after his return to a serenely peaceful Margaux, Robert died in a horrific accident at Le Mans.

Guy proposed marriage to Marie-Claude within weeks of their first meeting at the 1963 *Fête*; she accepted immediately. When informed of the engagement, his father was horrified: people like the de Bondés did *not* marry pieds-noirs. His wild threats of disinheritance, however, only served to strengthen Guy's resolve to marry Marie-Claude. It was a January wedding, and inside Sousson's unheated parish church the congregation exhaled clouds of steaming breath. For almost an hour after the service, while the customary photographs were snapped, Eric stood discontentedly on the church's steps in an icy wind howling across the Médoc from a tempestuous Bay of Biscay. Already suffering from a bad cold, he succumbed to bronchitis within three days, causing the newlyweds to speed home from their honeymoon at the Negresco in a windswept Nice. Marie-Claude said she perfectly understood Guy's desire to return, but deep down she was furious: acutely aware of Eric's strong opposition to the marriage, she suspected he'd deliberately made himself ill just to spoil the whole event. In truth, she was delighted when he swiftly died of pneumonia: she'd become a *baronne* far sooner than she'd ever imagined; her parents were over the moon.

Married life, alas, did not blossom at La Fayette. For one thing, Guy didn't appear to be as rich as any of the Lebruns had assumed. In consequence, Marie-Claude was prevented from undertaking many of the activities she'd planned, including a thorough refurbishment of the house, employing additional servants, shopping several days a week in Bordeaux to remedy the glaring deficiencies in her wardrobe, and lavishly entertaining the cream of Bordeaux society. Guy was sensible – too sensible for her tastes. He kept talking about tedious things like 'seigneurial duties', 'economic stringency', 'a weak market' and 'heavy capital expenditure programmes'. Furthermore, he expected her to 'muck in': her chores included sharing the lone gardener's heavy workload, and turning out in all weathers to distribute packed lunches to estate workers toiling in the vineyards. Thus, for a young woman who'd been used to an endless round of expatriate socializing facilitated by an Arab chauffeur, life in Margaux proved to be exceedingly dull.

It's possible that Guy could have won her over to his cause had he been prepared to compromise a little – a brief holiday here, a new dress there – but instead he made the fatal mistake of taking her through the château's accounts line by incomprehensible line. Guy, she concluded, was attempting to pull the wool over her eyes – and told him so – using obscenities he'd never heard a woman utter. The first of many tempestuous rows followed.

By contrast, Joséphine Bourjois adored her husband, Christophe. And although she was not a country girl by birth or upbringing, she was happy with her new life in Margaux; the old Bourjois cottage, though small, was a palace compared to the vermin-infested tenement she'd long suffered near the Gare St-Jean. She'd met Christophe at Bordeaux's great funfair held each October at the Place des Quinconces, the *Foire des Jambons*, where they'd found themselves standing next to each other at a shooting gallery. Christophe was an expert shot, thanks to his national service and years of rabbit shooting around Margaux. Joséphine was a disaster and made him laugh hysterically. They and their very different groups of friends – streetwise city girls and rustic vineyard workers – ended up doing the rides together. Christophe was enchanted: not only was Joséphine very pretty and vivacious; her clothes, language, humour and morals were decidedly contemporary – light years away from the Haut Médoc's dull, puritanical regimen. Joséphine, for her part, found Christophe good-looking, polite, kind, chivalrous and soft-spoken – very different to the Bordeaux boys she dated. He only had one defect – thick, curly black hair that covered almost his entire body: it seriously dampened her sexual desires. She knew the cause, but had never mentioned it to a living soul.

When Joséphine was ten, her mother had run off to Mozambique with a Portuguese sailor, leaving her two daughters with their violent alcoholic father. He was an ugly giant of a man, whose nickname at the Gare St-Jean was '*le Grand Singe*' – the Ape – because of his thick, all-encompassing black body hair. One afternoon, shortly before Joséphine's fourteenth birthday, he returned home drunk and in a foul mood from his shift at the station; her sister, Colette, was out playing with a school friend. Suddenly, the brute started yelling that Joséphine had always hated him and had poisoned her mother's mind against him. He punched and beat her. Then he raped her.

After two years of marriage, Christophe remained remarkably patient and considerate, even though sex with Joséphine was painfully problematic and incomplete. Things would start well, but at some stage he'd feel compelled to withdraw. He was no fool; it was clear Joséphine loved him dearly, which indicated that the problem probably stemmed from some traumatic event she'd experienced before they met. On several occasions he tried to coax the truth from her, but all his efforts proved hopeless. Finally, after much agonizing, he suggested psychiatric therapy. Joséphine refused: she was determined that no one would ever discover her terrible secret. And so, their frustrations became unbearable, particularly as they both fervently desired children.

*

By spring 1964, Guy's marriage was at breaking point: Marie-Claude spent much of her time complaining aggressively about something or other; Guy was generally on the receiving end, but domestic staff and estate workers were also subjected to her tantrums. Matters came to a crisis when she proclaimed that the lack of an Ocean residence at Arcachon or Cap Ferret was an intolerable social humiliation. One Wednesday morning in early June, following the Bondés worst row yet, Marie-Claude announced to all and sundry her departure for an indefinite stay at Pyla-sur-Mer, a select resort near Arcachon, where some old friends – a wealthy pied-noir family from Algiers – had treated themselves to an impressive late nineteenth-century villa. Resembling an oversized Swiss chalet, it was the sort of ostentatious beach residence which she expected Guy to buy for her.

It was common knowledge in Margaux that Guy would go for a long walk whenever he was stressed and needed to clear his head. His customary route was the lane which led down to the river at Port d'Issan, some two kilometres distant. Wednesday afternoons were when Christophe went into Bordeaux to study developments in viticulture at the university as part of Guy's ongoing staff training. That June afternoon, Joséphine had washed the lunch dishes and was sitting alone with a well-earned cup of coffee in her small front room, when she saw Guy walk past the window. Aware of his marital problems, she felt so sorry for him. He'd always treated Christophe and herself with respect and courtesy, as if the obvious class differences didn't exist. In truth, she couldn't help admiring his quasi-Nordic good looks – those amazing hypnotic blue eyes, the golden hair …

Suddenly, she was running upstairs to change her shoes and put on some lipstick.

By the time she'd passed the church, Guy was almost a kilometre ahead of her, striding purposefully down the straight road towards the river. She feared she'd never catch up with him, but when she reached the banks of the Gironde, he was sat cross-legged on the grass, staring at the water. Immobilized by strongly conflicting thoughts, she watched him for some minutes. Then, taking a deep breath, she walked over with her heart in her mouth.

'Hello!' she said, startling him.

'Good God! Joséphine! Sorry, I didn't hear you coming. I was lost in thought.' He motioned to her to sit down beside him. 'What are *you* doing here?'

'Such a lovely day! I couldn't bear being cooped up in the house. Sometimes I walk up to La Fayette after lunch, but with Christophe in Bordeaux … I don't know really. I walked down to the church and then just continued. I've never come this far before, would you believe? Lovely, isn't it?' As usual, Joséphine had difficulty in calling Guy by his Christian name; even after two years at Margaux, it still seemed wrong to be so familiar with a baron. And addressing him as *tu* rather than *vous*, also remained a mental hurdle.

Guy was nodding. 'Beautiful … so tranquil. I often come here.'

'Oh?'

'Good therapy.'

'Ah!' Joséphine wasn't sure what he meant, but assumed he was alluding to Marie-Claude. For a few minutes, they made polite conversation – the weather, an employee who'd had a minor car accident, gossip about a new supermarket opening in Pauillac. She began to feel acutely embarrassed – ashamed even. The plain truth was that she, a married woman, was flirting with a married man – her husband's employer! She couldn't imagine what had possessed her.

'I'd better be getting back,' she said through a forced smile. 'You won't be having any of that ... that therapy stuff with me gassing on.' She began to push herself up, but Guy caught her arm.

'Please don't go on my account, Joséphine. I'm enjoying our natter – honest!'

'I – I–'

'You *are* happy here, aren't you?' he asked, looking directly into her eyes.

'*Here*? Well, I ...'

'In Margaux – out in the wilds? Sometimes I think you must miss life in the big city. Sometimes you look' – he raised his shoulders – '... I don't know ... wistful. I worry about you – and Christophe, of course. Sorry, it's none of my business, but ... well, everything *is* all right between you two, isn't it? I mean, when you're walking alone along Margaux's back roads ... on a June afternoon, well ...'

Joséphine pursed her lips and settled back on the grass. 'Don't laugh, but what does ... "wistful" mean? Sorry, but I'm not much good with words.'

Guy smiled kindly. 'Wistful? Well now ... hmm, that's a good question. Wistful ... well, if someone looks wistful they've got an expression which says they're really longing for something – like *this*.' He did an impression and Joséphine laughed.

'Do I *really* look like that?'

Guy nodded. 'Yes, sometimes ... quite often, actually.' He stared across the river to the distant hilly shore of the Côtes de Blaye. 'What are *you* longing for, Joséphine? Is it a baby?'

Guy's genuine and heartfelt concern greatly touched her. He said that he was very fond of both Christophe and herself, and that if there was some impediment to their having children, then he'd be more than happy to do whatever he could to help. He'd pay for any necessary medical treatment – in absolute confidence, of course. If she wanted him to have a word with Christophe – he need never know of their chat – *never* – he'd be more than happy to do so. He'd known Christophe all his life. He loved him like a brother. He felt, therefore, that whatever the problem was, he was in a special position to help.

When Joséphine began to weep, Guy knew he'd hit a raw nerve. He put his arm around her shoulders and told her to cry as much as she wanted; she'd bottled up her emotions for far too long. Hesitatingly at first, but quickly gathering momentum, she told him everything. He listened in silence – and remained silent for some time after she'd completed her shocking tale. Then he whispered a few words and she kissed him.

They went into the woods, just a minute's walk along the riverbank. Without saying a word, Joséphine started to undress; Guy followed. With incredulity, she watched him extract a condom from one of his trouser pockets.

'Never go out without one,' he stammered, as if apologising. 'Force of habit. ... When I was in the army ... North Africa ...' *I must sound ridiculous. She must think I'm seducing employees' wives all day long.*

But Joséphine was relieved, and when she saw his near-hairless body, she experienced a surge of desire greater than anything she could ever have imagined possible. Guy's hesitation and overwhelming embarrassment remained until she drew him into her, whereupon he suddenly experienced a feeling of glorious liberation; it was as though a mass of tightly bound ropes which had long restricted his every movement had been made to disappear at a stroke. Such, then, was his rediscovery of the glorious sensations which he'd once enjoyed with the women he'd known before his disastrous marriage to Marie-Claude. At one point, he found himself imagining himself as Christophe, and it was with this vision still before him that he finally ejaculated as the wood resounded with Joséphine's cries of fulfilment.

She was still savouring her ecstasy when Guy withdrew and, with his back to her, made to remove the condom. He stared in horror: it had burst. He threw it into the undergrowth. He said nothing. There was no point in alarming Joséphine unnecessarily. With luck, there'd be no consequences at all.

They got dressed in silence. Joséphine assumed that Guy's post-coital coolness was – like hers – a product of intense guilt. She suggested that it might be sensible to walk back to Margaux separately. He didn't demur.

When Christophe returned from Bordeaux, Joséphine was still lying in the bath. Expressing some mock surprise that she wasn't in the kitchen preparing supper, he kissed her without ardour, and then proceeded to urinate in the toilet adjacent to the bath. As he was shaking off the final drops, Joséphine reached out with a soapy hand and grabbed his penis. He cried out in surprise and tried to jerk away, but before he knew what was happening, she was half out of the bath trying to pull his pants down. Fearing yet another one of their traumatic anticlimaxes, Christophe protested loudly with disingenuous good humour. But, without drying herself, Joséphine dragged him in a state of total confusion to the bedroom, stripped him in seconds, and then proceed to give him a sexual experience he'd never forget. Climaxing, she excited herself even further with an erotically charged vision of Guy suffused in a golden aura, while imagining the heavenly softness of his body against hers.

Christophe was also fantasising: he pictured the Elf filling station at Blanquefort, where he'd stopped to fill up on his drive into Bordeaux that afternoon. To his dismay, Guy's wife was standing on the forecourt beside her flashy new Citroën DS. Dressed in clinging yellow slacks and a turquoise décolleté short-sleeved blouse, she appeared to be arguing with the pump attendant; she was always arguing with someone. Feeling obliged to intervene, it transpired that *la baronne* had left La Fayette in such a flap that she'd forgotten her purse and only had a few francs on her. Her endeavours to procure credit, relying on her status as Guy de Bondé's wife, had cut no ice with the humble Elf employee: her voluble obscenities included references to his threats to summon the *gendarmerie*. Naturally, Christophe paid her debt. She gushed gratitude, told him to 'sort it out with Monsieur de Bondé', and then got back into her car. Reminding himself to do something about his addiction to strong black coffee as he walked to the men's washroom at the back of the service station, Christophe saw the Citroën pull away, and heaved a sigh of relief.

He was washing his hands when he heard the door behind him open. Glancing in the mirror above the washbasin, he gasped. 'What the *hell*–?' It was Marie-Claude. He spun round as she bolted the door behind her.

'Christ! she hissed, pulling down her slacks. 'I've wanted you since that bloody *Fête de la Fleur* last year. And don't tell me you're "a happily married man", because I know better.'

After two years of unbearable sexual frustration, Marie-Claude could have made Christophe do anything. Luckily, no one wanted to use the washroom during their five minutes of ecstasy.

*

In mid-July, when Joséphine discovered her pregnancy, she'd no reason to doubt Christophe's role. On the contrary, the guilt over her adultery with Guy instantly evaporated. And when she told Christophe the blissful news, he sobbed with joy. It was also remarkable how his own feelings of shame and treachery were now extinguished. There surely had to be some connection between his marriage's rebirth and his own seduction by Marie-Claude. It was just too much of a coincidence. Had something mystical happened that afternoon – maybe even supernatural? After all, he'd grown up on the land with country folk for whom superstition was a way of life.

Within half an hour of Joséphine's announcement, Christophe was running like an Olympic sprinter to La Fayette to give his employer the news in person, praying that Guy would be well enough to see him: word had come down from the house earlier in the day that he was ill with some kind of stomach upset and would be remaining in bed. In truth, a poisoned marriage had caused Guy's 'illness'. The night before, after more than a month's absence, Marie-Claude had returned unexpectedly from Pyla to inform her husband that she was pregnant; because of the timing, the father could only be Christophe Bourjois. Utterly bewildered by her bizarre accusation, Guy could not, and would not, believe her, even when she claimed that the Elf petrol station attendant at Blanquefort could verify their session in the men's washroom. Unless Guy complied with her demands, she'd tell Joséphine everything. And, bearing in mind the girl's imbecilic belief in papal infallibility, she suspected Joséphine would also be none too pleased to learn that she proposed to have Christophe's baby aborted.

Marie-Claude required a monthly allowance of ten thousand francs and a house of her choice at Pyla in the two hundred thousand francs bracket; these were not trivial sums in the mid Sixties. She'd convinced herself that Guy would accede to her demands, but she was genuinely surprised by the speed of his surrender. The next morning, after a sleepless night, Guy went to Marie-Claude's room and said that if she had the baby and kept her mouth shut, he'd double the allowance. She agreed instantly. Puzzled by his motives, she finally concluded that Guy's own lukewarm Catholicism had got the better of him. In fact, despite opposing abortion in principle, he would have countenanced it to preserve the purity and honour of his own noble line had the other party been anyone other than Christophe, whom he adored. In any event, due to his knowledge of the impediment in the Bourjoises' marriage, he couldn't blame Christophe for submitting to Marie-Claude's seduction.

When the major-domo, Navette, descended La Fayette's impressive staircase and informed Christophe that, notwithstanding his continuing illness, 'Monsieur le Baron' would be delighted to learn his 'incredible news', Christophe raced up to his master's room. Propped up in bed, Guy not only looked ten years older, but his eyes also gave every indication that he'd been crying. Clearly, this was no ordinary 'stomach upset'.

For a moment, Christophe forgot all about the baby. 'Oh my God!' he wailed, rushing to the bedside, '– you're not dying, are you?'

There was a dreadful silence as Guy stared into Christophe's terrified eyes. Then a smile began to form. 'Of course not, you bloody idiot!' Guy laughed as convincingly as he could manage and patted the bed. 'Now sit down and tell me all about this "incredible news."'

*

One day the following March, when she was eight months' pregnant, Marie-Claude instructed Navette to drive her over to the new house at Cap Ferret, which, in the event, she had decided was much more select than Pyla-sur-Mer. The car was loaded with a pile of swatches and pattern books containing the sort of things she had in mind for the '*grand salon*' so that she could make the final choices for the curtains and carpets. But when they arrived at the villa, Marie-Claude discovered that some of the swatches had been left behind at La Fayette. Navette received a brutal reprimand and was ordered back to fetch them. He argued it was unwise to leave his mistress alone in her 'delicate state', especially as the telephone had yet to be connected. Marie-Claude's riposte was, that unless she finalized matters immediately and got her orders placed with the suppliers, there was no way the house would be ready by the summer, and no 'sodding pregnancy' was going to foul up her plans. Against his better judgment, Navette drove off, leaving her in a cold, windswept and near-deserted Cap Ferret.

Marie-Claude was upstairs in what would be the main guest suite, when, within twenty minutes of his departure, the labour pains began. Her first thought was to get to one or other of the neighbouring villas, forgetting in her panic that they were all shut up for the winter. In desperate haste to make contact with someone, she lost her footing on the stairs, and fell head over heels, tumbling several times until she reached the hall's parquet flooring. Her head hit it with a tremendous crack.

Being a careful driver, it took Navette almost two hours to get to La Fayette, find the samples – they were in Marie-Claude's bedroom where she'd left them – and then drive back to Cap Ferret. When he found his mistress lying in a pool of bloody liquid at the foot of the staircase – conscious but delirious and in a well-advanced state of premature labour – the long-suffering servant didn't panic. Navette was a man who, like so many of his generation, had been subjected to the maturing experiences of war: during the Occupation he'd been forcibly removed from his humble clerical position in Bordeaux's Galeries Lafayette department store and ordered to Hamburg, where, due to the insatiable demands of Hitler's war machine, the city's hospitals were chronically short of personnel. He started as a porter, but as the RAF's bombing intensified and the city's infrastructure collapsed, rules and regulations ceased to have meaning. Within six months, he was delivering German babies in what was left of a once great hospital.

And so, at Cap Ferret that afternoon, Navette safely delivered a baby boy. But despite exceptional efforts to save his hated mistress, the loss of blood was too great and Marie-Claude died in his arms. Guy didn't await her burial before putting the villa back on the market. Indeed, in order to dispose of it quickly, he was even prepared to make a loss. Within six weeks, the accursed property was sold.

For the first three years of Henri de Bondé's life, Hector and Madame Lebrun were a constant thorn in Guy's side due to their efforts to control every aspect of his upbringing. Guy did not, therefore, shed any tears when the Lebruns, together with their surviving daughter, Thérèse, disappeared while sailing their yacht from Arcachon to Biarritz. The yacht was found; the bodies were not. It was presumed that a sudden and violent storm in the Bay of Biscay had caused the boat to capsize and that all three of them had drowned. Henri did not, however, inherit Hector Lebrun's vineyard, whether in trust or otherwise. Thanks to an inexplicable failure to update his will after Marie-Claude's death, the extinction of all four Lebruns brought into a play a testamentary provision under which all Hector's assets vested in an obscure orphanage for indigenous Algerians in Algiers.

Almost a month to the day after Marie-Claude's death, Joséphine Bourjois gave birth to Jean-Claude. Like his mother and Christophe, the baby was dark haired; in point of fact, he was one of the hairiest little chaps the attending medical personnel had ever seen. Despite the hair, however, everyone said he looked like his mother, which gave rise to many jokes at her expense. And yet, from the very moment she first set eyes on him, Joséphine knew he wasn't Christophe's. She kept telling herself that her intuition had to be at fault – that the condom couldn't have been defective. But when Guy came to visit her in the hospital, she immediately knew she was right: she could see it in his eyes as clear as daylight.

Guy had feared a blond baby and had initially been comforted by Christophe's call from the hospital that the new addition to the family was a 'chip off the old block'. But, despite the black hair and features inherited from his mother, when he held Jean-Claude in his arms for the first time, Guy felt a powerful surge of paternal love, and the enigmatic expression in Joséphine's eyes told him she knew what he was feeling. Christophe, on the other hand, didn't have the slightest reason to doubt 'his' boy's paternity – and nor did he, either then or at any time during the rest of his life.

At the time of Henri's birth, Guy had felt it would be a privilege to raise Christophe's boy; indeed, he swiftly came to regard Henri as his own son. By the time he was a toddler, however, Henri began to exhibit character traits which couldn't fail to remind Guy of Marie-Claude. In truth, as each year passed, the boy became ever more like her – bad-tempered, selfish, arrogant – even vicious. Whatever tenderness he'd originally felt for him, slowly yet inexorably dissipated. On more than one occasion the thought did cross Guy's mind that, for the purposes of her wicked blackmail, Marie-Claude had lied to him, and that Christophe was not, in fact, Henri's father. After all, why should she have restricted herself to one affair? And when Henri attempted to kill Jean-Claude by pushing him down the stairs at La Fayette, Guy finally convinced himself that there couldn't be a single one of Christophe's genes in the boy's evil body.

Nonetheless, there was always that fraction of one per cent of doubt. It was a dilemma which became an obsession. Then, during the mid-1980s, he read in the newspapers about a British geneticist called Alec Jeffrys, who'd developed something called 'DNA fingerprinting'.

CHAPTER 21

Jean-Claude was happy, an emotion he'd not experienced for a long time. It was not how he'd expected to feel on his last Monday morning drive to La Fayette, where he would collect his things and bade his farewells to all the colleagues with whom he'd served for so many years. As he drove along the familiar route through the Haut-Médoc, he kept telling himself that he should be feeling melancholy – even shame – over his severance of the long connection between his family and Margaux. To his surprise, however, he felt none of these things – far from it. Once the decision to leave had been made yesterday evening, a kind of euphoria had begun to creep over him, and as he got closer to Margaux on this overcast day, his resolve grew even stronger to bring this chapter of his life to a swift conclusion.

Having made an early start from Tante Colette's house – Sophie had insisted on remaining at Alexandre's bedside overnight in the Bordeaux clinic – Jean-Claude arrived in his humble office before eight. When the first of his colleagues began to turn up for work, he'd already filled the cardboard boxes he'd brought with him, and was loading them into the car. He quickly put them in the picture with a tale about 'an international consortium' which had great plans – still highly confidential – to create a new Bordeaux megastar. They'd made him an offer he couldn't refuse, and Henri had given his blessing to a swift, clean break. The news spread like wildfire.

At eight-fifteen, Jean-Claude put a call through to the house to inform Henri of his presence and to request an immediate interview. The housekeeper, Marie-Thérèse, answered the phone in tears: one of the estate workers had just burst into her kitchen with the news and she was devastated. She pleaded with him to stay, asserting he was the last symbol of 'the old order' – the only remaining brake on Henri's madness. Between sobs, she finally got round to disclosing that 'his nibs' had yet to make an appearance. Did Jean-Claude want her or Grégoire – her husband – to go up and tell him of his desire for an interview? Jean-Claude politely declined the offer, but said he'd come up to the house in any event if Henri hadn't materialized in the next thirty minutes.

As small groups of employees followed him around and helped with his boxes, Jean-Claude couldn't fail to wonder at the paucity of personal items he'd accumulated over all these years: some books, conference notes and diaries, and the usual hotchpotch of pens, pencils and cigarette lighters.

At nine, with no news from Marie-Thérèse, he made his way up to the house. Grégoire opened the front door.

'Dearie me, Jean-Claude,' the old retainer lamented, 'this is a sad day, a sad day indeed.' Instead of inviting him in, Grégoire came out and shut the door behind him. He shook his head, appearing both agitated and embarrassed, not knowing where to look. 'I haven't a clue what's going on, I'm sure, but his nibs is acting most peculiar. It were only a few minutes ago that I managed to wake him up, would you believe? I spotted a bottle of his wife's sleeping tablets on the bedside table.

'Well, when I says you're wanting to have a word with him, he goes bloody hysterical, shouting all sorts of rubbish about you being a dangerous criminal and not to let you in the house. Said you shouldn't even be here by all accounts. I can only think it were some bad dream or something, what with all them pills. Maybe he's going the same way as poor Monsieur Guy. … Anyway, his nibs was most insistent I wasn't to let you in – said you should wait out here.' He sighed heavily. 'I don't know what's going to become of us, Jean-Claude, I really don't. We – me and the missis – should have gone years ago, but who'd take us now? And then there's the pension Monsieur Guy promised us and … Oh, I don't know, I really don't. Poor Marie-Thérèse is at her wits' end. I mean, the house is too big for us to look after now, but his nibs won't get anyone else in and – and–'

Jean-Claude gripped Grégoire's arms as he began to tremble. 'Come on, Grégoire, this isn't like you. Look, the new place I'm going to … well, they might need someone – I can't promise anything – there's still a lot to be worked out, but–'

A deafening roar interrupted the peace as a powerful sports car roared through the gates, sped up the drive, and screeched to a halt. In open-mouthed horror, Grégoire glared at the skid marks across his finely raked gravel. Dressed in the frighteningly-expensive-yet-intensely-casual style favoured by the glitterati for the most formal of occasions, a young man with a sunbed tan and five-o'clock shadow, languorously extricated himself from the roadster and glanced at the two spectators through avant-garde sunglasses.

'Hi,' he mumbled.

'Hi,' Jean-Claude acknowledged.

Grégoire remained speechless.

'Er, I'm Patrick Audinette, the new *maître de chai*. Supposed to be here at eight.' He shrugged his shoulders. 'Traffic … you know how it is.' Moving like a giraffe, he glided to the foot of the steps. 'Is Henri around?' After a few seconds' silence, Audinette added: 'You know … Henri? – the Baron de Bondé?' He smiled broadly as if humouring two village idiots.

Finally, pulling himself up and clearing his throat, Grégoire declaimed: 'Monsieur le Baron *Guy* de Bondé, the proprietor of this château, sir, is indisposed due to a serious illness – and has been for some years. His *son*, Monsieur *Henri* de Bondé, who currently *manages* the estate as trustee, should be down presently. May I suggest, sir, that you take your ... *vehicle* round to the *chais* – where, for your information, *Monsieur* de Bondé expects *all* employees to park their cars – and await him there?'

Audinette opened his mouth, but before he could say anything, the study window opened and Henri stuck his head out.

'Hi, Henri,' Audinette drawled as if greeting an old friend. 'Sorry I'm slightly behind schedule, but–'

'Yes, yes,' Henri snapped, waving a hand dismissively, '– just a minute! I've got to deal with *him* first,' – he pointed at Jean-Claude – 'so go and introduce yourself to the people in the *chais* or something. I'll be over in a tick. Oh, and get that damned car off my forecourt.'

Audinette hesitated for a moment, but then it dawned on him that it might be unwise to antagonize his new employer on his first morning, particularly with an audience of minions hanging on his every word.

As Audinette nonchalantly got back into his car, Henri turned his attention to Grégoire. 'Brignard, it's no wonder the silver is in such a frightful state if you spend half the day gossiping. So, get inside and start polishing – *now!*'

The roar of Audinette's car, together with squealing tyres and flying gravel, served to drown out Grégoire's mumbled obscenities as he shuffled towards the front door. Before opening it, however, he turned, raised his eyebrows, and, using sign language, instructed Jean-Claude to come round to the kitchen later.

In keeping with many houses of the period and locality, La Fayette's apparent ground floor was effectively a basement, with the piano nobile above it – hence the long flight of steps leading from the forecourt to a balustraded terrace fronting the main doorway. Although the study window was, therefore, some three metres above the ground, Jean-Claude didn't descend the steps and position himself below it: instead, he moved to that side of the terrace which was closest to the window. It was not the position Henri had anticipated him to take. As a result, not only could he not look down on him, but because Jean-Claude was standing immediately to his right, he was also forced to lean out of the window and twist his head through almost ninety degrees.

'Do you have to stand there?' he barked.

'We could talk like sensible human beings in private – in the house – in the study – together.'

'Oh no,' Henri sneered, 'not after what you did to Tiquetorte on Saturday night – not after what you did to *me*, damn it, on Saturday morning!'

Jean-Claude shrugged. 'Have it your own way.' He took a deep breath. 'I suppose the new guy, the fashion model, is–?'

'I've been trying to phone you since yesterday. Bloody ridiculous not being contactable. What if there'd been a crisis here? A storm, a fire a–?'

'You've got your new *maître de chai*, haven't you? You must have been busy recruiting for weeks. I hope you don't expect me to hold his hand until he settles in because–'

'"*Hold his hand*"! Christ, no! The reason I was phoning you every five minutes was to tell you *never* to set foot on my land again. You're a homicidal maniac, Bourjois. I've seen Tiquetorte in hospital and–'

'You know perfectly well why he got taught a lesson.'

'Yes – yes, I *do*. Of course, it takes two to tango, Bourjois. Did you mete out similar punishment to your dear lady wife?'

Jean-Claude gripped the stone balustrade fiercely. After a few seconds, he said: 'Henri, I've cleared out all my things from the *chai*. I've said goodbye to almost everyone. Once I've seen the others, I'll be off. You see,' – he reached into his shirt's breast pocket for the cheque Henri had given him on Saturday morning – 'that new job–'

'You're *fired* – with *immediate* effect,' Henri interjected triumphantly, frantic to say the words he'd been rehearsing over and over with unrequited joy. Like a magician pulling rabbits out of a hat, he waved two envelopes above his head. 'There's a cheque for three months' salary in lieu – less that "*bonus*" you screwed out of me – which, in all the circumstances, is rather generous, I think. I'm telling the staff we've agreed to part on mutually agreeable terms, due to irreconcilable differences on – on … on matters of strategic policy. But believe me, Bourjois, if you start whingeing to any of your cronies in the press, like that little Miss Appleton, then a few references to your acts of violence, a clinically depressed wife seeking solace in another man's arms, a son who runs away from home, a – a – a …'

To Henri's consternation, his dismissed employee was laughing – vigorously! Even Jean-Claude was surprised, for deep down he knew that Henri's threats and slurs were not at all amusing. And yet the venom in the man's voice and the contorted expressions of anger and hatred on his face, coupled with his bizarre stance at the study window, conjured up an egocentric autocrat haranguing a press-ganged crowd gathered before the presidential palace of some dictatorship or other. And it was all for no purpose!

In silence, Henri stared nervously as his bête-noire appeared to suffer a nervous breakdown; he'd been absolutely right not to let the maniac into the house. He wondered whether he should summon assistance of some sort – Brignard, or even the police – but just as the possible consequences of involving the latter began to make Henri's heart beat even faster, Jean-Claude appeared to pull himself together.

'Have you quite finished, Bourjois?'

Jean-Claude nodded. 'Yes, thank you. You really have to be standing where I am – I mean in my shoes. ... The point is, I've been here since eight o'clock, Henri, clearing out my things. Do you want to know why?'

'A guilty conscience, no doubt. At least you had the common sense to realize you'd gone too far with Tiquetorte.'

'Oh, for Christ's sake, leave him out of it. You told me to find a new job on Saturday. I did – just a few hours later, would you believe? A fantastic offer which I certainly could *not* refuse. They wanted me to start right away – *today* in fact. I've already told everyone here.'

'You're – you're *bluffing* – trying to put a brave face on things.'

'Have it your own way, but you'll find out soon enough. And as for your 'bonus' cheque, Henri, you can have it back – or I can rip it up here and now. Which do you prefer?'

Henri stared at the piece of paper in Jean-Claude's hand. 'I – I ... I'm not writing out another cheque for your salary in lieu, so you'd better keep it.'

Jean-Claude sighed and then ripped up the cheque into tiny pieces. 'On reflection, I think it's best destroyed. And frankly, I don't give a damn about your bloody salary in lieu. The fact is, I don't want anything else from you.'

Henri grinned. 'Oh *really*? Are you sure?' He waved the second envelope at Jean-Claude. 'Perhaps you should read *this* first before being so cavalier about your ... your *wages*.'

Jean-Claude feigned exaggerated interest. 'What is it? A claim for damages from Tiquetorte?'

Henri shook his head slowly. 'No, it's not actually.' He threw the envelope onto the gravel beneath the study window, expecting Jean-Claude to go down and pick it up, but he stood his ground, not taking his eyes off Henri.

A few seconds passed.

'Well,' Henri continued acidly, 'whether you pick it up or not, you'll soon be receiving formal notification from my lawyers. It's about my demented father's barmy loan and the mortgage of your vile house at Le Porge and ... well, I'm exercising our powers to increase the monthly repayments to a commercial level. They'll be going up immediately by one *hundred* per cent. I'm not a bloody charity, Bourjois.'

Just for a few seconds, Jean-Claude was unnerved. How on earth would he be able to cope? After all, he'd nothing in writing from Laura yet, and the sale of Sophie's paintings was still wholly speculative. Then, almost involuntarily, he began to nod his head. 'OK,' he heard himself say, as if someone else was talking. 'Fair enough. It's only proper that the loan should operate on a completely arm's length basis, especially as we're now parting company, so to speak. In fact, Henri, I'd expected you to do something like this a long time ago.'

'I'm delighted you're taking it so well.'

'Actually, to be honest, Henri, we don't anticipate being in Le Porge much longer.'

Momentarily, Henri was taken aback. 'Oh? Divorce, I suppose – divvying up the Bourjois ménage's tacky assets and all that.'

'No, I don't think so.'

'Surely you're not trying to tell me that you've forgiven the dear lady's treachery, or that your display of brutality the other evening reawakened her long-dormant passion for you?'

Jean-Claude breathed deeply and told himself to remain calm. 'Let's just say, shit face, that the new job comes with a very pleasant house, so we won't be needing Le Porge. In fact, I anticipate seeing estate agents later today with a view to putting the property on the market. Hopefully, within a few months, at most, you should be getting the balance of your loan – *Guy*'s loan, that is – repaid.'

Henri was visibly stunned. 'Well, I must say it all sounds very ... *enterprising*. I don't suppose you'd care to throw in any names would you – a little flesh on the bones of your great new venture?'

Jean-Claude smiled and shook his head. 'Sorry, no can do – still confidential. The consortium will be going public when the time's right.'

'"*Consortium*"! My, oh my, how *very* grand! You must think I was born yesterday, Bourjois. Frankly, this farce has gone on long enough. I've got better things to do than to stand here listening to your fantasies.' He threw the other envelope out of the window. 'There's your salary cheque, if you want it. I won't have people saying that I don't honour contracts. And now, Bourjois, just get in your shitty car, drive out the gates, and never come back. ... Oh,' – he lowered his voice – 'one more thing. Don't bother trying any funny business with that printer chap in Pauillac. I've spoken with him this morning, and he knows which side his bread is buttered on. He's accepted that he made a mistake.'

In view of all that had happened since Friday afternoon, Jean-Claude had completely forgotten about Ducasse and his trip to Florida. In a sense, it now seemed irrelevant. Doubtless, Henri had blackmailed the poor guy with threats of taking his business elsewhere and bad-mouthing him to other vineyard owners. There were so many things Jean-Claude had planned to say at this parting of the ways, but now all he wanted was to leave. So, he merely said, '*Adieu*, Henri.' Then he turned, trotted down the steps, and, pointedly ignoring the two envelopes lying beneath the study window, strode across the forecourt towards the *chais*.

Henri watched him go, struggling to contain his anger over Bourjois's final performance. He was about to ring for Grégoire and instruct him to fetch the envelopes when he realized that he'd merely be sharing his humiliation. In the end, he ran out himself, cursing. Remounting the steps swiftly, he found Grégoire standing at the front door, polishing a silver candlestick. There was just a hint of a smile on his face.

'I could have picked up that *rubbish* for you, sir. You should have called.'

Henri grabbed Grégoire's collar so violently that the silver candlestick fell from his hands and clattered down the steps. 'Any more clever remarks from you, *old man*,' he snarled, 'and you'll end up like sodding Bourjois. And don't forget – as far as I'm aware, dearest Papa never put *anything* in writing about the bloody pension that you and your lazy wife hope to get one day.'

As soon as Jean-Claude reached the great cobbled courtyard, he cut round to the rear of the house and Marie-Thérèse's domain in the basement kitchen. Shaking her head, she was staring at various pieces of paper lying on the huge wooden table in the centre of the room.

'Oh, *there* you are, Jean-Claude. I was wondering where you'd got to. Instructions from his nibs,' she sighed, waving a hand over the pieces of paper. 'Some guests for dinner tonight – out of the blue. He expects me to rustle up this lot. I'm not bloody Michel Guérard – *I* wish! Anyway, you haven't come to hear me moan. Sit yourself down there. There's coffee in the pot. Help yourself – and pour me a cup while you're at it.' With a smile, Jean-Claude did as he was told.

She pushed a plate of home-made pastries in front of him. 'So,' she said, 'why are you *really* leaving us, love?'

Jean-Claude was economical with the truth. He just talked about the endless arguments with Henri over investment and marketing, the lack of a challenge, poor remuneration – she knew all about that! – and, thanks to that lot, there'd been some marital friction. He needed a change, and, out of the blue, he'd received a fantastic offer. No, he wouldn't be leaving Bordeaux – sighs of relief – only moving to Entre-Deux-Mers. Marie-Thérèse was shocked: even to her, it sounded like exile. He tried to convince

260

her to the contrary, but finally he rose, saying that Henri had ordered him out, and, no doubt, he'd soon be round at the *chais* checking up on him – if he wasn't already there.

There were hugs and kisses and promises to keep in touch, with Jean-Claude repeating his words to Grégoire about the possibility of a job in Entre-Deux-Mers – if, that is, they were prepared to move. Marie-Thérèse said that if it meant keeping house for Jean-Claude, she'd go to the ends of the earth. As he started to move towards the door, she pulled a handkerchief from her apron pocket to dab her eyes.

'I bet poor Baron Guy – Lord, bless him!' she sobbed, '– never thought he'd live to see the day when his beloved Jean-Claude would leave La Fayette.' The words could have been a dagger piercing his heart. 'Please don't be angry with me,' she continued softly, 'but I pray for the poor man's release from his torment. From the few snippets of information we get, I think it may not be long now.'

Jean-Claude opened the door. 'Yes, well I'd best be off before–'

'Me and Grégoire haven't seen him for … well, for years, I suppose. Everyone says it's for the best – that it would be too upsetting … a nightmare.' She shook her head. 'I don't know, I really don't. Such a lovely man, and then …'

Jean-Claude breathed in sharply. 'Sorry. I have to go – Henri …' He took a step back into the room. 'Look, I do honestly believe it *is* for the best that you remember Guy as he was. It's a terrible disease, Alzheimer's–'

'Oh, I know. My Tante Marguerite – my father's sister – went completely bananas. They put her in a lunatic asylum – as they called them in those days and–'

'Exactly. At least Guy is in a nice private clinic.'

Marie-Thérèse nodded slowly. 'I suppose so. That's what Grégoire and me keep telling ourselves. … Of course, you were always his favourite, you know.' Jean-Claude smiled warily and looked again at his watch. 'Oh yes, right from the start. To be honest,' – she lowered her voice almost to a whisper – 'you were the son he always wanted and never had – couldn't stand Henri … *never*. In fact, before they took him away, when he was still up in the attic an' all, I remember the nurse saying to me one day that the Old Boy – that's what she called him! – kept raving about a son called Jean-Claude who had to go to a lawyer in Paris who knew the truth. "Well," I says, "that's the son he never had, the apple of his eye – Jean-Claude Bourjois – the *maître de chai*." … I wonder what "truth" he could have been talking about – and which "lawyer"?'

Jean-Claude shook his head. 'No idea. I'm sure dear Guy didn't have a clue what he was saying.'

'Maybe, but it wouldn't at all surprise me if, when he finally pops his clogs, he's looked after you in his will. So, don't let that Henri tell you otherwise. It wouldn't at all surprise me if–'

The door that led into the service corridor opened and Grégoire shuffled in. 'Oh, Jean-Claude! Thank God! I feared I might have missed you. His nibs has been inspecting me polishing. It's like being back in the bloody army.'

After another bout of embracing and kissing of cheeks, all three of them came out into the small yard. With tears in his eyes, Jean-Claude turned and headed for the *chais*. On the way, he suddenly remembered the bottle of wine that Laura had brought over on Saturday. Something told him it was important, and that he should take it with him; in any event, it was Laura's property. As he entered the first-year *chai*, the sounds emanating from his former office indicated that the new *maître* was introducing himself to some of the staff. Within thirty seconds, he'd removed Laura's bottle from the wine fridge and was marching swiftly across the courtyard.

A few shell-shocked estate workers were standing around his car. As he approached, one of them said: 'Bloody hell, Jean-Claude, you should be leaving with half a dozen cases and not just one sodding bottle – Christ! – a bottle that's already been opened, to boot!'

Jean-Claude laughed. 'Ah, this is no ordinary bottle, Pierre. It's the very last wine I tasted here, and, in a way, I suppose, it changed my life.'

The puzzling remark was quickly forgotten as the final farewells were said. Then Jean-Claude was behind the wheel and driving across the cobbles. Had he looked in his rear mirror, he would have seen Henri emerge from the battered tasting room: trotting over to the *chais*, he'd taken refuge there on spotting his homicidal ex-*maître*'s tatty car. But Jean-Claude stared straight ahead until he was well away from La Fayette.

That afternoon, the Bourjois family visited Château Belle-Mère. Alexandre, who'd been discharged from the clinic with a clean bill of health, had initially been unhappy about missing a whole day at school; indeed, he'd derided the château's name with all the sarcasm at his disposal. He'd not been noticeably mollified by an assurance from his father that if things went according to plan, the vineyard's name would be changed: as far as Alexandre was concerned, the apparent warming of relations between his parents would do nothing to improve his chances of a new life in Paris. But, upon arrival, he found it impossible to conceal his admiration for Belle-Mère's glorious architecture. His vivid imagination conjured up exciting images of himself hosting birthday parties for his chums in the palatial dining room, and staging alfresco productions of Molière around the gazebo – suitably restored, of course. Sophie loved the house too. It had style – as did the Fontaines, whom Jean-Claude insisted on meeting despite Sue's protests. And the Fontaines treated the Bourjoises with great respect – almost too much for Jean-Claude's liking, albeit Sophie and Alexandre lapped it up. Even Richelieu loved the place, which everyone said was a very good omen. He had a wonderful time running through the woods and jumping into the lake with Humphrey and Pumphrey, who, by the end of the afternoon, were completely worn out. Sue said she'd never seen 'her boys' have so much fun, and looked forward to the canine trio sharing many more happy hours together, whether at Belle-Mère or Barrage.

Back at Tante Colette's, Jean-Claude reported to Laura by phone. A couple of hours later, together with Quincy and Sophie, they sat down for dinner at Le Noailles; as ever, the brasserie lived up to expectations, and by the end of the first course a festive mood was in full swing, the enthusiasm for Belle-Mère appearing to be both unanimous and unconditional.

Tante Collette was a heavy sleeper, but in the early hours of the morning even she was awakened by the unmistakable sounds of passionate lovemaking as her nephew and his wife experienced orgasm after orgasm in the adjoining guest bedroom. Nevertheless, comforted by this welcome evidence of marital bonding after months of worry, she was soon snoring once more. Alexandre heard nothing: bewigged as Louis XIV, he was busy welcoming ambassadors to his dreamy court at Versailles, which, oddly enough, bore a striking resemblance to Château Belle-Mère.

PART 2

CHAPTER 22

It was 11 November, and, on this frosty but sunny Armistice Day morning, Henri de Bondé was breakfasting in La Fayette's Morning Room while perusing *Le Figaro* – not that he was particularly interested in world events or current affairs – far from it – but the action in itself gave him intense satisfaction. It was, in his opinion, such a gentlemanly thing to do, especially in this day and age when, by the time he'd arisen from his exquisite eighteenth-century bed, even most professional people, including many of his own friends, would already have been sat in front of a ghastly 'desktop' for at least an hour.

Henri was feeling particularly content this morning. For a start, his wife, Nancy, wasn't sitting opposite him doing her very best to destroy the nostalgic charm of his breakfast ritual with endless witterings about society engagements, weddings, christenings, funerals and memorial services. Mercifully, she'd gone to spend a couple of days in Albi, where the Musée Toulouse-Lautrec was staging an exhibition of loaned works from various private collections. Neither she nor Henri knew much about Toulouse-Lautrec, but some Italian 'princess' was opening the bash, thanks to the generosity of her fourth husband; his cement company, a force to be reckoned with in the construction business from the Pyrénées Atlantiques to the Alpes-Maritimes, had somehow been persuaded to sponsor the exhibition.

Nancy and the 'princess' had met some years ago at a week-long course on Japanese flower arranging held at an exclusive hotel near Avignon. Although the 'princess' had invited Nancy to Albi as her 'guest', she'd dropped heavy hints that if Château La Fayette were to supply the wine for the lunch being given for the VIPs attending the exhibition's inauguration, it could prove a most useful marketing opportunity. Henri's opposition had only crumbled when the 'princess' emailed a copy of the VIP guest list: he'd found it difficult to believe that such a glittering battalion of wealthy do-gooders, titled dilettantes, and world-class art gallery bigwigs could materialize in such an obscure spot as Albi – and in November, to boot. He'd even been tempted to accompany Nancy, but the art world was a mystery to him, and he'd no desire to reveal his ignorance before such a gathering. Nancy could serve as an adequate ambassador:

through good old feminine charm and seemingly endless gushes of superlatives, she was excellent at making facile conversation and camouflaging her ignorance of almost any topic.

Unsurprisingly, the Département du Tarn's wine producers had been outraged when a whistle-blower in Albi's *hôtel de ville* spilled the beans that Bordeaux wine was going to be served at the Musée Toulouse-Lautrec. There were threats of demonstrations and boycotts, and the local media rallied to their cause. The story soon reached the Paris press; national television and radio followed. It was all wonderful publicity for La Fayette – and completely free! In the end, the museum and the municipal authorities negotiated a compromise: the Musée Toulouse-Lautrec would offer a choice of red wines, with three local offerings – chosen through a secret draw – in addition to the alien Bordeaux. Henri was sure which wine most VIPs would choose from the individual menu cards he'd also agreed to sponsor; pursuant to a discreet deal with the 'princess' to avoid sabotage, they'd only be placed on the tables shortly before lunch was served. Patrick Audinette had once again excelled himself: the menu cards and the 'deal' were his ideas.

Henri chuckled as he helped himself to another cup of coffee. Audinette certainly had a gift for marketing – such a contrast to stick-in-the-mud Bourjois! The chap was far better connected than he'd ever imagined, notwithstanding the constant blowing of his own trumpet. Indeed, his addiction to name-dropping could get on one's nerves, but he did have almost every French wine critic – and many others – eating out of his hands. It was hardly surprising: he could regale them with anecdotes about celebrities in the world of sport, cinema and popular music in a manner calculated to give the impression they were intimates and, therefore, admirers of La Fayette. Above all, Audinette was passionately proactive: he personally contacted critics, writers and journalists, proffering invitations to La Fayette with such charm that anyone would think he was in love with them – female or male. Henri had witnessed many of these telephonic gushings: Audinette had no compunction in taking calls on his overworked mobile even while 'in conference' with 'the boss'! But he got these loathsome characters down to Margaux, which was all that mattered. True, La Fayette's marketing budget had soared since Bourjois's departure, but it was a price worth paying.

Persuading Henri to offer accommodation to the wine hacks at the château itself had, however, proved an uphill struggle. Nevertheless, young Patrick's powers of persuasion had proved impossible to resist: 'the boss', he pointed out, would avoid the cost of putting up the hacks at local hostelries; anything below four-star standard would be counterproductive.

On the other hand, Henri did draw the line at accompanying Audinette to the nocturnal entertainments in Bordeaux selected for their guests, be they opera or ballet at the Grand Théâtre, or backstreet clubs accessed by plain steel doors with spy holes. Hitherto wholly unaware of almost all of them, Henri was amazed by the number of such establishments to which Audinette belonged. Indeed, this chameleon was revealing – vicariously and anecdotally – a side of Bordeaux that both surprised and oddly fascinated him.

Alas, Audinette did have defects: he could be very irritating with his Internet-age jargon; his flashy car and frighteningly expensive clothes occasionally made Henri feel managerially challenged. Above all, Audinette had found Bourjois's grim cubbyhole in the first-year *chai* wholly unsatisfactory. Sat in such an excuse for an office, he declaimed, no visitor would take him seriously. Campaigning vigorously for a room in the main house, he'd even had the temerity to suggest decamping to Henri's study, arguing that, as 'the boss' was away so often, he really didn't need it. Henri was unmoved. Audinette's second choice, the tasting room – with appropriate modifications, naturally – was also vetoed: after the small fortune expended on it, Henri was not going to have his chef d'oeuvre compromised. Finally realizing that there'd be no escape from the *chais*, Audinette went into overdrive and bombarded Henri with refurbishment plans for 'Bourjois's dump'. In the end, he sanctioned the 'ultra-modern' proposal bristling with halogen spots and oddly-shaped furniture. It all looked very artistic but proved to be extremely uncomfortable.

Nonetheless, now that he had 'a real team player' in the *chais*, Henri was prepared to tolerate these and other irritants. As for the day-to-day workings of the estate and the technical business of making wine, Audinette was like a breath of fresh air: there was none of Bourjois's 'roots-in-the-soil' rustic folklore nonsense – such as his insistence on racking the barrels when there was a new moon and a north wind. Audinette happily admitted that he saw wine production as a straightforward manufacturing process: behind the picturesque old stone walls of a Bordeaux château's *cuvier* were equipment and machinery performing the same functions as those found in any New World winery. He wasn't bothered about replacing La Fayette's ageing stock of equipment, or rebuilding the *chais*. On the contrary, he could see positive marketing advantages in maintaining their science-museum-like appearance: it all helped to generate an aura of tradition, craftsmanship and uncompromised standards. They certainly didn't need a battery of hi-tech microchip-controlled equipment to make wine that would please the critics. After all, thanks to his predecessors, La Fayette's 'production facilities' operated like a well-oiled machine and turned out a good product, but then being slap bang in the middle of Margaux, the Bourjois crowd would have been rather incompetent if they'd turned out anything less. All he had to do on the quality front, therefore, was to maintain these standards, and for this purpose there was an army of faithful retainers who knew their duties inside out.

In truth, the staff were bewildered. For decades, they'd known only the Bourjois clan's 'hands-on' management style – *maîtres* omnipresent in their supervision of everyone and everything. Audinette, however, had no intention of remaining a humble *maître de chai* for the rest of his life, overseeing all the humdrum day-to-day activities – pruning, ploughing, fertilizing, weeding, spraying, picking, sorting, fermenting, racking, tasting, assembling, bottling, labelling. And that was one of the reasons why he had to insinuate himself into every aspect of La Fayette's managerial operations and assume an aura of indispensability. In approximately two years' time, when he'd ask 'the boss' for a directorship and shareholding, Henri would have little choice but to agree, or risk a potentially disastrous hiatus.

Henri was already thrilled by Audinette's appreciation that his role was to assist him in boosting profits by making the first wine truly 'exclusive' – the wine everyone would be talking about – the wine the pretentious nouveau riche would die for. For these purposes, the stuff in the bottle had to be good – very good in at least a few vintages – but it didn't need to be mind-blowingly stupendous. It merely had to appeal to the most influential critics – particularly the Americans – when they visited Bordeaux every March for their first and all-important tastings of the latest vintage. And to achieve that, he just needed to 'tweak' the product during the first few months of its life.

The *assemblage*, therefore, was the one thing Audinette had no intention of delegating. Down to the last flickers of sensitivity on his well-honed taste buds and olfactory nerves, he knew exactly what sort of wine he wanted. La Fayette was to be rejuvenated. Who cared how the château's wine tasted in ten- or twenty-years' time? All that mattered was how it tasted for those March make-or-break tastings, when the château would make the bulk of its sales. He wanted a darker, fleshier, oakier wine to cater for the *goût Américain* – a 'Parker style' wine, one which could be drunk younger and would not, like most Cabernet Sauvignon-dominated Médoc wines, taste harsh and tannic during its first five years. After all, what proportion of wine drinkers indulged these days in the luxury of buying wines to lay down for ten or more years? How many had the space – let alone the cellars? Patience was a virtue few people exhibited in the twenty-first century: there just wasn't time for it.

Henri concurred wholeheartedly. His experiences in the USA confirmed that the average diner at a ludicrously overpriced restaurant was happy to splash out on a Pétrus, Haut Brion or Lafite which had only been in its bottle for a few years! – a complete waste, of course, but their producers were laughing all the way to the bank. They didn't care whether a vintage was consumed straight from the bottle when just four years old by a Denver advertising executive as an accompaniment to a Labour Day barbecue, or after twenty years from a Napoleon III Baccarat decanter by a bevy of wine freaks in a private dining room at the Waldorf Astoria. Anyway, who was to say that Audinette's new, softer, rounder, fruitier, oakier blend wouldn't mature into something very special?

For a few moments, as Henri polished off his last chunk of Armistice Day croissant and savoured the rich buttery taste in his mouth, he permitted himself the luxury of wondering why he felt so happy. In fact, on further reflection, he was forced to admit that he couldn't recollect a time when he'd felt happier. What truly excited him this morning were his interwoven images of Audinette's most enterprising innovation to date, and his predecessor's current bad fortune in Entre-Deux-Mers – what a fitting graveyard for a failure! – if the latest gossip weaving its way through the Bordelais bush telegraph was to be believed.

Henri looked admiringly at his Patek-Philippe. It was almost twenty-five past nine. Audinette would shortly be coming over from the *chais* with the artist's proofs of the *étiquette* for the latest addition to La Fayette's stable of wines – La-Fa, a jolly decent *rouge* with a generic Bordeaux *Appellation d'Origine Contrôlée*. Produced mainly from grapes grown at *petits châteaux* further north in the Bas Médoc, it would be Henri's answer to Mouton Cadet, the Rothschilds' generic Bordeaux produced at a factory-like winery on the outskirts of Saint-Laurent-Médoc. Well, if a third wine was good enough for that gang ... And then there was that pervert Vincent de Forgeron with his cheeky Forgeron Cub. He'd bloody knock the spots off both of them!

Turbocharged, Audinette had dashed around Aquitaine during the summer doing all sorts of enterprising deals, including a three-year lease on a Mouton Cadet-type winery near Pauillac built by an over-ambitious Moulis *crus bourgeois* that had got into difficulties. The lad had floated the idea that exports of La-Fa to the USA and the Far East could end up as General Lafayette, thereby enabling even more bottles of the real second wine to be transmogrified into the great *grand cru* itself. Pure genius! Of course, a loan – a rather large loan – had been necessary to finance the bulk supplies of grapes for the new winery, the extra staff, the marketing and so forth, but Audinette's butt-licking bank-manager father had been most obliging. OK, there were substantial start-up costs, but the margins on branded wine could be quite impressive. After all, Mouton Cadet was basically plonk – decent plonk, mind you – but plonk nevertheless, and look at the prices paid for it by idiots in the UK – and elsewhere – just because the names 'Mouton' and 'Rothschild' appeared on the label! What a farce! But then, as a leading producer in Bordeaux had said recently: 'Brands are designed for consumers who don't know a great deal.' How very true!

Yes, La-Fa was a masterstroke, and Henri congratulated himself on having the sense to put Audinette fully – well, almost – in the picture on the Château La Fayette/General Lafayette score within days of his employment's commencement. In any event, he was the sort of savvy wide boy who'd have quickly worked it out for himself. He was sharp – *very* sharp ... too sharp?

There was a knock on the door, and a frisson of excitement shot through Henri's body – Audinette, no doubt, early with the artist's proofs of the La-Fa *étiquette*.

'Enter!' he cried, rising from his seat with the intention of conducting the meeting in the study.

'Oh, *here* you are, Henri,' Audinette drawled, striding into the room dressed head-to-toe in autumnally beige Hermès, including an ensemble of sports jacket, polo-neck sweater and trousers in cashmere – yes, *cashmere*! Henri did some rapid arithmetic and wondered how the guy could possibly afford it all. 'I've been waiting for you in your office – *study* – sorry – for the last five minutes. I thought you said quarter past.'

'I–' but before Henri could put Audinette in his place, the phone rang. It was Geoffroy de Tiquetorte, a man who gave every impression these days of hovering on the borderline between normality and something that seemed worryingly close to the sort of eccentric behaviour one might expect from a retired admiral or general. The poor chap had never really recovered from the Bourjois debacle at Forgeron's *Fête de la Fleur* back in June; his front teeth implants had not helped, having given him not only a faint resemblance to Bugs Bunny, but also an odd lisp.

'Brathe yourthelf, old fruit,' Geoffroy intoned. 'The clinic'th jutht phoned me with the newth that Guy pathed away about half an hour ago.'

'What? ... Oh!'

After discussing all the tedious formalities for a few minutes, Henri put down the receiver and faced Audinette. 'My father's died,' he said brightly.

'So I gathered.'

What happened next became all rather dreamlike for the new *de jure* master of Château La Fayette and all the rights and privileges belonging or appertaining thereto. In an intoxicating cloud of Hermès Orange Verte cologne – a fragrance with which Henri had had a lifelong acquaintance – his *maître de chai* stepped forward, his face now a mask of compassion, and gripped Henri's arms as if in fear that his employer might at any moment slump grief-stricken to the valuable Persian carpet beneath his feet.

'My *dear* Henri, please accept my *very* sincere ... condolences. He was ... he was an *extraordinary* man.' The crushing embrace that immediately followed these ambiguous words felt almost passionate. 'Congratulations, *Baron*,' he added, whispering in Henri's ear, '– free at last!' A rare collapse of self-control ensued: the urge to kiss his employer on both cheeks couldn't be resisted.

CHAPTER 23

Jean-Claude's pouting reminded Quincy of a petulant child; it was no wonder he and Henri de Bondé had had such a turbulent relationship. Similar thoughts had also crossed Laura's mind during the board meeting, but even though they were on opposite sides of the argument, she'd found Jean-Claude's facial expressions and defensive body language rather touching. As usual, it was turning into another 'Anglo-Saxons-versus-the-French' confrontation, although so far, the opposing views had been expressed with decorum and in measured tones – in French, the language generally used at Belle-Mère's board meetings.

'Well, I'm sorry,' Quincy continued, looking from Jean-Claude to Charles Fontaine, 'but I'm completely with Laura on this one. If we're going to have any chance of making a success of this project, then we have to drag Belle-Mère by its bootstraps into the twenty-first century and produce wines which the mighty critics profess to like and the bloody punters will buy – at a decent price.'

'You sound like my old boss,' Jean-Claude protested. 'I don't see the point of making wine that tastes like something from California or Australia. Bordeaux has its own distinctive style, and if the English or the Americans don't like it, then that's *their* problem.'

A tremendous explosion of electric drilling from the floor above prevented Quincy from responding immediately. The appalling vibration caused more flakes of plaster from the dining room's ornate ceiling to descend to the table.

'Electricians or plumbers?' queried Laura.

'Both,' replied Fontaine, shaking his head. 'So much for all our careful scheduling.'

At any moment, Jean-Claude conjectured, *there'll be another diatribe against French workmen – Laura moaning about lengthy lunch breaks and Quincy championing the willingness of British 'workers' to put in as many hours as it takes to get a job done, even if it means working into the night and at weekends. Don't the Brits realize that even machines burn out, break down or explode if you overwork them?* Resolving to pre-empt the likely attack on his compatriots, he said proudly:

'The East Wing's almost finished. It looks *very* smart. There's a good chance we'll be OK for Christmas after all – us Bourjoises that is. Sophie will be thrilled when she gets back from Paris next week. No more choking dust or doubling up with you and Madame Fontaine in the West Wing, Charles.'

Involuntarily, Laura started drumming the tabletop. Did Jean-Claude have to sound so pleased about Sophie's goddam homecoming? Through a forced smile she said: 'I thought she wasn't due back for another fortnight – until Christmas Eve.'

Quincy noticed her fidgeting fingers and bit his lip. When the hell was Laura going to realize she was wasting her bloody time and bite the sodding bullet? Not only did Bourjois lack any sexual interest in her, he was also so naive and self-centred that he couldn't even spot her continuous flirting. Frankly, the more he saw of him, the more he thought their grandly styled '*Directeur Technique*' was a bit of a wally.

'She wasn't,' Jean-Claude replied merrily, 'but she needs to get back to work as soon as possible. *Les Orifices* have *all* been sold and Dominique' – Laura noticed that Jean-Claude always called the art dealer by his first name these days – 'wants her to resume production as soon as possible. He's procured a commission from a Korean shipping tycoon for ten *natures mortes* – dead fish, I think – and he – the Korean – wants them by the Chinese New Year. And now that her studio in the attic is finished–'

'Well, the all-important studio was *our* priority, wasn't it?' snapped Laura.

'Absolutely,' Jean-Claude replied, seemingly unaware of the sarcasm. 'She can't wait to see it. And she wants our first Christmas here to be *perfect* – decorations, a big tree – *everything*.'

'I'm sure dear Alexandre will really appreciate it,' Fontaine said warmly, like a doting grandfather. Then he glanced at Laura and winked, but the pursed smile on her face remained frozen.

As a tremendous banging broke out above, Fontaine glanced at the ceiling. 'I suppose that's the wall between the Yellow Room and the old nursery coming down ... to make space for your new office, Laura. Dear Mama was lamenting it yesterday evening over supper. ... Do you know, she slept in her old room last night for the first time? She decided that the smell of paint had finally evaporated. It brought tears to her eyes – the room not the paint. She never thought she'd sleep there again. You've made an old woman *very* happy, Laura. ... By the way, if the gatehouse isn't finished before Christmas, Mama says you're very welcome to spend it with us in the West Wing.'

'Or with us in the East Wing,' Jean-Claude said. 'I've checked with Sophie. Actually, it was her idea. I mean, now that they're working here on the château's central block, you can't live in the middle of a building site, can you? – not with all the dust and debris. It must be awful.'

'Unfortunately, my stables are nowhere near being finished,' Quincy chipped in. 'They haven't even started on the central heating. Thank God my Bordeaux apartment isn't sold yet. Of course, Laura, it goes without saying that *mi casa es tu casa*' – there's bags of room at Cours de Tournon, and they do a wonderful carol concert at Notre-Dame on Christmas Eve.'

'Actually, I'm thinking of going to Seattle and spending Yuletide with Dad.'

As if on cue, the racket above their heads ceased abruptly and a stunning silence fell upon Belle-Mère's large dining room. It was twenty-nine minutes after noon and the workers had downed tools for their customary partaking of the nine euro three-course *menu* – including wine – at their preferred café in Langoiran. They'd return shortly after two in their fleet of little white Citroën vans, only slightly inebriated.

'*Yule*tide?' Quincy wasn't sure whether she was joking. 'I thought – I mean–'

'Dad seemed a bit down when I last spoke with him on the phone. And with all the mess here ... And I really should go and have a chat with my publishers in New York and–'

'Ah yes, your publishers – *very* important.' Quincy had lapsed into English and sounded quite put out. 'Well, naturally I wasn't *planning* to spend ... "Yuletide" myself in Bordeaux, but I just thought that with you being at a loose end and the construction work here–'

'I won't be "at a loose end", Quincy.'

'Obviously not. Anyway, as I was saying, what with completion of Woopston Parva's sale scheduled for mid-February, there's a hell of a lot of clearing out to do – and deciding what's to go into storage and what to bring here. And my London chums always come down to Wiltshire for a few days at New Year. Well, being the last Christmas at Woopston, I thought I should organize something rather special. ... If you change your mind about Seattle, Laura, maybe you'd like to come to Woopston and–'

'I haven't made any final decision yet, Quincy.'

'Oh? Well, I–'

Fontaine cleared his throat exaggeratedly and looked at his watch. 'I'm not sure Jean-Claude is completely following all this,' he said in French.

The *Directeur Technique* appeared to come out of a trance. 'No, no. It's OK. I got the drift. I was just thinking about the *assemblage* and–'

'Quite,' Fontaine interrupted, 'the *assemblage*. That's what we were talking about – as per the agenda – before we were distracted by our dear workmen, who, no doubt, are now motoring to Langoiran for their well-deserved luncheon. Now, I hate to be a bore, but Mama has invited the

Comte and Comtesse de Gradignan for lunch, and they're expected around one o'clock, so I suggest we get a move on. I shouldn't keep Thierry and Isabelle waiting.'

Laura stared at Fontaine's smiling face and endeavoured to control her emotions. Suddenly, she had a recollection of a dazzling burst of light as she sat under a mighty tree and saw Fontaine on that June afternoon almost six months ago when he strode across Belle-Mère's lawn carrying his great silver tray. It truly was extraordinary how this bankrupt minion – Sue had treated him no better than a slave – had made good. She still found it difficult to understand how or why his rehabilitation had come about. Well, she knew something about the 'how' of course – Quincy, of all people, had in effect *insisted* on Fontaine being made part of the Belle-Mère project, a very important part. Oh, there'd been some plausible reasons for keeping him on as a consultant for a while, but making him a director with a five-year contract?

Quincy had argued that retaining him as a 'consultant' for just six months or so until Jean-Claude was au fait with the vineyard, as Laura had proposed, was neither sensible nor realistic. Jean-Claude was, of course, immensely talented, but he knew nothing about Belle-Mère. Charles, by contrast, knew every square metre of the *terroir*, every *barrique*, every item of equipment – each with its own idiosyncrasies – and every employee. They needed him for at least twelve months to take them through each season – from the beginning of one vintage to the next – and preferably longer. After all, as they planned to keep the red *en barrique* for up to eighteen months before bottling, their first vintage's *élevage* would take almost two years. And although there'd be a radical change in the marketing of Belle-Mère's wines, Fontaine was extremely well connected throughout Bordeaux. In particular, he knew the head honchos at CIVB – the *Conseil Interprofessionnel du Vin de Bordeaux* – and at UGC, the *Union des Grands Crus*, the top producers' association that organised the huge annual spring tastings for the press and trade. Quincy had reminded Laura that as UGC membership wasn't restricted to classed growths, they'd agreed Belle-Mère should join.

Then there were all Fontaine's contacts in Bordeaux's labyrinthine wine trade – the *place de Bordeaux* – with its hundreds of *négociants* and *courtiers*. The *négociants* constituted the conduit of brokers and merchants through which the vast bulk of Bordeaux's production was distributed. The *courtiers* were the agents operating at a level between the producers and the *négociants*, a professional interface unique to Bordeaux originating in the eighteenth century to obviate aristocratic producers from dealing directly with bourgeois merchants. Quincy repeatedly pointed out to Laura that neither of them had truly penetrated the *place*'s extraordinary complexities. Yes, they knew people at the leading *courtage* houses and firms of *négociants* – including Sichel and Barton & Guestier – but, when all was said and done, they were outsiders – like everyone else who was not born into the magic Bordelais circle. As for Laura's proposal to bypass the *place* and sell Belle-Mère's wines directly, Quincy pointed out that direct sales would take a couple of years to organise, so they needed to keep their options open for the present – another plus for Fontaine.

Furthermore, Quincy had opined that the Pronks' exiling of the Fontaines to the dilapidated gatehouse was intolerable. Laura had proposed the stables, but Quincy countered that as their conversion would be one of the biggest construction jobs, and Madame Fontaine was clearly in her twilight years, it seemed only honourable to provide accommodation in the main house. By a process that Laura had yet fully to understand, a two-bedroom ground-floor apartment had morphed into an allocation of an entire wing. The other wing had been allotted to the Bourjoises: neither Sophie nor Alexandre – 'Little Lord Fontleroy' as Quincy had swiftly nicknamed him – would settle for anything less. Additionally, they'd been granted preferential rights to use the central block's 'state rooms' – the dining room, blue drawing room, music room, library and three very grand bedrooms.

With his Cours de Tournon apartment, Quincy had no immediate need for accommodation at Belle-Mère. However, he had superb collections of paintings and antique furniture at Woopston Parva, and doubted they'd fit into Belle-Mère's gatehouse. The stables, on the other hand, would be 'adequate' In truth, the eighteenth-century neoclassical stone building was a stately home in itself: after all, it had been designed to accommodate some thirty horses, together with their feed and a corps of grooms. Left unstated were Quincy's romantic aspirations – that, being some distance from the main house, the stables would provide a discreet milieu for effecting Laura's long-planned seduction. In this connection, the sooner Sophie returned from her extended Parisian sojourn the better.

By all accounts, the bumptious Buffet had spent over two months parading Sophie before a gaggle of leading European, North American and Japanese art critics. She'd never eaten so many three-star Michelin meals in her life – or put on so much weight so quickly. But then, she had made an awful lot of money – as had Buffet. Indeed, he'd treated himself to a new summer residence – the Bourjoises' Le Porge house, so conveniently situated just a brief drive from one of Europe's finest gay beaches. He was already planning a glittering summer season; invitations had even been despatched to the likes of Elton John, Rupert Everett and, of course, 'dear' Sean Kunstmann. So far, only Sean had accepted.

In Paris, on the rare occasions Buffet had permitted a few hours respite from his aggressive marketing operations, Sophie had managed a couple of lunches and dinners with her parents. Through interrogating her about the financial implications of *Les Orifices* and Belle-Mère, the Charpentiers gleaned that their beloved daughter would soon be a real chatelaine – no more embarrassing smokescreen stories to their friends about her status at La Fayette. Sophie's father even telephoned Jean-Claude to congratulate him on his 'fantastic good fortune' – a partnership with such 'proactive investment opportunities' as Appleton and Dubloon. From time to time, he'd read about them in *The Financial Times* and *The Wall Street Journal*. In fact, with backers like them, he was interested in investing some 'loose change' in Belle-Mère himself.

'Love the brand name ... son,' Monsieur Charpentier had enthused down the phone. 'Tremendous marketing potential. Make sure you get it registered internationally before counterfeiters try to rip you off.'

Laura had exhaustively pondered the apparent contradiction between her status as the real Belle-Mère chatelaine and the bizarre process by which she'd ended up with the goddam gatehouse as her residence. However, she'd finally convinced herself that it was a blessing in disguise. For a start, she didn't want 'to live above the shop': after a day's toil at the château, it would be much healthier to walk out of her office and physically separate herself from work. But, more importantly, as the gatehouse was isolated, she and Jean-Claude would have far more opportunities for intimacy, especially when the wife and child were in residence in the East Wing. On that score, Laura had no doubts about what the future would bring: as with Le Porge, Sophie would quickly grow bored with Belle-Mère and rustic Entre-Deux-Mers. In any event, the way things were going, she'd be rushed off her feet, either churning out grotesque canvasses or flogging the crap in Paris, London or New York with Buffet. She'd be moving in a very different set, to say the least, and Bordeaux, along with her husband and weird child, would all become irrelevances. Just how many solitary nights in rustic isolation could a man with a healthy sexual appetite tolerate? Sophie had already been absent almost two months, and this was only the beginning of her new life as an international art celebrity.

Laura watched Jean-Claude doodling on his notepad. Although sitting immediately opposite her, he seemed so distant. It was not just the huge dimensions of the table; the dining room was ridiculously large for a meeting of just four people, but, yet again, Fontaine had taken it upon himself to make the arrangements. No, it was more than that: ever since the debate about the *assemblage* had started in earnest a few weeks back, an invisible barrier seemed to have existed between Jean-Claude and herself;

Fontaine's Gallic snootiness and Quincy's untypical aggression had not helped. Jean-Claude needed to believe he was winning an important point, and, with him on her side – *their* side – it would be three against one. Then Fontaine could go fuck himself. Sorry, but she was at the end of her tether.

Quincy's voice was noticeably louder, a sure sign he was beginning to get flustered. In truth, whenever he was defending a strongly held belief, be it the sanctity of the pound sterling, the evils of television or – as now – his views on the type of wine Belle-Mère should produce, his booming voice became even more theatrical than usual. With the dining room's acoustics accentuating the effect, the hint of a pained expression on Fontaine's face said it all. Laura considered a jokey intervention – reminding Quincy that no one was deaf – but thought better of it: he was shaking his head ominously.

'Honestly, you're not living in the real world – which, with all due respect, Charles, is probably why this vineyard has gone bust twice in the last ten years and the four of us are sitting around this table today.'

'I really don't think–'

'Let me finish, Charles. I've been very patient listening to you for the last fifteen minutes without interrupting.'

'I–'

'Here are some basic facts – facts that Laura and I had very much in mind when we bought Belle-Mère. Firstly, despite all the hype and wishful thinking, Bordeaux is in crisis.' Fontaine snorted dismissively. 'Yes, Charles, *in crisis*. The region has inflated a huge bubble around itself and there's a real risk of it bursting imminently. There are thirteen *thousand* of us wine producers churning out eight hundred *million* bottles annually. That's more than Germany's entire production! But out of all that lot, only about three miserable per cent come from the 'quality' producers that everyone associates with Bordeaux – the so-called *grands crus* and their equivalents. About half don't even merit a specific left- or right-bank *appellation d'origine* but are sold under the generic Bordeaux or Bordeaux Supérieures *appellations* – plonk in other words.'

'Oh, come on, Quincy, that's hardly fair.'

'No, Charles, it's bloody plonk – some is decent plonk, I grant you, but a hell of a lot is barely drinkable. Simon Farr of Bibendum, one of London's top wine merchants, has opined that most of Bordeaux's vineyards would be better planted with beetroot.'

'*Oh là, là!*' blustered Fontaine. '*Quel idiot!*'

'It's all very well scoffing,' Quincy boomed, 'but you and I know that at current prices, the lower end of the market – and that's a huge slice – can barely survive. Meanwhile, the miniscule top end, represented by the smug *grands crus* – like your alma mater, Jean-Claude – are greedily pushing up prices to astronomical levels. Some of these châteaux now produce wines that nobody can buy and nobody ever drinks, they're so bloody expensive. They're just investment commodities. It's a caricature of wine. If that isn't a crisis, I don't know what the hell is.'

Jean-Claude was nodding. 'I agree,' he said without looking up from his doodle. 'It's what Henri de Bondé is trying to do with La Fayette. It made my blood boil.'

Quincy glanced at him sympathetically but made no comment. 'As I see it, one of the major problems we have is trying to break into an international marketplace in which Bordeaux has a tarnished image – right across the board.'

'Oh *really*!'

'Yes, Charles – and what's particularly alarming is that you and most Bordelais either don't realise that or won't admit it. And whatever may be the size of Bordeaux's wine exports in volume or value terms, the fact is that in all major markets – the UK, Germany, Scandinavia, the Low Countries, North America – you're losing market share. In a nutshell, most consumers can only afford the plonk, and when they compare wines in the same price ranges, they conclude that those from the New World, Australasia, Iberia, South America, South Africa – even other parts of France – just knock the spots off Bordeaux.

'While standards everywhere have soared, Bordeaux – with some notable exceptions – has sat back and traded on its past. And matters have not been helped by the huge number of producers – most of them very small by international standards – continuing to rely solely on the *place* – the four hundred or so *négociants* – to sell their wine. Well, that system may be OK as long as there's a seller's market, but the *négociants* are *not* the producers' agents – in practice they're the *buyers'* agents. They source the wines sought by *their* customers – the wholesalers, shippers, importers, wine merchants and supermarket chains.

'The *négociants* do *not* promote the wines they deal in – except their own brands, of course. So, they don't have any interest in raising standards, undertaking market research, better labelling – *anything*. Frankly, I can't think of any other product that's marketed like this – if you can call it marketing – relying on a three-hundred-year-old connection with the name "Bordeaux" to sell a product. It's an incredible combination of arrogance and apathy. "Selling", "marketing", "promotion" – they're all dirty words for most of these thirteen thousand producers. It all smacks of "trade". Most of you never travel – never meet your ultimate trade customers. You just leave it to the *courtiers*, who, year after year, arrange the same old

278

deals with the same old *négociants* and who churn out the same old contracts to sign and automatically get paid their standard two per cent commission. And how do the *négociants* sell the *petits châteaux* and the nondescript wines that Bordeaux churns out and which no self-respecting client really wants to buy? They say, "Yes, Mr London importer, we can let you have some cases of Lafite or Pétrus, but only on condition that you also take one hundred cases of Château Filth and Château Piss."'

Fontaine was shaking his head and staring at the ceiling. 'I'm sorry, Quincy, but you're not being fair. I'm sure there are many producers in California who would be over the moon if they had a system like the *place* to sell their total production each year. You see, my dear chap, because they are comparatively small, most of the producers here simply don't have the resources to run a marketing operation – procuring customers across the world, negotiating hundreds of separate contracts annually, arranging the shipping, invoicing, debt collecting. They need the *place*, and, on the whole, it's worked well for them over many, many years. The *place* buys their wine each year, whether the vintage is good or bad, they get a fair price for it, they get paid *locally* by people they know and trust – and on time. It's not a perfect system, I grant you, but what is in this world?'

'Charles is spot on,' Jean-Claude said earnestly. 'Henri caused loads of problems at La Fayette by breaking ranks and abandoning the *place*. I mean, he set up his own *négociant* firm with a few of his cronies. And what happened? He ended up spending most of his time globe-trotting and losing touch with what was happening at home, *and* believing his own hype – all, no doubt, at great expense – money which, in my view, would have been better spent on the vineyard and improving the wine.'

'Exactly,' Fontaine snapped

'Oh, *come on*, Jean-Claude,' Quincy blasted. 'I don't think you can moan about the quality of La Fayette's wines. Naturally, I don't know *exactly* how Bondé's gone about marketing La Fayette, but I do believe that in principle he took the right decision to take control of his business and sever the connection with the *place*. Any sensible businessman – or woman – should be directly involved in the marketing of their products and in direct contact with trade customers. And as for Charles's point about the difficulties of setting up one's own marketing operation, I believe they're grossly exaggerated – it's just a bloody Bordelais cop out. Several châteaux have done it, and are doing very well, especially here in the Premières Côtes – and in St-Emilion ... and in Bourg and Blaye.'

'Mostly small fry,' Fontaine sniffed.

'Not so, Charles. Christ! – this is the *electronic* age – computers, websites, email. Once you've got your system up and running, you don't

279

need a sales force the size of an army to run it – everyone else in the world manages. So does much of the rest of France!'

'Quincy's absolutely right,' Laura said finally. 'And whatever the lack of expertise – real or imagined at other châteaux, he and I have worldwide contacts. We *do* speak several languages, and through our other interests we *do* know something about marketing. To be blunt, I've no intention of allowing Belle-Mère's wines to be abandoned to the whims of the *place*. We *will* promote *and* sell directly.'

Fontaine was again shaking his head. 'The Pronks thought they could bypass the *place*, and look where it got them.'

'Well, they don't seem to be doing too badly at Barrage, do they? And you tried hard, Charles, to upgrade Belle-Mère, and the *place* didn't exactly do a stunning job in trying to find *you* new customers. To be fair, the Pronks had to try and turn that mess around. Maybe they bit off more than they could chew. They were undercapitalized and didn't know the market you were aiming at. I believe *we* – Quincy and me … and Jean-Claude – *do*, especially overseas.'

'And *that*,' Quincy blasted, 'brings us back to the issue of our wine's style. I've no interest in producing just another "tasty" Premières Côtes with patronising comments from wine critics – you know the stuff, Laura, because we two have written it often enough.'

'"A surprisingly good effort for a *petit château*",' she intoned. '"Excellent value for everyday slurping." I want something *exceptional* – a seductively dark, fleshy, oaky wine bursting with fruit, a–'

'You want to produce another "exclusive", "exotic" wine,' Jean-Claude interrupted, 'a "jammy Californian–"'

'No!' shouted Laura, '– not "exclusive" … certainly not a mega-priced *garagiste*-type concoction selling at hundreds of euros a bottle.'

'Well, *that* – at least – is a relief,' Charles declaimed wide-eyed. He sighed sadly. '"*Garagistes*" – such a gimmick. I mean, here's a man, this Jean-Luc Thunevin over at St-Emilion, who comes from nowhere … well, Algeria to be precise, works in a bank, and then buys some miserable few hectares of vines. He gets a tiny crop of "superb" grapes through staggeringly low yields, crushes and even de-stems the crop *by hand* – years ago now – and makes the first vintage of his "Château Valandraud" in a garage because he didn't have the capital to construct a *cuvier* for his little venture. He puts his few thousand bottles on the market for over a hundred francs a bottle, and along comes your dear Robert Parker, Laura, and gives the stuff some super score in the upper eighties because it tastes like something from California. Thunevin never looked back. Now it retails at well over a hundred euros a bottle – obscene! My God, these "*garagistes*" are sprouting like mushrooms around St-Emilion and Pomerol. Their wines are nothing more than fashion accessories pampering to "*le goût Américain*" – a fad.'

Raising his volume even higher, Quincy boomed: 'Of course these miniaturist wines aren't worth the money paid for them by people with more money than sense. It may be a fad, Charles, but the *garagistes* are producing wines that people as eminent as Parker adore, and they're doing this with grapes grown in vineyards that, frankly, have little going for them. Yet in blind tastings, many top critics – and most consumers across the world with no specialist knowledge – prefer them to a hell of a lot of Bordeaux's output. So, all this guff that great claret – or Bordeaux whites – can only be produced in certain severely demarcated sacred spots in the Haut Médoc, Pessac-Léognan, Pomerol and Graves, is exactly that – guff. It's a myth propagated by the *grands crus* proprietors. The *garagistes*, Charles, have proved that rich, rounded wines bursting with fruit can be produced almost anywhere around Bordeaux – a fact that has sent shock waves through the *grands crus* stuffed shirts. They just pour scorn on these "new" wines with the ultimate insult – that they're alien Californian or Australian wannabes.'

'They're right,' Fontaine muttered.

Nodding, Jean-Claude said: 'I agree, Charles. Frankly, Quincy, I'm not sure what you're saying. Do you want Belle-Mère to produce a "*Parkerisé*" wine to appeal to "*le goût Américain*" or not? Sure, we could do it with very low yields through green harvesting – we did what we could to reduce yields as soon as we got the Pronks out in early July – plus rigorous selection at the *vendange*. Well, we did that too, not to the extent of the *garagistes*, of course – we can't afford to – but I did implement the best practices of a Margaux classed growth. And yes, we could go further – utilise all the new techniques to "enhance" and concentrate the flavours of a young wine and, in effect, make it taste maturer – rounder and softer, and, of course, oakier than a young Bordeaux would normally be expected to taste. We can opt for malolactic fermentation in barrel rather than in tanks, we–'

'Oh, my God!' exclaimed Fontaine. 'I most strongly advise against *malo en barrique*. It's terribly inefficient trying to monitor malolactic fermentation in hundreds of barrels rather than a few large tanks. It used to be common practice in Bordeaux right into the Fifties, before, that is, we really understood the secondary fermentation process and the conversion of nasty malic acid into lactic acid. I remember my father telling me the horror stories – the process not starting if the *chais* were too cold during the winter, and having to heat them up. If you were really unlucky, the

281

secondary fermentation might not start until after the wine was bottled. We don't want to go back to all that, do we?'

Smiling and reducing the volume, Quincy said: 'Technology's moved on a bit since the Fifties, Charles. Anyway, you're admitting that *malo en barrique* was a Bordelais tradition – that there's nothing "faddy" or Transatlantic about it.'

'That's true,' Jean-Claude said, 'but, arguably, putting the wine into barrels so early in its life destroys the distinctive hallmark of the wine's *terroir*, coarsens the tannins, and prejudices the wine's ageing potential. If you ask me, producers are going back to it for all the wrong reasons – to flatter a five- to six-month-old wine when the journalists invade Bordeaux in March for their annual tasting jamboree.'

Laura straightened her back. 'So what? If that helps to get an early thumbs up for your new wine, what's the problem – provided the wine, as bottled, is at least as good as it would have been if malolactic fermentation had taken place in tanks and only then poured into barrels?' Laura smiled her best smile at Jean-Claude. 'Come on, you know very well that there are many *maîtres* who believe that *malo en barrique* greatly improves the wine's ability to absorb the tannins and other compounds in the wood. OK, by March, when all those much-criticized journalists "invade", the wine is oakier, toastier – *torréfié* if you will – with even coffee aromas. But detailed experiments have been conducted – including at places as grand as Lafite and Latour – and after five years or so, they've hardly been able to detect any difference between wines from the same vintage that have undergone *malo en barrique* and those that haven't. And, as far as I'm aware, Jean-Claude, there's no hard evidence that the technique prejudices a wine's ageing potential. After all, *malo en barrique* was what you Bordeaux folks practised until fifty years ago, as Charles has reminded us – and it's what the Burgundians have *always* done. I believe we should go for it and start filling up those magnificent new oak *barriques* we've got out there. What do you say?'

Jean-Claude took a deep breath, but Fontaine got in first.

'Well, I remain of the view it's a step backwards – the risks involved are considerable. And I must again voice my dismay at the vast sums thrown at new oak. I accept that in Pronk times we weren't replacing *barriques* in sufficient numbers each year, but even at a classed growth only about half of each vintage goes into new *barriques*. I grant you that the likes of Château Margaux with their almost immortal wines can cope with so much oak, but wines lower down the pecking order, and particularly a wine like Belle-Mère ... well, the fruit will be completely dominated by damned oakiness. We're back to "*le goût américain*", the omnipotent and infallible Mr Parker, and the oak-besotted Anglo-Saxon market.'

Laura groaned and theatrically buried her head in her hands. When she looked up, Fontaine was staring pointedly at the clock on the mantelpiece, and Jean-Claude's face had visibly reddened. As her eyes met his, he quickly averted his gaze and began doodling again. He was adding more arrows to a large bunch of grapes that had already been struck by hundreds of Lilliputian archers.

Fontaine pushed his seat back and stood up. 'Well,' he said smiling, 'this is all *very* interesting, but Thierry and Isabelle will be arriving imminently and Mama will be wondering where I've got to. No doubt we can have another chat about–'

'This meeting,' Laura interjected, returning Fontaine's smile, 'is a formal meeting of the board of Société Civile du Château Belle-Mère, duly convened in accordance with its constitution, that is to say, a meeting of which each director – including you, Charles – was given seven days' written notice. We have a full agenda, and our deliberations are still in progress with several important and pressing matters to discuss and resolve. I'm afraid that you'll have to inform your mother that you're unavoidably detained. You can call her on the internal phone over there – one of the few things France Télécom have managed to get right.'

Fontaine remained stationary, the smile frozen on his face; he was staring at Quincy, who returned his gaze bemusedly. 'I don't think you quite understand, Laura. Mama's guests are the Comte and Comtesse de Gradignan. I'm expected. Thierry is a *very* important man in Bordeaux – isn't he, Quincy?'

Quincy nodded. 'Hmm, yes – *very* important. Pity, however, that Madame Fontaine had to invite him today – of *all* days, old boy.'

'Well, he's awfully busy, you know. Frankly, we were dashed lucky to get him over here at all – dashed lucky indeed. … And it's Armistice Day.' He began to edge slowly backwards towards the double doors. 'So–'

Laura slapped the table with the palm of her hand. 'Please, Charles, call Madame Fontaine and make your apologies. The sooner we finish here, the sooner you can join them for lunch. I would hope another half hour should be sufficient.'

Fontaine's smile finally evaporated. 'With all due respect, my dear, you have a lot to learn about how things are done in this part of the world. The Bordelais have certain *civilized* traditions, and finding time in the day to lunch and dine unhurriedly with family and friends is one of them. As the saying goes, "In Bordeaux it is difficult to eat alone." Moreover, Laura, as I trust you will soon appreciate, many of the most important transactions hereabouts are initiated, negotiated or concluded – or all three – around a dining table graced by good food and fine wine, and not in impersonal offices, down telephone lines or – horror of horrors – by "electronic mail". And now, my dear, if you don't mind–'

Laura slapped the table again. 'Charles, you wanted to be a director of this company. It is *not* an honorary position. It carries with it – as I'm sure you're aware – certain *legal* responsibilities with respect to the management of the company's affairs. You are *not* at liberty to abdicate them. This is our formal monthly board meeting. I will have minutes of its proceedings prepared. Decisions will be taken today on the matters set out in the agenda – taken, furthermore, by *majority* votes of those directors *present*.

'So, Charles, you have a choice. You can either stay and perform your duties, or go and have lunch with your "noble" guests – and, of course, be bound by any decisions the rest of us take in your absence. Is that clear?'

It was obvious from his demeanour that Fontaine was rapidly formulating a crushing response.

Smiling, Quincy cut in. 'I'm not sure, Laura, we need to be quite so … inflexible about all this. We're not the board of Bank of America. I dare say we could *all* do with a little break and a bite to eat. Couldn't we adjourn for lunch and reconvene around … say, three o'clock? I mean, old thing, Thierry de Gradignan can pull a lot of strings for us in the CIVB and UGC – so in a sense, you see, Charles's lunch *is* business, as the dear chap has been trying to explain.'

Laura wanted to knock the ear-to-ear condescending smile off Quincy's huge face. *What in Christ's name is wrong with him? Why is he always standing up for Fontaine – he's supposed to be on my side? … Sides? Less than six months into my venture, and our little board is already split into two opposing factions – three men against one woman! Just look at Jean-Claude! Even he's nodding his approval of Quincy's 'gentlemanly' compromise. At this rate we'll still be dithering at New Year about the* assemblage *and how to market our new wine. Compromise! A man's favourite word. Well, this isn't the UN Security Council or a European Union summit – those dickheads never get anything done either.*

Fontaine had reached the doors.

'Sorry, Quincy,' Laura replied acidly, 'no can do. I have appointments this afternoon – meeting the design people downtown at three to check out their proposals for the new Belle-Mère *étiquettes*, and the architects at four, *and* the guy from *Sud-Ouest* who wants to write a feature about us. He's fitting me in at five-thirty. That's why we're having a *working* lunch of sandwiches in here. Mind you, Marie-Thérèse was frantic this morning, wondering how she was going to cope in view of the *five*-course lunch she was having to prepare for Madame Fontaine, plus the last-minute cleaning of the West Wing, the arranging of enough flowers to stock a florist shop, and so on.

'Which reminds me. Before you leave us, Charles – the minutes will record that you were content to abide by any decisions reached in your absence – I want to make one further point *absolutely* clear to you – and please relay this message to your mother. Marie-Thérèse and Grégoire Brignard – like *you* – are employed and remunerated by our company. They are not *your* – or your mother's – personal servants available twenty-four hours a day at your beck and call. They've been employed by us for the purpose of providing catering, cleaning and maintenance services with respect to the *company*'s occupation of these premises. In brief – as you are so clearly anxious to leave us – that means looking after the central block of the château, where – once the work is finished – we shall have our few offices, our meeting room, and our hospitality suite – including this dining room, the new tasting room and the four guest bedrooms. Those of us who require the services of cleaners, housekeepers, cooks or other domestic staff – whether in this or any other wing, the stables or the gatehouse – must employ them *ourselves* and at *our* own expense.

'The Brignards have come here on Jean-Claude's recommendation, Charles. They are in their late fifties, and, having left one slave-driver of an employer at La Fayette, I'll not have their willing dispositions exploited or have them worked into early graves. In future, if you or your mother wish to make use of their services, kindly notify me or my secretary in advance and obtain *express* consent. Provided the Brignards have spare capacity at the relevant time, any such request would probably be granted. Understood?'

There was a deathly silence. Finally, almost in a whisper, a crimson-faced Fontaine said: 'I understand *perfectly* ... Laura. I shall communicate your edicts to my mother forthwith, although, in all the circumstances, one might have expected you to do so *in person*.' He walked out and slammed the door.

After a pregnant pause, Quincy said: 'Was that really necessary, Laura? He's not an errant schoolboy, for God's sake. I'm sure the Fontaines thought they were doing something very useful in inviting the Gradignans over for lunch. The old count is terribly well–'

'Oh, for Christ's sake, stop sucking up to Charles all the time. If it's so important for the business, how come *we're* not invited? *We're* the frigging controlling shareholders! ... I'll tell you why – because he wants everyone to think he's the big cheese around here. Well, I'm sick of it. He needs to be put in his place before he really starts taking liberties. And frankly, Quincy,

I'd welcome a bit more support. Anyone would think the guy has some hold over you.'

It was Quincy's turn to redden. 'And what the hell is *that* supposed to mean?'

But before Laura could explain, there was a knock on the door and Grégoire entered bearing a tray of cold cuts, cheeses and bread, mumbling apologies for the delay and that no one had had time to prepare sandwiches. After helping themselves, the three remaining directors returned to the vexed issue of the *assemblage*. Almost immediately, there was unanimity that Belle-Mère should produce red and white second wines, with only the estate's best lots being used for the '*grand vin*'. From their own tastings, it seemed likely that some sixty per cent of the production would end up as second wine; cash flow projections would need to be revised. Next year, there'd be even lower yields and more vigorous selection than anything yet seen in Entre-Deux-Mers. At the *vendange*, they'd take on far more students and do everything practicable to ensure that not an under-ripe or damaged grape would find its way into the crusher. As for the thorny issue of *malo en barrique*, there was further debate with continued scepticism from Jean-Claude. Finally, as the time approached for Laura to depart for her Bordeaux appointments, she came up with a 'compromise' proposal.

'OK,' she said, 'I accept that many producers have opted for *malo en barrique* simply to make their young wines taste better five months after harvest – just in time for the early tastings around March. And why do they take place at all, Jean-Claude?'

He looked puzzled, as if it was a trick question. 'Well, because about three-quarters of every new vintage is sold *en primeur* a couple of months later in June. You know that, Laura. People have to know what they're buying.'

'Of course she knows!' blasted Quincy. 'She's making the point that if you sell wine that's still at the beginning of its production process – as much as eighteen months away from being bottled, let alone ready for drinking – someone has to taste the stuff and say whether it's good, bad or indifferent. It's another dotty Bordelais tradition that doesn't stand up to logical scrutiny. It's like a woman going into Escada and ordering and paying for the summer collection for two years hence.'

Laura managed a chuckle. 'Very well put!'

'There you two go again,' Jean-Claude remonstrated, sighing. 'You know it all fits into the Bordeaux system of production being channelled through the *place*. It's a question of cash flow – selling *en primeur* gets cash into the producers' hands as soon as practicable. In the old days, when times were really hard, the *négociants* would buy wine that didn't even exist – when the grapes were still on the vine! They took huge risks.'

Laura sniggered. 'Yeah, Jean-Claude, they bought dirt cheap in return for taking those risks – and often made huge profits when they sold on. The merchants boomed and the producers languished. But you're talking about the days – before the Seventies – when the *négociants* were also the éleveurs – the blenders and bottlers. Most châteaux – even the top names – didn't bottle themselves – they couldn't afford to. The young wine was delivered to the *négociants*' vast cellars in Bordeaux, and that was the last they saw of it. So, the sooner the *négociants* got their hands on the wine they'd bought, the better.'

'But then came the boom years,' Quincy interjected, 'and the châteaux could afford to do their own bottling. So, they significantly reduced the risks of fraud by unscrupulous merchants, and also the vagaries in bottling quality from one *négociant*, importer or merchant to another for the same château's vintage. Huge quantities were even shipped in barrel to London for bottling.'

Jean-Claude smiled politely. 'Why are you telling me all this?'

'Because, dear boy, we're trying to illuminate the bizarre consequences of continuing to sell *en primeur*. When château-bottled wine became the norm in the Seventies, private and institutional speculators realised that buying it *en primeur* could be a jolly good investment. You were buying a very specific product – one produced from vines grown on a precisely delineated plot of land. You knew exactly – to within a few hundred square metres – where every aspect of its production had taken place – even the individuals who'd done all the work. Fantastic! And normally, the product would not only get "better" as it got older, but also rarer and more valuable because some of the production would have been consumed. Amazing! And what about this? – you could buy the stuff and not have to take delivery of it, or find space to store it, for at least two years, during which time you could always sell it on at a profit. It was as good as dealing in paper securities!

'But there was one teensy-weensy problem. As a private buyer in London or New York, how the hell could you tell whether this year's vintage of Château X was any good? Who were the independent experts? Cue Robert Parker and the like! Thus was born the Great Wine Critic, the new stars of the Wonderful World of Wine. Over to Bordeaux they trotted in early spring to do a massive round of tastings in order to get their verdicts published before the *en primeur* campaigns got under way in June. And naturally, speculators, traders, brokers – all business people – like simple things they can understand – numbers, scores out of a hundred – not a load of poetic verbiage.'

Laura was staring at her watch. She didn't want to rush Quincy – she knew the message he was trying to communicate to Jean-Claude – but time was running short. She didn't want to 'do a Fontaine' and duck out of the meeting.

'OK, guys,' she snapped. 'In a nutshell, we all know that tasting five-month-old Bordeaux is a bitch. It doesn't taste very nice, especially the left bank's predominantly Cabernet Sauvignon wines – the Médocs and the Pessac-Léognans, including all the megastars – Mouton, Lafite, Latour, Margaux and Haut Brion. Let's be honest, within these four walls ... they taste like shit.'

Jean-Claude looked as though he'd been hit in the solar plexus. Then he exploded with laughter. It proved infectious.

'Of course, in the old days,' Laura continued, with a huge smile across her face while the men still chuckled, 'when only the *négociants* bought *en primeur* – and controlled the bottling – *they* knew that. But they could tell good shit from bad shit, and being experts with claret in their veins, they could be fairly confident about how it would turn out after the élevage and bottling. Me and Quince go to the March tastings, Jean-Claude, and we get a general idea of what the vintage is going to be like, but, as you know, we never go public on what we think of individual wines at that stage. We know they're far too young and that over the following fifteen months plus, you *maîtres de chai* are going to do all sorts of things to your wines before they get bottled – more rackings, dumping barrels that don't eventually come up to scratch, et cetera.

'But today, *en primeur* prices hinge almost entirely on these March tastings. As soon as the first scores are published – and now there's a pathetic race by the critics to be the first – the producers start plotting their opening prices to test the market. The higher your score, the more you can charge and the stronger the demand. And when such important scores are being given to precocious wines that taste like shit, the less shitty they taste at that time the better. Hence the new popularity of *malo en barrique*, especially for less prestigious wines – I mean, no critic regularly fêted by a megastar is ever going to say that a glassful of any of *its* five-month-old wines would make you throw up. ... Maybe it's no wonder we spit them out. So, we have a stark choice at Belle-Mère. We either go for *malo en barrique* or we don't participate in the *en primeur* fiasco.'

Jean-Claude threw his head back. 'You can't be serious? – opting out of the system? It's unheard of – well almost. Yquem has never been sold

288

en primeur, but then as the world's greatest – and most expensive – sweet wine, it's in a class of its own. It can afford not to play the game.'

'I agree with you in principle, Laura,' Quincy said hesitantly, 'but it's a serious cash flow issue at present. We wouldn't get a penny for our new vintage for some considerable time. And there'd be all the league tables and media articles for new vintages with no mention of Belle-Mère – we'd be a kind of freak.'

'Is the superlative Yquem a "freak"?'

'It's *unique*, Laura, an exception.'

'Perhaps *we* should be "an exception", Quince. Maybe a vineyard owned by two "renowned" wine critics – and an illustrious *maître de chai* – that keeps its wine under wraps for a little while and turns its back on the whole *en primeur* farce, might generate the sort of interest – and, who knows, *respect* – that could do our fledgling venture a power of good. We start building up our client base through our worldwide contacts. We wet the appetites of the press with wisely crafted and timed press releases and hospitality – *here* – with tastings of our slowly maturing wines. And then, in twelve to eighteen months' time, we start accepting orders for our first vintage – under our new name, of course – whatever that's going to be, with the last Fontaine-Pronk vintages being sold off under the Belle-Mère name.'

'Sounds interesting,' Jean-Claude mused. 'Mind you, the financial implications would need to be assessed very carefully, wouldn't they?'

'Of course!' his fellow directors chorused with a consequent mutual chuckle.

Laura rocketed from her seat. 'Now I must dash if that's agreed.'

Startled, Jean-Claude mumbled, 'Oh … right.'

'Must dash too,' Quincy snorted, pushing his chair back. 'I'm sure I can sell that to Charles.'

Thrusting her board papers into a shoulder bag, Laura said: 'Tomorrow we can start work in detail on which lots of wine we're going to use for the first and second wines.'

Still dazed, Jean-Claude remained seated. 'Um … yes … sure. I …' He watched Laura and Quincy almost sprint to the room's double doors.

As Quincy opened them theatrically, Laura snapped: 'Any chance of a snack with you tonight in your comfortable East Wing, Jean-Claude? We could touch base on the artwork I'm picking up in town. Have you thought of any new names for Belle-Mère?'

'Er … OK. I mean, I'm just having some *confit de magret*, but you're welcome to join me. I'm not too sure about a new name though.'

'Fine. See you around eight.'

Jean-Claude opened his mouth but Laura swept out. For a moment, Quincy remained staring at him with a forced smile. Then he trotted after her with a cry of 'Hang on, Laura!'

'*Merde*,' Jean-Claude muttered, helping himself to another piece of cheese and a slice of Bayonne ham – he'd not eaten any breakfast. So much for all his plans for a quiet night in front of the TV with a tray watching the international between the Girondins and Real Madrid. Now he'd have to put up with Laura's superficial opinions on Europe, the world, and *everything* – not to mention the nightmare of having to repulse her amorous advances without hurting her tender feelings too much.

CHAPTER 24

Hesitating outside the door to the conference room, Monsieur Hubert Audinette detected the muffled voices of his two visitors and began fiddling with the knot of his silk tie, a rather striking crimson affair from Hermès. A few months ago, this expensive addition to his staid wardrobe had been a present to himself, when, after several years' penal servitude in Bordeaux's suburbs, his twenty-five years of blind loyalty to BIF – the mighty Banque Internationale de France – had finally paid dividends and he'd been promoted to manager of its prestigious Place des Quinconces branch. Now he had a position worthy of his abilities, with clients like the two titled big noises awaiting him on the other side of the door.

With a chuckle, Hubert pictured his wife glowing at dinner last night when she finally permitted herself to listen to the reasons for their premature departure from the BIF Senior Management Conference at Brantôme's renowned Moulin de l'Abbaye hotel. The drive home after Florence's eruption had been in total icy silence – not a single word all the way from the Dordogne to their new apartment in Allées de Tourny, the very expensive promotion gift to themselves that she'd demanded. But then, while she was thrashing around in the kitchen preparing their unplanned meal, her precious Patrick had phoned with the news that senile old Guy de Bondé had finally kicked the bucket and that his employer was now the new Baron de Bondé. So, when Florence's vow of silence crumbled over the dinner table in order to communicate their son's call, she in turn discovered that the loss of her four-star pampering at Brantôme was due to a request from none other than the Vicomte de Carbon Blanc for an urgent meeting. The noble lawyer had been somewhat reticent, but from what could be deciphered from his telephonic ramblings, recently promoted Hubert Audinette, no less, would be one of the executors of Guy de Bondé's estate! How Florence had had to eat humble pie!

By the end of dinner, not only had she specified every item of outerwear to be worn by her husband at the meeting, but she'd also begun to plan a chain of social events with the Carbon Blancs and Bondés, which, over the weeks and months to come, would graduate from an 'informal' drinks party to a sumptuous 'black-tie' dinner. What's more, at breakfast this morning, Florence presented him with an extensive shopping list, including a Limoges dinner service, a set of Baccarat wine glasses, *and* silver cutlery – that is, new *antique* silver cutlery: their modern Christophle set, a fairly generous gift to her husband from BIF to mark his quarter century of unblemished – albeit uninspiring – service to the bank, simply wouldn't do.

Wouldn't do, indeed! The woman was getting his promotion out of all proportion. Retirement was less than ten years away, and although the bank provided a generous pension, neither he nor Florence could rely on any other significant supplementary sources of income. They really had to start planning in earnest for those potentially long twilight years on a fixed income, plus a degree of inflation indexing. Saving, however, was not a word which struck any chords with profligate Florence; it didn't take a genius to work out where Patrick got his extravagant tastes from!

Sighing, Hubert returned to the hum of conversation within the conference room and allowed himself one further bout of self-inspection. Just as well: there was a scuffmark on his right shoe – John Lobb brogues – ludicrous! For the same price he could have got a half-dozen pairs of his favourite lace-ups from the Galeries Lafayette department store, but Florence had insisted. And this morning, of course, she'd gloated, pointing out how right she'd been: anyone who was anyone in Bordeaux wore *English* shoes, and Carbon Blanc and Henri de Bondé, no doubt, would be *most* impressed – and comforted – when they saw that the great Château La Fayette estate would be executed – or whatever it was that executors did – by a gentleman who wore 'the right sort of shoes' – indeed, who wore the right sort of suit too – in the English style – and made by that 'terribly exclusive' tailor in Rue Condillac, who, according to some of Florence's Lions Club friends, actually declined commissions from the 'wrong sort of people'.

'Is everything all right, Monsieur Audinette?'

'What? I– Oh, it's you, Madame Raffard. I – I–'

'You're not lost, are you?' interrupted the branch's chief cashier with a hint of sarcasm. Madame Raffard, in common with most of her colleagues, had felt quite shocked a few months back when the news came through that the powers-that-be at HQ in Paris had, in their infinite yet unfathomable wisdom, chosen such a common little man as Hubert Audinette to preside over the illustrious Place des Quinconces outpost of the BIF empire. She'd yet to be reconciled with their appalling decision, for everything that Audinette had so far done or said had confirmed her worst fears – and those of her ilk. The redecoration of both his own office and the conference room, for example, under the direction of his frightful wife had scandalized the branch's entire staff, but then, what could one expect from the offspring of trades people hailing from Blaye?

'*Lost*! No – of course not, Madame Raffard. Actually, I have a very important meeting with–'

'Well then, you've come to the right place,' she sneered, gesturing towards the sign 'Conference Room' – gold copperplate on an excessively shiny synthetic rosewood veneer that Madame Audinette had chosen. 'I would respectfully suggest that you do not keep Messieurs de Carbon Blanc and de Bondé waiting. With *my* many years of experience, I'm aware that they're rather particular about punctuality.'

Strutting away down the corridor, Madame Raffard heard her manager knock on his own conference room's door. 'Pillock!' she groaned.

Although the hushed conversation between Alain de Carbon Blanc and Henri de Bondé stopped abruptly as Hubert strode purposefully into the room, his carefully chosen words of greeting froze on his lips: half-rising from their chairs on the far side of the impressive table, the 'big noises' revealed the full extent of the funereal sombreness of their attire – dark, plain suits, white shirts and black ties. With reddening cheeks, he pictured himself in their eyes: the double-breasted suit in a gay Prince of Wales check, the red and blue striped shirt, the red Hermès tie – damn that tie! – *and* the tan shoes. Jesus! – the old baron hadn't been dead twenty-four hours, and here he was, a bloody executor, looking like – like … It was all Florence's fault. He should never have–

'Good morning, Monsieur … um … Audinette,' mumbled Alain, hesitantly holding out his right hand. 'So good of you to see us at such short notice. Do you know my client, Monsieur–?

Although Hubert seized the lawyer's hand, he stared with exaggerated compassion into the eyes of the bereaved. 'Morning, Monsieur le Vicomte de Carbon Blanc. … Um, Monsieur de Bondé – sorry – my apologies, Monsieur le *Baron* de Bondé … please accept my most sincere condolences … Baron.'

Henri managed a nod and was about to resume his seat, when, to his surprise, the bank manager lunged across the table and seized his hands.

'I feel I know you *so* well already, Baron de Bondé. My son, Patrick, never stops singing your praises. You must be devastated – about your father, that is. Such a wonderful man. I never had the privilege – I was only appointed manager of this branch a few months back, but … Anyway, the late *dear* Guy de Bondé was such a legend in Bordeaux – wasn't he? – such a respected pillar of our society, such a …' Hubert could feel Bondé sinking back into his chair and realized that if he didn't let go of his hands, he himself was in imminent danger of toppling over the table. He released his grip and, with an audible sigh of relief, Henri thumped into his seat.

Charming, sneered Hubert. *Grief? ... Hardly, not if Patrick's reports about the long history of animosity between father and son are true. And, according to Florence, Patrick said on the phone last night that Bondé had been 'absolutely over the moon' yesterday morning when he'd learned the old boy had finally snuffed it. Or is Bondé just miffed by my appearance? He's certainly avoiding my gaze.*

Hubert noted that Bondé seemed mesmerized by the file that he'd placed on the table just before launching his tactile condolences. Presumably, it contained the late baron's will, and Bondé was shitting himself in case it contained some nasty surprises. Christ! – if only he hadn't allowed Florence to experiment on him with all those different shirts and ties before breakfast, he might have got to the bank in time to examine the file and–

Quick! Improvise!

'Gentlemen, I must crave your forgiveness for both my appearance and for keeping you waiting a few moments, but I only got back from Brantôme – the Moulin de l'Abbaye – such a delightful hostelry, don't you think?' The question went unanswered; both visitors were now staring at the file. 'I mean – that is ... I was at Brantôme yesterday, Baron, when Monsieur de Carbon Blanc's sad news reached me–'

'Do call me Alain, Monsieur Audinette – it's so much easier.'

Hubert's mouth fell open. 'Oh – right – thanks. And I'm Hubert. *Do* call me Hubert – both of you – naturally. After all, we're probably going to be seeing quite a lot of each other over the coming weeks and months, aren't we?'

Alain smiled ambiguously.

Henri finally looked up. 'Are we?'

'Well ... yes, if I'm a co-executor. ... Actually, Monsieur – Alain – sorry! – I didn't quite follow on the phone–'

'Haven't you read the will yet?' hissed Henri, pointing at Hubert's file. 'I should have thought that's the first thing you would have done.'

'That's what I was trying to explain, Baron,' – Hubert paused for just a moment to give Henri an opportunity to invite use of his Christian name, but there was only silence – '... um, I was trying to explain that when ... *Alain* got through to me yesterday, I was up at Brantôme – attending the annual BIF Senior Managers' Conference – there were even some directors down from Paris – and, as I was giving one of the after-dinner speeches, Florence and I couldn't drive back to town until this morning. We set off *before* breakfast – came straight here – didn't even change – wasn't time. No disrespect intended.'

'"Florence"?' queried Alain, with raised eyebrows.

294

'"*Disrespect*"?'

Hubert stroked one of his lapels and then the other. 'My get-up,' he explained, '– fine for Brantôme, but hardly what one would have chosen for a meeting like *this*.' He shot a glance at Alain. 'Florence is Madame Audinette – my dear wife. Actually, she's got some very interesting suggestions for us all to get to know each other better ... round at our place ... in Allées de Tourny.' The address rolled of his lips with obvious pride.

'So, you haven't a clue what's in my father's file,' Henri snapped impatiently. 'That's what you're trying to tell us, isn't it?'

'Um–'

'Alain, let's not waste any more time. Put Audinette here–'

'*Hubert*, please, Monsieur – *Baron* de–'

'Please put him in the bloody picture. And let's be succinct, shall we?'

Being succinct had always been something of an ordeal for Alain, and he was already a few minutes into his discourse when he finally said: 'The point is ... *Hubert*, that my father–'

'The Comte de Pyla-sur-Mer?' queried Hubert rhetorically.

'My *father*,' Alain continued with a nod, 'drew up Guy's will some ten years ago – all pretty bog-standard stuff, thank God. Basically, subject to a few small legacies to some servants and employees,' – Henri groaned – 'and a rather generous bequest to a leading cancer charity,' – another groan – 'Henri here inherits the lot – or, in the event of Henri predeceasing Guy, any offspring of Henri's marriage–'

'We needn't bother with all that, Alain.'

'Sorry. No. ... Anyway, my father was to be an executor – or, in the event of him retiring, et cetera, the senior partner of his firm – that's me now, of course – together with the manager for the time being of this BIF branch – that's you ... Hubert.'

With a slight bow of his head, Hubert nodded acknowledgement.

'Of course, Audinette,' Henri interjected, '*my* father had your predecessor in mind, the late Louis de Montparnasse-Bourbon-Bainmarie. Frankly, Uncle Louis was not so much a bank manager, but ... well, one's meetings with him put one in mind of how a wise old courtier might have counselled his monarch at a private audience. Wonderful chap ... such a pity about the accident.'

'Yes, indeed,' Hubert empathised with apparent gravitas while flicking noisily through the surprisingly meagre contents of the Bondé file. 'And not that old really – only a year off the bank's compulsory retirement age. Still, skydiving was, perhaps, a tad reckless, albeit for charity.' *Reckless but most providential.*

'Indeed.'

'Anyway,' Alain continued, 'the point is that under Guy's will, you and I, Audi– ... *Hubert*, are indeed the two co-executors – assuming ... well, assuming two things, I suppose.'

'*Two* things?' repeated Hubert.

'Obviously! First, that you are prepared to act as–'

'Oh, I should be thrilled! I mean, it's an honour and–'

'– and, secondly,' – Alain and Henri exchanged nervous glances – 'that there are no codicils or ... or another will.'

Alain's final remarks hung in the air for some moments.

Finally, waiving a finger at the bank's file, Henri croaked: 'Nothing like that in there, I suppose, Audinette? Doesn't seem much from what I can see.'

'No, Baron,' Hubert agreed, 'not much at all. In fact, I don't seem to have a copy of the will, just–'

'The point is, Hubert,' Alain interjected, 'when I told my father yesterday about Guy's sad demise, he disclosed that about a week or two after the will was executed, Guy informed him – in the strictest confidence – that he'd left certain instructions with the bank – with Uncle Louis, to be precise ... actually he was a distant cousin but ... Anyway, Guy left instructions for a safe deposit box to be opened after his death. Papa says that Guy wouldn't tell him what was in the box, and, between you and me, nor would Uncle Louis.'

Hubert shrugged his shoulders. 'Naturally! That would have been a most serious breach of confidence and–'

'Whatever!' snapped Henri. 'So, Audinette, is there some blasted deposit box? – and, if so, what the hell's in the bloody thing?'

Hubert inhaled deeply. 'With all due respect, Baron, that was what I was about to tell you. Basically, from my quick flick through the file while you've been putting me in the picture, your father left instructions with my predecessor for the opening of *two* deposit boxes.'

'*Two*!' the others exclaimed.

'Indeed. I have the receipts here, and a written note of the late baron's instructions – they're signed and witnessed by Monsieur de Montparnasse-Bourbon-Bainmarie. In brief, one box is to be opened by the manager – apparently it contains just one sealed envelope.'

'Oh, God!' groaned Henri.

'The other, gentlemen, is to be opened only by yourself, Baron, and contains *two* sealed envelopes.'

'Can I see those instructions, Hubert?'

'In just a moment, Alain. ... However, in the event of your predeceasing your father, the manager was to open both boxes ... and destroy one of the envelopes – by burning it – and without opening it. Good Lord! – it's like something out of a novel, isn't it?'

Alain nodded. 'Maigret, or that English author, um … Agatha … Agatha–'

'Christie?' hazarded Hubert. '*Murder on the Orient Express* was one of hers, wasn't it?' Did you see the film – Ingrid Bergman was in it, wasn't she?'

'Was she? That was *Casablanca*, surely?'

Henri's fist hit the table. 'For God's sake, you two! Stop prattling on like a couple of bloody suburban housewives.'

Alain was used to these sorts of outbursts, but Hubert was taken aback. Such unwarranted sarcasm was not at all what he would have expected from a real gentleman. Still, there were moments when one had to swallow one's professional pride.

'Please excuse me, Baron. This is clearly a distressing time for you, but … but … Look, there's probably nothing to worry about. Actually, I'll let you in on a banker's little secret.' Hubert smiled coyly. 'Do you know what many gentlemen clients keep in their safe deposit boxes, hmm?'

There were blank expressions.

'Go on, have a guess.'

Silence.

'Oh well, I'll have to tell you – pornography. Hah! – I can see from your faces you don't believe me, but it's true – honest. Forget all those myths about stocks and shares, jewels, gold – absolute cobblers. Naturally, they don't want the little woman or the kiddies to find the stuff lying around at home – at the back of the wardrobe, under a floorboard, tucked behind a bag of fertilizer in the garage – it always gets found, doesn't it? No, they deposit it here. So, when the urge comes on, so to speak, they can pop round to the bank of a lunch hour, nip down to the strongroom, get the box out, and examine the contents in absolute privacy behind closed doors in one of the cubicles.

'I don't know whether you're familiar with our facilities, but they're *very* comfortable. Actually, to be frank, the strongroom and all the inspection facilities are on Florence's – *our* schedule for refurbishment. The furniture is a bit Eighties-ish – tubular steel and glass … that sort of thing – and we thought that here in Place des Quinconces something more classic would be appropriate. We've seen some repro Louis Quinze at a discount warehouse out at–'

'For fuck's sake!' roared Henri, thumping the table with both fists. 'I don't believe for one second that my father ever had the *slightest* interest in – in – in *pornography*, and, quite frankly, I regard your insinuation that–'

'No, no, no, my dear Baron, I didn't mean to insinuate–'

'Absolutely outrageous – defamatory!'

It took a few minutes for calm to be restored.

'I'm so glad we've got all that sorted out,' Hubert bleated humbly. 'I'm sorry if I keep repeating myself, but I only meant that whatever may be in your father's deposit boxes, will, in *all* probability, be quite ... innocuous, that's all. Treasured correspondence with an adolescent sweetheart, for example, or a wartime lover – that's another common one.'

'Jesus Christ!'

'I think we'd better go and open those boxes,' Alain suggested, rising from his seat, 'and put an end to all this absurd speculation, what?'

Hubert shot up like a jack-in-the-box. 'Absolutely! I'll lead the way. Would you like me to have some fresh coffee sent down to the strongroom?'

Alain shook his head. 'Not for me, old boy – I'll be dashing to the loo all morning.'

Now gripped by a strong sense of foreboding, Henri finally stood up. There were some beads of perspiration on his forehead. He stared fixedly at the door. 'Let's just get it bloody over with,' he muttered with as much interest in the bank's coffee as he had in its current manager.

Some ten minutes later, examining his faded surroundings, Hubert worried whether he might have been a bit pedantic in not allowing his co-executor to join him in the cubicle. They could have squeezed in another chair – just – but the instructions left by Guy de Bondé were quite explicit: the envelope addressed to 'Louis Charles Henri François de Montparnasse-Bourbon-Bainmarie, or to such other person as may occupy the position of Manager of the Place des Quinconces Branch of the Banque Internationale de France' was to be opened '**IN PRIVATE**', which Hubert took to mean exactly that – in the presence of no other person whatsoever. So, here he was alone at last in the three-metre-square room like a prisoner in a cell. Florence was right: the clinical strip of fluorescent lighting was absolutely awful. And the Eighties furniture was decidedly passé.

Anyway, getting back to the point, Alain's out there now in the strongroom surrounded by all that grubby cream-emulsioned woodchip wallpaper, waiting for Baron Toffee-Nose. Bloody Henri certainly wasn't going to have anyone leaning over his shoulders when he ripped open the old loony's sealed envelopes! If only Alain had a damned chair – so embarrassing! I could have fetched him one in a jiffy, but he'd insisted on standing. '"Been sat on my arse all bloody morning,"' Hubert mimicked softly. 'What a tit!' *Christ! I'd better get a move on. Toffee-Nose could be out any second.* He pressed an ear to the adjoining wall: nothing. *Bet it's porn – or an admission that he was queer and he wants his toy boy looked after … something like that.*

Playfully smacking a wrist, Hubert tore open the envelope. 'Right, so what have we got here?' After unfolding two pages of handwritten text, he unsuccessfully attempted to stifle a mischievous giggle. 'Bugger me! It *is* another will!' He cleared his throat: '"I, Baron Guy Louis-Philippe" – bla, bla, bla … Christ! – the names these toffs give themselves – "do hereby revoke all former wills" – dah-dee-dah, bla, bla, bla – "and, subject to the following bequests, legacies and exceptions, hereby bequeath all my property, whether moveable or immovable" – dah-dee-dah – "to Jean-Claude Bourjois of Rue de la Fraternité, Margaux" – what the hell? – "or, in the event of the said Jean-Claude Bourjois predeceasing me, to his children, whether legitimate or illegitimate, in equal shares, or, in the event there are no such children …"'

Simultaneously endeavouring to remember why the name of this Bourjois character rang a bell, Hubert read on, his voice becoming an incredulous whisper. By the time he reached the date and signature at the bottom of the page – comforted by the provisions appointing the two executors, himself as current branch manager, and Carbon Blanc as current senior partner of the Comte de Pyla-sur-Mer's law firm – he could hear sobbing on the other side of the partition wall.

Outside in the soon-to-be-redecorated chamber, Alain also thought he could detect sounds of emotional stress emanating from Henri's cubicle. After weighing up the pros and cons of tapping on the door, it seemed preferable to let his old friend be: ministering to overwrought clients had never been his forte; in any event, a chap had to do his blubbing in private. To be honest, he wouldn't be at all surprised if, notwithstanding all their ghastly arguments and scenes over the years, Guy had set down in writing just how much he'd loved his son, and how he'd always wanted to tell him to his face.

Inside his equally gloomy cubicle, Henri was striving to regain a degree of composure. He had dried his eyes, blown his nose, and reread the will for the third time; he'd yet to open the other envelope in the deposit box, the one melodramatically marked '**ABSOLUTELY PRIVATE AND CONFIDENTIAL. TO BE OPENED <u>ONLY</u> BY HENRI DE BONDÉ AND NO OTHER PERSON WHOMSOEVER.**' Repeating the words 'fucking bastards', which encompassed both his father and Bourjois, was proving therapeutic, as was the growing conviction that this handwritten gibberish was not worth the paper it was written on.

'I mean,' Henri blustered, thumping the top of the tubular steel desk, 'even *I* know that under French law you can't *totally* disinherit your own bloody family. That's one gaping defect in this – this – this *crap* for a start. Alain or, better still, a real wills expert – in Paris probably – should find more. What about handwritten? – unwitnessed?' A horrifying thought struck him: *Christ! That Audinette idiot will have read the same lunacy – Bourjois inheriting and – and … everything! He has to be put right before he sets the cat among the pigeons and – and …*

With his well-used handkerchief, Henri wiped the perspiration from his brow. Maybe the Old Man wanted Bourjois to have some kind of stick to keep beating him with for the rest of his life – endless litigation over the validity of this, that or the other will. He picked up the other envelope. It would tell all: loathing his only son; raking up the past – Bourjois's near-fatal accident all those years ago; rehearsing all the git's 'virtues'.

Henri ripped open the envelope. For a few moments, he shuffled the contents – a half dozen sheets of paper – trying to anticipate what might be the relevance of documents that at first sight appeared to be some kind of medical report from a Paris clinic, plus a gaudy marriage certificate … City of Las Vegas … Clark County in the State of Nevada. … What in God's name–? He pushed them aside. It *was* a sick joke after all. Obviously, the old loony had suffered from some kind of mental illness for years. The other few sheets were a letter written, like the 'will', in his father's distinctive careful hand.

Dear Henri, he began to read, but immediately stopped with a loud snort. '"Dear Henri," what a hypocrite!' For the first time, he noticed the embossed address, the George V, the Old Man's favourite hotel in Paris, and the date nine years ago. Was *that* before or after the real will? … *Dear Henri*, he continued …

*

Standing beside a window, Guy surveyed the crumpled sheets of paper littering the floor and wondered whether he could face yet another draft of the letter. He'd just torn up the fourth, believing it to be unnecessarily sentimental. The others had either been the opposite or simply unintelligible, such had been his haste to get the whole sorry business off his chest. Shaking his head from side to side, he pulled back the net curtains and watched the evening rush-hour traffic crawl along Avenue George V. Perhaps he should postpone things until after dinner, or even his return to Margaux? But then Henri would be around, triggering all the wrong emotions. And trying to find the time at La Fayette with so much to do. … No, this was the right time and place. He couldn't put it off any longer.

Guy poured himself another cognac and returned to the desk. He picked up a fresh sheet of hotel stationery and unscrewed the top of his faithful Mont Blanc. 'Be factual, unemotional and pertinent,' he told himself as he wrote the date below the hotel's address.

Dear Henri,

When you were a baby I loved you as much as I would have loved my own son. As far as I was concerned, you <u>were</u> my own son, even though your real father was Christophe Bourjois. I don't believe it would be helpful now to particularize how your mother, Marie-Claude, came to seduce Christophe. All I need say is, that for her own selfish and malicious motives, she informed me of the seduction long before your birth. There was, however, never any mention of it between Christophe and me; indeed, I've no reason to believe that he ever had the least suspicion that I was aware of it. Furthermore, I'm convinced that the thought never occurred to him that you might be his son. In this respect, nothing useful would have been achieved by any enlightenment on my part; on the contrary, not only would our friendship have been threatened, but also, more importantly, his happy family life would probably have been destroyed. You see, despite his momentary lapse of faithfulness, Christophe was very much in love with his wife, Joséphine, his feelings being wholly reciprocated.

With mounting horror, you're probably assuming that Jean-Claude is your half-brother. In fact, he is not related to you <u>at all</u>: I am his father. Undoubtedly, Christophe never knew or even suspected this. I will not relate how Joséphine and I came to commit our solitary act of adultery, although I can say that it was at a time when her marriage was experiencing problems of a most intimate nature. It had certainly not been our intention to conceive a child: the usual precautions were taken to avoid such a possibility, precautions which clearly proved defective. My lingering doubts were eliminated during the Eighties, when I read about DNA 'fingerprinting'. It took some time to get the various samples and to have them analysed discreetly, but the results were unequivocal: Joséphine and I sired Jean-Claude, and Christophe and my wife sired you, Henri. Indeed, as you grew older, you became more and more like your mother – selfish, greedy, petulant, malicious.

Just over a year ago, your father died at the Hôtel Dieu, here in Paris. I tried to persuade you to visit him during his long and painful treatment, and to attend the funeral in Margaux, if only as a mark of respect to one of our most loyal employees. You treated my requests, however, with contempt. You may remember that Joséphine had been battling heroically with multiple sclerosis for some time prior to Christophe's death, but his loss destroyed her will to live. She was buried beside him just a few weeks ago, another funeral you refused to attend.

I mention these matters because Christophe's death and her own illness crystallised Joséphine's thoughts concerning her son's security. Shortly after Christophe's funeral, she shared her concerns with me – concerns, I should say, which had also exercised my mind for some years. In brief, on my death, you would inherit both my estate and title, while my <u>real</u> son would get nothing – other than a relatively small legacy. Joséphine convinced me – although I needed little convincing – that this situation was inequitable. On the other hand, neither of us wanted to do anything which could expose the illegitimacy of either of you. Nor, I must confess, did I wish to take steps which might result in the extinction of a barony first granted to my ancestors by Louis XIII, a title which could not lawfully pass to an illegitimate son or his descendants.

My solution was to prepare a secret will, the very will that you have found with this letter. In effect, Henri, you are to keep you credentials as my son, and thus the barony you have now inherited. Jean-Claude, on the other hand, inherits the estate, including the vineyard that he so obviously loves – in contrast to yourself. It is not my intention to embarrass you publicly, or endanger the title by throwing you out into the gutter without a franc. In any event, when all is said and done, and despite all your character defects, you are the son of Christophe Bourjois, a man whom I loved.

Accordingly, you will have read in my will that for a period of twelve months following my death, you will continue to have the right to remain in residence at the château, rent free. You will also receive a legacy of 20,000 francs per month for five years, which, I trust, should help supplement the salary of the employment you will now need to secure, and for which your expensive education should have qualified you.

I have every confidence that my executors – Uncle Louis at the Bank, and dear Pyla, aided by his reputable law firm – will carry out my wishes. I have not informed them, or any living soul, of the contents of this letter, and, presumably, nor will you, for you have every incentive to keep these secrets to your grave.

There is one final matter of great sensitivity that I must disclose. When I explained the steps I had taken to provide for our son, Joséphine expressed a fervent desire for Jean-Claude's illegitimacy to be extinguished. She pointed out that Christophe's death now enabled us to do so by contracting marriage. On the other hand, a civil marriage here in France, however discreetly conducted, would be a matter of public record. I spoke with Jean-Claude and told him that at Christophe's funeral his mother had mentioned that she'd always longed to visit America. With his blessing, I arranged for her to make that trip – one that we rightly anticipated would be her last – accompanied by a qualified nurse. I also arranged to be on business in the USA and for our paths to cross.

And so it was that Joséphine and I were married in a brief ceremony in Las Vegas. She was radiant with the thought that our son's stigma of illegitimacy had been removed at last. Needless to say, the wedding has not been notified to the French authorities, but then, as long as your and Jean-Claude's antecedents remain secret, there'd be no need to do so.

In conclusion, Henri, I wish to express my hope that you will change your ways; it's not too late. Your father was a fine man. I beseech you to emulate him and thereby avoid the misery that will undoubtedly be your lot in life should you foolishly continue to follow in your mother's footsteps.

Yours as ever,

Guy

P.S. You would be wise to destroy this letter <u>immediately</u>.

Feeling emotionally drained, Guy put down his pen and finished his glass of cognac. A rumbling stomach told him dinner was long overdue. Looking at his watch, he was stunned to discover it was after ten. He rose from the desk, stretched and moved to the window. If only things had been different. If only ... But he couldn't tell Jean-Claude the truth – he couldn't turn his world upside down by revealing all the deception, lies, adultery. ... No, it would be cruel and selfish. Jean-Claude was happy, content with his lot – parentage, upbringing, home, job. And now he was a proud father himself.

A father himself? How foolish he'd been in not realising the implications before! Jean-Claude's baby boy, Alexandre, was his own grandson! Well, of course he'd realised that, but what if Henri's baby, Benoît, should never father a legitimate son? What if Benoît turned out to be Henri's only legitimate son? The barony would lapse on Henri's or Benoît's death! He was certainly unaware of any other possible heirs. What if–?

Guy stared hard at the writing table. All thoughts of a late dinner evaporated. He refilled his glass and snatched another sheet of stationery from the pigeonhole.

*

Hubert Audinette's heart was pounding: the meeting room had fallen silent again. It was all horribly embarrassing – not at all a good start to his first executorship of a great Bordelais estate. And now it was almost quarter to one, most of the bank's staff had beetled off for the *menu du jour* at their preferred local brasserie, and neither of his visitors had so far indicated the least desire to do likewise. But then in all the circumstances, that was perhaps unsurprising: Bondé had been dealt quite a body blow.

Hubert cleared his throat. 'Are you sure you wouldn't like some sandwiches sent in?'

Alain looked up from yet another rereading of what was now unanimously referred to as 'the so-called will' and shook his head. 'No thanks. Never touch the things if at all possible.'

Bloody hell! Anyone would think I was offering them sheep's eyes. 'To be honest, Alain, not my sort of thing either. I just thought – that is ...

303

Look, if you'd like a break from all this, I'd be more than happy to take you both out to lunch – a quiet table at–'

Henri hit the arm of his chair. 'Jesus Christ! Do you think you could possibly forget about sodding food for one moment, Audinette, and allow us to try and find a way out of this shit?'

'Keep your hair on, old fruit,' Alain chirped with exaggerated joviality. 'It's not *his* bloody fault that–'

'So, Alain, I take it then from your good humour that you can confirm – *finally* – that the so-called will isn't worth the paper it's written on, and that fucking Bourjois has no more of a valid interest in La Fayette, or any other part of *my* inheritance, than – than ... bloody Audinette here, hmm?'

Such venom, Hubert noted, relieved that Bondé's anger was now directed at one of the real villains of the peace.

'Well, Henri, I ... um ...' Alain smiled lamely at Hubert and rolled his eyes upwards as if to suggest that the fuming client was unbalanced and required humouring. Unwisely, Hubert returned the smile.

Jumping up abruptly, Henri roared: 'Oh, you find my predicament amusing, do you, Audinette? Well, I'll wipe that bloody smile off–'

'No, no! Of course not! You misunderstand, Baron. I–'

'Perhaps Bourjois is a customer of this bloody bank, Audinette – of your former *suburban* branch. Maybe you're old friends – in it together. Come to think of it, what a remarkable coincidence that you should be a client of Alain's law firm, and that *he*' – Henri prodded Carbon Blanc in the back – 'should have recommended *your* son to replace Bourjois as my *maître de chai*. Maybe you're *all* in it together – faking these documents in the deposit boxes and–'

'My *dear* chap,' Alain admonished, you don't know what you're saying.' He turned back to Audinette. 'Got any cognac? I think a stiff drink is in order – for *all* of us.'

After Hubert had left the room, Alain went over to one of the windows, where Henri was now peering through the Venetian blinds and muttering to himself.

'*Really*, Henri,' he said soothingly, 'not in front of the servants, so to speak. Sent the clot for some cognac. ... Sandwiches indeed! Couldn't believe it when the fellow suggested such things.' Henri made no acknowledgement. 'Let's sit down and discuss this sensibly, hmm? We'll find a way out, don't you worry.' He placed a hand on Henri's arm and tried to steer him back to the table.

As Henri resumed his seat, he looked into Alain's eyes. 'I wish I *had* killed him. I nearly did, you know ... years ago. I pushed him down the stairs at home. ... And then I killed his boy. ... Well, I thought I had, but it was some other boy … and he wasn't killed, I think. … He was on a bike … went into … or over the dyke … vanished in the forest … near Le Porge. … Never reported missing.'

Alain's face was a mask of incomprehension. 'Sorry? … You *"killed"* – *didn't* kill … a boy? … dyke? … disappeared? … Um, who–?'

A theatrical cough made both of them turn their heads towards the door. Holding a tray laden with a bottle of Courvoisier and three crystal tumblers, Hubert stood there with a facial expression suggesting that he'd just found the Holy Grail, not merely a bottle of cognac.

'Success! So, gentlemen, drinks all round. And I think I'll get some sandwiches sent in after all, OK?'

It had been a very long time since Alain had tackled half a baguette stuffed with *jambon de Paris*, but he had to admit to himself that it had proved quite enjoyable, despite the razor-sharp crust's damage to the roof of his mouth. With some form of masochistic pleasure, he gobbled the final chunk, and then, with a greasy finger, tapped the crumb-covered document on the table before him – a photocopy of the 'so-called will' which Audinette himself had made from his own copy.

'I'm sorry, Henri,' Alain said, 'but we can't attack its validity just because it's handwritten – perfectly valid under French law – provided the will's been written by the testator throughout and signed.'

'But–'

'Alain's absolutely right, *Henri*,' Hubert confirmed magisterially. 'I've dealt with plenty of manuscript wills over the years, and–'

'– and such wills,' Alain continued, 'don't need to be witnessed–'

'– or deposited with any official body – probated, that is.'

'Thank you, Hubert.'

'You're welcome, Alain.'

'Great! – so much for "the bad news",' Henri whined, pushing a ham baguette around his plate; he'd abandoned it after one small tentative bite. 'And "the good news"?'

'Ah, the *good* news, Henri,' Alain replied with a smile, 'is that the ability to dispose of property by will is limited by statute to protect a surviving spouse, children, and other descendants, as well as parents and grandparents, all of whom have to be allowed a certain proportion of the testator's estate. So, as all those categories are irrelevant in your case – all predeceased, thank God … other than "children", and you're the only one, you're legally entitled to at least one half of the estate … I think – maybe more. I need to check on that.'

Henri exhaled a deep sigh of relief. 'I knew *that* … naturally. What with the shock. … Frankly, the fact that the old bugger has tried to override the law confirms my conviction that he must have been batty at the time he wrote the so-called will. I mean, he was no novice when it came to wills and inheritance stuff.'

'I hope you don't think I'm being indiscreet, Henri,' Hubert ventured tentatively, 'but I've been wondering whether the *other* document your father left for you in the deposit box might be of some use in that respect – I mean the non compos mentis issue.'

Henri looked blankly at the loathsome bank manager. '*Non compos* ... What the *hell* are are you prattling about *now*?'

'Whether the Old Man was bonkers,' assisted Alain. 'I must say, Henri, the same point has crossed my mind. Perhaps we could take a look at it? – could be jolly important evidence, especially if we end up in court.'

'Absolutely,' Hubert concurred.

A frisson of horror shot up Henri's spine. He began to rub the lobe of his right ear. '*Court*? ... The "*other*" document"? ... I ... No, I'm afraid that's quite out of the question – *impossible*.'

Alain and Hubert looked at each other with furrowed brows. The latter was first off the mark. 'What isn't possible? – going to court or–?'

'– seeing the document?' interjected Alain.

The uneaten baguette was back in motion. Without looking up, Henri said: 'You certainly can't see the letter – that's what it was, a letter ... from Papa ... very personal stuff ... for my eyes only. Anyway, I've destroyed it.' There were more raised eyebrows. 'Tore the bloody thing up and flushed it down the loo – after I came out of that beastly cubicle thing in the strongroom.'

'Pretty drastic,' Alain suggested.

A master of understatement! thought Hubert. *Pretty drastic indeed! It must have been very upsetting stuff ... embarrassing maybe. Presumably, something so ghastly, Bondé wouldn't want anyone else to read it. But what? ... Logically, an explanation as to why his dad had cut his own son out of his inheritance and given the great La Fayette estate to a mere employee ... well, ex-employee, my Patrick's bloody predecessor! Come on, there's no smoke without fire. ... That's it! – a scandal! Either the old boy was queer and fancied this Bourjois, or ... or ... Jesus Christ! No, it couldn't be ... could it? I–*

'... and we simply can't get embroiled in that sort of litigation, Alain, not with sodding Bourjois, can we? Think, man, *think*!'

Alain shook his head in exasperation. 'That's all very well, Henri, but it's not just up to us, is it? Here is a will that, on the face of it, is perfectly valid, and, moreover, which specifies precisely how the executors are to dispose of the estate. So, when we inform Bourjois of the will's provisions, as we – Hubert and me – are obliged to do promptly, I can't see him saying, "Oh that's all right, chaps, I don't want a *grand cru* Margaux estate. My dear old chum Henri can keep it, bless him." His wife will certainly want to get her greedy hands on it, don't you think? I mean, Tiquetorte–' Alain checked himself just in time.

'Yes, well … anyway, Henri, when Bourjois is informed of his apparent inheritance, and is then told that you're going to challenge the will's validity on the grounds that it purports to override the statutory provisions on family inheritance, he's going to fight, isn't he? Unless we can prove that Guy was bonkers at the time he wrote the will – sorry, the *so-called* will – Bourjois could still be entitled to as much as fifty per cent of the estate – of the vineyard, the house … the lot.'

Henri's face appeared set in stone. 'No,' he croaked, 'impossible … unthinkable. We have to prove the Old Man was off his trolley. We *have* to.'

Hubert managed a theatrical empathetic sigh. 'Dear me, it's all a bit of a pickle, isn't it? Litigation, courts, public hearings … dear, oh dear, oh *dear*. I suppose, Alain, that in the event – as seems so likely – the will *is* contested, then, as an executor, you won't be able to act for Henri – conflict of interest and all that. Of course, you could relinquish your executorship. … And I suppose that if there were proceedings, we – all *three* of us – would have to give evidence – on oath – as to our knowledge of any documents left by the deceased that might cast any light on the will, or the testator's state of mind, like … well, like Henri's "letter". By the way, I wonder whether Baron Guy wrote a personal letter of some kind to Monsieur Bourjois, and, if so, where it might be. There was certainly nothing for him in the deposit box *I* opened.' With considerable interest, Hubert studied the effect his speculations had on Bondé; if he was not mistaken, he'd started to tremble.

Alain was not so observant: he was too busy analysing what he'd just heard, and feeling peeved that he'd not thought of such pertinent matters himself. 'Hmm … conflict of interest, a tricky one. And a note of some kind to Bourjois … possible, possible. Such a document might cast light on quite a few things – even prove that Guy was loopy. But where would it be? Certainly nothing in our files at the office. I'll have another look, and have a word with Papa, but I very much doubt … Um, I suppose Guy could have used another lawyer – several, even. Mind you, if he'd instructed someone in Bordeaux, I feel sure I'd have heard about it. You don't know of any other lawyers instructed by your father, do you, Henri? … in Paris, perhaps?'

Henri was as white as a sheet: the possibility had not occurred to him that the Old Man might have written directly to Bourjois, exposing the family's dirty linen. After all, he'd droned on and on in his vile letter about not throwing any spanners into the works of the peasant's precious family life, thereby exposing his nearest and dearest as adulterers and liars. It would utterly contradict all that stuff about the barony remaining with himself. Oh no, hypocritical 'Papa' didn't want to shatter any of Bourjois's precious illusions, and certainly not imbecilic images of either his former deceased employer or the bumpkin Christophe as paragons of virtue. Peasant or no peasant, if Bourjois discovered that Guy had married his slut of a mother, he'd be calling himself 'Baron de Bondé' before you could say 'Lafite Rothschild', and no two ways about it. But he obviously couldn't mention any of this to Alain or oily Audinette!

'No, Alain,' Henri hissed, seething with frustration, 'I'm *not* aware of the Old Man instructing any other lawyers. Anyway, I just don't believe he'd have written anything to Bourjois. Don't ask me why, it's ... it's just a very strong gut feeling.'

Clearly unconvinced, Alain shifted in his seat.

Impishly, Hubert said: 'Well, I suppose we'll just have to wait and see. The big question is – what do we do next?' He began to remove the plates. 'Are you sure you don't want your sandwich, Henri?' He shook his head. 'Sure? ... Oh, all right. I'll take it home for the dog.' As he moved towards a side table to deposit the crockery, he chuckled oddly. 'I bet we're all wishing that those nasty deposit boxes had been empty, hmm? It's truly amazing, isn't it, how a few sheets of damned paper can make life so bloody difficult? Incredible! Can you imagine, Henri, the reaction of Bordelais society, when – *if* – you have to move out of La Fayette? – the gossip about the late baron disinheriting his own son in favour of a former employee? There'd be loads of folk putting two and two together and making five, don't you think?'

'What on earth do you mean?' queried Alain, flashing a scowl at an open-mouthed Henri.

'Well, it's obvious, isn't it?' replied Hubert, returning to the table. Judging by the expression on Alain's ruddy face, it was certainly not. Nevertheless, Hubert was not ready to enlighten him. 'And then, you, Alain, are going to have to abandon our dear client here as his adviser in order to remain an independent executor, *and* seek independent legal advice, acting fairly and in the best interests of *all* beneficiaries under the will – the *so-called* will – or vice versa. ... Would I then be sole executor, or would we have to appoint a replacement?'

'I–'

'And I bet the Bordeaux legal community will be agog when they learn that, having instructed your father to prepare a will, Guy then went off and wrote his own, without – apparently – even telling him about it, let alone seeking legal advice. I mean, didn't you say that in all his subsequent dealings with your father – at least before the Alzheimer's destroyed his faculties – Guy always represented that the original will, the *first* will, was his one and only will? Well, that hardly indicates a profound relationship of trust between them, does it? The truth is, he deceived your father, Alain. … Why?'

'I–'

'Bloody damn obvious!' bellowed Henri. 'My father didn't want the Comte de Pyla-sur-Mer to know that he was dumping his son – *me* – in favour of a damned servant boy. The Old Man could never have looked him in the eyes again – the shame, the embarrassment, the fear. Pyla would think that Bourjois was … that – that …'

Alain was still all at sea. 'That Bourjois was what?'

'I … I don't know.'

'Come, come, gentlemen,' Hubert scolded gently, 'we're all men of the world. Surely you can see that such extraordinary behaviour would indicate to *some* people that, far from being insane, the late baron's testamentary dispositions merely reflected a blood relationship between testator and beneficiary.'

Alain was slowly tapping his fountain pen on the BIF notepad in front of him. '*Blood* relationship? … No, I'm still not following–'

'That this Bourjois, Alain, was Guy de Bondé's *son* – his *illegitimate* son – not that *I* would think such nonsense – not for one moment, naturally. Heavens no! Perish the thought! I'm just playing devil's advocate and suggesting how it might look to *some* people – people with warped minds … if it … got out.'

Alain's eyes bulged. 'Good Lord! I see what you mean. Oh, this is awful – *dreadful*!' He turned to face Henri, who seemed transfixed by a large and rather tastelessly framed colour photograph on the far wall of BIF's Paris headquarters. 'My dear, dear chap, Hubert's right, alas. People will think the worst. We can't let this get out – we just can't.'

Henri remained statuesque.

'But what can we do, Alain?' asked Hubert plaintively. 'We're executors. Bourjois has to be informed of the will, whether it's valid or not.'

'Well, yes, but … perhaps … in confidence … we could do some kind of … deal – buy the bugger out. We'd agree – that is, *Henri* would agree – not to start proceedings to have the will set aside in return for … for – I don't know – a lump sum – an annuity – a minority shareholding – his bloody job back!'

Down the corridor in her obsessively tidy office, even Madame Raffard, who'd just returned from the Café Bordelais and her daily ritual of consuming its *plat du joir*, heard Henri de Bondé's roar of protest.

In the event, Hubert's offer to forget all about 'the so-called will' in return for what he called 'a few perks' was rapidly accepted. There was unanimous agreement that Guy's estate would be distributed in accordance with the 'Pyla-sur-Mer will', and all documents evidencing the existence of any other will would be burned. Within a few days, Hubert had an account at the same Swiss bank patronized by Henri; a generous sum was promptly deposited in it – a most useful contribution to what Hubert called his 'pension fund'. Though the account was kept a secret from Florence, by the end of the month she'd dined no less than twice with the de Bondés – at La Fayette, to boot! – and once with the Carbon Blancs, whose palatial apartment just around the corner in Cours du Chapon Rouge convinced her that their own place in Allées de Tourny was too small after all.

PART 3
CHAPTER 25

In the small but tastefully furnished dining room of the Fontaines' Belle-Mère apartment, Madame Fontaine drained her glass of the estate's 1995 *rouge* and signalled to her son that she required a refill. 'Excellent,' she murmured, 'truly excellent. One of your best efforts, Charles. Just as we've been telling those three idiots for the last two years – that one has to be patient with wine, give it years to mature into splendid adulthood. Bourjois knows that, of course, but he's weak – pathetic almost.'

'You're so right, Mama, weak and spineless. … More lamb?'

'Most definitely, *chéri*. It's absolutely delicious! Now, come on – stop being a tease and tell me all about your meeting with those detective people. I do hope they had something juicy to report this time – they're costing enough. And with your cousin Bertrand on his deathbed, we may at last have our chance to put their intelligence to good use and get our property back – *and* at a very substantially discounted price.'

'He's been on his deathbed before, Mama. We thought we had a chance of buying it back from the receivers when the wretched Pronks got themselves into hot water, but–'

'I know, I know, *chéri*. But this is *quite* different. I have it directly from Dr Renoy at the clinic that Bertrand won't last the week.'

'Really? *Splendid!*'

'And so that mausoleum of a villa of his at Arcachon will soon be yours, and then you can sell it to those developers.'

Charles rubbed his hands together. 'Two blocks of luxury apartments replacing an art nouveau gem. A small price to pay, I think, to recover our home and vineyards.'

'*La Patrimonie* Fontaine!'

'Precisely!'

'All you have to do now, Charles, is to evict those parvenu interlopers. Is the pot still boiling nicely? Are their relationships continuing to cool, just as we predicted at the very outset?'

'Well–'

'No, no! That can wait. Tell me first about the cloak and dagger stuff.'

Charles licked his lips. 'Oh, all right then. It's really quite exciting. Well, where to begin? … Do you remember – about the time Appleton first came here – there was all that hoo-hah in town over Geoffroy de Tiquetorte having a nervous breakdown?'

'Oh yes. He was away from his practice for weeks, wasn't he?'

Charles nodded vigorously. 'And then, when he *did* go back to work, there were all those odd treatments, misdiagnoses and–'

'Tut, tut, tut – nasty allegations, *chéri*.'

'Three patients did sue, Mama. He came very close to being struck off.'

'I remember his father ... such a lovely man ... wonderful château at St-Estèphe ... or was it St-Julien? And then he made those foolish investments in Algeria. What a–'

'Mama! Never mind all that. The point is that Tiquetorte's "breakdown", those negligence claims, the loss of so many society patients, the divorce, the bankruptcy, *and* his unbelievable marriage to that ghastly Gravelier woman–'

'An *antiquaire*! Bizarre!'

'Bizarre indeed. Anyway, you'll never believe that all that was Bourjois's fault! – both of them, in fact, Jean-Claude *and* Sophie. I suspect they were after money. ... There's a video – not that you could possibly watch it – but it's dynamite. I bet the doting parents would do *anything* to ensure that a copy never comes to the attention of their precious Alexandre.'

'Charles, *chéri*, what *are* you talking about?'

'Oh, sorry. It's just that I still can't quite believe our extraordinarily good fortune. Well, apparently, poor Geoffroy's descent into the Bourjois hell all began when he first went to that Gravelier woman's shop – he was looking for some Empire dining chairs, would you believe? This would be almost three years ago now, and ...'

*

Jean-Claude put another log on the living room fire and then curled up again with Sophie on the sofa. Their early supper had been preceded by some feverish sex, a now standard ritual whenever she returned from one of her regular marketing trips to Paris. Earlier, he'd driven in to Bordeaux to pick her up from the Gare St-Jean, and when she stepped down from one of the TGV's first-class coaches, he'd glowed with pride: dressed in her latest purchases from the Rue du Faubourg St-Honoré, she was the most beautiful and desirable woman in the whole station. He'd hardly been able to wait to get her home.

'So, what else has happened?' asked Sophie, fondling his groin. 'Any more attempts by Laura to lure you into her lair and seduce you while I was away? Actually, I got to thinking on the train that we should really put her out of her misery and find her an eligible man. There was this nice young American wine merchant sitting next to me, and we got chatting–'

'As one does.'

'As one does, and somewhere between Angoulême and Poitiers, I thought – Christ, this is just the guy for frustrated old Laura! I even thought about exchanging phone numbers – inviting him down here – but then he started talking about the international situation – fatal mistake! – and how cowardly we French are in not supporting their "War Against Terror" and all that, and … well …'

'You didn't mince words.'

'Exactly.'

'Oh, Sophie, darling, thank God you didn't opt for a career in the *Corps Diplomatique*.' In protest, she squeezed Jean-Claude's testicles a little too tightly. After his mollification, thanks to some gentle massaging, he said: 'There was another tense board meeting this morning – very tense.'

'By "tense" I suppose you mean there was blood all over the carpet. I thought you sounded a bit uptight on the phone at lunchtime. Sorry I couldn't play nursie, but Dominique's American client was anxious to finalize things and get to the airport, and–'

'It's OK. At least you sold the painting.'

'One hundred and fifty *thousand* euros!'

'So you've said – at least twenty times since you got off the train. Ouch!'

The playful thumping, kicking and biting quickly turned to further sex.

About an hour later, Jean-Claude finally returned to the theme of boardroom belligerence. 'I think Laura's frustrated in more ways than one,' he posited. 'Our third *vendange* has just been harvested – even more rigorous selection of grapes than last year – and I believe we're going to produce our best wines yet, but bloody Laura's reopened all our battles over style. She's insisting that we're never going to break out of the prejudice against the Premières Côtes, or the whole E2M region, unless we produce – to use her words – "something so fricking mind-blowing it'll put Robert Parker into fricking orbit".'

'Good Lord! Americans and their expletives.'

'She uses far worse. Poor Charles often doesn't know where to look.'

'Well, he's such a mummy's boy.'

'Sophie! Don't be unkind. At least he's on my side – trying to stop her from turning Belle-Mère into a damned *"garagiste"* affair making tiny quantities of mega-concentrated trendy vanilla-scented alcoholic treacle selling at a thousand euros a bloody bottle.'

'Christ!'

'She says it's the only way to put Belle-Mère on the map – money talks.'

'In a way, she's right, darling. After all, if my paintings only sold for a thousand euros a throw, no one would take a blind bit of notice.'

Momentarily, Jean-Claude pondered this admission, but decided to say nothing undiplomatic. 'Yes, but if, for example, Dominique asked you to paint sunflowers like Gaugin–'

'Van Gogh.'

'– van Gogh, and then tried to flog them for a hundred thousand euros, you'd probably feel your integrity was being compromised, to say the least.'

'Too right!'

'Well, there you are then. It's the same with me. She's asking me to make caricatures of good wine for sale to a handful of philistines with more money than sense. Frankly, I've gone far enough down this road of compromising my principles. I'm damned if I'm going to make a wine that just mimics something made in bloody California.'

'Even at a thousand euros a bottle?'

'It's not a joke, Sophie.'

'I know, I know.'

In silence, they both stared into the flames.

After a while, Sophie said: 'So you told her that, did you? – so far and no further?'

'Yes. Charles was very supportive.'

'Hmm. ... And Quincy – what was his reaction? – or is he still sitting on the fence, hedging his bets?'

'Strangely enough, no. For the first time, as far as I can remember, he was quite sharp with Laura.'

'Perhaps he's finally realized he's never going to screw her.'

'Oh, here we go again!'

'Dear sweet boy, you're so deliciously naive. For years, you wouldn't accept that Laura was desperate for *your* body. Hell! – she was even prepared to–'

'Don't say it!'

'I will. She was even prepared to spend her last hard-earned dollar to get you into this business and into this house, her hope being–'

'Sophie!'

'Anyway, it was the same with Dubloon – in reverse. There's no fool like an old fool!'

'He's not that old.'

'Old enough to be her father.'

'Unkind.'

'But true. And now he's finally realized he's on a hiding to nothing. She just led him on to get his capital invested in Belle-Mère, to use his name and magazine for marketing. ... Maybe she slept with him once – who knows? – and promised more of the same if–'

'Pure speculation.'

'Nothing "pure" about it. ... Actually, the apparent breakdown in the Appleton-Dubloon entente cordiale may have something to do with cash flow problems.'

'Oh?'

'Papa was telling me over lunch in Paris that he'd heard a few things through the grapevine – no pun intended! – from a merchant bank that does something or other for Papa's publishing division.'

'I didn't know your father dabbled in publishing.'

'Papa doesn't "dabble" in anything, darling. To be honest, though, I don't think I knew about the publishing company – magazines or something. ... Anyway, the gossip in London is that Dubloon is trying to sell that rag of his, er–'

'*Wine Wisdom.*'

'Exactly, and that he's pretty desperate to sell.'

'I don't believe a word of it. *Wine Wisdom* means everything to Quincy. It's like ... well, like his own child.'

'Peasants in Thailand sell their kids to the sweatshops of Bangkok – and worse.'

'Oh *really*! Quincy's rolling in it. He had that huge castle in England, don't forget. He must have got millions for it.'

'Darling, he and Laura have *spent* millions buying this place and tarting it up – plus all your new oak *barriques*. And what about all those marketing trips halfway around the world, and – and ... Well, Papa's done some sums based on those accounts you sent him.'

'I really shouldn't have done that. I–'

'Papa says we're still making a thumping loss and–'

'I know that.'

'– and that a lot of extra capital is going to have to be pumped in for a few years yet until all your stocks of the first few vintages are sold, and you can then increase prices to reflect improved quality.'

'Now you're sounding like Laura and Quincy.'

'Well, there you are! They're both probably skint. No wonder she's so keen to go upmarket and into the stratosphere with a bloody thousand-euros-a-bottle lifesaver.'

Jean-Claude swallowed hard. 'Jesus! We're not going to go bust, are we? I'd always thought the two of them were absolutely rolling in it. I – they ... Now I come to think about it, Laura has been away a lot recently – two trips to the States in the last month alone. And I've hardly seen Quincy since ... well, the board meeting this morning must have been the first time since–'

'Papa also said that his contact at Time Warner in New York let it slip last week that Laura is negotiating with them to do some new TV series on the world's most expensive wines, and to write an accompanying range of books on exclusive wine accessories – antique crystal decanters and silver coasters – you know the kind of thing.'

'Oh, *come on*! How could she? She hasn't got the time. She can hardly–'

'Money, darling. She can't afford *not* to – Belle-Mère hasn't earned her a single dollar's profit yet. No money, no fame, no sex. No wonder she's become such a cantankerous bitch.'

'Don't gloat, Sophie. If she or Quincy – or both of them – pull out, where the hell will that leave us? I mean, this place' – Jean-Claude waved his arms graphically – 'comes with the job. And I've worked night and day, almost seven days a week, to turn the vineyard around. We love the house ... and the grounds – Alexandre loves them. You said yourself that the studio here is the best you've ever had. Christ! – it would be such a waste if–'

'*We* could buy it.'

Save for the crackling of the fire, the room was silent for a few seconds, the two of them staring into each other's eyes.

'You're crazy,' Jean-Claude finally managed to say. 'How on earth–?'

'We *could*.'

'Of course we couldn't! I know you've sold a hell of a lot of paintings and made a hell of a lot of money–'

'*We've* made a hell of a lot of money.'

'You know what I mean. ... Anyway, we don't have anything like enough to buy Belle-Mère, or to finance its operation until it starts making a profit. And I'm not going to borrow from a bank and–'

'Oh, *do* shut up, Jean-Claude, and listen to me. When I say *we*, I mean us and Papa. He's awfully keen to have a vineyard in Bordeaux – you know how businessmen love all that status and prestige stuff. I think he's got this guilty complex thing about never having given us a wedding present. ... Well, *you* remember. ... Darling, it's all in the past now. You'll have to talk to him – you know what I'm like with figures and everything. There'd be a new holding company ... in Luxembourg, I think, and we'd have shares

– almost half – and Papa's company, an affiliate in Liechtenstein, or somewhere – whatever – would have the others. You'd be in absolute charge of things, on a day-to-day basis, and Papa would be non-executive chairman and, and …

'Just think! No more Appleton – no more Dubloon! You'd be your own boss at last. And we'd have the whole house all to ourselves … just the occasional bigwig down here for entertaining – Papa's associates … people like that. Isn't it amazing how foreigners – particularly Americans and Japanese – Russians, even – go all gaga over vineyards, especially Bordeaux ones? And this place has such history – the Windsors! They're so easily impressed.'

Jean-Claude was shaking his head ominously. 'My, my, *my*, you and your father *have* been busy beavers up in Paris. How long have you two been hatching this little venture?'

'Papa only mentioned it to me this week – I swear. Obviously, he's been mulling it over for–'

'It's madness anyway – *madness*! I'm sure your father's been misinformed – about Laura … and Quincy. And yet … Hang on! Aren't you overlooking something rather important?'

'What?'

'The sitting tenants, so to speak, the Fontaines. They've got rights – a contract – and she's eighty-something. It's their home.'

'Oh, darling, you *are* silly. Papa says his legal people could easily get them out – just a small ex gratia payment. In any event, they'd be so much better off in an apartment in town – at her age, she needs to be close to good medical care. And from what I can make out, they already spend much of their time in Bordeaux at some social or cultural event of one kind or another. They'll be the least of our concerns. … To be honest, I think Papa has already … um … sort of started the ball rolling.'

＊

Alone in Belle-Mère's gatehouse, Laura was staring vacantly at the latest unaudited management accounts splattered around her on the sofa. She was imagining the scenes of intimacy probably unfolding at this very moment up at the château. Earlier, from her office window, she'd seen the two lovebirds return from Bordeaux; they'd even kissed when they got out of the car. It had been sickening – the final straw of a most unpleasant day.

'Fuck them! Fuck Bordeaux! Fuck the whole French nation! Fuck Europe!'

Yes, Laura was rather distraught. Her concerns over Belle-Mère's financial viability were certainly justified. But despite the blast of obscenities directed at third parties, she knew all too well that the person primarily responsible for the disaster was herself: she'd made one bad decision after another. Her judgment in all things had been at fault. And now she was stuck with an unprofitable vineyard in an area she'd never wanted to invest in, and with partners who were stabbing her in the back at every available opportunity. She knew her plan to turn things around dramatically was contentious – producing a *garagiste*-type wine would be something of a compromise of her principles too! – but even the very best Premières Côtes wines weren't retailing at much more than fifteen euros a bottle! Which, of course, was the crux of the problem, for although she'd known that from the outset, she'd still allowed herself to be hoodwinked into expending vast sums on converting the château into several very desirable residences – not to mention the smart offices and 'hospitality apartments'. All that lot could have waited – they could have slummed it for a few years – not her words – Quincy's! What a hypocrite! He'd never 'slummed it' in his life.

Well, be that as it may, she knew her *garagiste* plan could work – money, profit *and* fame. And was it such a shameful compromise of everyone's sanctimonious standards? Surely not: they'd only be producing a relatively small number of bottles of the stuff. The vast bulk of the estate's production would still be excellent, classic Bordeaux – and marketed as the estate's second wine. And there'd be such a demand for their mega deluxe brew that they'd be able to make its supply conditional on purchases of big consignments of the second wine. Naturally, she'd anticipated opposition from Jean-Claude, even forceful opposition – his self-confidence had certainly blossomed! – but Quincy's hostility had been beneath contempt.

*

Quincy arrived at the château well in advance of the board meeting. He went straight to Laura's office, where, as he'd correctly anticipated, she was hard at work dealing with emails that had come in overnight. After only the briefest of courtesies, he got down to business. It was all strictly confidential, he said, so, for the time being, he wanted it to go no further, and certainly not to Jean-Claude or Charles.

'Yesterday,' he announced, 'I received an email from a Paris merchant bank, Banque Bendix-Cohn, with an offer to purchase my forty-five per cent shareholding in Belle-Mère for five million euros. Presumably, old thing, they've been in touch with you too?' But it was quite obvious from the expression of disbelief on her face that Laura had received no such approach.

'What? ... No – I – I ... You *can't* sell, Quincy. I – you ... Under the company's constitution you can't sell your shares to an outsider without first offering them to me at the same price. And if I don't accept the offer within twenty-eight days, you then have to offer them to our other shareholder, Jean-Claude … with his ten per cent.'

'Don't go ballistic, old thing. I know all that, but the point is that if either of you don't want to buy my shares – or can't – I'm free to sell to this bank … not at a lower price, obviously. Frankly, I can't see Jean-Claude coming up with the dosh … but who knows?'

With her brain surging into overdrive, Laura was rapidly doing the necessary calculations, but there was simply no way she could get her hands on anything like five million euros! *Is Quincy spinning a yarn? After all, why hasn't this Paris outfit contacted me? … Have they approached Jean-Claude? … Anyway, assuming it's not a scam, if they were to offer to buy me out, would I be prepared to sell? … But how could I? It would be such an admission of failure. I'd be a laughing stock in the States. I just have to see this thing through. … Surely Quincy's in the same boat? He'll be a laughing stock in London if he walks away now.*

Nervously, Laura asked: 'Are you seriously considering this mysterious offer, Quince?'

'Yes.'

'Oh … right. … I know things have been a bit tough, but I've got a great plan and with just a bit of time and–'

'Yet more working capital?'

'Well, yes, but–'

'Laura, it's impossible. I can't put another euro, pound – whatever – into this venture. Almost all my capital has already been sunk in Belle-Mère. *Wine Wisdom* is not a milch cow – it's a niche publication. Most of the money I've made over the years has come from TV and my *How To* books. Well, old thing, it appears I'm over the hill.'

'What the hell do you mean?'

'For a start, it looks like the telly people will not be renewing my contract for *Let's Open A Bottle*.'

'Jesus!'

'And my dear publishers say the *How To* books are "passé" – "long in the tooth" – "not selling too well". I've offered to rewrite them, but they're just not interested. I'm in a pickle, Laura. I'm already negotiating to sell *Wine Wisdom* – very hush-hush. I probably won't get much, but the capital should help towards the old pension. I'm not that far off sixty, don't forget.'

She had forgotten: Quincy still looked fit; many men in their early fifties looked a lot older.

'Perhaps we've both bitten off more than we can chew, Laura. I – *we* – have to give this offer very serious consideration. It goes without saying that I'd rather sell to you – if you want to stay at Belle-Mère, but to be honest, I think you'd be wiser to call it a day.'

Call it a day! Laura had no intention of doing anything of the sort. Later, during the board meeting as she watched and listened to her three co-directors presenting their usual litany of criticisms of all her proposals – the undoubted products of a think-small European culture – she convinced herself that the only way to take Belle-Mère forward and, in the process, protect her international credibility and reputation, was by getting rid of the lot of them. All she needed was money. She'd made a start through her negotiations with *Time Warner* in New York, but that simply wouldn't be enough – and time wasn't on her side.

*

In the lonely gatehouse, as the evening wore on, Laura explored every conceivable avenue for procuring funds. She even considered eating humble pie and going cap in hand to the Two Moms: it was just possible that they could be interested in a Maison Blanche hotel and restaurant on this side of the Pond. Yes, she'd do anything to avoid another bank loan – the existing one from BIF was bad enough, what with the interest payments each month, and those nosy letters from the oily manager. Mental images of Hubert Audinette evaporated as the phone began to ring. It was Pierre Lampre.

'What a crazy coincidence,' Laura said. 'I was just thinking of you.'

'*How flattering!*'

'Yeah, I'm going through the latest statements of our accounts at BIF.'

'*Ah ... I see ... our friend Audinette.*'

'Exactly.'

'*And how are things at Belle-Mère, Laura?*'

'Fine.' It was rather late in the evening for this kind of mundane chit-chat. Something was obviously afoot. 'And how's the real estate business?'

'*Oh, can't complain, all things considered.*' There was a pregnant pause. '*Laura, it's been a long time since we've met up–*'

'Yes.'

'*– and I was wondering if you'd like to come into town tomorrow for dinner.*'

Laura's mind raced. *Either someone's cancelled at the last minute or– Hang on! Lampre's a bit of a deal fixer. Maybe he's got something to do with this Paris merchant bank business. In any event, he might know someone who'd like to invest in Belle-Mère.*

'Not sure, Pierre, if I'm ... Let me check. ... Tomorrow? Um, at your place ... with Madame–?'

'My wife's in Le Havre – a sick relative. No, this would be at the Tapés' – you know Madame Tapé and her daughter, Béatrice, don't you? Lovely people. They have that very smart florist's in Cours de Tournon – just across the road from Quincy Dubloon, actually.' Laura had a vague recollection. 'We're all Lions,' Lampre added proudly.

'That's nice.'

'Yes, the Bordeaux Lions Club is very active, and the Tapés play a most prominent role – have done for years. You'll like them – very down to earth. They throw regular dinner parties at their apartment and always assemble an interesting crowd. One's guaranteed a most stimulating evening, I can assure you. And the food's splendid – the wines too. The late Monsieur Tapé laid down an excellent cellar.'

Laura hesitated: it all sounded dire. She hated things like the Lions and the Rotary Club – invariably packs of bigoted bores scratching each other's backs.

'One can make some excellent contacts at the Tapés' dinners,' Lampre continued, 'business as well as social. They certainly know everyone in the wine business – producers, négociants … investors, even.'

The words hung in the air.

'I'd love to come,' Laura chirped. 'They won't mind, will they?'

'Who?'

'The Whatsits.'

'Tapés? Why on earth would they "mind"? They know I always bring … a friend. Anyway, they've scolded me often enough for not inviting you before now.'

*

Quincy had not been honest with Laura. It was not his disingenuousness, however, which now kept him pacing around the sitting room at Cours de Tournon. A far more serious matter lay heavily on his broad but weary shoulders. His financial predicament was genuine enough, but the crisis looming on the horizon had been precipitated a week ago by the receipt at *Wine Wisdom*'s offices of an airmail envelope incongruously bearing a Scottish stamp and an Orkney Islands postmark. It was also boldly marked '**PERSONAL – TO BE OPENED BY ADDRESSEE ONLY**'. Quincy's secretary had taken the initiative of forwarding it by courier to Bordeaux. The contents, alas, had proved most disturbing – a handwritten letter in green ballpoint and a photograph of two naked men on a double bed; there could be little doubt about the sexual activity being performed. After more than thirty years, Quincy's undergraduate days had finally returned to haunt him – and with a vengeance.

321

Pam Macdonald, née Hudson, and her third husband, 'Robbie', a disabled ex-trawlerman, were 'very hard up'. Pam thought Quincy could help by giving them £100,000. In return, she wouldn't send similar photographs of his Grantchester romps with Vincent de Forgeron to a certain tabloid newspaper. He had fourteen days to see sense.

When Quincy finally tracked down Forgeron to Bora Bora and learned that he'd received a similar communication from Pam, the relief of having a billionaire ally proved cruelly brief. Gripping the phone fiercely, he listened incredulously as Vincent languidly asserted that he was wholly unconcerned. Indeed, he found the threat of blackmail riotously amusing. He'd already told Pam to publish and be damned: his sex life had been an open book for decades. He advised Quincy to do the same and rang off.

Quincy had bristled with anger and resentment. How could he possibly 'do the same'? He was a household name! His TV contract, moreover, was currently being renegotiated, and, according to his agent, things were not going at all well. The BBC were hinting that they would prefer 'a younger person' – and female. Any whiff of scandal at this sensitive stage would give them the perfect excuse to dump him.

Standing in front of the tall living room windows, Quincy looked across the street towards Allées de Tourny. The elegant neoclassical buildings of the square's east side led to the massive floodlit grandeur of the Grand Théâtre. 'Just a facade,' he muttered sadly. 'That's Bordeaux, "all fur coat and no knickers" as Granny used to say.' Gradually, it dawned on him that the city was going to destroy him. The tiny seeds had been sown all those years ago by Forgeron – a sickly, corrupt, debauched and decadent youth who couldn't have kicked a rugby ball to save his life. Oh yes, full of charm, perfect manners, a polyglot dazzling one with literary allusions and discourses on the finer points of Renaissance art, but beneath that richly polished veneer of sophistication was an egocentric cowardly pervert. By all accounts, he was just like his father – an officer who'd abandoned his men at Sedan in May 1940 as the Germans bypassed the Maginot line and broke through the 'impenetrable' Ardennes. Faking orders, he commandeered a plane and had himself flown to Bordeaux, where, within hours of his arrival, he was bricking up thousands of bottles of his best vintages before the Bosch could get their hands on them. And how he collaborated when they did arrive! Oh yes, with the help of their German friends, the Forgerons made quite a packet buying up stocks of generic Bordeaux plonk and *petits châteaux* and relabelling them as 'Château Forgeron' and other *crus classés* for shipment to the Fatherland. Of course, nobody talked about the War in Bordeaux these days – too many skeletons in the closet.

Quincy's eyes were moist. He was pathetic – blaming Vincent for all his problems! No one had forced him to do those things back in that little house in Grantchester. And neither Laura nor anyone else – certainly no Bordelais – had put a gun to his head and forced him to invest in bloody Belle-Mère. How foolish! – how utterly pathetic to have ever imagined that Laura would fall for him, an Englishman on the wrong side of fifty-five in baggy corduroys, suede brogues and sporting a bloody Paisley cravat!

He opened the windows and was met by a rush of cool autumnal night air and the sounds of traffic four floors below. Leaning over one of his window boxes of rapidly fading geraniums, he reminded himself to tidy things up and plant something for a bit of colour in the spring. ... The spring! What nightmares would unfold between now and then? Would he be a disgraced and destitute has-been by Easter? ...

It really was quite a long way down. It would be quick, a couple of seconds at most, and then – **BAM!** All over. He leaned out a little bit further ... and closed his eyes.

A sudden burst of high-pitched wailing caused him to lose his balance. 'What the –! Oh, Jesus Christ!'

Grabbing the window box just in time, he pushed himself backwards into the room with all his might, falling heavily on the parquet. 'That bloody, sodding alarm! If those two silly cows don't get the bugger fixed, I'll – I'll ... Oh my poor back.' He lay on the floor for a while, staring at the open windows. Then he began to laugh.

Quincy loved the Tapés dearly, but both mother and daughter were walking disasters when it came to anything mechanical or electrical. The burglar alarm in their florist's directly opposite on Cours de Tournon had been going off for no obvious reason almost every night ever since the damned thing had been installed a fortnight ago. As usual, the cowboy who'd installed it was one of their Lions' chums. Well, enough was enough. Friends or no friends, some plain speaking was required.

Madame Tapé answered the phone. 'This is Quincy, Madame Tapé,' – he'd never heard anyone address her by a Christian name, and had certainly never been invited to do so, or get beyond the '*vous*' stage – 'Quincy Dubloon. I'm–'

'*Quincy–!*'

'I'm sorry, but I really must protest about–'

'*How* wonderful! *Telepathy! I was just about to call **you**.*'

'Good, because I've–'

'*Oh, don't be cross,* mon anglais favori. *You'll think it such a terrible breach of etiquette. I told her I was going to phone and invite you, and that it wasn't necessary for her to act as my proxy – you know how insistent*

Madame Pronk can be. But then Churchill bit Petit Boy, and during the fracas the phone got knocked over and … well, she must have beaten me to it.

'Anyway, dear Quincy, you **can** dine with us tomorrow evening, can't you? You're always such fun, and we've got some lovely people coming – including Madame Pronk, of course – Béatrice said we couldn't put off inviting her any longer. And Pierre Lampre tells me he's bringing a **very** special guest – it's a surprise – I **adore** surprises, don't you? Apparently, it's someone Béatrice has been dying to meet for ages. Oh, Pierre's such a tease! … You **are** coming, aren't you? I know it's short notice, but Pierre suddenly came up with this idea for a soirée with a wine theme only this afternoon. … Did I mention the young man from Margaux? He's just joined the Lions. I think he's quite struck on Béatrice. Could it be wedding bells at last? … My God, let's hope so! As a matter of fact, if you look out of your window, you'll probably be able to see her walking towards the shop. Apparently, that wretched alarm thing has gone off again – more trouble than it's worth! Can you hear it? … It's not that strange noise in the background, is it?'

'Um … "strange noise", Madame Tapé?' Shaking his head and laughing silently, Quincy held out his arm and directed the receiver towards the open window. After a few seconds, he added: '*I* can't hear any strange noise.'

CHAPTER 26

Although Henri de Bondé took for granted the need for Château La Fayette to have exquisitely manicured gardens in the classic French style, he had no other interest in things botanical; such matters were best left to Nancy and the gardeners. Nevertheless, over the last few years he'd been an occasional visitor to Bordeaux's Jardin Botanique, a fact made even more remarkable by reason of its situation in an insalubrious area on the edge of the city's north-eastern suburbs. The low-lying land bordering the Garonne was one of those very Sixties and Seventies landscapes dominated by out-of-town shopping complexes, sports stadia, nondescript office developments, exhibition halls, and vast car parks. The aesthetics of this twilight zone were not improved by the panoramic vistas of the Garonne's opposite bank, with its skyline of pylons, grain silos, oil tanks and chemical works.

More recently, however, a new generation of municipal planners had endeavoured to ameliorate some of their predecessors' errors by an extensive programme of landscaping; this was during the heady pre-euro days when the level of France's public spending was not the affair of bankers in Frankfurt. And so, seemingly dropped from the sky on those barren plots that hitherto had remained untouched by the developers, there materialized a golf course, a few highly speculative *réserves naturelles*, a veritable maze of *pistes cyclables*, and the Jardin Botanique.

All things considered, the Jardin was a creditable attempt to create something fairly pleasant, albeit the planned interconnected network of highly distinctive gardens – one from each of Bordeaux's twin cities across the world – had not been wholly successful: the effects of the region's erratic climate had, perhaps, not been sufficiently taken into account. Nonetheless, trees and shrubs had grown on the man-made hillocks and around the artificial lakes and ponds, the net result being numerous secluded and verdant oases where persons of a reclusive nature could enjoy peace and solitude in an otherwise bleak quasi-urban wasteland. Consequently, the Jardin Botanique was a popular venue with both local courting couples and the grubby raincoat brigade.

Although Henri didn't fall into either category, from time to time he did need to conduct sensitive 'business meetings' away from prying eyes and in locations where his chances of being recognized were remote. The Jardin Botanique admirably satisfied both criteria. Indeed, he couldn't imagine any friend who'd be seen dead there, or even within a kilometre of it. True, there was the golf club on the other side of the access road – the unimaginatively named Avenue du Golf – where Henri parked his car, but it was not the sort of club to which people like himself belonged. However, in the unlikely event of the car or himself being spotted, he could always claim that he'd just popped in to 'le Club House' to deal with an enquiry for supplies of economical La-Fa for a large function.

Sat in the 'Seville Garden' with its generous displacement of Andalusian-style fake gas lamps and garden seats, Henri was savouring the sunshine on this crisp, cloudless November morning, and rejoicing in the thought that it was highly unlikely he'd ever need to return to the wretched place again. He'd just strolled over from the 'Bristol Garden' – even drearier than usual at this time of year – where he'd rendezvoused with Quincy Dubloon – 'Albion' indeed! – who'd been told in no uncertain terms that La Fayette no longer required the services of his lousy magazine for 'promotion', and that if Dubloon thought he would pay ten thousand euros for a six-page feature on the 'glories' of the estate's most recent vintages, he had to be out of his tiny English mind.

What Henri had found particularly galling was the cheek of the man. For several years he'd lined Dubloon's pockets with crisp new bank notes for the occasional complementary comment in *Wine Wisdom*, and then, about two years ago, the tick had cut him dead, acting as though the very idea of paying for favourable references in his pedestrian rag was a monstrous insult. And now, after all this time, he'd dragged him down here with 'an offer you can't refuse'. Well, this morning the boot had been very much on the other foot! He'd told him straight: La Fayette didn't need *Wine Wisdom*; his wines were now an essential luxury product in North America – and in the important bits of Asia too; he even had to ration supplies to some of his best customers. No, La Fayette needed crappy *Wine Wisdom* as much as Latour, Lafite, Mouton or Haut Brion did. Dubloon could go to hell.

Perhaps he'd been mistaken, but, just for a moment, had he seen tears in Dubloon's eyes? He'd almost felt sorry for the old rogue. What an actor! It was obvious: Dubloon had bitten off more than he could chew with that pathetic vineyard in crappy Entre-deux-Mers. The fool – going into business with Bourjois – aargh! – *and* that self-important American bitch – aaaargh! Poor sod. ... Anyway, one down, one to go. Killing two birds with one stone in the Jardin Botanique – how delicious!

Henri looked at his watch – his third Patek Philippe, the latest gift to himself – and tutted. His next and final appointment was late. Par for the course: the fat queen was always bloody late. *Oh – talk of the devil!*

Maurice Revelle, a nurse in his late thirties who'd once worked at the clinic where Guy de Bondé had spent his twilight years, came waddling through the screen of stunted palms into the miniscule 'Plaza Juan Carlos' with its borders of near-leafless oleanders, and immediately collapsed on the bench. But when he finally got his hyperventilating under control, Henri made no attempt to respond to his fake pleasantries.

'Don't waste my valuable time, Revelle. I told you on the phone – I'm not paying you another euro.'

'I must have the money. I've a sick sister in–'

'You don't. You don't have any sick sisters, brothers, mothers, fathers, or any other sick relatives, for that matter. I know that for a fact. You're a heroin addict. It's why you lost your job at the clinic.'

'I – I ... I'll go to Bourjois – I know where he lives. I'm not bluffing. I really mean it. I'll tell him what the old geezer kept yelling just before he passed away – "Jean-Claude! My son! Monsieur Dumas! Paris! Jean-Claude! My son! Monsieur Dumas! ..." Over and over and–'

'Go and tell him what the hell you like. I'll give you the complete postal address, directions, email details.'

'I'll tell him how I came to see you a few days after the old bloke died and how you went bleeding mental – giving me a thousand euros on the spot and a guarantee of the same every month in return for not breathing a word of them ravings.'

'Look, Revelle, can't you get it through your thick faggy skull that I don't give a shit any more whether Bourjois knows that the Old Man kept babbling that crap about being his fucking father, or that he should go and see some lawyer in Paris?'

'You're lying. You're just trying to–'

Groaning loudly, Henri jumped up from the bench. 'You were useful to me once, Revelle, I grant you that – Bourjois could have made a lot of trouble – but that Paris lawyer was already dead when dearest Papa kicked the bucket, and now, after two years' silence, it's bloody obvious that no arrangements were ... that – that my father was senile.'

Finally grasping that Henri was not bluffing, Revelle began to panic: he needed cash desperately; he'd blown almost everything he had on the petrol driving down from Paris. Unless he had another fix soon ... 'Please, Monsieur de Bondé, I'm begging now. *Please*, for old time's sake, yeah? Just five hundred euros–'

'Go to hell! And take your grubby hands off my arm.'

'Three hundred–'

'I told you to take your fucking hands off me, you disgusting fat queer.' Henri wrenched Revelle's podgy fingers from the cashmere and pushed him away. Stumbling, the obese junkie lost his balance and fell backwards onto an ornate Spanish litter bin that promptly buckled and gave way under his considerable weight. For some moments, Henri watched him groaning on the ground, an almost humorous sight of heaving blubber, mangled metal, and crushed oleander.

'Pathetic, utterly pathetic,' Henri sneered. 'I just don't understand you working-class people. You moan about not having two cents to rub together – not being able to afford the basic necessities of life – and the next minute, you're spending what miserable earnings you do have on cigarettes, booze, tattoos and drugs. God help us! And, to cap it all, you expect us taxpayers to sort out the bloody mess you get yourselves into – "rehabilitation", medication, more sodding drugs, "sheltered accommodation", "therapy" – a load of headshrinkers who– Oh, I've wasted enough time!'

After Henri had exited the Plaza Juan Carlos, Revelle lay for some time amidst the destruction, feeling both overwhelming self-pity and incandescent hatred of his assailant. Oddly enough, the words that remained ringing in his ears were 'working class'. They were so unjust. 'Fat', 'queer', 'a junkie' – yes, he was all those things, but 'working class'? How dare he! He was a qualified nurse – a professional – he had certificates! They were framed and hanging on the wall of his 'studio' flat … on the tenth floor of a vandalized and terrorized tower block in one of Paris's worst slum districts.

He started to sob. He'd sunk pretty low – the bottom, really, if he was honest with himself. If only he hadn't gone on that holiday to Guadeloupe. Oh, it had started brilliantly – all those native boys! But then there was that party on the beach and … well, he'd drunk too much, one thing led to another and … At first, it had just been a bit of crack–

'And now I'm a fucking heroin junkie.'

In pain, Revelle shuffled back to the car park, intermittently sobbing and talking to himself, but wholly oblivious to the curious glances from the park's few visitors. As he approached his battered and untrustworthy twelve-year-old Renault 4, the thought struck him that if he did go to see Bourjois and tell him all that stuff that the old baron used to witter on about, he might think there was something in it and … well, he might just take pity on him and reward him generously for his trouble. Feeling a little less suicidal, he blew his nose and told himself it was worth a try. 'Château Belle-Mère,' he giggled, '– my butt!' All he needed now was an unvandalized phone box and a local telephone directory.

*

A few hours later, when Revelle brought his car to a halt before Belle-Mère's impressive facade, he was blear-eyed and totally exhausted. He'd driven through the night from Paris to make his early morning appointment in the Jardin Botanique, and, apart from a hamburger and a cup of black coffee snatched on the *autoroute*, he'd had nothing to eat or drink for the last twelve hours or more. Licking his parched lips, he studied the building and had a feeling that he'd struck gold. He mounted the steps and rang the bell.

To his surprise, the door was opened by a delicate teenage boy bearing all the hated hallmarks of aristocratic privilege, yet wearing some kind of uniform; Henri de Bondé immediately came to mind. 'Butler's day off, is it, sonny?' he sniggered, looking the youth up and down. 'Is Monsieur Bourjois back yet? The lady on the phone said he'd be back between one and two.'

Alexandre Bourjois held his ground. He'd only just got home himself and was not in the best of moods. It was Founder's Day at school, and, being a Friday, the traditional half-day holiday had resulted in him coming home early for the weekend. Although he could have taken the bus directly to Langoiran, Grégoire Brignard had been obliged to pick him up from the station across the river in Barsac: Alexandre found buses 'terribly plebeian', whereas the train had a first-class section; he treated himself in secret, paying the difference out of his pocket money, what he grandly called his 'allowance'. To be honest, public transport in general was really not his sort of thing at all, but neither Mama nor Papa had been able to come and collect him from school. They'd claimed to have 'some terribly important business' – to quote Mama's words – with the American Woman, and Brignard couldn't drive all the way into Bordeaux because he was needed at the château to help his wife prepare 'a working lunch' which the American Woman was having with some English wine merchants. And then, having subjected himself to all the inconveniences of public transport, he'd got home only to discover that Papa had gone into Bordeaux for 'an urgent meeting' with dotty Dubloon. So, Papa could have picked him up after all! Typical! He could have undertaken some research in the school library and awaited him, or gone to the Fragonard Exhibition at the Musée des Beaux Arts.

With a highly critical eye, Alexandre scrutinized the odd fellow sneering in front of him. He didn't like the look of him at all. His shoes – always a sure indication of a chap's class – were cheap and in desperate need of a good polish.

'The "lady" to whom you refer,' Alexandre intoned regally, 'would be my father's *secretary* in all probability,' – Laura's secretary, in truth – 'and, as a matter of fact, our *butler* is currently otherwise engaged – serving lunch to some distinguished foreign visitors, if you must know. *I* am

Alexandre Bourjois. My father has not yet returned from an extremely important engagement in Bordeaux. Did you make an appointment?'

'"*Appointment*"? No – I didn't even give me name, mate. It's confidential like.'

Alexandre sighed. 'Well, I doubt that he'll have time for *you*, but if you wish to await his return, I respectfully suggest that you take your' – he glanced disdainfully down the steps – '... your "*vehicle*" over to the *chais* and–'

Revelle's massive bulk was a force to be reckoned with, and Alexandre was pushed aside, squealing, 'Now just a minute, my good man!', but the visitor was already over the threshold.

'Look, sonny, I'm not here on vineyard business. It's personal, OK? I'll wait here.'

Charles Fontaine heard the raised juvenile voice as he strolled along the corridor which connected his wing of the house and the hall. 'Oh, dear God,' he muttered, 'not more strife between the little Dauphin and the servants.'

Late as usual, Fontaine was on his way to join Laura's 'working lunch' with the Englishmen, having already sadly concluded that it would be more 'working' than 'lunch'. Well, at least the English fellows were civilized: on their last visit a few months ago, they'd even shared some of his subtle jokes at Appleton's expense. All things considered, it had been quite an amusing meeting. As he emerged from the corridor and spied the 'Dauphin', he was devising some Anglo-French double entendres that could be lobbed into the discussions well over Laura's head.

'Now, now, young Alexandre,' he began good-humouredly, 'what's all this–?' He stopped dead in his tracks as the two verbal combatants turned to face him. Alexandre would later recall that Fontaine looked as if he'd seen his own ghost.

'*You*!' cried Fontaine, slapping a hand over his mouth.

Revelle's obvious puzzlement over his recognition by this stranger lasted just a few seconds. 'Well, well, well, well, *well*! It's ... Hang on, it'll come to me in a sec'.'

Alexandre launched into a pompous account of his dealings with the 'intruder', but neither Revelle nor Fontaine heard a word. Instead, they could both see sand dunes and intertwined naked bodies.

'Still pop down to Le Porge from time to time, do we, *Pierre*?' declaimed Revelle over the boy's babbling. 'It is Pierre, isn't it? – at least, that's what you used to call yourself.'

The expression of abject horror on Fontaine's face increased. 'Not here, you fool,' – he shot a glance at Alexandre – 'not in front of *him*, for God's sake. How did you–? ... I mean, it's impossible. I – I ...'

Looking from one man to the other, Alexandre finally sensed that a rather interesting situation was developing before him. He shut up.

'In *here*,' Fontaine snapped, moving swiftly over to the dining room's double doors, '– *now*!' He turned to Alexandre and made a Herculean effort to smile. 'Thank you, Alexandre. I'll handle this. Be a good b-boy, will you, and p-pop up to ... to the b-boardroom and tell M-Mademoiselle Appleton that I ... I'll be another few m-minutes, hmm? Some unexpected b-business – an old ... an old supplier of ... um ... corks. ... Go on! Cut along, boy!'

When he reached the top of the stairs, Alexandre stopped, listened, and fumed. '"Be a good boy",' he mimicked under his breath. 'Who on earth does he think he is? I'm not a damned servant at *his* beck and call!' He gasped wide-eyed: he'd said *that* word! He'd actually sworn like a grownup! He felt very mature – well, he *was* very mature – for his age. Indeed, all things considered–

Almost before Alexandre knew what was happening, he was already halfway back down the stairs. Tiptoeing past the dining room's closed doors, he crept into the adjoining library. Within seconds, an ear was pressed to the relevant wall; on the other side, voices were raised. If only he could hear what they were saying ...

Fontaine felt as though he was burning up with fever. He took off his tweed jacket and hung it on the back of one of the dining chairs. 'You don't understand, you idiot. I don't own this bloody place – not any more. I went bust – it's a long story.'

'I'm not in any hurry, mate.'

Fontaine waved a hand dismissively. 'This Bourjois fellow and his partners bought Belle-Mère from the receivers. They just kept me on as a consultant. My mother and I have a little flat ... in a wing. We're almost broke, for Christ's sake.'

Revelle snorted. 'You must think I was born yesterday.'

Both men were intermittently pacing clockwise around the long dining table, yet always managing to keep on opposite sides. Fontaine finally reached the end closest to the windows, and, looking out, caught sight of Revelle's tatty car parked on the broad sweep of the raked gravel forecourt. The wreck profoundly disturbed his aesthetic senses. God only knew what the Englishmen would think if they were to see it from the boardroom on the floor above. And Laura! She'd be furious!

Oh, concentrate, you bloody fool! If you pay him anything, he'll be back for more before you can–

'Old ... your mum, is she? ... Infirm? ... Does she know you're queer, "Pierre"? I've got snaps, you know.'

Turning away from the window, Fontaine was surprised to find Revelle standing by the door. If anything, the stupid grin on his fat ugly face was even wider. *What vile teeth! How could I have ever done it with ... with that? Be firm.*

'Get out – go on – clear off. You're wasting your bloody time.'

'Oh?' queried Revelle sardonically, opening the door. 'Really? I don't think so. You mull over everything I've said, love. I can write very graphically. Can you imagine the old dear's face – not to mention her dicky ticker – when she starts to read my letter over her breakfast coffee? Wouldn't surprise me if she–'

'Get out! Get out, you piece of shit!'

Next door, in Alexandre's hiding place, the unsavoury exclamation was unmistakable. The snooper was shocked: it was not at all like old Fontaine to resort to that kind of language. Now he could hear rapid movements, a door opening, footsteps on the hall's marble tiles, the front door's unmistakable clank. He dashed over to the window and peeked out. At a surprising rate of knots, the fat oik was wobbling down the steps to his horrid little car, with foul-mouthed Fontaine bellowing far worse obscenities – from the front door, presumably. The car spluttered into life and gravel was suddenly flying everywhere. Golly! – how on earth could such a heap of junk accelerate so quickly? Yet, within seconds, it disappeared from sight down the avenue of Lombardy poplars.

Returning to the dining room, Fontaine poured himself a glass of Armagnac and gulped a mouthful. He had to get to the damned boardroom or Appleton would– 'Oh, to hell with the bitch!' he hissed. 'I should have given that filth something. I'd never have seen him again. Now the bastard will be well and truly pissed off. Hell hath no fury like a vicious queen! – a creature capable of anything!' The sight of his jacket on the back of the chair where he'd left it made up his mind. 'A hundred euros,' he muttered. 'A drug addict – bloody obvious. A hundred euros would certainly do it. He'll be driving back to Bordeaux in that banger – easy to catch him up.' He grabbed the jacket, threw it on, and sprinted towards the door. 'Jesus!' he muttered, halting halfway across the hall, '– how much bloody cash have I got on me?' He thrust a hand into the jacket's inside breast pocket His brain seemed to explode. Nothing! He tried the other pockets. *My credit cards, driving licence, identity card! ... I'll have to report the theft to the police!*

'The bastard!' he screamed, dashing down the steps, '– I'll kill that fucking bastard!'

Inexplicably thrilled by the filthy expletives and homicidal threat, Alexandre watched spellbound from the library window as Fontaine jumped into his gleaming red Renault – a brand-new Belle-Mère company car – and raced away.

*

Jean-Claude changed gear and accelerated up the steep hill out of Langoiran. He felt exhilarated: the meeting with Quincy had gone very well, although, to be honest, the poor man had looked absolutely awful – puffy eyes, dishevelled hair, and, if he wasn't mistaken, he was wearing the same shirt he'd had on at yesterday's board meeting, which, of course, was not like Quincy at all. Sophie's dad was probably right: Quincy was short of cash; he was certainly very keen on the idea of selling his Belle-Mère shares!

Reliving their conference call with Paul Charpentier in Paris, Jean-Claude had to admit that Paul was a brilliant businessman. By the end of it, Quincy had agreed to make a formal written offer to sell Laura his shares for five million euros as soon as he'd spoken with his lawyers. She'd then have twenty-eight days in which to accept, failing which he'd be free to sell to the Bourjois-Charpentier consortium. They'd then have control of the company with fifty-five per cent!

'"Consortium",' Jean-Claude chuckled. 'I'm becoming quite a businessman myself.' Just another five minutes and he'd be able to tell Sophie all about it in person; Laura's 'working lunch' with a couple of representatives of a London wine merchant could wait a few minutes. He'd decided not to disturb Sophie by phoning from Bordeaux with a joyous report of Quincy's cooperation: having provided wonderful moral support during their heated discussions with Laura straight after breakfast, Sophie had then retreated to her studio; painting, she said, would calm her shattered nerves after all that unpleasantness.

In compliance with the CEDEZ LE PASSAGE sign, Jean-Claude pulled up at the crossroads with the D121, a minor road connecting Créon with Cambes. As was often the case, not a vehicle could be seen in either direction. Nevertheless, he hesitated: opposite, there was a stationery car – a decrepit white Renault 4 – with its left indicator blinking. Presumably, the guy was going to turn in front of him and head for Créon. He waited. Nothing. So much for courtesy! He was about to sound his horn, when he realized that the driver didn't even have his hands on the steering wheel; judging by his movements, the guy was counting bank notes – even kissing them!

Just as Jean-Claude depressed the clutch, there was a tremendous burst of horn blowing from somewhere. With a guilty, startled expression on his puffy face, the man in the Renault looked up and saw the car on the opposite side of the crossroads. Jean-Claude smiled and raised both hands

333

off the wheel as if to say 'It wasn't me, mate!' And then, like some deranged mechanical kangaroo, the Renault was bouncing towards him, turning right – then left – then right again. It stalled just metres from him, the driver frantically trying to restart the engine while simultaneously shooting glances over his shoulder and through the rear window. And there, up the road towards Belle-Mère, Jean-Claude could see it too – a red car rushing towards them – too fast – *far* too fast!

The red car was just seconds from the crossroads when there was the retort of a backfire, and, with a tremendous screeching of tyres, the Renault shot away down the D121 towards Cambes. Transfixed by the red car, now almost upon him, Jean-Claude shut his eyes and saw his own death. But the terrifying sounds of a speeding vehicle trying to stop were not followed by the horrific impact he was anticipating. When he opened his eyes, the red car – *I know it!* – *Fontaine?* – *Fontaine!* – was already Cambes-bound in frantic pursuit of the Renault.

With a pounding heart and taking deep breaths, Jean-Claude fleetingly thought of racing after the two mad drivers, but whatever Fontaine's problem might be, there was critical business to resolve at Belle-Mère. In his absence, Laura would probably fill the heads of the Larboard & Chitterling directors with all her '*garagiste*' plans for the estate's wines! He'd then look a complete fool when the consortium took over in a few weeks. And it was bad enough that he'd met one of the Englishmen – albeit briefly – at Forgeron's debauched party that traumatic night two years ago! So, Jean-Claude continued on his way to Belle-Mère, resolving to go straight to the boardroom – better to postpone seeing Sophie until the 'working lunch' was over and the English were safely off the premises.

In the event, when he let himself into Belle-Mère, a seething Laura was standing at the top of the main staircase; she'd heard his car on the gravel. 'You'd better get your ass up here *now*,' she hissed. 'I've been holding the fort for long enough while you've been in Bordeaux committing treason with Dubloon. Jesus! – if that wasn't bad enough, Fontaine has pissed off somewhere, driving like a bat out of hell! The Brits must think we don't give a shit about their visit!'

When they entered the boardroom, Larboard & Chitterling's Philip Rimmer and David Warbler were already tucking into Madame Brignard's heavenly vol-au-vents. Thirty minutes later, a red-faced and profusely perspiring Fontaine turned up. After effusive greetings to the visitors, he said:

'You won't believe it, but I was mugged – *downstairs*! – bloody thug passing himself off as a customer' – he'd already forgotten the cork salesman yarn, such was his state of barely controlled hysteria – '… um, asking to see you, Jean-Claude, actually. Young Alexandre let him in.

You'll have to have a word with him – needs to be more careful. Saw the bounder in the dining room. Told him to sling his hook after sussing out he'd no interest in buying anything. As soon as he'd gone, popped on my jacket to come up here – it was on the back of a chair – no bloody wallet! – must have pinched it when my back was turned! Thought I could catch him up – bounder driving an old banger – bit foolhardy with hindsight! Bloody lost him – must have turned off the main road somewhere. ... Was that you I passed down at the crossroads, Jean-Claude? Couldn't be sure – I was going like the proverbial clappers. I–'

'Yes. I thought it was you, Charles. You almost killed me. In fact, it's amazing you didn't kill yourself driving like that.'

'*So* sorry, dear boy, but–'

'*Charles*! *Enough*! We're here to discuss our *wines*, not your goddam frigging wallet!'

Laura's explosion was the worst Jean-Claude had witnessed; even Philip and David ceased masticating their mouthfuls of vol-au-vents.

Just after four, as the meeting was on the point of breaking up, the Langon police finally arrived in response to Fontaine's notification by phone of the larceny. There were, however, more officers than might have been expected to investigate the theft of a mere wallet, but then a junior *gendarme* let it slip to Marie-Thérèse that there'd been a car crash and the suspected thief was dead. They interviewed Fontaine first – in the dining room, the scene of the 'mugging'. Unwisely, he failed to tell the truth at the outset – not just about his past relationship with Revelle, but also that he'd caught up with him on a dirt road in the forest, that he'd witnessed Revelle's collision with a chestnut tree when he lost control of the unroadworthy Renault, and that he'd realized Revelle was dead when he examined him: having been thrown through the windscreen, he'd received horrific injuries. He would finally confess all in the days to come – condemned by forensic tests on his shoes and car tyres, together with the evidence of a farmer who'd seen Fontaine's red car emerge from the track and rejoin the D121.

Advised by an excited Marie-Thérèse of the officers' presence at the château, Sophie emerged from her studio to join Jean-Claude and Alexandre in the library; they were interviewed separately. Sophie knew nothing, of course; Jean-Claude just repeated what he'd said earlier that afternoon in the boardroom. Alexandre, however, was closeted with the detectives for almost an hour. When his parents were finally invited to join him, the senior officer, looking very serious, said:

'I'm afraid we'll have to take Alexandre into Langon to make a formal statement.'

Sophie exploded. 'What *is* this,' she protested, '– the Inquisition? He's only twelve, for God's sake!'

'It's all right, Mama,' Alexandre said calmly. 'I've told them *everything*.'

And 'everything' turned out to be quite a story.

Shortly after six o'clock, Madame Fontaine suffered a massive heart attack. The news that her son had been arrested on suspicion of having caused the death by dangerous driving of one Marcelle Revelle, a homosexual male nurse who, it was believed, had been blackmailing him, had been bad enough, but when she saw a sobbing and handcuffed Charles being led down the steps to the awaiting police van, it all proved too much for the octogenarian. Several officers, well trained in first aid, did their very best – to no avail, alas.

After the ambulance had departed with her body, the subdued Bourjois trio retreated to their East Wing apartment for a family debriefing session over coffee and, in due course, cognac for the adults. As soon as they were all comfortable in front of the living room fire, Alexandre said:

'I should assume that, despite some initial bad publicity concerning the unconventional predilections of Monsieur Fontaine, his exit – and Madame Fontaine's – from the Belle-Mère stage, so to speak, might just facilitate our acquisition of absolute legal title in, and to, the whole of the estate, don't you think?'

Struck dumb, Sophie and Jean-Claude merely stared at their sanguine son.

'Yes, I know it was somewhat ungentlemanly of me to look, but when I got back from school, the kitchen table was still littered with breakfast debris. ... We really must hire some full-time servants of our own – the Brignards are positively antediluvian. ... Well, the table was a shambles, and amidst the debris lurked a bundle of photocopied emails from Grandpapa about the proposed takeover, together with your notes, Papa, and ... Well, let's be candid. As things have turned out, it was rather fortuitous that I *did* read them, hmm? – *and* that it was *I* who let that queer chap into the house, and not anyone else. ... By the way, I denied Fontaine's allegation that the deceased wanted to see *you*, Papa. Do you think that was wrong of me?'

CHAPTER 27

Although Laura was shocked by Fontaine's arrest and his mother's death, these events did not weaken her resolve to accompany Lampre to the Tapés' dinner: she couldn't afford to leave any stone unturned now that Jean-Claude had revealed his treacherous hand. The bottom line was a powerful motivator: unless she procured the necessary funds to purchase Quincy's shareholding, the vile Bourjois-Charpentier conspirators could be in control of Belle-Mère in the very near future. Lampre might just have some solution up his sleeve.

When the police finally took their leave, however, Laura had barely enough time to get down to the gatehouse to shower and change. She was halfway into town when it occurred to her that as a matter of common courtesy, if nothing else, Quincy should be told that Fontaine was in custody and that his mother had kicked the bucket. But there was no reply at his apartment and she could only get his mobile's message service; seeing her number on his screen, he was probably refusing to pick up. When she phoned the Bourjoises to check whether they'd thought to tell him, Jean-Claude answered. He sounded smug, announcing that he'd already called Quincy at Cours de Tournon – just as he was about to go out for dinner with some neighbours – and put him in the picture.

'I bet he has!' she hissed, slamming the mobile on the front passenger seat. 'Scheming, fuckers – the two of them.'

The plan had been to meet Lampre at his Cours de l'Intendance apartment at around quarter to eight for an aperitif; apparently, it was only a five-minute stroll over to the Tapés' place. However, due to road works on the Pont de Pierre compounding her delay, there was no time for a drink after all, so she called and arranged to meet Lampre outside the entrance to his building. When she arrived, he was effusive with his embracing, kissing of cheeks, and praise over Laura's appearance and outfit – one of Escada's latest creations in black leather.

'They're in Rue Vital-Carles,' Lampre fizzed, feeling that unmistakable stirring in his loins as he steered her across the road. 'You'll love the Tapés – Tapette and her daughter, Béatrice. Not top drawer or anything – pieds noirs between you and me ... Casablanca. The late Monsieur Tapé – Robert – was in tobacco there. To be honest, Laura, they're rather hard up,' – she groaned inwardly – 'but they still manage to enjoy life to the full – always have a fascinating mixture of guests. ... I don't know how they do it, really. Food's first class – Béatrice is a *wonderful* cook. She'd make some lucky fellow a damned good wife, even at her age ... fine woman – Tapette too. You'd never think she was ... Sorry! – that would be indiscreet.'

After a few minutes of spouting potted biographies of their prospective hosts, Lampre halted before a large stone building redolent of nineteenth-century neoclassicism. 'Ah, here we are!' he announced. 'Of course, they're a bit eccentric,' he admitted, lowering his voice as he searched for the right buzzer in the gloom of the street lighting. 'Then there are the dogs. And they can't afford help these days, so don't be surprised if–'

A distorted '*Allo!*' crackled through the ancient intercom.

'*Bonsoir*! *C'est moi*, Pierre!'

The building's vast entrance hall, a form of enclosed porte cochère designed to accommodate carriages, smelled of rotting refuse. Ahead of them, adjacent to the foot of the staircase, and as if to confirm Laura's worst suspicions, a huge black plastic bin bag lay on its side. As they approached, something furry scuttled away and disappeared behind it.

Laura squealed and clutched Lampre's arm. Seemingly oblivious to the rat, he said: 'There's a young American couple with two children on the floor below Tapette. You ought to meet them. He's in computers or something. Not sure they've got the hang of our way of disposing of rubbish yet.'

Cautiously, Laura pulled open a diminutive lift's door. She was on the point of saying something in defence of her fellow countrymen, when Lampre shook his head. 'We'd better take the stairs,' he advised. 'They're only four floors up.'

Laura sighed: the feeling that she'd been duped into participating in a wild goose chase was intensifying by the minute. There'd certainly be no investor with a fat cheque book in this dump.

When they reached the second floor, Lampre said: 'I don't know all the guests tonight, but apparently you'll be in good company as a *viticulteur*.'

Laura raised her eyebrows. Here it comes, she prayed: the first hint of his role as an intermediary – a deal fixer. 'Oh *really*?'

'Hmm, quite a contrast. At one end of the spectrum there's a very dynamic young chap from the Médoc – Margaux to be precise. I think Tapette said Margaux. ... Anyway, he's just joined the Lions. Very entrepreneurial by all accounts, and Béatrice can't keep her eyes off him.' Lampre sighed. 'Poor Béatrice, if only she wasn't so ... so big boned.'

'And at the other end ... of the spectrum?' prompted Laura.

'The other end? ... Ah yes. Well, you're old friends – dear Sue – Sue Pronk – I mean *Olivier*. She's threatened to kill anyone who doesn't use her maiden name in future. Such a tragedy – Eric drowning like that, wasn't it?

And such a good fisherman too. Mind you, the Dordogne can be a treacherous river, especially when in full flood. Still, let's not spoil our evening.'

They'd reached the fourth-floor landing, where Lampre stopped in front of massive double doors, one of which stood slightly ajar. From within came the sounds of 1930s dance music and barking dogs. '*Voilà!*' he cried, sweeping an arm theatrically before him as if they'd just reached the summit of Everest.

Laura remained fixed to the spot. '*Sue?*' she queried incredulously.

'Hmm? ... 'Hello! Anyone at home? ... Where on earth–? Tapette! *There* you are, and as beautiful as ever, my darling.'

*

Quincy had arrived at the apartment at seven-forty, a polite ten minutes after the time specified by Madame Tapé in their telephone conversation the previous evening. He'd hoped to be one of the last guests, thereby avoiding the Bordelais custom of awaiting the full complement before anyone gets sight of an aperitif – always champagne – or any nibbles, which chez les Tapés was invariably pâté spread very slowly by Tapette herself on savagely toasted bread before the assembled company. It quickly transpired, however, that only two other invitees had preceded him, the aged Comte Christian de Salleboeuf and his wife, Céline; they resided nearby in a vast and magnificently furnished apartment overlooking the Garonne. For the last thirty years, Céline had been a regular customer at the Tapés' shop: having spent most of her life in a gilded cage, she revelled in Tapette's most un-Bordeaux-like informality. As for her husband's toleration of the Tapés, he lusted after Béatrice. In fact, despite his seventy-three years, he still spent one week every month with his long-suffering mistress in Biarritz, a custom the equally long-suffering Céline had come to accept as a fact of life, even though she still wept volubly on each occasion he exited their front door with his battered Vuitton suitcase.

Quincy encountered Christian while strolling unannounced along the wide and lengthy hall that ran down the centre of the Tapés' apartment: he was on his hands and knees rummaging through a cupboard piled high with dusty bottles, muttering obscenities about the total absence of order in 'this damnable excuse for a wine cellar'.

'Evening, Christian. Are we the first?'

'What? Oh, Quincy! This should be your bloody job. If only you'd arrived a few minutes earlier. They've got Médocs mixed up with Graves, whites with reds, and vintages all over the bloody place! Some of this lot should have been drunk up bloody *years* ago. Christ only knows what I should get out. They should have had something upright and opened *hours* ago to let it breathe, what? But as usual here, total bloody chaos – *women!*'

'Hmm. I'll give you a hand if you like.'

'No, no! You're on fire duty. They've got Céline laying the bloody table, would you believe? You'd better report to the kitchen post haste.'

The Tapés had abandoned the Comtesse de Salleboeuf in order to finish getting dressed. When Quincy entered the kitchen, she was merrily ransacking drawers to find a sufficient number of clean napkins, acting as though she was Marie-Antoinette in apocryphal milkmaid mode. After embracing, she said with an engaging grin:

'I've been left very clear instructions that immediately upon your arrival, Quincy, you are to be directed to the living room, where you'll find all the essentials for making a jolly good blaze.'

Despite a mountain of firelighters, old newspapers and kindling, Quincy was still failing to get the logs burning when, to his consternation, Patrick Audinette walked into the room, armed with a huge bouquet of red roses. By the time Sue Olivier arrived, laden with a large and ominously heavy cardboard box, Patrick had managed to create a roaring inferno; he wasted no time in cracking a joke about Quincy's soot-covered hands and red face, and how, in all probability, the English were as good at making fires as they were at making love. Until he uttered those words, Sue had found Audinette quite attractive, but they stirred up within her a small but still potent residue of patriotism.

'Well,' she retorted, 'from what I've 'eard, if your bleedin' generals 'adn't spent so much time shaggin' their mistresses in May 1940, you might 'ave put up a better show against the bleedin' Krauts.'

With Patrick momentarily lost for words, Quincy picked up Sue's box, saying, 'Come on, I'll show you to the kitchen, old thing, before we have to resort to the UN. Jesus! – what the hell's in this?'

'Wine, of course,' Sue replied, rolling her eyes. 'I've brought twelve bottles – four of each colour. I know those two are a bit short of the readies, so I offered to supply the old vino. So proud these old dames, aren't they? By all accounts, Madame Tapé is … Bloody 'ell! – what *is* 'er bleedin' first name, Quince?'

'I've always called her "Madame Tapé", Sue. *Very* close friends are permitted to address her as "Tapette", but I wouldn't–'

'Tapette will do fine. Any road, Tapette said not to bother with bringin' any wine – they 'ad some old bottles somewhere. Well, it sounded right pathetic, so I just 'ad to 'elp out. And you never know who might be at one of these dos, do you?'

Quincy glanced at Audinette and raised his bushy eyebrows.

340

The Tapés' living room was large and tall, but in common with every other room in the apartment, it was generously stuffed with furniture, paintings, objets d'art, and down-to-earth knick-knacks – the treasured fruits of decades of trawling at the Sunday flee market held around the magnificent medieval church of St-Michel. Thus, for a most economical outlay, the duo had created a form of antique decor which, although not visually displeasing, was claustrophobic.

When Madame Tapé herself ushered the final two guests into the furnace-like room – it was a mild autumnal evening and Patrick's fire was now verging on the volcanic – her proud announcement that they now had no less than *two* of the world's greatest wine writers in their midst sent such a seismic shock through a sufficient number of the guests that all conversation ground to a halt. By chance, it was at this moment that the Tapés' most recent and contentious acquisition – a 1930s standard lamp in the form of a life-size boy of Afro-Caribbean origin decked out in a fanciful red and gold servant's costume clutching a bare sixty-watt bulb in one hand – finally lived up to Céline de Salleboeuf's worst fears, just as she'd predicted some weeks ago upon first setting eyes on it. This evening, ever since she'd entered the room, it had been flickering ominously, which was hardly surprising in view of the lamp's age and the Tapés' reckless inattention to basic electrical safety standards. In truth, the apartment was a death trap: it was common for up to six power-hungry appliances to be connected to one wall socket through the injudicious use of twin and triple plugs.

In any event, upon all conversation ceasing due to Tapette's announcement, leaving only Jean Sablon's voice booming around the apartment on the temperamental Seventies music centre in the hall, the black boy's bulb flickered for the last time and then exploded. There were several cries of '*Oh là, là!*' in the ensuing apartment-wide blackout, with Sablon rapidly grinding to a deep bass halt. Then Lampre stood on Churchill's tail, the outraged yelping dog bit his ankle, and 'big-boned' Béatrice knocked over the side table bearing the Tapés' de rigueur pâté and toast. In the non-illuminated bedlam, each dog attempted to eat the lion's share, and those who could understand English heard Laura shout, 'Why the fuck didn't you tell me Quincy was coming, Pierre?'

Recklessly, Patrick volunteered to accompany Béatrice to the fuse box; they were gone some time.

The Tapés' grand dining room had long ago been converted into a 'bedsit' for their mysterious student lodgers – always young men – who were never seen by guests, nor even alluded to by the hosts. Dining had, therefore, been relegated to a cosy room that led directly off the commodious but antiquated kitchen, and which in former times had served as the housekeeper's quarters; the Tapés had bade their farewells to servants when they departed Casablanca. The problem of seating large numbers of diners around the rectangular table had been resolved by acquiring two refectory-style benches, each of which could – albeit with considerable discomfort – cope with four average-size adults; Tapette and her Amazon daughter always sat in comfortable dining chairs – with arms – one at each end. Tonight, they only had seven guests: notwithstanding the invitation to do so, Sue had not brought a 'partner'; Tapette had ensured that Patrick came alone. Clearly delighted, Béatrice firmly steered him to the seat at her right side. Despite blocking manoeuvres, Laura grabbed the seat at her left: she was anxious to be as far away as possible from Quincy, who, as Tapette's favourite Englishman, had been seated next to her.

They were well into the first course of *coquilles St-Jacques*, when, for some reason best known to herself, Céline de Salleboeuf began waxing lyrical in her sing-song voice on the superiority of French butter over all others. It was a topic she stuck to doggedly, despite Sue's vociferous attempts to procure everyone's agreement that her 2004 Barrage *blanc* was not only the perfect accompaniment for seafood and fish of every kind, but also an infinitely superior product to 'the old stuff' that the hosts had been forced to serve up. She was sat next to Quincy, who'd kicked her under the table while expressing his thanks to the hosts for spoiling them with no less than two bottles of the heavenly 1987 vintage of Haut Brion's very limited production of white wine. Laura and Patrick were still analysing it with technical jargon that meant little to Béatrice, but all three of them were unanimous in their preferences; the Barrage was, accordingly, ignored. Béatrice, as was her wont, managed to add insult to injury when, reaching for the bread basket, she managed to knock over her glass of abandoned Barrage. Laura and Patrick, who'd been exchanging the occasional conspiratorial expressions of the what-the-hell-are-we-doing-here? variety, exploded with howls of laughter.

As Béatrice dabbed at the pool of spilt wine, Céline, who was completely unphased by the 'accident', resumed her butter monologue. 'There's this dear little creamery near our place in Normandy where ...'

'Stuck up old cow.' Sue muttered, leaning close to Quincy. Nodding, he kept smiling at Céline: in truth, he was very fond of her, and French butter was his favourite too. 'So,' Sue continued under her breath, 'you and the Yank seem to be at daggers drawn. Things got bloody worse at Belle-Mère, 'ave they?'

Still smiling, Quincy leaned a little closer to her. 'Frightful, actually,' he replied over suddenly raised voices: tongue in cheek and winking at Laura,

Patrick was claiming that butter from Charente knocked the spots off even Normandy's best. 'To be honest, Sue,' Quincy whispered in her ear, 'and this is absolutely confidential, I'm probably going to call it a day and sell out. Jean-Claude's tycoon father-in-law has made an offer to buy my shares.'

Sue's heart seemed to miss a beat.

Laura swirled the magnificent Haut Brion around her mouth and felt the ultimate sensation of sublime satisfaction which she only experienced when savouring a truly world-class wine. If only for that, it had been worth coming to this crazy dinner. She flashed a smile at Patrick, and he smiled back as he mischievously warmed to his Charente butter theme.

OK, Laura mused, *maybe he's just a bit too good-looking in that stereotypically French way – like champion-winning dogs over-bred into parodies of the species – but he's definitely hot, and, for a Bordelais, he seems to have a good sense of humour.* She shot a glance sideways to her left down the table towards Lampre two seats away. *Is this Patrick guy somehow involved in his scheme? – if there is a scheme. Does he have money? He certainly oozes it with his flashy clothes.*

Notwithstanding her mother's frowns of disapproval, Béatrice had almost finished her third glass of the rapidly diminishing supply of Haut Brion and was moving into emotional overdrive. By now, even she had lost interest in the butter debate. 'Are your parents enjoying living in town, Patrick?' she asked with exaggerated interest and an oily smile – she possessed a very large mouth and a complete set of formidable teeth to go with it. Before he had time to answer, she added, half-turning to Laura: 'They have a *lovely* new apartment in Allées de Tourny – quite small but *ever* so nice furnishings. Monsieur Audinette – Hubert – has been a Lion for *years*. It's taken absolutely *ages* to get him to persuade Patrick to join.' Béatrice patted his hand. 'He's a bank manager, you know – BIF – Place des Quinconces.'

Laura felt both confused and oddly electrified. 'Patrick or Hubert? I mean–'

'Don't be *silly*,' Béatrice sniggered girlishly, staring at Laura with a patronizing smile, 'Patrick's the *maître de chai*–'

'*Directeur*–' Patrick began to correct.

'– at Château La Fayette in Margaux.'

Laura's mouth fell open. For just a second, her brain froze. What the hell was afoot? 'So, you're Patrick *Audinette*,' she croaked, desperately trying to smile broadly, 'and your dad's Hubert – *my* bank manager – Belle-Mère's bank manager. I'm so sorry – we weren't properly introduced. Nobody told me that ... I mean–'

'I should be the one apologising, Laura,' Patrick interjected, chuckling. 'I just assumed you knew that I'm the La Fayette guy! Amazing about you and Dad. He's never mentioned it, but then he's *very* discreet.'

Béatrice was nodding vigorously. 'I'll say!' She ran her fingertips over Patrick's hand again. 'Oh! – remember those holiday snaps I mentioned at the Lions the other evening, Patrick?' The smile froze on his face. 'We can have a look at them after dinner. There're quite a few of me by the pool – our old friends in Burgundy, Laura, have a *super* château with a *huge* pool – and Mama snapped me a few times – *topless*!' The revelation prompted more hysterical giggling and an equally animated bust.

The second course, *ris de veau*, came in a wonderful creamy white wine sauce. Earlier in the hall cupboard, Salleboeuf had unearthed three bottles of 1986 Pape Clément, which he suspected needed to be drunk up and would prove a perfect accompaniment. To keep the old philanderer happy, Tapette, who'd no idea of their value, had happily concurred with two being opened. There was something of an unseemly scramble as Salleboeuf and Sue competed for the one red wine glass allotted to each diner. Quincy, who couldn't help feeling something akin to pity for her, offered to start with the Barrage *rouge* and then move on to the Pape Clément. Graciously, Tapette agreed to do likewise. Had they been present, it was a scene that would have amused Laura and Patrick. However, while Béatrice had been fetching the *ris de veau* from the kitchen – Tapette never moved from her seat during any of her dinner parties – Laura had asked for directions to 'the bathroom' and Patrick had said that he would check on the living room fire. Returning, they met each other in the hall, where the tinny hi-fi was now belting out the Andrews Sisters' wartime hits.

'Incredible!' chuckled Laura, pointing at the distant appliance festooned in a web of electric cabling.

Nodding and smiling, Patrick said: 'Those old songs probably remind them of Casablanca – Vichy – liberating American GIs–'

'"*You must remember this*",' Laura sang, but she was no match for the Andrews Sisters' cacophony.

Patrick looked bemused. 'Yeah. ... Anyway,' – Laura began moving towards the dining room door – 'you and Dubloon seem a bit frosty. Everything OK at ... er–?'

'Belle-Mère.'

'Sure ... yeah, Belle-Mère,' – he sniggered – 'or is Bourjois making your lives a misery? Sorry! That's none of my business, but ... well, I know he was a real pain in the ass at La Fayette. Technically first rate, of course, but–'

'Come on, you two,' boomed Salleboeuf from the doorway, '*ris de veau*'s getting cold!'

'Round Two!' chuckled Patrick under his breath. 'Maybe we could have a drink afterwards, Laura ... at Le Noailles. I'd like to hear more about how you're trying to create a rising star in Entre-deux-Mers and–'

'Premières Côtes *actually*.'

'Whatever.'

They were on the dining room's threshold. Béatrice had her back to them as she served the *ris de veau* with gay abandon and scant regard for the wine glasses in her vicinity.

'Oh, *do* be careful, Béatrice!' admonished her mother from the far end. 'This week alone, you've already broken three glasses, a cup and the kitchen clock.'

Everyone laughed, except Béatrice.

As the two guests resumed their seats, Laura, with her voice raised, said: 'Yes, I'd love to join you for a drink later, Patrick, at Le Noailles,' whereupon Béatrice, who, by design, was serving the American last, managed to drop her diminutive helping of the *ris de veau* on the wine-stained tablecloth.

'It's like a bleedin' *Carry On* film,' Sue said giggling, but Quincy barely managed a smile: he could already picture how Laura's evening would end after those drinks. Sue studied his profile and guessed correctly what he was thinking. She'd long known of his infatuation, and Laura's total lack of reciprocity. To be blunt, he'd invested in Belle-Mère for all the wrong reasons, allowing his heart to rule his head – fatal in business. It was not that the vineyard couldn't be turned around, but rather that the three current partners were, in her opinion, trying to make a silk purse out of a sow's ear. On several occasions over the last couple of years, she'd tried to warn Quincy, but he just wouldn't listen. His wine snobbery – as she saw it – coupled with the infatuation had been a fatal combination. And now Laura was flirting with this young smartarse from snooty Margaux, and poor old Quince was dying with jealousy.

Perhaps she was going soft in the head, but she actually felt sorry for him. It was more than that: to her surprise, she wanted to touch him – hug him – show the old coot a bit of tenderness. All impossible really: after all, their one-night stand had indirectly led to a business arrangement which made any kind of friendship between them rather tricky. He'd been summoned from Bordeaux in the middle of the night, and there in Belle-Mère's kitchen, with the incriminating mobile lying on the table in front of the three of them, she and Fontaine had agreed to keep their mouths shut about Quincy's 'unprofessional' dealings with Château La Fayette – and, no doubt, other vineyards around the world. Fontaine had got some cash and a promise of a directorship in any Belle-Mère joint venture; Château Barrage was 'discovered' by *Wine Wisdom* and received lavish praise for its 'products'. Presumably, therefore, it was still impossible for Quincy not to associate her with 'blackmail'– his word not hers. On the other hand, at least she hadn't pushed her luck, having the common sense not to kill the goose that was laying her golden eggs. Mind you, she didn't really see his moneymaking sideline as something unprofessional at all.

Squashed together on the communal bench, Sue could feel Quincy's massive left thigh pressing against her. She relived that night of lust in one of Belle-Mère's guest rooms and felt deliciously aroused. It would be lovely to have him again. Could he really hate her? He'd always been so polite about the 'blackmail', but then his class were like that – they only said and did the nasty things behind your back. She thought of the long drive back to Barrage, and how, despite all those shutters and the security system, it was a big, empty, lonely house. Pronkie had been a pain in the *derrière*, but at least she'd felt safe with him around the place. Even after all these years, she'd still wake up in terror in the dead of night, imagining herself back in Kinshasa and–

Perhaps, if she played her cards right, Quincy might ask her to spend the night at his place. The opening gambit would be some crap about a spare room, but once through the front door–

Spotting Madame Tapé's right hand reaching for the adjacent bottle of Pape Clément, Sue grabbed her Barrage just in the nick of time. 'Oh no, love, don't drink no more of that old stuff. You want somethin' young – somethin' with a bit of a kick in it.' Before Tapette could protest, her glass was full to the brim with red Barrage. 'Quince has said some smashin' things about my 2004s in his *Wine Wisdom* thing – that's the top British wine mag, love – *ever* so influential – so they must be good, mustn't they?'

Tapette's enigmatic smile evinced that, as always, she was bewildered by Sue's cockney French. At the other end of the table, Patrick and Laura halted their exchange of eye-to-eye views on the attributes of a truly great wine and how their respective vineyards should respond to commercial realities, a discussion from which a now pouting and taciturn Béatrice had been unintentionally yet fortuitously excluded.

'Ah yes,' declaimed Patrick languidly, '*Wine … **Wisdom***. I used to flick through that now and then.' He flashed a smile at Laura. 'To be honest, Monsieur Dubloon, in view of the lamentable state of English literature these days, I've often wondered why, with your extraordinary skills at *creative* writing, you've never attempted to write *real* fiction – or do you have a string of unpublished novels up your sleeve? Perhaps you *have* published some – under a *nom de plume.*'

Initially, the true import of these remarks was lost on everyone except Quincy himself, albeit Laura, who thought they sounded very clever and wonderfully 'European', tittered. Not to be outdone, Béatrice, emboldened by the wine and anxious to curry favour with her putative boyfriend, exploded like a braying mule.

Salleboeuf nodded his head solemnly. 'I must say, Quincy,' he said over Béatrice's racket, 'one does wonder what has happened to the land of Shakespeare, Scott and Dickens. Apart from Waugh, and, perhaps Greene, the twentieth century seems a bit of a void on the old literature front. I mean, are there *any* contemporary English authors of literary fiction being read internationally these days? They all seem to be damned Americans.'

'Exactly,' Patrick agreed, albeit he had about as much interest in literature – be it French, English, or otherwise – as he had in Gregorian chant.

Still reeling from the innuendo contained within Audinette's barb, Quincy remained unable to frame a sensible reply. Sue, however, stepped into the breach.

'What a load of bleedin' crap! There's that what's-her-name, the one who's written all them '*arry Potter* books. They're read *every*where – even in toffee-nosed Bordeaux. She's made a bleedin' fortune.'

There was a ripple of polite laughter.

'My dear Sue,' Salleboeuf purred, stroking her hand, 'I would humbly suggest that you've just made my point – *Harry Potter* indeed!'

'Well, I think they're wonderful books,' Tapette enthused above the chuckling of her non-British guests, '– very complex. And I love the films.'

'Oh, Tapette!' scolded Céline. 'I don't know how you can watch those dreadful foreign films dubbed into French – ghastly!'

Quincy hardly uttered another word until after Béatrice had deposited the cheese board on the table with a deafening thud. In the meantime, he'd stared either at his plate or diagonally across the table at Laura, who, despite the day's mayhem at Belle-Mère, appeared to be in excellent spirits. Well, she'd be delighted to have got rid of Fontaine – and his poor mother. But surely, she must be concerned about Charles being charged with manslaughter – or worse? When the news broke – it would certainly be in tomorrow's papers – had it already made the regional TV news? – Bordeaux society would have a field day. On the other hand, wasn't it Oscar Wilde who'd said that there was only one thing worse than being talked about – not being talked about? It was time to deflate Laura's bubble.

Noisily, Quincy cleared his throat. 'Oh, by the way,' he boomed, silencing the conversation – but not Edith Piaf, who'd taken over from the Andrews Sisters down at the far end of the corridor – 'although neither Laura nor I would wish to dampen the proceedings, I fear that when you read all about it in tomorrow's papers, you'd think it very strange of us not to have mentioned that' – Laura scowled at him murderously – 'our co-director Charles Fontaine was arrested by the local constabulary this afternoon at Belle-Mère on suspicion of killing his gay ex-lover, who, apparently, was blackmailing him.'

Béatrice threw up her hands with a gasp of excited incredulity, knocking over both her own and Laura's water glasses. For once, Tapette was too shocked to scold her.

'I'm afraid there's worse,' Quincy continued gravely. 'Poor old Madame Fontaine had a fatal heart attack when she saw Charles led away in handcuffs. I wasn't there, but Laura witnessed the whole tragic spectacle.'

Just for a moment, the other diners – with the exception of Laura and childlike Béatrice – wondered whether Dubloon's announcement was just classic English black humour. Within seconds, however, Laura pulled herself together and launched into a heroic attempt at damage limitation. Béatrice's magnificent *tarte tatin* was sadly eclipsed by the Fontaine drama and the warfare that broke out between the Belle-Mère contingent as Quincy pulled out all the stops in ridiculing Laura's attempts to argue that in all probability the police had made a ghastly mistake and would soon be on the receiving end of a suit for wrongful arrest.

When all of the *tarte* had finally been devoured, there was no offer of coffee, but then neither Tapette nor Béatrice drank it in the evening. In any event, Tapette's seemingly boundless resources of energy always evaporated around eleven, when she'd announce that it was her intention to 'retire' and only the most hard-skinned of guests would fail to realize that they were expected to depart.

The Salleboeufs left first, rapidly followed by Laura and Patrick. As they walked up Rue Vital Carles in the direction of Le Noailles, Laura said:

'Where did you leave your car, Patrick? Le Noailles isn't out of your way, is it? We can forget the drink if–'

'Absolutely not. I came by taxi. I never drink and drive.'

Laura liked the sound of that – very responsible – almost unique in Bordeaux. Without a second thought, she said: 'Oh, right. I'll drive you home then. It's not far, is it – the Parc Bordelais, I think you said?'

'That's very kind of you, but there's a taxi rank just–'

'No sweat.'

'Well, if you insist.'

'To be honest, I think I've had enough booze for one night, but I could kill for a cup of coffee.'

'Perfect! Actually, even though I say so myself, I make excellent coffee. But you won't have to kill for it. Anyway, one murderer sounds more than enough for any board of directors. Ouch! That hurt!'

*

Having rooted out the unopened bottles of Barrage from the Tapés' kitchen, and dragooned an embarrassed Quincy to remove them from the premises and carry them back to her car, Sue and her involuntary porter waited to cross Vital Carles.

'I'll drive you round to Cours de Tournon,' Sue said, as if she was doing him a big favour.

'That's very kind of you, Sue, but I could really do with the fresh air. Anyway, with the one-way system, it's quicker to walk.' That sounded ungracious. 'I mean–'

'I do 'ave a Ferrari, Quince. … Didn't you know? I thought it were all the gossip round town. Treated meself a fortnight ago with Pronkie's life insurance.'

'Oh, yes. … I did hear something. I just meant–'

At that moment, Pierre Lampre – the last to leave the Tapés', as usual – exited the building. 'Hello, you two. Still loitering? What a dinner! Always a damned good experience here, eh?' Walking my way, Quincy? … Suzanne?'

'No,' Quincy snapped. 'I'm carrying Sue's … *things* back to her car.'

Lampre stared pointedly at the cardboard box cradled in Quincy's arms. 'Ah … yes, such a quaint English custom. Well, goodnight, Suzanne.' He kissed her cheeks, and then held out his hand to Quincy. 'We'll be in touch soon, I shouldn't be surprised.'

When Sue screeched to a halt in front of Quincy's building after a white-knuckle drive around the city centre, he felt honour bound to invite her up for a nightcap. 'I've got a bleedin' long drive back to Barrage,' she replied. 'How's your coffee though?'

Around ten the next morning, Quincy awoke to the smells of fried bacon and eggs. It was reassuring evidence that last night had really happened. On the way to the kitchen, he passed the living room, and, looking through the open door, smiled at the pile of dishevelled clothes on the floor, and the array of bottles and glasses on the coffee table. It was a bloody miracle he didn't have a hangover!

349

In the kitchen, dressed in one of his silk dressing gowns with the sleeves rolled up, Sue was standing over the cooker, quite oblivious to the spitting fat. 'Mornin', darlin',' she chirped, looking up from the frying pan. 'I 'ope yer 'ungry!'

'Ravenous!' Quincy came to stand right behind her and put his hands around her waist. 'I could even eat you.'

'Careful, big boy! I'll knock the bleedin' pan over. Ooh ... that's nice.'

By the time they came to be eaten at the kitchen table, the eggs and bacon were cold. Holding a cup of coffee in both hands, Sue said: 'I've been thinkin' 'ard about everythin' you told me last night, Quince, and do you know what I'd do?'

Quincy felt the glorious glow of contentment within him instantly dissipate. 'Oh ... *that*. I'm sorry. I shouldn't have burdened you with, um ... Look, forget all about it. It's all so ... so–'

'Shut your bloody posh gob and listen. For a start, sell out – to Jean-Claude – that Charpentier geezer – whoever – and as soon as poss'. And sell that stupid poncey magazine of yours as well – always thought it were a load of crap – more effort than it's worth, I should think.'

'Charming! You seemed keen enough to get your bloody Barrage on its pages.'

Sue snorted dismissively. 'As for that effin' Pam cow and her blackmail, do a Forgeron!'

'What the hell do you mean?'

'Easy! Tell the bitch to eff off – publish and be damned – isn't that the expression? Look, Quince, it was thirty bleedin' years ago, and anyway, these days that kind of dirt does wonders for celebs' images. I bet you anythin' you like, that far from cockin' up your chances of a new TV contract, a load of stuff in the tabloids about you and three-in-a bed romps would put you back on the map. Your publishers would probably want you to write your own biography thingy – turn the tables on that blackmailin' scumbag – tell all about Forgeron and them wild parties at Oxford and Arcachon.'

'Cambridge and Cap Ferret, for Christ's sake!'

'Don't split 'airs. Go further, darlin' – rip the lid off 'the Wonderful World of Wine' – reveal all them bribes and backhanders from the big noises, the scams – the rip-offs – name names – 'cept mine, of course! Mind you, I never paid nothin' for them rave reviews.'

'I couldn't, Sue.'

'Couldn't what?'

'Do any of those things. It wouldn't be ... wouldn't be–'

350

'Cricket? Give me an effin' break, darlin'! If you want to avoid years of misery – bankruptcy – if you want to make a bleedin' fortune, then get on the blower to your agent geezer now and tell 'im to get off his fat arse and start lookin' for a publisher – and a paper that'll pay the most for the serialization rights. Attack is the best form of defence, as some general said, Quince. Eric and me learned that lesson the 'ard way, thanks to them soddin' stuck-up Fontaines and their dirt-diggin' in the Congo.'

Quincy managed a smile. 'Thanks for sharing all that with me last night. I must say that if anyone should write an autobiography, it's you, Sue. Rags to riches via Kinshasa – it's one hell of a tale.'

Sue grinned back. 'Now there's a thought, darlin'! Maybe you could ghost it – or whatever the expression is.'

Quincy was about to reply when a canine cacophony erupted in the street below.

'What the–?' quizzed Sue, standing up to peer out the window.

Quincy roared with laughter. 'It's just Churchill and Petit Boy arriving to take up their daily residence at the florist's. Another late start for the Tapés! Of course, if they see you exiting the front door downstairs, they'll be able to dine out on the news for a month.'

With mounting hilarity, Quincy and Sue – with his arm around her waist – watched the spectacle as Tapette and Béatrice fiddled about with a remote control and then unlocked their premises' front door. As soon as the dogs shot in, the burglar alarm began wailing, and the two snoopers across the road collapsed on the kitchen floor in hysterics.

CHAPTER 28

It was a Saturday afternoon, and, on a gentle hillside at Belle-Mère, Patrick Audinette and Laura were walking arm-in-arm between rows of merlot vines, their grapes picked weeks ago. In the November sunshine, the leaves were a dazzling display of rich autumnal colours – golden yellows, reds and russet browns. The vines were dying back, and soon the labourers would be pruning them savagely and making great bundles of kindling tied up with twine for lighting the fires in monumental fireplaces. How Laura loved those crackling winter blazes! They reminded her of old black-and-white movies bubbling with gentle comedy and wholesome romance – Cary Grant and Katharine Hepburn marooned without a chaperone in a snow-bound Connecticut 'cottage'. For the last two years, Laura had rarely had anyone with whom to share these atmospheric blazes, but all that, she prayed, was about to change.

A cold gust of wind blew through the vineyard, rustling countless thousands of leaves. Patrick pulled Laura closer to him. 'You should have put some gloves on,' he admonished, looking up at the few wispy clouds scudding across the sky. 'The wind's moving round to the north-west. There's a cold front on the way – could even be some snow overnight if the temperature continues to drop at this rate.'

Laura stared into his tanned face – *he has to use a sun bed, surely?* – and surprised herself with the observation that Patrick did bear some resemblance to Cary Grant.

'You have to give credit where credit's due, Laura. Bourjois has done a first-rate job here – in the vineyard, the *chais*, the *cuvier* – everything. One could almost imagine being back in Margaux, and not at a *petit château* in the Premières Côtes.'

Laura beamed, seemingly oblivious to the sting in the tail. 'I never said he hadn't done a good job, but–'

'But his solid professionalism is – *was* – never going to make Belle-Mère famous.'

Laura nodded. 'It's a pity you and me didn't meet two years ago.'

Patrick thought that sounded like another cue for a kiss. Obligingly, he pressed his lips against hers, and the fragrance of Orange Verte instantly generated kaleidoscopic images in Laura's mind of some of the climactic moments from their lovemaking during the last ten days. Patrick satisfied her sexual desires as no man had ever done, and although he didn't possess

Jean-Claude's powerful physique or his deliciously hairy chest with its thick black curls, he was lean and wiry and, above all, endowed with a penis of impressive proportions.

And so, the post-Tapé night of passion in Patrick's surprisingly impressive apartment overlooking the exclusive Parc Bordelais had whetted what would prove to be an insatiable appetite. Thereafter, driving into Bordeaux after a hard day's slog had proved no obstacle for Laura. In truth, since the Tapés' dinner party, they'd only missed one night together, when Patrick had flown to Zurich to finalize the arrangements for the acquisition of Dubloon's forty-five per cent shareholding in Belle-Mère.

Unlike Quincy and Sue, Laura had not unburdened herself to Patrick on the occasion of their first feverish coupling. After all, he'd replaced Jean-Claude at La Fayette, and she knew all too well what Henri de Bondé had been up to at the time. Unfortunately, it was quite possible that fraudulent activities of one kind or another had continued, and that Patrick would be involved, whether tacitly or actively. Be that as it may, to the outside world he had an excellent track record at La Fayette: since his arrival the château's reputation had rocketed, fraud or no fraud, and it was common knowledge that the introduction of the highly successful La-Fa had been his idea. Yes, he was refreshingly proactive for a Bordelais, and he knew so many useful people – celebrities, trendsetters, the media crowd. What a contrast to her partners! Naturally, she'd never expected Jean-Claude to do much on the marketing side, but Dubloon had been a different matter. Frankly, he'd been a big disappointment. Two years back, she'd simply failed to spot that he'd reached his plateau of achievement and was about to slide off. He was one of yesterday's men – and most of his contacts fell into the same dismal category. Fontaine, of course, had been hopeless.

It was not long before the Parc Bordelais pillow talk turned to personal revelations. One thing led to another, and by the end of the first week of their relationship, highly tentative possibilities for Jean-Claude's removal from Belle-Mère had firmly crystallised. Indeed, on more than one occasion, Laura had had to reassure herself that she really was in control of events – that she was not being manipulated by a man – a Bordelais, moreover – whose private life was still something of a black hole. And when she did finally broach the subject of Belle-Mère going down a kind of *garagiste* road, Patrick proved wholly supportive – not naively so, but with practical advice and relevant facts. Casually – almost flippantly – he floated the idea of investing in Bell-Mère himself: he'd finally realised that Henri was too much of a snob to ever make him a partner in the business. If he could procure the finance to enable Laura to buy Dubloon's shares, then, with her own holding, she'd have the magic figure of ninety per cent and the right under the company's constitution to buy out the minority compulsorily – Bourjois's irksome ten per cent. In return, he'd expect an equal partnership.

Laura experienced a flicker of concern – and indeed, sadness – that Patrick had only seen her as some kind of meal ticket, a most fortuitous escape route from the rut into which he now claimed to have found himself at La Fayette. But she didn't dwell on these negative thoughts for long. If anything, revealing his true colours provided further evidence of his entrepreneurialism. And whatever might be his motives in having sex with her, they didn't diminish the pleasure. In truth, what choice did she really have? During what remained of the twenty-eight-day option period, her chances of getting hold of five million euros to defeat the Bourjois-Charpentier takeover were minimal. The Two Moms weren't interested, and when, notwithstanding all her best intentions, she'd contacted some banks in town during the last few days – Hubert Audinette's BIF included – they'd all scoffed at the idea of a *garagiste* megastar in the Premières Côtes ever generating sufficient profits to pay off the size of loan she was seeking.

Laura didn't probe too deeply about the source of Patrick's capital. He mentioned Hong Kong businessmen he'd met in Bordeaux who collected rare vintages and who were awash with cash from mainland China. He talked about share mortgages, nominee companies and trust holdings. If he could come up with the greenbacks, she concluded, it was really no concern of hers. So, their respective lawyers burned the midnight oil preparing draft contracts, and a stunned Quincy was presented with a confidential 'tax efficient' acceptance of his formal invitation to purchase his shares. Patrick then flew to Zurich with powers of attorney to open bank accounts for Laura and Quincy through which the purchase monies would be channelled. Everything was now set for Monday, when Patrick would return to Zurich with Quincy for the deal's closure: the crediting of Quincy's account and his handing over of the share transfer documents were to be effected personally and simultaneously. It had all sounded rather exotic to Laura, but the words 'French tax' had been enough to convince her that the Swiss escapade was perfectly understandable.

When Laura and Patrick reached the end of the row of vines, they turned and gazed at the splendid view from their vantage point – the glorious château, the park with its lake, and beyond, the rolling countryside of Entre-deux-Mers. Patrick glowed inwardly: despite its idiotic name, Belle-Mère was a stunning house; it would make a most fitting residence for himself ... and Laura, although, in all probability, what with the marketing of their wines in the States and her new TV series, she'd be spending a great deal of time on the other side of the Atlantic. Yes, she'd be away a lot. So, there'd be plenty of scope for 'enterprising activities', which would greatly please his backers in the Far East. Together, they'd make Henri de Bondé look like a complete amateur! He felt Laura shiver. 'Oh, darling, you must be freezing. We'll go back. I just didn't want to talk business where anyone might overhear us.'

'I told you, the Bourjois duo have gone to Paris for the weekend – all that shit about Sean Kunstmann turning up suddenly at Buffet's gallery and demanding to see talentless Sophie in person to place a commission! They must think I was born yesterday. Why they couldn't just admit they were going to see old man Charpentier to finalize their "takeover" and–'

'OK, but that creepy kid's around.'

Laura sniggered. 'Yeah, Alexandre's one hell of a weirdo. You know, it wouldn't at all surprise me if he was up on the roof now, watching us through binoculars.'

'Hah! He'll probably have a breakdown when he learns he's going to have to move out of "Versailles"!'

'Oh, Sophie's got enough money to buy a goddam château of her own.'

'Maybe, but to find a house like Belle-Mère – such elegance, such exquisite proportions, such–'

'Jesus! You sound as if you're more in love with that pile of stone than with me.'

'Shit! You've discovered my secret! But I can't have sex with a pile of stone. ... Do you think the fire will still be burning in the living room?'

'Probably. You're so good at it.'

'I know.'

Laura groaned, but before she could reply, she found herself running hand-in-hand with a laughing Patrick down the rows of vines towards the house.

From his lookout on the roof, Alexandre ducked behind one of the massive chimney stacks and let go of the binoculars hanging around his neck. 'Hmm, suspicious,' he murmured, '... *most* suspicious.'

*

Although Laura was correct in her assumption that Jean-Claude and Sophie would be discussing the Belle-Mère takeover plans in Paris with Paul Charpentier, the trip had indeed been prompted by the unexpected arrival of Hollywood star Sean Kunstmann armed with a request for Sophie to paint his portrait. Sophie had told him by phone that she didn't paint portraits. Sean was most displeased, announcing on the spot that if she refused his commission, he'd put his entire collection of her works up for auction. Buffet was horrified: if more than a dozen of Sophie's canvasses came on the market en masse and were sold at prices below the going rates for her new works, or – heaven forbid! – didn't reach their reserve prices at auction, a 'rather delicate' situation could arise. The Bourjoises dropped everything and flew to Paris. In the event, Sean was placated over a sumptuous lunch at the Crillon. Sophie would do the portrait, but they compromised over the venue for the sittings: Paris and Los Angeles lost out to New York.

'But, Dominique, I *can't* paint portraits,' Sophie whined after the star had dashed off to Charles de Gaulles.

'Oh, darling, if you present Sean with a plain canvass smeared with a lump of shit, that dickhead would think it a masterpiece. Don't worry!'

Sophie and Jean-Claude flew home on Sunday evening. They were both in buoyant moods when they finally pulled up before Belle-Mère's impressive facade. As she got out of the car, Sophie stretched out her arms, and, mimicking Sean's Californian drawl, declaimed: 'One day – very soon, in fact – all this will be yours, my boy.'

Jean-Claude exploded with laughter. '*Ours, chérie,*' he corrected, '*ours.*'

Ours and your father's, he thought, with just a hint of irritation.

They found Alexandre in the library. 'Oh, you're back,' he intoned, looking up from a large leather-bound volume. 'You may be interested to learn that Monsieur Patrick Audinette has been here all weekend with Appleton. They appeared extraordinarily pleased with themselves, I must say. And *he* examined every nook and cranny of both the house and the estate like a chartered surveyor. I should hazard to suggest that the two of them are up to something.'

The smiles on his parents' faces evaporated.

'In fact,' he continued, 'when Audinette finally left a couple of hours ago, I heard them talking about some flight tomorrow morning to Zurich – Audinette and Dubloon – *together*. ... Oh, and that half-witted inspector from Langon phoned yesterday afternoon. Fontaine's been formally charged with Revelle's manslaughter, and they need more statements from us. The inspector asked me if Revelle had said anything about the late Baron Guy de Bondé. Apparently, he was a "nurse" at the baron's nursing home or something. The point is that Fontaine is now claiming that's why Revelle came here in the first place – to talk to you, Papa, about something the baron told him just before he died – I can't imagine what. Anyway, Revelle certainly did *not* say anything of the sort to me. I think Fontaine's making it up. I believe the bounder was just after money – that he remembered you visiting the baron several times and hoped you'd take pity on him and give him something for having cared for your deranged former employer during the final traumatic months of his life. Of course, Fontaine's still alleging that I'm a liar. Well, we'll see about that in court.' He tapped the volume in front of him. 'Do you remember all those stories about the Duke and Duchess of Windsor coming here in 1937? ... Absolute poppycock! – and that's just for starters.'

That night, Alexandre's parents didn't sleep well, having failed to get hold of Quincy by telephone – either at Cours de Tournon or on his mobile. The next morning, Jean-Claude was in his office before dawn. After a couple of frantic hours of repeatedly phoning Quincy's numbers, he rang *Wine Wisdom*: a helpful secretary confirmed that 'Mr Dubloon' was 'on business' in Switzerland.

As one o'clock approached, Jean-Claude was in the first-year *chai* debating whether to join some of his junior colleagues for lunch and avoid eating alone: Alexandre was back at school; Sophie was brooding in her studio. He was making his way along one of the long rows of *barriques*, when Laura appeared out of the gloom. To his surprise, her face was graced with the sort of smile she'd not exhibited in his presence for some time.

'Hello, Jean-Claude. I might have known you'd be ... Look, I just wanted you to know as soon as things were finalized. ... A short while ago I acquired Quincy's stock. So, as I'm now the holder of ninety per cent, I'm exercising my right to buy you out compulsorily in accordance with the company's constitution. I've left the formal notice on your desk. Once you – and Sophie – have had time to digest the implications, we'll need to have a chat to sort things out – say nine o'clock tomorrow morning ... in the boardroom? OK?'

*

Despite Sophie's oft-repeated resolution during the flight back from Paris not to watch the DVDs of Kunstmann's films that Buffet had given her, she'd moved the player into the studio. When Jean-Claude tapped hesitantly and popped his head around the door, she was glued to *Abattoir Cats*. She waived him in with an expression of intense relief.

'Thank God! Saved from a nervous breakdown by lunch. How anyone can watch this mind-numbing crap I'll never know. So much for Dominique's hopes for inspiration!' As she pressed the STOP button on the remote control, she noted that her husband looked even worse than he'd done at breakfast. 'Oh God! What's happened? Have you finally managed to get through to Dubloon?'

Some two hours later, Jean-Claude and Sophie had yet to eat anything.

'It's not the end of the world,' he said soothingly.

'God! You sound like a stuck bloody record.'

He tried to ignore the bitterness: she was understandably upset. 'We'll find another vineyard,' he persevered, '– another château. There are plenty on the market – and in better *appellations*.'

'If I've told you once I've told you a hundred times – to find a house as magnificent as this – and in such a heavenly setting – and so close to Bordeaux – and a studio like *this*!' She flapped her arms despairingly. 'Papa said we'd be getting a bargain – a palace for peanuts, a–'

'Darling, a fine house is all very well, but for me the vineyard–'

'This *is* supposed to be a good vineyard! – or were you deceiving me and Papa?'

'Of course not! I–'

'Papa had great plans for putting this place on the map – all that stuff about "exceptional medium-term investment" – "profit margins" – whatever. I mean, just to buy some crappy dump in your precious Médoc with a poky Victorian brick villa masquerading as a château would be beyond my means, let alone to tart it up. There are only so many canvases I can turn out in a year, you know.'

'I know. I–'

'Image is terribly important for Papa. His partners have to be impressed – made to feel important – made to think that *Papa* is important … financially sound … powerful. After a weekend in a tatty dump in the shadows of Château Margaux and the like, Papa would look cheap.'

'Well–'

'Alexandre, the poor boy, will be heartbroken. He worships this place. He had such plans for restoring it to its former glory.'

'"*Plans*"? What sort of plans?'

Sophie stared at her husband incredulously. 'Don't you *ever* listen to *anything* he says?'

'Of course I do!'

'Oh yes! You certainly listened carefully enough when he recounted what he'd told those policemen – especially who Revelle came to see.'

'I – he–'

'Oh, this is pointless. We'll have to go to the lawyers and find out how quickly she can boot *you* off the board and *us* into the street.'

'Come on, *chérie*, I'm sure Laura wouldn't do anything vindictive. She–'

'For Christ's sake, Jean-Claude, don't be so pathetically naive! She's putty in the hands of that louche Audinette. He's behind all this, mark my words. You said yourself that he had a shady reputation, even before he arrived at La Fayette.'

'Well–'

'La Fayette! That shit hole follows us around like a curse. It's … it's almost supernatural.'

'Hardly super–'

'And then Appleton shacks up with your successor, who – surprise! surprise! – just happens to be the son of Belle-Mère's bank manager!'

'I just can't believe that BIF could have loaned Laura the money to buy out Dubloon.'

'Me too … unless Audinette senior is as crooked as his son.'

Silence ensued until Jean-Claude, cocking his head to one side, said: 'Maybe Henri is the secret investor – out of sheer spite – jealous of my – *our* success … or something.'

Sophie's artistic mind was more muddled than ever. 'Frankly, Jean-Claude, nothing would surprise me anymore. Christ! – Henri bloody de Bondé! How I hate that man and his sodding château. May he rot in hell, and may plagues and tempests and – and … *fire* destroy every last stone and vine of his stinking estate!'

By four o'clock, Jean-Claude was sitting in his elegant office, staring at the telephone. Back in the studio, there'd been a final heated debate as to who should inform Alexandre and Sophie's father of the Belle-Mère debacle. Jean-Claude had argued that Sophie was closer to both of them, and, moreover, more of 'a telephone person'. She'd said he was a coward. In the end, they'd tossed for the dubious honour.

So, Jean-Claude now had to phone his son and inform him that there'd be no summer season of alfresco Molière around Belle-Mère's restored *source* and 'temple' after all. He took a deep breath and began a countdown: at zero, he'd dial the school's number. There was always a chance that Alexandre might be on the playing fields … or, more likely–

The landline phone burst into ear-piercing life. Gasping, Jean-Claude grabbed the receiver. 'Yes?' he croaked.

'*Monsieur Bourjois?*'

'Yes.'

'*Monsieur Jean-Claude Bourjois?*'

'Yes.'

'*Excellent! At last! I've tried a few times to get hold of you today. This morning, I spoke with your colleague, a Mademoiselle Appleton, and then, I think, with her secretary. Didn't you get the messages?*'

'Er … you are …?'

'*Sorry! I'm Fabrice Canet of DPM – Duplan, Papageorge, Molinard – in Paris. I'm Monsieur Adolphe Lafosse's assistant.*'

Jean-Claude groaned audibly. It had to be more bad news. 'Oh ... right. ... I suppose you're phoning about Laura's compulsory purchase of my ten per cent shareholding?'

'*Sorry? ... Laura? Um, no – I think you must be confusing me with ... Look, before I go any further, would you mind awfully if I just ask you a couple of personal questions – for security purposes?*'

'Um–'

'*Splendid! Could you confirm your date of birth and your mother's maiden name, please?*'

In view of the day's events, Jean-Claude was too shell-shocked to be anything other than wholly compliant.

'*Jolly good, Monsieur Bourjois. Now ...*' Momentarily, Canet's confident patter appeared to run out of steam. '*Well now, I'm not absolutely sure where to start, but perhaps I should do so by offering Monsieur Lafosse's apologies – he would have liked to talk with you himself, but ... well, he's had to go ... abroad – on urgent client business. ... Look, to be frank, Monsieur Bourjois, we seem to have made a bit of a cock up at our end.*'

'Oh?'

'*Terribly, **terribly** sorry. It's always the same, isn't it? There are always those odd few files where one little mistake sets off a whole chain reaction, and before one knows where one is ... well, **you** know?*'

'Er ...?'

'*And I'm very sorry to say that that is* precisely *what happened here. My predecessor's fault, actually. She's in our London office now.*'

'Ah.'

'*And the* Faculté d'Avocats *sat on the enquiry for absolutely* ages – *such a pack of pen-pushers, I can tell you.*'

'Um, "enquiry" ...?'

'*Apparently a relative phoned them – of the deceased – a couple of weeks back. Some chap called Revelle – got killed in a car crash – and when they searched his Paris flat, they found a piece of paper with the name of a Monsieur Dumas on it. ... Well, something like that. The nitwits at the* Faculté *were a bit vague.*'

'Ah – oh, Revelle ... I see. But what's that got to do with me?'

'*You might well ask! Well now, the point is that when Dumas died five or six years ago, my firm – DPM – you've probably heard of us – we're one of the largest law firms in Paris – France, I suppose. ... To be honest, family law and wills aren't really our sort of thing at all. We're mainly corporate chaps – mergers, acquisitions, anti-trust. ... Anyhow, Monsieur Bourjois,*

Monsieur Dumas had a jolly decent private client list – oodles of millionaires – so, when he passed away, we bought his goodwill and took over most of his files. One of them concerned Baron Guy de Bondé – of Château La Fayette – super wine! – do you know it? Silly question, I suppose, being in Bordeaux and everything!'

'I–'

'Well, from my reading of the file, it seems that periodically, the baron put Monsieur Dumas in funds to operate a system whereby every month, he – Dumas – would check to ensure his client was still alive – sounds a bit macabre really, doesn't it? I gather he used to phone the château and ask to speak to him!'

'I–'

*'Well, the system was still running when we took over the file, and, by my reckoning, my predecessor carried on with it for a while. But then, just at the time the diary system came up for renewal – a fresh injection of funds on account was required – Eugénie got posted to London, and her diary systems were **unfathomable** – well, I certainly couldn't make sense of them on the WP. The file got sent over to Securities for storage – they're in a separate building on the other side of Rue Montaigne, and … well, I … we – it got overlooked. So easy to happen, really, and everything's computerized now, so–'*

'Of course, perfectly understandable.'

As a corporate lawyer by training, Canet was somewhat taken aback by Jean-Claude's apparent understanding. *'Oh … right. … Well, when we got this query from the* Faculté *about Dumas and this Revelle character, I got volunteered to go through the old files, and when I came to read the Bondé file, um … The baron died some years ago,'* Canet said brightly.

'I know. He was my former employer.'

'Really? Golly! How … interesting.'

'There was a will.'

'Oh goody! I thought there would be.'

'I received a generous legacy of two hundred thousand francs – well, the equivalent in euros … eventually.'

'Splendid! … Well now, it's a bit of a puzzle really, but the point is that in old Dumas's file there's a letter for you – at least, I assume it's a letter – there's no indication in the file what the envelope contains. You were supposed to get it when he – Guy de Bondé – passed away. It's marked, and I quote, "<u>TO BE OPENED BY MONSIEUR JEAN-CLAUDE BOURJOIS ONLY</u>*" in whopping block capitals with lashings of underlining.'*

'Well, just post it, and–'

'No, no – impossible. The instructions are quite explicit. The envelope must be delivered into your hands **personally** by Monsieur Dumas, or, if you predeceased the baron, to be destroyed.'

Jean-Claude sighed with exasperation. 'But Dumas, you say, is *dead*, for God's sake.'

'*Quite so, but I think a court would interpret that as meaning, "by him or his lawful heirs or assigns". That's us.*'

'Well, I haven't got time to come to Paris at the moment. Can't you come down here? After all, you're the ones responsible for the two-year delay.'

Canet could suddenly see trouble looming after all. '*Oh, I'm sure we can agree to pay for a courier. I just need to pop across the hall and get the approval of Monsieur Lafosse, but–*'

'I thought he was abroad.'

'*Um … oh yes – I meant check by phone, naturally. But if delivery is to you upon presentation of your passport or identity card, I think we'll have satisfied the late baron's requirements. Anyway, who's to know?*'

'Exactly. So, some time tomorrow–'

'*No, no – **tonight**! The premium service we use here in Paris guarantees delivery to any major French city within hours. They're not cheap, but … well, it's the least we can do … in all the circumstances. Now, let's see … it's half past four, so, if I phone them immediately, you should have the package well before midnight. Where are you exactly?*'

After Jean-Claude had given Canet the details, he said: 'By the way, have you told Revelle's relative about this?'

'*Good Lord no! It's confidential – client privilege and all that.*'

At fifteen minutes past midnight, Jean-Claude gave up the vigil and joined Sophie in bed.

'Bloody ridiculous!' he moaned, snuggling up to her. 'I knew they wouldn't come. Whatever the hell it is, it could have waited until tomorrow – today now. After all, he's been dead and buried–'

The front door bell rang.

'Jesus! It can't be?'

'Let the servants get it,' Sophie muttered.

'Can't. I have to show my bloody passport!'

As Jean-Claude opened one of the massive double doors, a young unsmiling man in a blue uniform hissed: 'Talk about the back of beyond! Thought you was that place down by the gates. No one in. Got a delivery for your boss, mate. You'd better get him out of the four-poster. Some crap about a passport–'

Jean-Claude was still fuming when he got back to the bedroom.

Half asleep, Sophie moaned: 'What the hell was all that shouting about?'

'He thought I was a bloody servant!'

Sophie groaned: it was the very nightmare she'd been having just before Jean-Claude woke her up again. 'So, what the hell is it then – that package?'

'No idea.'

'After all that, you're not going to open it?'

'No. I can't keep my eyes open. It can wait until the morning.'

CHAPTER 29

Henri de Bondé was holding court in his bedroom. He had a nasty dose of flu and a spot of fever, but enjoyed telling everyone that it was an occupational hazard when one was constantly jetting around the global market place. After breakfast, and with his wife on an upmarket tour of Vietnam with a herd of other titled Bordelaise chatelaines, he'd anticipated a leisurely morning, flicking through a mountain of catalogues from Cartier, Hermès, Patek-Philippe and the like. It was not to be, however. Shortly after half past nine, Patrick Audinette had insisted on an interview to discuss a matter of 'momentous importance.'

Henri had been expecting some smug, self-congratulatory announcement – Audinette had finally secured a delivery of La Fayette to the cellars of the Élysée Palace, or something along those lines. The receipt, therefore, of the man's resignation had come as a shock – a shock, moreover, that was compounded by an earnest request for his six months' notice to be waived! Between coughing and sneezing fits, Henri huffed, puffed and blustered, his voice becoming ever hoarser. And yet, at the back of his mind the thought was gestating that Audinette's resignation could prove rather propitious. The mountebank had become too big for his designer boots – demanding a shareholding, the ludicrous title of 'Deputy Managing Director' and an even bigger office! The tick never stopped. And now that La Fayette was so clearly in the limelight, all that 'shady business' stuff really had to stop. Yes indeed, Audinette had served his purpose.

But as Henri continued to go through the motions of protest while formulating a compromise deal that would require Audinette to stay until the end of the week, the wind was completely taken out of his sails when, in an attempt to lighten Henri's mood, he broke his word to Laura to keep things under wraps and disclosed the identity of the pastures new to which he'd be moving. Almost immediately, Henri's initial shock gave way to delight. Bourjois was being kicked in the teeth, stabbed in the back, dragged through the mud! It was the delicious icing on the cake, what with Revelle being 'bumped off' by that old fag Fontaine – well, there'd been rumours about him in Bordeaux for years.

Henri was half-listening to Patrick's gleeful account of Jean-Claude's failed attempt to acquire control of Belle-Mère with financial backing from his father-in-law, when there was a tap on the bedroom door.

'I'm terribly sorry to disturb you, Monsieur le Baron,' said the butler, Sabot, without conviction as he entered, 'but there's a Monsieur Bourjois down in the hall asking to see you – very insistent, I must say.'

'Christ!' chuckled Patrick. 'He doesn't waste any time, does he?'

'No, no, *no*,' Henri fumed, 'it can't be *me* he wants to see, surely, Sabot? He wants Monsieur Audinette here. Patrick, be a good fellow and pop down to see him – in the *chais* please. If he's come to pick a fight with you, I don't want him doing any more damage to my property.'

Patrick shrugged his shoulders and sighed. 'If you insist, Henri, but I can't imagine why–'

'I'm sorry, Monsieur le Baron,' Sabot interjected, 'but the gentleman was *most* specific, most specific indeed. He said that if you were "difficult", I should inform you that the matter concerns the late Baron Guy de Bondé and, um ... Las Vegas.'

Although Henri could hear himself speaking, and the other two men replying and moving about, the world around him had ceased to make sense. Now they were asking him things, and he was shaking his head. They were walking out, leaving him ... leaving him!

*Please, God, don't let him know about the will, or anything else – not the **real** reasons. ... Perhaps he's merely discovered they shared a hotel room in Las Vegas, that's all. ... But how could he have possibly found **that** out? **How?***

Exiting the bedroom, Patrick and Sabot gasped and stopped dead in their tracks: Jean-Claude was standing outside in the corridor; ashen-faced and ominously silent, he held a slim attaché case.

'This is *most* improper,' Sabot proclaimed. 'You were asked–'

'It's all right,' Patrick interjected. 'I'll deal with this. Go downstairs.' With feigned grumbles of discomfort, Sabot swiftly complied.

Momentarily irresolute, Patrick's mind raced: Laura was supposed to have met with Bourjois this very morning to discuss the formalities for his departure from Belle-Mère. Had she stuck to their agreement to keep his own name out of things until he'd confirmed putting Bondé in the picture? Maybe she hadn't. Or had Bourjois just jumped to conclusions about the financing of Dubloon's buyout? But how could he have met Laura at nine and got to Margaux by – Patrick glanced at his watch – just a few minutes before ten?

Resolving to phone Laura as soon as he was alone, Patrick said: 'Now look, Bourjois – sorry, *Jean-Claude* – if you're all worked up about Belle-Mère, it's me you should be seeing, not Henri. It's nothing to do with him – believe me. He's not involved – no way. Surely, Laura told you that?'

Jean-Claude didn't appear to hear. 'It's personal,' he finally mumbled, '– *very* personal ... between me and Henri.'

'Oh ... I see. Well, I'll be waiting just down the corridor. ... You have a bit of a reputation, you know. The merest hint of trouble and–'

'Don't worry. There won't be any fisticuffs – at least, not on my part.'

As soon as Jean-Claude had shut the bedroom door behind him, Patrick made his way to the first-floor landing. Below in the hall, Sabot was chatting excitedly to one of the cleaners. Patrick smiled, got out his mobile and phoned Laura.

In the bedroom, as Jean-Claude approached the foot of the bed, Henri, through a fit of coughing spluttered: 'Whatever the purpose of your damned visit, Bourjois, you should see Audinette. I'm poorly – *very* – with influenza.' It was a performance worthy of an actor playing an invalid revealing a terminal illness.

'I'm sorry to hear that,' Jean-Claude said quietly as he opened the attaché case and removed an A4-size envelope. Henri's laboured breathing became noticeably faster. 'Do you want to read these documents, Henri, or would you prefer me to read them to you?'

Henri was transfixed by the envelope. 'I – I don't understand. What's all this about?'

'Come on, let's not waste time playing games.' Jean-Claude began extracting the envelope's contents. 'Well, for a start, I presume there's no point in reading you the will – you'll have the original – or one of the originals. You see, Guy wrote it out in duplicate and instructed a lawyer in Paris to protect my interests.'

Henri tried to grab a tissue before sneezing. He failed and ended up with phlegm all over his hands.

'Here – let me help you.' Jean-Claude pulled a couple of tissues out of the box and handed them to Henri, saying: 'And how did you deal with the executors, Carbon Blanc and that pillock Hubert Audinette? I remember the letter signed by them jointly when I finally received my legacy under the will – the *duff* one. Was Patrick in on it? I'm even beginning to wonder whether Laura ...'

Shaking his head sadly from side to side, Jean-Claude sat down heavily at the bottom of the bed. 'Did Guy warn you too, Henri, that his letter explaining the will – the *real* one – could be "painful", and that if you didn't want any illusions destroyed, to burn it unread?'

'I–' Henri broke off and paused a few seconds. 'I still haven't the faintest idea what you're prattling about.'

Thumping the bed, Jean-Claude cried: 'Oh *please*! Guy may have been crazy two years ago, but ten years back he was as sane as you or me. Do you honestly think he made it all up? – concocted the DNA results? – the marriage certificate? … *Do* you? Hell! – do you imagine for one moment that I like it any more than you? – being illegitimate? – adulterous parents? – all the lies, year after year after year?'

Tears were beginning to trickle down Jean-Claude's cheeks. 'Guy never even had the guts to acknowledge me as his son,' he sobbed. 'And he kept Christophe in the dark about–'

Henri rasped a maniacal cough. 'You sanctimonious hypocritical bastard! What the hell are *you* whingeing about? – being a de Bondé? – not a fucking peasant's son after all? – inheriting my–?'

Down the corridor, Patrick detected Henri's raised voice. 'I just heard Bondé shouting, Laura. Should I nip back and make sure he's OK?'

'*No! Wait! It's none of your business. Don't interfere. If I were you, I'd beat a quick exit – or go and clear out your office.*'

'I did that first thing this morning.'

'*Impressive! … Is Henri still shouting?*'

'Um … no. All quiet again.'

'*Good. Well, stay out of it. There's a long history between those two – since they were kids.*'

Another bout of coughing had arrested Henri's outburst. When he finally got his breathing back under some semblance of control, Jean-Claude said: 'I wouldn't carry out your threat to challenge the validity of the will if I were you, or allege that any of these documents are forgeries. Any handwriting expert could–'

'Experts! One can always find experts who'll say anything.'

'And the marriage certificate?'

'The parties are dead! *They* can't give evidence. And the magistrate – or whatever they're called – in Las Vegas died *years* ago. I had it all checked out. I'll allege that the whole thing was a fraudulent conspiracy between you and your mother.'

'You're insane! The evidence is overwhelming. And there are the DNA tests. You can't–'

'We don't know what samples Guy gave to that laboratory. … He *always* hated me.'

'He didn't, at least not at the start.'

'He *did* … *always*. He would have done anything to destroy my life. You don't know what he was like – the beatings, the constant criticism – physical and mental torture from my earliest recollections.'

'You're mad!'

'Oh? You think so? We'll see about that when we get into court – should you dare make a claim.'

'Court? You'd actually be prepared to have all *this*' – Jean-Claude pointed at the documents – 'read out in court?'

Henri smiled. 'Would *you*? Your mother and Guy? … Your "*father*" – your precious Christophe – and my *mother*? … You're a peasant trying to usurp a Bordelais aristocrat's title and estate. Who do you think is going to be believed at the Palais de Justice? I'll give you three guesses.'

Jean-Claude had not anticipated such obstinacy. Back at Belle-Mère that morning, when he and Sophie had attempted to digest the staggering contents of the couriered package, they'd both assumed that after an initial protestation of ignorance and denial, Henri would be relatively compliant in order to avoid a scandal and to keep his all-important title. But now it appeared he'd be prepared to endure a courtroom battle. Would he himself have the stomach for such an ordeal? Did he really want La Fayette so much? Sophie certainly did – she'd even made a sick joke about having bodies exhumed.

Trying hard to concentrate, Jean-Claude stopped tracing the swirls of the Paisley patterned counterpane, and stared at Henri. He was smirking: clearly, he thought he'd won – game, set and match. All those years of supercilious sniping and criticism came flooding back. *Jesus Christ! – and all the time, I was the de Bondé, not him!* Something snapped inside him.

'I'll have the bodies exhumed,' Jean-Claude said coldly, '– Guy, Marie-Claude *and* Christophe. I'll get court orders. I'll have you forced to submit samples. I'll prove your Christophe's bastard and have you stripped of your title.'

'*You?*' scoffed Henri, '– Saint Jean-Claude? Give me a break! You *wouldn't* – you *couldn't* – it's just not in your nature.'

'Oh? I've already taken legal advice from my father-in-law's lawyers. Paul is real mad thanks to your *maître de chai* cocking up all our plans to buy Belle-Mère. They say that in a case like this, I'd have no difficulties getting the necessary orders – especially with so much evidence in the testator's own handwriting.' He was lying: there'd been no time yet to speak with any lawyers.

Henri was no longer smirking. 'Your father-in-law? I can't imagine Charpentier would want his precious business empire tarnished by a squalid tale about you and your–'

'Oh, "Dad" is quite chuffed with the idea of his daughter becoming a baroness – well, you know what these nouveau riche types are like. He's promised to fund any litigation – all the way to the Court of Appeal in Paris if necessary.' Willing himself not to lose his temper, Jean-Claude added: 'Look, I really *do* want to be reasonable.'

'"*Reasonable*"–!' but Henri's retort was cut short by another coughing fit.

'I don't want you or your family humiliated, Henri. Guy believed I wouldn't want the barony, and he was right. I'll honour the will – allow you to live on here for a year–'

'Too generous!'

'– and pay the annuity–'

'Hah!'

'– and you'll keep your name, title, "*honour*". … You must have some savings. You could buy another estate. We could both keep quiet and say you'd sold me La Fayette. Christ, Henri, when all's said and done, I *am* Guy's son! He married *my* mother. I was made legitimate. You've no valid claim to the château at all – or the title – *anything*. I think I'm being pretty generous, really'

At first, Jean-Claude thought that Henri was merely coughing again, but he quickly realized that he was sobbing. It was a pitiful sight. Standing up, he said: 'I'm sorry. You're not well, and naturally you need time to think. But once you've digested everything, I'm sure you'll accept that to go quietly is much the best course of action. You'll still be the Baron de Bondé. … It's … it's not the end of the world, Henri. I'll phone … tomorrow morning … around eleven. OK?'

When Jean-Claude reached the door, he turned. 'Look, Henri, now that we both know the truth – that we're sort of related … well … perhaps' – he wished he'd never started this pseudo-Freudian gibberish – '… um … perhaps we could become … friends.' Feeling sick, he added: 'Shall I shut the door, or …? I'll leave it open.'

Audinette was standing at the end of the corridor. Jean-Claude felt magnanimous. He strode purposely towards him: it was time for some more honesty – Belle-Mère this time.

Back in the bedroom, Henri blew his nose violently. '"Friends"!' he croaked. '"*Friends*"! He threw his aching, burning head back into the deep pillows. 'Jesus sodding Christ! – exhumed corpses!' It was all too much. Today – of all days – in bed – with a fever – Nancy away on some damned jaunt in God-awful Vietnam. … *Nancy*! How would he ever be able to tell her that he was the son of a– Impossible! She'd want a divorce – she'd want *money*! – lots of money! 'I hope that evil, wicked old man,' he rasped, 'rots in agony for ever in–!

Henri distinctly heard laughing, and, if he wasn't mistaken, the culprits were Audinette and Bourjois – the Bondé usurper! 'He'll never be a Bondé,' he muttered, '– over my dead body! … What are they up to out there? Are they in it together? After all, Audinette's dimwit father at BIF–'

Chanting 'traitor' as he fumed over the sums he'd paid Hubert Audinette to buy his silence, Henri forced himself out of bed and shuffled barefooted towards the open door. There they were, down at the far end of the corridor, the two of them with their backs to him, chatting away like a couple of washerwomen at the village pump. Birds of a feather! It *was* a fraudulent conspiracy – most definitely. The Audinettes, Bourjois – maybe even Dubloon and Appleton were in on it too. Bourjois, of course, had hatched the whole thing. They'd forged everything – of course! – organized the deposit boxes, and … Carbon Blanc? Was he a traitor too? Had he made up all that stuff about Guy telling his father about the deposit boxes? Money? Blackmail? Oh, nothing would surprise him anymore.

Now halfway along the corridor, and despite the thumping in his head, Henri could pick out much of what the conspirators were saying.

'… only just told Henri,' Audinette said. 'Took it really well, actually. I was expecting fireworks, I can tell you.'

'You'll like Belle-Mère, Patrick. You've done a good deal.'

'Oh, I'm relieved you think so, Jean-Claude. Laura and I feared you wouldn't want to leave and that you'd dig your heals in, but … well, it sounds like you've got a pretty exciting time ahead of you. You'll have to tell us all about your plans once you've dotted the i's and crossed the t's.'

In fact, Patrick was wondering whether all Bourjois's talk of 'an exciting new venture in the Médoc' was just putting on a brave face over his humiliation at Belle-Mère. He was certainly being very cagey about giving any details. Yet, Jean-Claude was actually feeling a flicker of contentment, notwithstanding the trauma of his interview with Henri. Audinette was so full of himself, what with becoming some kind of partner with Laura at Belle-Mère, but just wait until he discovered that, far from being humiliated professionally and evicted from his home, he, Jean-Claude – the real Baron de Bondé! – would soon be returning in triumph to La Fayette! Laura would be pretty pissed off too!

Down in the hall, the cleaner had resumed her vacuuming, and Sabot had turned his attention to straitening the pictures she'd disturbed while dusting. Upstairs, Henri, hovering a few metres behind Patrick and Jean-Claude, his wheezing drowned out by the vacuum cleaner's racket, was burning with both fever and fury. He'd heard enough. The conspirators were as thick as thieves – they *were* thieves! They – and the others – were trying to steal everything he owned – even his title! And they thought they'd got away with it!

'*Never!*' he hissed.

Jean-Claude glanced at his watch and said something in Patrick's ear. Patrick nodded and put an arm around Jean-Claude's broad shoulders. Then they moved off the landing onto the first stair. As they did so, Henri could see Jean-Claude making the same move more than thirty years earlier. That had been after another humiliation, when the *maître de chai*'s uncouth 'son' had thoroughly defeated the master's 'son' in a game of Cowboys and Indians in the attic. ... And then the saintly oik was tumbling over and over, down towards the marble–

Despite his painfully sore throat, Henri roared a tremendous war cry as he rushed towards the landing. Mystified by the strange sound just discernible over the vacuum cleaner's shrill whine, both Jean-Claude and Patrick faltered and reflexively looked back up the stairs, just as Henri burst out of the corridor onto the landing.

'What the–?'

Before Patrick could finish, Henri was flying through the air.

'Grab him!' yelled Jean-Claude as he instinctively seized the banister at his side with one arm, and simultaneously flung out the other to arrest Henri's fall. Patrick, however, was too stunned to react. With an ear-splitting scream, he ricocheted off Henri and went tumbling down the stairs towards the hall's gleaming chequerboard tiles.

PART 4

CHAPTER 30

In order to keep cool on this blisteringly hot day in late May, Quincy and Sue were wallowing side-by-side at the water's edge. Like the half dozen other people enjoying this stretch of the beach, they were naked.

'I 'ope this sun cream's water resistant,' Sue said lazily, a wavelet breaking over her stomach.

'You've certainly put enough on.'

'I 'ave to be careful with me skin.'

Quincy shook his head. 'I still can't believe that in all the years you've lived in Bordeaux, you've never been to the bloody beach.'

'Never 'ad the time, and Pronkie wasn't a beach person. Any'ow, Le Porge is a long way from Barrage.'

'All work and no play ...'

'I enjoy me work.'

'Don't I know it!'

'Oooh – look at that huge wave breakin' out there! We're goin' to get swept away in a minute.'

'It'll have dissipated by the time it reaches us.'

'Gawd love us! Speak English, Quince.'

Quincy rolled his eyes. 'I often suspect that you're not half as daft as you look – or sound, darling.'

'Charmin'! Take that!'

After a few minutes of frolicking about in the shallow water like a couple of young seals, they lay on their stomachs looking up the beach towards the massive dunes and the dense pine forest beyond.

'It's smashin' 'ere, isn't it? enthused Sue. 'I'd no idea the beaches were like this – so wide and straight – you can't even see the end of 'em – in either direction! And the sand's so ... so *white*. It's like a great silver ribbon.'

'Very poetic, darling. Maybe that's why it's called the Côte d'Argent.'

'What? ... Oh, I see – *argent* – got it!' Sue playfully smacked Quincy's buttocks.

'More! More!'

'Well, of course *you'd* want more, you've got your kinky reputation to live up to now, 'aven't you?'

Quincy propped himself up on his elbows and pretended to scan the horizon. 'Do you see any hacks from Fleet Street lurking in the dunes? – any sunlight reflected off concealed lenses?'

'I 'ope not. I don't want to see meself in me bleedin' birthday suit in *The Sun*, thank you very much.'

'Chance would be a fine thing.'

'Oh, give over!'

'No, I don't think we were followed, darling – the roads out here are so straight, we'd have spotted anyone tailing us.'

'To be honest, Quince, I don't give a toss about the papers, but them poison letter things you've 'ad from round 'ere, well, that's a different kettle of fish.'

Quincy laughed heartily. 'Oh, I don't worry about *them* – bit of a lark really.'

'A *lark*! There was a death threat in one. And what about that car that almost forced you off the road near Barsac last week?

'A simple accident, my sweet – nothing to worry about.'

'Well, I *do* worry.'

'I'm touched.'

Quincy received another slap across the buttocks, but this time gave as good as he got.

Later, after they'd rinsed the sand out of each other's crevices, Sue said: 'You know, Quince, I could really get to like this place.'

'Good. That's what I was hoping. We'll come again then.'

'Definitely! Fancy some lunch? I'm bleedin' starvin'. I've brought a great picnic.'

'Food! Now you're talking! And some wine, I hope – maybe some superlative Barrage.'

When they were comfortably ensconced on Quincy's tartan rug sipping chilled Barrage rosé, Sue said: 'You know, I've been wonderin' whether any of them letters could 'ave come from that Henri de Bondé bloke.'

'Why on earth would you think that?'

'Well, by all accounts, he's barmy enough.'

'Somehow, Sue, I don't think that in itself would be sufficient to convict him. Anyway, what would be his motive? *I* haven't done anything to harm him. I certainly wasn't responsible for his unexpected departure from La Fayette.'

'Maybe he sees it differently. Maybe he thinks you're goin' to name 'im in your biography as–'

'*Auto*biography, my sweet.'

'– *auto*biography as one of them Bordeaux bigwigs who paid you for "favours". When will it be finished anyway?'

'It *is* finished.'

'Blimey! Already?'

'I don't hang about, Sue. The manuscript is with my editor now. We hope to get it in the bookshops by late October – in time for the Christmas market, and just after the launch of my new TV series, *Sick as a Claret*.'

'What a bleedin' name! Did you see that bit in *Sud-Ouest* last week re-'ashin' the BBC's advance publicity?'

'Ah yes ... a wee bit threatening.'

'*Threatenin*'! The Bordelais have declared war on you, Quince – before you've even fired a single shot. I mean, all that stuff about bitin' off the 'and that's fed you for so long, well ...'

'Hmm. I've heard through the grapevine that there's intense lobbying of the TV companies not to broadcast the series here.'

'Why did *Sud-Ouest* call you "Albino Perf-somethin'"? Is it very rude?'

Quincy choked back the laughter. '*Perfide Albion*!' he corrected.

'Whatever. I don't like it when you laugh at me like that, Quincy boy.'

He took another chicken leg from the hamper. 'I'm not laughing at you, darling. It was just ironic that they should have chosen that name. You'll understand when the book's published. Anyway, to get back to the point, I don't think Henri is up to reading newspapers, let alone understanding them. When I saw Jean-Claude at La Fayette last week, he said that the poor man was still in the psychiatric hospital and ... well, he hasn't spoken to anyone for months now. Obviously, he's suffered a complete nervous breakdown. He's not violent – quite the opposite – no reaction to anyone or anything, apparently. It's as though he's in some kind of trance. ... So, darling, that's why I don't believe Henri can be the source of the letters.'

'No, probably not. What about Jean-Claude? I mean, if you're goin' to name La Fayette as one of them dodgy châteaux–'

'Of course it's not Jean-Claude! Don't be ridiculous. Anyhow, he's not bothered – he told me straight out. It all happened under Henri's reign – the last time about three years ago now. ... Is that right? ... Yes, three years. And he's the new broom that's swept the place clean – well, sort of. I've tasted his latest vintage and he's certainly not done anything to undo Audinette's work.'

'He'd be mad to, if that smarmy geezer's La Fayettes are selling as well as you keep telling me.'

'Quite. There'll be no going back to the traditional Bourjois Margaux style when he was just La Fayete's *maître de chai*.'

As she refilled their glasses, Sue said: 'I still don't get it.'

'What?'

'Why that Henri sold out. The whole thing was so fishy – especially with Audinette's involvement. The two of them swappin' places like that – and his dad being Belle-Mère's bank manager.'

'*And* one of the executors of Guy de Bondé's – Henri's father's – will.'

Sue whistled. '*Really*? You never told me that.'

'I'm sure I did.'

'I don't think so.'

Quincy inhaled deeply. 'The air's so good here … the salt, the scent of pine resin and–'

'Do you know what I think?'

'Hmm? … Sorry?'

'I think they blackmailed him into sellin' La Fayette.'

'What? … Who?'

'Jean-Claude and smarmy Patrick.'

'You really don't like him – "smarmy Patrick" – do you?'

'No. He gives me the creeps.'

'*Really*? … Anyway, blackmail? You're not suggesting they found out about Henri's contributions to my pension fund, are you?'

'Maybe. … I don't know.'

'I think it was much more straightforward, Sue. Laura met Patrick at the Tapés' do, right? Like Bourjois before him, he'd finally realized that Bondé was never going to take him into partnership, and so, he was looking around for a new job. He chats up Laura, and she tells him she's about to lose control of her precious Belle-Mère because of the Bourjois-Charpentier consortium's offer to buy me out. So, Audinette sees an opening for himself at Belle-Mère if he can get rid of Bourjois. He knows that dear Jean-Claude would kill to own La Fayette, so he tells him that Bondé is massively in debt – his dad's bank had loaned him a small fortune to set up that third wine operation – and BIF is about to pull the plug. *And* Nancy – Henri's long-suffering spouse – is about to divorce him – the louse must have had more mistresses than I've had hot dinners – and sue him for a few million euros.

'So, Jean-Claude beetles off to Bondé, and, with the millions his father-in-law had earmarked for the Belle-Mère acquisition, offers to buy the place before the shit hits the fan and Bondé is forced into receivership – bankruptcy – debtors' prison. It was an offer he couldn't refuse. I bet you anything you like that the consortium bought at a great price. A public sale would have been so humiliating for Bondé, even if he could have got more money.'

Sue looked doubtful. 'Bondé could 'ave put out confidential feelers – to insurance companies, multinationals – all the usual investors in *grand cru* properties that come up for sale these days, and got an 'igher price, and avoided sellin' out to his despised ex-employee.'

Quincy shrugged his massive shoulders. 'Henri wouldn't have wanted mega firms of international auditors going through his accounts with a fine toothcomb. Well, maybe there was a spot of extortion – whether over the extent of Bondé's indebtedness, his dealings with me, or–'

'I'm sure it was somethin' like that. And then, when Bondé realized the full 'orror of what they'd forced 'im into, 'e blew a fuse and tried to kill 'em both. I mean, wasn't it fishy that Patrick and Jean-Claude were there together and–'

'Oh, Sue, spare me that nonsense again!'

'It was all round Margaux, for Christ's sake – all round Bordeaux!'

'Patrick tripped and fell down the stairs.'

'Tripped my fanny!'

'That cleaner and the butler saw it all. They said–'

'They said one thing in Margaux's local boozer, and somethin' totally different to the *gendarmes*.'

'Patrick himself said he slipped. Jean-Claude confirmed it.'

'That's because they didn't want the cops snoopin' into 'ow Jean-Claude ended up with La Fayette.'

'For heaven's sake, darling – conspiracy theories gone mad! Enough! I'm roasting. Let's go for a swim.'

'Well, a paddle maybe – them Atlantic rollers–' Sue broke off, removed her sunglasses and stared northwards along the beach. 'What the 'ell are them two lads doin' over yonder, Quince? They're not–? They can't–?'

'They *are*. Don't look, Sue. The French have no shame – and such hypocrites too. In the Jardin Public, just around the corner from me in Cours de Tournon, if you so much as take your bloody shirt off for a spot of sunbathing, the park police are in there before you can say Jancis Robinson, quoting by-laws and threatening to evict you if you don't cover up immediately. While here at Le Porge–'

Sue put a hand over his mouth. 'Oh, shut your gob for Christ's sake!' Gripping Quincy's penis with her other hand, she added: 'I don't know whether it's me rosé or the sight of them two gays 'avin' it off, but I feel dead randy.'

Several hours later, with the vast beach all to themselves as the sun sank towards the distant Atlantic horizon, Sue and Quincy untwined their bodies and reluctantly agreed it was time to make the long trek back over the dunes and through the forest to the car. It took them almost half an hour, and when Quincy was finally driving at speed along the straight empty road between Le Porge and Le Temple, Sue said:

'That was one of the 'appiest days of my life, Quince.'

He was about to laugh when he shot her a sideways glance and saw tears running down her cheeks. He reddened with embarrassment. 'Oh ... good. It *was* wonderful, wasn't it? I'm so glad you enjoyed it.'

To his intense relief, Sue managed a chuckle. 'Gawd Almighty! You're so ... so *British*! – even after all we've done on that beach today!'

'Yes, that's me.' He took a hand off the steering wheel and squeezed her knee. 'Give me your hand, Sue.' She looked surprised, but complied. He gripped it tightly. 'I've ... I've decided not to buy that apartment in Kensington,' he said. 'I think it would be wiser to *rent* in London for the time being – the new TV show could bomb – the book as well. I'll keep Cours de Tournon pro tem.'

Sue guessed what 'pro tem' meant and reciprocated his grip. 'I'm so glad,' she said softly. After a brief silence, she added: 'What do you think about changin' Barrage's name to "Château Olivier-Dubloon"?'

*

At that moment, on the other side of the Atlantic, several thousand miles almost due west of Le Porge, Laura was lunching Jean-Claude and Sophie at La Maison Blanche de New York; Daniel Mombrier, who was also in the Big Apple for the New York Wine Event, had been delighted to accept her invitation to join them; Mrs Mombrier was back in Los Angeles 'holding the fort'. Laura was deliciously happy: she'd enjoyed a wonderful morning at the Wine Event, hobnobbing with the superstars of the international wine scene and being treated like one herself. Ignoring Mombrier's incessant chatter about the celebrities who'd been lucky enough to get a table at 'his' Los Angeles restaurant during the last week, she relived the praise from both merchants and critics alike for Belle-Mère's pedestrian wines, thanks to the extraordinary hype that she and Patrick had been able to generate during the last few months for their new micro-treasure, the gestating 'Château Laurinette'.

Back in March, they'd managed to get several of the world's top wine writers over to taste their new baby, and minds had been blown. One of them, having declaimed that it promised to be 'the archetypical hedonistic wine', returned to the States to repeat the praise on network television and his website. And then, when Laura and her 'partner' announced that they anticipated producing only six hundred cases – 7,200 bottles – and that they'd be seeking a price of around a thousand dollars a bottle when released after twenty-one months' ageing, the U.S. media were banging on Belle-Mère's doors for interviews. The Europeans – slow off the mark as usual – led by the British, had eventually fallen into line. A few weeks ago, the first emails from Far Eastern billionaire wine collectors had started arriving.

Yes indeed, Laura reminded herself, she and Patrick had been right all along: thanks to Laurinette – as predicted – everyone wanted to know about folksy Château Belle-Mère's second wines – all three colours, as the dreaded Sue used to say! One minute they were barely saleable nonentities outside Bordeaux; the next, one would think they were the products of a respectable Médoc *cru bourgeois*, or even a fifth growth *cru classé*! Well, as several New York merchants had discovered this morning, if they wanted a case of Laurinette next year, they were going to have to take quite a few cases of dear old Belle-Mère – and they wouldn't come cheap – thirty euros a bottle, ex-château ... maybe more. And then, just a couple of hours ago, while she was talking to one of the Rothschilds, Patrick had phoned on her mobile with the icing on the cake, saying he'd been up all night and couldn't wait until she came home, and–

On the other side of the tall menu she was still failing to study, Laura heard Mombrier say in French: 'Well, have we all decided?' A few heads at a neighbouring table turned to investigate the source of the non-American voice. 'Laura, what have we been able to tempt you with?'

After all these years since their bust up in Margaux, she still found him obnoxious. Making up to him and Mom had been an ordeal, but Patrick's advice had been spot on: the two Maison Blanche restaurants would be marketing flagships for Laurinette; pride had to be swallowed. Smiling sweetly, Laura closed the menu and deposited it on the impressive silver underplate before her. 'Oh, Uncle Daniel,' she cooed, 'it's just *so* difficult to choose. What are *you* all having?'

Before the Bourjoises could respond, Mombrier said: 'Look, unless you have any strong feelings, chef has suggested a little *menu* to me that might possibly appeal to you all – *écrevisses à la Bordelaise, faisan rôti à la Périgourdine*, and a *soufflé aux pruneaux*. How does that sound?'

There was unanimity that it sounded just fine.

When the sommelier arrived, Mombrier went overboard introducing 'his' guests. 'Craig, this is Sophie Bourjois, the great contemporary artist, over in New York to paint Sean Kunstmann's portrait – yes, dear Sean, one of our most beloved LA clients. ... Her husband Jean-Claude, the world-famous viticulturist and owner of glorious Château La Fayette. ... And last – but not least – the illustrious wine writer and TV star herself, Laura Appleton, who has stunned the industry with her staggering transformation of an Entre-deux-Mers vineyard from utter obscurity to international acclaim in just the winking of an eye.'

Mombrier's faux pas went through Laura like an electric shock – she spotted the Bourjoises exchanging smirks across the table – but at least he hadn't referred to her as his stepdaughter. Before she could recover her composure, he was already suggesting wines.

'I think we should start with a fresh, crisp white – and nothing fits the bill better than the delightful 2004 Belle-Mère.'

'Oh no!' cried Laura, feigning embarrassment, '– not my own wine!'

There were thin smiles on the Bourjoises' faces, a mixture of surprise that Belle-Mère should now be on the restaurant's wine list, and injured pride: the 2004 was Jean-Claude's 'baby'.

'No, no, Laura,' Mombrier continued, 'it will be a perfect accompaniment with the *écrevisses*, and with so *many* bottles of the stuff down in the cellars, it's about time we cracked open a case. ... And to follow ... Of course! In honour of Jean-Claude we should enjoy the glories of the 1990 La Fayette ... yes?'

It was Jean-Claude's turn to be modest. 'Oh ... well,' – he glanced sheepishly at the sommelier – 'when in Rome ... What about something Californian?'

But Mombrier was insistent. 'Well now, Sophie,' he steamrollered on as the sommelier took his leave, 'you paint.' It sounded like an accusation. Momentarily, she was taken aback.

'Yes – yes I do, although portraits are not really my – my–'

'You normally do landscape things,' Mombrier prompted. Art was not at all his forte.

'Well, I–'

'Oh no, Uncle Daniel, she's really an abstract painter.'

Mombrier's face was a mask of neutrality. '*Really*? How interesting. ... Anyway, Sophie, you must be finding Sean a *wonderful* subject – such a lovely man. Did you see him in *Abattoir Cats*? Fantastic performance – so talented. Presumably you'll have seen his latest movie, *Gutted*?'

Sophie had; she'd been forced to. It was the most repulsive film she'd ever seen. She nodded with a forced smile.

A silent type, Mombrier concluded. He'd try the husband. 'So, Jean-Claude, how are you settling in at La Fayette? Did Laura's guy leave it in good shape? Too bad about Bondé. If you ask me, he was heading for a breakdown – burned himself out marketing – always on some whistle-stop tour across the States. But it wasn't really him. He wasn't a natural salesman – those foppish aristocrats never are. You closed your deal just in time – before the guy cracked. I suppose you were lucky to have a tycoon like Charpentier behind you.'

'Yes,' Jean-Claude agreed, nodding, 'Sophie's father was most ... supportive.'

Mombrier turned on a toothpaste advertisement smile. 'Ah yes. Sorry, I was forgetting the family connection.' He picked up the wine glass into which Craig the sommelier had just poured a mouthful of the Belle-Mère, swirled it around, and began sucking and slurping. Nodding sagely, he said: 'Very ... pleasant – there's a decadent bouquet of honeyed super-ripe melons, a nuance of smoky oak ... a great deal of charm ... and character.' With both Laura and Jean-Claude wondering whether he was taking the piss, Craig began moving around the table with the approved bottle.

'I suppose the 2004 must be one of my husband's efforts,' Sophie announced proudly.

'Well remembered!' chirped Laura. 'Goodness! Is it only *six* months since you left Belle-Mère?' She shook her head. 'It seems like an eternity – as if you'd never been there at all really. I mean, so much has happened in the meanwhile – for *all* of us.'

As Jean-Claude tasted the wine and found himself pleasantly surprised, he reflected on Sophie's ability to amaze him. Despite loathing Laura, it was she who, shortly after their arrival at La Fayette, had suggested the ex-partner as the estate's U.S. marketing consultant: Laura had all the right connections and the flair. And, whatever her failings, there'd never been the least hint of dishonesty in her business dealings.

The Bourjoises' approach had stunned Laura, but on reflection, and having talked it over with Patrick, she realized that acting as a consultant for a Margaux *grand cru* – her alma mater, moreover – would be quite a feather in her cap, and, in all probability, would help to promote the Laurinette/Belle-Mère stable: the trade would reason that an illustrious name like La Fayette would only allow itself to be associated with other top-quality wines. And because of the huge difference in price, their premium brands could hardly be in competition. There might be some overlap between their respective second and third wines, but they were mainly sold on the back of the first wines in the States. In any event, Patrick had his sights very much set on the Far Eastern trade: he was convinced profit margins would be even better.

So far, both sides had been satisfied with the arrangement. In fact, many in the trade had already assumed that there was some commercial tie-up between the two estates – common shareholders, or a joint venture – in view of Jean-Claude's connections with both of them.

And, as Laura had conjectured more than once, given time, perhaps some kind of merger might take place: all those thousands of uneconomic little producers couldn't continue operating Bordeaux's vineyards much longer.

'How's Patrick, Laura?' asked Mombrier. 'Still on crutches? And when are we – your mom and me – going to meet this smart young fella? Bondé never used to bring him over.'

Laura noticed the Bourjoises exchanging another one of their sly looks, and wondered how she could ever have fancied Jean-Claude. 'Well, Uncle Daniel, you could always come over to see *us*, you know. Patrick would have loved to accompany me, but he only threw away those damned crutches last week and–'

'Great!' roared Mombrier, slapping the table.

'At last,' added Jean-Claude. 'I was beginning to fear that broken leg would never mend.'

'Me too,' Laura said, nodding. 'The crutches were driving him crazy – you know how active he is.'

Four waiters dressed in morning suits, each one no less handsome than the sommelier, began removing the remains of the first course.

Watching them like a sergeant-major, Mombrier said: 'You know, there were some crazy rumours I heard over here that Bondé tried to kill Patrick – or you, Jean-Claude – or both of you. Something about–'

Theatrically, Jean-Claude burst out laughing. 'Oh, that old chestnut!'

'Ridiculous!' scoffed Sophie.

Shaking her head, Laura added: 'Some people have got nothing better to do than–'

'Patrick and I,' Jean-Claude interjected firmly, 'were at La Fayette for business reasons. Poor Henri had a severe dose of flu – with a fever and everything. We should really have postponed the meeting, but he insisted. … Anyhow, when I went into his bedroom to talk figures – our offer to buy La Fayette – I asked Patrick to wait for me outside in the corridor. Well, afterwards, we stood for a while chatting at the top of the stairs. The cleaner was down in the hall vacuuming. … I guess Henri remembered something important he wanted to be included in the draft contract and got out of bed to tell me – he must have heard us talking down the corridor. Well, just as we began to go downstairs, we heard this strange cry behind us, and there was Henri at the top of the staircase gesticulating for us to wait.'

Jean-Claude tutted. 'What with his flu – I really shouldn't have seen him – it could have waited. … He must have had a dizzy turn and lost his balance, because the next thing, he was falling down the bloody stairs and … I was lucky. I had the hand rail on my side, so I'd something to hold on to when I grabbed him. But poor Patrick had nothing – just the wall and all those family portraits. I think he was too stunned to react, and down he went when Henri slammed into us. Christ! – when he hit that marble floor, I thought he was a goner.'

The sommelier, who'd returned to serve the red wine, was standing obediently to attention, looking from Mombrier to Laura, and from her to Jean-Claude. 'Um, may I enquire who would like to taste the 1990 La Fayette?' he asked delicately.

'The owner,' Mombrier and Laura chorused. Everyone laughed.

Jean-Claude shook his head. 'Lack of objectivity. I think Laura should – both as our host and as an ex-pupil, so to speak.'

In the mistaken belief that Jean-Claude was attempting to put Mombrier in his place, Laura smiled at him sweetly. Just for a brief moment, Sophie experienced a flashback to the dark little cellar at the old Margaux house – the two of them down there embracing, a broken bottle with its blood red contents at their feet. *How bizarre life is*, she thought as she watched Laura perform her farcical tasting ritual. *Just look at her! Thank God Jean-Claude doesn't indulge in such nonsense. ... I wonder if she'll marry that Audinette conman.*

Solemnly, Laura scanned the expectant faces. 'Hmm,' she murmured. 'I don't know ...'

Mombrier's smile evaporated. 'Not corked, surely? To be honest, Jean-Claude, I didn't like to say anything, but on a few occasions over the last year – both here and in Los Angeles – a few clients have expressed disappointment over the most recent La Fayettes. Of course, *we* all know that they're not ready for drinking yet, but you have to stock wines that people can afford. ... And then there are those Americans – sorry, Laura – who think the younger the wine, the better it is – mad, I know! Anyhow, some bottles of the 98s and the 99s are ... well, to be frank, a little thin on top – not at all like the massive wines young Patrick has been developing – or *your* best, Jean-Claude, before you went to Belle-Mère. To me they tasted ... well, more like your second wine, Maréchal – General–'

'Christ, Uncle Daniel, I was just teasing! The wine's *perfect* – La Fayette at its *very* best.' She nodded to the nervous sommelier. 'It's fine, Craig.'

As the others sipped and expressed their pleasure, Laura suddenly realized what she'd said. What a jerk! – La Fayette 'at its very best' indeed. If Patrick got to hear of it, he'd ... he'd what? He'd probably agree. After all, when all was said and done, he was a Bordelais who loved classic claret but who had the common sense to realize that in order to survive you had to give the market what it wanted. And now it seemed that even stick-in-the-mud Jean-Claude had learned that tough lesson. Yep, there'd be no more La Fayettes like this 1990. It was sad in a way.

I wonder if I should ask gorgeous Craig to fetch a bottle of vintage Bollinger and announce the engagement? … Or should I tell Mom and Dad first? … No, Patrick's right. I'll get even more attention at the Wine Event if I go public immediately.

*

Alexandre Bourjois had kept the secret all these months, but his resolve was failing. Life at school had become impossible. Today had been the final straw. Led by the vile Carbon Blanc urchin, the usual gang had seized him during morning break as he was making his way to the library, pushed him into the washroom, subjected him to the usual filthy insults, punched him, and then thrust his head down one of the lavatories. Well, this time they'd gone too far. He'd dragged himself to the principal's office, ignored his half-witted secretary's remonstrances, and gone straight in. Despite a meeting with three departmental heads being in progress, the bedraggled pupil secured a private audience thanks to a rapidly developing black eye and impressive threats of legal action against the principal himself, the entire board of illustrious governors and a bevy of aristocratic parents, coupled with pertinent references to vicarious liability and three cases pending before the European Court of Human Rights.

What Alexandre told the principal came as no surprise: the scandalous allegations made against the boy and his victimization reflected the attitudes prevailing amongst Bordeaux society. Although the principal found the allegations too fantastic for words, when all was said and done, one day the Baron Henri de Bondé was a highly successful and respected owner of a Margaux *grand cru*, and the next, he was selling his heritage to a former employee, being dragged through the divorce courts, and suffering a nervous breakdown. Now the poor man was in a psychiatric institution, apparently without a euro to his name.

It was quite possible, of course, that Bondé had been a gambler – the casinos at Arcachon and Biarritz had a lot to answer for – or had squandered his fortune on a mistress – jewels, an apartment on the Riviera – who knew? But, be that as it may, Alexandre Bourjois was an obnoxious youth who hated sport and acted as though he was bloody royalty. Consequently, it was difficult to empathize with his plight. He'd speak with the parents and advise them that in the boy's best interests, he should attend another school, preferably far from Bordeaux – ideally abroad.

Oblivious to the principal's interjections, Alexandre was in full flow. Such was his animation, he'd come very close to revealing both his true

383

identity and the whole extraordinary Bourjois-Bondé saga during his account of its latest bizarre twist.

'Before leaving for New York, sir, my misguided father made arrangements for the destitute Monsieur Henri de Bondé to be brought from his lunatic asylum and installed with a nurse in our château's attic! When Papa informed me of such arrangements, he attempted to diffuse my outrage with biblical quotations – or rather misquotations – and some nonsense about rebuilding bridges with "the Great and Good of Bordeaux". Indeed, I firmly told *both* my parents that they were naive. Far from rehabilitating themselves, the local aristocracy and their hangers-on would regard the provision of a complimentary rooftop home as the rubbing of salt into the lunatic's wounds.'

As Alexandre droned on about the commodious facilities that were being installed for 'Monsieur de Bondé' at La Fayette in an attempt to emphasize the injustice of his own persecution by fellow pupils, 'rubbing salt into the wounds' was precisely the principal's verdict.

'I think I should phone your father – *immediately*,' he snapped.

'My parents are in New York until the weekend, sir.'

'Oh ... I see. Well, you should go home, Bourjois, until their return. With your eye and ... It's for the best. I assume there are people to look after you at Margaux?'

'Naturally – the housekeeper, the butler, the–'

'Quite.'

And so, while Quincy and Sue were frolicking in the Atlantic at Le Porge, Alexandre took the train to Margaux, the only occupant, as usual, of the diminutive first-class section. The nurse who'd arrived that morning to prepare for Henri's transfer from the 'lunatic asylum' offered to dine with Alexandre, but, to her surprise and subsequent anger, he firmly rejected her unforgivable presumption. Clad in jacket, shirt and tie, he dined stylishly on his own in what he insisted on calling 'the State Dining Room'; with the cheese, he'd even helped himself to a glass of port. Throughout the solitary meal, as Alexandre relived the events of the morning, his sense of injustice became ever stronger, the port serving to stoke up the fire smouldering within him. When old Brignard came to clear away and, with one eye on the wine glass, asked with an all too obvious sneer whether 'Master Alexandre' would care to partake of coffee in the library, the lad replied that he would take it in the study.

'I have a rather important history project to complete,' he said, little realizing that the principal had already spoken with a majority of the governors and secured the green light for his removal from the school. 'Oh, and *this* time, Brignard, make sure the coffee is made with water that's just *off* the boil.'

As the old retainer hobbled away mouthing obscenities, Alexandre withdrew to the study. Although he had his own 'study' upstairs complete with a desktop – it had formerly been Benoît de Bondé's bedroom – the wood panelling of *the* study was most impressive, as were the magnificent Louis XVI desk, the state-of-the-art desktop and laser printer, and, above all, the portraits of long-deceased Bondés. Indeed, as Alexandre tapped away at the keyboard, he couldn't help glancing at them, joyously reminding himself that these people were *his* people – his own ancestors. His dream had come true: he wasn't a commoner after all! He was an aristocrat, and there, behind the portrait of the late Guy de Bondé – his grandfather, no less – was the safe which contained the proof.

Oh, it was so unfair! All those beastly, ludicrous, infantile allegations about his parents that he had to put up with all day long at school – 'communists', 'blackmailers', 'thieving scum', 'scheming peasants', kidnapping and torturing Henri's vile children! – slowly poisoning Henri with mercury over several years! – witchcraft even! Alexandre could feel tears welling up. He couldn't go back to all that. And yet, those very same cretins would grow up and inherit their families' estates and businesses – just as he would inherit La Fayette one day – but they'd never forget or forgive Papa's and Mama's 'crimes'. He'd have to live with their vile gossip, lies and innuendo for ever.

Alexandre stared once more at his grandfather. He'd only taken the portrait down to check on the painter's signature. There was a whole set of the Bénézit in the library, and when they'd first moved in, he'd wanted to find out as much as possible about the paintings in order to produce a definitive catalogue. But behind Guy de Bondé, he'd discovered a safe, an old-fashioned thing with a keyhole. Had his parents known about it, they would surely have told him, wouldn't they? Perhaps it contained something exciting. If so, it would be *his* discovery!

There'd been rather a lot of keys in the desk, but by trial and error he'd eventually identified the right one. To his dismay, however, the safe contained all sorts of dreary documents which made no sense to him – stock certificates of nominee companies in New York, and records of payments to 'Albion'. But then he'd been stunned to find an envelope bearing the name of his own father … then another. And as he read the contents, he'd experienced shock, horror, disgust, excitement, and, at one point, a most perplexing and yet not unpleasant stirring in his groin. The full import of it all had been difficult for a thirteen-year-old boy to comprehend, but despite frightening words like 'illegitimacy' and adultery', one thing was crystal clear: his father was Guy de Bondé's *son* – not barmy Henri! Papa had lied – so had Mama: they hadn't bought La Fayette from Henri – Henri *Bourjois* – they'd *taken* it from him – taken what was rightfully theirs from a common thief and thrown him out! And now everyone thought *they* were the thieves – the Bourjois family – except that they weren't horrid Bourjoises at all!

'Papa and Mama will thank me … eventually,' Alexandre whispered as he shut down the desktop and opened one of the desk drawers. 'They'll see that it was all for the best.'

The key wasn't in the same place. He finally found it inside a box of paper clips; clearly, his father had tried to conceal it. While the photocopier produced copies of Grandpapa's will and letter, Alexandre addressed envelopes in block capitals with the help of the local telephone directory. He knew all their names and the châteaux where they lived. That was enough – one didn't need a postcode if one lived in a château! He couldn't wait to see their faces when he got back to school! They'd have to grovel! And, on reflection, illegitimacy and adultery could fairly be regarded as indicia of aristocratic blood. After all, the French royal houses – English too – all of them if truth be told – had been awash with such matters. The de Bondés, therefore, were in very good company.

It was well after ten when Alexandre finished addressing the last envelope – it was to *Sud-Ouest*'s editor – and began sticking on the stamps he'd removed from the stock kept in the desk's top drawer. Then it was just a ten-minute walk to the postbox beside the Margaux *mairie*. No one was about when he returned and let himself in. He'd just removed his coat and was about to climb the stairs to his room when Madame Brignard appeared from the direction of the kitchen, holding a glass of warm milk in one hand and a plate of biscuits in the other.

'Oh, just off to bed Master Henri? – *Alexandre* – silly me! I *am* sorry, Master Alexandre. I – I … It was just that …'

'What?'

'Oh nothing. I must be losing my marbles, that's all.'

'No, *please*. What were you going to say?'

'Well, I … I was thinking about Monsieur de Bondé as I was preparing your supper here – your mum and dad have done a smashing job of making the attic nice and comfy, I must say – and how ironic it is that he's coming back and … To be honest, Master Alexandre, you remind me of the baron.'

A hint of a smile appeared on Alexandre's face. '*Really*? – the late Baron Guy de Bondé?'

Madame Brignard laughed. 'Oh *no* – of course not! You remind me of Monsieur *Henri*. I think it's the tone of your voice, and the way you stand, and …' *And now you're scowling like him.* 'Yes, it's silly. I'm sorry. I'm *very* tired.' She began to mount the stairs; Alexandre remained immobile. Passing him, she asked: 'Aren't you going to bed then?'

He appeared not to hear. 'Hmm? … What? … Um, yes – in my own good time. I just have to check on … check on something.'

Madame Brignard was on the point of uttering some motherly words of warning about late nights, but stopped herself just in time. 'Well, good night then,' she said coldly.

'Oh, by the way, Marie-Thérèse, please use the back stairs in future.'

When the Bourjoises had first arrived at the château, a framed photograph had stood on the grand piano in the music room. During the happy trio's tour, Sophie had immediately removed it and placed it in a drawer of a Louis XVIII commode that stood a few metres away. Alexandre doubted that the memento would still be there, but he was in luck. It was lying at the back of the middle drawer under a pile of Chopin sheet music bought by Nancy de Bondé in naive anticipation of a miraculous development of her daughter's lamentable musical skills. Alexandre took the photograph over to a table lamp and scrutinized it closely. It was a family group – Henri, his dim-looking wife, and the two ghastly children. Henri appeared to be staring back at him with a supercilious grin.

He brought the photograph even closer to the light. There was something oddly familiar about the counterfeit baron, but why? Certainly, he'd seen him a few times at school before the beastly Benoît had been removed, but it wasn't just that. … For a fraction of a second, there was an image of a dazzling ball of light hurtling towards him. Gasping and swaying, he almost lost his balance.

'Bed,' he advised earnestly. 'You've had a pretty eventful day, old boy.' Concealing the silver-framed photograph under his jacket, he exited the library and swept regally across the great hall's chequerboard marble floor.

That night, with the photograph standing on his bedside table, Alexandre dreamed again of the hideous house at Le Porge. It was always the same dream, but this time as he pedalled his diminutive bicycle along the straight road through the forest, he recognized the face of the silver motor car's driver. It wasn't an accident! He'd tried to kill him, and when the lunatic shouted across the dyke's stagnant waters, he'd told him why:

'It's the tone of your voice, Alexandre, and the way you stand.'

THE END